The Superhero Illustrated Guidebook

A Review of Superhero Series On Television

Edited by William E. Anchors, Jr.

Credits...

Writers of this volume include William E. Anchors, Jr.; David W. Dietz, III; Howard T. Konig, Craig W. Frey, Jr., Robert Alan Crick, Doug Snauffer and Jim Faerber. The editor wishes to express his appreciation for everyone who contributed to this book.

The material in *The Superhero Illustrated Guidebook* previously appeared in *Epi-log*, *Epi-log Special* and *Epi-log Journal* magazines. See the end of this book for more information on our magazines, or write to the address below.

Additional copies of this book can be ordered at $14.95 each + $6.00 postage and handling by writing to the above address. Wholesale prices are available for lots of 20 or more copies (write for pricing).

INDEX

The Dynamic Duo: Burt Ward as Robin, Adam West as Batman.

Batman

review by William E. Anchors, Jr.

Production credits:

Executive Producer	William Dozier
Producer	Howie Horwitz
Story Consultant	Lorenzo Semple, Jr.
Director of Photography	Howard Schwartz
Makeup	Ben Nye
Music	Neal Hefti (theme)
	Nelson Riddle

Regular cast:

Batman/Bruce Wayne	Adam West
Robin/Dick Grayson	Burt Ward
Police Commissioner Gordon	Neil Hamilton
Chief O'Hara	Stafford Repp
Alfred	Alan Napier
Aunt Harriet Cooper	Madge Blake
Batgirl/Barbara Gordon	Yvonne Craig

Number of episodes: 120 one half hour segments

Premise: The crime-fighting adventures of the caped crusader, his sidekick Robin, and a new member of the Dynamic Duo, Batgirl.

Editor's comments: The adventures of everyone's favorite crime-fighting hero, in the ultra-camp super-hit program of the 1960s. Played by square-jawed Adam West, his ultra-straight portrayal of Batman and the camp style of this show made a tremendous influence on programs of the era. The stories can be described as fun, or ludicrous beyond belief, depending on one's point of view.

SEASON ONE

Hey Diddle Riddle - Smack in the Middle (airdates: Jan. 12, 1966; Jan 13, 1966). A riddle is released from a cake, leading Batman and Robin to the Peale Art Gallery where they arrest the Riddler - who sues them for false arrest. The Riddler knows that Batman will be forced to reveal his secret identity if he goes to court, which the Caped Crusader must prevent. So Batman and Robin catch the Riddler and his henchmen in a real crime, which they do by concealing themselves inside a gigantic paper-mache mammoth and arriving Trojan-horse-style. **Guest cast:** Frank Gorshin as Riddler, Jill St. John [*Diamonds Are Forever*] as Molly, Allen Jaffe, Michael Fox as Inspector Basch, Damian O'Flynn as Gideon Peale, Ben Astar as Moldavian Prime Minister, Jack Barry as the newscaster, Dick Reeves as the doorman, William Dozier as the Maitre d'. **Writer:** Lorenzo Semple, Jr. **Director:** Robert Butler.

Fine Feathered Finks/The Penguin's a Jinks (airdates: Jan. 19, 1966; Jan. 20, 1966). After being released from prison, the Penguin pulls off ingenious robberies, but cannot be arrested as he never actually takes anything. Bruce visits the evil genius' umbrella factory, where he tries to hide a listening device that sets off an alarm and gets Bruce put on a conveyer belt leading to a blast furnace. **Guest cast:** Burgess Meredith as the Penguin, Leslie Parrish as Dawn, Dan Tobin as Mr. Jay, Walter Burke as Sparrow, Lewis Charles as Hawkeye, David Lewis as Warden Crichton, Alex D'Arcy as the jewelry shop owner, Johnny Jacobs as the assistant shop owner, Robert Phillips as the cellmate named Swoop. **Writer:** Lorenzo Semple, Jr. **Director:** Robert Butler.

The Joker Is Wild/Batman Gets Riled (airdates: Jan. 26, 1966; Jan. 27, 1966). Joker escapes from prison to obtain revenge for his not being included in the Gotham Art Museum's Comedian's Hall. He begins looting the museum, but is surprised by Batman and Robin. After escaping, Joker creates his own utility belt, used in assisting his men in capturing Batman and Robin, who are now about to be unmasked on live television. **Guest cast:** Cesar Romero as the Joker, Nancy Kovack as Queenie, David Lewis as Warden Crichton, Jerry Dunphy as Fred, Jonathan Hole, Merritt Bohn as the assistant Warden, Dick Curtis as the inebriate, Al Wyatt as the first henchman, Angelo DeMeo as the second henchman. **Writer:** Robert Dozier. **Director:** Don Weiss.

Instant Freeze/Rats Like Cheese (airdates: Feb. 2, 1966; Feb. 3, 1966). Mr. Freeze, a super-villain who can exist only in freezing temperatures because of an accident involving Batman, is planning revenge on the Caped Crusader. After pulling off a diamond heist, he goes after the famous Circle of Ice diamond, owned by a princess. Batman and Robin figure out Freeze's next caper and rush there to save her and the diamond, but are instead turned into instant ice cubes by the dastardly bad guy. **Guest cast:** George Sanders as Mr. Freeze, Selby Grant as Princess Sandra, Troy Melton as Chill, Guy Way as Nippy, Roy Sickner as Mo, Robert Hogan as Paul Diamante, William O'Connell as Mr. Perkins, John Zaremba as named Kolevator, Don Hannum as Art Rogers, Ken Del Conte as Al Scott, Dan Terranova as Dr. Vince, John Willis as the newscaster, Bill Hudson as the photographer, Teri Garr [*Close Encounters of the Third Kind*] as the girl. **Writer:** Max Hodge. **Director:** Robert Butler.

Zelda the Great/A Death Worse Than Fate (airdates: Feb. 9, 1966; Feb. 10, 1966). Every year Zelda the Great robs a Gotham City bank of $100,000 on April first, but no one ever catches her or knows who commits the crimes. Batman sets a trap by publishing in the newspaper that her most recent theft was made up of counterfeit money. This creates problems for her when a scientist she owes money too will not accept it. She plans another theft, but becomes aware of another Bat-trap, so she kidnaps Aunt Harriet and holds her over a boiling vat of oil, then demands a ransom from millionaire playboy Bruce Wayne. **Guest cast:** Ann Baxter as Zelda, Jack Krushen as Eivol Ekdol, Barbara Heller as Hillary Stonewin, Frankie Darro as the newsman, Jim Drum as Officer Clancey, Stephen Tompkins as the bank guard, Victor French as the first hood, Bill Phillips as the second hood, Jerry Doggett as the announcer, Douglas Dumbrille as the doctor. **Writer:** Lorenzo Semple, Jr. **Director:** Robert Heller.

A Riddle A Day Keeps the Riddler Away/When The Rat's Away

BATMAN-15

8

The Batmobile in the Batcave.

The Mice Will Play (airdates: Feb. 16, 1966; Feb. 10, 1966). The Riddler is back in town, and presents the visiting King Boris with an exploding bouquet of roses. A series of clues lead Batman and Robin to the Riddler's hide out, where they are captured and the villain plans to destroy the Dynamic Duo by shackling them to huge, spinning wheels connected to a giant generator drive shaft. **Guest cast:** Frank Gorshin as the Riddler, Susan Silo as Mousey, Tim Herbert as Whiskers, Reginald Denny as King Boris, Marc Cavell as Fangs, Roy Jenson as Whitey, William Kendis as the newsman, Joy Harmon as Julia Davis, Johnny Magnus as the M.C., Tris Coffin as the Ambassador, John Archer as the guest, John Hubbard as the Maitre D', Marvin Miller as the TV announcer. **Writer:** Fred De Gorter. **Director:** Tom Gries.

The Thirteenth Hat/Batman Stands Pat (airdates: Feb. 23, 1966; Feb. 24, 1966). Mad Hatter is back, and plans revenge on Batman and the twelve jurors who sent him up the river. After kidnapping the jurors and stealing their hats, he plans to add Batman's cowl to his collection. When the Hatter tries to fake Batman into removing his cowl to make a plaster bust, a fight breaks out and the Masked Crimefighters find themselves encased in Super-Fast Hardening Plaster. Holy Plaster of Paris! **Guest cast:** David Wayne as the Mad Hatter, Richard La Starza as Cappy, Sandra Wells as Babette, Diane McBain as Lisa, Gil Perkins as Dicer, George Conrad as Turkey Bullwinkle, Albert Morin as Octave Marbot, Monique Le Maire as Madame Magda, Ralph Montgomery as the silver shop manager, Bob Legionaire as the sporting goods manager, Norma Varden as Mrs. Monteagle, John Ward as the citizen. **Writer:** Charles

Hoffman. **Director:** Norman Foster.

The Joker Goes to School/He Meets His Match, the Grizzly Goul (airdates: Mar. 2, 1966; Mar. 3, 1966). The Joker is recruiting dropouts from Gotham City High School for his gang. He rigs the school vending machines, then has a female gang member steal some papers to commit blackmail. When the Caped Crusader arrives to straighten out the situation, he and Robin are trapped by the Joker and his new gang, then are placed in electric chairs connected to a slot machine that, when the right combination comes up, will bring the case to a shocking conclusion. **Guest cast:** Cesar Romero as the Joker, Donna Loren as Susie, Sydney Smith as Vandergilt, Kip King as Nick, Bryan O'Byrne as Shoolfield, Tim O'Kelly as Pete, Cheri Foster as the first cheerleader, Linda Harrison as the second cheerleader, Glenn Allan as Herbie, Donna Di Martino as the third girl, Dick Bellis as Joe, Joan Parker as the fourth girl, Breeland Rice as the cop, Jim Henaghan as Fulton. **Writer:** Lorenzo Semple, Jr. **Director:** Murray Golden.

True or Falseface/Super Rat Race (airdates: Mar. 9, 1966; Mar. 10, 1966). False Face, the ultimate master of disguise, steals a jeweled crown and replaces it with a fake. Later, Batman arrives at an armored car theft, but False Face gets away. One of his gang who was captured squeals on his boss and takes Batman and Robin to his hideout. But it is a trap: Falseface knocks out the crimefighters with gas and they are glued to some subway tracks where a train is due at any second. **Guest cast:** Malachi Throne as Falseface, Myrna

9

Fahey as Blaze, S. John Launer as George W. Ladd, Larry Owens as Bevans, Joe Brooks as the fat man, Billy Curtis as the midget, Patrick Whyte as the curator, Brenda Howard, Mike Ragan as the cowboy, Michael Fox as Leo Gore, Gary Owens as the TV announcer. **Writer**: Stephan Kandel. **Director**: William Graham.

The Purr-fect Crime/Better Luck Next Time (airdates: Mar. 17, 1966; Mar. 18, 1966). The Catwoman arrives in town, where she is looking for the Captain Manx treasure. She steals one of a pair of gold cat statues, a key to the treasure, but Batman sets a trap when she steals the second statue. Tracking her to her hideout at a local fur

Julie Newmar as Catwoman, Michael Rennie as the Sandman.

factory, the Dynamic Duo fall through a trapdoor into a pit with a tiger. **Guest cast**: Julie Newmar [*My Living Doll*] as the Catwoman, Jock Mahoney [*Tarzan*] as Leo, Ralph Manza as Felix, Harry Holcomb as Mark Andrews, Pat Zurica as the guard, Alex Sharp as the henchman. **Writers**: Stanley Ralph Ross and Lee Orgel. **Director**: James Sheldon.

The Penguin Goes Straight/Not Yet, He Ain't (airdates: Mar. 23, 1966; Mar. 24, 1966). Has the Penguin turned into a crime fighter? It seems so, as he thwarts one crime after another, then sets up Batman to appear as though he was caught in the act of committing a burglary. With the police now looking for Batman and Robin, the ex-crimefighters search for the Penguin at an amusement park. But they end up being captured and tied up behind a shooting gallery where, at that very moment, Commissioner Gordon and Chief O'Hara are ready to fire their guns at the targets. **Guest cast**: Burgess Meredith as the Penguin, Kathleen Crowley as Sophia Starr, Al Checco as Dove, Harvey Lembeck as the Eagle-Eye, William Beckley as Reggie Rich, Bill Welch as the newsman, Jim Drum as the policeman, Hope Sansberry as Mrs. Van Climber, Ed McCready as Crook, Douglas Bank as Lt. Coppie. **Writers**: Lorenzo Semple, Jr. and John Cardwell. **Director**: Les Martinson.

The Ring of Wax/Give 'Em the Axe (airdates: Mar. 30, 1966; Mar. 31, 1966). The Riddler returns to Gotham City, where he dramatically gives the Caped Crimefighters riddles to his next caper. They arrive at the public library, where the Riddler is stealing an old

book on Inca treasures. When Batman and Robin pursue the Riddler and his henchmen, they are captured and are in danger of being turned into giant candles after being tied above a vat of bubbling wax, where they are at their wit's end as to how to escape the trap. **Guest cast**: Frank Gorshin as the Riddler, Elizabeth Harrower as Miss Prentice, Linda Scott as Moth, Michael Greene as Matches, Ann Myers as Mme. Soleil, Joey Tata as Tallow, Al McGranary as the Mayor. **Writers**: Jack Paritz and Bob Rodgers. **Director**: James B. Clarke.

The Joker Trumps an Ace/Batman Sets the Pace (airdates: April 6, 1966; April 7, 1966). The Joker returns to commit nutty crimes, including stealing hairpins and a hole from a golf course. Batman figures Joker will make a play for a visiting Maharajah's set of gold golf clubs, so he heads to the local course, where the stolen hole is being used to release colored immobilizing gas. The big Maharajah is fork-lifted to a waiting van that Batman arrives just in time to pursue, but the van disappears. Later, they catch up with the Joker and his henchmen, but are overpowered and stuck in a huge chimney that is being filled with poison gas. **Guest cast**: Cesar Romero as the Joker, Dan Seymour as the Maharajah, Jane Wild as Jill, Tol Avery as Prescott Belmont, Angela Greene as Mrs. Belmount, Norm Alden as Lookout, Jacques Roux as the manager, Bebe Louie as the clerk, Owen Buch as the caddy, Byron Keith as Mayor Linseed, Johnny Seven as the second henchman, Bebe Louie as the girl clerk. **Writers**: Francis and Marian Cockrell. **Director**: Richard C. Sarafian.

11

The Curse of Tut/The Pharaoh's in a Rut (airdates: April 13, 1966; April 14, 1966). King Tut, a college professor who, after being struck in the head, believes he is the reincarnation of an Egyptian king, is planning a takeover of Gotham City. He intends to to turn it into a modern version of Thebes, and places a huge sphinx in Gotham Central Park where he begins to make demands. One of his commands includes a permanent exit of the Dynamic Dunderheads, leading to a fight between the crimefighters and King

Cesar Romero as the Joker.

Tut's Tutlings, but the criminals get away. A plan to trap Tut backfires and Bruce is kidnapped and held for ransom, and while being transported up a mountain in an ambulance, the rear door opens and the gurney rolls out the back - where it heads right for a cliff, and a drop in Batman's career. **Guest cast:** Victor Buono as King Tut, Ziva Rodann as Queen Nefertiti, Don "Red" Barry as Vizier, Olan Soule as the newscaster, Frank Christi as Scrivener, Emanuel Thomas, Bill Quinn as a board member, Emanuel Thomas as the reporter, Bill Boyett as the policeman. **Writers:** Robert C. Dennis and Earl Barret. **Director:** Charles R. Rondeau.

The Bookworm Turns/While Gotham City Burns (airdates: April 20, 1966; April 21, 1966). The Bookworm, a criminal who specializes in plots stolen from books, arrives in Gotham and arranges a fake assassination of Commissioner Gordon while he is dedicating a new bridge. Batman and Robin see this on TV and head into town, where Bookworm leaves a clue at the Batmobile indicating he intends to destroy the new bridge. Batman uses one of Bookworm's captured underlings to set a trap, but instead Robin is captured and fastened to a huge bell, where the nasty nitwit schemes to wring his neck. **Guest cast:** Roddy McDowall as the Bookworm, Francine York as Lydia Limpet, John Crawford as the Printer's Devil, Byron Keith as Mayor Linseed, Jan Peters as Typesetter, Jerry Lewis as himself, Tony Aiello as Pressman, Jim O'Hara as the sergeant. **Writer:** Rik Vollaerts. **Director:** Larry Peerce.

Death in Slow Motion/The Riddler's False Notion (airdates: April 27, 1966; April 28, 1966). The Riddler is up to no good again, and he and his gang arrive at a silent film festival dressed like Charlie Chaplin and the Keystone Cops. After they steal the receipts from the box office, a riddle left behind leads Batman to another robbery - and another riddle. This time Batman shows up and gets into a free-for-all fight at a temperance party. Meanwhile, Robin is kidnapped while waiting for Batman, and is tied down to a huge buzzsaw that may lead to a split personality. **Guest cast:** Frank Gorshin as the Riddler, Sherry Jackson as Pauline, Frances X. Bushman as Van Jones, Theo Marcuse as Von Bloheim, Richard Bakalyan as C.B., Walter Woolf King as the manager, Jim Begg as the baker, Burt Brandon as Wolf, Alex Bookston as the guard, Virginia Wood as Sylvia, Judy Price as the cashier. **Writer:** Dick Carr. **Director:** Charles R. Rondeau.

Fine Finny Fiends/Batman Makes the Scene (airdates: May 4, 1966; May 5, 1966). Alfred has been kidnapped by the Penguin, and is brainwashed to help the batty bird rob an upcoming Multi-millionaire's Annual Award Dinner. Back at stately Wayne Manor, Batman and Robin notice that Alfred is acting strangely, and receive a clue from him that enables the crimefighters to locate Penguin's hide-out at a fishing pier. But the fowl fiend captures the Caped Crusader and the Boy Wonder, and puts them in a vacuum tank that is slowly removing all their oxygen. **Guest cast:** Burgess Meredith as the Penguin, Julie Gregg as Finella, Victor Lunden as Octopus, Dal Jenkins as Shark, Louie Elias as Swordfish, Howard Wendell as the millionaire, Bill Williams as the multi-millionaire, Lisa Mitchell as Miss Natural Resources, Frank Wilcox as the million-aire, Charles La Torre as the manager, Ann Reece as Beauty. **Writer:** Sheldon Stewart. **Director:** Tom Gries.

SEASON TWO

Shoot a Crooked Arrow/Walk in the Straight and Narrow (airdates: Sept. 7, 1966; Sept. 8, 1966). A new bad guy is in town,

Shown clockwise from top left: Neil Hamilton as Police Commissioner Gordon, Stafford Repp as Chief O'Hara, Yvonne Craig as Barbara Gordon/Batgirl, Alan Napier as Alfred.

the nefarious Archer, who robs Bruce Wayne's wall safe at stately Wayne Manor. Batman and Robin later capture and put in jail the Archer and his gang, but they are bailed out by common citizens whom the Archer has been giving stolen money to. Batguy tracks the Archer to his hangout in an attempt to find out what the criminal is up to, but they accidentally set off an alarm that gets the duo captured in a huge net. Archer has the crimefighers tied to stakes, then he and his men begin to take turns running at them with lances - intending, no doubt, to prove their point. **Guest cast:** Art Carney as Archer, Sam Jaffe as Albert A. Aardvark, Barbara Nichols as the maid Marilyn, Robert Cornthwaite as Alan A. Dale, Loren Ewing as Big John, Doodles Weaver as Crier Tuck, Arch Moore as Everett Bannister, Dick Clark, Steve Pendleton as first guard, Lee Delano as second guard, James O'Hara as cop, Myran Dell as pedestrian.

Writer: Stanley Ralph Ross. **Director:** Sherman Marks.

Hot Off the Griddle/The Cat and the Fiddle (airdates: Sept. 14, 1966; Sept. 15, 1966). The wicked Catwoman has returned to Gotham, where she begins a school for cat burglars. A trap set by Batman backfires and they are ambushed by Catwoman's Catmen and are thrown from an upper-story window, but miraculously survive the fall. The Dynamic Duo track the cat to her lair, where they are gassed to unconsciousness, then are strapped to aluminum sheets under giant magnifying lenses, where Batman's temper soon boils over. **Guest cast:** Julie Newmar as the Catwoman, Jack Kelly as Jack O'Shea, George Barrows as Charles, Charles Horvath as Thomas, Buck Kartalian as John, David Fresco as Zubin Zucchini, Edy Williams as the hostess, James Brolin as Ralph Staphyloccus, George Neise as Cramer. **Writer:** Stanley Ralph Ross. **Director:** Don Weis.

The Minstrel's Shakedown/Barbequed Batman (airdates Sept. 21, 1966; Sept. 22, 1966). Batman runs into a new villain known as the Minstrel, a sinister singer who swoons while committing crimes. He launches a scheme to extort stock exchange members who must make blackmail payments or he will cause the market to crash. Batman and Robin capture him, but Minstrel escapes after blinding them with a clever device. Knowing that the Dynamic Duo will follow him to his lair, Minstrel moves to another part of town and sets a trap, which they fall into. Now that they are caught, Minstrel puts them on a huge electrical spit, where he plans to grill them for information. **Guest cast:** Van Johnson as the Minstrel, Leslie Perkins as Amanda, John Gallaudet as Courtland, Norm Grabowski as Treble, Remo Pisani as Bass, Army Archerd as Putman,

James O'Hara as the policeman in the basement, Del Moore as the TV newsman, Eddie Garrett as the first broker, Herbert Moss as the second broker, Stu Wilson as the third broker, Tom Anthony as the first waiter, Vince Dedrick as the second waiter, Phyllis Diller as the scrubwoman. **Writers:** Francis and Marion Cockrell. **Director:** Murray Golden.

The Spell of Tut/Tut's Case is Shut (airdates: Sept. 28, 1966; Sept. 29, 1966). A couple of Egyptian-dressed thieves steal a string of amber beads from their wealthy owner, a pretty good clue to Bruce and Dick that King Tut has returned. A clue leads them to Tut and a battle with his gang, and Tut escapes - but not before leaving behind part of his latest project to place Gotham City under his spell. Batman sets a trap by leaving Tut's pyramid (see **The Curse of Tut**) on the grounds of Wayne Manor with the Boy Wonder hiding inside. Tut takes the bait, but he traps Robin in a pit filled with alligators. **Guest cast:** Victor Buono as King Tut, Michael Pataki [*Spiderman*] as Amenophis Twefik, Mariana Hill as Cleo Patrick, Sid Haig as Royal Apothecary, Peter Mamakos as Royal Lapidary, Boyd Santell as Sethos, Bea Bradley as Susan Smith, Rene Paul as the Man of Distinction, Van Williams and Bruce Lee as the Green Hornet and Kato. **Writers:** R.C. Dennis and Earl Bennet. **Director:** Larry Peerce.

The Greatest Mother of Them All/Ma Parker (airdates: Oct. 5, 1966; Oct. 6, 1966). Ma Parker and her gangster family arrive in Gotham to give Batguy some trouble. After robbing the audience at the Ladies Auxiliary's Mother of the Year Award ceremony, Batman and Robin catch up with her brood, but the family escapes capture. As they commit more crimes, members of the family

Shown clockwise from top left: Art Carney as the Archer, Roddy McDowell
as Bookworm, Van Johnson as the Minstrel, and David Wayne as the Mad Hatter.

continue to be caught, until Ma and Legs are captured and are taken
to the state prison. Unknown to Batman, Ma has been replacing the
prison staff with her own men, and now controls the institution.
Meanwhile, a bomb has been put in the Batmobile that will blow up
when the car reaches sixty miles per hour - Holy Detonation! **Guest
cast:** Shelly Winters as Ma Parker, Tisha Sterling as Legs, Mike
Vandever as Mad Dog, James Griffith as Tiger, Robert Biheller as
Pretty Boy, Peter Brooks as Machine Gun, David Lewis as Warden
Crichton, Julie Newmar as the Catwoman, Fran Ryan as Chairlady,
Budd Perkins as the prison guard, Milton Berle as Lefty. **Writer:**
Henry Slesar. **Director:** Oscar Rudolph.

Batgirl on her Batcycle.

The Clock King's Crazy Crimes/The Clock King Gets Crowned (airdates: Oct. 12, 1966; Oct. 13, 1966). Batman is pitted against the Clock King, a strange criminal who does things in his own time. He and his Second Hands rob a jewelry store after gassing everyone inside, bringing the duo rushing to the rescue. Batman catches up with the King of Crime at another caper, but he and his men escape when Batman and Robin are surrounded by giant-size clock main springs. Freeing themselves, the crimefighters track the King to a factory where they are led into a trap. Clock King removes their utility belts and places them in a huge hourglass that is rapidly filling up with the sands of time. **Guest cast:** Walter Slezak as the Clock King, Eileen O'Neil as Millie Second, Herb Anderson as Harry Hummert, Ivan Triesault as Benson Parkhurst, Jerry Doggett as Forbes, Sammy Davis, Jr., Linda Lorimer as the car hop, Roger Bacon as the boy, Sandra Lynn as the girl. **Writers:** Bill Finger and Charles Sinclair. **Director:** James Neilson.

An Egg Grows in Gotham/The Yegg Foes in Gotham (airdates: Oct. 19, 1966; Oct. 20, 1966). Egghead arrives in Gotham, where he plans to take over the town by stealing the city charter and preventing Gotham from fulfilling its obligation to make payment on city property. If his scheme works, he can forclose on Gotham and take over the sprawling metropolis. Before Batman and Robin can go into action, Dick and Bruce are kidnapped with several other people, and all are taken to Egghead's hideout. Once there, he reveals that he knows one of the men is Batman - and decides it is Bruce Wayne. **Guest cast:** Vincent Price as Egghead, Gail Hire as Miss Bacon, Edward Everett Horton as Chief Screaming Eagle, Steve Dunne as Tim Tyler, Ben Welden as Foo Long, Albert Carrier as Pete Savage, Gene Dymarski as Benedict, Bill Dana as Jose Jimenez, Ben Alexander as the plainclothes cop, Mae Clark as the lady, George Fenneman, Byron Keith as Mayor Linseed, Grant Woods as the tour

guide, Burt Mustin as MacDonald, George Fenneman as the newsman, Anthony Brand as the motorcycle cop, Jonathan Hole as the jewelry store clerk, George McCoy as the motorist. **Writer:** Stanley Ralph. **Director:** George Waggner.

The Devil's Fingers/Dead Ringers (airdates: Oct. 26, 1966; Oct. 27, 1966). Evil pianist Chandell arrives in Gotham, a musician who is plotting to get rid of Dick and Bruce so he can marry Aunt Harriet for her fortune. Meanwhile, the millionaire playboy and his ward have been on vacation, but become suspicious of Chandell and return to Gotham. At Chandell's concert, he gives the signal for his three female accomplices to rob an import company. When the Dynamic Duo arrive they are led into a trap, where they are captured and tied to a perforation machine that will turn the crimefighters into rolls of music for a player piano. **Guest cast:** Liberace as Chandell/Harry, Marilyn Hanold as Doe, Edy Williams as Rae, Sivi Aberg as Mimi, James Millhollin as Alfred Slye, Diane Farrell as Sally, Jack Perkins as the piano mover henchman. **Writer:** Lorenzo Semple. **Director:** Larry Peerce.

Hizzoner the Penguin/Dizzoner the Penguin (airdates: Nov. 2, 1966; Nov. 3, 1966). The Penguin plans, of all things, to go straight and become the mayor of Gotham City. As the Penguin wages a massive campaign to win the race for the political position, Batman realizes that the only good defense is an offence, so he runs for office as well. Knowing that Batman may ruin his plans to run the city, the Penguin's G.O.O.N.'s grab the duo and tie them up to a sulphuric acid vat, where they prepare to take a final dip. **Guest cast:** Burgess Meredith as the Penguin, Woodrow Parfrey as Rooper, Cindy Malone as Lulu, George Furth as Gallus, Allen Ludden as David Doodley, Chet Huntley, Jack Bailey as the moderator, Paul Revere and the Raiders, Byron Keith as Mayor Linseed, Murray Roman as Trendek, Joe Besser as Collector, Pat Tidy as the little old lady, Don

17

Julie Newmar as Catwoman.

Wilson as Walter Klondike, Dennis James as Chet Chumley, Little Egypt as the belly dancer, Peg Shirley as Mother, Fuzzy Knight as the blind news dealer, James O'Hara as the cop, John Indrisano as the prisoner, Benny Rubin as the man. **Writer:** Stanford Sherman. **Director:** Oscar Rudolph.

Green Ice/Deep Freeze (airdates: Nov. 9, 1966; Nov. 10, 1966). Mr. Freeze escapes prison in an ice cream truck, then kidnaps Miss Iceland from the Miss Galaxy contest, and plans to make her his frigid wife. Meanwhile, the frozen fiend conducts a campaign to make Batman look both crooked and foolish, resulting in Batman's locating Mr. Freeze's cold storage plant hideout - where he and Robin are frozen by the freeze gun and are transported to a nearby factory to be turned into giant Frost Freezies. **Guest cast:** Otto Preminger as Mr. Freeze, Marie Windsor as Nellie, Dee Hartford as Miss Iceland, Byron Keith as Mayor Linseed, Nicky Blair as Shivers, Kem Dibbs as Chill, Charles O'Donnell as the TV newsman, James O'Hara as the police sergeant, Robert Wiensko as the Iceman, Mike Durkin as the little boy, Joan Twelve as the bathing beauty. **Writer:** Max Hodge. **Director:** George Waggner.

The Impractical Jokers/The Joker's Provokers (airdates: Nov. 16, 1966; Nov. 17, 1966). The Joker is using a mysterious black box that allows him to control time to commit successful robberies. But when Batman and Robin catch up with the villainous clown, they capture the box - which contains nothing except a light and battery, as the Joker had only been hypnotizing his victims. Batman traces Joker to his latest hide-away, where they are caught and Robin is locked inside a spray wax machine, and Batman is strapped down to a giant key-duplicating machine. **Guest cast:** Cesar Romero as the Joker, Kathy Kersh as Cornelia, Christopher Cary as Angus Ferguson, Louis Quinn as Latch, Larry Anthony as Bolt, Howard Duff, Alan Napier as Egbert, Nalerie Szabo as the little girl, Larry Burrell as the first commentator, Clyde Howdy as the second commentator. **Writer:** Jay Thompson. **Director:** James B. Clark.

Marsha, Queen of Diamonds/Marsha's Scheme of Diamonds (airdates: Nov. 23, 1966; Nov. 24, 1966). Chief O'Hara has been placed under the spell of Marsha, the Queen of Diamonds - a situation that allows her to steal a famous diamond. While the Caped Crusaders try to understand the Chief's strange behavior, Commissioner Gordon is also drugged to become her pawn. Marsha uses Gordon to lead Batman into a trap, where Marsha shoots Batman with a love dart to bring him under her spell as well. He overcomes the drug, but her gang captures Robin, and unless Batman marries her Marsha will have the Boy Blunder put to death. Holy shotgun wedding! **Guest cast:** Carolyn Jones [*The Addams Family*] as Marsha, Estelle Winwood as Aunt Hilda, Woody Stode as Grand Mogul, James O'Hara as Sgt. O'Leary, H. Douglas as the announcer, Joyce Nizarri as the girl, Charles Stewart as the clergyman, Ben Gage as the clerk. **Writer:** Stanford Sherman. **Director:** James B. Clark.

Come Back Shame/It's the Way You Play the Game (airdates: Nov. 30, 1966; Dec. 1, 1966). A conniving crooked cowboy known as Shame steals a race car in order to build a vehicle that will outrun the Batmobile. Batman has broadcast that some new hot rod parts are being installed in the Wayne limousine, and sets a trap to catch Shame. Batman allows Shame to steal the car, then follows the crook to his amusement park hideout. In an all-out brawl with Shame's men, the crimebusters are knocked out by a falling chandelier, then are staked outside in front of a herd of stampeding cattle. **Guest cast:** Cliff Robertson as Shame, Joan Staley as Okie Annie, Jack Carter as Hot Rod Harry, Timothy Scott as Messy James, John Mitchum as Rip Snorting, Milton Frome as Laughing Leo, Eric Shea as Andy, Kathryn Minner as the little old lady, James McHale as the guard, Werner Klemperer as Colonel Klink. **Writer:** Stanley Ralph Ross. **Director:** Oscar Rudolph.

The Penguin's Nest/The Bird's Last Jest (airdates: Dec. 7, 1966; Dec. 8, 1966). The Penguin opens a restaurant to obtain handwriting samples from wealthy clients. Once placed back in prison, the villain plans to have a fellow prisoner, a master forger, fill out fake checks in their handwriting. But no matter what he does, the Penguin can't seem to get arrested. Finally, his gang takes Chief O'Hara prisoner, and when Batman and Robin try to save him, they are pinned down by murderous machine gun fire. **Guest cast:** Burgess Meredith as the Penguin, Grace Gaynor as Chickadee, Voltaire Perkins as Judge Moot, Vito Scotti as Matey Dee, Lane Bradford as Cordy Blue, James O'Hara as officer Hoffman, David Lewis as Warden Crichton, Marvin Brody as the bailiff, Violet Carlson as the lady, Stanley Ralph Ross as Ballpoint Baxter, Ted Cassidy [*The Addams Family*] as Lurch. **Writer:** Lorenzo Semple, Jr. **Director:** Murray Golden.

The Cat's Meow/The Bat's Kow Tow (airdates: Dec. 14, 1966; Dec. 15, 1966). The Catwoman's back, this time with a device that can steal voices, and she plans to take those belonging to rock stars Chad and Jeremy. Using the device on Gordon, she learns that the British duo are at Wayne Manor, where she arrives to knock everyone out with a gas. After reawakening, Batman and Robin fight back by rounding up all of Catwoman's thugs, but when they go to arrest her she knocks them out by scratching them with drug-coated claws, then plans to drive them mad with a leaky faucet inside a giant echo chamber. **Guest cast:** Julie Newmar as the Catwoman, Joe Flynn as Benton Belgoody, Tom Castronova as Meanie, Chuck Henderson as Miney, Sharya Wynters as Eenie, Chad Stuart as himself, Jeremy Clyde as himself, Judy Stragis, Ric Roman as Moe, Jay Sebring as Mr. Oceanbring, Peter Leeds as Harry Upps, Maurice Dallimore as Sir Sterling Habits, Anthony Eustrez as the British butler, Steve Allen as Allen Stevens, Calvin Brown as the newsman, James O'Hara as the policeman, Don Ho. **Writer:** Stanley Ralph Ross. **Director:** James B. Clark.

The Puzzles Are Coming/The Duo is Slumming (airdates: Dec. 21, 1966; Dec. 22, 1966). A new villain, a master criminal known as the Puzzler, gives Batman a clue that leads the crime fighter to conclude that multimillionaire Artemus Knab is in danger. Actually the Puzzler is only using Knab to gain entrance at a shindig full of wealthy individuals that he and his thugs rob. When the Dynamic Duo arrive they are gassed and the Puzzler escapes. Later, a new puzzle leads the crimefighters into a trap at his headquarters, where they are placed in the basket of a hot-air balloon that will release the gondola when the airship reaches 20,000 feet. **Guest cast:** Maurice Evans as the Puzzler, Barbara Stuart as Rocket O'Rourke, Paul Smith as Artemus Knab, Robert Miller Driscoll as Blimpy, Alan Emerson as Glider, Jay Della as Ramjet, Santa Claus. **Writer:** Fred De Gorter. **Director:** Jeff Hayden.

The Sandman Cometh/The Catwoman Goeth (A Stitch in Time) (airdates: Dec. 28, 1966; Dec. 29, 1966). A foreign criminal known as the Sandman arrives in Gotham, and teams up with the fatal female, Catwoman. The two plan to pull a fast one on wealthy insomniac J. Pauline Spaghetti. Their scheme works and Sandman knocks out Pauline with gas, then copies her financial records just as Batman comes to the rescue. Sandman escapes, but is followed to his lair by the Caped Crusaders, who are trapped by the Sandman's gang, and Robin is placed under Sandman's spell and is ordered to murder his partner. [Note: The episode named **A Stitch in Time** is a syndicated alternate version of **The Catwoman Goeth**.] **Guest cast:** Michael Rennie [*The Day the Earth Stood Still*] as the Sandman, Julie Newmar as the Catwoman, Richard Peel as Snooze, Spring Byington as J. Pauline Spaghetti, Tony Ballen as Nap, Gypsy Rose Lee as the female newscaster, Pat Becker as Catti,

In the original Batman movie, the Dynamic Duo faced the Penguin, the Joker, the Riddler, and Catwoman.

Jeanie Moore as Catarina as Policewoman Mooney, Lindsey Workman as Tuthill, Ray Montgomery as Officer Dan Dietrich, James Brolin as Officer Reggie Hogan, Valerie Kairys as Kitty. **Writers:** Ellis St. Joseph and Charles Hoffman. **Director:** George Waggner.

The Contaminated Cowl/Mad Hatter Runs A Foul (airdates: Jan. 4, 1967; Jan. 5, 1967). The Mad Hatter returns to Gotham, where he has stopped stealing hats and now uses them to pull off crimes. He steals 700 hat boxes to store his collection, but the crime alerts Batman, who uses the Batcomputer to discover what next crime will be committed by the devilish thief. Batman arrives at the Top Hat Room just as the Mad Hatter steals a valuable ruby, but he manages to escape after covering Batman's cowl with a radioactive spray. Batman is forced to change to another mask after it turns pink from the spray, but he and Robin are captured by the Mad Hatter's men, who place them in a fluoroscope cabinet where X-rays threaten to turn them into glowing corpses. **Guest cast:** David Wayne as Jervis Tetch (the Mad Hatter), Jean Hale as Polly, Barbara Morrison as Hattie Hatfield, Lennie Breman as Benny, Victor Ames as Skimmer, Leonid Kinskey as Prof. Overbeck, Jesslyn Fax as Bonbon, Paul Bryar as Jennings, Gil Stewart as the American operator, Margaret Teele as the British operator, Richard Collier as Otto Puffendorfer, Ivy Bethune as Maudie. **Writer:** Charles Hoffman. **Director:** Oscar Rudolph.

The Zodiac Crimes/The Joker's Hard Times/The Penguin Declines (airdates: Jan. 11, 1967; Jan. 12, 1967; Jan. 18, 1967). The Joker and Penguin join together to launch a crime wave on Gotham City. Joker plans to commit the zodiac crimes - twelve criminal acts based on the signs of the zodiac. Penguin and Joker try to trap Batman and Robin, but are nearly caught themselves. By following some

clues, Batman discovers the location of the Joker's lair, but when he gets there it is empty except for one female assistant, who leads them to a caper in progress. The Penguin is captured while the Joker escapes, but when Batman and Robin arrive to stop the Joker's theft in the Gotham City Museum, they are captured and tied up to an alter below a huge meteor that is rigged to fall on them, with crushing consequences. **Guest cast:** Burgess Meredith as the Penguin, Cesar Romero as the Joker, Terry Moore as Venus, Joe Di Reda as Mars, Hal Baylor as Mercury, Dick Crockett as Neptune, Charles Fredericks as Leo Crustash, Charles Picerni as Uranus, Eddie Saenz as Saturn, Howard Wendell as Basil Bowman, Louis Cordova as the salesman, Vincent Barbi as the truck driver, Rob Reiner as the delivery boy. **Writers:** Stanford Sherman and Steve Kandal. **Director:** Oscar Rudolph.

That Darn Catwoman/Scat, Darn Catwoman (airdates: Jan. 19, 1967; Jan. 25, 1967). Catwoman's assistant, Pussycat, uses a hypnotic drug on Robin, turning him into a criminal and part of her gang. He helps Catwoman steal $200,000 from a safe at Wayne Manor, then Catwoman phones Batman and tells him that she will kill Robin if he or the police try to interfere with her crime spree. Batman tracks Robin and Catwoman to her hideout, where he is captured and Robin begins cutting a rope that will release the hammer of a giant mousetrap that Batman is tied to. **Guest cast:** Julie Newmar as the Catwoman, Leslie Gore as Pussycat, J. Pat O'Malley as Pat Pending, Jock Gaynor as Spade, George Sawaya as Templar, Allen Jenkins as Little Al, Tony Epper as Marlowe, Steve Franken as Rudy, David Renard as Price Ibn Kereb, Rolla Altman as the girl teller. **Writer:** Stanley Ralph Ross. **Director:** Oscar Rudolph.

Penguin Is a Girl's Best Friend/Penguin Sets a Trend/Penguin's

Disasterous End (airdates: Jan. 26, 1967; Feb. 1, 1967; Feb. 2, 1967). When Batman and Robin see the Penguin pulling off a holdup they try to stop him. But the fiend is only shooting a movie, and Batman is forced to agree to take part in the film in order to avoid false-arrest charges being leveled at him. The Penguin forces Batman to do a hundred of kissing Marsha, Queen of Diamonds, then sets up the Dynamic Duo to be trapped when they arrive to prevent a theft. While still on camera, they are attached to a giant catapult that is about to launch them into oblivion. **Guest cast:** Burgess Meredith as the Penguin, Carolyn Jones as Marsha, Estelle Winwood as Aunt Hilda, Alan Reed, Jr. as Gen. MacGruder, Bob Hastings as Beasley, Kimbery Allen as Miss Patterson, Frank Baron as the first henchmen, Milton Stark as Mr. Tambor, Ted Fish as the truck driver, Frank Conte as the second henchman, Brad Logan as the workman. **Writer:** Stanford Sherman. **Director:** James Clark.

Batman's Anniversary/A Riddling Controversy (airdates: Feb. 8, 1967; Feb. 9, 1967). Batman and Robin answer a distress call from Gordon, only to find themselves arriving at an anniversary dinner for Batman. When a gift for charity is presented, the Riddler and his men arrive to steal it from under the very noses of the fearless fighters of freedom. As usual, the criminal leaves behind a riddle before making a successful escape, and it is deciphered by Batman, who, with Robin, ends up in an underwater battle against the Riddler and his men. They escape again, so Batman tends to other business: posing for a marshmallow figure on top of a giant three-story cake that he is lifted upon with Robin, where they find the topping substituted with quicksand by the Riddler. **Guest cast:** John Astin [*The Addams Family*] as the Riddler, Deanna Lund [*Land of the Giants*] as Anna Gram, Martin Kosleck as Prof. Charm, Ken Scott as Down, Jim Lefebvre as Across, Bryon Keith as Mayor Linseed, Eddie Quillan as Newsie, Bud Furillo as the reporter, Tom Kelly as the TV announcer. **Writer:** W.P. D'Angelo. **Director:** James Clark.

The Joker's Last Laugh/The Joker's Epitaph (airdates: Feb. 15, 1967; Feb. 16, 1967). Commissioner Gordon is being driven crazy by the Joker, who has attached a loudspeaker to his jacket playing hysterical laughter. Meanwhile, Batman and Robin arrive at a bank where the Joker has been passing counterfeit money, and after following a series of clues he is led to the offices of the Penthouse Comic Book Publishers - Joker's latest hideout. Bruce arrives at the office to try to trick Joker into printing some phony currency, but the Prince of Crime catches on that something is up when he sees Robin and has the Boy Blunder tied up to a giant printing press. Joker then orders Bruce to throw the switch to activate the printing machine - a pressing problem for Robin. **Guest cast:** Cesar Romero as the Joker, Phyllis Douglas as Josephin Miller, Lawrence Montaigne as Mr. Glee, J. Edward McKinley as Mr. Flamm, Clint Ritchi as Boff, Ed Deemer as Yock, Hollie Haze as Miranda Fleece, Oscar Beregi as Dr. Floyd. **Writer:** Lorenzo Semple, Jr. **Director:** Oscar Rudolph.

Catwoman Goes to College/Batman Displays His Knowledge (airdates: Feb. 22, 1967; Feb. 23, 1967). After being released from prison, Catwoman enrolls at college and takes a course in criminology. While there, she steals a statue of the Caped Crusaders, bringing the crimefighters to the scene. She is using the statue as a uniform pattern for one of her thugs, who dresses up as Batman and holds up a supermarket. Later, the real Batman is arrested for the crime, but a disguise allows him to escape from jail. Now a wanted man, Batman goes looking for Catwoman, but she captures him and Robin, then places them in a huge coffee cup below a monstrous percolator full of acid. **Guest cast:** Julie Newmar as the Catwoman, Paul Mantee as Cornell, Sheldon Allman as Penn, Jacques Bergerac

as Freddy the Fence, Whitney Blake as Amber Forever, Paul Picerni as Brown, Art Linkletter, David Lewis as Warden Crichton, Jan Burrell as Alma Mater. **Writer:** Stanley Ralph Ross. **Director:** Robert Sparr.

A Piece of the Action/Batman's Satisfaction (airdate: Mar. 1, 1967; Mar. 2, 1967). The Green Hornet and Kato have arrived in Gotham City, and Batman isn't sure if they are friends or foes. The Green Hornet is trying to end the activities of a criminal named Colonel Gumm, and Batman arrives to do the same thing, but all four are trapped by Gumm and his men. While Batman and Robin stand by to await their turn, the Green Hornet and Kato are attached to a huge perforation machine that is about to turn them into human postage stamps. **Guest cast:** Van Williams as the Green Hornet, Bruce Lee as Kato, Roger C. Carmel as Col. Gumm, Diane McBain as Pinky Pinkerston, Edward G. Robinson, Alex Rocco as Block, Seymour Cassel as Cancelled, Harry Frazier as Mr. Stample, James O'Hara as police Sergeant Semple, Angelique Pettyjohn as the first model, Jan Watson as the second model, Dusty Cadis as the waiter. **Writer:** Charles Hoffman. **Director:** Oscar Rudolph.

King Tut's Coup/Batman's Waterloo (airdates: Mar. 8, 1967; Mar. 9, 1967). King Tut returns to steal a sarcophagus from the Gotham City Museum, then prepares to kidnap the daughter of a wealthy socialite to make her his queen. Batman is hoodwinked and sent to the wrong location to capture Tut, while he kidnaps the girl, who is a look-alike of Cleopatra. Batman later tracks Tut down to his lair, but is captured and placed inside an Egyptian casket, where he is being lowered into a pool of boiling oil. **Guest cast:** Victor Buono as King Tut, Grace Lee Whitney [*Star Trek*] as Neila, Lee Meriwether [*The Time Tunnel*] as Lisa, Tim O'Kelly as Jester, Suzy Knickerbocker, Tol Avery as Deputy Mayor Zorty, Lloyd Haynes as Lord Chancellor, James O'Hara as the Irish cop, Joseph Abdullah as the guard, Nelson Olmsted as John E. Carson, Walter Reed as the officer, Tommy Noonan as Jolly Jackson, Richard Bakalyan as Fouad Sphinx, Terri Messina as Penny, Barry Dennen as the valet. **Writer:** Stanley Ralph Ross. **Director:** James B. Clark.

Black Widow Strikes Again/Caught in the Spider's Den (airdates: Mar. 15, 1967; Mar. 16, 1967). The Black Widow is in town pulling off bank robberies by using a brain short-circuiting weapon. Batman sets a trap for her, and thanks to some Anti-Short-Circuiting Batelectrodes they are immune to her device. But she is able to use spider venom to escape, where they have the sleuths trail her to her underground hideout, only to become entangled in a giant spiderweb and are being approached by two giant black widow spiders. **Guest cast:** Tallulah Bankhead as Mrs. Max Black, Don "Red" Barry as Tarantula, Grady Sutton as Irving Cash, Mike Lane as Daddy Long Leggs, Al Ferrara as Trap Door, Meg Wylie as Grandma, George Raft, Pitt Herbert as Irving Leghorn, George Chandler as Grandpa, Walker Edmiston as the teller, Milton Stark as Irving Bracken, Don Briggs as Irving Irving, Richard Krisher as the motorcycle cop. **Writer:** Robert Mintz. **Director:** Oscar Rudolph.

Pop Goes the Joker/Flop Goes the Joker (airdates: Mar. 22, 1967; Mar. 23, 1967). The Joker arrives in town and begins destroying works of art, but the criminal's efforts are hailed as artistic triumphs. Batman is unable to do anything against him, so he waits until the Joker announces that he has opened an art school for millionaires only. Bruce signs up while the Joker kidnaps the entire class and holds them for ransom - until Robin arrives, and is aided in a fight with Joker's men by Bruce. But they are overpowered and Bruce is tied up while the Boy Wonder is in danger of being cut to shreds by

some rotating knives. **Guest cast:** Cesar Romero as the Joker, Diana Ivarson as Baby Jane Towser, Reginald Gardiner as Bernie Parks, Jan Arvan as the judge, Jerry Catron as the first henchman, Jack Perkins as the second henchman, Fritz Feld as Oliver Muzzy, Jody Gilbert as Mrs. Putney, Owen McGiveney as Charles, Gail Ommerle as the first browser, Milton Stark as the second browser. **Writer:** Stanford Sherman. **Director:** George Waggner.

Ice Spy/The Duo Defy (airdates: Mar. 29, 1967; Mar. 30, 1967). Cold-blooded Mr. Freeze has a new hideout inside an iceberg, and he uses giant magnets to stop the *Gotham Queen* and kidnap an Icelandic scientist. The doctor has a formula for instant ice that Mr. Freeze needs, then after taking it he holds the scientist for ransom in his new headquarters below a skating rink. Batman and Robin locate his hideout, but are captured and placed in a Sub-Zero Temperature Vaporizing Cabinet, where they will be vaporized into oblivion. **Guest cast:** Eli Wallach as Mr. Freeze, Leslie Parish as Glacia Galze, Elisha Cook, Jr. as Prof. Isaacson, H.M. Wyant as Frosty, John Archer as Carlisle, Anthony Aiello as the first officer, Alfred Daniels as the second officer, Ron Riley as the usher, Eddie Nesh as the Coast Guard officer. **Writer:** Charles Hoffman. **Director:** Oscar Rudolph.

SEASON THREE

Enter Batgirl/Exit Penguin (airdate: Sept. 14, 1967). The Penguin kidnaps Commissioner Gordon's daughter Barbara in hopes of avoiding run-ins with the police. She is naturally reluctant to go along with his marriage plans, particularly when she is getting ready to launch her own crime-fighting career as Batgirl. **Guest cast:** Burgess Meredith as the Penguin, Elizabeth Harrower as Drusilla, Jonathan Troy as Reverend Hazlitt, Jon Walter as the first henchman. **Writer:** Stanford Sherman. **Director:** Oscar Rudolph.

Ring Around the Riddler (airdate: Sept. 21, 1967). The Riddler is back, this time launching a scheme to control prize fighting in Gotham. Aided by the Siren, she tries to use her wail to knock out Batgirl when the female crimefighter tries to interfere with the Riddler's plans, but she escapes Siren and her thugs. Meanwhile, Batman is tricked into a boxing match in Gotham Square Garden with the Riddler. **Guest cast:** Frank Gorshin as the Riddler, Joan Collins as Siren, Peggy Ann Garner as Betsy boldface, Jerry Quarry, Armando Ramos, Paul Rojas, James Brolin as Kid Gulliver, Nicholas Georgiade as Kayo, Gil Perkins as Cauliflower, Peggy Olson as the cashier. **Writer:** Charles Hoffman. **Director:** Sam Strangis.

The Wall of the Siren (airdate: Sept. 28, 1967). The Riddler has been hauled off to the pokey, but the Siren remains in town to cause the Dynamic Duo and Batgirl further problems. The Siren, actually named Lorelei Circe, places Police Commissioner Gordon under her hypnotic spell when she lets go with her seven-octave wail. She orders the friend of Batman to locate the crimefighter and discover his true identity. **Guest cast:** Joan Collins as Siren, Mike Mazurki as Allergro, Cliff Osmond as Andante. **Writer:** Stanley Ralph Ross. **Director:** George Waggner.

The Sport of Penguins/A Horse of Another Color (airdates: Oct. 5, 1967; Oct. 12, 1967). Batgirl foils a robbery by the Penguin, but he leaves behind an umbrella-bomb that must be disarmed by Batman and Robin. Later, the Penguin teams up with Lola Lasagne in a scheme to enter a horse in the Bruce Wayne handicap. When Lola and Penguin learn that the proceeds of the race will go to charity, they plan to fix the race so they will both end up winners. **Guest cast:** Burgess Meredith as the Penguin, Ethel Merman as Lola Lasagne, Horace McMahon as Glu Gluten, Lewis Charles as Armband, Joe Brooks as Visor, Herbert Anderson as the racing secretary, Constance Davis as Myrtle, Allen Emerson as the photographer, Gary Owens as the radio announcer. **Writer:** Charles Hoffman. **Director:** Sam Strangis.

The Unkindest Tut of All (airdate: Oct. 19, 1967). Tut arrives in town, no longer a criminal, but a predictor of crimes - capers that he is actually behind. When Batman and Robin try to crimp his style, Tut plants a homing device on the Batmobile and learns that the Batcave is below Wayne Manor. Making a quick deduction, he challenges Bruce Wayne and his alter-ego to appear in public at the same time. **Guest cast:** Victor Buono as King Tut, Patti Gilbert as Shirley, James Gammon as Osiris, Cathleen Cordell as the librarian, James Ramsey as the TV announcer. **Writer:** Stanley Ralph Ross. **Director:** Sam Strangis.

Louie the Lilac (airdate: Oct. 26, 1967). Louie the Lilac plans to take over the minds of groovy Gotham City's mellow flower children. Their leader is kidnapped, and a clue is left for Batman and Robin to come to her rescue - and a trap. Arriving at a flower shop, the Dynamic Duo are knocked out by potent poseys and are surrounded by giant, man-eating lethal lilacs. **Guest cast:** Milton Berle as Louie the Lilac, Lisa Seagram as Lila, Dick Bakayan as Arbutus, Karl Lukas as Acacia, Schuyler Aubrey as Princess Primrose/Thelma Jones, Jimmy Boyd as Dogwood. **Writer:** Dwight Taylor. **Director:** Sam Srangis.

The Ogg and I/How to Hatch a Dinosaur (airdates: Nov. 2, 1967; Nov. 9, 1967). Egghead is back, and kidnaps Commissioner Gordon in order to obtain a ransom from Gotham City. Meanwhile, Egghead's partner Olga is planning a theft, which she pulls off with the help of her cossack warriors. However, Batman and Robin are hidden inside the samovar she stole, and when they try to surprise her they are knocked out by a gas. Later, after avoiding being captured by Batman and Batgirl, Olga and Egghead prepare to hatch a million-year-old dinosaur egg and unleash the beast on Gotham City. **Guest cast:** Vincent Price as Egghead, Anne Baxter as Olga, Alfred Dennis as Omar Orloff, Alan Hale, Jr. as Gilligan, Violet Carlson as the old lady, Billy Corcoran as the boy scout, James O'Hara as the policeman, James Lanphier as the Indian man, Par Becher as the technician, Mary Benoit as Petula, Jon Lormer as Prof. Dactyl, Donald Elson as Tendor. **Writer:** Stranford Sherman. **Director:** Oscar Rudolph

Surf's Up! Joker's Under! (airdate: Nov. 16, 1967). The Joker is back, and is trying to run Gotham Beach with the help of some muscle-bound beachcomber thugs. Joker kidnaps a surfing champion - a friend of Barbara Gordon - and uses a device to transfer the surfer's skills to himself. Now it's up to Batman to prevent the Joker from winning a surfing contest. **Guest cast:** Cesar Romero as the Joker, Sivi Aberg as Undine, Skip Ward as Riptide, Ron Burke as Wipeout, Ronnie Knox as Skip Parker, John Mitchum as Hot Dog Harrigan, Joyce Lederer as the girl surfer, Johnnie Green and His Green Men. **Writer:** Charles Hoffman. **Director:** Oscar Rudolph.

The Londinuim Larcenies/The Foggiest Notion/The Bloody Tower (airdates: Nov. 23, 1967; Nov. 30, 1967; Dec. 7, 1967). A series of baffling crimes require the services of Batman, Robin and Batgirl in Londinium. Once there, they learn that Lord Phogg and Lady Penelope Peasoup plan to steal the crown jewels. But Batman and Robin may be off the case permanently after a bomb is attached to the Batmobile, set to go off when they arrive at the Londinium branch of the Batcave. **Guest cast:** Rudy Vallee as Lord Phogg,

Left: Frank Gorshin as the Riddler, Right: Burgess Meredith as the Penguin.

Glynis Johns as Lady Penelope Peasoup, Lyn Peters as Prudence, Lynley Lawrence as Kit, Stacey Maxwell as Rosamond, Aleta Rotell as Daisy, Larry Anthony as Digby, Maurice Dallimore as Watson, Monty Landis as Basil, Harvey Jason as Scudder, Nannettte Turner as Sheila, Gil Stuart as the bobby. **Writers:** Elkan Allan and Charles Hoffman. **Director:** Oscar Rudolph.

Catwoman's Dressed to Kill (airdate: Dec. 14, 1967). Catwoman's theft of some high-fashion gowns is thwarted by Batman, Robin, and Batgirl, but the girl crimefighter is caught and kidnapped. Batman is informed by Catwoman that Batgirl is tied to a pattern cutting machine that threatens to bisect her - giving the crimefighter a choice of saving Batgirl's life or stopping Catwoman's next theft. **Guest cast:** Eartha Kitt as the Catwoman, Rudi Gernreich as himself, James Griffith as Manx, Dirk Evans as Angora, Karen Huston as Queen Bess, Jeanie Moore as the woman, Gerald Peters as the attendant. **Writer:** Stanley Ralph Ross. **Director:** Sam Strangis.

The Ogg Couple (airdate: Dec. 21, 1967). Egghead and Olga, Queen of the Cossacks, return to Gotham, where they raid the Gotham City Museum. Batman predicts they will next rob a bank, but arrive too late to catch the criminals. Batgirl, meanwhile, has convinced Egghead to doublecross his partners, but she actually is being led into a deadly trap when the villains try to drown her in a vat of caviar. **Guest cast:** Vincent Price as Egghead, Anne Baxter as Olga, Violet Carlson as the old woman, Billy Corcoran as the boy scout, Donald Elson as the bank manager, Ed Ling as the museum guard, Penelope Gillette as passerby. **Writer:** Stan Sherman. **Director:** Oscar Rudolph.

The Funny Feline Felinies/The Joke's on Catwoman (airdates: Dec. 28, 1967; Jan. 4, 1968). After serving his prison term, Joker is picked up by Catwoman, and they begin plans to blow the vault in the Federal depository in Gotham. While Catwoman and the Joker go after a cache of gunpowder to be used in the robbery, Batgirl is following a clue that puts her on their trail. But Batgirl becomes captured and tied up with quickly-contracting Cat Whiskers which will soon squeeze the stuffings from the girl crimefighter. **Guest cast:** Eartha Kitt as the Catwoman, Cesar Romero as the Joker, Kick Kallman as Little Louie Kallman, Ronald Long as Karnaby Katz, Sandy Kevin as Giggler, Bobby Hall as Laughter, David Lewis as Warden Critchen, Pierre Salinger as Lucky Pierre, Rusty Lane as the judge, Dick Kallman as Little Louie Groovy, Joe E. Ross [*It's About Time*] as Louis Groovy's agent, Louis Quinn as Mr. Keeper, Christine Nelson as Mrs. Keeper. **Writer:** Stanley Ralph Ross. **Director:** Oscar Rudolph.

Louie's Lethal Lilac Time (airdate: Jan. 11, 1968). Bruce and Dick are kidnapped by the henchmen of Louie the Lilac, a situation discovered by Batgirl, who tells Commissioner Gordon. But the Commissioner, for some strange reason, cannot locate the Caped Crusaders. At the Batcave, loyal butler Alfred uses the Batcomputer to discover the location of his boss. Knowing Batgirl's identity, he contacts her to rescue the millionaire playboy and his ward. When she and the police arrive at Louie's headquarters, Batgirl sneaks in, only to be caught and placed in a vat being filled with boiling oil. **Guest cast:** Milton Berle as Louie the Lilac, Nobu McCarthy as Lotus, Percy Helton as Gus the janitor, Ronald Knight as Sassafras, John Dennis as Saffron. **Writer:** Stanford Sherman. **Director:** Oscar Rudolph.

Nora Clavicle and Her Ladies' Crime Club (airdate: Jan. 18, 1968). Mayor Linseed is forced by his wife to appoint Nora Clavicle, a woman's rights spokesperson, as the new commissioner of Gotham City. The whole police force is replaced with females, and a trap is set for the three Caped Crimefighters. Nora's female thugs rob a bank, and Batman pursues them to their hideout, accom-

24

panied by Robin and Batgirl. The three are caught and are tied into a human knot - if they move in the slightest they will be strangled. **Guest cast:** Barbara Rush as Nora Clavicle, June Wilkinson as Evelina, Inga Neilson as Angelina, Byron Keith as Mayor Linseed, Larry Gelman as the bank manager, Jean Byron as Mrs. Millie Linseed, Judy Parker as the telephone operator, Ginny Gan, Rhea Andrece, Alyce Andrece and Elizabeth Baur as the policewomen. **Writer:** Stanford Sherman. **Director:** Oscar Rudolph.

Penguin's Clean Sweep (airdate: Jan. 25, 1968). Penguin and his henchmen take a guided tour of the U.S. Mint in Gotham, but when Batman arrives he finds they have stolen nothing. Unfortunately, while he was there, the quacking villain has contaminated the money, making it impossible to use. While Batgirl heads to a bank which part of the currency was already shipped to, Batman and Robin go to the hospital that holds the rare vaccine for the infectious disease left by the Penguin. When they arrive, they discover that the Penguin and his men have vaccinated themselves and destroyed the remaining drug. As they escape the hospital, Penguin and his thugs leave behind three contaminated flies to infect and finish off the Dynamic Dimwits. **Guest cast:** Burgess Meredith as the Penguin, John Vivyan as the bank director, John Beradino as the doctor, Monique Van Vooren as Miss Clean, Charles Dierkop as Dustbag, Newell Oestreich as Pushbroom, William Phillips as the Mint supervisor, Richard Jury as the bank teller, Pam McMyler as the teenage girl, Len Felber as the policeman. **Writer:** Stanford Sherman. **Director:** Oscar Rudolph.

The Great Escape/The Great Train Robbery (airdate: Feb. 2, 1968; Feb. 8, 1968). Shame has broken out of prison and returns to Gotham, where he joins his new gang and gives Batman a puzzling riddle as a clue to his next crime. Batgirl solves the riddle and meets Batman and Robin downtown, just as Shame and his gang are robbing the Gotham City Opera House. When the Terrific Trio try to stop Shame, the sinister cowboy uses fear gas on the crimefighters, turning them into sniveling cowards as Shame escapes with a kidnapped Batgirl. **Guest cast:** Cliff Robertson as Shame, Dina Merrill as Calamity Jan, Hermione Baddeley as Frontier Fanny, Barry Dennen as Fred, Dorothy Kirnstein as Leonora Sotto Voce, Brian Sullivan as Fortissimo Fra Diavolo, Victor Lindin as Chief Standing Pat, Jerry Mathers as Pops the doorman, Arnold Stang as Peter the gun shop owner. **Writer:** Stanford Sherman. **Director:** Oscar Rudolph.

I'll Be a Mummy's Uncle (airdate: Feb. 22, 1968). King Tut escapes from a psychiatrist's office, and rejoins his gang to launch a new crime wave on Gotham. He has located a deposit of the world's hardest metal below Wayne Manor, and he plans to pull off robberies to buy a piece of property near the mansion, where he will sink a shaft that will cross onto Bruce Wayne's property and uncover the Nilanium. Unfortunately, the shaft being dug is aimed right at the Batcave, and if Tut breaks through he will discover the secret identities of Batman and Robin. **Guest cast:** Victor Buono as King Tut, Angela Dorian as Florence of Arabia, Henry Youngman as Manny the Mesopotamian, Joey Tata as Suleiman the Great, Kathleen Freeman as Rosetta Stone, Tony Epper as Tutling, Jock Mahoney [*Tarzan*] as H.L. Hunter. **Writer:** Stanley Ralph Ross. **Director:** Sam Strangis.

The Joker's Flying Saucer (airdate: Feb. 29, 1968). While in prison, the Joker steals the plans for a flying saucer from a mad scientist's cellmate. Once out of prison, Batman learns his intentions

of building the U.F.O. and throwing Gotham City into a panic. But what the crimefighter doesn't know is that the Joker has hidden a powerful explosive aboard the Batmobile, set to go off at midnight - finishing off the troublesome two. **Guest cast:** Cesar Romero as the Joker, Corinne Calvet as Emerald, Richard Bakalyan as Verdigris, Jeff Burton as Shamrock, Byron Keith as Mayor Linseed, Tony Gardner as Chartruese, Fritz Feld as Prof. Greenleaf, Ellen Corby as Mrs. Green. **Writer:** Charles Hoffman. **Director:** Sam Strangis.

The Entrancing Dr. Cassandra (airdate: Mar. 7, 1968). Invisible crooks have robbed Gotham City Bank, sending the Dynamic Duo to investigate the crime. Commissioner Gordon is warned by the invisible Dr. Cassandra that the police can do nothing to stop her crimewave, but he warns Batman about her next threatened robbery. Arriving at a jewelry store they find Cassandra stealing a fabulous diamond - but are shot with her Alvino-ray gun, that turns them into flat, two dimensional creatures. The three flattened foes of crime are then taken to the police department and slipped under Commissioner Gordon's door. **Guest cast:** Ida Lupino as Dr. Cassandra, Howard Duff as Cabala, David Lewis as Warden Critchen, Bill Zuckert as the prison captain, G. David Schine as himself. **Writer:** Stanley Ralph Ross. **Director:** Sam Strangi.

Minerva, Mayhem and Millionaires (airdate: Mar. 14, 1968). A villain known as Minerva is using her health spa to learn the secrets of her wealthy customers by placing a hairdryer over their head that is actually a mental-eavesdropping device. When Bruce Wayne goes to her spa for a treatment, his brain is picked and Minerva obtains the combination to the Wayne Foundation safe. When Batman discovers what she is up to, he and Robin arrive at the Minerva's Mineral Health Spa to give her a piece of their mind - only to be placed in a huge pressure cooker. **Guest cast:** Zsa Zsa Gabor as Minerva, Jacques Bergerac as Freddie the Fence, Bill Smith as Adonis, Mark Bailey as Apollo, All Ferrara as Atlas, Yvonne Arnett as Aphrodite, William Dozier as Adonis, Boyd Santell as the security guard, George Neise as Mr. Shubert, Howie Horwitz as himself. **Writer:** Charles Hoffman. **Director:** Sam Strangis.

MOVIES

Batman (Release date: August 3, 1966, a theater-released movie based on the TV series). An anonymous tip nearly turns Batman into shark food, but the trusty Shark-repellent Batspray wards off the attacking predator. A nearby boat has disappeared, and Batman does not yet know that its mysterious loss is tied into a plot launched by the greatest group of villains ever put together: Catwoman, the Joker, the Riddler, and the Penguin. When Batman discovers Penguin has bought a preatomic submarine from the Navy, he knows the criminal was involved with the ship - proven when a missile from the sub skywrites a warning to Batman from the four evil-doers. At their hideout, the crooks are scheming to kidnap the United World Security Council, who are due to meet in Gotham City, and hold them for ransom. But their most immediate task is to eliminate the Dynamic Duo! **Guest cast:** Lee Meriwether [*The Time Tunnel*] as Catwoman, Cesar Romero as the Joker, Burgess Meredith as the Penguin, Frank Gorshin as the Riddler, Reginald Denny as Commodore Schmidlapp, Milton Frome as Vice Admiral Fangschleister, George Sawaya as Quetch, Dick Crockett as Morgan, Gil Perkins as Bluebeard, Maurice Dallimore as the British delegate, Teru Shimada as the Japanese delegate, Ivan Triesault as the West German delegate, Jack La Lanne. **Writer:** Lorenzo Semple Jr. **Director:** Leslie H. Martinson.

Captain Power
and the Soldiers of the Future

review by William E. Anchors, Jr.

Production credits:

Executive Producers	Gary Goddard
	Tony Christopher
	Douglas Netter
Created by	Gary Goddard
	Tony Christopher
Music	Gary Guttman

Regular cast:

Captain Jonathan Power	Tim Dunigan
[Leader of the Soldiers of the Future]	
Major Matthew "Hawk" Masterson	Peter MacNeill
[Master of aerial combat]	
Lt. Michael "Tank" Ellis	Sven Thorsen
[Ground assault unit]	
Sgt. Robert "Scout" Baker	Maurice Dean Wint
[Espionage and communications]	
Corporal Jennifer "Pilot" Chase	Jessica Steen
[Tactical systems expert]	
Mentor	Bruce Gray
[The Soldiers' computer hologram]	
Colonel Cypher	Lorne Gossette
[Resistance leader of Angel City]	
Lord Dread	David Hemblen
[Leader of the Bio Dread Empire]	
Soaron, the Sky Sentry (voice)	Deryck Hazel
Blastarr (voice)	John Davies
Overmind (voice)	Tedd Dillon
Overunit Wilson	Kelly Bricher
Laccki (voice)	Don Franks

Number of episodes: 22 one half hour segments

Airdates: Syndicated beginning in the fall of 1988, finishing up all new episodes by the summer of 1989. The actual airdates for each varied from station to station.

Premise: In the year 2147 humanity has been nearly wiped out after the Metal Wars, where machine battled man - and machines won. Out of the ashes of the defeat have come Captain Power and the Soldiers of the Future, masters of combat with their fantastic power suits, becoming humanity's only hope of defeating Lord Dread and his Bio Dread Empire.

Editor's comments: Although intended for younger viewers and created primarily to sell toys, the stories featured in this show were very adult and entertaining, and except for some occasional animation, the special effects and model work were excellent. It is a shame the program didn't last longer, but Captain Power was ultimately cancelled when its toy company sponsors withdrew support. Why doesn't someone digitize Mattel?

Shattered. Scout infiltrates an Energy Substation, and although nearly caught, manages to destroy the installation. Dread is upset over Power setting back his New Order plans, and decides to use someone from his past to destroy Power: an old girl friend, Athena Samuels. The Soldiers regroup back at headquarters, where they receive a message from Athena, whom Power has not heard from in years. She had been his father's lab assistant, and he had fallen in love with her, but lost track of the girl when the Metal Wars began. Now Pilot is flying him there, not realizing that Athena has been digitized (a method Dread uses to convert people into computerized versions of their former selves, putting them in his power) and is part of a trap to digitize the leader of the Soldiers of the Future. **Guest cast:** Ann-Marie MacDonald as Athena. **Writer:** Larry Ditillio. **Director:** Larry Azzopardi.

Wardogs. Scout has monitored a transmission regarding raids by persons unknown on Dread's forces in sector 24. Power knows of no resistance units in that area, and wants to contact the group in hopes of enlisting their aid against Dread. The group in question turns out to be the "Wardogs", led by a Cherokee warrior who guides highly-effective assaults on Dread's units. While Hawk watches, the Wardogs attack a Dread supply train, destroying it, or so they think. As they walk away a hidden laser cannon opens up nearly obliterating them, but the Wardogs are saved by Hawk when he blasts the cannon. When the Wardogs see him, they shoot the flying soldier down, not realizing he was on their side. Meanwhile, Tank and Scout locate a hidden Dread installation, possibly part of the New Order operation that Dread is working on. **Guest cast:** Kate Trotter as Vi, Graham Greene as Cherokee, Jane Luk as Keiko, Michael Woods as Overunit Webber. **Writer:** Larry Ditillio. **Director:** George Mendeluk.

Abyss. A communications signal is picked up at headquarters - an obsolete military code from sector 42. Power feels that it may be a signal from a resistance unit, so they fly there to investigate. At Volcania, Dread is alerted to the signal as well, and orders the flying sentry Soaron to investigate. When Power and Hawk arrive at the signal location, they are attacked and knocked out by a group of human soldiers. When they awake, they find themselves in the underground headquarters of a military installation run by a deranged General Briggs, who is waiting for orders from the President (killed years earlier in the Metal Wars) to use his soldiers to counter-attack Dread. Briggs is convinced Power and Hawk are traitors, and after torturing and interrogating the men, he orders his second in command to execute them. **Guest cast:** Michael J. Reynolds as Gen. Briggs, Hardee T. Lineham as Masters, Victor Ertmanis as the interrogator, Ray Prisley as Hamilton Price, Tim Koetting as the soldier. **Writer:** J. Michael Straczynski. **Director:** Larry Azzopardi.

Sven Thorsen as Lt. Michael "Tank" Ellis [Ground assault unit].

Final Stand. To learn what Dread's next operation will be, the Soldiers lure in some Dread warriors and trap them, allowing Power to make off with a Bio Dread transmitter. The soldiers fly to the location mentioned in the memory of the computer, hoping to stop an attack on the humans who live there. When they arrive, they find marauders terrorizing their fellow humans. Their leader is a genetically engineered super-human (as is Tank) named Hasko. The oversized warrior tells Power that he is holding hostages with a bomb that will explode in one hour. He will allow it to go off unless Power allows Tank to remove his armor and face Hasko in a fight to the death in order to settle an old grudge. **Guest cast:** Charles Seixas as Hasko, Susan Conway as the woman. **Writer:** J. Michael Straczynski. **Director:** Doug Williams.

Pariah. Dread has his Troopers out looking for a human, but the teenager escapes. Nearby are Pilot and Power, also searching for something, but Soaron arrives and temporarily interrupts their operation. They manage to elude Soaron, while elsewhere Dread warriors are closing in on the boy they have been hunting. Hawk sees them and attacks. He is badly outnumbered and tries to fly away with the teenager but is shot down. Hiding among the ruble, the boy tells Hawk that the Dreads have been experimenting on him in a lab - probably having to do with a new plague that allows Lord Dread to knock out humans for hours, so that they can be more easily digitized. But there is a reason why the boy is being pursued - *he* is the prototype of a new weapon against the humans. While immune himself, he carries the plague that renders humans, and now Hawk, unconscious. **Guest cast:** Gordon Woolvett as Mitch, Wayne Best as Commander Lorek. **Writer:** Marc Scott Zicree. **Director:** Otta Hanus.

Mirror in Darkness. Captain Power arrives in a desolate city area, where humans that knew he was coming to help them rush out to greet him. Only the arriving man isn't Power, but a fake being used by Dread to lure humans out hiding and digitize them. Elsewhere, Power is informed of movements of Dread's soldiers and an unusual amount of radio transmissions in sector 9, and the team heads there to investigate the activity - and why humans there are mysteriously disappearing. **Guest cast:** Tom Diamond as the man, Dwayne McLean as the second man, Colin O'Merr as Fal. **Writers:** Marc Scott Zicree and J. Michael Straczynski. **Director:** Otto Hanus.

The Ferryman). Power plans a dangerous, but much-needed raid on Epsilon Station. They launch the attack and manage to steal a Bio Dread memory bank just before becoming surrounded by Dread warriors, and they narrowly manage to escape. Lord Dread is furious, as the memory banks hold information on the New Order operation that Power and his group are trying to find out about. Meanwhile, Power realizes that they have the information on hand to stop Lord Dread's latest project, designed to launch a whole new legion of mechanical warriors - to begin that very night. But Power and his Soldiers may be unable to stop Dread after one of his technicians sends a self-destruct signal to the memory bank, destroying it - along with the computer holograph personality Mentor, who was connected to the bank at the time. **Guest cast:** Peter Snider as the commander, Ric Sarabia as Riwih. **Writer:** J. Michael Straczynski. **Director:** Otta Hanus.

Gemini and Counting. A powerful form of influenza is sweeping through the ranks of humans, so Power rushes a vaccine to the doctor caring for the stricken remains of humanity. But there isn't nearly enough of the drug for everyone, and Pilot recommends that she infiltrate Dread's Chem Factory Med-Lab One in order to steal the necessary vaccine. Having worked there before the Metal Wars, she knows the building well, but Power is still reluctant to send her in among Dread's dedicated workers. When Pilot does manage to get into the building she is confronted with a female worker who is loyal to Dread, and has no intentions of allowing Pilot to escape. **Guest cast:** Laurie Holden as Erin, Ana Ferguson as the doctor. **Writers:** Christy Marx and J. Michael Straczynski. **Director:** Otta Hanus.

And Study War No More. The one-of-a-kind, immensely-powerful evil mechanical being Blastarr [created in **The Ferryman**] is on the loose. Meanwhile, Power and his team are heading towards sector 12, where unusual activity has been detected. Arriving there, they find themselves surrounded by a large number of Dread Troopers - they have fallen into an ambush planned by Lord Dread. Fighting off the attackers, they enter a cave that is the source of unusual power readings - just before Tank is knocked out by a bazooka-like weapon. But he survives and wipes out the last of the attackers. Heading into the cave, they discover Haven - a complete community and sanctuary being run by Miles Williamson, who tells them that they will never leave the underground society. **Guest cast:** Graeme Campbell as Miles Williamson, Tonya Williams as Chelsea Chandler. **Writer:** Michal Reaves. **Director:** Jorge Montesi.

The Intruder. While delivering some medical supplies, a man breaks into Power's shuttle and hides aboard. After they return to base, the man, Andy Jackson, leaves the ship and sets off an alarm. Power catches him and he and his soldiers interrogate Jackson, who claims to be a member of an underground resistance force that wants to team up with Power and the Soldiers. Unknown to any of them, Lord Dread has had the group under surveillance and sees Jackson leave on the shuttle. He sends out a party of Dread Troopers and Blastarr [last seen being buried alive in a cave in **And Study War No More**], intending to find the location of Power's base and annihilate the Soldiers of the Universe. **Guest cast:** Barry Flatman as Andy Jackson, Ted Simonett as Jim Mitchell, Steve Whistance Smith as scavenger #1. **Writers:** Marc Scott Zicree and J. Michael Straczynski. **Director:** Jorge Montesi.

And Madness Shall Reign. An intercepted message leads Power to believe that a resistance group lead by Cipher is being targeted by Dread for an experiment. Power and his men arrive at Cipher's underground base, but find all the people there either dead or raving lunatics. Meanwhile, Dread watches their movements with a hidden camera, and orders his Troopers to surround and capture Power and his men. Just after Cipher is found, Pilot warns Power that Dread's men are closing in, so he grabs the resistance leader and fights his way back to the shuttle. Dread sends in Soaron to destroy the shuttle, but Hawk manages to shoot him down. Back at base, Mentor discovers that a chemical was used in the water at the resistance base to cause insanity. The only problem is Tank drank some of the water before they left, and he is already turning on his companions. **Guest cast:** None. **Writer:** Larry Ditillio. **Director:** Jorge Montesi.

Judgement. Captain and Pilot have found important data on Project New Order, but their sky-speeder is intercepted and shot down by Soaron, who is also damaged in the battle and will be incapacitated for hours. Lord Dread demands the data tape be returned, so he sends

Captain Power and his Soldiers prepare to activate their power suits.

out Blastarr to retrieve both it and Captain Power. Now stranded in the desert and out of communication with their team-mates, Pilot and Power regain consciousness only to find that the captain has a broken leg. He sends Pilot to a nearby community who has been known to help the resistance. But it's the worst possible place for her to go, as she is recognized as a woman who, years earlier while working for Dread, helped send to their death members of the families who live in the remote desert community. Upon seeing her, they demand revenge. **Guest cast:** Hans Jason Engel as Randall, William B. Davis as Arvin, Jan Filips as Clegg, David Gardner as Gaeian, Rich Parker as Martin, Kerry Rosall as Jack. **Writer:** Larry Ditillio. **Director:** Jorge Montesi.

A Summoning of Thunder, part one. At the same time every year Captain Power returns to visit the gravesight of his father, Dr. Stuart Gordon Power. His memories take him back to his teenage years during the Metal Wars, when he is training at his Father's lab, knowing that he will soon be involved in the war between machine and man. Meanwhile, still-human Dread takes commands from Overmind, believing the machine must be the evolutionary future of mankind. Back at his lab, Stuart Power is upset over his involvement in the creation of Overmind, but is determined to stop Dread and the computer. Unknown to him, Overmind has just created the first Bio Dread creature, Soaron. **Guest cast:** Anthony Dean Rubes as Landry, Vincent Orle as the commander, Jonathan Wilson as Soldier Jack, Dylan Neal as the young Jonathan Power, Bruce Gray

[Mentor] as Dr. Stuart Power. **Writer:** J. Michael Straczynski. **Director:** Otto Hanus.

A Summoning of Thunder, part two. Dr. Power has created the incredible power suits to battle with Liomon Tagert (after the war known as Lord Dread), but the evil leader of the mechanical forces has captured Jonathan, and gives the doctor one hour to come to his headquarters or his son will be killed. Matthew Masterson discovers Stuart has left, and is confronted by the Doctor's image in a computer hologram known as Mentor. The computer tells Matthew of the power suits, although they are untested and may kill the user. But Matthew decides the risk is worth an attempt to save Jon and Stuart; meanwhile, Tagert is trying to get Dr. Power to join his side and work with Overmind. Back at the lab, Matthew tries on the flying suit, and is nearly killed in the process. But the suit works, so he sets out to rescue his friends. **Guest cast:** Dylan Neal as the young Jonathan Power, Bruce Gray as Dr. Stuart Power and Mentor. **Writer:** J. Michael Straczynski. **Director:** Otto Hanus.

The Eden Road. The shuttle is bringing to headquarters a blind-folded resistance leader, who has something important to tell Captain Power. He has come to inform him of a Eden 2, a place that the Soldiers consider a myth. The leader insists that the resistance has set up an underground network to smuggle humans to Eden 2, where they are safe from Dread. But there has been a leak regarding their operations, leading to Dread wiping out some resistance workers that were shuttling the people. Now the leaders of Eden 2 will trust no one - except Captain Power and his men. They have asked the Soldiers to come to a secret place where only they could survive, and as proof of their good faith they send part of a Wardog uniform with a handwritten message from Vi to Matthew, saying that she made it Eden 2 [see **Wardogs**]. **Guest cast:** Brent Stait as John, Kate Trotter as Vi. **Writer:** J. Michael Straczynski. **Director:** Ken Girotti.

Freedom One. Freedom One is the voice of the East Coast resistance movement, a radio broadcast that tells humans of their victories over Dread's forces. The woman who reads over the air includes a secret message to Power during her latest program: "A summoning of thunder", the signal for Captain and his Soldiers to come to the rescue. They arrive to wipe out some attacking Dread Troopers who homed on on her signal. Once they are finished, Captain meets Christine Laraby, and she explains that she plans to use her transmitter to bring together the heads of all the resistance movements - a plan Power considers unduly dangerous. And he should, as Laraby is in league with Dread. **Guest cast:** Gwynth Walsh as Christine Laraby, Raymond O'Neill as Elzer, Nich Nichols as Gundar, Laing Maybee as Overunit. **Writers:** Christy Marx and J. Michael Straczynski. **Director:** Rihen Scherberger.

Flame Street. Power and his men are disguised while visiting Tec City looking for information on Project New Order, and are searching for a woman named Mindsinger. But an informant for Dread recognizes Power and contacts his master, who sends Blastarr to kill the resistance leader. Meanwhile, Power tells Mindsinger that he wants to enter the Web, a highly-dangerous computer system that directly links with the human mind. Just as Power connects with the machine, Blastarr and Dread warriors arrive to attack the town - and if Power is disconnected before completion of the program that is running, he will be killed. Worse still, Overmind and Lord Dread are linking with the Web, and they intend to take over his mind. **Guest cast:** Laurie Paton as Mindsinger, Brock Johnson as the zone boy, Bruce Gray as Dr. Stuart Power. **Writers:** Michael Reeves and J. Michael Straczynski. **Director:** Otto Hanus.

A Fire in the Dark. Lord Dread is after a woman to help him design the perfect mechanical warriors, and Soaron and Dread Troopers are sent out to find Jessica Morgan. When the elders of a village refuse to tell where she has gone, they are digitized. Power and his Soldiers are trying to find out why the artist - blinded fifteen years earlier in Dread's attack on the town she lived in - is wanted by Dread. Jessica is alive and well, hiding in a nearby cave, and Power arrives to take her to safety. Back at headquarters, the Soldiers receive a communication from Dread: unless Jessica is turned over, one of her friends will be killed every hour she is in their protection. While Power and his crew try to figure out what to do, Jessica takes matter into her own hands when she steals a sky-speeder, earlier computer-attuned for flight by her voice command, and flies to the coordinates given by Dread. **Guest cast:** Patricia Collins as Jessica Morgan, Gerry Pearson as Arthur, J.R. Zimmerman as Henry, Robert O'Ree as Adam. **Writer:** Marv Wolfman. **Director:** Doug Williams.

New Order part one: The Sky Shall Swallow Them. Scout and Power are meeting an informant named Locke, who has knowledge of Project New Order, but the meeting is broken up by the arrival of Soaron and Blastarr, who have orders to kill Power and retrieve the stolen data. They manage to escape, and back at headquarters Power learns that a platform has been launched into space, where a huge digitizer will mass-eradicate the remaining human population. To further destroy anything remaining from the human civilization, a series of depots will be exploded, causing a plasma storm that will burn everything on the surface of the Earth. Unless Captain Power and his Soldiers can stop Dread, humanity will be destroyed in only a few hours. **Guest cast:** Todd Waite as Overunit Gerber, Paul Humphrey as Locke. **Writer:** Larry Ditillio. **Director:** Otto Hanus.

New Order part two: The Land Shall Burn. The space digitizer has been defeated, and is plummeting towards Earth - right at Volcania. If the two-hundred-ton mass strikes Dread's headquarters, it will stop him from releasing the plasma storm. Soaron is sent to intercept the falling platform, where it collides with the flying machine and Soaron is destroyed, then moments later Volcania is struck. But the Prometheus section, where the plasma is to be launched, survives the onslaught, as do Dread and Overmind. Power and his soldiers now have twenty-one minutes to destroy Dread, even though their power suits are at a dangerously low power levels, and could malfunction at any time. **Guest cast:** Todd Waite as Overunit Gerber, Paul Humphrey as Locke. **Writer:** Larry Ditillio. **Director:** Otto Hanus.

Retribution, part one. Captain Power and his Soldiers are jubilant after defeating Project New Order and putting Dread on the run, but Power is concerned where Dread will strike next. Taking turns dancing with her fellow soldiers, Pilot, who has always been attracted to Power, is falling in love with him. Meanwhile, Dread manages to restore Soaron and Blastarr, and plans to become a machine himself. But his first objective is the total destruction of Power, and then to eliminate the rest of mankind. Dread launches an all-out offensive with the remainder of his army, killing everywhere and never taking prisoners. Power is helpless to stop the carnage, and can only sit back and wait for an opportunity to arise to make a move against Dread. **Guest cast:** None. **Writer** J. Michael Straczynski. **Director:** Jorge Montesi.

Retribution, part two. Using a device that will track Power's ship, Dread contacts his troops around the globe to be on the lookout for Power. When the captain's ship is spotted, Soaron is sent to track it with a device that will reveal where the Soldier's teleportation device sends them. The mission is completed, and Dread now knows the location of Power's headquarters. Back at their mountain fortress, Pilot is about to reveal to Power that she loves him, but Scout interrupts before she reveals her feelings. The Soldiers meet with informant Locke again, and he sells them troop movements and one other piece of information: Colonel Cypher has been captured and the Soldiers must rescue him before he can be delivered to Dread's headquarters. But Locke is lying - it is all a trap to finish off the Soldiers when Power's ship arrives at the location he is supposed to be at. Arriving there, the soldiers are ambushed and stranded when their ship is blasted out of commission. Back at headquarters, Pilot is alone when Blastarr and Troopers arrive to destroy Power's fortress. Pilot sets the self-destruct, but it fails after after Blastarr attacks. After sending out a sky-speeder with a computer backup of Mentor, she receives a call from Jonathan. She tells Power she loves him, then hits the manual self-destruct, killing herself and Blastarr. **Guest cast:** Paul Humphrey as Locke [not credited], Tom Quinn as Overunit. **Writer** J. Michael Straczynski. **Director:** Jorge Montesi.

The Green Hornet (Van Williams) and Kato (Bruce Lee).

The Green Hornet

review by William E. Anchors, Jr.

Production credits:

Executive Producer	William Dozier
Producer	Richard Bluel
Associate Producer	Jerry Thomas
Creator	George W. Trendle
Music	Billy Man
Theme song by	Al Hirt

Regular cast:

Britt Reid/Green Hornet	Van Williams
Kato	Bruce Lee
Lenore "Casey" Case	Wende Wagner
District Attorney F. P. Scanlon	Walter Brooke
Mike Axford	Lloyd Gough
Newscaster	Gary Owens

Number of episodes:	26 one half hour segments

Premise: The adventures of the crime-fighting team of the Green Hornet, who uses clever schemes to outsmart his opponents, and Kato, a master of karate and judo. Unlike most super-heroes, the Green Hornet did not use superpowers to overpower crooks, but utilized a few select weapons and natural brilliance - along with a knack at playing his opponent's games better than they could.

Editor's comments: Another show created only to cater to the *Batman* craze, *Hornet* was a tedious flop that only lasted as long as it did because of its tie-in with *Batman*.

The Silent Gun (airdate: Sept. 9, 1966). District Attorney Frank Scanlon receives an urgent call from a man who wants to meet him at his father's funeral, although he doesn't say why. Not long after arriving the son is murdered by a man with a very unusual pistol: it produces no sound or muzzle flash whatsoever. The following day Britt Reid, publisher of the Daily Sentinel, receives a call from Scanlon and fills him in on the details of the case. About that time he finds out that the murdered man's girlfriend wants to sell her story, so a reporter, Mike Axford, is told to talk to her later that evening. Meanwhile, Britt returns home where he learns the gun was used again in a theft, so he and his chauffeur dress in their costumes, and make the first appearance of the Green Hornet and his judo-expert sidekick, Kato. **Guest cast:** Charles Franciso as Al Trump, Lloyd Bochner as Dan Carley, Henry Evans as Renner, Kelly Jean Peters as Jackie, Ed McGrealy as Olson, Max Kelvin as Stacey, L. McGranary as the minister, Breland Rice and Bob Harvey as the policemen. **Writer:** Ken Pettus. **Director:** Leslie H. Martinson.

Give 'Em Enough Rope (airdate: Sept. 16, 1966). After two men meet in a darkened alley, one is strangled to death by the other - a sinister man in black. The same killer attacks Mike, who was there to have a secret meeting with the dead man, an informant who was going to give him damaging evidence on someone committing insurance fraud. But before the strangler can kill Mike, the Green Hornet arrives, causing the man in black to flee while the Hornet puts Mike to sleep with his gas-emitting Hornet gun. Looking into the insurance scam, Hornet investigates the man who is pretending to be hurt in an accident. But the accident "victim" gets paranoid and orders the kidnapping of his attorney, who was seen working with the Hornet. Now Reid and Kato must find both the man in black, the kidnapped attorney, and prove the man with the insurance claim is a fake. **Guest cast:** Diana Hyland as Claudia Bromley, Mort Mills as Alex Colony, Jerry Ayers as Pete, Joe Sirola as Charley, David Renard as Joe Sweek, Ken Strange as the big bruiser. **Writers:** Gwen Bagni and Paul Dubov. **Director:** Seymour Robbie.

Programmed For Death (Sept. 23, 1966). Daily Sentinel reporter Pat Allen phones Reid to tell him he has found something important, but the man is killed by a leopard before he can reveal what it is. The police find on his desk an expensive diamond, which Scanlon tells Reid might be counterfeit. When Britt remembers a scientist who, years earlier, had developed a process to manufacture diamonds, he decides to go see him and possibly find a clue as to why Pat was murdered. **Guest cast:** Signe Hasso as Yolanda de Lukens, Richard Cutting as the charwoman, Barbara Babcock as Cathy Desmond, Sheila Leighton as the D.A.'s secretary, Don Eitner as Pat Ellen, John Alvar as Mark. **Writer:** Jerry Thomas and Lewis Reed. **Director:** Larry Peerce.

Crime Wave (airdate: Sept. 30, 1966). Two men board an aircraft to repair its air conditioner, but actually are thieves who knock out the crew and passengers with a sleeping gas, then steal a briefcase of diamonds. Before they leave, they drop a sticker at the scene of the crime with the Green Hornet logo - someone is trying to frame the Hornet! To make matters worse, publisher Britt Reid receives a letter dated a day before the crime describing the robbery in the detail. The man who wrote the letter claims his computer predicted Green Hornet's theft of the diamonds Furthermore, he can predict more future Hornet crimes, all of which is believed by the police. **Guest cast:** Peter Haskel as Abel Marcus, Sheila Wells as Laura Spinner, Ron Burke as Joe, Denny Costello as the detective, Jennifer Stuart as the stewardess, Wayne Sutherland as the clown, Breland Rice as the policeman, Wilkie de Martel as the jeweler, Dee Sutherlin as the woman. **Writer:** Sheldon Stark. **Director:** Larry Peerce.

The Frog is a Deadly Weapon (airdate: Oct. 7, 1966). A pair of frogmen kidnap Nat Pyle, who had contacted Britt Reid to sell him information about the return of a crime kingpin, thought to have died

The Black Beauty: a rolling arsenal of crime-fighting weaponry.

years earlier. That night the Green Hornet goes in search of the man, but while visiting Pyle's home, he finds clues that indicate that Lenore Case, Britt's secretary, has been kidnapped as well. Unfortunately, there are no leads as to where Case or Pyle could be - until the police inform Britt that a woman answering his secretary's description has been found dead, floating outside the harbor. **Guest cast:** Victor Jory as Charles Delaclaire, Thordis Brandt as Nedra Vallen, Barbara Babcock as Elaine, George Robotham as Nat Pyle, Ruby Hansen as the fisherman, Roger Heldfond as the attendant. **Writer:** William L. Stuart. **Director:** Leslie H. Martinson.

Eat, Drink and Be Dead (airdate: Oct. 14, 1966). After a gangland style killing of two men, Britt is infuriated, and that night he goes to the bar the murdered men had been at and grills the owner: the Hornet learns that a bootleg liquor gang has been forcing tavern owners to buy their product. With some persuasion, Hornet is given the clues he needs to pursue the case. **Guest cast:** Jason Evers as Henry Dirk, Harry Lauter as Brannigan, Harry Fleer as Evans, William McLeannan as Winfield, Eddie Ness as Crandall, Shep Sanders as Carney, Jo Ann Milam as the copy girl. **Writer:** Richard Landau. **Director:** Murray Golden.

Beautiful Dreamer, parts one and two (airdates: part one, Oct. 14, 1966; part two, Oct. 28, 1966). The Green Hornet is racing to contact a Professor Wylie after learning the man's life is in danger, but arrives just as his car explodes in flames, with the poor doctor still inside. Britt figures out that the call warning his newspaper that the man was going to be murdered came from the Vale of Eden Club, but he is unable to get ahold of the woman who phoned. That

night, Hornet and Kato use the Hornet Sting to force the doorlock at the club, and enter to search the premises for clues to the killer. They obtain the informant's address, but when they arrive at her home she is being kidnapped. When they give chase, the woman - a former Sentinel employee - is thrown from the car. Britt decides that more detective work is needed at the club, which caters to a wealthy clientele, and when he goes there as a customer he learns that the establishment is brainwashing clients to pull off crimes, and later the people have no memory of the event. Now Hornet must figure out who is behind the operation and how far it has spread. **Guest cast:** Geoffrey Horne as Peter Eden, Pamela Curran as Canessa, Henry Hunter as Wylie, Jean-Marie as Dorothy, Maurice Manson as Cavanaugh, Barbara Gates as Mary, Victoria George as Harriet, Fred Carson as Joel, Chuck Hicks as Cork, Jerry Catron as Johnny, Sandy Kevin as Phil, Marina Ghane as Helga **Writers:** Ken Puttus and Lorenzo Semple, Jr. **Director:** Allen Reisner.

The Ray is for Killing (airdate: Nov. 11, 1966). Wealthy Britt Reid is holding a celebrity art show at his home, and although he cannot be there himself, the program is being monitored by cameras. Suddenly, thieves crash the show and steal the most important paintings, and when the police try to pursue the crooks their car is blown up by a laser beam. Later, Britt Reid receives a $1,000,000 ransom demand for the return of his stolen art collection. To pay the money would ruin the publisher financially, so he is left only one alternative: the Green Hornet must find and corral the criminals and retrieve his paintings. **Guest cast:** Robert McQueeney as Richardson, Bill Baldwin as Dr. Karl Bendix, Mike Mahoney as the policeman, Grant Woods as Steve, Bob Gunner as the detective, Jim

35

Raymond as the driver. **Writer:** Lee Loeb. **Director:** William Baudine.

The Preying Mantis Kills (airdate: Nov. 18, 1966). Britt Reid is told of a vicious protection racket operating in Chinatown, so that night the Green Hornet goes into action at the Golden Lotus Cafe, where thugs are making threats to the owner. They try to make the informant look like a member of their gang, and Kato is knocked out when the thieves flee. But now the informant, Jimmy Kee, is in trouble because he can identify the thugs, so Kato and Hornet pick up Jimmy to protect him and find out who is behind the extortion racket. **Guest cast:** Mako as Low Sing, Tom Drake as Duke Slate, Allen Jung as Wing Ho, Al Huang as Jimmy Kee, Lang Yun as Mary Chang. **Writers:** Ken Pettus and Charles Hoffman. **Director:** Norman Foster.

The Hunters and the Hunted (airdate: Nov. 25, 1966). The Green Hornet meets a gangster who tells him that they are both on a list of criminals to be assassinated. Hornet doesn't believe him at first, but the man is suddenly killed with a poison dart - and now the killer is after the Hornet. After missing the crimefighter, the killer takes off, but crashes his car and is killed when the Black Beauty pursues him. The next day Britt learns from Scanlon that the dead man was a respected businessman with no record. That night, the Green Hornet goes into action again, and pursues some clues that lead him to believe that members of the Explorers Club, a group of wealthy big-game hunters, are the ones who have taken it upon themselves to kill the city's top gangsters. **Guest cast:** Robert Strauss as Bud Crocker, Charles Bateman as Quentin Crane, Douglas Evans as Leland Stone, Rand Brooks as Conway, Bill Walker as the bartender, Frank Gerstle as Mel Hurk, Dick Dial as Del, Gene LeBell as Barney. **Writer:** Jerry Thomas. **Director:** William Baudine.

Deadline for Death (airdate: Dec. 2, 1966). The police run down a burglar who turns out to be Mike Axford. In the home they believe he just robbed, they find a butler who was beaten, then dies, resulting in Mike being charged with murder. When the police investigate, they discover that every home Mike has been in for an interview has later been robbed, further incriminating the reporter. But the Hornet knows better, and sets out to learn the truth. He and Kato discover that at each interview Mike had the same photographer, but Mike refuses to believe the girl - the daughter of an old friend - is guilty. But he is mistaken, as the photographer's boyfriend has been knocking off the homes using information he receives from her. **Guest cast:** James Best as Yale Barton, Lynda Day [George] [*The Return of Captain Nemo*] as Ardis Ralston, Jacques Aubuchon as policeman #1, Kirby Brumfield as policeman #2, Annazette Williams as the telephone operator, Glen Wilder as Murf, Roydon Clark as Aldo. **Writer:** Ken Pettus. **Director:** Seymour Robbie.

Secret of the Sally Bell (airdate: Dec. 9, 1966). The Green Hornet is keeping a freighter, the Sally Bell, under observation as he suspects it is being used to smuggle drugs into the city. Hornet and Kato catch a known criminal leaving the ship, but during the scuffle he is knocked unconscious. Unfortunately, the man is the only one who knows where $2,000,000 in narcotics are hidden, so they take him to a local hospital. After the Hornet leaves, the criminal is kidnapped by thugs who know of the shipment and want it for themselves. Unless Hornet can relocate the man, he and Kato will be unable to stop the drugs from entering the city. **Guest cast:**

Warren Kemmerling as Bert Seldon, Beth Brickell as Dr. Thomas, Jacques Denbeaux as Gus Wander, Greg Benedict as Carlos, Dave Perna as Wolfe, Ann Rexford as the nurse, Timothy Scott as Honeyboy, James Farley as Carmichael. **Writer:** William L. Stuart. **Director:** Robert L. Friend.

Freeway to Death (airdate: Dec. 16, 1966). Mike Axford is investigating a construction racket, but gets into trouble when his informant is killed and he is being chased by a bulldozer - until missiles from the Black Beauty stop the piece of equipment. Mike is convinced to share the information he has with the Hornet, and it leads the crimefighter to Emmet Crown, who is with the construction company. When Britt questions him, the man denies everything - then orders his men to arrange an "accident" before Britt leaves the property, one that will insure the death of the nosey newspaperman. **Guest cast:** Jeffrey Hunter [*Star Trek*] as Emmet Crown, John Hubbard as Giles, Reggie Parton as Spike, David Fresco as Wiggins, Harvey Parry as Lefty, Fred Krone as Rook. **Writer:** Ken Pettus. **Director** Allen Reisner.

May the Best Man Lose (airdate: Dec. 23, 1966). Frank Scanlon is running for election again and narrowly avoids being murdered when his car explodes, killing an aide. That night, the Green Hornet and Kato meet a hood who can tell them who is after Scanlon, but the man won't talk. Later that evening, political rival Calvin Ryland is grilled on tv by Mike, who asks him if he is behind the murder attempt, but Scanlon insists his adversary is beyond reproach. However, Ryland's campaign manager, his corrupt brother, is far from being guiltless. When the Hornet follows Ryland's brother - the thug who wouldn't reveal his identity - he's sure he has the attempted assassin. **Guest cast:** Harold Gould as Calvin Ryland, Linden Chiles as Warren Ryland, Robert Hoy as Woody, Troy Melton as Pete, Bill Phupps as Jack Starkey. **Writers:** Judith and Robert Guy Barrows. **Director:** Allen Reisner.

Seek, Stalk and Destroy (airdate: Jan. 6, 1967). At a military supply depot, a tank is stolen. The next day, a prison warden contacts Britt saying that a condemned prisoner wants to see him. When Britt arrives, the prisoner tells him that he knows why the tank was stolen: one of the prisoners who is due to be executed is about to be busted out of prison by the tank crew that he served with in Korea. When the Hornet tries to confirm the story, he finds himself face-to-face with the stolen armored vehicle, and it becomes a fight to the finish between the powerful tank and the Black Beauty's formidable arsenal. **Guest cast:** Ralph Meeker as Earl Evans, Raymond St. Jacques as Hollis Silver, Paul Carr as Eddie Carter, John Baer as Bradford Devlin, E.J. Andre as Paul, Harvey Parry as Bill. **Writer:** Jerry Thomas. **Director:** George Waggner.

Corpse of the Year, parts one and two (airdates: part one, Jan. 13, 1967; part two, Jan. 20, 1967). While out on a date, Britt sees the Black Beauty round a corner and fire a rocket at a Daily Sentinel delivery truck, killing the driver, then speeding off. Later, the Green Hornet enters the Daily Sentinel office and throws a bomb, then continues attacks on the newspaper trucks with the Black Beauty. Someone is obviously pretending to be the Green Hornet, but who? When Britt/Green Hornet continues to investigate, he learns that the people working for a competing newspaper, the Daily Express, may be involved. **Guest cast:** Joanna Dru as Sabrina, Celia Kaye as Melissa Neal, J. Edward McKinley as Simon Neal, Cesare Danova

as Felix Garth, Tom Simcox as Dan Scully, Barbara Babcock as Elaine, Nora Marlowe as Apple Annie, Jack Garner as the doorman, Sidney Smith as Willoughby, Sally Mills as the secretary, Angelique Pettyjohn as the girl. **Writer:** Ken Pettus. **Director:** James Komack.

Bad Bet on 459-Silent (Feb. 3, 1967). When the Green Hornet hears about a jewelry store break-in during a police call over the radio, Kato heads the Black Beauty to the store. The police arrive first, and find the safe open - but steal some jewelry themselves. Hornet arrives after they leave, and he becomes suspicious when he finds a button from a police uniform on the floor. But just then another police car arrives, and they open fire and hit the Hornet, thinking he was the thief. He and Kato manage to escape, but the Hornet has a bad shoulder wound and he knows that his identity will be revealed if he goes to a hospital. Somehow he must return to work the next day, and create an explanation for the wound. Worse still, while the Green Hornet is out of action the crooked cops continue pulling more capers. **Guest cast:** Bert Freed as Sgt. Bert Clark, Jason Wingreen as the doctor, Brian Avery as Jim Dixon, Nicolas Coster as Gregory, Barry Ford as Lawson, Bud Perkins as the dispatcher, Dick Dial as the reporter. **Writer:** Judith and Robert Guy Barrows. **Director:** Seymour Robbie.

Ace in the Hole (airdate: Feb. 10, 1967). When the Hornet meets with two underworld crime bosses, the unconscious body of reporter Mike Axford is brought in. Guards found him snooping and knocked him out, but when Mike wakes up and tries to escape he is shot and killed, or so the crooks think. Hornet volunteers to dispose of the body, but he is actually hiding Mike while he begins a plan to make both of the kingpins think that the other is out to get them - hopefully wiping out both crime rings in the process. **Guest cast:** Richard Anderson [*The Six Million Dollar Man*] as Phil Trager, Richard X. Slattery as Steve Grant, Percy Helton as Gus, Tony Epper as Nixie, Bill Couch as Carns, Bill Hampton as Jess. **Writers:** J .E. Selby and Stanley H. Silverman. **Director:** William Baudine.

Trouble for Prince Charming (airdate: Feb. 17, 1967). The Green Hornet is aware that a dignitary arriving at the airport may be heading for trouble, so he and Kato rush there in the Black Beauty. Another person is on her way to the airport to meet the man, a girl named Janet Prescott, the prince's fiancee. As Prince Rafil starts to leave the plane, a van with assassins pulls up to shoot him, but the Green Hornet stops them in time. Later, while visiting Reid to tell him of the Hornet's exploits, the Prince has Janet go to answer the phone, but she is grabbed and kidnapped. When the kidnappers call with their demands, Green Hornet learns that they want the prince to abdicate as ruler of his country, or they will kill Janet. Now the Hornet has just 48 hours to find the girl before the prince renounces his throne. **Guest cast:** Edmund Hashim as Prince Rafil, Susan Flannery as Janet Prescott, Alberto Morin as Abu Bajr, James Lanphier as Sarajek. **Writers:** Ken Pettus. **Director:** William Baudine.

Alias the Scarf (airdate: Feb. 24, 1967). Wax museum owner James Rancourt adds two new figures to his Chamber of Evil: the Green Hornet and Kato. Another figure is 'The Scarf', a murderer who garrotes his victims with a white scarf, but who had disappeared

twenty years earlier. Unfortunately, the killer returns that night and strangles Rancourt's partner, then tries to kill a woman, but she escapes and tells the Daily Sentinel that the Scarf is back in town - a situation the Green Hornet will soon rectify. **Guest cast:** John Carradine [*The Howling*] as James Rancourt, Patricia Barry as Hazel Schmidt, Ian Wolfe as Peter Willman, Paul Gleason as Paul Garret. **Writers:** William Stuart. **Director:** Allen Reisner.

Hornet, Save Thyself (airdate: Mar. 3, 1967). An old enemy attends Britt's birthday party, but Britt wants nothing to do with him. As Britt is examining a gun he was given as a gift, it goes off, killing the man. With a roomful of people witnessing what looks like murder, the police cannot believe his story that the gun went off on its own, which happens to be the truth. Realizing he must escape to prove his innocence, Britt knocks out Scanlon, and escapes by the secret entrance to the Black Beauty. Now it is up to the Green Hornet and Kato to prove that the weapon was fired by remote control. **Guest cast:** Michael Strong as Dale Hyde, Marvin Brody as Eddie Rich, Frank Marth as the police lieutenant, Ken Strange as the policeman, Jack Perkins as the desk sergeant. **Writer:** Don Tait. **Director:** Seymour Robbie.

Invasion From Outer Space, parts one and two (airdates: part one, Mar. 10, 1967; part two, Mar. 17, 1967). While Britt Reid is watching TV, an announcement comes on saying that a UFO has crashed near town. Moments later, silver-clad people arrive at his home and claim they are space travellers who crashed nearby. They demand safe passage to the city, so Britt calls Scanlon to let him block certain roads so the aliens will not be interfered with. Before leaving, the aliens knock out Britt and Kato and take Britt's secretary, Lenore Case, prisoner. But the hoax doesn't last long, for when Britt awakens he remembers meeting one of the "aliens" before: he is Doctor Mabouse, a renegade scientist. Furthermore, the route to town the aliens want cleared is the same one the U.S. Air Force is using to transport a nuclear bomb! **Guest cast:** Larry D. Mann as Dr. Eric Mabouse, Arthur Batanides as Shugo, Linda Gaye Scott as Vama, Christopher Dark as Martin, Denny Dobbins as the colonel, Joe di Reda as Corman, Britt King as Major Jackon, Frank Babich as the task force sergeant, Lloyd Haynes as the military policeman, Troy Melton and Jerry Catron as the henchmen, Tyler McVey as the police chief, Richard Poston as the Air Force captain, Bennie Dobbins as the Air Force colonel. **Writer:** Art Weingarten. **Director:** Darrel Hallenbeck.

The Hornet & the Firefly (airdate: Mar. 24, 1967). A firebug is plaguing the city, setting new fires every night. The Green Hornet and Kato go out on the town each night looking for the arsonist who calls himself the Firefly, but without any success. The next night they follow a man in a fire-protection suit and capture him after he starts a fire. But he escapes while they save a knocked-out guard. While the Green Hornet seems to be going nowhere on the case, reporter Mike Axford may be on to something: he suspects a fire department employee who was forced into retirement after he is hurt in an accident. Mike is correct - except that the ex-employee now plans to kill Mike and blame the fires on him. **Guest cast:** Gerald S. O'Loughlin as Ben Wade, Russ Conway as Commissioner Dolan, Buff Brady as the guard. **Writer:** William Stuart. **Director:** Allen Reisner.

William Katt as superhero Ralph Hinkley, with Connie Sellecca as Pam Davidson, and Robert Culp as Bill Maxwell.

The Greatest American Hero

Believe It or Not... He's a Superhero

article by David W. Dietz, III

It's a bird! It's a plane! It's...Ralph Hinkley?

With that same expression of disbelief, one of the most unique superhero sagas in the history of television began. On March 18, 1981, as the television promotional spots proudly announced, *The Greatest American Hero* had come to save us. And for three seasons after the series' pilot movie first aired, *The Greatest American Hero* waged a continuous crusade against the forces of evil. Not bad really, when one stops to consider that he never really wanted to be a superhero in the first place.

If the series' leading protagonist, Ralph Hinkley (as played by William Katt) ever in his childhood fantasized about swooping down from the sky onto unsuspecting evildoers, he certainly never gave any indication of it. He even had to have a small boy teach him the correct way to fly! Nevertheless, Ralph Hinkley proved to be an effective force against the wrongdoers that threatened society.

The Greatest American Hero was the brainchild of writer/producer Stephen J. Cannell, the man responsible for such other television series as *The A-Team* and *21 Jump Street*. When the ABC network first commissioned the pilot for the series, they were undoubtedly trying to cash in on the success of the then-popular *Superman* movies. What the network got was something more interesting and entertaining.

The Greatest American Hero was based on the premise of what would happen to the life of an ordinary Joe if he were suddenly given super powers and told that he alone had the power to save the world? Save the world? Someone who couldn't keep his own checkbook balanced?

Nevertheless, that was what was expected of Ralph Hinkley the night he wandered off into the desert surrounding Palmdale, California searching for help with a stalled school van. Hinkley's already topsy-turvy life was only further complicated by the appearance of an alien spacecraft which descended to earth and presented him with a strange suit possessed of super powers. The aliens obviously felt that the meek, mild-mannered school teacher had the right combination of humility and compassion to successfully carry out the assignment they presented him. Unfortunately, the aliens hadn't counted on Ralph's own natural human foibles getting in the way.

Ralph's uncertainty at the prospect of becoming a superhero was clearly in evidence throughout most of the first few episodes of the series. So much so, that on more than one occasion Ralph nearly decided to give up being heroic all together and resume what most would consider a normal life. Not surprising seeing how the night of his close encounter, Ralph not only managed to lose a vital instruction book for his strange new super-powerful suit, but the aliens also decided to team him with a volatile FBI agent named Bill Maxwell (wonderfully portrayed by Robert Culp).

Ralph had met Bill Maxwell hours before the encounter and not under the best of circumstances. Maxwell's partner had been killed by a radical terrorist group and he was drowning his sorrows in a bottle of booze when Ralph and his group of students came upon him in a small restaurant. Maxwell was unimpressed with Ralph and his horde of students and ended up pulling a gun on one of them when their taunts got to be too much for him. In fact, he ended up nearly running Ralph over with his car which he had lost control of due to alien intervention. When the aliens finally descended, it was Maxwell's recently-deceased partner who appeared to present them with the suit and tell them of their assignment before leaving with the aliens.

Maxwell's personality was in complete contrast to that of Ralph. He was the gung-ho, rough-and-tumble action man who would rather let his gun, or Ralph's super-powers, do the talking. He was fiercely loyal to the "Good ol' U. S. of A.," and may have still held to the McCarthyan awareness of the "Red Menace". Many times it was apparent that Maxwell had his own ideas for using the suit to further his own petty-minded schemes and better his record as a law enforcer, but always it was Ralph's high-minded idealism which kept Maxwell's passions in their proper perspective.

Perhaps that is what made these two characters likable as well as work so well together on the screen. Like *Star Trek*'s Captain Kirk and Mister Spock, they represented the opposite extremes of the human psyche: Maxwell the action-driven id, and Ralph the ever-thoughtful ego. Like everything else in life, there is always more than one interpretation of a situation, and through Ralph and Bill, the audience is able to perceive a situation from two angles rather than one. It was kind of fun to realize that in certain episodes it turned out that Bill Maxwell was the one with the correct solution to the problem.

More often than not though, the one person who was able to keep these two on a straight course had to be Ralph's cool-headed and patient girlfriend - and eventual wife - Pamela Davidson (Connie Sellecca). Like Ralph, Pam was an idealistic character. She would have to have been to put up with a boyfriend who runs around in red leotards and a black cape, as well as a Fed who was always trying to do things his way. Pam was not immune to human frailty, however. In a couple of episodes it seemed that she was growing tired of Ralph's seeming neglect of her and was preparing to end her relationship with him. However, her love for the hapless hero had to have been at least as powerful as Ralph's suit because it always brought her back. It often appeared that Pam was actually the mediating force that kept Ralph and Bill together. This is most

clearly evident in the episode **Train of Thought** in which Ralph's inability to fly straight causes him to have a literally head-on collision with a runaway freight train and lose his memory. It is only through Pam's cool-headedness that Ralph is able to regain his memory and continue his escapades.

Together, these three made quite an effective and unique crime-fighting combination. Their closeness and loyalty to one another seemed to grow with each subsequent episode. So strong was their bond, that in the episode *Heaven is in Your Genes*, we see Ralph and Pam not only mourn the apparent death of their friend Bill Maxwell, but when through Ralph's super powers - they discover that he is alive, the pair set off on a crusade to find him when all others had given up hope.

With a premise like that and three such intriguing lead characters, it would seem that a show like *The Greatest American Hero* had basically all that anyone could ask. But the success of the series didn't solely rest there. Along with other classic programs such as *Star Trek* and *The Twilight Zone*, the format of *The Greatest American Hero* was fairly open-ended allowing a writer to tell any kind of story that he or she wanted to.

And did the series ever have a diversity of stories! One week a viewer could tune and see typical crime fighting story like in the series' first one-hour episode **The Hit Car**. The next week one could see a hostile alien life form on a rampage through Los Angeles as seen in **The Shock Will Kill You**. These very different kinds of tales, combined with the presence of the three leading characters always made for an entertaining hour of television which few series seem to achieve anymore.

From a production standpoint, it seemed that the actors themselves really enjoyed what they were doing every week. So great was their enjoyment, that Robert Culp was permitted to write and direct two episodes of the series. Many fans believe that in no two other episodes were the characters as real and alive as they were in

both *Lilacs, Mr. Maxwell* and *Vanity, Says the Preacher*.

The Greatest American Hero was also a showcase of talent, both young and old. William Katt is the son of *Perry Mason* star Barbara Hale who appeared in the episode **Who's Woo in America** playing, you guessed it, Ralph's mother. Katt himself had only begun to make his mark as an actor when he landed the role of Ralph Hinkley. He had been previously seen playing a teenage tormentor of Stephen King's *Carrie*, and after his tenure on *The Greatest American Hero*, Katt went on to star in the film *House*, as well as land a recurring role as a private investigator in the revival of *Perry Mason*.

Robert Culp had a long and varied career in Hollywood films as well as in the dawn of television. His previous outings in science fiction included such series as the *Man from U.N.C.L.E.*, *The Twilight Zone, The Outer Limits,* and a failed pilot for the late Gene Roddenberry called *Spectre*. The role of FBI man Bill Maxwell fit Culp like a pair of old shoes since he had previously starred in *I Spy* for three seasons during the espionage craze of the late 1960's.

Connie Sellecca admitted to never being a big science fiction fan, yet her career is littered with appearances in the genre. Before *The Greatest American Hero*, she had starred in the short-lived *Beyond Westworld*. Her life has also been touched by the genre, having been previously married to former *Buck Rogers* star Gil Gerard, she recently married *Entertainment Tonight* and *One on One* host John Tesh, who had a small role in *Star Trek: The Next Generation*. Her last project was the CBS drama *P.S. I Luv You*.

Two of Ralph Hinkley's students graduated to film and TV careers which also brushed shoulders with the science fiction universe. Faye Grant, who played Rhonda Blake, went on to star in *V* as well as the TV movie *Omen IV*. Michael Pare (Tony Villiconna) left *The Greatest American Hero* to star in films such as *Streets of Fire, The Philadelphia Experiment*, and *World Gone Wild*.

Even the series guest artists gave some stunning and memorable performances. William Windom had made an impact years ago in the *Star Trek* episode **The Doomsday Machine**, and delivered another spectacular performance as corrupt newsman and political hopeful Henry Williams in **Live at Eleven**. *Designing Women* star Dixie Carter noted a top performance under her belt as O'Neil, the troubled FBI efficiency expert in **Lilacs, Mr. Maxwell**. And frequent guest star James Whitmore, Jr., turned in great performances as the evil mercenary Gordon McCready in **Here's Looking at You, Kid** the sadistic IRS agent Byron Bigsby in **There's Just No Accounting...**, and the nerdy game designer Norman Fakler in **Wizards and Warlocks**. *Lost in Space*'s June Lockhart did a great job as Pam's mother in several episodes.

After its cancellation, *The Greatest American Hero* went into syndication where it found a resurgence in popularity. So great was the impact, that plans were made to revive the series in a new format. This was first attempted in a pilot called *The Greatest American Heroine* in which Ralph is finally exposed as a secret superhero and is forced to give away his suit to another: in this case a woman named Holly Hathaway (played by Mary Ellen Stuart.) Hathaway and Bill Maxwell would have continued the fight for justice had the networks decided to make a series out of the pilot. At one point there were also plans for an animated version of the series, but they never came to fruition.

All in all, *The Greatest American Hero* can be looked upon as a success. It provided a not-too-mind-numbing, entertaining hour of television with stories and characters that were just real enough to be understood by an audience yet fantastic enough to provide an escape from reality for awhile. No doubt fans of the series, both young and old and yet to come will continue to enjoy the adventures of America's most unusual superhero.

Greatest American Hero Biographies

article by Howard T. Konig

Ralph Hinkley/Henley (William Katt): Ralph was just a normal guy until a trip out to Palmdale and a visit by aliens left him with a super powered suit and partner in heroics named Bill Maxwell. The red suit (which includes a black cape and a silver belt) gives Ralph a number of super powers including: super strength, super speed, the ability to fly, invisibility, telekinesis, pyrokinesis, and invulnerability. Ralph, who is unaware of the suit's full potential as he lost the instructions, can also see visions known as holographs which allow him to tune in on the "vibes" of an item and see a person's past, present or future location.

Ralph is a teacher of special education at Whitney High School in California. His class, who call him Mr. H, includes problem students as well as kids with learning disabilities. He was briefly promoted to vice principal as part of a special program that allowed the students to elect their favorite teacher to that post.

Ralph, who drives a green station wagon with brown wooden panels, lives at house number 13216 with his second wife, Pamela. Their phone number is 555-4365. Ralph has a son named Kevin from his ex-wife Alicia. His mother, Paula Hinkley, is a widow.

Using the suit, Ralph has excelled at a number of sports including tennis and skiing. He has played professional football (using his friend's name). As part of a case, Ralph also had a brief career as a professional baseball player (#1) with the California Stars.

Robert Culp as F.B.I. agent Bill Maxwell.

Before being graduated from Union High School in 1972, Ralph was elected most likely to succeed. His high school girlfriends included Gloria Corwin and Wendy DeFazio (who was dating another guy at the time). As a kid, Ralph loved magic. His hero was the Lone Ranger.

Ralph's predecessor in the "super hero business" was James J. Beck (and partner Marshall Dunn). After retiring, Ralph turned the suit over to Holly Hathaway.

(Hanley was Ralph's last name for a brief time after John Hinckley attempted to assassinate President Reagan.)

William Maxwell (Robert "I Spy" Culp): Bill Maxwell, a special agent with the Los Angeles office of the Federal Bureau of Investigation (FBI) was investigating the murder of his partner (John Mackie) when he ended up in the desert teamed up by "the little green guys" with Ralph Hinkley and the "magic jammies".

Bill has been a federal agent for twenty to thirty years. His second collar, in 1953, was the capture of the Barefoot Mugger. He went from a mediocre service record to a 98% "kill" record after meeting Ralph and receiving the suit. Bill, who has previously served in the Detroit and Phoenix offices, shows up late to work and keeps a messy desk. His first partner was Harlan Blackford.

Carlisle, Bill's current supervisor, dislikes Maxwell, whom he considers a "burnout". It is probably due to Carlisle that Bill went from working in a cubicle (17B) to a small desk in a large room shared by many agents. Under former supervisors Ace Aarons and Palmer Bradshaw, Bill ran the FBI baseball gaming pool.

Bill normally drives a beige government issue Dodge Diplomat. His license plates have included 973-QSN and his unit designation is X-Ray 6. However, Bill constantly needs to exchange cars as he has a habit of destroying them. At one point, he was criticized for having totaled five cars in the past eighteen months.

Previous to his career as a Federal agent, Bill was a sergeant in

43

Korea. He served under Capt. Tracy Winslow in the 72nd Armored Division. Tracy, who once saved Maxwell's life, was Bill's hero until years later when Tracy (then a police lieutenant) broke the law. Bill, who was shot in the chest while in Korea, played the accordion while in the Army.

While growing up, Bill always wanted to be a Federal agent. His mother, who had a drinking problem, spent a lot of time away from home and criticized Bill's early career choices. Bill was once married but no further details about his wife are known. Among his dislikes are ketchup, tomatoes, rock music and cats (which he is allergic to). He wears an American flag pin on his left lapel, usually wears a loose tie (with his top shirt button unbuttoned), and likes to snack on Milkbone dog biscuits.

In 1945, "Wild Bill" Maxwell played on a state championship football team (as #43). A knee injury prevented him from pursuing an athletic career.

After Ralph gave up the suit, Bill teamed up with Holly Hathaway.

Pamela Davidson Hinkley (Connie "Hotel" Sellecca): Pam, Ralph's fiance and eventual wife is initially the only person besides Bill who is aware of the super suit and its origins. In fact, Pam almost decided not to marry Ralph because of the suit.

Pam, an attorney, initially practiced family law (she handled Ralph's custody fight for Kevin.) She later practiced corporate law. Her law firms have included Carter, Bailey & Smith and Selquist, Allen, & Minor. She also worked as the only female attorney for a firm run by Sherwood Dawes.

She drives a white Volkswagon convertible (license plate 793 LAF) and briefly owned a stray cat named Lefty. In college, Pam belonged to a sorority and minored in theater arts.

Pam's parents, Alice and Harry Davidson, own a hardware store. Additionally, Harry Davidson serves as the mayor of Deerlick Falls, Minnesota.

Anthony J. Villicana (Michael Pare): Tony, one of Ralph's students, plays on the Whitney High School basketball team. He is manager of the band LA Freeway (made up of Ralph's students) and had the male lead in the school's production of *The Taming of the Shrew*. Tony, who drives the Villicana Parana, briefly worked at Cameron's Auto Recovery (in a job that Ralph helped him get). His favorite actor is Brando and his girlfriend's name is Rhonda Blake.

Rhonda Blake (Faye "V" Grant): As the predominant female member of Ralph's class, Rhonda serves as the lead vocalist in LA Freeway. She played the female lead in *The Taming of the Shrew* and occasionally babysits for Kevin Hinkley. Her mother, Rose Harris, is a cocktail waitress and a part-time file clerk. Rhonda, who was born when her mother was sixteen, dates Tony Villicana. She diets in order to maintain her figure.

Paco Rodriquez (Don Cervantes): Paco, a member of Ralph's class, plays guitar for LA Freeway. He also plays on the Whitney High School basketball team.

Cyler Johnson (Jesse D. Goins): Cyler, who worked one summer loading freight on a dock, is a member of Ralph's class and plays basketball on the Whitney High School basketball team. He plays keyboard for LA Freeway.

Carlisle, Norm/Les (William Bogert): Carlisle, Bill's FBI supervisor, has been with the bureau for twenty years. It was with the first name of Norm that Carlisle was temporarily relieved of his duties after filing a report about a flying man in a red suit (i.e. he saw Ralph fly and crash through a wall.) Carlisle, who later used the first name Les, is currently married.

Kevin Hinkley (Brandon Williams): Kevin the son of divorced parents Ralph and Alicia Hinkley, was the subject of a bitter custody battle. Although initially custody was given to Ralph, the fact that Kevin disappeared in later years seems to indicate that Alicia (an actress/model) finally received custody.

Ray Buck (Robby Weaver): Ray, who spent eight months teaching special education before Ralph took over the class, is currently the coach of the Whitney High School basketball team. His dream is to coach for a professional team.

Joey (Paul Carafotes): As the inheritor of Tony's Parana, Joey

filled the role left void when Tony Villicana left Ralph's class.

Tammy (Deborah Mays): Tammy, Joey's girlfriend, is the predominant female student in Ralph's class after the departure of Rhonda Blake. At one time, Tammy considered becoming a nurse.

Chaffee (Benny Medina): Chaffee, another member of the special education class, once found himself reluctantly running for student council president as part of a scheme devised by Tony Villicana.

David Knight (Edward Bell): Mr. Knight is the principal of Whitney High School and, thereby, Ralph's boss.

Holly Hathaway (Mary Ellen Stuart): Holly, who received the supersuit after Ralph retired (when his identity was revealed to the world), is an environmentalist and kindergarten teacher. She drives a red Cabriolet (license plate 5Q8 HPQ) and has a foster daughter named Sarah. Her partner in the "super hero" business is FBI agent Bill Maxwell.

Sarah (Mya Akerling): Sarah, the only person besides Bill and the Hinkleys' that knows about Holly and the suit, is Holly's seven-year-old foster daughter.

Profile: Stephen Geyer
interview by Doug Snauffer

In 1981 producer Stephen J. Cannell succeeded where many before him, and after, have failed. He managed to create and produce a fantasy series for television which became both a critical and commercial success. Titled *The Greatest American Hero,* the show dealt with an average Joe chosen by aliens to be Earth's last hope against her domestic enemies. He's given a bright red super-suit complete with an instruction book, which he promptly loses, and proceeds to leap into tall buildings in a...oops, better not get into that.

The show was given a spring tryout on ABC and soared in the Nielsen ratings. While much of the program's success was certainly due to fine performances by the actors and generally well-written scripts, it certainly did not hurt the series when the main title song, *Believe It or Not*, rose to number one on the pop charts. The tune, blared from beach radios, was released as a best-selling single, and vocalist Joey Scarbury was invited to perform on *Solid Gold*. Not bad for a TV theme, particularly one banged out in a matter of hours.

Cannell had hired music master Mike Post to produce both the theme song and weekly score for his series. Post subsequently turned to musician and lyricist Stephen Geyer to put the words to his music. As Geyer recalls, "Mike and I sat down together one weekend, we discussed the project briefly, and then Mike proceeded to write the music in what couldn't have been longer than an hour or two. Then it was my turn to go off and write the lyrics."

He remembers doing so without the benefit of having read the pilot script or having seen any film footage. "All I'd done is heard what the show was about," he continues. "I was told it had a sense of humor to it, and a sense of wonder with a little bit of fantasy. I figure I spent probably a couple of hours working on the lyrics." He went back to it now and then to sharpen it and hone it here and there, but the foundation was set. "I wish I could say there was more to it," he jokes. "Because then maybe I could justify the fee I got paid."

Today Geyer, 41, lives in the San Fernando Valley with his wife Erin, a real estate broker, and their two-year-old son Devon. He spent an early May morning reminiscing with *Epi-log* about his work on *The Greatest American Hero* and how it paved the way to his current distinction of being perhaps the most prolific songwriter in television history.

Back in 1981, Geyer, then 29, had already written songs for

Still, Cannell must have sensed something. He decided he wanted more of the same for his fledgling series. He wanted *The Greatest America Hero* to be peppered with songs that would not just serve as background noise, but would fit the plotline, would help move the story, add impact to certain scenes, and entertain viewers. Rather than buying the rights to popular songs and re-recording them with another vocalist like many series do, Cannell opted to have a new, original song written every week, and wanted Geyer to do it.

And Geyer said yes. "Having a producer of Cannell's caliber approach you in that manner was incredible. Me being in that position, I couldn't say no, although I wasn't really sure I could do it. I'd never written songs on demand before, with that kind of regularity."

Did Cannell have any doubts? "No, absolutely not," the producer told *Epi-log*. "Stephen had done work for us before *The Greatest American Hero*. I had known him for a while and was confident he could handle it."

The songs ranged in length from one to three minutes. Geyer did receive a little more of an edge this time around, being given the opportunity to see first drafts of most scripts, "I never got to see an episode first, because we were always working so far ahead of the production company's shooting schedule," he remembers. "I would read the script, write the song, demo it, and then go in and play it for Stephen personally.

As Cannell remembers, "Stephen would come over and play these songs for me and I was just knocked out. They were just so innovative and right for what I was trying to do with the show. I really thought he managed to find a completely different style and essence for each one that was in keeping with the episodes. He would bring the demos over to me and they would generally be just him playing a guitar and singing. And I would just sit there and be thinking the songs were so cool. Stephen doesn't have what you would call a traditional voice, but he really does sing his own material very well. And I was always saying, 'God, you should sing this, this is great!" But of course, Post, who was calling the shots from that end, was trying to establish Scarbury, who did all the on-air vocals.

The songs would be recorded on a soundstage at Universal, once Cannell approved, which he did on nearly every occasion. "Strangely enough," says Geyer, "the only song that wasn't approved was the first song I wrote for the first episodic show. I wrote a song that was a little bit too mellow. It was similar in tone to a Paul Simon song. I went in very happy about it, and Stephen said 'No, I think we need something a little more up'. Luckily, from there on in I never had another song declined."

His personal favorite for the show was a soft number titled *Once Upon A Time* for the first year episode **Saturday on Sunset Boulevard**, which dealt with two Russian lovers attempting to defect, who get separated and become lost in Los Angeles with the KGB in pursuit. "All the songs had some kind of message or story in them. Sometimes you had to listen more closely than other times, but it's like that for most songs."

Cannel recalls specifically a song Geyer did for *The Greatest American Hero* episode **The 200 Mile an Hour Fastball**, which Cannell himself had written. Says Cannell, "He wrote a song called

several major artists and a year earlier had penned a number three hit, *Hot Rod Hearts*, for Robbie Dupree. He and Post had already done the theme for a previous Cannell series, *Richie Brockelman, Private Eye*, as well as a package of songs for a Ron Howard film, *The Locust*. But Geyer was looking for the kind of long-term security a hit series could provide, and found that opportunity in *The Greatest American Hero*.

"I remember one of my major considerations about it was, did the songs have to be called *The Greatest American Hero*, did that phrase actually have to be in the song. I was concerned because I knew that would be absolutely impossible to do," he laughs. "Fortunately, Mike gave me the free reign to go where ever I needed to go, so I started writing it with the hook, "Believe It or Not." Once it was completed, we then had to get Stephen's approval." Which they did, with one stumbling block to go.

"We began to worry about whether we had the right to use that title since there was such a famous series of books by the same name. I think the way it worked out was that we actually had to pay *Ripley's Believe It or Not* some fee." Geyer admits to being extremely relieved that a compromise could be worked out. "I was really happy to find out we didn't have to change it, because we'd of had to trash the entire song."

When they went into the studio to record it, Post brought in Joey Scarbury to do the vocal track. Post had been managing Scarbury and was trying to get his career off the ground, so this was quite an opportunity for national exposure, although Geyer says that as they listened back to *Believe It or Not*, no one guessed it would ever become as popular as it did.

The Game Goes On and it was really heroic. It was just perfect for the episode, which was about Hinkley putting the suit on because he'd always wanted to be a major league pitcher, and throwing these 200-mile an hour fastballs and actually breaking into the major league. It was sort of like 'Damn Yankees' in that respect, and the song just really made a huge difference in the episode."

Obviously Cannell was closely involved with the music portion of the show, and Geyer's opinion of the producer is indeed high. "Stephen Cannell is a real maverick. You hear a lot about the way the business is and the way people in the business are, and all I can say is that he is a real gentleman and I couldn't respect him more. I couldn't have had a more pleasurable working experience."

Cannell's feelings are mutual. "Stephen's a pretty terrific guy. We always got along very well, and he was always every easy to work with." Early in their relationship, before *The Greatest American Hero*, Cannell admits he thought of Geyer solely as a lyricist, but "I was surprised by what a great songwriter he turned out to be. Which really shouldn't of surprised me, because he was always a great poet."

Making the experience even more enjoyable was the fact that Geyer also immensely enjoyed the show he was working on. "I thought it was a lot of fun just to watch. There's not a person I've run into who've said they didn't really, really enjoy the show. Everybody thought it was either funny, or cute, or appealed to them in some way. I was proud to have had the opportunity to work on the show.

Geyer, Post and Cannell's working relationship continued well beyond *The Greatest American Hero*. In the fall of 1982, as that series was heading into it's third and final season, scheduled opposite *Dallas* on CBS, Cannell began work on a sister series that would air immediately afterwards on Friday nights. Titled *The Quest*, it followed the zany exploits of four Americans who were found to be heirs to the throne of a small European kingdom. They were dispatched on a noble journey that would take them around the globe and give each the opportunity to prove their worthiness to rule.

Post and Geyer again teamed up for the main title, *Kings & Queens*, which was performed by Lisa Lee. Geyer then began turning out a second weekly tune for this series, which was pulled from ABC's schedule after only five of it's nine episodes were broadcast. *The Greatest American Hero* was laid to rest a short time later.

Since that time, Geyer and Post have authored several more popular TV themes, including Ronnie Milsap songs for *The Rousters* (1983) and *J.J. Starbuck* (1987). They turned to hard rock for *Hardcastle & McCormick*'s popular *Drive!* (1983), and most recently collaborated on the song from NBC's *Blossom*, which is performed by Dr. John. Although Post alone composed the instrumental opening theme for *Stingray* (1986), Geyer wrote the dark, macabre tunes that haunted a majority of the series 23 episodes. In the spring of 1986, Geyer teamed with composer Charles Fox on *Together Through the Years*, sung by Roberta Flack for *The Hogan Family*. His movie credits include *The River Rat* with Tommy Lee Jones and *Zapped* with Scott Baio.

Geyer's biggest challenge, though, may have been his involvement two years ago with Steven Bochco's ill-fated, but ambitious *Cop Rock*, on which Geyer was head songwriter. "I loved that show," he says. " I loved the idea of the show and I'm sure if it would have had another year it would have been absolutely spectacular. As it was, when it was good it was just extraordinary and when it was bad it was terrible."

So what went wrong? "I wish I could tell you. A lot of people have told me they just didn't get the idea of having people sing during dramatic action. And the only thing I can say is that I don't understand that point of view, because it's happening in Broadway musicals, which is the American art form, for years, for decades. And I can't understand why they didn't want to see it on their televisions. But I'm very proud of the work that I and the other songwriters did." He was involved in writing at least two or three songs per show. "It was a brilliant failure," he concludes.

Overall, quite an impressive resume for someone who never took a music lesson. Geyer was born in Lima, Peru. His father was in the CIA, and the family moved quite frequently. Remembers Geyer: "I lived in Cyprus, the Philippines, Okinawa, and England." Of his father's career he jokes, "That's probably where I got the ability to put the hidden messages in my songs." He feels that seeing so much of the world at such a young, inquisitive age helps him in writing his music.

At the time, Geyer did enjoy music, specifically folk music. He listened to the Kingston Trio, The Limelighters, The Highwaymen, Ray Charles and The Beach Boys. But still, he wasn't necessarily pursuing a musical career. "Basically, my older brother played guitar, and was popular, particularly with the ladies, and that really caught my interest," he says. "I was eleven at the time, and I began sneaking into his room and practicing on his guitar, figuring it would help me get girls."

He eventually bought a banjo, "I was so inspired by the Kingston Trio," and got into Flatt & Scruggs, country and bluegrass picking. He studied art in college in Maryland, and in 1972 he drove out to California in a VW bug, with one hundred dollars in his pocket and intentions of becoming "the next Jackson Browne, the next Paul Simon, or James Taylor. For whatever reason, that didn't happen, but luckily I was able to go in a different direction."

He spent quite a few years living in a $100 a month apartment with a Murphy bed and struggled to get by. But he did have a glimmer of hope on his horizon. In 1973 he attended an open audition titled "The Songwriter's Alternative Showcase", which offered unknowns the opportunity to play for industry people. The vice-president of BMI heard and liked Geyer's playing, and introduced him to Mike Post, who also publishes music.

From there, Geyer turned to his magic bag of talent and began writing songs, which began selling for other artists. What was the first song he ever sold? He hesitates, laughs, and confesses, "I hate to admit it, but I think it was the *Ballad of Linda Lovelace*". From there his credits include *You Turn the Light On* for Kenny Rogers; *Dreams* for John Denver; *Love Brought Us Here Tonight* for Smokey Robinson; and his most prized composition, *Blood Line*, a title cut on a 1976 Glen Campbell album, which "was kind of a John Ford epic Western in song."

Later, he began writing for television while continuing to do road work as a lead guitarist and background singer for acts like Carole Bayer Sager and Jonathan Edwards. When *Greatest American Hero* took off, he was more than happy to settle down in Los Angeles. "I had had plenty of the road so I was glad to get a steady thing. It was a very unusual job for a songwriter to have something that steady. It provided me with a real good foundation to stay in town and build myself as more of a songwriter both for assignment writing on television and for records."

And what makes for a good lyricist? "It's a craft," says Geyer, although "there is an X-factor, you know, somewhere between being born with it and developing it as you experience life. It's a way of looking at the world and making connections. You see the connections between words and between things and places. You see the irony and you build on that to create memorable phrases or ideas

Faye Grant as the beautiful Rhonda.

within a song. In terms of the craft it's much like doing a crossword puzzle, not only with words but with sounds and phonetics, searching for the right sound, word, or phrase for a specific point in the song."

Can it be learned? Is life experience a prerequisite? "Again, I got to see a lot of the world while I was growing up, but I don't think you have to be Rhodes scholar to write great lyrics. I mean there are some absolutely terrific lyrics in some folk songs and country songs that have nothing to do with scholarship. It can be learned, but frankly that X-factor is a real special ingredient in it. It's what you can bring to a craft that anybody can learn. Anybody can learn to put a brush in the paint and put the paint on the canvas, but what are you going to say with that comes from somewhere else." Geyer sits down with nothing more than his guitar and a pad of paper when he writes. What about the money? "Well, good money is all so relative. I don't think that the money is nearly as good as it should be. Music is an extremely important part of television and movies, but unfortunately it often goes ignored to a large extent, at least consciously. I'll tell you this, you won't get rich. The odds are stacked way against you. If you want to make a lot of money, don't become a songwriter."

Geyer himself is expanding his horizons. "The truth is that at this point I have basically switched my attentions from writing music to writing TV and movie scripts," he said. Which he's actually been involved with for a number of years. In 1988, Cannell gave him a staff scriptwriting position on his NBC series *Sonny Spoon* and more recently Geyer has written an episode of the CBS late-night crime-time series *Silk Stalkings*. He's sold a number of screenplays, which have not yet been produced, and has at least one project showing some really nice potential, which he is unable to comment on at the moment. "But that's where my focus is right now," he says.

"I prefer writing drama that encompasses a bit of humor, just as life does," he comments. And with his ability to capture everyday ironies, the results should be intriguing to say the least.

Believe It or Not (Theme from *The Greatest American Hero*) by Stephen Geyer - Music by Mike Post. Copyright (c) 1981 by Stephen J. Cannell Productions

Look at what's happened to me
I can't believe it myself
Suddenly I'm up on top of the world
It should have been somebody else

Believe It or Not
I'm walking on air
I never thought I could feel so free
Flying away on a wing and a prayer
Who could it be
Believe It or Not, it's just me

Just like the light of a new day
It hit me from out of the blue
Breaking me out of the spell I was in
Making all of my wishes come true
This is too good to be true
Look at me, falling for you

The Game Goes On from *The 200 Mile an Hour Fastball* Music and Lyrics by Stephen Geyer Copyright (c) 1981 by Stephen J. Cannell Productions

Everybody has a dream
When everyone is young
Lookin' back, we wonder about
The Things we might have done
The chances that we didn't take
The breaks that never came
Oh, play me coach
I'll bring 'em home
Just put me in the game
And it's one, two, three strikes and you're gone
But the game, oh the game, the Game Goes On

Trouble On Wheels from **Hog Wild** Music and lyrics by Stephen Geyer Copyright (c) 1981 by Stephen J. Cannell Productions

I got my hand on a throttle
And my eyes on a thin white line
Gonna burn a little rubber
Wanna listen to the engine whine
I got a dirty job to do
Ain't gonna quit until I'm through
'Cause I'm a mean motor scooter
And I'm feelin' mean all the time
Oh, here comes trouble
I ain't makin no deals
I'm danger in motion
Trouble on Wheels

Geyer's driving tips, the hook from *Hardcastle & McCormick*'s *Drive*

Drive!
Push it to the floor 'til the engine screams
Drive!
Drive it like the demon that drives your dreams

Music of

The Greatest American Hero

article by Howard T. Konig

Although most people remember the opening theme song to their favorite show, not many are conscious of the background music that is played during the action of the actual show. *The Greatest American Hero* is no exception, for besides its well known theme song (*Believe It or Not* - #2 on Billboard's charts in 1981), *The Greatest American Hero* also included a wonderfully composed background soundtrack courtesy of Mike Post and Pete Carpenter. In fact, *The Greatest American Hero* took this all one step further with most of the episodes featuring originally composed songs (by Mike Post and Stephen Geyer). Therefore, this article provides the reader with a summary of all the originally composed songs. (Please note that this list excludes previously written songs, such as *Eve of Destruction* in **Operation Spoilsport** or *Taxman* in **There's Just No Accounting**, that were reperformed for *The Greatest American Hero*.

Episode
Song
Incident

The Hit Car
Hang on Sister
Ralph and Bill escort a female witness.

Here's Looking at You, Kid
Nothin's Gonna Bring Me Down
Ralph searches for a missing plane.

Saturday on Sunset Blvd
Once Upon a Time
The FBI searches for a couple from an Eastern Block country.

Reseda Rose
Anytime You Need Me
Ralph helps Bill with an assignment.

My Heroes Have Always Been Cowboys
Heroes are Human
Ralph considers his hero responsibilities.

Fire Man
Your Friend
Ralph helps to clear Tony of an arson charge.

The Best Desk Scenario
Sum of My Old Friends
Pam and Ralph receive career boosts while Bill ponders his own stalled career.

The 200-Mile-An-Hour Fastball
The Game Goes On (later used in an episode of *Hardcastle and McCormick*).
Ralph plays major league baseball.

Hog Wild
Trouble on Wheels
A motorcycle gang rides the road.

The Lost Diablo
Pieces of Gold
Ralph and the kids search for a gold mine.

Plague
Don't Let Me Down
Ralph saves Bill after the FBI agent is dropped from a helicopter.

Train of Thought
Where Do We Go From Here
Ralph suffers from amnesia.
My Friends
Ralph remembers Bill.

Now You See It
Scramble
The Air Force tries to shoot down a stolen plane.

Just Another Three Ring Circus
Secrets
Ralph and Bill join the circus.

It's All Downhill From Here
Free to Fly
Ralph uses the suit to ski.

Dreams
Dreams
Ralph makes a friend's dream come true.

The Good Samaritan
Sometimes
Bill and Ralph search for a missing boy.

Capt. Bellybuster and the Speed Factory
Good Guys
Capt. Bellybuster fights against injustice.

Divorce Venusian Style
Opposites
Bill and Ralph clash.

The Price is Right
Big Shot
Ralph attends his high school reunion.

This is the One the Suit Was Meant For
A Bicycle Built For Two
Ralph and Bill ride a two person bike.

The Newlywed Game
Everything You Dream
Ralph flies north on a mission.

Desperado
Desperado
Wild horses run free.

The 200-Mile-Per-Hour Fastball: (left to right) Michael Pare, Faye Grant, William Katt, Don Cervantes, and Jesse D. Goins.

50

The Greatest American Hero

review by William E. Anchors, Jr.

Production credits:

Executive Producer	Stephen J. Cannell
	Juanita Bartlett
Co-Executive Producer	Jo Swerkling, Jr.
Supervising Producer	Frank Lupo
Producer	Alex Beaton
	Christopher Nelson
	Babs Greyhosky
Creator	Stephen J. Cannell
Music	Pete Carpenter, Mike Post
Theme	Mike Post, Stephen Geyer
Sung by	Joey Scarbury

Regular cast:

Ralph Hinkley*	William Katt
Bill Maxwell	Robert Culp
Pam Davidson	Connie Sellecca
Tony Villicana	Michael Pare (years 1-2)
Rhonda Blake	Faye Grant (years 1-2)
Clyer	Jesse D. Goins
Rodriquez	Don Cervantes
Kevin Hinkley	Brandon Williams (year 1)
Agent Norman Carlisle	William Bogert
Joey	Paul Carafotes (year 3)
Tammy	Deborah Mays (year 3)
Chaffee	Benny Medina (year 3)

Number of episodes: pilot movie, 43 one hour shows

*In a typical case of network ingenuity, Ralph Hinkley's name was changed to "Hanley" for a few first season episodes (conveniently bleeped out in syndication) after a real person named Hinkley tried to assassinate President Reagan. After all, viewers are too stupid to tell the difference between a guy who flies around in a red suit and an insane assassin, right?

Premise: *Greatest American Hero* started out as a cross between Superman (DC Comics sued over the similarities) and *Welcome Back Kotter*. The character of Ralph Hinkley was that of a well-meaning do-gooder high school teacher just assigned the worst class in the system: a group of delinquents and misfits that everyone else had given up on, but a situation Ralph saw as a challenge. His life became more complicated after being given the alien super-suit and teaming up with super-straight, ultraconservative F.B.I. agent Bill Maxwell, after which he became a somewhat reluctant superhero. Luckily, the misfit kids (including Faye Grant, soon to be a star on *V*) were gradually phased out of the stories and more action was brought in.

Comments: Most of *The Greatest American Hero* are episodes are quite good, and the characters are a delight. Towards the end of the series the stories became weaker, and the decision to air it on Friday night - the "killer" time period that has led to the cancellation of *Star Trek, Highwayman, Starman, Something is Out There, The Phoenix, Nightmare Cafe, Dark Shadows*, etc. - condemned it with the poor ratings all sci-fi series receive on Friday evenings.

The Greatest American Hero (airdate: Mar. 18, 1981, two-hour pilot, not in syndication). A group of baldheaded religious fanatics hunt down and kill F.B.I. agent John Mackie. Elsewhere, Ralph Hinkley is a new teacher at Whitney High School, and is given the worst class in the system - a group of disobedient misfits that everyone has given up on, but whom Ralph sees potential in. After nearly getting into a fist fight with the hard-nosed Tony, Ralph informs the class he has arranged a class trip. They can't believe anyone would trust them outside the classroom, but they leave for the desert, and on the way there stop at a diner for lunch. Also at the diner is straight-laced F.B.I. agent Bill Maxwell. Tony starts an argument with Maxwell, and pulls a knife on him. The rowdy teenager stops when Bill pulls out a gun, causing Ralph to send him back to the rest of the kids, then proceeds to apologize to the gun-wielding Maxwell, who wants no explanations. Back on the road, Ralph and the kids are stranded in the middle of the desert at night when the electrical system on the bus suddenly goes out. Ralph starts walking to go for help, and is nearly run over by Bill Maxwell, whose car goes out of control as it swerves all over the road. When the vehicle comes to a stop Ralph runs over to it and finds an unconscious Maxwell, who has been looking for his missing F.B.I. friend, not knowing that John Mackie is dead. As Ralph and Bill talk and try to figure out what went wrong with the car's steering, a huge UFO suddenly appears overhead. Jumping inside the car to leave, Bill and Ralph find it won't start, the doors suddenly lock on their own, and the radio comes to life with a message that they are to listen to an important message. Next they hear the voice of Mackie, who presents Ralph and Bill with a super-suit, designed to give one specific wearer a wide range of powers to help humanity. It will only work on Ralph and if he doesn't wear it within two weeks it will automatically disintegrate. The ghostly form of Mackie shows up, places the suit in the trunk, and tells Bill he has been dead for six hours and is now starting a new life living with the aliens. Ralph and Bill are both in a daze as the spacecraft disappears. They go to the trunk and look over the suit, which Bill wants no part of and leaves. Ralph, standing alone in the desert, doesn't notice the instruction book drop into the sand as he walks back to the bus. Once there, Rhonda gets upset with Ralph because she has a crush on him and she won't accept his explanation that he can't get involved with a student.

As Ralph and the kids drive home, elsewhere is Nelson Corey, the leader of the militant fanatics, and a millionaire who has spent a fortune to move Adam Taft into the presidency so that Corey can overthrow the government. Taft goes on TV to announce his running for office just as Ralph arrives home to check out his suit, which he doesn't build up courage to try on until the next day. He is nearly seen in the suit by his young son, who is the subject of an upcoming court battle with Ralph's ex-wife. Ralph is trying to keep custody of the child, which his ex-wife is contesting. Meanwhile, Ralph is falling in love with his attorney, Pam Davidson. Ralph just wants to forget the suit, but is reminded of it when he arrives at school and is told that a "friend" is in the boy's bathroom throwing up! Ralph has no idea who it is until he reaches the restroom, and finds Bill Maxwell, who is getting over a drunken spree he went on after their alien encounter. Bill is all in favor of starting their partnership - until learning the instruction book was lost. The "team" begins with a major confrontation when Ralph refuses to drop everything and follow Bill's orders. Ralph agrees to meet him in two days. Later, after trying on the suit again it gives him a holographic image in which he sees Maxwell captured and in danger of being killed by the fanatical group who killed the other agent. Convincing Pam that he really does have super powers, she and

Ralph save Bill, and form an alliance to go after Corey. **Guest cast:** Richard Herd [*V*] as Adam Taft, G.D. Spradlin as Nelson Corey, Bob Minor as John Mackie, Ned Wilson as Shackelford, Robby Weaver as Buck, Edward Bell as David Knight, Jeff MacKay [*Tales of the Gold Monkey*] as the police officer, Hank Salas as Brother Michael, Robert Dunlap as the accountant, Jeff MacKay as Cowan, Jason Corbet, Roberta Jean Williams, Jody Lee Olhava, Robbie Kiger, Carol Jones, Ed Deemer, James King, Corkey Ford, John Caliri, Lydia Fernandez, Cheryl Francis. **Writer:** Stephen J. Cannell. **Director:** Rod Holcomb.

The Hit Car (airdate: Mar. 25, 1981). When an F.B.I. agent tries to deliver a witness to a courthouse where she is to testify, they are attacked by a steel-plated, machine-gun-equipped car, and the agent is killed. The next day Ralph is trying to talk the class into putting on a Shakespearian play, which they are against. Ralph won't take no for an answer and "volunteers" the kids and Pam to put on the production. As they work on the various parts, Bill arrives and demands that Pam and Ralph drop whatever they are doing and Ralph prepare to fly to San Francisco on their next assignment: delivering show girl Scarlet Wild to Los Angeles, where she is a witness in the trial of Johnny Damanti, an underworld crime leader whom Bill has been trying to bust for fifteen years. Pam resents being dragged into the "team" to perform menial tasks, and Ralph doesn't want to abandon the kids, but realizes the chance to get the dope dealer off the streets is a deserving task. While they head to San

Francisco, Damanti orders that the hit car be sent to take care of Maxwell. Bill and Ralph's first problem comes up when the star says her astrology chart indicates she cannot fly the next few days, so she must be driven to the trial - which will make them a perfect target for the killer car. As Bill tries to convince her it will be safer to take a plane, a sniper opens up, barely missing Bill and Scarlet as bullets come through a window. Ralph puts on the suit and flies from the upper story window across the street, but misses the roof and crashes through a window into a couple's bedroom. He apologizes and goes in search of the sniper, who is long gone. Going back to Scarlet's room, the three leave in Bill's car, and once on the road Scarlet reveals that, according to her astrological chart, she can only spend the night in Santa Barbara. Bill is against it, wanting to stay at a nearby F.B.I. safe house. Ralph finds a compromise by phoning Pam and arranging to stay at her employer's beach house. Pam meets them there, not realizing Damanti's men have followed them. The next day thugs surround the house, so Bill goes out the front to draw their fire while Ralph sneaks around behind them in the suit. Before Ralph can reach them Bill is shot in the hand, but Ralph soon rounds up both men while Bill calls the police to arrest the assassins. Damanti is furious to learn his men are now staying in a mental institution after claiming a "flying super guy" stopped them. Knowing the route Maxwell will be using to leave the beach house for Los Angeles, Damanti sends the hit car to attack Maxwell and Scarlet. It catches up with them as they reach the courthouse where she is to testify, launches an attack that leaves Bill shot in the leg, and gets away - just before Scarlet refuses to testify now that she is appearing before the grand jury. It now appears Scarlet's claiming to want to testify was only a ruse for Damanti to murder Bill - which he is still determined to do. **Guest cast:** Gwen Humble as Scarlet Wild, Gianni Russo as Johnny Damanti, Kene Holliday as Arnold Turner, Ernie Orsatti as Bob Baron, Bob Goldstein as the maitre d', Virginia Palmer as the woman, Quin Kessler as the hat check girl, W.T. Zacha, Anthony Charnoto as Mike, Arnold Turner as Billings, Ernie Orsatti as Bob Aaron, Melvin F. Allen as the man, James Arone as the waiter. **Writer:** Stephen J. Cannell. **Director:** Rod Holcomb.

Here's Looking at You, Kid (airdate: April 1, 1981). At the Palmdale, California research branch of Beller Aircraft, a new computer-controlled gunsight is being tested on a jet fighter. The aircraft takes off to test the sight, but the pilot refuses to answer radio calls, then heads off course as the jet dives below radar detection and disappears altogether. The Beller Aircraft executives and government officials are informed that the real test pilot was found knocked out, so they are led to believe a foreign agent has stolen the aircraft to obtain the sight - a great blow to U.S. national security. The aircraft lands in the desert, where the pilot turns over the gunsight to enemy agents, who then camouflage and hide the plane. When the Air Force cannot locate the aircraft, Bill thinks he knows where the jet might be, so he arrives at school to grab Ralph, who is due to meet Pam's parents for the first time. He doesn't want to hear about another of Bill's "big ones", but finally agrees to help if he can get back in time. A reluctant Ralph leaves to help, and uses Bill's car phone to inform Pam he may be late for the meeting - a fact she clearly is not pleased with. While Pam greets her parents at the airport, Bill and Ralph arrive in the desert where Ralph uses the suit to search for the aircraft. Still not able to master flight, Ralph spends as much time crashing as flying, but finally discovers the camouflaged aircraft. Bill arrives and they find the pilot's helmet, which Ralph uses to holograph in on the pilot's thoughts. He learns that a mercenary stole the gunsite, and Bill believes he knows who it might be. Before they leave, Bill gets the idea that the suit may have telekinetic powers, so he talks Ralph into concentrating to see what might happen. Something goes haywire with the suit causing him to keep turning invisible, and the only way he can regain visibility is to take off the suit. Going to the mercenary club, Ralph suddenly becomes visible and has to hide so he won't be seen in the suit. Before they can decide what to do next, Ralph flickers in and out of invisibility, and finally disappears again. He holographs on a man inside the club, where he sees Gordon McCready negotiating to sell the site to foreign agents. He is going to hold an auction and sell the top secret device to the highest bidder. Ralph reports to Bill that the site is being sold at a foreign embassy, which Maxwell realizes is foreign territory outside of U.S. jurisdiction. But, with Ralph using his new power of invisibility, he might just get in that evening and steal the site. However, Ralph's immediate problem is meeting Pam's parents - which will be tough, since Ralph cannot become visible. **Guest cast:** James Whitmore, Jr. as Gordon McCready, June Lockhart [*Lost in Space*] as Mrs. Davidson, Bob Hastings as Harry Davidson, Red West as Cliff, Thomas W. Babson as Colvin, Will Gill, Jr. as the African representative, Gerald Jann as the Asian representative, Eric Forst as the European representative, Roger Etienne as the captain, Daniel Chodos as the aide, Al Dunlop as the mechanic, Nick Ginardo as the consul person, Bert Hinchman as the bus driver, Blake Clark as the policeman, Zitto Kazann as the consul general, F.J. O'Neil as Van Kamp, Laurence Haddon as Gen. Morehead, Denise Halma as Carrie. **Writer:** Juanita Bartlett. **Director:** Bob Thompson.

Saturday on Sunset Boulevard (airdate: April 8, 1981). Carlisle

and other F.B.I. agents surround and capture a Russian citizen and his wife, a wealthy heiress. But before they go very far their car is run off the road by some Russian hit men trying to get the Valenkovs, who escape during the ensuing gunfight. The Russian assassins continue to look for the woman, as they need an island she owns to establish a missile base for use against the U.S. Meanwhile, Ralph is getting frustrated trying to teach his kids, who cannot understand why they should waste their time in school. Furthermore, Ralph is told that maybe the reason he is stuck teaching misfits is because he is a misfit himself. Ralph ponders the situation while Bill, at F.B.I. headquarters, is in trouble because he cannot answer a lie detector test truthfully without revealing Ralph and the suit. Bill finds himself suspended after he fails the test, and is given two days to reconsider his answers. If he cannot pass then he will be off the force permanently with no benefits. Pam, Ralph, and Bill meet at a restaurant where Ralph tries to explain why he is no longer sure of his job choice, but Bill is only interested in his immediate problem - saving his twenty-year career in the F.B.I. - and has a plan to salvage the situation: he knows that both the F.B.I. and the Russians are after the heiress and her husband, and if Ralph uses the suit to help them crack the case it will get Bill off the hook. Ralph agrees to help, flies to the Federal Building, steals the F.B.I. records on the Russian citizens, then returns to see Bill and Pam. Going through the file, they learn the truth about the Valenkovs. Bill realizes there is little time for an extensive search to find the man and wife, who are each hiding in a different location. Ralph volunteers to have his kids search for the Valenkovs, an idea both the students and Bill are against. Nevertheless, both parties agree to compromise, and the search begins while Bill operates a command post to receive any news the kids might phone in. As the search progresses, no trace of the Valenkovs is found, but Tony makes peace with Ralph after having criticized him in class. Later, while in the van, Tony and Ralph see Serge Valenkov and follow him. He picks up Theresa, but some Russian agents arrive and kidnap the husband and wife. Ralph changes into his super suit just as Pam arrives, but when he tries to stop the kidnapping the Russian agents grab Pam and threaten to kill her if Ralph intervenes. He can do nothing but stand by and watch as the Russians drive away with a kidnapped Pam, along with the Valenkovs. **Guest cast:** Alexa Hamilton as Theresa, Kai Wulff as Serge Valenkov, David Tress as Mikhail, Mal Steward as Sherman, Ian Teodorescu as the Russian official, Lev Mailer as Frederic, Will MacMillan as Kerner, Christopher Thomas as Craig, Lawrence Benedict as Hellinger, Richard R. Holley as the helicopter pilot, Glenn Wilder as the Kavolstock, Joseph Warren as Harlan Cain. **Writer:** Stephen J. Cannell. **Director:** Rod Holcomb.

Reseda Rose (airdate: April 15, 1981). Five miles off the California coast, a submarine is cruising the waters of the Pacific. It sends a message to the mainland by radio to an agent and informs him that instructions will be transmitted that night. Elsewhere, Rose Blake, Rhonda's mother, works as a waitress full time, but has a part time clerk job with Technitron, the manufacturer of top-secret weapons systems. Russian agents who have infiltrated Technitron find one of Rose's ear rings where it dropped in a drawer containing top-secret papers. They assume that she has been stealing some of the documents and kidnap her just after leaving her apartment. The next day Ralph is upset over dealing with his ex-wife and custody of their little boy, Kevin, after she ruins their weekend by refusing to keep Kevin as planned. Pam and Ralph cancel their trip and prepare to take Kevin to Marineland, only to have Bill stop by and remind Ralph that he and the suit were supposed to help him crack a case. Ralph agrees to go after Bill assures him it won't take more than three hours, and Pam leaves to take Kevin to a movie. Just as they are about to leave, Rhonda arrives after her mother didn't return

Ralph and Bill find a stolen jet in "Here's Looking at You Kid".

home, and asks Mr. Hinkley for help. Ralph talks Bill into stopping at the saloon where Rose works, and finds the owner irate after Rose didn't show up for work, then two thugs beat him up to see if he had the documents she was supposed to have taken. Since the hoods already knew about Technitron, Ralph and Bill head there, where Ralph holographs in on a break-in on the third floor. Bill runs to the building as Ralph flies through the third story window and puts both men out of action. Ralph "persuades" one of them to reveal where Rose is by flying him to the top of a ledge on the building, then after getting the address he flies there while Bill heads to the residential home in his car. Neither Bill or Ralph realize that the kidnapping ties in with a case they were already working on - a ring of Russian agents operating in the U.S. Ralph arrives at the home and sees Rose in a holograph, then disarms the Soviet agent just before he transmits a message. Putting him out of action, Ralph finds Rose and looks for clothes to put on over his suit so Rose won't see him in it. Ralph doesn't notice the agent flip a switch that turns on an outside light, so when a second agent, Simpson, arrives with the stolen papers, he immediately leaves. Bill arrives moments later and sees the light, making him realize Ralph slipped up. Going in the house, he and Ralph untie Rose and question her. They learn that Simpson, whose real name is Semenenko, has been stealing secrets from Technitron. Now they just have to find Simpson and the rest of the ring - and Ralph has to get back home to Pam and Kevin, who have already returned from Marineville, and deal with his ex-wife as

well, as she is having a fit because Ralph didn't spend the day with Kevin. **Guest cast:** E.J. Peaker as Rose Blake, Simone Griffeth as Alicia Hinkley, Peter White as Semenenko/Simpson, Kurt Grayson as Vladimir Zorin, Jens Nowak as the submarine seaman, Don Dolan as the Technitron guard, George Ganchev as the submarine captain, Dave Shelley as Manny, Al White as the station attendant, Nicholas Worth as Leonard, Stephen Kahan as Merv. **Writer:** Juanita Barlett. **Director:** Gabrielle Beaumont.

My Heroes Have Always Been Cowboys (airdate: April 29, 1981). Ralph and Bill are out chasing two bank robbers, and Ralph is having a lot of trouble with his flying. He keeps landing near police officers, who are all now chasing the "nut case in red pajamas". He finally stops the robbers, causing a bus to nearly goes off the side of a cliff while trying to avoid hitting the thieves' car, but Ralph saves the photo-snapping Japanese tourists. The thieves take off again, but Bill catches up and runs them off the road and arrests them. Ralph arrives and explains what happened. Nearly causing the death of innocent people depresses Ralph; later, a good Korean War buddy of Bill's tells him he is fed up with the law enforcement system and is leaving the police force. Cap realizes he can't make a difference any more, and has given up trying. He can't deal with the system, and tells Bill that he and four other cops are going to rip off a jewel theft ring, then head to Argentina. He has it all planned out and wants Bill to join in, but Maxwell thinks Cap is joking. Only later, after he realizes Cap was telling the truth, does Bill become disillusioned that his friend is turning into a thief himself. At his house, Ralph puts away his super suit in disgust, but when his son wants to see a local appearance of Ralph's childhood idol, John Hart, Ralph agrees to go and it gives him much to think about since the Lone Ranger had always been his hero. Meanwhile, unknown to Bill, his friend Tracy "Cap" Winslow tells his partners about Maxwell, and agree he must be gotten rid of. Bill arrives at Ralph's house and tells him that Cap, his hero, may be going bad, and he wants Ralph and the suit to help stop Winslow from making a mistake. Ralph hasn't had a chance to tell Bill he doesn't want to wear the suit anymore, and reluctantly agrees to go along. They soon catch up with Cap's accomplices stealing the jewels, but Bill's car breaks down and Ralph is on his own to catch the crooked cops. Once again, Ralph catches up to the car, but has to save an old woman from getting run down while Cap's accomplices escape. This is the final straw for Ralph, who wants nothing to do with the suit from here on in. After returning to Ralph's house, Cap shows up and tries to make Bill feel guilty for trying to implicate him in the robbery when Cap had carried Bill across fifteen miles of frozen real estate in war-torn Korea. He leaves, and Bill agrees to drop his investigation. The next day, Ralph goes to see John Hart again, and an inspiring talk with the actor gives Ralph an idea on how to take care of his and Bill's situation. **Guest cast:** Jack Ging as Tracy Winslow, John Hart [*The Lone Ranger*] as himself, Ferdy Mayne as Abe Figueroa, Frank McCarthy as Edward McAstelli, William Woodson as the announcer, Brandon Williams, Joseph Chapman as Tim Carson, Robert Gooden as Sam Watson, Bruce Tuthill as Norm Woods, Glenn Wilder as Pete King, William Woodson as the announcer, Charles Walker as the man, David Clover as the policeman. **Writer:** Stephen J. Cannell. **Director:** Arnold Laven.

Fire Man (airdate: May 6, 1981). An arsonist burns a warehouse using a flame thrower, and as the culprit escapes a guard is nearly run down by the arsonist's speeding car. The guard gets the license number of the car, a vehicle that is about to cause Ralph Hinkley much concern. Later, Tony is working in the job Ralph helped get him - repossessing cars. But the first night he picks up the car used by the arsonist at the warehouse. Police stop him after seeing the maroon Ford, and find a flame thrower in the trunk. They start to arrest him for the torch job, but he takes off, resulting in a high-speed chase right past Whitney High School as Ralph is preparing to go home. After getting caught changing into his super-suit, Ralph takes off and enables Tony to escape. Afterwards Tony disappears, and the next day his fellow students refuse to say where he is. Bill arrives at school and accuses the teenager of being the arsonist who torched the warehouse. Even worse, the same arsonist is believed to have burned some other buildings, including one with Federal records. Now both the police and the F.B.I. want the student, making Ralph realize he must find out who the real arsonist is before the man kills Tony to protect his identity. Returning home, Ralph finds the teenager waiting for him, having broken into the house. Pam also arrives, hears his story, and approaches Federal authorities to learn why they suspect Tony. The representative she speaks to claims that Tony never had a job repossessing cars according to the people he was supposed to be working for. They believe he was paid to destroy important records needed to convict someone on an upcoming case. She doesn't believe it and leaves - with several F.B.I. men following her. Back at his house, Ralph learns that he got Tony a job with hoods, so he goes to Cameron Auto to confront the owner, Mr. Cameron, who is already fed up with questions from the Feds and the police. He and an assistant throw Ralph off their property, so he changes into he suit and uses his power of invisibility to enter Cameron's garage to "liberate" papers signed by him that author-

ized Tony to pick up the car. Meanwhile, a Treasury agent is accusing Bill of hiding Tony, hinting that Maxwell may have been in on the fires. Bill leaves after denying everything, but is fed up with the flak he is taking over being a friend of Ralph and Pam. Arriving at Ralph's house, a confrontation occurs and ends with an ultimatum: either Bill helps clear Tony or Ralph will end their partnership. Reluctantly, Maxwell agrees to cooperate, but only then do they realize that Tony has run away again. **Guest cast:** Sandy Ward as Lt. Rafferty, Timothy Carey as Cameron, Woody Eney as Moody, Mark Withers as Shaeffer, Raymond Singer as Kaufman, Steven Hirsch as Lane, Paul Cavonis as Thompson, Henry Sanders as the policeman, Duane Tucker as the fireman, Scott Thompson as the young boy, Gayle Vance as the young lady, Mercedes McCloskey as the woman, Danny Glover [*Predator II*] as Joyner, Robby Weaver as Ray Buck. **Writer:** Lee Sheldon. **Director:** Gabrielle Beaumont.

The Best Desk Scenario (airdate: May 13, 1981). Bill and Ralph meet in the desert to practice the suit's powers. Bill insists Ralph try to burn a bush with his telekinesis power, but he instead accidentally torches Bill's official government vehicle - the third totaled that year. He doesn't know how he will explain the latest snafu. Elsewhere, Pam is having lunch with Clarence Carter, a high-powered attorney who offers her the position of junior partner in his prestigious law firm. She agrees to take the job after he assures her that she is not being hired just because she is a woman. But when Pam takes a ride with the head of the firm in his limousine, they are run off the road by two thugs who threaten Clarence if he doesn't back off a case. Pam suspects something is wrong, but doesn't realize yet that the attorney is also an underworld leader. Meanwhile, Ralph returns to Whitney High and finds that he has been made an assistant principal, a temporary position that he obtains because so many students voted for him. He is excited by the job, but it doesn't turn out quite like he planned - particularly when his first disciplinary case turns out to be Tony. Elsewhere, Bill's having totaled three cars in six months results in his being demoted to a desk job, where he meets Palmer Bradshaw, an upcomer in the F.B.I. who is advancing his meteoric career at the expense of others. Later, Bill arrives at Ralph's house where they are supposed to meet Pam. Bill has been concerned that not only is he getting older - a fact driven home when he keeps seeing friends listed in the obituary column of the newspaper - but that his career, unlike Pam and Ralph's, seems to be going nowhere. Pam arrives nearly in tears, and explains what has happened - unaware that the men who threatened Clarence thought Pam was his daughter, and now that they have found out differently they plan to kill her. The trio go to Pam's new office to try to investigate Clarence, where Ralph uses his holograph power to learn about a record company Carter is involved with. As they leave the two thugs show up and grab Pam, so Ralph jumps out a window and catches up with the hoods as they drive away. Bill takes them away in handcuffs after catching up, but when he arrives at the Federal Building Bradshaw cannot figure out why Bill was involved in a police-jurisdiction crime, and has no idea what to make of the hoods babbling about a super guy in red underwear. He assumes it was another mistake on Bill's part, and leaves for a dinner with the mayor. Later, Bill, Pam, and Ralph meet for supper and try to sort out their lives, which all seem to fallen apart in a matter of hours. The next day Clarence asks Pam to sit in his car so he can explain the previous incident - but instead finds herself a kidnapping victim again. When Ralph cannot find Pam, he joins up with Bill and they decide to use the suit to save Pam and help Bill outsmart the young up-and-coming Palmer Bradshaw. **Guest cast:** Eugene Peterson as Clarence Carter, Duncan Regeher [*Wizards and Warriors, V*] as Palmer Bradshaw, Michael Ensign as Principal Kane, Tom Pletts as Agent Genesta, Eric Server as Kyle Morgan, Rod Colbin as Theo-

Ralph has to save Rhonda's mother in "Reseda Rose".

dore Svenson, William Frankfather as Chet Kanaby. **Writers:** Juanita Barlett and Stephen J. Cannell. **Director:** Arnold Laven.

SEASON TWO

The 200-Mile-an-Hour Fastball (airdate: Nov. 4, 1981). A couple of thugs beat up an important baseball player so that his team will lose an upcoming game - the third player put out of commission. Bill contacts Ralph to convince him to join the team where, with the help of the suit, he can help them win the next game. Ralph is reluctant to join the team, but agrees to throw a few balls to Bill to see if he can make it as a pitcher. His first fast ball breaks Bill's hand and throws him twenty feet! They go to the stadium for a try out, strike out the best hitter, and set a record for the world's fastest speedball. That afternoon, Bill and Ralph go to the team owner's home to sign Ralph up, and while he is talking to the owner, Debbie Dante, Bill arranges a contract with an army of attorneys and accountants - and only later finds out the contract he negotiated is nearly worthless. Meanwhile, the hoods trying to fix the games are preparing a major illegal-arms deal. They plan to buy ten million dollars in arms to finance a revolution, and are aware they will be killed if they fail in their task of sabotaging the baseball team to obtain the funding for the weapons. Back at the Dante mansion, Debbie tries to make it clear to Ralph that he shouldn't let "stardom" get the best of him, as she has seen it ruin many others. A producer from the *Mike Douglas Show* phones to arrange Ralph's appearing on TV and afterwards he heads home where he is attacked by the thugs who have been beating up other members. They warn Ralph to stay away from the team, but after they leave Ralph changes into the suit to chase the hoods. Unfortunately, Ralph has to stop a speeding bus from crashing into a car, during which the thugs escape. Later, Bill shows up with the contract, and tell his partner he will be making three million dollars a year. Only after Ralph starts playing in his first game does Bill find out that the only payment Ralph will receive is an insurance policy that will pay only if Ralph dies - which is a definite possibility, as the thugs have seen him play despite their warnings, and they plan to make an example of the team's new star. Even after only one game, the stardom is going right to Ralph's head, although the manager of the team seems reluctant to use him. And for good reason: the manager is working for the thugs, so when the next game comes up and Debbie orders the manager to allow Ralph to pitch, the thugs attack and kidnap her. Ralph sees this on a holograph, notifies Bill, and flies after the hoods. He soon catches them, and after Bill arrives and is unable to get them to talk, Ralph takes one of them on a flight, scaring him into revealing the gun deal that will help overthrow several Latin American countries. To avoid this, Ralph must get back to the game and save it for his team - if there is enough time left. **Guest cast:** Markie Post as Debbie Dante, Carmen Argenziano as Nick Castle, Michael J. London as Raymond Sloat, Richard Gjonola as Russ Decker, Bruce Kirby, Hector Elias, William Marquez, Stanley Brock, Ralph Maura, Charles McDaniels, Porfirio Guzman Berrones, Hank Robinson, Mike Douglas as himself, Richard Guonola as Russ Decker, Ralph Mauro as the man, Hank Robinson as umpire #1, Porfirio Guzman Berrones as Manuel Cortez. **Writer:** Stephen J. Cannell. **Director:** George Stanford Brown.

Operation: Spoilsport (airdate: Nov. 11, 1981). Something has gone wrong at the Twin Peaks Missile Base: a Titan missile prepares to fire all on its own. Within seconds of lift-off it deactivates and returns to its silo. It appears that someone has tapped into the U.S. Air Force defense computer, and within twenty four hours a base-load of nuclear missiles will be launched at Russia, starting World War III. Elsewhere, Ralph is already unhappy because Pam is out of town on a long case, and his day continues to go downhill as Tony crashes his junker into Ralph's car. Naturally he has no insurance, and to make matters worse, Tony's radio suddenly plays a message to Ralph that the aliens want to meet him and Bill in Palmdale. Meanwhile, Bill is working on the case of a missing

computer expert, but military intelligence takes him off the case. Ralph is finally able to convince a reluctant Bill to drive to Palmdale, where they are met by a dead Air Force missile operator who was killed earlier that day when trying to deactivate the launch system. The aliens use him to give Bill and Ralph a warning that the total destruction of Earth is imminent. After they are told about the activated missiles preparing to fire on Russia, the dead man walks away and is beamed up by a flying saucer just like the one that gave Ralph his suit. Afterwards, Bill explains Operation Spoilsport: a system designed to fire missiles on Russia automatically the day after World War III ends, designed to finish off any survivors. Unfortunately, with sixteen hours to accomplish an impossible mission, they have no idea where to start on the task or even how to accomplish it. Since their car is broken down Bill and Ralph have to start walking home, and even after catching a ride they have lost four hours just getting back to Ralph's house. They realize the missing Charles Ratner must be tied in with the military's computer problems; meanwhile militant Gen. Stocker is promoting the idea of a pre-emptive strike against the U.S.S.R. to wipe out the Russians before they can get off a counter-strike. Ralph and Bill go to a Federal building and break into a computer system to learn more about Ratner and Spoilsport, but while Ralph waits in his car outside, soldiers who were alerted by the computer being activated arrive on the roof of the Federal building by helicopter. Before Ralph can reach Bill to help him, the helicopter leaves and is out of sight when Ralph arrives on the roof. Ralph is now on his own to stop a nuclear war. **Guest cast:** John Anderson as Gen. Stocker, Dudley Knight as Charles Ratner, James Burr Johnson as Major Dyle, Robin Riker as Nancy Ratner, John Di Fusco as Sgt. Jenson, John Brandon as Adm. Bailey, Al White as Capt. Reilly, Don Maxwell as the motorcycle cop, Russ Martin, Arnold Spivey as Smitty, John Bristol as the guy who lives under the bridge, Dein Wein as the spiral computer, Rex C. Yon as the man near the phone booth. **Writer:** Frank Lupo. **Director:** Rod Holcomb.

Don't Mess Around with Jim (airdate: Oct. 18, 1981). The death of billionaire J.J. Beck makes the news everywhere - except that he isn't dead. While Ralph and his class watch a documentary about Beck, elsewhere Bill is trying to do the same at a bar, but gives up when he can't hear the telecast over the noisy clientele. Going outside, he is attacked and kidnapped by two thugs. Later they grab Ralph as he is leaving school, and both are taken to Beck Industries where they meet the "dead" J.J. Beck. The wheelchair-bound Beck has arranged to steal the super suit as well, and when Ralph and Bill arrive, he tells them he knows all about the suit and how they got it. He has spent months following them and collecting proof that he can use to expose their secret if they refuse to help him. It seems that Beck went through considerable trouble to fake his death and give his fortune to charity, but now that he is "dead", Beck's physician is selling his will to some crooks who want his fortune. Bill and Ralph realize that the money can help many people, so they agree to assist the old man. They are flown to Las Vegas, and are told to use the suit's telekinetic power to win at gambling. Ralph wonders how the attorney could know how to use a super-power that he wasn't aware the suit had, and only later do they learn that many years earlier Beck had been given a suit by the aliens, but he foolishly misused it for personal gain. After they arrive in Vegas, Ralph sees in a holograph Beck's attorney get kidnapped, but Ralph arrives too late to stop their flying away on a 747. Afterwards they go to the casino where Beck's physician, Dr. Springfield, is gambling. Ralph tries to jinx his game, but is distracted by pretty girls and causes him to win. Moments later Bill is confronted by an ex-con that went to prison because of Bill's F.B.I. work. The thug leaves after threatening to kill Maxwell, and Ralph returns to the table and uses his powers to overcome a fixed table to make Springfield lose considerable sums of money. This ruins the casino owner's plans of paying off Springfield for the will by winning at the table, so he has some employees grab Ralph and drag him away. Bill can do nothing to help, as he has already been captured by

Operation Spoilsport: Michael Pare as Tony Villicana, Don Cervantes as Rodriguez, Jesse D. Goins as Cyler.

several ex-cons who Bill sent up, and they proceed to beat him up in an alleyway. They are putting him in a car to take Bill out into the desert and kill him when Ralph arrives. By the time he gets into the suit the car is out of sight. Unless he can find it, Bill is as good as dead and their mission will come to an end. **Guest cast:** Joseph Wiseman as James J. Beck, Byron Morrow as Marshall Dunn, Stan Lachow as Jordan Heath, Bernard Behrens as Dr. Springfield, Barry Cutler as the cab driver, Michael Alldredge as Vern, W.T. Zacha, Luke Andreas, Bernard Behrens, Fred Lerner, Jerry Dunphy as himself, Chuck Bowman as Keith Asherman, Barry Cutler as the cab driver, Barry Davis as Croupler, Phyllis Hall as girl #1, Zan Dres as girl #2, Don Pulford as Gil, Dave Ziletti as Phil, Sonny Shields as Diggs, Carl Wickman as the pilot. **Writer:** Stephen J. Cannell. **Director:** Robert C. Thompson.

Hog Wild (airdate: Nov. 25, 1981). Driving through the desert, Ralph is trying to make Bill understand the basics of human communications, which the agent considers to be limited to the use of a gun and a badge. As they debate his inability to grasp the feelings of people around him, a motorcycle gang drives past their car. As usual, Bill doesn't know when to shut up, so he pulls over the gang and tries to bust the dozen members he's annoyed with. Ralph has no success in getting Bill to shut up - a condition that would be helpful since Ralph's suit is in the trunk. The gang ends up jumping and beating up both Bill and Ralph, then leaves them unconscious in the desert. When they wake up it turns out that Bill has three fractured ribs, so they go to a nearby doctor's office, where the agent still cannot get the punks off his mind. He refuses to listen to Ralph's lectures or consider changing his ways. When Bill assures Ralph that he will go alone after the gang if need be, Ralph agrees to put on the suit and help his friend, who will surely get in trouble over his head. They drive back out to the desert and Bill has Ralph fly around looking for the motorcyclists, who are busy planning to get revenge against a small town that had put the gang leader in jail. When they see Ralph flying past Bill, they realize the agent must have a special device that enables Ralph to perform his stunts - a perfect weapon for their revenge against the town. They grab Bill and threaten to kill him if Ralph doesn't agree to cooperate. He realizes they aren't bluffing, and gives in to their first demand: handing over the super-suit to Preacher, leader of the gang. Bill and Ralph are tied up and the suit is given to "Bad B", a not-too-intelligent gang member. He is unable to perform any super deeds, so Bill informs Preacher that Bad B only needs to launch from a higher location if he wants to fly. He climbs to the top of a barn and jumps - only to fall and break his arm. Ralph reveals the truth, that the suit only works on him. Preacher agrees to give the suit back and ░░░ helps them attack the town, to which he ░░░ ading towards the town they stop and take ░░░ after given sufficient threats, offers to help ░░░ they talk, Ralph tries to talk to a girl prisoner ░░░ kept doped up. She is unable to speak ░░░ ns nothing before Preacher grabs him to head ░░░ ver. While Bill is busy back in the barn trying ░░░ imprisoned farmers, Ralph realizes that their ░░░ is to convince the townspeople to stand up ░░░ uest cast: Gregory Sierra as Sheriff Vargas, ░░░ Preacher, Paul Koslo as Bad B, Marianne ░░░ elle as Stella, Tony Burton as Curley, Dennis Fimple as Cile Kane, Marland Proctor as Basil, Hoke Howell, Terrence Beasor as the county sheriff, Kerrie Cullen as Flo. **Writer:** Stephen J. Cannell. **Director:** Ivan Dixon.

Classical Gas (airdate: Dec. 2, 1981). An assassin named Hydra is preparing to kill 10,000 Americans with poison gas. After meeting with a foreign agent paying the hitman, Hydra kills him to eliminate the only person who knows of his presence. Meanwhile, Ralph is getting his kids' rock band an audition with a man who is putting on a "Classical Gas" concert, in protest of the government's transporting truckloads of toxic nerve gas through populated areas - the same gas the assassin plans to steal. The teenagers play at the club, owned by Charley Wilde, a rock promoter client of Pam, who is annoying Ralph with his romantic overtones towards Pam. Ralph would be even more upset if he knew the promoter was involved in the scheme to spread nerve gas through the crowd at the concert. After the performance Pam leaves with Charley, but once in his limousine he gets a call from Hydra that she overhears. Meanwhile, after taking the kids to his house for a party where he gives them the news that they will be singing at the Classical Gas concert, Ralph contacts Bill to see if he found out anything about Wilde. The only thing the agent could come up with is that Charley had changed his name, and a year earlier had been dead broke. After the students leave, Ralph uses the suit for unethical purposes: he holographs in on Pam at her home. He is furious after seeing her have a drink with Charley, so he flies to her house and accidentally crashes through the roof. Pam runs up to the attic after hearing the crash, and her suspicions are proven correct - Ralph has been spying on her! She is even madder than he is, and informs the teacher that maybe it's time to reconsider their relationship. Ralph leaves after Charley's limo drives away, and follows him to a meeting with Hydra. Taking a photo of the terrorist, he takes it to Bill, who develops the film and is amazed to see it really is Hydra - who is supposed to be in a German prison. This seems to indicate Wilde is up to no good, but they have no idea yet what scheme he has in mind. After putting the entire F.B.I. on alert to find Hydra, Bill returns to his office, where he finds he is in big trouble: the German prison has sent a photo of Hydra in prison - and he obviously can't be in two places at once. Unless Agent Maxwell does something fairly incredible, his career may be over. Elsewhere, Hydra prepares to steal the poison to murder the concert-goers. **Guest cast:** Edward Winter [*Project: UFO*] as Charley Wilde, George Loros as Hydra, Garnett Smith as Hanson, Blake Clarke as Sgt. Crane, Christopher Thomas, Joe Horvath as Doug, Steve Liebman as Huey, Dennis Madalane as the biker. **Writer:** Frank Lupo. **Director:** Bruce Kessler.

The Beast in the Black (airdate: Dec. 9, 1981). Ralph goes to see a house that has been empty for years, and will soon be torn down. He has until the following Monday to bring in the kids and haul off anything of value, which the owner is donating to the school. But while looking over the house some strange things happen, so he returns that night with Bill to open a hidden safe he found earlier. Wearing the suit, he plans to break into the safe, but before doing so Ralph begins seeing things Bill doesn't. Writing it off as an optical illusion, the safe is opened, and inside are stocks of ownership in an oil company. Next, Ralph sees through a bricked-up doorway a fire burning in a hearth. Bill only sees a brick wall. Ralph walks over to the wall and steps through after watching an old woman inside. But it is far more than a woman: a terrifying beast attacks Ralph and throws him through the wall. He survives only because of the suit, but Ralph is covered with welts and Bill has to take his friend to the hospital. While Ralph is busy telling Bill he wouldn't go back in the house for a million dollars, the teacher remembers his kids are due to arrive at the old mansion at any minute. Racing to the house, Ralph finds two teenagers missing, and while he goes to look for them a chandelier falls and kills Bill. Ralph returns after hearing the kids screaming, and finds Bill with no pulse but, strangely, he suddenly revives, but remains unconscious. Waking up in the hospital, Ralph notices that Bill's eyes have changed color - he not yet knowing that Bill has been possessed by a dead woman's spirit so she can return to the living. After the doctor leaves, the truth of Bill's death and sudden revival is revealed to Ralph, who is told that if he gets in the way, she will use Bill's body to kill him. After Bill leaves Ralph contacts Rhonda, who knows a psychic who may be able to explain what has happened to his friend. He meets the woman in the morning, and is told the old woman's spirit would be destroyed when the house is demolished, so she is using Bill's body as a vessel to continue her existence. To save Bill, Ralph must enter a weird forth dimension where the suit doesn't work, and is the home of a monstrous beast that is out to kill Ralph. **Guest cast:** Christine

Train of Thought: Pam, Ralph, and Bill.

Belford [*Outlaws*] as Sheila Redman, Jane Merrow as Betty, Rae Allen as Edith, Jeff MacKay [*Tales of the Gold Monkey*] as Dr. Weinstein, Vince Howard as Workman, John Macchia as Arnold. **Writer:** Juanita Bartlett. **Director:** Arnold Laven.

The Lost Diablo (airdate: Dec. 16, 1981). Bill talks Ralph into taking the kids prospecting near the trailer of his old friend and first partner, Harland Blackford. After they have been driving through the desert for hours, Pam finally asks the obvious: are they lost? Of course they are, but Bill won't admit it. They continue driving and finally find where they must park the bus to hike to the campsite - unaware that they are being watched by someone on top of a nearby mountain. Once set up at their camp, Bill almost accidentally reveals he is tricking Ralph and his students into looking for a gold mine, the Lost Diablo. As Bill, Ralph, Pam and the kids get some sleep they are still unaware they are being watched by a group of murderous mountain men. Ralph finally gets Bill to tell him about his gold mine map, which he swears was given to him by Harland on his deathbed. Ralph refuses to use the suit to find the mine unless the kids will get part of the gold, but after Bill gives in Ralph is able to holograph in on the mine in a nearby gulch. The entrance has been long-since buried under rubble and boulders, but Ralph is easily able to clear the opening with the use of the suit. Once inside to look around, he finds an ore car that confirms the mine is the Diablo, but the beams holding it are very unstable and may collapse at any moment. Ralph returns to tell the kids, Pam, and Bill that he found the mine, but after they return to the entrance the kids don't listen to Ralph's warnings that it is dangerously unstable, and go wild inside, resulting in Tony nearly being killed by an old booby-trap he tripped. Seeing an ore car with gold inside, the students go crazy, unaware that the danger that exists outside, where the mountain men are tracking down Ralph and the teenagers. That night the kids and adults return to the camp, where they make plans for a "golden" future. The following morning Ralph, Pam, and Bill wake up to find Tony and the others have already gone to the mine, where their fooling around causes a cave-in - with them still inside. Ralph tries to use the suit to dig them out, but only causes more of the mine to collapse. Flying to the top of the mountain, he finds an upward shaft - and immediately falls down it. However, he gets into another tunnel that enables him to clear a passage for them to escape. After they are out Ralph flies out of the upward shaft, changes clothes and rejoins the kids. They all head back to the camp, where Ralph discovers the teenagers stupidly filled their canteens with gold instead of water. Arriving at the bus, Bill can't get it to start. Opening the hood, Ralph finds out why: the engine was stolen by the mountain men - who moments later arrive and surround Ralph and the kids and take them prisoner. **Guest cast:** Fred Downs as Pop Casco, John Miranda as Fletcher, Gary Grubbs as Doyle, Bill Quinn, Joseph Whipp. **Writer:** Juanita Bartlett. **Director:** Lawrence Doheny.

The Plague (airdate: Jan. 6, 1982). Near Faultline Junction, California, a gunrunner/mercenary named Harvey Locke is found dieing from a plague after he passes out and crashes his truck. Later, Carlisle briefs his agents about the case, one that no one wants to touch as Locke may be dieing from a germ-warfare bacteria. You-know-who isn't afraid of nasty germs and takes the case. After getting some inoculations, Bill arrives to pick up Ralph, who is busy playing basketball with his students. Tony swings at another student and floors Ralph instead, so Bill offers to arrest Tony. Ralph declines, and upon hearing about the case, is more than a little reluctant to get involved. Bill drags him away to grab the suit, although after they pick it up Ralph wonders if the aliens built the suit to be plague-resistant. Arriving at a gun firing range used by known mercenaries, Bill and Ralph start asking questions about Harvey Locke, but find out nothing and leave. They don't realize several of the mercenaries have followed them as they arrive at the hospital Locke is being held at. Ralph is surprised to find Pam there, who arrived to meet the rest of the team after the kids told her where the men were heading. Bill is furious about the security leak, and leaves to make a phone call. While doing so, the mercenaries break into the room and Bill is kidnapped. Ralph hears his cries for help and flies after the car, but loses him after running into a flock of birds. Bill arrives at a mercenary training center lead by a fanatic who threatens the agent to reveal what he knows about Locke. Maxwell won't tell him anything, but when Bill's vaccination mark is seen the mercenaries are aware the Federal government is on to their plan to release deadly plague germs. Meanwhile, Ralph finally catches up and sets off perimeter defenses at the training center. Making his way through a mine field, Ralph closes in on the headquarters as the mercenaries grab Bill and evacuate the base by helicopter. This doesn't stop Ralph, who chases the helicopter just as the mercenaries throw Bill out for not talking about Locke. Ralph catches him after falling thousands of feet, and they make a not-too-gentle landing in the desert. Returning to the hotel where Pam is staying, Ralph begins to show the first symptoms of having smallpox. **Guest cast:** Ed Grover as Bunker, Arthur Rosenberg as Kelly, Jeff Cooper as Reo, Glenn Wilder as Harvey Locke, Melvin F. Allen as Arnold Diggs, Richard Brand as Dr. Keene, James Dybas as the medic, Hand Salas as the cadre man, Robert Curtis as the truck driver, Blake Marion as the radar operator, J.P. Bumstead, Chip Johnson. **Writer:** Rudolph Barchert. **Director:** Arnold Laven.

Train of Thought (airdate: Jan. 13, 1982). Bill is after some terrorists, but ends up captured and tied up by them. While they question Bill, others from the group secure the Lancaster Switching Yard to steal a train load of radioactive waste and crash it into a small town. They order Bill to use his communicator to bring in Ralph, who bursts through a door and knocks out the terrorists. But Bill is too late: the switching yard has already been hit, a worker shot, and the train taken over as well. As they get away the terrorists send some cars in the opposite direction on a collision course with an oncoming train, and Ralph has to stop the runaway cars before a head-on collision occurs. Disaster is averted by a matter of seconds but, unfortunately, Ralph collides with the train head first, resulting in amnesia. Bill arrives in his car and picks his partner up then rushes him to a nearby hospital, where Pam soon arrives. When Ralph awakens he has no memory of Bill or the suit. He thinks Bill is a nut when he tries to explain their working together, and Pam is afraid to tell him the truth. His doctor believes Ralph is trying to suppress a deep psychological trauma - which Bill and Pam realize he received when the aliens gave him the suit - but cannot reveal this to anyone, least of all Ralph. Bill agrees to back off and give Ralph time, not realizing that the terrorists are making preparations to launch the attack with the train load of nuclear waste. Back at Ralph's house, Bill shows his partner the suit and why they must find and stop the train, but Ralph considers Maxwell to be completely insane. He throws Bill out of the house and tosses the suit into a trash can. Bill is on his own. After he is gone, Ralph spends time with Pam trying to catch up on where their relationship has gone over the past eight months. The counselor cannot reveal that their lives have been

disrupted by the arrival of the suit, and tries to explain what has happened without mentioning any of their super-adventures. Later, Bill returns after discovering what the terrorists are up to, and insists Pam make Ralph believe the truth. She does so, and after Ralph finally agrees to try the suit on, only then do they realize the suit has been picked up and has already been transported to a dump. They go to the landfill just as the garbage truck arrives and manage to retrieve an extremely smelly super suit. Next, they take Ralph into the desert to learn how to use his super powers again. They finally prove that the suit works and Ralph has a holograph that leads them to the terrorists. After eliminating all opposition, the trio realize the train is already gone, so Ralph gets a holograph off the track the nuclear waste car had been sitting on. Seeing where it is heading, Bill, Ralph, and Pam use the agent's car to catch up with the train and "launch" Ralph - who immediately has another head-on collision with the train. **Guest cast:** Milt Kogan as the doctor, James Lydon as McGivers, Judd Omen as Mohammed, Nick Cinardo as Sylvester, Sonia Petrovna as Sonja, Nick Shields, Robert Alan Browne, Warren Munson as the engineer, Perry Cook as Carter. **Writer:** Frank Lupo. **Director:** Lawrence Doheny.

Now You See It (airdate: Jan. 20, 1982). A Russian sub enters U.S. waters off the coast of California, where they put ashore a Cuban team near Malibu. They meet some comrades and dress as ranchers, then leave for a nearby airport. Meanwhile, Pam has a hectic schedule, so she dumps her vicious cat, Lefty, off with Ralph. The feline immediately begins to make his life miserable. He has no choice but to drag it along on a ride with Bill - who's allergic to cats - as they head out into the desert to try to work out kinks in the suit. Bill has had a friend do research on making the human body aerodynamically stable in flight, resulting in some wings that attach to Ralph's legs to help him fly. But, once tried, Ralph's flying is even worse than usual. However, his crash landing activates a new power in the suit - it enables Ralph to see into the future, and he has just seen a jet transport plane crash. The only problem is he is the only one who can see it, until he touches Bill and the agent gets a vision as well. Bill goes to alert the fire department while Ralph examines the wreckage - except that there *is* no crashed plane. Bill and the fire department arrive and he has to do some quick talking to get he and Ralph out of trouble - and explain Ralph's suit as well. Bill begins babbling about the Federal Fire Inspection Drill, and as he and Ralph leave, Bill promises to give the department an excellent report. Going to a secluded park, Ralph shows Bill the jet's flight recorder he is still carrying by touching Maxwell's hand. They finally realize Ralph is seeing a future event, and head to the airport to prevent the accident from happening. Elsewhere, Pam is being hassled by Richard Beller, who is in a hurry for her to complete a project. He and Senator Henderson explain that the paperwork must be in Washington in a matter of hours, so she agrees to fly with them in their private plane and complete the work on board. At the airport, Bill and Ralph receive no cooperation in trying to find the plane, and no one believes their story. Learning where the aircraft is, they head to Beller Aircraft, but before they arrive the Cuban agents kill and replace the pilots so they can steal the prototype aircraft. They enter the plane - the same one Pam and her employers are using - and take the three passengers hostage. Elsewhere, Bill is racing towards Beller Aircraft after Ralph gets a holograph of the plane Pam is taking a business trip on - and unless he can change the future, Pam is doomed. **Guest cast:** Christopher Lofton as Sen. Henderson, Jon Cypher as Beller, Charles Bateman as Col. Cullen, Laurence Haddon as Burke, Robert Covarrubias as De Jesus, Richard Beauchamp as Phillipe, Joe Mantegna as Juan, Matthew Faison, David Clover, Patrick Cameron as Smitty, Dennis Haskins as Trigg, Glenn Wilder as Capt. Fredericks, Gary Jensen as Capt. Williams. **Writer:** Patrick Burke Hasburgh. **Director:** Robert C. Thompson.

The Hand-Painted Thai (airdate: Jan. 27, 1982). During the Vietnam War in 1970, several U.S. soldiers are captured in Cambodia where they are told they will pay for their crimes for attacking

Just Another Three-Ring Circus: Pam and the kids watch Ralph's "Human Cannonball" act.

the Asian country. Twelve years later, the man threatening them, now living in the U.S. as Shawn Liang, a successful businessman, puts them to use. His superior arrives to tell him it is time to deliver the Platinum Rosebud - a code word for a project that involves destroying a dam, killing important scientists at a meeting (along with millions of other people), and the destruction of hundreds of thousands of acres of prime farm land. Gen. Chow leaves after ordering that the ex-soldiers be contacted to commit acts of sabotage once a phrase is given to them that activates the programming they were given during a POW brainwashing session. Bill and Ralph become involved when Ralph accidentally picks up a call intended for one of the saboteurs, an F.B.I. friend of Bill. Timothy Lider goes into a trance after the call and when Bill tries to help he opens fire on Bill, Ralph and Rhonda. Going outside, Tim sees the school bus with Ralph's class and Pam aboard, and hijacks the vehicle to head towards an unknown destination. Since Ralph's suit is in the bus, he and Bill grab a car to follow the kids, hoping that none of them will be hurt. Forcing the bus off the road, Tim runs with Ralph and Maxwell just behind. Tim reaches the roof of the skyscraper where he thinks he is in Vietnam, and runs off the edge of the roof. Ralph catches him at the last second, and Gen. Chow is furious when he doesn't show up with the others. If the ex-soldiers fail in their task, he promises Liang a slow and painful death. The three men are given instructions on how to blow the dam - and kill themselves afterwards. Elsewhere, Tim has been placed in a psychiatric unit of a local hospital, where Bill is trying to find out what happened to his friend. The only thing the agent can remember are the words "Platinum Rosebud" - the same word Ralph heard when he answered the phone. Ralph and Pam surmise that Tim is a victim of some kind of deep hypnosis. Bill doesn't believe a word of it, but he goes along with his partners to see a night club performer who is an

expert in hypnosis. Erika Van Damm meets with them after her act, and confirms Tim's condition. Unknown to them, Bill has been accidentally hypnotized during the performance and every time the word "scenario" is mentioned (which Bill uses in every other sentence) he falls asleep. Meanwhile, they return to see Tim to question him further - just as he receives a phone call from Liang commanding Tim to commit suicide. As Bill and his friends are walking through the hospital parking lot they see Tim jump from an upper story window, and this time Ralph can't save him in time. They are determined to avenge Tim's death, and Ralph starts by getting a holograph vision that will lead him to Liang. **Guest cast:** James Shigeta as Shawn Liang, John Fujioka [*Tales of the Gold Monkey*] as Gen. Vin Chow, Kurt Grayson as Tim Lider, Hilary Labow as Erika Van Damm, J.P. Bumstead, Kurt Grayson as Tim Lider, Terrance O'Hara, Charles Lanyer, Hilary Labow, Terrance Evans, Michael Cornelison, Chris Hendrie as Marv Keegan, James Saito as Kelly Kim, Odesa Cleveland as the nurse, Lori Michaels as Shirley. **Writers:** Frank Lupo, Stephen J. Cannell and Burke Hasburgh. **Director:** Bruce Kessler.

Just Another Three-Ring Circus (airdate: Feb. 3, 1982). At a nearby circus, a clown is followed, caught, and kidnapped by a couple of thugs. Meanwhile, Bill is in trouble with his F.B.I. boss again, so Carlisle gives him the worst assignment he can find: that of finding the clown. Because the circus performer is a foreign national, it has become a Federal case. As Bill leaves he is informed that, because of the number of cars he has trashed, he has been given a new vehicle. Outside Bill finds a bright red, dilapidated Volkswagon Beetle. Bill is in a foul mood when he catches up with Ralph, who is equally bent out of shape because his kids failed an extremely important test that reflected poorly on him. Feeling his students don't care about their future and he isn't making a difference, Ralph is ready to quit his job. They both leave after Bill explains their latest case, and once at the circus, Ralph, who has always loved being around a big top, is mistaken for the new human cannonball the missing clown was supposed to have hired, so he accepts the position. He is even able to wear his suit without appearing abnormal, pretending it is part of his costume. Meanwhile, Maxwell continues to investigate on his own. After questioning a suspect, two masked men use acrobatic maneuvers to gain entrance to the apartment and kidnap the man. When Bill chases the kidnappers to the top of the skyscraper, he is shot and falls off the side of the thirty story building. Luckily, Ralph had already been on his way there and catches Bill just before they both land in a dumpster. After checking out of the hospital where he had a bullet removed from his arm, Bill leaves with Ralph and Pam and meets Carlisle at the apartment building where he was shot. Bill takes his supervisor to where the kidnapping occurred, only to find a party in process and the missing man replaced by an impostor who convinces Carlisle that no kidnapping ever occurred. Now Bill is in more trouble than ever, but while in the apartment Bill picks up a matchbook advertising a dating club - the same kind of matchbook found in the missing clown's tent. Meeting Pam and Ralph back at the car, they go to Ralph's house, where Bill formulates a plan to go undercover at the circus as a laborer, Ralph will question his co-workers while being the human cannonball, and Pam is to go to the date center to find out what she can while pretending to be looking for her "ideal mate". Things do not go well: a tiger is released into the cage Bill is cleaning; Ralph is fired out of the cannon with too much of a charge and disappears from sight, and Pam finds herself hounded by men desperate for a date - none of the trio realizing the dating club is actually an undercover debriefing center for the C.I.A. **Guest cast**: Catherine Campbell as Erica, David Winn as John, Kai Wulff as Peter, Alex Rodine as Klaus, Derek Thompson, Richard Doyle as Uri Yovanovitch, Patrick Stack as Chuck, Chip Johnson as Sharp, Jourdan Fremin as Lisa, Derek Thompson as Spielman, Gene Lebell as Yuri. **Writer**: Stephen J. Cannell. **Director**: Chuck Bowman.

The Shock Will Kill You (airdate: Feb. 10, 1982). Something has gone wrong with a space shuttle trip: all electrical power is out and the astronauts cannot be contacted by radio - the same problem that plagued a satellite they picked up. NASA expects the shuttle to fall to Earth, where it will hit in the middle of the city of Bakersfield, California. Ralph, Bill, and the counselor head for Bakersfield, where Ralph is concerned he'll end up like "road pizza" if the shuttle falls on him while he diverts it away from the city into a desert landing. Nevertheless, he manages to divert the shuttle and land it east of town. Ralph is driven several feet into the ground upon landing, and after he regains consciousness, he finds himself electrically-charged with sparks flying off his body and his hair sticking straight up. Pam and Bill arrive in his car, where they discover Ralph was charged by something electrifying the hull of the shuttle - and that the astronauts were already dead long before returning to Earth. They get the idea of Ralph grounding himself out on some railroad tracks to dispel the excess voltage. It works, but now Ralph has been turned into a super-magnet that attracts anything within yards, and creates havoc with Bill's car. Going to a motel, the trio watch on TV the shuttle being unloaded and investigated. Ralph is afraid to take off the suit as the magnetic energy may kill him. Needless to say, Ralph has no intention of going through life as a super-magnet, so they try to learn what caused the situation in the first place. Elsewhere, the shuttle is being examined by technicians in protective suits, but when one of the men enters the space craft he is attacked and killed by an alien electrically-charged creature - that begins heading towards Los Angeles, killing anyone that gets in its path. When all electricity fails in the area of their motel, Bill takes Pam and Ralph with him to Edwards Air Force Base, where the shuttle is being checked. When the trio arrives at the base they find the power is out there as well, so Ralph makes himself invisible

(although his magnetic field still sets off horns every time he nears a car) and enters the headquarters building. His presence powers all the lights in the room, where top brass are trying to figure a way to contain the creature, until it is found that the alien has entered power cable tunnels heading towards Los Angeles. Ralph returns to the car and reveals what transpired during the meeting, and there appears little choice but to try to intercept the alien at the spot the creature is most likely to head for: the hydroelectric plant powering Los Angeles. **Guest cast**: Don Starr as Crocker, Rod Colbin as Gen. Enright, Ray Girardin as Col. Nelson, Leonard Lightfoot as the lieutenant, Bert Hinchman, Doug Hale, Ned Ballamy as R.J., Randy Patrick as Rider, Bert Hinchman as the guard. **Writers**: Patrick Burke Hasburgh, Frank Lupo and Stephen J. Cannell. **Director**: Rod Holcomb.

A Chicken in Every Plot (airdate: Feb. 17, 1982). Ted McSherry, an old friend of Bill's, invites him, Ralph, Pam, and the kids to the Caribbean, but Ted runs into problems before they arrive: he has been investigating a voodoo cult on the island, and its members surround his house one night to terrorize then kill him. Although he makes a valiant effort to escape, he is chased down in the woods and executed. Ralph, Pam, Bill, and the kids soon arrive, where Bill is perplexed when Ted, an old F.B.I. buddy, isn't there to meet them. He tries to get some information from a couple of aircraft mechanics, but they claim to know nothing. After antagonizing the locals, Bill grabs the rest of the group and heads into the airport, where they obtain a guide who takes them to Ted's address. When they arrive at his salvage company they find it burned to the ground. Ralph discovers a burned voodoo doll that is shown to the guide, who recommends they leave the island immediately. Going to Ted's home, they find it ransacked, with more signs of voodoo inside, including dead chickens. While there, Rhonda is nearly killed by a falling battle-ax and only then finds a voodoo doll in her purse that looks just like the teenager. Now Pam suspects the voodoo killers are after them as well. Bill finally reveals to Ralph that they are there to help salvage a ship. Ralph decides to put on the suit while Bill checks out Ted's boat, but the agent is knock unconscious by a stranger who pilots the boat out of the harbor. Ralph flies out to the boat, knocks out and ties up the stranger, and returns the vessel to dock. He instructs Pam to take the students back to the airport to fly home, but before they leave the police arrive, led by Col. Felipe Augereau. He informs Bill that his help is not wanted or needed, and that Ted McSherry is dead. Furthermore, Col. Augereau reveals that the "prisoner" is Gen. Louie Devout, the Caribbean nation's president's security officer. He orders both Bill and Ralph arrested, which Augereau has no choice but to obey. Once the General is gone, Augereau reveals that Bill and Ralph are in grave trouble, and after being imprisoned, they learn that they are to be transported somewhere else. Meanwhile, Pam tries to free the boys with some legal firepower, but Augereau makes it clear that he has no power to release the men, who will soon be tortured and killed. Only later do they learn that the general is involved in the voodoo cult and is out to take over the island's government. **Guest cast**: Ron O'Neal [*Bring 'Em Back Alive*] as Col. Felipe Augereau, Thalmus Rasulala as Victor Suchet/Etienne, Lincoln Kilpatrick as Le Masters, John Hancock as Gen. Louie Devout, Todd Armstrong as Ted McSherry. **Writers**: Danny Lee Cole and Jeffrey Duncan Ray. **Director**: Rod Holcomb.

The Devil in the Deep Blue Sea (airdate: Feb. 24, 1982). Five miles off shore of St. Croix in the Bermuda Islands, a small boat named the *Contrail* is attacked by gunmen in a speedboat, but just as the thugs start to take over the ship it is attacked by something very large and strange. The ship is nearly destroyed and a passenger is thrown overboard with a life preserver. Nearby is Ralph, Pam, and the kids, who have taken a Caribbean vacation. While the kids pay for their expenses by having their rock group sing at a club, Tony works as a totally inept waiter who spills more drinks than he serves. After Ralph gets a drink in the lap from Tony, he and Pam take a walk on

The Hand-Painted Thai: Bill arrests a Thai secret agent.

the beach, where Ralph hears the overboard passenger crying for help. Seeing her, Ralph swims out to rescue her, gets the pretty young girl back to the beach, and listens to what happened. When he hears her story he calls Bill and tells him to come right away to stop "It". Bill nearly loses his job getting there, only to have Ralph explain that he thinks "It" is an ancient dinosaur which is prowling the water and sinking the ships within the Bermuda Triangle. Bill is furious, particularly when he questions the survivor - who claims to have seen the beast - and discovers she is a drug junkie. However, Ralph is able to holograph off the girl and he knows she is telling the truth about the highjackers. Seeing a chance to salvage his career, the three go out in a motorized raft. They immediately get lost, then are almost run down by the "missing" *Contrail*. After jumping off the raft just before it sinks, Bill and Pam are stranded in the water while Ralph swims at super speed to catch the *Contrail*. Getting the boat under control, he picks up his friends and informs them that no one is aboard the boat. Taking it back to port, they give a report to the police, not aware that the officer they speaking to is working with the pirates. He resents their asking questions about why so many boats have disappeared in the area, and becomes belligerent after hearing Ralph mention Devereaux, a name he hologramed off of the ship. Unknown to them, Devereaux is not only the warden of a local penal institution, but is also leader of the pirates. Captain Le Clerc leaves on his police boat and reports Ralph and Bill's questions to Devereaux, who is furious that the officer came in broad daylight to visit him. After Le Clerc admits that no one saw him arrive on the penal island, Devereaux decides the answer to all his problems is to get rid of the pesky officer - along with Bill, Pam and Ralph. **Guest cast:** Jeremy Kemp as Devereaux, Glynn Turman as Le Clerc, Michael Halsey as Collins, Anne Bloom as Linda, Will Hare. **Writer:** Frank Lupo. **Director:** Sidney Hayers.

It's All Downhill from Here (airdate: Mar. 3, 1982). A skiing competition is being held at Squaw Valley, California, where Ralph and Pam are vacationing during a pleasant break from Bill. However, their vacation begins going downhill when Ralph runs into an old flame, Samantha, who hangs all over Ralph. This doesn't go unnoticed by Pam, particularly after Ralph leaves her behind to ski with Samantha. Matters take a definite turn for the worse when they

become involved in a plot to kill the U.S. contestant, Scotty Templeton. The Czechoslovakian entry, Yuri, wins the event because of a foreign agent, Talenikov, shooting a lethal drug into the young skier. Seeing this, Ralph, who is dressed in his super-suit to keep warm, races to catch the assassin, but Talenikov gets away by sending a tracked vehicle towards a group of skiers then jumping out and running away while Ralph keeps the children from being killed. The doctor examining the skier claims he died from a heart attack, but Ralph knows he was shot, even though he was unable to catch the sniper. He phones Bill and tells him exactly what happened, making the agent decide to leave for Squaw Valley immediately. Meanwhile, Ralph and Pam come to the attention of Blandin, a federal agent who threatens to send both to Washington for "extensive questioning" if they don't make themselves scarce. Later, while waiting for Bill, Samantha, a left-wing environmental extremist, proceeds to make a nuisance of herself until Maxwell finally shows up. Shortly after arriving Bill and Ralph head to the bar and run into "Bobo" Blandin, a C.I.A. agent and good friend of Maxwell's. Or at least Bill thinks so until Blandin tells him it would be best for everyone concerned if he, Ralph, and Pam should ship out immediately. Blandin leaves, but shortly afterwards Ralph gets a holograph of the agent being beaten for information. He and Bill jump in a Jeep and race to the locker room Blandin is in, but arrive too late: Blandin is found dead. As they get his body out of a locker, C.I.A. agents arrive and arrest both men until they can be identified. After being taken to an office, Bill finds that they are about to be questioned by Robert Klein, a high-up senior C.I.A. official who plans to have both men arrested for Blandin's murder unless they leave immediately. Knowing who Klein is and the power at his control, Maxwell grabs the reluctant Ralph and leaves. But they aren't ready to leave yet: Ralph becomes invisible and goes back into the office, where he learns enough that he is able to determine that Blandin was involved in a foreign plot to prevent the Czechoslovakian skier from defecting. **Guest cast:** Red West as Blandin, Sandra Kearns as Samantha, Bill Lucking [*Outlaws*] as Klein, Norbert Weisser as Yuri, Michael Billington [*UFO*] as Talenikov, Stefan Gierasch as Karpov, Sara Torgov as Anna, Craig Schaeffer as the boy in the lift line, Dan Shurwin as Scott Templeton, Stan Howard as lift attendant. **Writer:** Patrick Burke Hasburgh. **Director:** Sidney Hayers.

Dreams (airdate: Mar. 17, 1982). A crook that Bill and Ralph helped convict is trying to get an early parole by pretending to be a religious fanatic and a model citizen. At a San Quentin Prison parole meeting, he states that his previous claims of seeing a "flying man in a red suit" was only an attempt at receiving an insanity verdict. They agree to release him, not realizing he actually plans to murder Bill and Ralph once out of prison. Elsewhere, Ralph uses the suit to land on the top of a building containing a toy company, where he leaves a message for the head of development. After he leaves he sees a Federal bank being robbed and knocks out the culprit before calling Bill to nab him. Bill arrives just before the police and claims to have made the bust, and once the officers leave Ralph heads to a meeting with Pam, but cannot enter the restaurant after losing his clothes during the flight to the bank. Later, after arriving at school, the janitor, Duffy, reveals that his dream has come true: a toy company has offered him hundreds of thousands of dollars for the game idea he sent them (which he doesn't know Ralph helped with). Ralph is pleased at his friend's "luck", but would be less cheerful if he knew that Johnny Sanova has just left prison, where he meets four old accomplices, and they go in search of the men that put the fanatic away: Bill and Ralph. Meanwhile, Ralph's professional and personal life seems to be falling apart: while helping Bill he misses important meetings, and after giving a teacher friendly advice, Margaret loses her job. Another friend, Evan Thoman, takes a suggestion Ralph made to extremes when he cashes in his insurance and life savings to enter a high-stakes poker game. The math teacher has invested 25,000 hours in a computer program that will insure his success - or so he thinks. Bill arrives in a total state of panic with the news about Johnny, and although he won't admit he is scared, Bill won't let Ralph or the suit out of sight. Before Ralph leaves with Bill he tries to save Margaret's job, but is too late - she has already been fired. Meeting Bill and Pam again, they are concerned about surviving an encounter with Johnny (who is already following them around) but Ralph is preoccupied with the state of his fellow employees. Ralph arrives at the bank Evan is arranging a loan from so he can try to talk him out of what is sure to be a disaster, but Johnny and his men arrive with plans to grab Pam to force the "super guy" to do their bidding. As luck would have it, a robbery occurs across the street from the bank, resulting in Ralph, Pam, and Bill going in pursuit. The crooks are caught, and while Bill waits for the police arrive, Pam and Ralph return for his clothes that were left behind in an alley, then return to Ralph's high school to stop Evan. But Evan refuses to listen to reason, and leaves for the game, not realizing that it is rigged so he will lose every cent he owns. **Guest cast:** Michael Baseleon as Johnny Sanova, Elizabeth Hoffman as Margaret Detwiller, Robby Weaver as Ray Buck, Fred Stuthman as Evan Thoman, Nicholas Worth as Norm, James Costy as Duffy Magellan, Johnny Crear as Matty, John LeBouvier as Irma Keeler, Charles Hutchinson as Ted Keeler, Peter Trancher as the seminar guest speaker, Edward Bell, Nick Pellegrino, Milt Kogan. **Writer:** Stephen J. Cannell. **Director:** Sidney Hayers.

There's Just No Accounting... (airdate: Mar. 24, 1982). Bill is trying to help some parents free their daughter from three kidnappers, and he goes against Carlisle's orders in convincing the family to pay the ransom. Bill leaves to drop off the ransom and retrieve the little girl with the help of Ralph and his suit, but Ralph is currently preoccupied with surviving an upcoming IRS audit from an extremely abusive and obnoxious agent. As Bill and Ralph reach the drop off site, Ralph goes in pursuit of the kidnappers, who plan to kill the kid once they get back to the freighter she is imprisoned in. Ralph crash lands on the ship but the two men and a woman accomplice escape again with their victim. The crooks get away when Ralph has to prevent the little girl from being killed after they drop her off, and when Bill closes in on them the kidnappers shoot his windshield out - stopping his pursuit and blowing out the window all of Ralph's receipts for the audit. Although the daughter has been rescued, Ralph has to go back and find the ransom money while Bill returns the child to her parents, then, after returning home with the case of ransom money, Ralph leaves it in his living room - where it is seen by the pesky IRS man - who is already bent out of shape over Ralph's not having the receipts as promised. Byron assures Ralph his life has taken a turn for the worse. Back at F.B.I. headquarters, Carlisle reads Bill the riot act: Bill guaranteed the return of the money without F.B.I. approval, and he will have to pay it himself if he cannot return it to the parents. But when he arrives at Ralph's house, Bill finds IRS agents leaving - after they confiscated the ransom payment of $250,000. Byron promises to audit Ralph for the past seven years, and as he and Ralph argue over the matter a car drives by with a passenger who blows out the windows of Ralph's house with a shotgun. Everyone presumes the driver and passenger were the kidnappers who returned to kill Ralph as revenge for his rescuing the money. Later, Byron drags Bill and Ralph into Carlisle's office where he makes both men appear to have been working with the kidnappers to steal the money. Pam gets Ralph temporarily off the hook but Bill is suspended. The three leave and discuss their alternatives, of which there are few. Since the kidnappers are trying to get even by killing Ralph, it is decided to use the suit to track them down. As the team continue working on the case, they find out that the would-be killers are not the kidnappers, but men paid to eliminate the ever-resourceful Byron. **Guest cast:** James Whitmore, Jr. as Byron Bigsby, Jerry Douglas as Jack Martel, Marc Alaimo as Donnie Armus, Emily Moultrie as Debbie Sherwin, Cloyce Morrow as Penny Sherwin, Carole Mallory, Eugene Peterson, Ted Gehring, Ryan MacDonald. **Writer:** Frank Lupo. **Director:** Ivan Dixon.

The Good Samaritan (airdate: Mar. 31, 1982). Bill is trying to catch two escaped prisoners, but the cons use firebombs to set fire to a building and sidetrack the police and Bill. Ralph arrives with the suit to help, but is sidetracked when he has to rescue a blind woman. After flying her down from an upper story, Ralph turns her over to a stranger whom the blind girl believes saved her life. When news cameras and reporters arrive the man takes full credit for assisting the helpless woman, while the cons escape, resulting in Carlisle giving Bill just 36 hours to find them. Later, Ralph, Pam, and Bill get together, and Ralph can barely talk because of smoke inhalation. Ralph reveals he is tired of combating crime. Instead of "tagging and bagging" criminals for Bill, he wants to fight for environmental causes and similar problems. Bill wants nothing to do with Ralph's do-gooder ideas, but unless Bill will get involved in something with human interest, Ralph will not put on the suit again. The change of priorities results in Ralph going to the aid of Ira Hagert, an old man fighting for his home when the government tries to take everything he owns for missing one house payment many years earlier. Once they run him off, they plan to use the property to lengthen the city airport. Ralph persuades Ira not to shoot at the police, and when the S.W.A.T. team surrounding the home fires tear gas into it, Ralph inhales the gas and leaves after promising to help. At his home, Ralph discusses with Pam and Bill as to how they can assist Ira, and Pam decides to approach a city counselor in hopes of resolving the problem. Meanwhile, Pam notices an article in the paper about Dave Tanner saving the blind girl. Hearing the name, Bill realizes he is a thief who robs burning buildings. "Torchy" Tanner already has a twenty-year record, and Bill insists this latest blunder during Ralph's help-society crusade is ample proof that they need to return to crime fighting - particularly since he will be fired without Ralph's help. Bill proves his point by taking Ralph and the counselor over to Tanner's apartment, where Torchy reveals he was in the building to rob it. He also claims that he has had a change of heart ever since people started looking at him as a hero. His whole life has been turned around, and Tanner plans to enter the priesthood. Now Ralph is convinced he is finally using the suit for its true purpose, much to the aggravation of Bill. Later, Ralph attempts again to help Ira, who is now convinced the teacher-turned-superhero is a figment of his imagination. **Guest cast:** Keenan Wynn [*Return of the Man From U.N.C.L.E.*] as Ira Hagert, Dennis Lipscomb as Dave Tanner, Carmen Argenziano as Murph, Harry Grant as Nino, Sandra McCully as Judy, Bill Quinn as Harlan, Ron Thompson, Will MacMillan, Wendy Wessburg as the TV reporter, Pat Wilson as the woman, Joshua Miller as Jonathan. **Writer:** Rudolph Borchert. **Director:** Bruce Kessler.

Captain Bellybuster and the Speed Factory (airdate: April 7, 1982). Mickey is Captain Bellybuster, the super-hero spokesperson for Hamburger Heaven, a hamburger chain. He really believes in his "good-guy" image with the kids, and is appalled when he learns that the company's factory is turning out more than meat: they are also transporting truck loads of illegal drugs. As soon as he finds this out, he phones Bill Maxwell to inform him of a shipment that just left the plant. The pushers realize their mascot has discovered the drug shipment, and they must eliminate him. Bill and Ralph leave in pursuit of the shipment, but Mickey has also called an unethical reporter, who witnesses Ralph's stopping the truck, revealing his secret. As Bill and Ralph open the trailer up to inspect it they find they have been set up - it is empty. As Ralph flies away the newspaper reporter takes photos of him that are published in the next day's newspaper. The text claims that the flying man's identity will be revealed the next day, so Ralph and Bill leave to see the reporter, Bruce, but they fail to intimidate him. In fact, now that he knows who Bill and Ralph really are, Bruce claims he plans to expose them in the next newspaper. After a display of Ralph's power, Bruce decides it might be in his best interests to scrap the story, and agrees to keep their secret quiet. However, the next day he does just the opposite and Carlisle calls Bill in for a chewing out, and to tell him that he will soon be up for a psychiatric exam if he cannot prove Ralph exists.

The Shock Will Kill You: Ralph is in trouble.

Bill and his friends return to see Bruce and find the reporter has just been shot, and before he dies he mentions the name of Captain Bellybuster, who is currently being hunted down by the drug traffickers. Ralph and Bill become the primary suspects in the murder and, unknown to them, only Captain Bellybuster knows who the real killer is. Later, the mobster looking for Bellybuster waits for him to arrive at a grand opening ceremony for a new restaurant, knowing that he won't want to disappoint the kids attending the opening. He shows up, as do Bill, Ralph, and Pam to question him. The thugs grab Bellybuster first, so Ralph flies after the limo he is in and slows it down long enough for him to get away. He is nearly hit by a truck but Ralph saves him, and after returning to Ralph's house, the captain reveals everything to Bill, who realizes they must grab the mobster before his men can knock off Bellybuster - and somehow clear themselves of the suspicion of killing the reporter. **Guest cast:** Chuck McCann, Anthony Charnoto as Mike, Colin Hamilton, Stanley Grover, Danny Wells, Rex Ryon, Jim Greenleaf, John Roselius as the passenger, Janet Winter as the receptionist, Bob Jacobs as the kid. **Writers:** Stephen J. Cannell and Frank Lupo. **Director:** Arnold Laven.

Who's Woo in America (airdate: April 14, 1982). In Hawaii, an attempt to steal a top-secret computer chip is made when its owner, an Oriental driver, is forced off the road. It turns out Dr. Woo already sent the chip to the mainland with a courier, so several hitmen are sent to intercept the unknown courier flying to Los Angeles. As it happens, Ralph's mother was in Hawaii at the same time, and she arrives back in town to tell Ralph she is getting married to Phillip Kaballa, an "international consultant" who turns out to be Ralph's own age. But when Pam and Ralph are supposed to meet the husband-to-be for dinner, he doesn't show up on time, resulting in Ralph being mistaken for Kaballa by a stranger. Kaballa finally shows up and acts very suspicious. After eating Ralph has Bill do a check on Kaballa, after which Ralph goes home and is taken hostage by the stranger and a thug who want information from Kaballa. Ralph tries to explain who he is, with little success before Bill arrives and helps him escape. Prentice Hall and his strong-arm man get away - until Ralph puts on the suit, stops Hall's car, and finds he is a senior president of a petroleum company. The next day Bill

reports a clean record on Kaballa, not knowing that he is working with the C.I.A. Ralph leaves to meet Phillip to play racquetball - where he is taken hostage again by another group looking for Kaballa. The real Phillip finally shows up and both thugs chase him out of the building. By the time Ralph reaches the outside, all three men are gone. Ralph reports the situation to Bill, who has been ordered from someone "high up" to stay off the case; meanwhile, Kaballa is preparing to deliver the chip at the Devine Light Mission, the same place he is supposed to marry Mrs. Hinkley the next day. Ralph and Bill meet Mrs. Hinkley and Pam for lunch, where the second group of kidnappers see Ralph's mother and decide to continue following her in hopes of catching Phillip. As they talk a phone call comes in saying that Hall and his assistant, after Bill and Ralph caught and jailed them, have been freed on bail. Driving to the home of Hall, they find the man floating face down in his swimming pool just before a sniper opens up and hits Ralph. The bullet bounces off of the suit, and Ralph goes in pursuit of the would-be killer and his colleagues after they leave in a helicopter. Unfortunately, they get away when Ralph has to catch a falling sniper after his comrades throw him out of the high flying helicopter. Elsewhere, Mrs. Hinkley and Pam prepare for the wedding, not realizing Phillip is using the marriage as a cover for delivering the chip to C.I.A. operatives at the Devine Light Mission. **Guest cast:** Barbara Hale (William Katt's real mother) as Mrs. Hinkley, Tom Hallick [*The Return of Captain Nemo*] as Phillip Kaballa, Michael Prince as Prentice Hall, Jon Cedar as Heller, Hugh Gillin as C.C. Smith, Dave Cass as Goodwin, Daniel Chodos, Don Maxwell as Brockman, Daniel Dayden as Haffa, Gerald Jann as Dr. Woo, Milt Tarver as the computer clerk, Terri Hanaver as Jill, Ted Richards as the waiter, Brian Sheehan as the racquetball clerk, Dinah Lindsey Smith as the woman. **Writer:** Patrick Burke Hasburgh. **Director:** Bob Bender.

Lilacs, Mr. Maxwell (airdate: April 28, 1982). In the early hours of the morning, Bill has Ralph help him break into the district headquarters of the F.B.I. They find working in the basement efficiency expert O'Neil, placed there with her desk for criticizing Carlisle's choice of office colors. After getting her out of the way, Bill finally locates what he is looking for: a huge room containing artifacts from unsolved crimes, which he plans to solve by using the holographic images from the suit. When Ralph picks up a machine gun, however, they become involved in a very modern case when he sees a man being murdered by one of the missing guns from the case. Using the super-suit, Ralph arrives and captures the murderers, who turn out to be a pair of master spies. On his way there, Bill swerves his car and crashes to avoid hitting a dog, and only escapes from the car by seconds before it explodes. The next day Bill is hailed as a huge hero, which gets him the attention of the snoopy efficiency expert, who, unknown to Bill, has been ordered by the KGB to kill him. Later, after seeing Bill on TV, Ralph gets a holographic image of a sniper preparing to shoot the agent, so he flies to Bill's address and captures the would-be assassin and his partner just before Bill arrives with the romantically-inclined O'Neil. The next day, Pam and Ralph meet Bill and O'Neil for lunch, and Bill reveals that he is helping O'Neil train to be a top-notch agent. Pam and Ralph can both see Bill is getting emotionally involved with the efficiency expert, who doesn't understand Bill and Ralph's relationship. After telling Ralph he wants to reveal to O'Neil the truth about the suit, Bill leaves with his friend to dig up some guns buried on a beach. Once there, Bill easily locates the weapons, but is beaten up by two thugs who knew he was coming. Elsewhere, Ralph, suspicious of O'Neil, breaks into her apartment and tries on a hat to holograph any information about her - just as she and Bill return to her apartment. Ralph hides as his friend and O'Neil enter her apartment, where he sees an upset O'Neil hide a pistol in some towels she is taking to Bill - who is obviously going to kill the agent. **Guest cast:** Ted Flicker as David, Adam Gregor as Yuri, Arnold Turner as the insurance man, Dixie Carter as O'Neil, Gay Rowan, Trisha Hilka, Gary Pagett, Craig Shreeve, Judd Omen, Robert Alan Browne, James Lydon, Dabbs Greer, Nick Shields, Stefanie Faulkner as Jane,

Ralph Clift as Mr. Bunker, Gary Pagett as Mr. Rogers, Craig Shreeve as Mr. Newton, Trisha Hilka as Annie. **Writer:** Robert Culp. **Director:** Robert Culp.

SEASON THREE

Divorce Venusian Style (airdate: Oct. 29, 1982). Bill and Ralph are slowly driving each other crazy while on a stake out, hiding in a motel to watch for some felons who are supposed to arrive. But they are being watched as well - by a group of modern-day Nazis who are planning the comeback of the Fourth Reich, and who plan to kill them both. Ralph finally gets tired of Bill's arrogant style and walks out, but moments later Bill sees the men they have been looking for, and calls Ralph to go in pursuit. He catches the felons, but another argument breaks out, and Ralph hands over the uniform to Bill and retires. After he walks away two American Nazi members open fire on Bill, and when Ralph races back to help, the teacher is critically wounded by machine gun fire. Bill manages to get Ralph to safety in a hot dog vendor's van, which he takes to escape the Nazis and rush Ralph to a nearby hospital. But when they arrive at the emergency room, the van suddenly has a mind of its own: it not only locks Bill and Ralph inside, but starts driving itself at high speed for some unknown destination. Meanwhile, Pam arrives at the motel to pick up Ralph, but her can is taken over as well, and is headed out into the desert. Elsewhere, Bill realizes the aliens have returned when he sees a roadsign for Palmdale, where they received the suit. Once in the desert the flying saucer returns, beams Bill and a dieing Ralph aboard, where the agent encounters several aliens who give him a language translator to tell him Ralph will be healed. Moments later, Ralph appears and seems to be returned to normal. He and Bill are shown around the ship as it flies to the alien's home world. Once there, the humans see it is nothing but a burned-out cinder. The message is clear: Bill and Ralph must work harder, stop quibbling, and save the world. Taken back to Earth, Ralph is given another instruction book and both men are beamed down to an awaiting Pam. Despite what they've been through, both men still get into an argument over who will get to read the book first. Bill ends up with it, but finds it is in an alien language that Ralph obviously needs the suit to read. The only problem is that Bill left the suit back in his car with the Nazis - who are currently testing the indestructible material in hopes of duplicating it. **Guest cast:** Jeremy Kemp as Franz Zedlocker, Dean Santoro as Jackson, Kurt Grayson as Hertzog, James McIntire as Billy Boy Floyd, Jason Bernard as Morgan, Shane Dixon as the ranch guard, Wayne Storm as the police officer, Robert Gray, Al W. Coss, Joe Clarke, Frank Doubleday, Eugene Brezany. **Writer:** Patrick Burke Hasburgh. **Director:** Ivan Dixon.

The Price is Right (airdate: Nov. 5, 1982). As Bill is watching on TV his favorite pro football player, Price Cobb, Ralph mentions that he saved Price's career back when they went to high school together. Price was flunking algebra so Ralph helped him out, making it possible for him to go on to pro-sports. Bill doesn't believe a word of it until Ralph proves it by phoning Cobb. Before the matter can be discussed further, the trio have to leave to save two F.B.I. agents under fire. Arriving at the shoot-out, the criminals take off in a maroon Ford, resulting in a high speed chase. Ralph uses the suit to stop the car while Bill arrests both men. After returning home, Ralph gets a call from Cobb about attending their high school class reunion. Cobb invites Ralph, Pam, and Bill to a practice game, then after getting off the phone finds himself confronted by thugs who have entered his home making threats and ordering the player to throw his team's next game. Later, Bill, Ralph, and Pam arrive at the practice where Maxwell gets an old football autographed and, as they leave, Bill sees Cobb in the parking lot talking to an ex-con he busted years ago. Ralph uses the suit to follow Cobb and several hoods in a car, but loses them after nearly being hit by a helicopter, causing him to crash face first into a picnic lunch. Afterwards, Ralph and Pam prepare to go to the reunion, and are horrified when they have to use a purple limousine Bill rented. Ralph had wanted to

impress his ex-classmates, but when he shows up in a purple Cadillac his intentions don't worked out as planned. As soon as he leaves the car he is met by Price's wife Wendy, and ex-girlfriend that is all over him. As Ralph mingles with his ex-schoolmates he becomes furious after finding out Price was dating Wendy at the same time he was, and apparently everyone by Ralph was aware of their secret meetings. Minutes later, Bill sees Price arrive and confronts him about leaving in the car with the hoods. Seeing Bill's badge Price knocks him down and takes off in his car, with Bill in pursuit with the 'pimpmobile' and Ralph flying in his suit. Ralph catches Cobb as his car nearly goes off a cliff, and when he touches the player, Ralph gets a holograph of the truth: his wife has been kidnapped and she is being held prisoner until Price throws the game. [The chase scenes of Bill and the maroon Ford Fairlane are taken entirely from another episode. In fact, this same car is seen in many different episodes, usually being used by crooks making getaways.] **Guest cast:** Stephen Shortridge as Price Cobb, Jack Andreozzi as Florenzia, Don Pulford as Miller, Patrick Collins as Gertmanian, Martin Speer as Stan Hawn, Heather Lowe as Wendy Cobb, Chip Johnson as Deke, Dick Butkus as the coach, Anthony Davis, Doug France as Caprice, Tom Harmon, Edith Fields, Cathryn Hart as Gloria, Louise Hoven as Roberta, Susan Duvall as Angie. **Writer:** Stephen J. Cannell. **Director:** Ivan Dixon.

This is the One the Suit Was Made For (airdate: Nov. 11, 1982). A new automated Mach-6 interceptor, the Zephyr 1, is launched from Cape Kennedy, but not long after takeoff it is thrown off course by hijackers sending powerful radio transmissions from a ship in international waters. It drops below radar height and disappears. Elsewhere, Bill and Ralph are stopping a gang from robbing a bank, and Ralph has to force open a vault door before the employees locked inside die from lack of oxygen. Once all the crooks are rounded up Ralph leaves in a big hurry to see Pam, who is furious over him being late for the millionth time. He has missed an important party, the guests having already left. Pam is ashamed that he stood her up, and believes the super-suit is destroying their relationship. Ralph proposes they take a week off and go on a vacation, leaving the suit and Mr. Scenario behind. Bill is equally ticked off when Ralph reveals he is taking a week off, particularly since he should be working on the "one the suit was made for". When Ralph's plans fall through (the cabin he wanted to use has burned down), he has to reveal what has happened to Pam, who doesn't believe a word of it. Just as Pam and Ralph are about to get into a major argument, Bill gives them a set of tickets to a remote Bermuda island. As it so happens, the island is where the missing aircraft is being held for the Russians. Not knowing any better, Pam and Ralph accept the tickets and have a great time - until Ralph, getting a bad sunburn on the beach, is given a message to come back to his room. Expecting to find Pam, he instead is confronted by Bill, who expects Ralph to use the suit to find the Zephyr 1. Ralph refuses to get involved, but after much argument agrees to holograph off a photo to give Bill information he needs. Ralph sees it under a tent where it is hid on a military base. Pam shows up, forcing Ralph to hide in the bathroom while Bill (hiding in the shower) continues to plead for his help. Ralph refuses and goes with Pam to a tennis match they were scheduled for. Afterwards, Bill gets alone with Ralph and convinces him to help locate the aircraft, which they do, then round up the guards with the use of the suit. Thinking he is out of potential trouble with Pam now that the case is solved, Ralph returns to his hotel room, but once there is attacked by a female who has had her eyes on Ralph. She begins ripping off his clothes - revealing the super-suit in the process - when Pam walks in. She is furious over both the suit and Ralph's involvement with the girl, and as far as she is concerned their relationship is over. **Guest cast:** Bo Brundin as Stanislov, Pepe Serna as Cortez, Jay Varela as Fernandez, Loyita Chapel as Bunny, Dean Wein as Mitchell, Randall Nazarian, Bob Basso, Randall Nazarian, Dean Wein as Mitchell, Maurie Lauren as Sandy, Bobby Don McGaughey as the employee. **Writer:** Babs Greyhosky. **Director:** Ivan Dixon.

67

Devil in the Deep Blue Sea: Ralph and Bill confront a modern-day pirate (Michael Halsey as Collins).

The Resurrection of Carlini (airdate: Nov. 18, 1982). Ralph is trying to decide what he can come up for entertainment for a teacher's function when Bill arrives to tell Ralph and Pam to watch a tv program describing an upcoming annual magician's banquet, this year's meeting being devoted to the fabulous Carlini. Carlini died under suspicious circumstances, just after his assistant was murdered. Carlini himself was believed to have been involved, but just as Bill and other F.B.I. agents arrived to arrest him he died in a fiery act. Three magicians will be performing at the banquet three of Carlini's exclusive tricks - on the night Carlini swore he would return from the dead. Watching the show, Ralph is inspired to perform magic acts at the function, however, Bill has a more important matter to discuss: he has received a letter saying that Carlini's four greatest enemies - the three competing magicians who will perform his tricks, and Bill, who was pursuing him for the murder of his assistant - are named in his will, and they are to show up at the dead magician's home. Bill suspects that Carlini's second assistant, Blachard, may be out to kill all four of them in revenge. Knowing Blachard is not dealing with a full deck and has been making threats, Bill takes along Ralph and Pam to Carlini's closed mansion for a reading of the will. The other magicians hope to receive information or material on other acts Carlini was developing at the time of his death, so they eagerly show up at the home. Even though the attorney hasn't arrived yet, Ralph and Bill enter the house with the suit - even though the magicians and Bill swore the door was locked and Ralph is certain it wasn't. The magicians are spooked by this, and even more so when a fireplace and candles suddenly light themselves. While the escape artists try to find a way out of the room they become locked in, the room suddenly bursts into flames and Ralph has to use the suit to escape. He sees a car driving away and pursues it, and once catching up Ralph finds it contains the old assistant of Carlini. Bill arrests Blachard and

questions him, but the man swears he was there for the will too, so the unbalanced man is let go for lack of evidence. That night, Bill, Ralph, and Pam arrive at the banquet, where the three competing magicians are nearly killed - seemingly by the dead Carlini. **Guest cast:** Andrew Robinson, Jack Magee, Timothy Carey, Ferdinand Mayne, Randi Brooks [*Wizards and Warriors*] as Beverly, Sandy Martin as the woman, Troy Slater as the little boy, Robert Aberdeen as the magician. **Writer:** Frank Lupo. **Director:** Arnold Laven.

The Newlywed Game (airdate: Jan. 6, 1983). On the day before Ralph and Pam's wedding, Ralph accompanies Bill to meet an informant, but they are met with automatic-firing machine guns, self-launching grenades, and a driverless truck - someone is obviously trying to kill Bill. They return to Ralph's house, where Pam's mother is preparing a spectacular wedding, when all Pam and Ralph want is something small and intimate. Ralph would be further horrified if he knew Bill and some friends have prepared a stag party for him over his objections that he doesn't want one. Even worse, neither man is aware that Ralph was filmed at the barn where he had bullets bouncing off his chest, stopped a huge truck single-handedly, and flew home. The Russian agents watching the film want to know how this is possible, so agents are sent to grab both Ralph and their target, Bill Maxwell. Before Ralph can iron out any problems, Bill arrives to take his friend to the bachelor's party, while Bill pretends to be on a case. On the way to the hotel the party is to be held at, they are kidnapped prior to arriving at their destination. Both men are blindfolded, picked up by a helicopter on the hotel roof, and taken to an underground installation guarded by Marines. While Pam is trying to learn where Bill and Ralph have gone, they are met by a former U.S. secretary who reveals that the government knows all about the suit, and Ralph is now working for him and the President. Ralph is aware that Matthew Powers was removed from office under an official explanation of "failing health", but Powers claims that he left the office to find out who was performing super deeds, which led him to Ralph. Now Ralph is to work from the underground Utah installation and will report only to the White House. Furthermore, Bill is not needed and is to return to his normal F.B.I. work. Powers agrees to let Bill stay after Ralph explains their teamwork. To obtain the suit to perform his first mission, Ralph phones Pam, who is hungover from a stag party of her own. She agrees to deliver the suit to a limousine, and it soon arrives (with Pam) for Ralph's use. Now Ralph is told that his first assignment is to take photographs of missile launch sites near the North Pole - not realizing that the mission is a hoax by the Russians, and when he returns with the film he will be giving away valuable military secrets. **Guest cast:** Hansford Rowe as Matthew Powell, Norman Alden as Mr. Davidson, Woody Eney as Martin, Terrence McNally as Campbell, Pamela Bowman as Boom Boom, Dan Peterson as the stripper, Alice Backes as Eleanor Pilburn, Frank K. Wheaton as the videoman, Robby Weaver as Ray, Cynthia Steele. **Writer:** Babs Greyhosky. **Director:** Chuck Bowman.

Heaven is in Your Genes (airdate: Jan. 13, 1983). Bill is being chased by two thugs in a truck trying to run him off the highway, and his car finally skids off the road into a gas station where it explodes. The next day Pam and Ralph attend his funeral, where they are the only ones who show up except for some strangers who discover they are at the wrong funeral. No one from the bureau shows up, a situation that makes Ralph upset. He and Pam decide to go to Bill's apartment, where they find a diary Bill had been keeping about their adventures. While listening to Pam reading the diary, Ralph puts on Bill's fishing hat on and immediately receives a holographic image - Bill is alive! Seeing Bill pick up a menu in a closed restaurant in Rio Cava where he is being held, Ralph decides to try to track down his partner, and flies to the airport where Bill is being flown out of the country by the men who faked his death - thugs working for a former Nazi genetic engineer who plans to use Bill in an experiment. Ralph locates the closed diner Bill was being held in, but Maxwell is already on a plane heading south. Pam arrives, and so do police who rapidly come to the conclusion that Ralph is crazy. Ralph gets a holograph of Bill on the aircraft and leaves after tieing up the belligerent police officer and telling Pam to catch the next flight south. Meanwhile, Bill is taken to the island where the experiments are taking place, being conducted by the ruthless Kris Peterson and her reluctant assistant, Tom, who objects to their work. Unfortunately, he faces charges back in the U.S. and cannot return home, so is in no position to stop the work being supervised by Dr. Striegel. Bill is soon informed that he is going to be the subject of an experiment, and was chosen because of his brilliant arrest record, the scientist not knowing the credit actually belongs to Ralph and the suit. Striegel, having been trained by the late Nazi physician Dr. Mengele, is now working at creating clones of brilliant or gifted people. So far his only attempts have resulted in disaster, but he is certain the work on Maxwell will be more successful. Elsewhere, Ralph arrives in Mexico and uses the suit to "muscle" some answers out of locals as to where Bill is. As Ralph continues his search, Tom Gardener tries to escape the island, not wanting to see Maxwell killed. When Striegel learns he has run away, the scientist has Bill injected with a virus that will kill him if he is not given the antidote - which he will only receive upon the return of Gardener. Bill leaves to locate the missing scientist, realizing he has little chance of finding him without Ralph's help. Later, when Ralph finally arrives and locates Bill, he must face a genetic horror created in an earlier experiment. **Guest cast:** William Price as Dr. Striegel, Dennis Lipscomb as Tom Gardener, Andre the Giant as the monster, George McDaniel as Rutter, Carolyn Seymour as Kris Peterson, Rick Barker as Bradley, Ted Gehring as Lutz, Richard Fullerton, Gene Ross as Plummer, Patricia Wilson as Barbara Lutz, Ruben Morino as the gas station attendant, Gina Alvarrado as receptionist. **Writer:** Patrick Hasbough. **Director:** Christian I. Nyby, Jr.

Live at Eleven (airdate: Jan. 20, 1983). As usual, Ralph is late for an appointment to see Pam because Bill is holding him up. When he finally arrives at the plush retirement party for an extremely popular TV anchorman, Henry Williams, whom Ralph greatly admires, he is pleased to get the chance to meet Williams - whose friends are trying to get him to run for president. But while at the party Ralph touches the briefcase of a man working for Williams, and gets a holographic image of men breaking into a nearby nuclear power-plant. When Ralph tries to stop some mercenaries from stealing radioactive material, the container is overturned and they run as plutonium rods are exposed - causing Ralph to glow. Bill, after being contacted by radio, arrives and panics upon seeing Ralph place the radioactive rods back in their container. Guards arrive and try to arrest both men, but Ralph discovers the suit has a new power: he suggests they leave and they immediately follow his order. Meanwhile, the real culprits get away. Bill is placed in a hospital to be checked for radioactive poisoning, a situation made worse when hypochondriac Bill sees Williams give a newscast on all the symptoms the thieves will have after being exposed to the nuclear rods. Ralph uses the power of suggestion again to convince Bill he isn't sick, while elsewhere the men who broke into the nuclear plant report that they are getting sick to their boss, Chuck Cole, the person working on William's future election plans. He promises to take care of them, while Bill finds himself trying to explain the communicator he and Ralph use to contact each other after Carlisle heard it in action, and Ralph finds that his new power of suggestion (brought on by the radioactivity) works well on his students. As he convinces them to read classical literature, Ralph finds a business card from Williams in his pocket, and receives an image of the anchorman being assassinated. Ralph arrives in time to save him from being murdered by one of the mercenaries who was exposed to plutonium at the nuclear plant, and as Ralph goes to arrest the assassin, the man dies of radioactive poisoning. Bill arrives with Carlisle, who heard Ralph's warning over the radio, but Ralph gets rid of the nosey F.B.I. chief by using his mind control power again. With him gone, both Ralph and Bill are led to believe that there is a connection between Williams and the nuclear plant, but it remains a mystery as to what it is. **Guest cast:** William Windom as Henry Williams, Alan Fudge [*Man from Atlantis*] as Chuck Cole, Miguel Fernandes as Canton, Will MacMillan as Fields, Eugene Peterson as Sherwood Davis, Melvin E. Allen as the security guard #1, Debra Mays as Tammy, Charles Walker as Shelton, Woody Skaggs as Coursey, Victoria Boyd as Vicki, Mary York as the policeman, Eileen Saki as the nurse, Amanda Harley as Gladine, Dudley Knight as the foreman, Terrence Beasor as Schneider, Will MacMillian. **Writer:** Babs Greyhosky. **Director:** Arnold Laven.

Space Ranger (airdate: Jan. 27, 1983). An unknown person has been contacting and giving information to the C.I.A. under the name "Space Ranger", a genius at telecommunications. The C.I.A. keep trying to catch him, but are always unsuccessful. Lately he has been tapping in on Russian satellites, and KGB agents, like the C.I.A., are determined to find the boy - except they plan to kill him before he can turn over his system to the U.S. government. It turns out that Space Ranger is actually Allen, a student of Ralph's, who ended up in his class because of his secluded nature. All of the other kids treat him like a geek, even though he is obviously a genius - a fact that Ralph has noticed, and cannot understand how he could be placed in a Special Education class. His classmates try to get him to work on a science project with them, but Allen figures it is another trick to make him look foolish. Ralph arrives for class and joins in convincing Allen in assisting in the science fair. He announces that he has perfected a radio telescope to decode messages from spy satellites. Since the gear must be brought to school and set up, Ralph goes along with Allen in the teenager's electronics-filled van to his dilapidated home, where two KGB agents break through the front door and attack Allen and Ralph. While Allen runs, Ralph changes into the suit and puts both agents out of commission, then has to save the nearly-blind Allen when he loses his glasses and walks in front

A Chicken in Every Plot: Faye Grant as Rhonda.

of a truck. Returning to school, the equipment is set up and works perfectly, although the class doesn't seem to be impressed when they contact a weather satellite at 20,000 feet. Taking him home for supper, Ralph questions Allen about the earlier incident, as does Bill when he arrives. Pam cooks their meal after Allen repairs her microwave, and the boy manages to get a phone call in to the C.I.A. Before Allen can offer many explanations to Bill and Ralph, who have learned that there is no Allen Smith and the house the boy lives in is an empty condemned home, the KGB agents break into Ralph's house and open fire, which Bill returns. The C.I.A. also arrive, having traced the call to Ralph's. Allen gets away to his van and takes off with Bill in tow while Ralph, now in the suit, goes after the KGB men and, believing a second car with C.I.A. men are part of the same group attacking Allen, he stops their car only to find himself under arrest when they think he is Space Ranger. **Guest cast:** Douglas Warhit as Allen Smith/Longstress, Joe Santos [*Blue Thunder*] as Fetchner, James Beach as Oscar, Alex Rodine as Proslov, Jan-Ivan Dorin as Zatkoff, Billy Zabka as Clarence Mortner, Jr., Evonne Kezios as Zelda, Steve Alterman as Milton, Kene Holliday, Jay Gerber, Edward Bell, James Beach. **Writer:** Rudolph Borchert. **Director:** Ivan Dixon.

Thirty Seconds Over Little Tokyo (airdate: Feb. 3, 1983). Ralph, Pam, and Bill are going out to dinner, where they are to meet a blind date for Bill - something he is exceedingly unhappy about. Ralph is already upset about an upcoming tenure meeting, while Bill is horrified to arrive at his favorite eating place only to learn it has been changed into a Japanese restaurant. Going inside, Dotty, the lady Bill assumes will be an ogre, turns out to be very attractive but extremely headstrong, and immediately locks horns with the agent when she seems to know more about football than he does. Meanwhile, a Japanese youth gang, led by a teenager with dreams of becoming a samurai, reports that he has located Isoroku Shikinami. He is ordered to kidnap the man, who is the uncle of a young scientist who has invented a deadly particle weapon that a Japanese criminal society wants. Unfortunately for the kidnappers, the uncle works at the restaurant being used by Ralph and friends. Just as the dinner is completely falling apart, the gang breaks in and kidnaps the Japanese waiter, but he is freed by Ralph as the gang escapes. Isoroku is

so grateful over Ralph saving him that he begins paying back the favor by trimming Ralph and Pam's bushes all night, among other things, and is rapidly driving the couple crazy. He refuses to stop "helping" Ralph, as it will mean dishonor to him. Ralph decides to visit Isoroku's nephew Ernie to try to get Isoroku to cease his activities. Before this can be done, Ralph has to try to survive his tenure meeting, where Bill breaks in with big plans to find the kidnappers. Ralph is furious over Bill's intervention, which results in Ralph being ordered to provide a written explanation within twenty-four hours of his involvement with the F.B.I. They leave to search for the kidnappers at a karate studio, where Bill antagonizes everyone before discovering Ralph doesn't have the suit, and both are badly beaten. Returning to Ralph's house, Pam is upset over Isoroku having rearranged all her pans, and Bill tries to recover from his injuries while Ralph attempts to get a holograph off of Isoroku's clothing to find out who is after him. Moments later kidnappers bust into the house, grab Isoroku while he was giving Ralph a bath, and nearly kill the arriving Dotty. After they leave Ralph fails to get a holograph from Isoroku's belongings, so they go in search of his nephew Ernie, who turns out to be an important engineer and the person the gang is really after. They plan to use Isoroku as leverage to get to Ernie and the high-tech weapon he is working on for the government. **Guest cast:** Soon-Teck Oh as Ernie Shikinami, Mako as Master of Flowers, Lloyd Kino as Isoroku Shikinami, Christine Belford [*Outlaws*] as Dotty, Peter Kwong as Tanaka, Dana Lee, Edward Bell, Robert Alan Browne, John Wyler as Benning, George Paul as the landlady, Bert Henchman as the security guard. **Writers:** Danny Lee Cole and J. Duncan Ray. **Director:** Arnold Laven.

Wizards and Warlocks (airdate: syndicated). On a college campus, a group of students are involved in a Wizards and Warlocks role-playing game. One of the students is a Middle East prince that has been marked for assassination by a man who also tried to kill his father. Later, a sheik arrives to see agent Maxwell: he is looking for Prince Ahad, his son, who has been missing for over twenty-four hours after entering the Wizards and Warlocks game. Much to Carlisle's horror, King Shalabim wants no other agent than Bill to take the case, and explains that an assassin is after both him and the prince. After the king leaves, Bill contacts Pam and Ralph and explains the scenario, none of them realizing that the prince's disappearance is tied into playing the role game. Going to the prince's university, Ralph tries to convince Bill not to go overboard and flash his badge at everyone, but it only takes two minutes for Bill to pull a J. Edgar Hoover routine. A leader of the Warlock game finally admits he knows where Ahad is, but as they return to the boy's room for information, three Middle-East thugs jump through the door and grab him. Opening fire on Bill, Ralph, and Pam, they take cover until Ralph gets his suit on, but the kidnappers escape when Ralph hits a tree. Later, they meet another boy involved in the game, and he sends them to the only person who might be able to determine Ahad's location: Norman Fakler, the nut case who devised the game. Arriving at his office, they find he is more interested in marketing games. Only after he hears his game may receive some "bad press" does he agree to help. Returning to the school, they are given clues leading them to underground tunnels, where the thugs and the kidnapped teenager are already searching for Ahad. The prince carefully avoids both groups who fail to do the same when they get involved in a shoot-out that ends with Ralph attacks with the suit. The hoods are arrested and taken in, but Ahad is still missing - and the nearly blind Norman has gotten lost in the underground maze after his glasses are broken. **Guest cast:** Steve Peteman, Shunil Borpujari, Nicko Minardos, James Whitmore, Jr. as Norman Fakler. **Writer:** Shel Willens. **Director:** Bruce Kessler.

Desperado (airdate: syndicated). Pam and Ralph spend a weekend in the country taking photos of wild horses in a protected area. When they see the horses being herded up by cowboys, Ralph - without his super-suit - goes to the rescue, only to receive a severe beating. They go to the local sheriff, who tells them the horses are captured to be sold to a dog food company. He refuses to help, so Pam calls Bill with a fake story so he will bring the suit and help them on another "caper". After he arrives at their motel, they explain the situation, but the agent isn't terribly sympathetic. Since the horses are protected by Federal law, Bill joins the crusade to stop the rustlers. Ralph uses the suit to find stallion leading the herd. It is captured and taken by trailer to the local veterinarian, where they learn that the cowboys are really working for Justin King, a man with a grudge. It seems that the stallion they caught, named Desperado, used to belong to him. While trying to break the horse it threw King and he has been crippled ever since, so he put a bounty of $1000 on the horse's head. Now he wants the horse back to kill it. While they discuss the situation to the vet, Bill goes to the sheriff's office and, not finding him there, leaves a message for the man to contact Bill at the motel. Hearing a commotion near Ralph's station wagon, Bill runs outside and is joined by Ralph and Pam, who find one of King's men, Charley, and an accomplice trying to steal Desperado. They are stopped, and Ralph gives Charley a free ride to the pinnacle of a nearby mountain until he reveals where the stolen horses are. King, who has the horses on his ranch, soon makes an appearance and Desperado nearly kills him. The wealthy rancher returns to his home and castigates his boys for wanting to make a little money on the side by rounding up extra mustangs - against King's orders, who wants them to return Desperado to him no matter what it takes - something Ralph is determined to prevent. But the trio soon find themselves surrounded by armed masked men who steal the stallion and threaten to kill it if they intervene - exactly what King wants. **Guest cast**: John Vernon as Justin King, James Hampton the sheriff, Red West as Charley, Luke Askew as Matt, Rick Lenz, Conlan Carter, Linda Hoy as Martha Wells, Beach Dickerson as the judge. **Writers**: Stephen J. Cannell, Frank Lupo. **Director**: Christopher Nelson.

It's Only Rock and Roll (airdate syndicated). The crew aboard a private jet are informed that a bomb may be aboard, one that is set to go off when the aircraft descends to a certain altitude. At F.B.I. headquarters Bill is told of a threat to destroy the rock band Elvira by blowing up their aircraft. While Bill leaves to pick up Pam and Ralph, they are busy trying to deal with disgruntled neighbors who want the couple to take better care of the appearance of their lawn. Bill arrives with squealing tires, picks up the Hinkleys, and heads to the airport - only then Bill finding out that he is supposed to save a "pinko rock group". At the airport they are told that the device has been set to explode as the plane lands in order to blow up the leader of the rock group in front of his fans. As the aircraft gets low on fuel Ralph flies to it to investigate, locates the bomb inside a cargo compartment, and removes it from the plane. Flying away, the bomb goes off while Ralph is holding it, knocking him into the ocean. He flies back to the airport, changes clothes, and meets Bill and Pam at the aircraft, while elsewhere a pair of motorcycle riders watch the plane and are upset that it didn't blow up. Rock star Dak Hampton is told what happened, and his manager insists the F.B.I. provide security for Dak. Pam suggests Bill take him to a safe house where he can hide out, which he reluctantly agrees to do. Unfortunately, when Bill gets out of sight Dak makes a phone call to the rest of his group, tipping off his location. Later, a group of bikers arrive to kill the band leader, and Bill suddenly finds the house being turned into Swiss cheese by heavy gunfire. After being called Ralph arrives and chases off the gang members, but he and Bill discover Dak took off during the fight. A holograph leads them to a night club where Dak has agreed to play a few songs. They pick him up, but as they leave Ralph doesn't notice some of his students in the audience who follow to see where they are taking Dak. Meanwhile, the rock star finally admits that the motorcycle gang financed his first album, and now owns him since he made it big. He wants out, but they don't see it that way. Bill heads to Ralph's house to leave Dak there, not realizing the kids have followed them and are telling everyone where the rock star is. Soon the rest of the rock band arrives, trashes the house, and before long everyone in town seems to know where Dak is. **Guest cast**: Judson Scott [*The Phoenix*] as Dak Hampton,

Anthony Charnoto as Mike Christopher, Robert Dryer, George Dickerson, Lesley Woods, Dennis Stewart, Andy Wood, Michael Mancini, Sheila Frazer, Rick Dees as announcer, David Sage as the official. **Writer**: Babs Greyhosky. **Director**: Christian I. Nyby, Jr.

Vanity, Says the Preacher (airdate: syndicated). Ralph and Pam attend a "Man-of-the-Year" ceremony for Bill Maxwell put on by a small foreign country. But the ceremony is only a complex plan to kidnap the F.B.I. agent. He is flown to the banana republic where, thirty years earlier, he had helped establish a democratic government. Now the government is falling apart, and the family Bill worked with before wants his help. Reliving his earlier days of practically running the country goes to Bill's head, until he tries to stop two arguing brothers from conducting a duel, and is shot himself. Critically injured, he is saved by the arrival of the aliens who provided the power suit. But the aliens are ready to take back the super suit, feeling that Bill is making too many "screw ups". **Guest cast**: Isela Vega, Julio Medina, Dehl Berti, Joseph Culp, Jason Culp, Luis Moreno, Frankie Pesce as the bartender. **Writer**: Robert Culp. **Director**: Robert Culp.

[*The Greatest American Hero* was cancelled by ABC before any of the previous four episodes were shown, but they are included in syndication. This is probably just as well as these last four all feature terrible writing, with **Vanity** being the worst episode of the entire series. Among other problems, **Vanity** uses scenes of Bill and the aliens taken from a previous episode. But even this abysmal entry is surpassed by the truly horrendous **Greatest American Heroine**, now shown in syndication. In 1986, the following new pilot was filmed with a female version of Ralph Hinkley, but it was never sold or shown on tv until it suddenly turned up in syndication. Thankfully, the new series was never made.]

The Greatest American Heroine (airdate: syndicated, pilot for unmade series). F.B.I. agent Bill Maxwell is sitting in a lonely, darkened office recounting to a tape recorder how he and Ralph Hinkley got together, and their various exploits. All of this came to an end when secret super-hero Ralph is exposed from coast to coast as the "greatest American hero", who is now greeted by the President, guest stars on the Johnny Carson show, and is a national celebrity - a movie is even being made about him, called "The Ralph Hinkley Story". But the aliens have had enough, and they take over Pam's VW (with her and Ralph inside) and drive it to a secluded spot, where the flying saucer arrives. The aliens explain that the situation isn't working out, and they have decided to give the suit to someone else. Ralph, Bill, and Pam will be allowed to retain their memories of the suit, but everyone else in the world will be made to forget the greatest American hero. Meanwhile, Ralph is given the job of finding his replacement, someone wholesome and caring who can use the super suit for good. Bill is mad that he wasn't picked to get the suit, but he agrees to aid in the search. Ralph finds Holley Hathaway, a day school worker, a girl dedicated to the betterment of the world. Ralph and Pam meet Bill out in the desert where they received the suit, and Bill is furious that Ralph has passed on the suit to a "skirt". After Bill is introduced to Holley, goodbyes are said between Pam and Ralph and Bill, now that the old team has ended. Holley and Bill begin training with the suit, until Holley announces that she has picked their first case: investigating the sinking of a ship involved in a "save the whales" campaign. They fly to Newfoundland, but Holley's naive style of asking direct questions in a rowdy bar gets them both in trouble - a situation rectified by Holley in the suit. After wiping up the bar, one of the men tells what he knows of the ship that was sank. The next day, back at home, Holley reveals her super-identity to her foster daughter Sarah, a precocious seven-year-old. When Bill finds out he can only cringe [As does the audience!]. **Guest cast**: Mary Ellen Stuart as Holley Hathaway, Mya Akerling as Sarah, John Zee, Jerry Potter, Wayne Grace, Jeffrey Markel as Timothy. **Writer**: Babs Greyhosky. **Director**: Tony Mordente.

The Incredible Hulk

review by William E. Anchors, Jr.

Production credits:

Executive Producer	Kenneth Johnson
Creator for tv by	Kenneth Johnson
Character created by	Stan Lee
Music	Joe Harnell

Regular cast:

Dr. David Banner	Bill Bixby
The Hulk	Lou Ferrigno
Jack McGee	Jack Colvin

Number of episodes: 6 two hour movies, 79 one hour segments

Premise: Dr. David Banner, physician and scientist, is searching for a way to tap into the hidden strengths that all humans have. An accidental overdose of gamma radiation alters his body chemistry. Now when David Banner becomes angry or outraged, a startling metamorphosis occurs. He turns into a creature driven by rage, and is pursued by an investigative reporter, Jack McGee. The creature is wanted for a murder he didn't commit, the world believing David Banner is dead. And he must make them believe he is dead until he can find a way to control the raging spirit within him.

Editor's comments: In a sort-of science fiction version of *The Fugitive*, Banner goes on the run from those who would enslave him, meeting and helping new people in each episode while being pursued by reporter Jack McGee. Although the series and movies have little to do with the Marvel comic strip character, they remained highly popular for many years and attracted a large following.

SEASON ONE

The Incredible Hulk (airdate: Nov. 11, 1977, two hour pilot movie). While out for a drive, David Banner is involved in an accident that flips his car, causing the death of his wife when he cannot get her out of the burning vehicle. Ever since, the research scientist has buried himself in his work: research in finding ways to tap and control the hidden reserves of strength in humans that come out in moments of crisis. But during a test he is subjected to an accidental overdose of gamma radiation that triggers the hidden force and transforms the scientist into something incredible: a huge, hideous, rampaging beast of limited mental abilities - and turns into this beast whenever experiencing extreme pain, fear, or anger. Later, Dr. Elaine Marks is killed in a laboratory fire. She had been a good friend of Banner, as well as a colleague until her death. A reporter, Jack McGee, sees the Hulk for the first time and assumes that the creature started the fire that killed the doctor. Meanwhile, Banner is believed to be dead, so he leaves to begin a journey to find a cure to prevent his transformation into his alter-ego, while the reporter makes it his life's ambition to capture the Hulk. **Guest cast:** Susan Sullivan as Dr. Elaine Marks, Susan Batson as Mrs. Jessie Marie, Lara Parker [*Dark Shadows*] as Laura Banner, Mario Gallo as Martin Bram, Charles Siebert as Ben, Eric Devon as B.J. Maier, Jake Mitchell as Jerry, June Whitley Taylor as Mrs. Epstien, Eric Server as the policeman, William Larsen as the minister, Olivia Barash as the girl at the lake, George Brenlin as the man at the lake, Terrence Locke as the young man. **Writer:** Kenneth Johnson. **Director:** Kenneth Johnson.

Death in the Family (airdate: Nov. 28, 1977, two hour episode). After obtaining a new job, Dr. Banner learns that his boss is giving a drug to her crippled step-daughter that may be worsening her condition. The young girl is an heiress and it appears that her stepmother may be after her wealth. With David becoming a friend of the girl, he becomes angered by the way she is being treated and turns into the Hulk. While in the body of his other self, Banner keeps rescuing the girl while they are both being pursued by hired killers using bloodhounds and a helicopter. **Guest cast:** Laurie Prange, Dorothy Tristan, Gerald MacRaney, William Daniels [*Knight Rider, Captain Nice*]. **Writer:** Kenneth Johnson. **Director:** Alan Levi.

The Final Round (airdate: Mar. 10, 1978). David is attacked by a pair of muggers, but is saved by an unemployed boxer that he becomes friends with. But as Banner gets close to Rocky, he realizes that the prizefighter is being used in a dope deal - one in which he could end up dead. **Guest cast:** Martin Kove as Rocky, Al Ruscio as Sariego, Johnny Witherspoon as Tom, Fran Myers as Mary. **Writer:** Kenneth Johnson. **Director:** Kenneth Gilbert.

The Beast Within (airdate: Mar. 17, 1978). David's latest place of employment is the zoo, and he makes friends there with Claudia, a pretty young scientist. The girl is doing genetic research similar to what turned Banner into the Hulk, and he hopes to turn her in another direction in her research. But David becomes involved in bigger problems when he discovers a smuggling operation. In an enraged state he becomes the creature again, and ends up in a battle with a gorilla. **Guest cast:** Caroline McWilliams as Claudia, Dabbs Greer as Dr. Malone, Richard Kelton as Carl, Charles Lampkin as Joe, Jean Durand as Jagger, Billie Joan Beach as Rita. **Writers:** Karen Harris and Jill Sherman. **Director:** Kenneth Gilbert.

Of Guilt, Models And Murder (airdate: Mar. 24, 1978). David's new job is that of being a valet for a wealthy playboy. But something goes wrong and he turns into the Hulk. Later, when he awakes, he has no recollection of what occurred during his period as the beast - except that he finds himself near the body of a murdered young scientist. Now he must find out what happened during his alter-ego state. **Guest cast:** Jeremy Brett as Joslin, Loni Anderson as Sheila, Deanna Lund [*Land of the Giants*] as Terri Ann, Ben Gerard as

Bill Bixby as Dr. David Banner, Lou Ferrigno as the Hulk.

Sanderson. **Writer:** James D. Parriott. **Director:** Larry Stewart.

Terror in Times Square (airdate: Mar. 31, 1978). Arriving in New York, David becomes friends with an arcade owner and the man's daughter - until he finds out that a murder is about to occur, a situation that may destroy his friendship and activate the Hulk. **Guest cast:** Jack Kruschen as Norman, Pamela Shoop as Carol, Arny Freeman as Leo, Robert Alda as Jason. **Writer:** William Schwartz. **Director:** Alan Levi.

747 (airdate: April 7, 1978). David is on board an aircraft that will soon be pilotless: the pilot and a stewardess, his girlfriend, knock out the crew with drugs and parachute out of the aircraft with some extremely valuable artifacts they have stolen. Realizing their situation, David tries to pilot and land the aircraft, with the help of a little boy. But the tension of the situation builds up until it activates the Hulk. **Guest cast:** Brandon Cruz (Bixby's co-star on *The Courtship of Eddie's Father*) as Kevin, Edward Power as Phil, Sondra Currie as Stephanie, Shirley O'Hara as Mrs. MacIntire, Howard Honig as Jack, Susan Cotton as Cynthia Davis. **Writers:** Tom Szollosi and Richard Christian Matheson. **Director:** Sigmund Neufield, Jr.

The Hulk Breaks Las Vegas (airdate: April 21, 1978). David drifts to Las Vegas, where he obtains a job in a casino. When a journalist starts doing an investigative report, David agrees to help him. Unfortunately, it turns out that the man's partner is none other than Jack McGee - the reporter who is determined to imprison Banner's alter-ego. **Guest cast:** Julie Gregg as Wanda, Dean Santoro as Campion, Don Marshall [*Land of the Giants*] as Lee, Simone Griffith as Kathy, John Crawford as Tom Elder, Paul Picerni as Charlie. **Writer:** Justin Edgerton. **Director:** Larry Stewart.

Never Give A Trucker An Even Break (airdate: April 28, 1978). David helps out a beautiful woman trucker, not realizing what trouble it will get him into. He ends up in the middle of a road chase when the woman goes in pursuit of her father's stolen tank truck. He and the female trucker finally find themselves trapped, leading to a transformation into the Hulk, who takes on the oncoming semi-truck. **Guest cast:** Jennifer Darling, Frank Christi as Ted, Grand Bush as Mike, John Calvin [*Tales of the Gold Monkey*] as the Irishman, Charles Alvin Bell as the gas station man. **Writer:** Kenneth Johnson. **Director:** Kenneth Gilbert.

Life and Death (airdate: May 12, 1978). David Banner agrees to take part in a DNA experiment at a local hospital. On the way there he runs into a pregnant young lady and becomes friends with her - both of them not realizing that their lives will depend on the fury of the Hulk. **Guest cast:** Diane Civita as Carrie, Andrew Robinson as Dr. Rhodes, John Williams as Dan, Julie Adams as Ellen Harding, Carl Franklin [*Fantastic Journey*] as Crosby, Al Berry as the trucker. **Writer:** James D. Parriott. **Director:** Jeffrey Hayden.

Earthquakes Happen (airdate: May 19, 1978). David decides that he may be able to reverse his split-personality condition if he has the use of some gamma ray equipment. He learns that such a device is at a nearby nuclear facility, so he masquerades as an inspector to gain entrance to the research lab. He is unaware that the establishment has been under considerable criticism as it is located over an earthquake fault line. Later, after his cover is blown, an earthquake erupts causing a disaster to occur that is only averted by the timely arrival of the Hulk. **Guest cast:** Peter Brandon as Hammond, Sherry Jackson as Diane Joseph, Kenne Holiday as Paul, Lynne Topping

as Nancy, Pamela Nelson as Marsha, John Alvin as Dr. Patterson. **Writer:** Jim Tisdale. **Director:** Harvey Laidman.

The Waterfront Story (airdate: May 31, 1978). Banner arrives in Galeveston, Texas, where he becomes employed at a bar. While working at the waterfront tavern, there is a battle brewing within the dock worker's union that he becomes drawn in to. The previous president of the union had been murdered, and the crime was never solved. Now someone is coming after the president's widow, who has become a friend of David, and the beast is released when Banner becomes upset over the killers attempt on her life. **Guest cast:** Sheila Larken as Josie, Jack Kelly as Tony, James Sikking as McConnell, Candice Azzara as Sarah, Ted Markland as Marty, William Benedict as Vic. **Writers:** Paul M. Belous and Robert Woltersoff. **Director:** Reza Badiyi.

SEASON TWO

Married (airdate: Sept. 22, 1978, special two hour episode). David learns that a woman psychiatrist has developed new uses for therapeutic hypnosis. He travels to Hawaii to meet Dr. Caroline Fields, who is on leave at the time from her job. Trying to figure out how to ask her for help, he follows her home, where he finds her having a seizure and saves the woman's life. In return for his assistance, she agrees to help him, and while they try to learn how to reverse the effects of the gamma rays, the two scientists fall in love. Although they realize they will have many problems, they decide to marry. **Guest cast:** Mariette Hartley [*Genesis II*] as Dr. Caroline Fields, Brian Cutler as Brad, Duncan Gamble as Mark, Meeno Peluce [*Voyagers*] as the young boy, Diane Markoff as the girl, Joseph Kim as the Justice of the Peace. **Writer:** Kenneth Johnson. **Director:** Kenneth Johnson.

The Antowuk Horror (airdate: Sept. 29, 1978). David turns into the creature and is seen by locals while he is in a down-and-out resort town. The people living there are quick to realize that if they can publicize the monster being in their town they can bring back plenty of tourists. And it works - would-be big-game hunters arrive in droves, with everyone wanting a piece of the creature. To make sure interest in the beast remains high, a fake monster is sent into the nearby hills by the townspeople, who don't take into consideration the trigger-happy tourists. **Guest cast:** William Lucking [*Outlaws*], Debbie Lytton as Samantha, Lance LeGault [*Werewolf*] as Brad, Dennis Patrick as Buck, Myron D. Healey as Cotton, Gwen Van Dam as Mayor Murphy. **Writer:** Nicholas Corea. **Director:** Sig Neufeld.

Ricky (airdate: Oct. 6, 1978). David arrives in New Mexico, where he lands a job at a race track. He becomes friends with the retarded brother of one of the race car drivers, who is talked into driving in a demolition derby with a defective car - a situation that causes the beast to return. **Guest cast:** Mickey Jones as Ricky, James Daughton as Buzz, Robin Mattson as Irene, Eric Server as Ted Roberts, Gerald McRaney as Sam Roberts. **Writer:** Jaron Summers. **Director:** Frank Orsatti.

Rainbow's End (airdate: Oct. 13, 1978). Banner takes a job at a race horse track, but he is looking for more than employment: he has learned that a trainer there is experimenting with a formula to calm a wild race horse. Banner believes the formula may help stop him from transforming into his other self, but before he can proceed with his investigation David becomes emotionally involved with the

protection of the horse from an abusive employee. **Guest cast:** Ned Romero as Logan, Craig Stevens as Carroll, Michele Nichols as Kim, Gene Evans as Kelley, Larry Volk as Andy Cardone, Warren Smith as the guard. **Writers:** Karen Harris and Jill Sherman. **Director:** Kenneth Gilbert.

A Child In Need (airdate: Oct. 20, 1978). After taking a job as a school gardener, David befriends a little boy who claims to have a lot of accidents, but Banner suspects parental abuse. When this turns out to be the case, the beast intervenes. **Guest cast:** Dennis Dimster as Mark Hollinger, Sandy McPeak [*Blue Thunder*] as Jack Hollinger, Sally Kirkland as Margaret Hollinger, Rebecca York as Mary Walker, Marguerite De Lain as the reporter. **Writer:** Frank Dandridge. **Director:** James D. Parri.

Another Path (airdate: Oct. 27, 1978). A Chinese philosopher has given David Banner hope that he can conquer the beast within: the Oriental man can provide lessons that can place a control on the the nervous system, a possible counter to Banner's wild experiences as the Hulk. But the experience instead releases the monster, who rescues Li Sung and preserves his wise influence within the community. **Guest cast:** Mako as Li Sung, Tom Lee Holland as Frank Silva, Irene Yah-Ling Sun as Simon King, Jane Chung as Stamma Loo, Joseph Kim as Fong. **Writer:** Nicholas Corea. **Director:** Joseph Pevney.

Alice in Disco Land (airdate: Nov. 3, 1978). David obtains a job in a disco, where he becomes pals with one of the dancers. The young girl, who is suffering from a drinking problem, is being used by the ruthless proprietor of the nightclub. The beast is ultimately unleashed to save the teenager from the owner, while the more sedate Dr. Banner works with her on her alcoholism. **Guest cast:** Donna Wilkes as Alice, Jason Kincaid as Louie, Freeman King as D.J., Mo Malone as Rosalyn Morrow, Marc Alaimo as Ernie, Julie Hill as Molly, Betty Ann Rees. **Writers:** Karen Harris and Jill Sherman. **Director:** Sigmund Nuefeld.

Killer Instinct (airdate: Nov. 10, 1978). David accepts a job at a high school, where he will be working as an assistant trainer with a football team. At the school, a physician is studying aggressive behavior by watching the team, which David hopes will bring some results that will help his case. Unfortunately, the Hulk is unleashed to save a player, a troubled teenage boy who believes in winning at any cost. **Guest cast:** Denny Miller as Tobey, Barbara Leigh as June Tobey, Rudy Solari as Dr. Stewart, Wyatt Johnson as Bowers, Herman Poppe as J.P. Tobey, Tiger Williams as J.P. Tobey as a child. **Writers:** Joel Don Humpreys and William Whitehead. **Director:** Ray Danton.

Stop the Presses (airdate: Nov. 24, 1978). David is working at a restaurant that is exposed by the National Register, a trash tabloid that specializes in untrue stories. Unfortunately, the newspaper includes a photo of David, which David fears may be seen by Jack McGee. His highly-emotional state releases the creature, who makes a clean sweep of the National Register's publication offices. **Guest cast:** Mary Frann as Karen, Julie Cobb as Jill, Sam Chew, Jr. as Joe Arnold, Art Metrano as Charlie Watts, Pat Morita as Fred, Richard O'Brien. **Writer:** Susan Woolen. **Director:** Jeff Hayden.

Escape from Los Santos (airdate: Dec. 1, 1978). After leaving his restaurant position, David heads towards Phoenix, and while hitchhiking he is given a ride by a policeman. The situation gets out of hand and David finds himself in jail with a girl being framed for a murder she didn't commit. But the timely arrival of a certain green monster allows them to break out of jail and prove their innocence. **Guest cast:** Shelly Fabares as Holly, Lee de Broux as Deputy Evans, Dana Elcar [*MacGyver*] as Sheriff Harris, W.K. Stratton. **Writers:** Bruce Kalish and Philip Taylor. **Director:** Chuck Bowman.

Wildfire (airdate: Jan. 17, 1979). David is hired on at an oil rig run by an independent owner. He isn't there long before someone sabotages the operation by setting a fire at the well, and while David helps put the fire out he comes under attack by the saboteur. The Hulk is unleashed while Banner is being confronted by the would-be murderer, resulting in an end to the fire. **Guest cast:** John Anderson as Mike Callahan, Billy Green Bush as Thomas, Dean Brooks as Adler, Ernie Orsatti as Haze, John Petlock as Wade, Cristine Belford [*Outlaws*]. **Writer:** Brian Rehak. **Director:** Frank Orsatti.

A Solitary Place (airdate: Jan. 24, 1979). Banner decides he wants to get away from civilization for awhile, so he moves to a remote area, but his isolation doesn't last long. A woman on the run accidentally finds his camp, and stays for awhile. Although suspicious of each other at first, David and Gail gradually begin to feel friendship - neither of them realizing that reporter Jack McGee is looking for them both. **Guest cast:** Kathryn Leigh Scott [*Dark Shadows*] as Gail, Jerry Douglas as Frank, Bruce Wright as Richard, Hector Elias as Raul. **Writers:** Jim Tisdale and Migdia Varela. **Director:** Jeff Hayden.

Like A Brother (airdate: Jan. 31, 1979). David becomes involved in a fight between his co-worker friend and the man's brother, while a pushy preacher complicates matters. But the continuing battle ends up releasing Banner's beast. **Guest cast:** Stuart Stoker as Rev. Williams, Dale Pullum as Bobby, Ernie Hudson as Lee. **Writers:** Richard Christian Matheson and Thomas E. Szollasi. **Director:** Reza Badiyi.

The Haunted (airdate: Feb. 26, 1979). David is helping a young lady move to another town after accepting a job as a driver. She had lived there years earlier, until her twin sister was accidentally drowned. But the death wasn't an accident, which Banner finds out when he decides to stay with her for a few days - and now the Hulk is going to settle accounts for the murder of the twin. **Guest cast:** Carol Baxter as Renee, John O'Connell as Bernard, Johnny Haymer as Fred Lewitt, Jon Lormer as Dr. Rawlins, Randi Kiger as Renee as a child, Iris Korn as the woman. **Writers:** Karen Harris and Jill Sherman. **Director:** John McPherson.

Mystery Man, part one and two (airdates: part one, Mar. 2, 1979; part two, Mar. 9, 1979). After being involved in an accident, David loses his memory. Jack McGee finally locates Banner, whose face is still covered with bandages from the accident. They make arrangements to be flown home, but the plane crashes and Banner and McGee are the only survivors. Now stranded in the middle of nowhere, their lives are threatened by a forest fire, but they are saved when the beast emerges from David - and the transformation is witnessed by the reporter. **Guest cast:** Victoria Carroll as Rose, Aline Towne as Nurse Phalen, Howard Witt as Bob Cory, Bonnie Johns as Helen. **Writer:** Nicholas Corea. **Director:** Frank Orsatti.

The Disciple (airdate: Mar. 16, 1979). Banner visits with Li Sung

again, hoping to bring his inner beast under control. But the Chinese philosopher, the leader of a cult, has had his faith badly damaged over a recent incident. Because of this, he turns over the reigns of his cult to a police officer, a situation Banner is trying to rectify. [This episodes is a sequel to **Another Path**.] **Guest cast:** Mako as Li Sung, Rick Springfield as Michael, Gerald McRaney as Colin, Stacy Keach, Sr. as Tim, George Loros as Lynch. **Writers:** Nicholas Corea and James G. Hirsh. **Director:** Reza Badiyi.

No Escape (airdate: Mar. 30, 1979). On the road again, David is arrested and is being sent to jail as a vagrant, and on the way there he meets a strange couple, a man and a wife who consider themselves freedom fighters. Before they can reach the jail, events transpire that turn David into his alter-ego, freeing them all from the police van they were being transported in. **Guest cast:** James Wainwright as Tom Wallace, Mariclare Costello as Kay, Sherman Hemsley as Robert, Thalmus Rasulala as Simon, Skip Homeier. **Writer:** Ben Masselink. **Director:** Jeffrey Hayden.

Kindred Spirits (airdate: April 6, 1979). Banner travels to some Indian grounds when he hears about the finding of some bones of an ancient creature similar to the Hulk, believing he may find a key to control his aggressive other self. But while there, a woman recognizes his true identity - and he learns that Jack McGee will soon arrive. **Guest cast:** Whit Bissell [*The Time Tunnel*] as Prof. Williams, Kim Cattrall as Dr. Gabrielle White, Chief Dan George as Lone Wolf, A. Martinez as Rick Youngblood. **Writers:** Karen Harris and Jill Sherman. **Director:** Joseph Pevney.

The Confession (airdate: May 4, 1979). The National Register, the cheap tabloid that had caused David trouble earlier, sends an aggressive young reporter to assist McGee in locating the Hulk, but they are thrown off track by a strange person claiming to be the opposite identity of the Mean Green Machine. **Guest cast:** Markie Post as Pamela, Barry Gordon as Harold, Richard Herd [*V*] as Mark Roberts. **Writer:** Deborah Davis. **Director:** Barry Crane.

The Quiet Room (airdate: May 11, 1979). An unethical scientist is experimenting with mind-controlling drugs on helpless victims - including Dr. David Banner, who has been taken in as a deranged mental patient strapped in a straight jacket. The situation infuriates David, which unleashes the Hulk. **Guest cast:** Joanna Mills as Dr. Joyce Hill, Philip Abbott as Dr. Murrow, Sian Barbara Allen as Kathy, Robert F. Lyons as Sam. **Writers:** Karen Harris and Jill Sherman. **Director:** Reza Badiyi.

Vendetta Road (airdate: May 25, 1979). David finds himself between a rock and a hard place after he is caught in a struggle between corrupt cops and a pair of renegades who are blowing up gas stations. It seems that the renegades' father was run out of business and died because of an unscrupulous competitor, and they want revenge. Meanwhile, David tries to contact the press to have the truth be told, but instead runs into Jack McGee. **Guest cast:** Ron Lombard as Ray Floyd, Christina Hart as Cassie Floyd, Morgan Woodward as Madrid, Chip Johnson as Greg Bantam. **Writer:** Justin R. Edgarten. **Director:** John McPherson.

SEASON THREE

Metamorphosis (airdate: Sept. 21, 1979). David's new job is working for a bizarre New Wave rock group. While at a concert to operate the sound equipment, Banner becomes involved with help-

ing a fan who is hurt during a riot that breaks out. Afterwards, the lead singer who hired David feels guilty that her performance caused the serious injury, so she tries to commit suicide on stage. As the creature is unleashed to save her, the fans cheer on, believing it is all part of the performance. **Guest cast:** Mackenzie Phillips as Lisa Swan, Katherine Cannon as Jackie Swan, Gary Graham as Greg. **Writer:** Craig Buck. **Director:** Alan Levi.

Blind Rage (airdate: Sept. 28, 1979). Banner and a friend are dying after they have been exposed to a deadly biological weapon when an accident occurs at a chemical warfare research station. While a blind Dr. Banner tries to come up with an antidote, they are hindered by a local TV station who broadcasts denials that the accident ever occured. **Guest cast:** Tom Stechschulte as Lt. Jerry Banks, Lee Bryant as Carrie Banks, Nicholas Coster as Colonel Blake, Don Dubbins as Sgt. Murkland, Jack Rader as Major Anderson, Michelle Stacy as Patty Bank. **Writer:** Dan Ullman. **Director:** Jeffrey Hayden.

Brain Child (airdate: Oct. 5, 1979). While on the run himself, David comes in contact with a teenage runaway, a highly-intelligent young girl who is looking for her mother. But the law is now looking for them both, and it is doubtful that they can reach her mother before being trapped by the authorities. **Guest cast:** Robin Deardon as Jolene Collins, June Allyson as Dr. Kate Lowell, Lynn Carlin as Elizabeth Collins, Henry Rowland as Dr. Saltz, Madeleine Taylor Holmes as La Bruja, Fred Carney as Mr. Sweeney, Stack Pierce as the cop. **Writer:** Nicholas Corea. **Director:** Reza Badiyi.

The Slam (airdate: Oct. 19, 1979). David is once again arrested for vagrancy, but this time does not escape before being imprisoned in a tough work camp. The other prisoners look up to Banner because of his style and education, and try to talk him into airing their complaints to newspaper reporters. But they become upset when he refuses, not realizing that contacting the press will bring in Jack McGee. However, when David turns into his alter-ego, the camp and its inmates receive all the attention from the press they could ever ask for. **Guest cast:** Charles Napier [Outlaws] as Blake, Marc Alaimo as Captain Holt, Julius Harris as Doc Alden, Robert Davi as Radar, Skip Riley as Roth, Brad Dexter as the sheriff, Charles Picerni as Harris. **Writer:** Nicholas Corea. **Director:** Nicholas Corea.

My Favorite Magician (airdate: Oct. 26, 1979). An old magician takes on a new partner, Dr. David Banner, when he works at a benefit. But the greatest performance comes when the beast makes an appearance. **Guest cast:** Ray Walston [Bixby's co-star on *My Favorite Martian*] as Jasper Dowd, Anne Schedeem as Kimberley, Robert Alda as Giancarlo, Scatman Crothers [*Twilight Zone: The Movie*] as Edgar McGee, Joan Leslie as Lily, Bill Capizzi as Bill, Archie Lang as the Justice of the Peace, Fritzi Burr as Rose Brown, Franklin Brown as Maurie Brown, Bob Hastings as Earl. **Writer:** Sam Egan. **Director:** Reza Badiyi.

Jake (airdate: Nov. 2, 1979). Banner is working in a rodeo when he becomes friends with an overage cowboy. The man is well past his prime, but continues putting on shows with a sickness that could kill him at any time. Meanwhile, cattle rustlers are using the cowboy's brother for illegal activities. **Guest cast:** L.Q. Jones as Jake White, James Crittenden as Leon White, Sandra Kerns as Maggie, Jesse Vint as Terry, Richard Fullerton as Buford, Buck Young as Bob Long, Sandra Kerns as Maggie Burbank, Fred Ward as Marv. **Writer:** Chuck Bowman. **Director:** Frank Orsatti.

Behind The Wheel (airdate: Nov. 9, 1979). David is hired as a taxi driver by a lady who owns the taxi company, hoping that he can help her put an end to a drug-smuggling operation that is destroying her operations. **Guest cast:** Esther Rolle as Coleen Jenson, Jon Cedar as Sam Egan, Michael Baseleon as Michael Swift, John Chandler as Eric, Margaret Impert as Jean, Albert Popwell as Calvin, Richard O'Keefe as the owner, Jim Staskel as the dealer, Ed Reynolds as the driver. **Writer:** Andrew Schneider. **Director:** Frank Orsatti.

Homecoming (airdate: Nov. 30, 1979). Although knowing it is a great risk, David gambles that he will not be caught and returns home at Thanksgiving. He cannot chance seeing his family, but accidentally meets his sister, who tells him their father is about to go broke and lose his farm because of a crop-destroying plague. Although David doesn't get along with his father, he decides to stay and try to create an antidote to the plague. **Guest cast:** Diana Muldaur [*Star Trek: The Next Generation*] as Dr. Helen Banner, John Marley as D.W. Banner, Regis J. Cordic as Dean Eckart, Guy Boyd as Steve Howston, Richard Armstrong as the entomologist, Claire Malis as Mrs. Banner, Barbara Lynn Block as the newscaster, Reed Diamond as young David, Drew Snyder as Cross, Bob Boyd as the pilot. **Writer:** Andrew Schneider. **Director:** John McPherson.

The Snare (airdate: Dec. 7, 1979). David is on an island owned by a strange wealthy man, where a game of chess leads to David being turned into a human quarry during a hunting trip. **Guest cast:** Bradford Dillman as Michael Sutton, Bob Boyd as the pilot. **Writers:** Richard Christian Matheson and Tom Szollosi. **Director:** Frank Orsatti.

Babalao (airdate: Dec. 14, 1979). David is working with a young lady doctor in New Orleans, where she is trying to overcome ancient superstitions still being used by modern people. Dr. Renee Dubois and Banner end up having a close encounter with a local witch doctor and his gang of thugs, but the Hulk arrives during Mardi Gras to enliven the celebrations. **Guest cast:** Louise Sorel as Dr. Renee Dubois, Jarrod Johnson as Louie, Bill Henderson as Antonio Moray/Babalao, Michael Swan as Luc, Paulene Myers as Celine, Christine Avila as Denise, Morgan Hart as the girl, John D. Gowans as the local, Patti Jerome. **Writer:** Craig Buck. **Director:** Richard Milton.

Captive Night (airdate: Dec. 21, 1979). David's latest job is that of a clerk in a department store, but he gets into trouble over a discrepancy in stock. Before he can correct the problem, the store is taken over by thieves while he is working late, and to protect two fellow employees he must join the crooks. A not-amused Banner activates the beast, who manages to rearrange the store before the night is over. **Guest cast:** Anne Lockhart [*Battlestar Galactica*] as Karen Mitchell, Parley Baer as Raymond, Paul Picerni as Jim, Stanley Kamel as Gary. **Writer:** Sam Egan. **Director:** Frank Orsatti.

Broken Image (airdate: Jan. 4, 1980). The police are looking for a hood who could be a twin of David Banner, and they mistake David

for the real criminal. Banner ends up having to run from the police as a revenge-seeking gangster - and reporter Jack McGee, who cannot figure out who's who. **Guest cast:** Karen Carlson as Lorraine, John Reilly as Steve, Jed Mills as Teddy, George Caldwell as Pete. **Writers:** Karen Harris and Jill Sherman. **Director:** John McPherson.

Proof Positive (airdate: Jan. 11, 1980). National Register reporter Jack McGee has spent two years searching for Dr. David Banner and his monstrous other self, but when a new owner takes over the paper, McGee's job of finding his obsession is given the ax. Disgusted when he is no longer allowed to pursue Banner, McGee quits to find Banner on his own time - and prove once and for all that the Hulk is not a product of his imagination. [Bill Bixby does not appear in this episode.] **Guest cast:** Caroline Smith as Pat Steinhauser, Walter Brooke as Mark Roberts, Charles Thomas Murphy as Dick Garland, Wayne Storm, Isabel Cooley. **Writers:** Karen Harris and Jill Sherman. **Director:** Dick Harwood.

Sideshow (airdate: Jan. 25, 1980). David becomes a stage manager for a traveling carnival, and finds himself becoming romantically involved with a lady named Nancy. His real job turns out to be more of a bodyguard for the show, which sports an all-female cast. Wherever the carnival has gone disaster seems to strike, but the constant problems are really being caused by a mind reader working at the carnival and the lunatic who is out to get her. **Guest cast:** Marie Windsor as Belle Starr, Judith Chapman as Nancy, Robert Donner as Benedict, Bruce Wright as Jimmy, Louisa Moritz as Beth, Allan Rich as Luther Mason, Tam Elliot as Candy, Essex Smith as Cox, Terence Evans as Cecil. **Writer:** Len Jenkin. **Director:** Nicholas Corea.

Long Run Home (airdate: Feb. 1, 1980). David makes friends with a motorcycle gang member, and faces ostracism when he is thought to be a member of the group. Worse still, he becomes involved in a dispute between gang members - a situation quickly resolved by the arrival of the Hulk. **Guest cast:** Paul Koslo as Carl Rivers, Robert Tessier as Johnny, Mickey Jones as Doc, Stephan Keep as Fitzgerald, Edward Edwards as Bob, Albert Popwell as the doctor, Pamela Bryant as Ann, Nina Weintraub as Abigail, Galen Thompson as the foreman. **Writers:** Allan Cole and Chris Bunch. **Director:** Frank Orsatti.

Falling Angels (airdate: Feb. 8, 1980). David truly enjoys his new job of working with orphans, but has some problems getting a group of children under control who are placing a criminal influence on several of his favorite kids. David's life is further complicated by the untimely arrival of ex-reporter Jack McGee. **Guest cast:** Annette Charles as Rita Montoya, Timothy O'Hagan as Peter Grant, Anthony Herrera [*Mandrake the Magician*] as Don Sipes, Deborah Morgan-Weldon as Jodie, Cindy Fisher as Mickey, William Bronder as Jeff, Earl Billings as Lee, Arline Anderson as Mrs. Taylor, George Dickerson as George, Vincent Lucchesi as Tom. **Writers:** Eric Kaldor, D.K. Kremien and James Sanford Parker. **Director:** Barry Crane.

The Lottery (airdate: Feb. 15, 1980). David is taken advantage of by a friend, who collects and uses his lottery winnings in a scheme to make more money. The friend is in big trouble by the time David finds out about what he has done, and a fake shooting transforms David into his alter-ego to save the friend's life. **Guest cast:** Robert Hogan as Harry Jefferson, Peter Breck as Hull, David McKnight as

Clark, Adam Thomas as Steve, Jimmy Hayes as the guard, Luis Avalos as the official, Russell Arms as the announcer. **Writer:** Dan Ulman. **Director:** John McPherson.

The Psychic (airdate: Feb. 22, 1980). After meeting David, a psychic has visions of the beast - who is being sought for the murder of a young boy. When she meets Jack McGee she tells him that she can see his future - one of death at the hands of the real killer. **Guest cast:** Brenda Benet (the late Mrs. Bill Bixby) as Annie Caplan, Stephen Fenning as Johnny Wolff, Jason Ross as the cop, David Anthony as Robbie Donner. **Writers:** Karen Harris and Jill Sherman, George Bloom. **Director:** Barry Crane.

A Rock and a Hard Place (airdate: Feb. 29, 1980). Banner is once again caught between opposing forces: a woman who hires him as a handyman ends up forcing him into a gang of bank robbers, while a brutal FBI agent gets ahold of David and makes him reveal the gang's movements. Both groups are aware of his alter-ego of the Hulk, so he has no alternative but to do as they order. **Guest cast:** Jeanette Nolan as Lucy Cash, John McIntire as Preston Dekalb, Eric Server as Randolph, J. Jay Saunders as Granett Simms, Robert Gray. **Writer:** Andrew Schneider. **Director:** Chuck Bowman.

Deathmask (airdate: Mar. 14, 1980). In a new town David is living in, young girls are being murdered, and their deaths are being blamed on Banner after a girl the Hulk saves mutters David

Banner's name. David is arrested by the real killer, a mentally-unbalanced cop, and when the town decides to take justice into its own hands, the killer turns over David to their mercy. **Guest cast:** Gerald McRaney as Frank Rhodes, Frank Marth as Mayor Fowler, Lonny Chapman as J.J. Hendren, Melendy Britt as Joan Singer, Marla Pennington as Miriam Charles, Don Marshall [*Land of the Giants*] as the man, Dennis Bowen as Dale Jenks, Michael Bond as Sid Fox, Kieran Millaney as the young man, Desiree Kerns as the young blonde woman, Robert Luney as the newsman. **Writer:** Nicholas Corea. **Director:** John McPherson.

Equinox (airdate: Mar. 21, 1980). Banner becomes employed on an island estate belonging to a rich heiress. The spoiled girl insists that he attend a masquerade party, which he is reluctant to do as Jack McGee will be in attendance. Later that evening, someone tries to kill the obnoxious female, but the arrival of the Hulk changes the killer's plans. **Guest cast:** Christine DeLisle as Diane, Paul Carr [*Voyage to the Bottom of the Sea*] as Allan Grable, Louis Turenne as Pierce, Henry Polic II as Donald, Joy Garrett as Tina, Bob Yannetti as Carlo, Mark McGee as Sir Francis Drake, Kathie Spencer-Neff as the Inquisitor, Alexis Adams as the girlfriend, Danny Dayton as Skipper, Christine Delisle as Diane Powell. **Writer:** Andrew Schneider. **Director:** Patrick Boyriven.

Nine Hours (airdate: April 4, 1980). Now employed in a hospital, David teams up with an ex-police officer with a drinking problem to rescue a kidnapped child and a former criminal. **Guest cast:** Marc

Alaimo as Joe Franco, Sheila Larken as Rhonda Wilkes, David Comfort as Timmy Wilkes, Sam Ingraffia as Slick Monte, Phil Rubenstein as Fats, Doris Dowling as Nurse Grasso, Frank De Kova as Sam Monte, Dennis Haysbert as the guard, John Medici as Danny, Hal Bokar as Capt. Deeter. **Writer:** Nicholas Corea. **Director:** Nicholas Corea.

On The Line (airdate: April 11, 1980). David is put to work stopping a forest fire after nearly dying in it - a fire being blamed on Banner's arch enemy, Jack McGee. But the reporter is trapped in a fireline with a female firefighter, and David transforms into the Green Meanie to rescue the pair. **Guest cast:** Kathleen Lloyd as Randy Phelps, Don Reid as Eric Wilson, Joe Di Reda as Mackie, Peter Jason as Bennett, Tony Duke as the reporter, Bruce Fairborn as Weaver. **Writers:** Karen Harris and Jill Sherman. **Director:** L.Q. Jones.

SEASON FOUR

Prometheus, parts one and two (airdates: part one, Nov. 7, 1980; part two, Nov. 14, 1980). A strange meteor that crashes to Earth has grave effects on David Banner: while changing into the Hulk, he becomes frozen in an in-between state. After he finally finishes changing into the creature, he is caught by the Army, who believes he is an alien. They transport Banner/Hulk to Project Prometheus, a fantastic underground bunker complex where they plan to study the beast. **Guest cast:** Laurie Prange as Katie Maxwell, Monte Markham as the colonel, Whit Bissell [*The Time Tunnel*] as Dr. John Zeiterman, Carol Baxter as Charlena McGowan, Arthur Rosenberg as Sr. Jason Spath, Stack Pierce as the sergeant, Roger Robinson as Captain Welsh, John O'Connell as Col. Appling, John Papais as the corporal, Chip Johnson as the pilot, Jill Choder as the lieutenant, Steve Bond as the young man, John Vargas as the soldier, Charles Castillan as the man, J.P. Bumstead as the second man. **Writer:** Kenneth Johnson. **Director:** Kenneth Johnson.

Free Fall (airdate: Nov. 21, 1980). David's next job gets him involved in a fight between two parties, a sky diver friend and the son of a crooked politician. **Guest cast:** Sam Groom [*The Time Tunnel*] as Hank Lynch, Jared Martin [*Fantastic Journey, War of the Worlds*] as Jack Stewart, Sandy Ward as Max Stewart, Kelly Harmon as Jean, Michael Swan as Woody Turner, Ted Markland as Ike, Erik Holland as Mead, John Zenda as Fowler, George Brenlin as Hughes. **Writers:** Chris Bunch and Alan Cole. **Director:** Reza S. Badiyi.

Dark Side (airdate: Dec. 5, 1980). David tries drugs again as a cure for his other self. But the experiment goes awry and causes the evil portion of his personality to grow, and when he transforms into the beast again, the monster may turn murderous. **Guest cast:** Bill Lucking [*Outlaws*] as Mike Schilte, Rosemary Forsyth as Ellen, Philece Sampler as Lori, Jonathan Perpich as Jimmy, Taaffe O'Connell. **Writer:** Nick Corea. **Director:** John McPherson.

Deep Shock (airdate: Dec. 12, 1980). David Banner becomes psychic after receiving a bad electrical shock. But the future he envisions is that of a rampaging hulk causing continual destruction, so he takes steps to prevent it from happening. **Guest cast:** Sharon Acker as Dr. Louise Olson, Edward Power as Frank, Tom Clancy as Edgar Tucker, Bob Hackman as Walt, M.P. Murphy as the first security officer, Charles Hoyes as the second security officer, Helen Boil as the nurse, Saundra Sharp as the reporter, Harriet Matthew as

the receptionist, Robert Alan Browne as the foreman, Stefan Gierasch. **Writer:** Ruel Fischman. **Director:** Reza S. Badiyi.

Bring Me the Head of The Hulk (airdate: Jan. 9, 1981). An unbalanced mercenary-type decides to stalk, capture, and kill the ultimate prey: the invincible Hulk. **Guest cast:** Jed Mills as La Fronte, Jane Merrow as Dr. Jane Cabot, Walter Brooke as Mark Roberts, Sandy McPeak [*Blue Thunder*] as Alex, Laurence Haddon as Hines, Murray MacLeod as Lubin, Barbara Lynn Block as Pauline. **Writers:** Alan Cole and Chris Bunch. **Director:** Bill Bixby.

Fast Lane (airdate: Jan. 16, 1981). David has been hired to drive a car, not knowing that he is transporting a suitcase full of money that several parties will do anything to obtain. **Guest cast:** Robert F. Lyons as Joe, Dick O'Neill as Callahan, Victoria Carroll as Nancy, Alex Rebar as Clyde, Lee de Broux as Leo, Frank Doubleday as Danny, Ben Jeffrey as Clint, John Finn as the merchant. **Writer:** Reubon Leder. **Director:** Frank Orsatti.

Goodbye, Eddie Cain (airdate: Jan. 23, 1981). Private detective Eddie Cain encounters David Banner while investigating a scheme to murder someone. **Guest cast:** Cameron Mitchell as Eddie Cain, Donna Marshall as Norma Crespi Lang, Anthony Caruso as Dante Romero, Jennifer Holmes as Victoria Lang, Gordon Connell as Mac, Thomas MacGreevy as Sheehan, Ray Laska as Jack Lewis, Rosco Born as Sheldon, Virginia Hahn as Mrs. Stauros. **Writer:** Nick Corea. **Director:** Jack Colvin.

King of the Beach (airdate: Feb. 6, 1981). David's new place of residence gets him involved with Carl Molino, a fellow restaurant worker who is a fanatical body builder. **Guest cast:** Lou Ferrigno as Carl Molino, Leslie Ackerman as Mandy, Charlie Brill as Sol Diamond, Goerge Caldwell as Rudy, Nora Boland as the lady, Angela Lee as the little girl, Ken Waller as the King, Kimberley Johnson as the King's girlfriend, Leo de Lyon as the trainer. **Writer:** Karen Harris. **Director:** Barry Crane.

Wax Museum (airdate: Feb. 13, 1981). David accepts a position at a wax museum. While there, he becomes worried about Leigh Bamble, the young lady who hired him. She seems to be becoming mentally unbalanced, a situation caused by her father dying in a fire that she may have accidentally caused. **Guest cast:** Christine Belford [*Outlaws*] as Leigh Bamble, Ben Hammer as Kelleher, Natalie Masters as the woman, Kiki Castillo as Andy, Michael Horsely as the news vender. **Writer:** Carol Baxter. **Director:** Dick Harwood.

East Winds (airdate: Feb. 20, 1981). David is living in Chinatown in an apartment with a solid gold bathtub. When some gangsters go after Banner, a near-retirement age policeman named Jack Keele comes to his aid. **Guest cast:** William Windom as Sgt. Jack Keeler, Richard Loo as Kam Chong, Richard Narita as William, Tony Mumolo as Officer Bill Menning, Irene Yah Ling Sun as Tam, Beulah Quo as the landlady, Del Monroe [*Voyage to the Bottom of the Sea*] as the Lieutenant. **Writer:** Jill Sherman. **Director:** Jack Colvin.

The First, parts one and two (airdates: part one, Mar. 6, 1981; part two, Mar. 31, 1981). David travels to the hamlet of Visaria after he hears rumors of a creature that sounds similar to his own alter-ego, a beast that is supposedly terrorizing the countryside. **Guest cast:**

The Hulk and Daredevil.

Harry Townes as Dell Frye, Lola Albright as Elizabeth Collins, Billy Green Bush as Sheriff Carl Decker, Jack Magee as Walt, Bill Beyers as Case, Dick Durock [*Swamp Thing*] as Frye's creature, Kari Michaelsen as Linda, Hank Rolike as the janitor, Julie Marine as Cheryl. **Writer:** Jill Sherman. **Director:** Jack Colvin.

The Harder They Fall (airdate: Mar. 27, 1981). David Banner finds himself permanently crippled after being involved in a car accident, but he believes that by bringing out his alter-ego he can transform back to his previous self. **Guest cast:** Denny Miller as Paul, Peter Hobbs as Dr. Hart, Diane Shalet as Judy, Joe Dorsey as Al, Hugh Smith as Bernie, Alan Toy as Bobby, Ralph Strait as the bartender, William Bogert. **Writer:** Nancy Faulkner. **Director:** Mike Vejar.

Interview With the Hulk (airdate: April 3, 1981). Banner has a run-in with another reporter, a desperate individual who takes some information from Jack McGee and decides to find the creature and obtain the greatest interview of all time. **Guest cast:** Michael Conrad as Emerson Fletcher, Jan Sterling as Stella Verdugo, Walter Brooke as Mark Roberts. **Writer:** Alan Cassidy. **Director:** Patrick Boyriven.

Half Nelson (airdate: April 17, 1981). Banner's latest home brings him in contact with Buster Caldwell, a midget wrestler he becomes friends with, and David helps him cope with life among big people. **Guest cast:** Tommy Madden as Buster Caldwell, H.B. Haggerty as Gregor Potemkin, Elaine Joyce as Mitzi, Sandy Dryfoos as Marsha, Paul Henry Itkin as Channing, Joey Forman, David Himes. **Writer:** Andrew Schneider. **Director:** Barry Crane.

Danny (airdate: May 15, 1981). Now working on a farm, David becomes involved in disputes between three people who turn out to be farm-machinery thieves, and it takes an intervention of the Hulk to settle their squabbles. **Guest cast:** Don Stroud as Nat, Bruce Wright as Ben, Robin Dearden as Rachel, Taylor Lacher. **Writer:** Diane Frolow. **Director:** Mark A. Burley.

Patterns (airdate: May 22, 1981). David takes a job in the garment industry, but while there his employer tells some loan sharks that are after him for money that Banner is his partner who can settle his debts - which the creature does. **Guest cast:** Eddie Barth as Sam, Laurie Heineman as Liz, Paul Marin as Malamud, Robert O'Reilly as Sonny, Joshua Shelly as Solly. **Writer:** Ruebon Leder. **Director:** Nich Hazinga.

SEASON FIVE

The Phenom (airdate: Oct. 2, 1981). David's latest employment brings him in contact with a rookie pitcher, a man needing the services of the Hulk. **Guest cast:** Anne Lockhart [*Battlestar Galactica*] as Audrey, Robert Donner as Devlin, Dick O'Neil as Cyrus, Brett Cullen as Joe Dunning, Ken Swoffard. **Writer:** Ruebon Leder. **Director:** Bernard McEveety.

Two Godmothers (airdate: Oct. 9, 1981). Three women convicts, one of them pregnant, have made a prison escape, and when they run into David, they hold him captive. **Guest cast:** Suzanne Charny as Barbara, Penny Peyser as Lannie, Sandra Kerns as Sondra, Kathleen Nolan as Hackett, Gloria Gifford as Grubb, John Steadman as Phil Giles, Gay Hagen as the matron. **Writer:** Rueben Leder. **Director:** Mike Bejar.

Veteran (airdate: Oct. 30, 1981). David goes to the aid of a Vietnam War hero that is set up for assassination by a sniper, a situation that puts his secret identity in danger. **Guest cast:** Paul Koslo as Doug Hewitt, Wendy Girard as Lisa Morgan, Richard Yniguez as Frank Rivera, William Boyett as R. Harnell, Bruce Gray [*Captain Power and the Soldiers of the Future*] as Harrison Cole. **Writer:** Nicholas Corea. **Director:** Reubon Leder.

Sanctuary (airdate: Nov. 6, 1981). Banner befriends an immigrant while pretending to be a minister. **Guest cast:** Diana Muldaur [*Star Trek: The Next Generation*] as Sister Anita, Henry Darrow as Patrero, Gillermo San Juan as Roberto, Fausto Barajas as Rudy, Edie McClurg as Sister Mary Catherine. **Writer:** Deborah Davis. **Director:** Chuck Bowman.

Triangle (airdate: Nov. 13, 1981). David and a lumberyard owner named Jordan become involved with the same woman. **Guest cast:** Andrea Marcovicci as Gale Webber, Peter Mark Richman as Jordan, Mickey Jones as George, Charles Napier [*Outlaws*] as Bert, Jerry Sloan as Lyle, Don Maxwell, Bill Cross. **Writer:** Andrew Schneider. **Director:** Mike Bejar.

Slaves (airdate: May 5, 1982). An embittered negro ex-con turns the tables on David Banner when he turns him into a slave. **Guest cast:** John Hancock as Isaac Ross, Charles Ryner as Roy, Faye Grant [*V, Greatest American Hero*] as Christy, Jeffrey Kramer as Marty. **Writer:** Jerri Taylor. **Director:** John Liberti.

A Minor Problem (airdate: May 12,1982). Banner finds himself in an isolated, deserted town. While there, he becomes afflicted by a sickness from a contaminated bacteria strain. **Guest cast:** Nancy Grahn as Patty, Linden Chiles as Cunningham, Lisa Jane Persky as Rita, Kander Berkeley as Tom, John Walter Davis as Mark, Gary Vinson. **Writer:** Diane Forlov. **Director:** Mike Preece.

MOVIES

The Incredible Hulk (syndicated). This is the syndicated pilot movie. **Guest cast:** See description of pilot. **Writer:** Kenneth Johnson. **Director:** Kenneth Johnson.

Return of the Incredible Hulk (syndicated). This syndicated movie is a retitled version of **Death in the Family**. **Guest cast:** See descrption of **Death in the Family.**. **Writer:** Kenneth Johnson. **Director:** Alan Levi.

Bride of the Incredible Hulk (syndicated). This is a syndicated version of **Married**. **Guest cast:** See the descrption of **Married**. **Writer:** Kenneth Johnson. **Director:** Kenneth Johnson.

The Incredible Hulk Returns (airdate: May 22, 1988). It's been two years since David has transformed into the Hulk. He is seeing Maggie Shaw, whom he spends most of his time with. He is working on a new machine, a gamma transponder, that may make it possible for him to return to human form forever. David's boss, John Lambert, has allowed the brilliant scientist to work on the device without asking questions about David's mysterious background. When the night comes that David plans to use the transponder to rid himself of the beast inside, he is interrupted by the arrival of Donald Blake, an old friend who has no idea that Banner is also the monster. He has spent a long time tracking David down to tell the scientist about problems of his own: on a distant mountain Donald found a cave

The Hulk and Thor.

with a casket inside containing a Viking hammer. By calling on the Norse gods, the legendary Thor can be brought to Earth. David finds this hard to believe, so Donald summons the overgrown Thor, who proves to be both hostile and belligerent over being called. He manages to trigger David's own monster, resulting in a battle between the two mighty beings. When the fight is over neither is a clear-cut winner, leaving both David and Donald to solve their mutual dilemmas. Meanwhile, the publicity surrounding the battle brings back newsman Jack McGee, who hopes to finally catch the monster. **Guest cast:** Steve Levitt as Donald Blake, Tim Thomaerson as Col. Jean LeBeau, Eric Kramer as Thor, Lee Purcell as Maggie Shaw, John Gabriel, Jay Baker, William Riley, Tom Finnegan, Donald Willis, Carl Nick Ciafalio, Bobby Travis McLaughlin, Burke Davis, Nick Costa, Peisha McPhee, William Malone, Joanie Allen. **Director:** Nicholas Corea. **Director:** Nicholas Corea.

Trial of the Incredible Hulk (airdate: May 7, 1989). In this made for TV movie, David Banner rescues a young woman in a subway from two thugs, which results in his being arrested and put in jail. A most unusual lawyer comes to his aid, a blind attorney named Matt Murdock that just so happens to be a super-hero known as Daredevil. Once Banner is released from jail, he and Daredevil become involved in thwarting the plans of a criminal who is scheming to create a crime empire. **Guest cast:** Rex Smith [*Streethawk*] as Matt Murdock/Daredevil, John Rhys-Davies as Wilton Fisk, Nancy Everhard as Christa Klein, Richard Cummings, Jr. as Al Pettiman, Nicholas Hormann as Edgar, Linda Darlow, John Novak, Dwight Koss, Meredith Woodward, Mark Acheson, Richard Newman, Don McKay, Doug Abrahams, Mitchell Kosterman, Beatrice Zeilinger, S. Newton Anderson, Ken Camroux, Charles Andre, John Curtis. **Writer:** Gerald DiPego. **Director:** Bill Bixby.

Death of the Incredible Hulk (airdate: Feb. 18, 1990). In another made for TV movie, Banner is again trying to be free of his alter-ego. He obtains a job as a janitor at the lab of Dr. Ronald Platt, a scientist whom David believes may be helpful in getting rid of the beast. In the evenings while the lab is closed, Banner begins sneaking into the high-security lab and altering the research work Platt is doing. But he is eventually caught and must tell Dr. Platt the truth, and the scientist agrees to help David. Meanwhile, David becomes involved with a beautiful foreign agent, who is interested in Platt's DNA work, believing that the scientist is trying to develop the perfect soldier for the government - and she plans to steal the secret work or destroy it. **Guest cast:** Elizabeth Gracen as Jasmin, Andreas Katsulas as Kasha, Chilton Crane as Betty, Carla Ferrigno as the bank teller, Duncan Fraser as Tom, Dwight McFee as Brenn, Lindsay Bourne as Crane, Mina E. Mina as Pauley, Marlane O'Brien as Luane Cole, Garwin Sanford as Shoup, Justin DePego as Dodger, Fred Henderson as Aaron Colmer, Judith Maxie as Carbino, French Tickner as George Tilmer, Anna Katerina, John Novak. **Writer:** Gerald DiPego. **Director:** Bill Bixby.

Lynda Carter as Wonder Woman, Lyle Waggoner as Major Steve Trevor.

Wonder Woman

reviews by William E. Anchors, Jr.

About The Show: Wonder Woman could have been titled "The Show That No One Wanted". It's original pilot starred Cathy Lee Crosby, set in modern times, but response was poor. Over a year later ABC tried again with Lynda Carter, Miss World-USA for 1973, and the show was dated during World War II. This version, titled *The New, Original Wonder Woman*, was more interesting and truer to the comic, and while the ratings were good, it was erratically shown by ABC who used it as filler material for *The Bionic Woman*, which was temporarily off the air while Lindsay Wagner was recuperating from injuries received in a car accident. When it was cancelled, the production company went to CBS, where it was picked up and had a successful two year run under the title *The New Adventures of Wonder Woman*. In this third version, Wonder Woman (still Lynda Carter) was again set in modern times. The CBS was by far the best of the three, and has remained the most popular.

Wonder Woman

(First Pilot)

Wonder Woman (airdate: March 12, 1974, 90 minute pilot movie). In the first pilot film, Wonder Woman leaves her home of Paradise Island among an amazing race of Amazon women, and moves to America, where she assists the U.S. government in combating a villainous spy ring that is plaguing the country. **Cast:** Cathy Lee Crosby as Wonder Woman, Ricardo Montalban [*Star Trek*] as Abner Smith, Anitra Ford as Ahnjayla, Andrew Prine [*V*] as George Calvin, Charlene Holt as Hippolyte, Kaz Garas as Steve Trevor, Richard X. Slattery as Col. Henkins, Sandy Gaviola as Tina, Beverly Gill as Dia, Donna Garrett as Cass, Jordan Rhodes as Bob, Roberta Brahm as Zoe, Robert Porter as Joe, Ronald Long. **Writer:** John D.F. Black. **Director:** Vincent McEveety.

The New Original Wonder Woman

(ABC series)

Production credits:

Producer	Wilfred Baumes
Executive Producer	Douglas S. Cramer
Characters created by	Charles Moulton
Developed for tv by	Stanley Ralph Ross
Music	Artie Kane, Charles Fox
	Norman Gimble

Regular cast:

Wonder Woman	Lynda Carter
Major Steve Trevor	Lyle Waggoner
Gen. Phillip Blankenship	Richard Eastham
Yeoman Etta Candy	Beatrice Colen
Drusilla	Debra Winger
The Queen Mother	Cloris Leachman
	Carolyn Jones
Magda	Pamela Shoop
Dalma	Erica Hagen

Number of ABC episodes:	1 90 minute pilot movie,
	12 one hour segments

Premise: Wonder Woman, under the guise of Diana Prince, leaves her home on Paradise Island - located in the Bermuda Triangle - to fight crime and evil. The first twelve episodes are set in the World War II era, where she battles Nazis and other bad guys. She works with Steve Trevor, U.S. Army flying ace who meets Wonder Woman when he is shot down over Paradise Island. Wonder Woman takes him back to the U.S., and remains with him under her secret identity of secretary Diana Prince.

The New Original Wonder Woman (airdate: Nov. 7, 1975, second 90 minute pilot movie). U.S. Army fighter pilot Steve Trevor is shot down in a remote section of the Atlantic by Germans, and he crash lands on an uncharted island. But while the island may be uncharted, it is definitely inhabited - by a race of beautiful and amazingly strong Amazon women who rescue him. He is nursed back to health by Princess Diana, and it is decided to return him to the United States. Olympic games are held to determine who is the greatest warrior, and the contest is won by Diana, so she is sent to stay and help protect the U.S. as Wonder Woman (Steve is given a drug to remove his memory of Paradise Island). Before leaving she is given a golden belt to preserve her strength away from her home, and a golden lariat that will obey her command. Arriving in America, she is not there long before being pitted against Nazi spys who are trying to steal a highly-advanced bomb prototype. **Guest cast:** Red Buttons [*Five Weeks in a Balloon*] as Asley Norman, Kenneth Mars as Col. Vonblasko, Stella Stevens as Marsha, Eric Braeden as Kapitan Drangal, Fanny Flag as the Amazon doctor, Henry Gibson as Nicholas, Severen Darden as the bad guy, Ian Wolfe, Fritzi Burr, Helen Verbit, Tom Rosqui. **Writer:** Stanley Ralph Ross. **Director:** Leonard Horn.

Wonder Woman Meets Baroness Von Gunther (airdate: April 21, 1976). The Amazon princess must defeat the Baroness Von Gunther, an ingenious female Nazi and head of a spy ring endangering the country. **Guest cast:** Christine Belford [*Outlaws*] as Baroness Von Gunther, Bradford Dillman as Arthur Deal/Thor, Christian Juttner as Tommy, Ed Griffith as Hanson, Edmund Gilbert as the warden. **Writer:** Margaret Armen. **Director:** Barry Crame.

Fausta, The Nazi Wonder Woman (airdate: April 28, 1976). To retaliate for Wonder Woman's interference with their operations, the Nazis create a superwoman of their own to oppose her. And it appears Fausta has been successful when she defeats Princess Diana and takes her back to Germany as her prisoner. **Guest cast:** Lynda Day-George [*The Return of Captain Nemo*] as Fausta, Christopher George [*The Immortal*] as Rojack, Bo Brundin as Kesselmann. **Writers:** Bruce Shelby and David Ketchum.

Beauty on Parade (airdate: Oct. 13, 1976). German agents acting as saboteurs are using a traveling beauty contest as a cover for their activities. **Guest cast:** Anne Francis [*Honey West*] as Lola Flynn, Dick Van Patten [*When Things Were Rotten*] as Jack Wood, Bobby

Van [*Lost Horizon*] as Monty Burns, Christa Helm as Rita, Jennifer Shaw as Suzan, William Lanteau as Col. Flint. **Writer:** Ron Friedman. **Director:** Richard Kinom.

The Feminum Mystique, part one and two (airdates: part one, Nov. 6, 1976; part two, Nov. 8, 1976). Wonder Woman must come to the rescue when Nazi scientist Professor Radl kidnaps Diana's sister Drusilla, also known as Wonder Girl. Holding her prisoner, he hopes to find the secret of the bulletproof metal used in the bracelets of the Amazon Wonder Woman and her younger sister. **Guest cast:** John Saxon as Radl, Charles Frank as Peter Knight, Paul Shenar as Wertz, Pamela Shoop as Magda, Erica Hagen as Dalma, Kurt Kreuger as Hemmschler, Curt Lowens as Gen. Ulrich. **Writers:** Jimmy Sangster, Barb Avedon and Barb Corday. **Director:** Herb Wallerstein.

Wonder Woman vs. Gargantua (airdate: Dec. 18, 1976). Nazi Hans Eichler has specially bred a powerful gorilla to eliminate the Amazon Princess. **Guest cast:** Robert Loggia [*T.H.E. Cat*] as Hans Eichler, Gretchen Corbett [*Otherworld*] as Erica Belgard, John Hillerman as Conrad Steigler, Mickey Morton as Gargantua, Tom Reese as Carl Mueller. **Writers:** David Ketchum and Tony DiMarco. **Director:** Herb Wallerstein.

The Pluto File (airdate: Dec. 25, 1976). A scientist finishes a document that details the formation of volcanoes, but the secret papers are stolen. However, the thief, Sean Fallon, is unaware that he is a carrier of the bubonic plague. **Guest cast:** Robert Reed as Sean Fallon, Hayden Roarke as Prof. Warren, Kenneth Tigar as Dr. Barnes, Albert Stratton as Charles Benson, Michael Twain as Frank Willis, Jason Johnson as James Porter. **Writer:** Herb Wallerstein. **Director:** Herb Wallerstein.

Last of the $2 Bills (airdate: Jan. 8, 1977). The latest Nazi threat comes from a counterfeit ring that plans to flood the market with fake two-dollar bills. **Guest cast:** James Olson as Woton, Barbara Anderson as Maggie, Richard O'Brien as Frank Wilson, John Howard as the doctor, David Cryer as Hank, Dean Harens as Dan Fletcher, Victor Argo as Jason. **Writers:** Paul Dubob and Gwen Bheni. **Director:** Stuart Margolin.

Judgement From Outer Space, part one and two (airdates: part one, Jan. 15, 1977; part two, Jan. 17, 1977). An alien from a distant planet arrives on Earth. The man, known as Andros, explains that unless mankind stops their constant state of warfare he must destroy the planet to eliminate humanity's war-like nature before it develops the ability to wreak havoc on other worlds. But Nazis kidnap the alien and hide him behind their lines, and now only Wonder Woman can save him. **Guest cast:** Tim O'Connor [*Buck Rogers*] as Andros, Scott Hylands as Paul Bjornsen, Kurt Kasznar [*Land of the Giants*] as Von Dreiberg, Janet MacLachlan as Sakri, Vic Perrin as Gorel, Arch Johnson as Gen. Kane, George Cooper as Gen. Clewes, Hank Brandt as Graebner, Christopher Cary as Mallory, Fil Formicola as the sergeant, Patrick Skelton as Gormsby, Christine Schmidtmer as Lisa Engel. **Writer:** Stephen Kandel. **Director:** Alan Crosland.

Formula 407 (airdate: Jan. 22, 1977). A scientist, Professor Moreno, has perfected a means to produce rubber as strong as steel. But Nazis are after the formula, so Trevor and Diana follow German agents to Buenos Aires to stop them. **Guest cast:** Nehemiah Persoff as Prof. Moreno, Marisa Pavan as Maria, John Devlin as Major Keller, Charles Macaulay as McCauley, Peter MacLean as Schmidt, Maria Grimm as Lydia Moreno, Armando Silvestre as Antonio Cruz. **Writer:** Elroy Schwartz. **Director:** Herb Wallerstein.

The Bushwackers (airdate: Jan. 29, 1977). A new threat to the U.S. war effort comes from German cattle rustlers who are raiding ranches in Texas. Mr. Hadley contacts the government and request their and Wonder Woman's help in combating the thieves. **Guest cast:** Roy Rogers as Mr. Hadley, Henry Darrow as Walter Lampkin, Lance Kerwin as Jeff Hadley, Tony George as Emmett Dawson, David Clarke as Sheriff Bodie, David Yanez as Charlie, Christoff St. John as Linc, Justin Randi as Freddie, Carey Kevin Wong as Sen, Rita Gomez. **Writer:** Skip Webster. **Director:** Stuart Margolin.

Wonder Woman In Hollywood (airdate: Feb. 16, 1977). Heroes of the U.S. armed forces are brought home to Hollywood to film a movie about their exploits, but the men are being kidnapped by ruthless Nazi agents. **Guest cast:** Harris Yulin as Mark Bremer, Robert Hays [*Starman*] as Jim Ames, Christopher Norris as Gloria Beverly, Charles Cyphers as Kurt, Alan Bergmann as the director. **Writer:** Jimmy Sangster. **Director:** Stuart Margolin.

The New Adventures of
Wonder Woman
(CBS series)

Production credits:

Executive Producer	Douglas S. Cramer
	Wilfred Baumes
Developed for tv by	Stanley Ralph Ross
Characters created by	Charles Moulton
Music	Artie Kane
Theme	Charles Fox
	Norman Gimbel

Regular cast:

Wonder Woman	Lynda Carter
Steve Trevor, Jr.	Lyle Wagner
Joe Atkinson	Normann Burton
The Queen Mother	Beatrice Straight

Number of CBS episodes:	1 90 minute pilot movie,
	45 one hour segments

Premise: After the war has ended, Princess Diana returns home to Paradise Island. Thirty-two years later, she decides the country needs her again, and the ageless superheroine comes to the aid of the U.S. as Wonder Woman, where she teams up with Steve Trevor's son under her civilian identity of Diana Prince. Steve Trevor, Jr., is the head of the Inter-Agency Defense Command, where Wonder Woman becomes an operative. They are assisted by IRAC, the agency's talking computer.

FIRST CBS SEASON

The Return of Wonder Woman (airdate: Sept. 16, 1977, third 90 minute pilot). Thirty-two years after her return to Paradise Island at the end of World War II, the ageless Diana Prince becomes involved with the outside world again after a U.S. aircraft carrying government agents is disabled by a knock-out gas delivered by an enemy agent. The plane wanders out of control and enters the airspace of Paradise Island, where the Amazon women rescue those on board. Princess Diana is startled to see a young Steve Trevor after so many years, but finds out that he is Steve Trevor, Jr., who is an agent of

the Inter-Agency Defense Command. Diana realizes the country is opposing evil forces once again, so she receives permission to return to the U.S. as Diana Prince. Her queen mother gives her powerful weapons to fight evil, including a lariat, a magic belt, a set of bullet-reflecting wrist bands, and a tiara containing a special ruby that allows her to contact Paradise Island at any time. Steve is hypnotized to forget Paradise Island and to believe Diana is a replacement assistant he was supposed to meet on his trip to Latin America. The aircraft is sent aloft with Diana at the controls and the rest of the passengers and crew are awakened after Diana leaves via an escape hatch and enters her own invisible plane, which she uses to fly to Steve's destination in Latin America. Once there, the hypnotized Steve accepts Diana upon seeing her at the airport. She quickly becomes involved in helping Steve overcome an international terrorist. Later, when they return to the U.S., Diana updates her personnel files on a computer, and takes her place as Steve's assistant in the Inter-Agency Defense Command, lead by Steve Trevor, Jr. **Guest cast:** Fritz Weaver as Dr. Solano, Jessica Walter as Gloria, Beatrice Sraight as the Queen, Bettye Ackerman as Asclepia, Russ Marin as Kleist, Dave Knapp as Maj. Gaines, Frank Killmond as Logan, Dorrie Thompson as Evadne, Brooke Bundy as Beverly. **Writer:** Stephen Kandel. **Director:** Alan Crosland.

Anschluss '77 (airdate: Sept. 23, 1977). In a South American country where Nazi's took refuge after World War II, the Germans are planning a comeback with the establishment of a Fourth Reich. Their plan: to clone der fueher, Adolf Hitler. **Guest cast:** Mel Ferrer [*Robocop*] as Fritz Gerlich, Julio Medina as Gaitan, Leon Charles as Von Klemper, Kurt Kreuger as Koenig, Barry Dennen as the cloned Hitler, Peter Nyberg as Strasser. **Writers:** Dallas L. Barnes and Frank K. Telford. **Director:** Alan Crosland.

The Man Who Could Move the World (airdate: Sept. 30, 1977). Wonder Woman's return to activity against criminals in 1977 revives an old grudge from a previous operation in World War II. It seems that an ex-Japanese soldier has sworn to obtain revenge for Wonder Woman's interference thirty-five years earlier. **Guest cast:** Yuki Shimoda as Ishida, J. Kenneth Campbell as Taft, Lew Ayres as Dr. Wilson, James Long as Oshima, Peter Kwong as Massake. **Writer:** Judy Burns. **Director:** Bob Kellijan.

The Bermuda Triangle Crisis (airdate: Oct. 7, 1977). Wonder Woman returns to the area of her home, Paradise Island in the Bermuda Triangle, after an aircraft disappears there. To locate the surveillance plane, Steve and Diana go undercover as a wealthy vacationing couple. **Guest cast:** Charles Cioffi as Manta, Larry Golden as Lt. Mansfield, Herman Poppe as the sergeant. **Writer:** Calvin Clements, Jr. **Director:** Seymour Robbie.

Knockout (airdate: Oct. 14, 1977). Has Steve been kidnapped? The head of the Inter-Agency Defense Command has disappeared while in Los Angeles, so Diana Prince goes in search of her boss. **Guest cast:** Ted Shackelford as Pete, Jayne Kennedy as Carolyn, Frank Marth as the tall man, Arch Johnson as John Kelly, Burr DeBenning as Tom Baker, K.C. Martel as Ted, Abraham Alvarez as Officer Fernandez, Frank Parker as Lane Curran. **Writer:** Mark Rodgers. **Director:** Seymour Robbie.

The Pied Piper (airdate: Oct. 21, 1977). A rock musician is using special music to place young women under his power, then he sends them out to pull off thefts. When Wonder Woman discovers who is behind the crimes, she tries to arrest Hamlin Rule, but the special frequency of music he uses to hypnotize females may be too strong even for Wonder Woman. **Guest cast:** Martin Mull as Hamlin Rule, Eve Plumb as Elena Atkinson, Bob Hastings as the gatekeeper, Denny Miller as Carl Schwartz, Sandy Charles as Louise. **Writers:** David Ketchum and Tony DiMarco. **Director:** Alan Crosland.

The Queen and the Thief (airdate: Oct. 28, 1977). Steve wants to capture an internationally-wanted thief. He believes Robley may

appear at a foreign embassy, so he and Diana go undercover: Steve pretends to be the leader of a foreign country, while Diana takes the job of a maid. **Guest cast:** Juliet Mills as Queen Kathryn, David Hedison [*Voyage to the Bottom of the Sea*] as Evan Robley, John Colicos [*Battlestar Galactica*] as Ambassador Orrick. **Writer:** Bruce Shelly. **Director:** Jack Arnold.

I Do, I Do (airdate: Nov. 11, 1977). Foreign agents are operating out of an exclusive spa that caters to the wives of important government officials, and while there they are forced to reveal secrets that could prove damaging to the U.S. **Guest cast:** Celeste Holm as Dolly Tucker, John Getz as Christian Harrison, Simon Scott as Sam Tucker, Kent Smith [*The Invaders*] as Justice Brown, Henry Darrow [*The Invisible Man*] as David Allen, Steve Eastin as Johnny. **Writers:** Brian McKay and Richard Carr. **Director:** Herb Wallerstein.

The Man Who Made Volcanoes (airdates: Nov. 18, 1977). An eccentric scientist, Dr. John Chapman, has discovered a way to activate volcanic disturbances - and begins a scheme that will cover the planet with artificially induced volcanic eruptions. **Guest cast:** Roddy McDowall [*Planet of the Apes*] as Dr. John Chapman, Roger Davis [*Dark Shadows*] as Jack Corbin, Irene Tsu as Mei Ling, Richard Narita as Lin Wan, Milt Kogan as Kalanin, Ray Young as Tobirov. **Writers:** Dan Ullman and Wilton Denmar. **Director:** Alan Crosland.

The Mind Stealers From Outer Space, parts one and two (airdates: part one, Dec. 2, 1977; part two, Dec. 9, 1977). Diana reteams with Andros, an outer space alien she met thirty years earlier [see **Judgement From Outer Space**], in an effort to overcome a group of villains known as the Skrills. The outlaws are staging kidnappings all over the country, collecting, for some sinister purpose, the most brilliant scientists and intellectuals the nation has to offer. **Guest cast** Dack Rambo as Andros, Vincent Van Patten as Johnny, Kristin Larkin as Debbie, Barry Cahill as General Miller, Allan Migicovsky as Dr. Rand, Sol Weiner as Capt. Parelli, Earl Boen as Chaka, Pamela Mason as Carla Burgess, Curt Lowens as Nordling. **Writer:** Stephen Kandel. **Director:** part one, Michael Caffey; part two, Alan Crosland.

The Deadly Toys (airdate: Dec. 30, 1977). Dr. Hoffman, a sinister toymaker, designs full size toys in the form of androids, mechanical creatures so real they can pass as human. Steve and Diana go into action when the toymaker uses them to rip off the top-secret plans for a new weapon being designed for the government. **Guest cast:** Frank Gorshin [*Batman*] as Dr. Hoffman, John Rubinstein as Major Dexter, Ross Elliott as Dr. Lazar, James A. Watson, Jr. as Dr. Prescott, Donald Bishop as Dr. Tobias, Randy Phillips as the doctor. **Writer:** Anne Collins. **Director:** Dick Moder.

Light-Fingered Lady (airdate: Jan. 16, 1978). When the Agency learns of plans for a fifty million dollar theft, Diana is sent undercover to become a member of the ring planning to steal the money. **Guest cast:** Greg Morris [*Mission: Impossible*] as Anton Caribe, Joseph R. Sicari as Leech, Christopher Stone as Tony Ryan, Titos Vandis as Michael Sutton, Gary Crosby as Grease, Larry Ward as Adler, Bubba Smith [*Blue Thunder*] as Rojak, Rick DiAngelo as Ross, Stack Pierce as the desk sergeant, Saundra Sharp as Eve, Judyann Elder as Marge Douglass. **Writer:** Bruce Shelley. **Director:** Bruce Shelley.

Screaming Javelin (airdate: Jan. 20, 1978). A nutty "dictator" of an imaginary country decides he can receive recognition by winning

that year's Olympics, so he begins kidnapping top-notch athletes to win the games for Mariposalia. **Guest cast:** Henry Gibson as Marion Mariposa, E. J. Peaker as Lois Taggart, Melanie Chartoff as Nadia Samara, Robert Sampson as Bo Taggart, Rick Springfield as Tom Hamilton, Vaughn Armstrong as Eric. **Writer:** Brian McKay. **Director:** Mike Caffey.

Diana's Disappearing Act (airdate: Feb. 3, 1978). The Agency learns of a scheme to radically raise oil prices in the Mid-East. A Black Arts master, Count Cagliostro, is planning a scheme involving selling fake gold to the greedy president of a foreign country. **Guest cast:** Dick Gautie as Count Cagliostro, Ed Begley, Jr. as Harold Farnum, Brenda Benet as Morgana, Aharon Ipale as Emir, Saundra Sharp as Eve, J.A. Preston as Jazreel, Andy Williams as Hutchins. **Writer:** S.S. Schweitzer. **Director:** Michael Caffey.

Death in Disguise (airdate: Feb. 10, 1978). Armed killers are after Diana Prince when she accepts a job guarding a wealthy industrialist from a group of assassins. **Guest cast:** George Charkiris as Carlo Indrezzati, Charles Pierce as Starker, Joel Fabiani as Woodward Nightingale, Jennifer Darling as Violet, Lee Bergere as Marius, Arthur Batanides as Krug, Christopher Cary as Beamer. **Writer:** Tom Sawyer. **Director:** Alan Crosland.

IRAC is Missing (airdate: Feb. 17, 1978). Computer genius Bernard Havitol plans to rule the world by taking over the memory banks of the world's most powerful computers, and seems to be succeeding - unless Wonder Woman can stop him. **Guest cast:** Ross Martin [*The Wild Wild West*] as Bernard Havitol, Tina Lenert as Cori, Lee Paul as Dirk, W.T. Zacha as Dick, Jim Veres as Sgt. Dobson, Lloyd McLinn as the guard, Cletus Young as the official. **Writer:** Anne Collins. **Director:** Alex Singer.

Flight to Oblivion (airdate: Mar. 3, 1978). A traitorous officer who used to serve within NATO forces is sabotaging U.S. Air Force operations by using his incredibly strong hypnotic powers. **Guest cast:** Alan Fudge [*The Man From Atlantis*] as Major Cornell, Corinne Michaels as Capt. Ann Cornell, John Van Dreelan as Edmund Dante, Michael Shannon as Lt. Stonehouse, Mitch Vogel as Drummer, David Sak Cadiente as the first heavy. **Writer:** Patrick Mathews. **Director:** Alan Crosland.

Seance of Terror (airdate: Mar. 10, 1978). After years of work, an international peace conference is arranged. But the talks are being sabotaged by a child who is able to influence the behavior of the delegates with his "psychic photographs". **Guest cast:** Todd Lookinland as Matthew, Rick Jason as Koslo, Kres Mersky as Theodora, Hanna Hertelendy as Ms. Kell, John Fujioka as Yamura, Adam Ageli as Bakru. **Writer:** Bruce Shelly. **Director:** Dick Moder.

The Man Who Wouldn't Tell (airdate: Mar. 31, 1978). Company scientists havn't been able to find the correct ingredient needed for a powerful new explosive, but a bungling janitor, Alan Akroy, manages to discover it. Unfortunately, a rival company is now after Alan and the formula. **Guest cast:** Gary Burghoff as Alan Akroy, Jane Actman as Meg, Philip Michael Thomas as Furst, Michael Cole as Ted, Millie Slavin as B.J. **Writer:** Anne Collins. **Director:** Alan Crosland.

The Girl from Ilandia (airdate: April 7, 1978). Tina, a beautiful young lady found floating on a raft at sea, proves to have unusual telekinetic powers - just the thing that makes her wanted by underworld thugs. **Guest cast:** Julie Ann Haddock as Tina, Harry Guardino as Simon Penrose, Allen Arbus as Bleaker, Fred Lerner as Davis, Buck Young as the doctor. **Writer:** Anne Collins. **Director:** Dick Moder.

The Murderous Missile (airdate: April 21, 1978). While on her way to a missile site to perform an assignment, Diana is taken prisoner in a deserted old desert ghost town. **Guest cast:** Warren Stevens as Sheriff Beal, James Luisi as George, Steve Inwood as Mac, Mark Withers as Luther, Lucille Benson as Flo, Hal England

as Hal Shaver. **Writer:** Dick Nelson. **Director:** Dick Moder.

SECOND CBS SEASON

One of Our Teen Idols is Missing (airdate: Sept. 22, 1978). Wonder Woman must save Lane Kincaid, a teenage idol that has been kidnapped, and replaced with a convincing double. **Guest cast:** Leif Garrett as Lane Kincaid/Mike Kincaid, Dawn Lyn as Whitney Springfield, Michael Lerner as Ashton Ripley, Albert Paulsen as Raleigh Crichton, Michael Baseleon as Morley. **Writer:** Anne Collins. **Director:** Seymour Robbie.

Hot Wheels (airdate: Sept. 29, 1978). Diana Prince is searching for a Rolls Royce that has been stolen, as its hood ornament contains some top-secret microfilm. **Guest cast:** Peter Brown as Tim Bolt, Lance LeGault [*Werewolf*] as Otis Fiskie, John Durren as Alfie, Marc Rose as Slim. **Writer:** Dennis Landa. **Director:** Dick Moder.

The Deadly Sting (airdate: Oct. 6, 1978). For some reason, highly-skilled college football players are bungling and losing important games. When Diana investigates, she discovers that someone is subconsciously manipulating the players to cause their teams to lose. **Guest cast:** Harvey Jason as Prof. Brubaker, Ron Ely [*Tarzan*] as Bill Michaels, Scott Marlowe as Angie Cappucci, Danny Dayton as Louis the Lithuanian, Marvin Miller as Beamer, Roman Gabriel, Deacon Jones, Lawrence McCutcheon, Eddie Allen Bell, Gill Stratton. **Writer:** Dick Nelson. **Director:** Alan Crosland.

The Fine Art of Crime (airdate: Oct. 13, 1978). A group of art thieves are mysteriously able to rob without being caught by the authorities. When Wonder Woman tries to catch them, she finds herself in the position of being transmuted into a work of art. **Guest cast:** Roddy McDowall [*Planet of the Apes*] as Henry Roberts, Michael McGuire as Moreaux, Ed Begley, Jr. as Harold Farnum, Gavin MacLeod as Ellsworth, Patti MacLeod as Mrs. Ellsworth. **Writer:** Anne Collins. **Director:** Dick Moder.

Disco Devil (airdate: Oct. 20, 1978). Someone is stealing vital government secrets, and when Wonder Woman investigates she finds a psychic who is using his disco to lure in government workers and rob their minds of secret information. **Guest cast:** Paul Sands as Del Franklin, Wolfman Jack as Infrared, Michael DeLano as Nick Moreno, Russell Johnson as the Colonel, Ellen Weston as Angelique. **Writer:** Alan Brenner. **Director:** Les Martinson.

Formicida (airdate: Nov. 3, 1978). Dr. Irene Janus becomes "Formicida", a being with incredible power and the ability to control thousands of insects. Now she is using her powers to stop the manufacture of a deadly pesticide. **Guest cast:** Lorene Yarnell as Dr. Irene Janus/Formicida, Robert Shields [*Wild Wild West Revisited*] as Doug, Robert Alda as Harcourt, Stan Haze as Cawley. **Writer:** Katharyn Michaelian Powers. **Director:** Alan Crosland.

Time Bomb (airdate: Nov. 10, 1978). A scientist from the year 2155 uses a time travel device to return to 1978. But she has no intention of furthering science; instead, she plans to use her knowledge of the future to become a billionaire. **Guest cast:** Joan Van Ark as Cassandra Loren, Ted Shackelford as Adam Clement, Allan Miller as Dan Reynolds, Fredd Wayne as J.J. MacConnell. **Writers:** Kathleen Barnes and David Wise. **Director:** Seymour Robbie.

Skateboard Whiz (airdate: Nov. 24, 1978). Skateboard wiz Cynthia Eilbacher is being used for blackmail and extortion by her godfather, a Mafia kingpin. **Guest cast:** Jaime O'Neill as Cynthia

WN-12

94

Eilbacher, Eric Braeden as Donelson, Ron Masak as Duane Morrisey, Art Metrano as Friedman, John Reilly as Skye Markham, James Ray as John Key. **Writer:** Alan Brennert. **Director:** Les Martinson.

The Deadly Dolphin (airdate: Dec. 1, 1978). Criminals have kidnapped a trained dolphin and sent him out on a suicide mission: the animal is carrying explosives that will detonate when they strike an oil tanker carrying 50,000 barrels of crude oil, the release of which will cause an ecological disaster. **Guest cast:** Penelope Windust as Dr. Sylvia Stubbs, Nicolas Coster as Silas Lockhart, Britt Leach as Billy, Albert Popwell as Gaffer, Brian Tochi as Darrel, Michael Stroka as Henry. **Writer:** Jackson Gillis. **Director:** Sigmund Neufield.

Stolen Faces (airdate: Dec. 15, 1978). To learn what she is up to, Diana is following a fake Wonder Woman who is performing good deeds; but finds that more duplicates are being made of other people, including one of Steve. **Guest cast:** Joseph Maher as Edgar Percy, Kenneth Tigar as John Austin, Bob Seagren as Roman, John O'Connell as Todd Daniels, Diana Lander as Nancy. **Writer:** Richard Carr. **Director:** Les Martineson.

Pot O' Gold (airdate: Dec. 22, 1978). Wonder Woman goes to the aid of a leprechaun to help him recover his stolen gold. **Guest cast:** Dick O'Neill as Pat O'Hanlon, Brian Davies as Thackery, Steve Allie Collura as Bonelli, Arthur Batanides as Maxwell, Ric De Angelo as Raucher, Sherrie Wills as Lisa. **Writer:** Michael McGreevy. **Director:** Gordon Hessler.

Gault's Brain (airdate: Dec. 29, 1978). Billionaire Harlow Gault is alive and well, or at least his brain is. The disembodied brain is looking for a new body as a home to continue Gault's existence. **Guest cast:** John Carradine [*The Howling*] as the voice of Gault, Lloyd Levine as Stryker, Kathy Sheriff as Tara London, David Mason Daniels as Morton Danzing, Mark Richman as Dr. Crippin, Erik Stern as Turk. **Writers:** Arthur Weingarten and John Gaynor. **Director:** Gordon Hessler.

Going, Going, Gone (airdate: Jan. 12, 1979). A group of criminals who specialize in stolen nuclear hardware is being infiltrated by Diana Prince to put a stop to their thefts. **Guest cast:** Hari Rhodes as Como, Bo Frundin as Zukov, Kaz Garas as Lucas, Mako as Brown, Charlie Brill as Smith, Marc Lawrence as Jones, Milton Selzer as Captain Louie. **Writer:** Patrick Mathews. **Director:** Alan Crosland.

Spaced Out (airdate: Jan. 26, 1979). Two rival groups will do anything to obtain a stolen laser crystal, but it has been hidden somewhere at a science-fiction convention. **Guest cast:** Rene Auberjonois as Kimball, Paul Lawrence Smith as Simon Rohan, George Shung as Mr. Munn, Bob Short as Robby the Robot. **Writer:** Bill Taylor. **Director:** Ivan Dickson.

The Starships are Coming (airdate: Feb. 2, 1979). Is Earth being invaded by aliens? Someone has pulled off a fantastic hoax to make Wonder Woman and the rest of the world believe that hostile starships are heading towards our planet. **Guest cast:** Andrew Duggan as Mason Steele, Jeffrey Byron as Henry Wilson, Tim O'Connor [*Buck Rogers*] as Col. Robert Elliott, David White as the general, James Coleman as the aide, Sheryl Lee Ralph as Bobbie, Frank Whiteman as the newsman. **Writers:** Glen Olson and Rod Baker. **Director:** Alan Crosland.

Amazon Hot Wax (airdate: Feb. 16, 1979). Diana goes undercover as a singer to put an end to an extortion scheme being used by someone in the record industry. **Guest cast:** Kate Woodville as Adelle Kobler, Bob Hoy as Marty, Sarah Purcell as Barbie, Curtis

Credel as Eric Landau, Martin Speer as Billy Dero, Rick Springfield as Anton, Danil Torpe as Jerry, Michael Botts as Kim, Judge Reinhold as Jeff Gordon. **Writer:** Alan Brennert. **Director:** Ray Austin.

The Richest Man in the World (airdate: Feb. 19, 1979). Wonder Woman and the rest of the country are trying to find a wealthy recluse. The man has disappeared after obtaining a top-secret missile-guidance system scrambling device, but no one can find him. **Guest cast:** Jeremy Slate as Marshall Henshaw, Roger Perry as Lawrence Dunfield, Barry Miller as Barney, Marilyn Mason as Lucy DeWitt. **Writer:** Jackson Gillis. **Director:** Don MacDougall.

A Date with Doomsday (airdate: Mar. 10, 1979). What does a computer dating service have to do with the theft of a government-produced biological warfare germ? Wonder Woman must find out after the deadly virus is stolen from the lab it was produced at, and has been traced to the dating service. **Guest cast:** Hermione Baddeley as Mrs. Thrip, Donnelly Rhodes as Ward Selkirk, Carol Vogel as Dede, Taaffe O'Conell as Val, Arthur Malet as Prof. Zander, Michael Holt as John Blake. **Writers:** Dennis Landa and Roland Starke. **Director:** Curtis Harrington.

The Girl With The Gift For Disaster (airdate: Mar. 17, 1979). A pretty young girl, Bonnie Murphy, always seems to be at the center of one calamity after another. But the latest situation is not her doing: a thief is using her as an unwilling accomplice to steal some priceless historical documents. **Guest cast:** Jane Actman as Bonnie Murphy, James Sloyan as Mark Reuben, Raymond St. Jacques as William Mayfield, Ina Balin as Elizabeth Koren, S. Newton Anderson as Pete Phillips, Charles Haid as Bob Baker, Dick Batkus [*Blue Thunder*] as Neil, Dulcie Jordan as the receptionist, Nina Weintraub as Abby. **Writer:** Alan Brennert. **Director:** Alan Crosland.

The Boy Who Knew Her Secret, parts one and two (airdates: part one, May 28, 1979; part two, May 29, 1979). Metallic pyramids are falling onto Earth from outer space, and anyone who touches them has their mind trapped by the beings that exist inside the pyramids. While Wonder Woman investigates the situation, humans whose minds have been taken over begin to search for an alien criminal. To avoid capture, the being can transform into anything, including Wonder Woman. **Guest cast:** Clark Brandon as Skip Keller, Michael Shannon as Cameron Michaels, John Milford as Mr. Keller, Lenora May as Melanie Rose, Tegan West as Pete Pearson, Burt Remsen as Dr. Eli Jaffe, Joyce Greenwood as Mrs. Keller. **Writer:** Anne Collins. **Director:** Les Martinson.

The Man Who Could Not Die (airdate: Aug. 28, 1979). Wonder Woman is faced with two threats: a criminal genius with incredible powers, and a super-man who is her match in power. **Guest cast:** Bob Seagren as Bryce Kandel, Brian Dawles as Joseph Reichman, James Bond III as T. Burton Phipps III, John Durran as Dale Hawthorne, Robert Sampson as Dr. Martin Akers, John Aprea as Durpis. **Writer:** Anne Collins. **Director:** John Newland.

Phantom of the Roller Coaster, parts one and two (airdates: part one, Sept. 24, 1979; part two, Sept. 11, 1979). Diana investigates an amusement park that seems to be the hideout for the leader of a group of foreign spies. Wonder Woman follows him back to the theme park in Washington, but both she and the foreign agent are confronted by a phantom that haunts the park - a disfigured veteran who lives there under the roller coaster. **Guest cast:** Joseph Sirola as Harrison Fynch, Jared Martin [*Fantastic Journey*] as Leon Hurney/David Gurney, Ike Eisemann [*Fantastic Journey*] as Randy, Marc Alaimo as Pierce, S. Newton Anderson as Roberts, Jocelyn Summers as Ms. Patrick, Jessica Rains as the secretary, Mike Kopsha as the sergeant, Judith Christopher as the receptionist. **Writer:** Anne Collins. **Director:** John Newland.

Thomas Hill as King Baaldorf, Jeff Conway as Prince Erik Greystone.

96

Wizards and Warriors

review by William E. Anchors, Jr.

Production credits:

Producer	Bill Richmond
	Robert Earl
Created by	Don Reo
Supervising Producer	S. Bryan Hickox
Music	Lee Holdridge

Regular cast:

Prince Erik Greystone	Jeff Conway
Marko	Walter Olkewitz
Prince Dirk Blackpool	Duncan Regehr
Wizard Vector	Clive Revill
King Baaldorf	Thomas Hill
Queen Lattinia	Julie Payne
Princess Ariel	Julia Duffy
Geoffrey	Tim Dunigan
Justin Greystone	Jay Kerr
Bethel	Randi Brooks
Wizard Tranquill	Ian Wolfe
Cassandra	Phyllis Katz

Number of episodes:	8 one hour segments

Premise: A sword and sorcery fantasy-comedy with the medieval forces of good (Greystone, Baaldorf, Marko, Ariel, Justin, Tranquill), opposing those of evil (Blackpool, Geoffrey, Vector, Bethel).

Editor's comments: What a waste of a terrific cast. *Wizards and Warriors* was an obvious attempt to cash in on the "swords and sorcery" nonsense that was popular at the time, but the audience interested in such a subject was far too limited to support a series. *Wizards* primary problem is its silly premise, otherwise the stories were well written and produced, and featured a popular cast.

The Unicorn of Death (airdate: Feb. 26, 1983). Vector plans to send a gift to Princess Ariel, a unicorn that contains an immensely-powerful explosive, hoping to blow up her, her father King Baaldorf, and a large part of their kingdom. Blackpool has his brother Geoffrey deliver the bomb, as he is smitten with the princess. Pretending to be a subject paying tribute, Geoffrey delivers the unicorn to Baaldorf's castle. Later, Blackpool and Vector arrive with an ultimatum: surrender their kingdom or be destroyed. But all may not be lost, as the key that sets off the explosive is in Blackpool's castle, and Greystone and Marko leave to face the countless dangers of Blackpool's castle to steal the key. **Guest cast:** Joseph Robert Sicari as Goz Dunder, Christine DeLisle as Beldonna, Phyllis Datz as Cassandra, Ken Hixon, Brent Huff, Lonnie Wun, Kathleen McIntyre, Mark Douglas Sebastian, Steven Strong, Nancy Thiesen. **Writer:** Bill Richmond. **Director:** Bill Bixby.

The Kidnap (airdate: Mar. 5, 1983). Wizard Tranquill is telling a young boy of an adventure that happened years before: on their way to Castle Baldor, Marko and Greystone save a woman and her son who are being attacked by thieves. Meanwhile, Blackpool's forces are attacking the kingdom of Camarand, but his warriors are losing the battle. Vector arrives to offer his power to assist Blackpool, in exchange for a powerful amulet. Prince Greystone arrives to meet Ariel for the first time, but his marriage to her is postponed while he is committed to defend her kingdom. Back at his castle, Blackpool schemes with witch Bethel to steal Vector's monocle - the source of his black power - to place the wizard under his control. **Guest cast:** Christine De Lisle as Beldonna, George McDaniel as Hook, Robert Allan Browne as the general, David Ankrum, Michael Crabtree, Elyse Donaldson, M.C. Gainey, Emerson Hall, Chuck Hicks, Fred Lerner, George Marshall Ruge, Steven Strong, Steven Williams. **Writer:** Don Reo. **Director:** Richard Colla.

The Rescue (airdate: Mar. 12, 1985). In a continuation of **The Kidnap**, Princess Ariel has been kidnapped by Blackpool and Vector after they use black magic to enter Baaldorf's castle. King Baaldorf sends Greystone and Marko to Blackpool's castle to save the princess, knowing that they will encounter many traps and dangers along the way set by Vulkar. The prince and his friend come under attack by a lightning hawk, but manage to escape and head into the Forest of Gloom. Meanwhile, as Blackpool and Vulkar are on their way to a hidden castle in the Land of Storms with their captive, the incessant chatter from Princess Ariel is getting on everyone's nerves. Blackpool is getting fed up with Greystone's pursuing him, and orders Vulkar to kill the emissaries of King Baaldorf - or Blackpool will put the wizard to death. **Guest cast:** Art La Fleur as Michael, Piper Perry as Lucille, Tara Perry as Margaret, Bobby Porter as Lender, Prof. Toru Tanaka and Lonnie Wun as Baaldorf's aides. **Writer:** Don Reo. **Director:** James Frawley.

Night of Terror (airdate: Mar. 19, 1983). Erik and Ariel are out on a courtship picnic near a haunted castle. Greystone would rather be somewhere else, but the princess insists she likes the area. She also insists on hearing stories about the cursed castle, and she and Eric end up in the castle itself after her dog runs away and they follow him inside - all of which was orchestrated by Vector, who is going to let the curse of the castle - that marks transgressors for death at the hands of a friend - finish them off. While Eric and Ariel are being terrorized in the castle, her dog escapes and returns to King Baaldor's castle, where the canine alerts the king and Marko to the fate of the prince and princess. Marko leaves immediately to help, but once in the castle he becomes a crazed killer who is trying to fulfill the castle's curse by murdering his friends. **Guest cast:** None. **Writer:** Bill Richmond. **Director:** Bill Bixby.

Skies of Death (airdate: April 9, 1983). Prince Greystone and Marko are leading an assault of King Baaldor's men against Blackpool's castle, but the army is nearly wiped out by an explosion. It seems that Blackpool is using a new weapon that fires an

Julia Duffy as Princess Ariel.

Jeff Conway as Prince Erik Greystone.

Duncan Regehr as Prince Dirk Blackpool.

Walter Olkewicz as Marko, Jeff Conway as Prince Greystone.

immensely-powerful explosive. Now Vector informs Blackpool he has a new scheme: he will use black magic to alter the powder so it will wipe out all life within Baaldor's kingdom, but will leave all structures unscathed. Learning that Baaldor's kingdom is about to be destroyed, Prince Erik mounts a suicide mission up the dreaded Cliffs of Death, to destroy the medieval version of a neutron bomb. **Guest cast:** Robert Gray as the injured soldier, Robert Carnegie as guard #4, Chris Hendrie as guard #3, Warre Munson as the peasant, Alex Daniels, George Marshall Ruge, Lonnie Wun. **Writer:** Don Reo. **Director:** Bill Bixby.

Dungeon of Death (airdate: April 30, 1983). During a night battle, Marko is captured while being sent on a secret mission to obtain a list of a hundred of King Baaldorf's agents operating in the north. The king sends Prince Erik to rescue Marko before he can reveal to Blackpool who the agents are, but breaking into the evil prince's lair is sure to be immensely dangerous. And Blackpool is already setting a trap for Greystone, to be activated by Bethel. Meanwhile, Eric employs a rag-tag carnival troupe whose special abilities will be needed to break into the castle and rescue Marko before his torture session begins. **Guest cast:** Jerry Maren as Floyd the Feather, John Bennett Perry as Colter, Monique Van de Ven as Thalia, John Ratzenberger as Archie, Stephen Nichols as Ogden, Alan Shearman, Patrick Wright, Chuck Hoyes, Ron House, Ryland G. Allison, Troy Evans, Rodger Bumpass. **Writer:** Judith Allison. **Director:** Kevin Conner.

Caverns of Chaos (airdate: May 7, 1983). Wizard Tranquill needs a rare fruit from the Caverns of Chaos to cure a fatal crimson fever

that Vector has cast on King Greystone. Eric volunteers to go there, knowing that no one has ever returned alive from the cave. Mark stays behind to guard the kingdom against attack; meanwhile, back at Blackpool's castle, Blackpool is angry with Vector as he has been affected by the crimson fever as well. Blackpool sets out to retrieve the fruit first, but is warned by Vector not to use violence in the cave, as the magic that exists there will bind him to whatever he tries to kill. But, once inside the caverns, he forgets the wizard's warning and attacks Greystone when Prince Eric grabs the fruit first. Back at Blackpool's castle, Vulkar reveals to Bethel that he is scheming to eliminate Blackpool to regain his monocle, and gain power over King Greystone's kingdom. **Guest cast:** Michael Currie as King Richard Greystone, Richard Fullerton as card player #1, Steven Strong as the grox. **Writer:** Don Reo. **Director:** Paul Krasny.

Vulkar's Revenge (airdate: May 14, 1983). The Kingdom is being ravaged by Rains of Death after King Tronan dies. That night, King Baaldorf has two unexpected guests arrive under a flag of truce: Blackpool and Vector, who are seeking shelter from the Rains of Death when a bridge washes out and they cannot reach Blackpool's castle. But while Blackpool schemes to murder Greystone, Vector has bigger plans during his stay at Baaldorf's castle: he raises from the dead a killer zombie named Vulkar to assassinate Blackpool the next day, so the wizard can retrieve his monocle. However, Vulkar goes out of control and lays siege to Baaldorf's castle with his barbarian hord, and plans to kill everyone to avenge his own death. **Guest cast:** Richard Blum, Lonnie Wun. **Writer:** Robert Earll. **Director:** Kevin Conner.

George Reeves as Superman/Clark Kent with Phyllis Coates as Lois Lane.

Superman

review by William E. Anchors, Jr.

Production credits:

Executive Producers	Robert Maxwell
	Bernard Luber
	Whitney Ellsworth
Creator	Jerome Siegel
Special Effects	Thol (Si) Simonson

Regular cast:

Superman/Clark Kent	George Reeves
Lois Lane (season 1)	Phyllis Coates
Lois Lane (seasons 2-5)	Noel Neill
Jimmy Olsen	Jack Larsen
Perry White	John Hamilton
Inspector Henderson	Robert Shayne
Professor Oscar Quinn	Sterling Holloway
Professor Pepperwinkle	Philip Tead

Number of episodes: 104 one-half hour segments

Premise: A native from the planet Krypton is sent to Earth as his home world explodes. The rocket carrying the baby from another world crashes near Smallville, where he is found and adopted by the Kent family. Because of the differences in the sun and size of planets, Clark Kent is gifted with incredible powers, which he uses to fight crime as Superboy, and later as Superman.

Editor's comments: A show only a child could love. Actually, I grew up with it, and while I was an avid reader of the comics I thought the series was horrendous.

SEASON ONE

Superman on Earth (airdate: Feb. 9, 1953). Just before the planet Krypton self-destructs, the planet's leading scientist, Jor-El, sends his infant boy from his home world aboard a small, one person spaceship. The baby crash lands on Earth, a planet that is smaller than Krypton and has a yellow sun, two elements that give Kal-El fantastic powers. Found by Ma and Pa Kent just after the crash, they adopt the boy and raise him in the rural town of Smallville. When he becomes a teenager he dons a special invulnerable costume made of Krypton cloth, and calls himself Superboy - a champion of justice and fearless foe of crime. Growing into an adult, he moves to Metropolis, where he becomes a reporter on the Daily Planet newspaper, working with his friends Lois Lane, Jimmy Olsen, and Perry White, and continues his super-adventures as Superman. **Guest cast:** Robert Rockwell as Jor-El, Herbert Rawlinson, Stuart Randell as Gogan, Aline Towne as Lara, Tom Fadden as Eben Kent, Frances Morris as Sara, Dani Nolan, Dabbs Greer as the rescued man, Ross Elliott. **Writers:** Richard Fielding and Whitney Ellsworth. **Director:** Thomas Carr.

The Haunted Lighthouse (airdate: Feb. 16, 1953). Jimmy Olson's life is in danger when he visits his aunt. He has heard stories of a haunted lighthouse, and when he investigates he becomes a prisoner of smugglers using the structure for their operations. **Guest cast:** Jimmy Ogg as Chris, William Challee as Mack, Maude Prickett as Aunt Louisa, Allene Roberts as Alice, Sarah Padden as the real Aunt Loisa, Steve Carr as the commander. **Writer:** Eugene Solow. **Director:** Thomas Carr.

The Case of the Talkative Dummy (airdate: Feb. 23, 1953). Jimmy gets involved with a ventriloquist who is using a dummy to relay positions to rob armored cars. However, Jimmy makes a not-so-bright move by locking himself in a safe with a rapidly-diminishing air supply, a situation that must be rectified by Superman. **Guest cast:** Tris Coffin as Mr. Davis, Syd Saylor as Marco, Pierre Watkin as Harry Green, Phil Pine, Robert Kent as the usher. **Writers:** Dennis Cooper and Lee Backman. **Director:** Thomas Carr.

The Mystery of the Broken Statues (airdate: Mar. 2, 1953). Lois is tracking down crooks who, for some strange reason, keep finding then destroying plaster statues. But what they are looking for are keys that will solve a puzzle enabling them to unlock a post office box containing a fortune. **Guest cast:** Tris Coffin as Paul Martin, Michael Vallen as Mr. Bonelli, Maurice Cass as the shop owner, Phillip Pine, Joey Ray, Wayde Crosby as Pete, Steve Carr as the shopkeeper. **Writer:** William C. Joyce. **Director:** Thomas Carr.

The Monkey Mystery (airdate: Mar. 9, 1953). Superman obtains the assistance of a monkey belonging to an organ grinder to obtain a valuable piece of information about an atomic formula from a communist nuclear scientist. **Guest cast:** Allene Roberts as Maria, Michael Vallon as Tony, Harry Lewis as the boss, William Challee as Max, Steve Carr as the doctor. **Writers:** Ben Peter Freeman and Doris Gilbert. **Director:** Thomas Carr.

A Night of Terror (airdate: Mar. 16, 1953). Lois has gotten herself in trouble again while pursuing a story. She is being held captive by gangsters after stumbling onto a murder at the Restwell Tourist Camp. Jimmy tries to rescue her but becomes a prisoner as well, and it will take Superman to rescue them before Baby Face Stevens can silence them permanently. **Guest cast:** Frank Richards as Solley, John Kellog as Mitch, Ann Doran as Mrs. King, Almira Sessions as Miss Bacharach, Joel Friedkin as Oscar, Steve Carr as Mr. Quinn,

Richard Benedict as Baby Face Stevens. **Writer:** Ben Peter Freeman. **Director:** Lee Sholem.

The Birthday Letter (airdate: Mar. 23, 1953). A crippled girl wants more than anything to see Superman, but gets into trouble when she is phoned and given important information by mistake. The hoods who were supposed to receive the information kidnap her by using a fake Superman. **Guest cast:** Isa Ashdown as Cathy Williams, John Douchette as Slugger, Virginia Carroll as Mrs. Williams, Paul Marion as Cusak, Maurice Marsac as Marcel Duval, Nan Boardman as Marie, Jack Daly as Perkins. **Writer:** Dennis Cooper. **Director:** Lee Sholem.

The Mind Machine (airdate: Mar. 30, 1953). A crime boss will do anything to win his trial, so he forces a scientist to use a fantastic invention - a weapon that burns out people's brains - to dispose of the witnesses who planned to give damaging testimony at a federal court. **Guest cast:** Dan Seymour as Cranek, Ben Weldon as Curley, Griff Barnett as Dr. Stanton, James Seay as Senator Taylor, Steve Carr as Dr. Hadley, Harry Hayden as Al, Frank Orth as Wagner, Lester Dorr as the bus driver. **Writesr:** Dennis Cooper and Lee Backman. **Director:** Thomas Carr.

Rescue (airdate: Apr. 6, 1953). Lois enters a coal mine with an old prospector, but it collapses and seals them inside. It seems to take Clark forever to discover their predicament, but when he does he goes into action as his super other self. **Guest cast:** Houseley Stevenson, Sr. as Pop Polgase, Fred E. Sherman as Sims, Ray Bennet as Stan, Edmund Coff. **Writer:** Monroe Manning. **Director:** Thomas Carr.

The Secret of Superman (airdate: Apr. 13, 1953). Lois and Jimmy have been kidnapped by an unethical scientist. The doctor uses mind-bending drugs on Superman's friends to discover the Man of Steel's secret identity, but Clark/Superman saves them by faking amnesia. **Guest cast:** Peter Brocco as Dr. Ort, Larry Blake as the henchman, Helen Wallace as Mrs. Olsen, Joel Friedkin as the waiter, Steve Carr. **Writer:** Wells Root. **Director:** Thomas Carr.

No Holds Barred (airdate: Apr. 20, 1953). A devious professional wrestler is crippling his opponents - permanently, by using a new grip he learned from a captive from India. A college wrestler friend of Lois' goes into the ring with him to expose his criminal acts. **Guest cast:** Malcolm Mealey as Wayne as Sam Bleaker, Richard Reeves as Bad Luck Branningan, Richard Elliott, Herbert Vigran as Murray, Tito Renaldo as Ramm, Henry Kelky as Crusher. **Writer:** Peter Dixon. **Director:** Lee Sholem.

The Deserted Village (airdate: April 27, 1953). Snoopy Lois is out to solve a mystery concerning her hometown, where the last few people living there seem to be guarding a horrible secret. They are telling strangers they are being terrorized by a sea serpent, but they actually plan to make huge profits from the mining of a rare mineral. **Guest cast:** Maude Prickett as Matilda Taisey, Fred E. Sherman as Dr. Jessup, Edmund Cobb as Peter Godfrey, Malcolm Mealey as Alvin. **Writers:** Dick Hamilton and Ben Peter Freeman. **Director:** Thomas Carr.

The Stolen Costume (airdate: May 4, 1953). A crook hides in Clark's apartment and finds his Superman costume. The uniform falls into the hands of a more ambitious gangster, who tries to extort Superman for the return of his uniform, whose secret identity has been exposed by a the criminals. Until he can undue the damage he strands the crook and his girlfriend on a peak of ice in the frozen Artic. **Guest cast:** Norman Budd as Simms, Frank Jenks as Candy, Dan Seymour as Ace, Veda Ann Borg as Connie, Bob Williams as the policeman. **Writer:** Ben Peter Freeman. **Director:** Lee Sholem.

Mystery in Wax (airdate: May 11, 1953). A weird female sculptress specializes in the bizarre: her latest additions are all of prominent people she predicts will die at their own hands - including the Daily Planet editor, Perry White. When snoopy Lois tries to find the woman's secret, she is captured and held prisoner. **Guest cast:** Myra McKinney as Madame Selena, Lester Sharpe as Andrew, Steve Carr as Dr. John Hurley. **Writer:** Ben Peter Freeman. **Director:** Lee Sholem.

Treasure of the Incas (airdate: May 18, 1953). Clark, Jimmy and Lois head to the steamy jungles of South America while following a clue they believe will lead them to something incredible, which it does: inside a dark cave they find an Inca treasure. But they also find a group of criminals already there - who have no intention of allowing the reporters to live. **Guest cast:** Leonard Penn as Mendosa, Martin Garralaga, Juan DuVal as Dr. Questa, Hal Gerard as Prof. Laverra, Juan Rivero, Steve Carr as Anselmo. **Writer:** Howard Green. **Director:** Thomas Carr.

Double Trouble (airdate: May 25, 1953). Superman gets mixed up with a pair of identical twins when he has to fly overseas to retrieve a batch of stolen radioactive material, obtained by some Nazis who have taken it from an Army base in Germany. **Guest cast:** Howard Chamberlin as Fischer and Dr. Schumann, Selmer Jackson as Col. Jake Redding, Rudolph Anders as Dr. Albrecht, Jimmy Dodd as Jake, Steve Carr as Otto Von Klaben. **Writer:** Eugene Solow. **Director:** Thomas Carr.

The Runaway Robot (airdate: June 1, 1953). An ingenious inventor has created a fantastic robot named *Hero*, but it is stolen by criminals who use it in criminal activities. **Guest cast:** Dan Seymour as Rocko, John Harmon as Mousie, Lecien Littlefield as Horatio Hinkle, Russell Johnson as Chopper, Robert Easton as Marvin, Herman Cantor. **Writer:** Dick Hamilton. **Director:** Thomas Carr.

Drums of Death (airdate: June 8, 1953). Clark, Lois, and Jimmy are assigned to a story in Haiti, where people are being scared out of the jungle. While there, they encounter a voodoo cult involved in criminal operations, secretly led by their own jungle guide. **Guest cast:** Harry Corden as William Johnson, Leonard Mudie as Leland Masters, Milton Wood as Mr. Bardarier, Mabel Albertson as Kate White, George Hamilton as Dr. Jerrod, Smoki Whitfield. **Writer:** Dick Hamilton. **Director:** Lee Sholem.

The Evil Three (airdate: June 15, 1953). Perry and Jimmy go on a fishing trip together, but while staying at a remote hotel they are terrorized by three deranged individuals who will do anything to keep their secret safe. **Guest cast:** Rhys Williams as Macey Taylor, Jonathan Hale as Col. Brand, Cecil Elliot as Elsa. **Writer:** Ben Peter Freeman. **Director:** Thomas Carr.

Riddle of the Chinese Jade (airdate: June 22, 1953). In the Chinatown district of Metropolis, a young man becomes involved in the theft of an oriental jade statue, a coveted family heirloom that belongs to his future wife's father. But when the man and his fiancee nearly drown before being saved by Superman, he decides to go straight. Meanwhile, Lois is kidnapped again. **Guest cast:** Victor Sen Yung as Harry Wong, James Craven as Greer, Gloria Saunders as Lilly, Paul Burns as Lu Sung. **Writer:** Richard Fielding. **Director:** Thomas Carr.

The Human Bomb (airdate: June 29, 1953). A thief has kidnapped Lois in hopes that Superman will not interfere while he is robbing a museum - if he should do so, Lois will be blown up. **Guest cast:** Trevor Bardette as the butler, Dennis Moore as Conway, Marshall Reed as inspector Hill, Lou Lubin. **Writer:** Richard Fielding. **Director:** Lee Sholem.

Czar of the Underworld (airdate: July 6, 1953). A movie company contacts Clark Kent and police inspector Henderson in hopes that they will assist in the production of a crime expose on a mafia kingpin. They agree to do so - until their lives are threatened for getting involved with the film. **Guest cast:** Paul Fix as Ollie, John Maxwell, Tony Caruso as Luigi Dinelli, Roy Gordon, Steve Carr. **Writer:** Eugene Solow. **Director:** Tommy Carr.

The Ghost Wolf (airdate: July 13, 1953). Clark, Lois, and Jimmy are in the wild woodlands of Canada when they encounter a howling wolf - and a professional arsonist. **Guest cast:** Jane Adams as Babette, Stanley Andrews as Sam Garvin, Lou Krugman as Olivier, Harold Goodwin as the railroad worker. **Writer:** Dick Hamilton. **Director:** Lee Sholem.

The Unknown People, parts one and two (airdate: part one, July 20, 1953; part two, July 27, 1953). Perry has sent to Silsby his top two reporters, Clark and Lois, to do a feature on the world's deepest oil well after it is shut down. While they are there they encounter weird mole men who live in the subterranean depths. The local townspeople fear the underground creatures may be radioactive, and set out to destroy them. When one of the mole men is captured, Superman releases him and returns him to his underground world. [This two part Superman episode is actually a revised version of *Superman and the Mole Men*, a theater-released movie.] **Guest cast:** Jeff Corey as Luke Benson, Walter Reed as Bill Corrigan, Stanley Andrews as the Sheriff, Billy Curtis as the Mole Man, Jack Branbury as the Mole Man, Jerry Marvin as the Mole Man, Tony Baris as the Mole Man, Florence Lake, Ed Hinton, J. Ferrell MacDonald as Pop Shannon, Frank Reicher as Chief Administrator, Paul Burns, Hal K. Dawson, Ray Walker as Craig, Beverly Washburn, Steve Carr as the man, Margia Dean, Byron Foulger, Irene Martin, John Phillips, John Baer as Dr. Reed, Andrienne Marden. **Writer:** Richard Fielding. **Director:** Lee Shelem.

Crime Wave (airdate: Aug. 3, 1953). A crime boss has targeted Superman for destruction after the Krypton native vows to clean up crime in the city. A fantastic display of electrical fireworks is set off on Dover's Cliff, where the crime boss has set a trap for Superman. **Guest cast:** John Eldredge as Walter Canby, Phil Van Zandt as Nick, Al Eben as Ed Bullock, Joseph Mell as the Professor, Barbara Fuller as Sally, Bobby Barber as Tony, Bill Kennedy as the radio announcer. **Writer:** Ben Peter Freeman. **Director:** Thomas Carr.

SEASON TWO

Five Minutes to Doom (airdate: Sept. 14, 1953). An innocent man has been tried and sent to prison, where he awaits the electric chair. The governor reprieves his sentence when the truth is discovered, but Superman has only a short period of time to get the governor's letter freeing the man to the prison where the execution will momentarily take place. **Guest cast:** Dabbs Greer as Joe Winters, Sam Flint as the warden, Lois Hall, John Kellogg, Jean Willes as the secretary, Lewis Russell as Wayne, Dale Van Sickel as Baker, William E. Green as the governor. **Writer:** Monroe Manning. **Director:** Thomas Carr.

The Big Squeeze (airdate: Sept. 21, 1953). An ex-convict tries to go straight, but when an ex-partner in crime starts blackmailing him he is assisted by Superman. **Guest cast:** Hugh Beaumont as Dan Grayson, John Kellogg, Aline Towne as Peggy, Harry Cheshire as Mr. Foster, Bradley Mora as Tim Grayson, Ted Ryan, Reed Howes. **Writer:** David Chantler. **Director:** Thomas Carr.

The Man Who Could Read Minds (airdate: Sept. 28, 1953). The police are baffled as to the identity of a highly-successful phantom burglar, so Jimmy and Lois pursue the man themselves - which may result in their being killed. **Guest cast:** Larry Dobkin as the Swami, Veola Vonn as Laura, Richard Karlan as the phantom, Tom Bernard as Duke, Russell Custer. **Writer:** Roy Hamilton, **Director:** Thomas Carr.

Jet Ace (airdate: Oct. 5, 1953). A top-notch, heroic test pilot is highly valued for his work for our country. But his deeds mark him for kidnapping by foreign agents who need his services in there home land. **Guest cast:** Lane Bradford as Chris White, Selmer Jackson as Gen. Summers, Richard Reeves as Frenchy, Jim Hayward as Tim Mollory, Sam Balter, Larry J. Blake as Martin, Mauritz Hugo, Bud Wolfe, Ric Roman as Nate. **Writer:** David Chantler. **Director:** Thomas Carr.

Shot in the Dark (airdate: Oct. 12, 1953). A teenage photographer trying out his new camera accidentally stumbles onto an incredible secret - he has taken a picture of Superman changing into Clark Kent. The photo is obtained by a criminal who supposedly died years earlier, who plans to put it to good use. Now Superman must decide how to acquire the photograph without giving away his identity. **Guest cast:** Billy Gray, Verde Marshe as Harriet Harper, John Eldredge as the tulip man, Frank Richards, Alan Lee as Bill. **Writer:** David Chantler. **Director:** George Blair.

The Defeat of Superman (airdate: Oct. 19, 1953). Some criminals have gotten a hold of Kryptonite, a rare mineral that is from Superman's home world, whose radioactive properties do not harm humans but will kill anyone from Krypton. The gang manages to lure Superman into a trap by taking Lois and Jimmy hostage, and putting them in a basement with the deadly rock. The Man of Steel's only hope is if Lois and Jimmy can somehow remove the Kryptonite from his presence. **Guest cast:** Maurice Cass as Meldini, Peter Mamakos as Happy King, Nestor Paiva, Sid Tomack as Ruffles. **Writer:** Jackson Gillis. **Director:** Thomas Carr.

Superman in Exile (airdate: Oct. 26, 1953). Superman has been exposed to a high level of Gamma radiation. While the rays do not

affect the Man of Steel, until they wear off he is a danger to any human he goes near. Meanwhile, a hood takes advantage of his absence by pulling off a jewel heist. **Guest cast:** Leon Askin as Ferdinand, Joe Forte as the director, Phil Van Zandt as Regan, John Harmon as Skinny, Robert S. Carson, Sam Balter, Gregg Barton, Don Dillaway. **Writer:** Jackson Gillis. **Director:** Thomas Carr.

A Ghost For Scotland Yard (airdate: Nov. 2, 1953). A magician/illusionist will supposedly be resurrected from the dead, a situation that will threaten a friend of Perry's. Clark and Jimmy are sent to England to cover the story, but Jimmy is captured by the magician - who was alive all along - and threatens to blow up the cub reporter with a bomb. **Guest cast:** Leonard Mudie as Brookhurst, Colin Campbell as Sir Arthur, Norma Varden as Mabel, Patrick Aherne as Farrington, Clyde Cook as the vendor, Evelyn Halpern as Betty. **Writer:** Jackson Gillis. **Director:** George Blair.

The Dog Who Knew Superman (airdate: Nov. 11, 1953). A criminal owns a pooch that is too smart for its own good, as it has taken a glove that belongs to Superman's secret other self. Realizing it can recognize Superman's alter-ego, the crook follows the dog, but the only thing he finds is a peeved superguy. **Guest cast:** Billy Nelson as Louie, Ben Weldon as Hank, Lester Dorr, Dona Drake as Joyce, John Daly as the dog catcher, Corky as the little dog. **Writer:** David Chantler. **Director:** Thomas Carr.

The Face and the Voice (airdate: Nov. 16, 1953). A hoodlum has had his features changed to match Superman, and begins to commit crimes to make the Man of Steel look bad. The man pulls off such a good impersonation that he has everyone fooled - until he makes a mistake. **Guest cast:** Hayden Rorke as the psychiatrist, Stanford Jolley, George Chandler as Scratchy, Percy Helton as Hamlet, Carlton Young as Fairchild, Nolan Leary as the watchman, Sam Balter, William Newell as the store clerk. **Writer:** Jackson Gillis.

Director: George Blair.

The Man in the Lead Mask (airdate: Nov. 23, 1953). Both the police and the press are dumbfounded when a criminal seems to have found a way to change his fingerprints. But the man in the iron mask is really a crook pulling a fast one on other criminals. **Guest cast:** Frank Scannell as Canfield, John Crawford as Doc, Louis Jean Heydt, Paul Bryar and John Merton are the gangsters, Joey Ray as Marty Mitchell, Lynn Thomas, Sam Belter, Paul Bryar is also Morrell. **Writers:** Leroy H. Zehren and Roy Hamilton. **Director:** George Blair.

Panic in the Sky (airdate: Nov. 30, 1953). Superman must destroy a meteor that is on a collision course with Earth, but he is unable to stop the huge object - and is unaware that it contains Kryptonite until he loses his memory. **Guest cast:** Jonathan Hale as Prof. Roberts, Jane Frazee as the farmer, Clark Howat, Thomas Moore. **Writer:** Jackson Gillis. **Director:** Thomas Carr.

The Machine That Could Plot Crimes (airdate: Dec. 7, 1953). Superman meets for the first time the brilliant but erratic Prof. Oscar Quinn after crooks take control of an advanced room-sized computer that will enable them to plot bank robberies - and may be able to determine what Superman's secret identity is. **Guest cast:** Billy Nelson as Larry McCoy, Sherry Moreland, Stan Jarman, Ben Walden, Sam Balter as the announcer, Russell Custer, Sterling Holloway as Uncle Oscar. **Writer:** Jackson Gillis. **Director:** Thomas Carr.

Jungle Devil (airdate: Dec. 14, 1953). Superman must save a jungle expedition after they lose a gem from the eye of a pagan idol, an act that has infuriated the primitive local natives. **Guest cast:** Doris Singleton as Gloria, Damian O'Flynn as Dr. Harper, Al Kikume, James Seay as the pilot, Leon Lontoc, Steve Calvert, Bernard Gozier, Henry A, Escalante, Nacho Galindo as Alberto. **Writer:** Peter Dixon. **Director:** Thomas Carr.

My Friend Superman (airdate: Dec. 21, 1953). The operator of a small restaurant is approached by hoods trying to extort money from him for a protection racket. But the owner finds himself in hot water after constantly bragging about what a great personal friend Superman is. **Guest cast:** Tito Vivolo, Yvette Dugay as Elaine, Paul Burke, Terry Frost and Joseph Vitale as the gangsters, Ralph Sanford, Edward Reider and Ruta Kilmonis as the teenagers, Frederick Berest. **Writer:** David Chantler. **Director:** Thomas Carr.

The Clown Who Cried (airdate: Dec. 28, 1953). Unless Superman intervenes, a charity telethon may be robbed by a small-time thief who is going to appear on the show as a circus clown. But the real clown arrives, and chases his replacement to a nearby rooftop, where they both fall from the tall building while struggling. **Guest cast:** Mickey Simpson as Hercules, Peter Brocco as Crackers, Harry Mendoza, George Douglas as the guard, Charles Williams Tim, Richard D. Crockett, Richard Lewis, Harvey Parry, William Wayne as Rollo. **Writer:** David Chantler. **Director:** George Blair.

The Boy Who Hated Superman (airdate: Jan. 4, 1954). A misguided young man worships a common criminal that Clark Kent helps have arrested. The boy vows to get even, so he uses Jimmy in retaliation - but both end up being kidnapped by some hoods. **Guest**

cast: Roy Barcoft as Duke Dillion, Leonard Penn as Fixer, Tyler McDuff as Frankie, Charles Meredith, Richard Reeves as Babe. **Writer:** David Chantler. **Director:** George Blair.

Semi-Private Eye (airdate: Jan. 11, 1954). When they suspect Clark is really Superman, Lois, accompanied by Jimmy, hires a private detective to follow Superman's alter-identity. Later, Jimmy sees the detective and Lois being kidnapped, so he decides to play private eye himself - and he ends up kidnapped as well. **Guest cast:** Elisha Cook, Jr. as Homer Garrity, Paul Fix as Fingers, Richard Benedict as Cappy Leonard, Alfred Linder as Morrie, Douglas Henderson as Noodles. **Writer:** David Chantler. **Director:** George Blair.

Perry White's Scoop (airdate: Jan. 18, 1954). Perry White decides to cover a story himself when he investigates a dead man found in a diving outfit, and the clues lead him to a boxcar full of paper used for counterfeiting money - and to a firey death, unless the Man of Steel can save him. **Guest cast:** Steve Pendleton as Lynch, Jan Arvan as Max, Robert J. Wilke as Bingham, Bibs Borman as Maria, Tom Monroe as the diver. **Writer:** Roy Hamilton. **Director:** George Blair.

Beware the Wrecker (airdate: Jan. 25, 1954). A super saboteur pulls off one caper after another, always eluding the police. But the villain is actually a leading citizen getting rich on filing phony insurance claims. **Guest cast:** William Forrest as Mr. Crane, Pierre Watkin, Tom Powers, Denver Pyle, Renny McEvoy as the carnival barker. **Writer:** Royal Cole. **Director:** George Blair.

The Golden Vulture (airdate: Feb. 1, 1954). After finding a note in a bottle washed onto the shore, an investigation leads to Clark, Jimmy, and Lois being held captive. Now Superman must figure out a way to get his friends free from a deranged sea captain without giving away his secret identity. **Guest cast:** Peter Whitney as Capt. MacBain, Vic Perrin as Scurvy, Robert Bice as Bennet, Murray Alper as Sanders, Wes Hudman as the dock worker, Saul M. Gross, Carl H. Saxe, Dan Turner, William Vincent. **Writer:** Jackson Gillis. **Director:** Thomas Carr.

Jimmy Olsen, Boy Editor (airdate: Feb. 8, 1954). Jimmy has pulled off the impossible: he manages to get Perry to trade jobs with him for one day. In a scheme to draw a criminal out into the open, he publishes a false story in the Daily Planet. And it does get his attention, as the thug is now trying to kill the Cub Editor. **Guest cast:** Herb Vigran as Legs Leemy, Keith Richards as the henchman, Dick Rich, Anthony Hughes as the hospital director, Jack Pepper, Ronald Hargrove, Bob Crosson. **Writer:** David Chantler. **Director:** Thomas Carr.

Lady in Black (airdate: Feb. 15, 1954). Jimmy visits an old house plagued with strange images and unusual noises - could it be haunted? But the unusual happenings are actually the doing of a landlord who is using a hole knocked in the basement wall to break into an art gallery. **Guest cast:** Frank Ferguson as Mr. Frank, Virginia Christian Mrs. Frank, John Doucette as Scarface, Rudolph Anders as Glasses, Mike Ragan, Frank Marlowe. **Writer:** Jackson Gillis. **Director:** Thomas Carr.

Star of Fate (airdate: Feb. 22, 1954). A scientist desperately needs a poisonous sapphire, and he turns to murder and theft to obtain it. When Lois gets near the gem, she falls victim to the poison it contains, and she will die unless Superman can find the cure from a plant found only in Egypt. **Guest cast:** Lawrence Ryle as Dr. Barnak, Jeanne Dean as Alma, Arthur Space as Dr. Wilson, Paul Burns as Mr. Whitlock, Tony McMario March, Ted Hecht as Ahmed. **Writers:** Roy Hamilton and Leroy G. Zehren. **Director:** Thomas Carr.

The Whistling Bird (airdate: Mar. 1, 1954). Prof. Oscar Quinn has returned, this time having created a super explosive. The only problem is that his pet bird is the only one who knows the correct ingredients. **Guest cast:** Otto Waldis as the scientist, Marshall Reed as the agent, Allene Roberts as Nancy Quinn, Toni Carroll as Dorothy Manners, Jerry Housner, Sterling Holloway as Uncle Oscar, Joseph Vitale as Speck. **Writer:** David Chantler. **Director:** Thomas Carr.

Around the World With Superman (airdate: Mar. 8, 1954). A blind girl's dreams come true when she wins a trip around the world in a contest, which brings her in contact with Superman, who restores her sight and flies her around the globe. **Guest cast:** Kay Morley as Elaine Carson, Patrick Aherne as the man, Raymond Greenleaf as Dr. Anderson, Judy Ann Nugent, Ann Carson, Max Wagner. **Writer:** Jackson Gillis. **Director:** Thomas Carr.

SEASON THREE

Through the Time Barrier (airdate: Sept. 13, 1954). The erratic Prof. Quinn has created, of all things, a time machine. Unfortunately, he has managed to send the Daily Planet staff, himself, and a vicious gangster back into prehistoric times. [This is the first color Superman episode.] **Guest cast:** Jim Hyland as Turk Jackson, Florence Lake as the cavewoman, Ed Hinton as the caveman, Sterling Holloway as Prof. Twiddle. **Writer:** David Chantler. **Director:** Harry Gerstad.

The Talking Clue (airdate: Sept. 20, 1954). When Inspector Henderson's son uses his new tape recorder, he mistakenly records the sounds of the inspector's safe's tumblers at work. Now a criminal has gotten ahold of the tape and plans to steal some evidence from the safe that will incriminate him on a crime. The boy is kidnapped, but leaves behind a recording to help Superman rescue him. **Guest cast:** Billy Nelson as McGurk, Richard Shakleton as Ray, Brick Sullivan as the officer, Julian Upton as Claude James. **Writer:** David Chantler. **Director:** Harry Gerstad.

The Lucky Cat (airdate: Sept. 27, 1954). Superman gets involved with the members of an antisuperstition society, who have been receiving threats and are in danger of sabotage and murder. **Guest cast:** Harry Tyler as Botts, Carl Harbord as Mr. Fredericks, Ted Stanhope as Charlie King, John Phillips, Charles Watts as Bill Green. **Writer:** Jackson Gillis. **Director:** Harry Gerstad.

Superman Week (airdate: Oct. 4, 1954). Metropolis is holding its annual celebrations during Superman Week. However, two criminals have obtained a block of Kryponite, and plan a very special surprise for the Man of Steel. **Guest cast:** Herb Vigran as Si Horton, Tamar Cooper as the artist, Jack George, Paul Burke as the partner, Buddy Mason. **Writer:** Peggy Chantler. **Director:** Harry Gerstad.

Great Caesar's Ghost (airdate: Oct. 11, 1954). Is Perry going crazy? It looks that way when he starts seeing the ghost of Julius Caesar. Actually, a criminal has been faking the ghost in hopes that Perry will be rejected as a witness at his trial. The plot seems to be having the desired affect of making the editor look insane, but the timely arrival of Superman saves the editor from ruin. **Guest cast:** Trevor Bardette, Jim Hayward as the delivery man, Olaf Hytten as Jarvis. **Writer:** Jackson Gillis. **Director:** Harry Gerstad.

Test of a Warrior (airdate: Oct. 18, 1954). An Indian chief must undergo a dangerous ritual to test his courage, but isn't up to the rigors of the event. Jimmy tries to help until Superman can arrive and salvage the situation. **Guest cast:** Ralph Moody as the medicine man, Maurice Jara, Francis McDonald as Great Horse, George Lewis as John Tall Star, Lane Bradford. **Writer:** Leroy H. Zehren. **Director:** George Blair.

Olsen's Millions (airdate: Oct. 25, 1954). After Jimmy saves her cat from a locked safe, a kindly old woman gives the cub reporter one million dollars! But crooks hear about the reward money, and send a fake butler to work for Jimmy as an insider until they can figure out how to relieve Master Olson of his dough. **Guest cast:** Elizabeth Patterson as Miss Peabody, George E. Stone as Big George, Richard Reeves as Stacey Tracey, Leonard Carey as Herbert, Tyler McDuff as the delivery boy. **Writer:** David Chantler. **Director:** George Blair.

Clark Kent, Outlaw (airdate: Nov. 1, 1954). Clark fakes being an outlaw to join a gang of thieves, who let him in after witnessing his great safe-cracking abilities. He wants to bring the leader of the gang, a top-notch criminal, out of hiding, but Perry blows Clark's cover. **Guest cast:** John Doucette as Foster, Sid Tomack as Curtis, Tris Coffin as Stoddard, George Eldridge as Wingate, Patrick O'Moore as Bennet, Lyn Thomas. **Writer:** Leroy H. Zehren.

Director: George Blair.

The Magic Necklace (airdate: Nov. 8, 1954). An archaeologist has discovered a necklace that will make the wearer invulnerable. But the devious doctor is pulling a fast one hoping to make money to finance future trips. Unfortunately, a gangster becomes interested in the necklace and has no plans on paying for it. **Guest cast:** Leonard Mudie as Prof. Jody, Frank Jenks as Lazy, John Harmon as Clicker, Paul Fierro, Lawrence Ryle as Jake Morrell, Ted Hecht, Cliff Ferre. **Writer:** Jackson Gillis. **Director:** George Blair.

The Bully of Dry Gulch (airdate: Nov. 15, 1954). Jimmy and Lois stop in an old western town while on a road trip. They find a bully running Dry Gulch, and his henchmen throw Jimmy in jail when he rubs the boss the wrong way. But when the bully sets out to conquer Lois, Superman arrives to save the day. **Guest cast:** Raymond Hatton as Sagebrush, Myron Healey as Gunner Flinch, Martin Garralaga as Pedro, Eddie Baker as the bartender. **Writer:** David Chantler. **Director:** George Blair.

Flight to the North (airdate: Nov. 22, 1954). A backwoodsman who claims to be Superman accepts an assignment to fly a lemon meringue pie to a woman's fiance working in Alaska, not knowing that it is in the best interests of a gangster to stop him. **Guest cast:** Chuck Connors [*Werewolf*] as Sylvester J. Superman, Ben Welden as Leftover Louie Lyman, Richard Garland as Steve, Ralph Sanford as Buckets, Marjorie Owens as Margie, George Chandler as the manager. **Writer:** David Chantler. **Director:** George Blair.

The Seven Souvenirs (airdate: Nov. 29, 1954). In the first episode with Prof. Pepperwinkle, a set of thefts involving some unusual daggers has occurred - knives that were supposed to have been damaged when used to attack Superman. The crime boss who arranged their theft believes that if Superman will use his x-ray vision on them, they will be turned into highly-valuable pure radium. **Guest cast:** Arthur Space as Mr. Jasper, Rick Vallin as Scar Man, Steve Calvert as Louie, Louise Lewis as the lady, Lennie Breman, Jack O'Shea, Phil Tead as Mr. Willie. **Writer:** Jackson Gillis. **Director:** George Blair.

King for a Day (airdate: Dec. 6, 1954). Jimmy is involved in political intrigue when he agrees to take the place of a European prince for a day. While Jimmy pretends to be the ruler of the country, the real prince is out nabbing the people who planned to assassinate him. **Guest cast:** Peter Mamakos Marcel, Leon Askin as Valance, Phil Van Zandt as Maral, Jan Arvan as Rigor, Steven Bekassy, Carolyn Scott as the Baroness, Chet Marshall as Prince Gregory. **Writer:** Dwight Babcock. **Director:** George Blair.

SEASON FOUR

Joey (airdate: Sept. 12, 1955). The father of a young girl is forced to sell her horse to the Daily Planet to save their farm. The paper plans to race the horse and give the winnings to charity, but as the little girl tries to inspire the race horse to victory, some crooks are working for just the opposite. **Guest cast:** Janine Perreau as Alice, Mauritz Hugo as Luke Palmer, Tom London as Pete Thomas, Billy Nelson as Sulley, Jay Lawrence, Willard Kennedy. **Writer:** David Chantler. **Director:** Harry Gerstad.

The Unlucky Number (airdate: Sept. 19, 1955). A group of gangsters are running a contest that has been rigged, but when Clark guesses the correct number of jelly beans in the bottle, he wins and gives the prize money to an old woman. Now the gangsters who run the contest think that the member who arranged it double crossed them, and want him dead. **Guest cast:** Elizabeth Patterson as Clara Exbrook, Henry Blair as Bobby, John Beradino Dexter, Russell Conklin as Slippery Elm, Jack Littlefield as Boots, Alan Reynolds as Mr. Kelly, Tony DeMario as the newstand operator, Alfred Linder as collector. **Writer:** David Chantler. **Director:** Harry Gerstad.

The Big Freeze (airdate: Sept. 26, 1955). As it nears election time in Metropolis, a crooked politician hires a scientist to keep Superman out of the way, accomplished by freezing him in a powerful refrigerator. **Guest cast:** Richard Reeves as Little Jack, George E. Stone as Duke Taylor, John Phillips as the citizen, Rolfe Sedan as Dr. Watts, Eddie Baker as the guard. **Writer:** David Chantler. **Director:** Harry Gerstad.

Peril by Sea (airdate: Oct. 3, 1955). Perry White's scientific research results in a secret formula being developed that will allow uranium to be taken from ordinary sea water. Trying to give the Chief the credit he deserves, Jimmy runs a story about the discovery, resulting in Perry's formula being stolen by a pair of master criminals who escape in a submarine. **Guest cast:** Claude Akins as Ace Miller, Julian Upton as Barney, Ed Penny. **Writer:** David Chantler. **Director:** Harry Gerstad.

Topsy Turvy (airdate: Oct. 10, 1955). Professor Pepperwinkle returns; this time he comes to Superman's attention after inventing a kooky mirror that makes everything look upside down. The mirror is obtained by a crooked carnival owner who uses it to pull off bank heists. **Guest cast:** Ben Welden, Mickey Knox as Yoyo, Charles Williams as the man. **Writer:** David Chantler. **Director:** Harry Gerstad.

Jimmy The Kid (airdate: Oct. 17, 1955). A young con who has just escaped from prison kidnaps his look-a-like twin: Jimmy Olson. With the real Olson out of the way, the fake goes to work at the Planet where he tries to divert an investigation by Clark Kent. In doing so, he breaks into Kent's apartment - and finds his Superman outfits. **Guest cast:** Damian O'Flynn as J. W. Gridley, Diana Darrin as Macey, Florence Ravenel as Mrs. Cooper, Jack Larson, Steven Conte and Rick Vallin as the thugs. **Writer:** Leroy H. Zehren. **Director:** Phil Ford.

The Girl Who Hired Superman (airdate: Oct. 24, 1955). A wealthy socialite manages to hire Superman to entertain at a party, but she finds herself involved in criminal activity. Meanwhile, Superman does not realize he will be doing some smuggling. **Guest cast:** Gloria Talbott as Mara Van Cleaver, Maurice Marsac as Aristo, George Khoury, Lyn Guild as Milly, John Eldredge as Jonas Rockwell. **Writer:** David Chantler. **Director:** Phil Ford.

The Wedding of Superman (airdate: Oct. 31, 1955). Romance blossoms between the Man of Steel and Lois, who dreams of when he will pop the all-important question. When he courts the girl reporter, Henderson becomes jealous, and Kent is upset when he is asked to attend their wedding as their best man. **Guest cast:** Milton Frome as Mr. Farady, Julie Bennet as Mabel, Doyle Brooks as Poole, John Cliff as the assistant, Nolan Leary, Dolores Fuller. **Writer:** Jackson Gillis. **Director:** Phil Ford.

Dagger Island (airdate: Nov. 7, 1955). The Daily Planet staff have three brothers transported to a desert island, where they begin looking for a treasure they are supposed to inherit from a dead relative. However, the relative is alive and well, and is planning to kill Lois and Jimmy. **Guest cast:** Myron Healey as Paul, Dean Cromer as Mickey, Raymond Hatton as Jonathan Scag, Ray Montgomery as Jeff. **Writer:** Robert Leslie Bellem. **Director:** Phil Ford.

Blackmail (airdate: Nov. 14, 1955). Some evil bad guys plan to zap Superman with a new weapon. To keep Inspector Henderson busy, they plant stolen money on the detective, and he is accused of taking a bribe. **Guest cast:** Herb Vigran as Arnold, Sid Tomack as Eddie, George Chandler as Bates, Selmer Jackson as the commissioner. **Writers:** Oliver Drake and David Chantler. **Director:** Harry Gerstad.

The Deadly Rock (airdate: Nov. 21, 1955). Jimmy sees an FBI agent react to Kryptonite the same as Superman, even though the rock should not affect Earth people. Meanwhile, a scientist finds a piece of the meteor that brought the Kryptonite to Earth, and wants to sell it to the highest-bidding criminal who wants to kill the man from Krypton. **Guest cast:** Robert Lowery as Gary Allen, Lyn Thomas, Steven Geray as Van Wick, Robert Foulk as Big Tom Rufus, Ric Roman as Snorkel, Vincent G. Perry as the doctor, Sid Melton as a thug, Jim Hayward as baggage man. **Writer:** Jackson Gillis. **Director:** Harry Gerstad.

The Phantom Ring (airdate: Nov. 28, 1955). The "Phantom Ring" is a group of criminals who carry coins that can make them invisible. Kent is offered a membership in the gang, but when he refuses they throw him out of a moving aircraft. **Guest cast:** Paul Burke, Peter Brocco as the Specter, Lane Bradford, Ed Hinton, Henry Rowland, George Brand as the clerk. **Writer:** David Chantler. **Director:** Phil Ford.

The Jolly Roger (airdate: Dec. 5, 1955). The Navy is planning to destroy a small Pacific island, but when the Daily Planet staff are sent there to witness the event, they find it is inhabited by a group of cut-throat pirates who will not believe that their days are numbered on the island. When the navy ships open fire, Superman must catch all the incoming ordinance to save the lives of Jimmy and Lois. **Guest cast:** Leonard Mudie as the pirate captain, Myron Healy, Patrick Aherne, Jean Lewis, Pierre Watkin, Eric Snowden, Ray Montgomery as Riffles, Dean Cromer as Tyler, Chet Marshall. **Writer:** David Chantler. **Director:** Phil Ford.

SEASON FIVE

Peril in Paris (airdate: Sept. 10, 1956). Superman and Jimmy are in France, where the Man of Steel agrees to help an actress escape from behind the Iron Curtain. But Superman unwittingly becomes a jewel thief because of the woman, who wants to recover some family heirlooms. **Guest cast:** Lilyan Cahuvin as Anna Constantine, Peter Mamakos as Gregor, Albert Carrier as Inspector Lamont, Charles LaTorre as Officer Gerard, Franz Roehn as Jacques Ducray, Robert

Shayne as Inspector Lonier. **Writers:** Robert Drake and David Chantler. **Director:** George Blair.

Tin Hero (airdate: Sept. 17, 1956). A meek and mild accountant accidentally stops a bank robber from making a getaway. Now he thinks he is a great crime fighter, and is hired by Perry as a consultant. Some hoods scheme to capture the man, but end up kidnapping Jimmy instead. **Guest cast:** Carl Ritchie as Frank Smullens, Sam Finn as Fingers Danny, Frank Richards, Paula Houston as Celia, Jack Lomas as Big Jack. **Writer:** Wilton Schiller. **Director:** George Blair.

Money to Burn (airdate: Sept. 24, 1956). Some crooks have cooked up a great gimmick: as fireman try to put out fires at buildings owned by corporations, they offer coffee and donuts to the fire fighters. Meanwhile, they break into the burned buildings and steal the holdings inside the corporate safes. After the rash of recent fires, Perry becomes suspected of committing insurance fraud, so he investigates the fires and learns the truth behind the safe heists. **Guest cast:** Mauritz Hugo as Slim, Dale Van Sickel as a partner, Richard Emory. **Writer:** David Chantler. **Director:** Harry Gerstad.

The Town That Wasn't (airdate: Oct. 1, 1956). Enterprising crooks are using a phony town that can be broken down and moved in order to set up speed traps around the interstate, and pull over people passing through to give them phony traffic tickets. Jimmy has the misfortune of traveling through the town while on vacation and gets ticketed. Once back home, he tells Lois and Clark about the racket, and they decide to check it out. **Guest cast:** Frank Connor, Charles Gray as a policeman, Richard Elliot as the judge, Terry Frost as the policeman, Jack V. Littlefield as the waiter, Michael Garrett, Phillip Barnes as the truck driver. **Writer:** Wilton Schiller. **Director:** Harry Gerstad.

The Tomb of Zaharan (airdate: Oct. 8, 1956). Two Middle-Eastern dignitaries visiting Metropolis see that Lois and believe that she is the reincarnated ruler of their country. To trap her, they invite her to visit them for an interview. She takes Jimmy along, and the two find themselves being sealed into a tomb to fulfill the men's ancient religious prophecy. **Guest cast:** George Khoury as Inspector Henderson, Jack Kruschen as the villain, Ted Hecht as Abdul Ben Bey, Gabriel Mooradian as the villain, Jack Reitzen as Ali Zing. **Writer:** David Chantler. **Director:** George Blair.

The Man Who Made Dreams Come True (airdate: Oct. 15, 1956). A con man convinces an aging European king that he can make his wishes come true. Preying on his superstitious nature, he plans to usurp the throne. **Guest cast:** Cyril Delevanti as King Leo, Keith Richards as the Dreamer, John Banner as Bronsky, Sandy Harrison as Ruby, Hal Hoover as Mike, Laurie Mitchell as Nancy Boyd. **Writer:** David Chantler. **Director:** George Blair.

Disappearing Lois (airdate: Oct. 22, 1956). Lois will do anything to get a story first, so in order to beat Clark to a big scoop, she fakes her disappearance from her apartment. While the confused Clark tries to find her, she sneaks into a gangster's hotel suite for an interview. But she and Jimmy accidentally stumble across some hidden stolen cash, and her desire for an exclusive story gets them both kidnapped. **Guest cast:** Milton Frome as Garrett, Ben Welden

as Lefty, Andrew Branham, Yvonne White as Sara Green. **Writers:** David Chantler and Peggy Chantler. **Director:** Harry Gerstad.

Close Shave (airdate: Oct. 29, 1956). Jimmy overhears a strange conversation while waiting for a haircut. It seems that the barber is using the power of suggestion to reform an old gangster. But the hood's friends are not amused, and Jimmy and the barber find themselves in a close shave with death. **Guest cast:** Rick Vallin as Rick Sable, Richard Bendict as Tony, Jack V. Littlefield as Mickey, Missy Russell, John Ferry as Trigger, Donald Diamond, Harry Fleer. **Writer:** Benjamin B. Crocker. **Director:** Harry Gerstad.

The Phony Alibi (airdate: Nov. 5, 1956). Professor Pepperwinkle's latest invention helps some criminals establish perfect alibis for their crimes. The device, a machine that can dematerialize human beings, sends them through a telephone line then rematerializes them on the other end, allowing the crooks to show up miles from the scenes of their crimes. Lois and Jimmy get involved in the situation, but are materialized in the frozen wastes of the Artic. **Guest cast:** John Cliff as Ed Crowley, Frank Kreig as Benny, Harry Arnie as Moe, William Challee as Clippy. **Writer:** Peggy Chantler. **Director:** George Blair.

The Prince Albert Coat (airdate: Nov. 19, 1956). A young boy pleads for Superman's help after he gives away his great grandfather's old coat to charity, not knowing that it contained the old man's life savings. While working on the case, the Man of Steel saves Jimmy and Lois from certain death and stops a devastating flood. **Guest cast:** Raymond Hatton as Mr. Jackson, Stephen Wooton as Bobby, Daniel White as Mike, Ken Christy as Mr. McCoy, Phil Arnold as Cueball, Jack Finch as Tom Summerfield, Claire DeBrey as Mrs. Craig, Frank Fenton as Mortimer Vanderlip. **Writer:** David Chantler. **Director:** Harry Gerstad.

The Stolen Elephant (airdate: Nov. 19, 1956). Some crooks have stolen a circus elephant that they hide in the barn of an old farm. Later, the boy who lives there finds the elephant and thinks it is a birthday present from his mother. Telling Clark about the wonderful gift brings a visit from Superman and the rounding up of the thieves. **Guest cast:** Gregory Moffet as Johnny Wilson, Thomas Jackson as Mr. Haley, Eve McVeigh as Mom, Gregg Martell as the butcher, Stanford Jolley as Spike. **Writer:** David Chantler. **Director:** Harry Gerstad.

Mr. Zero (airdate: Nov. 26, 1956). Mr. Zero, a small green alien from Mars, arrives on Earth and uses his power to paralyze people by pointing his finger at them. But he is still captured by criminals, bringing about Superman's first encounter with an alien. **Guest cast:** Billy Curtis as Mr. Zero, Herb Vigran as Georgie Gleap, George Barrows as Souchy Magoo, Leon Alton as the clerk, George Spotts as the Martian leader. **Writer:** Peggy Chantler. **Director:** Harry Gerstad.

Whatever Goes Up (airdate: Dec. 3, 1956). Jimmy playing the role of amateur scientist, which seems to pay off when he discovers an antigravity fluid. When some crooks find out that Olson can defy gravity, they figure they can defy the law and steal the secret formula to pull off some grand crimes. **Guest cast:** Tris Coffin as Major Osborne, Milton Frome as Gannis. **Writer:** Wilton Schiller. **Director:** Harry Gerstad.

SEASON SIX

The Last Knight (airdate: Sept. 16, 1957). While investigating the activities of a knighthood society, Lois and Jimmy are kidnapped by the secret association. Kent begins his own investigation, and discovers a plot to defraud an insurance company. **Guest cast:** Marshall Bradford as Sir Arthur, Paul Power as Sir Gwaine, Andrew Branham, Pierre Watkin as Sir Lancelot, Jason Johnson as Sir Henry, Ollie O'Toole, Thomas P. Dillon as the guard, Ronald Foster. **Writer:** David Chantler. **Director:** Thomas Carr.

The Magic Secret (airdate: Sept. 23, 1957). A Metropolis criminal is working with a scientist to devise a Kryptonite ray gun. Lois and Jimmy are kidnapped to lure Superman into a trap, one that features rapidly-closing walls to surround the superhero. **Guest cast:** Freeman Lusk as Grizwald, George Selk as Prof. Vom Bruiner, Jack Reynolds as a criminal, Buddy Lewis as Eddie, Kenneth Alton as a criminal. **Writers:** Robert Leslie Bellem and Whitnety Ellsworth. **Director:** Phil Ford.

Divide and Conquer (airdate: Sept. 30, 1957). Lois, Clark, and Perry are in a South America country when they see Superman rescue a political leader from certain danger. But the people who oppose the ruler arrest Superman and place him in jail. Since he cannot break the law, he devises a way to leave the cell by splitting his molecular structure into two Supermen. **Guest cast:** Everett Glass, Donald Lawton as President Bateo, Robert Tafur as Hernando Obregon, Jack Reitsen as Philippe Gonzales, Jack V. Littlefield as the jail keeper. **Writers:** Robert Leslie Bellem and Whitney Ellsworth. **Director:** Phil Ford.

The Mysterious Cube (airdate: Oct. 7, 1957). A criminal who has been wanted for seven years devises a way to beat the statute of limitations by hiding away in an impenetrable cube, made of an unusual concrete. But Superman tricks the crook into leaving his enclosure too early. **Guest cast:** Everett Glass as Prof. Lacerne, Ben Welden as Jody, Keith Richards as Steve, Bruce Wendell, Paul Barton, Joel Riordin, John Ayres as the admiral. **Writers:** Robert Leslie Bellem and Whitney Ellsworth. **Director:** George Blair.

The Atomic Captive (airdate: Oct. 14, 1957). A famous nuclear scientist defects to America, where he goes into hiding after being exposed to a high dose of radiation. Unaware of this, Lois and Jimmy are tracking the man down for an interview, while foreign agents - also ignorant of the danger of getting too close to the scientist - are trying to locate him in order to force him to return to their country. Worse still, none of them know they are in an area where a nuclear bomb is about to be exploded at any moment for a government test. **Guest cast:** Elaine Riley as Agent x-29, Jan Arvan as Agent x-249, Walter Reed as the general, Raskin Ben-Ari as Latilov, George Khoury as Nicoli, Mark Sheeler as Igor. **Writers:** Robert Leslie Bellem and Whitney Ellsworth. **Director:** George Blair.

The Superman Silver Mine (airdate: Oct. 21, 1957). A rich Texan is kidnapped by his criminal lookalike after he donates a silver mine to charity. Superman gets involved after the Texan's double has taken over his identity and kidnaps Lois and Jimmy. **Guest cast:** Dabbs Greer as Mr. Pebble and Dan, Charles Maxwell as Boris. **Writer:** Peggy Chantler. **Director:** George Blair.

The Big Forget (airdate: Oct. 28, 1957). Does everything Professor Pepperwinkle invent end up being used for crime? It seems so, because his latest concoction, an antimemory vapor, is stolen by thugs who use it to commit perfect crimes - ones where no one can even remember them happening. Superman also uses the spray to save his secret identity after it is exposed. **Guest cast:** Herb Vigran as Mugsy Maple, Billy Nelson as Knuckles Nelson. **Writer:** David Chantler. **Director:** George Blair.

The Gentle Monster (airdate: Nov. 4, 1957). Professor Pepperwinkle puts together a highly-advanced robot. The only problem is its source of power: a piece of Kryptonite, which Pepperwinkle is unaware of, and Superman doesn't find amusing when he discovers it. **Guest cast:** Ben Welden as Blade, John Vivyan, John Bennes, Orville Sherman as the scientist, Wilkie DeMatel as Mr. McTavish. **Writer:** David Chantler. **Director:** Howard Bretherton.

Superman's Wife (airdate: Nov. 11, 1957). A policewoman fakes a marriage to Superman to go undercover and trap a group of criminals. **Guest cast:** Joi Lansing, John Eldredge as Mr. X, John Bennes, Harry Arnie, Wayne Heffley as Duke Barlow. **Writers:** Robert Leslie Bellem and Whitney Ellsworth. **Director:** Lew Landers.

Three in One (airdate: Nov. 18, 1957). Three circus performers, the Strong Man, the Human Fly, and the Escape Artist, pull off incredible crimes that seem to take super-powers to commit, so Superman becomes the natural suspect. **Guest cast:** Sid Tomack, Rick Vallin as Pallini, Buddy Baer as Atlas, Craig Duncan as Tex Dawson. **Writers:** Wilton Schiller and Whitney Ellsworth. **Director:** Lew Landers.

The Brainy Burro (airdate: Nov. 25, 1957). Superman heads south to Mexico where a mind-reading donkey is forced to help commit crimes. **Guest cast:** Mark Cavell as Pepe, Ken Mayer as Albert, Marritz Hugo as Tiger, Edward LeVegue as Senor Luki, Mativitad Vacio as Tomeo, Sid Cassell. **Writers:** Wilton Schiller and Whitney Ellsworth. **Director:** Lew Landers.

The Perils of Superman (airdate: Dec. 2, 1957). Superman must save the Daily Planet staff (Lois from a locomotive, Perry from a huge saw, and Jimmy from a runaway car) when a gang of lead-masked criminals sets them up for murder. **Guest cast:** Michael Fox, Steve Mitchell, Andrew Branham, Missy Russell, Yvinne White. **Writers:** Robert Leslie Bellem and Whitney Ellsworth. **Director:** George Reeves.

All That Glitters (airdate: Dec. 9, 1957). Professor Pepperwinkle has devised a way to turn lead into gold, but the device knocks Jimmy unconscious. While asleep Jimmy dreams that he and Lois have somehow acquired the powers of the Man of Steel. **Guest cast:** Len Hendry as Mitchell, Jack Littlefield as Boots, Myrna Fahey, Richard Elliot as Mr. Colby, George Eldredge as Mr. Salem, Paul Cavauagh as Mr. Carter. **Writers:** Robert Leslie Bellem and Whitney Ellsworth. **Director:** George Reeves.

The Amazing Spider-Man year two cast: Ellen Bry as Julie Masters (left), Nicholas Hammond as Peter Packer (bottom), Robert F. Simon as J. Jonah Jameson (above), Chip Fields as Rita (right) and Nicholas Hammond as Spider-Man (top).

The Amazing Spider-Man

A Look Back at
The Amazing Spider-Man

article by Craig W. Frey, Jr.

I remember waiting with great excitement when CBS announced that it would be airing a two hour *Spider-Man* movie. It was 1977, and the science fiction/fantasy genre was basking in the glow caused by the box office explosion of *Star Wars*. Television was following suit with shows like *Battlestar Galactica*, *Salvage 1*, *Wonder Woman*, and *Project UFO* either already on the air, or in production.

And then there was *Spider-Man*. I had been a fan from the time I had first learned to read. My father brought home comics for me, and I was an avid watcher of the animated *Spider-Man* series. I was forever drawing him in the margins of my school notebooks, so it was no surprise that I was sitting in front of the television at 7:59 pm on September 14, 1977 turning the dial (remember those?) to the local CBS affiliate. And I watched as my favorite comic book hero came to life.

I was only ten years old when the film aired, and I was too thrilled with the prospect of *Spider-Man* becoming a series to be critical. Sixteen years later, however, it's hard to look at the show with the same exuberance. As a fan, I still have a soft spot for *The Amazing Spider-Man*; it is the only live-action version of the web-slinger around, after all. Even so, the series wasn't all that it could have been. Most of the stories were woefully simplistic and uneven, and except for the pilot, the Spider-Man costume worn by Nicholas Hammond was substandard. Looking back at the individual episodes, as will be done here, it becomes clear that although the show had its good points, *The Amazing Spider-Man* stands as another example of how a production's ambitions can be beyond the reach of its budgetary and storytelling abilities.

The pilot film, simply titled **Spider-Man**, while substantially changing the character's comic book origin, still remained basically true to the character. Peter Parker is a down-on-his-luck graduate physics student who is bitten by a spider which has absorbed violent amounts of radiation. In a freak twist of fate, Peter gains the proportionate strength and abilities of the spider. Later, when the father of one of his classmates is charged with a robbery he can't remember committing, Peter dons a costume and becomes Spider-Man in order to discover who's really behind the robberies.

Spider-Man works well in some respects. Nicholas Hammond makes a good Peter Parker; shy, beleaguered and confused when given powers beyond his imagination. The plot, while cliched, moves at a good pace and the production values were good for television. They also got the costume right.

The film fails, though, when it dramatizes Peter's motivation for becoming Spider-Man. In the comics, when Peter first gains his powers, he uses them to make money. He only becomes a costumed hero after neglecting to apprehend a thief who would later murder his Uncle Ben. The grief he feels over ignoring the responsibility his powers have thrust upon him drives him to fight against evil. This facet of Spider-Man's origin is discarded in the pilot film. Peter creates a costume and becomes Spider-Man "just because". He has these powers, why not use them to thwart the plans of evildoers? That and an anti-climactic ending mar an otherwise laudable attempt to bring Spider-Man to the screen.

Seven months later, the pilot film **Spider-Man** spawned the television series *The Amazing Spider-Man*. The series began with the two-part episode **The Deadly Dust**. The episodes started well, with Peter and some of his fellow students protesting their professor's decision to bring a canister of radioactive uranium on campus. A few of these students steal the uranium and build an atomic bomb just to show the professor how easy it is. An international illegal arms dealer named White finds out about the bomb, and plans to get his hands on it then sell it to the highest bidder. Peter, as Spider-Man, must stop White from obtaining the bomb while trying to save his friends, and keep his identity a secret from an attractive and nosey newspaper reporter sent from Florida to dig up dirt on Spider-Man.

The plot point of Peter Parker juggling problems as himself and as Spider-Man is pulled straight from the comics and works throughout the episodes to great effect. Unfortunately, that's about the only thing that does work. The uranium plot unravels when one of the students gets radiation poisoning. She is rushed to the hospital, then forgotten. Also, White, who is a wealthy and brilliant arms dealer, hires mindless thugs to obtain the bomb; a big lapse in judgment to say the least, not to mention an overused television cliche. Finally, someone, somewhere decided to make some changes to Spider-Man's costume. The skin-tight gloves and leggings were replaced with wide gauntlets and gaudy, plastic looking, wedge-soled boots, and his web-shooter and utility belt were worn outside the costume. This makes the character look clumsy and less dramatic than in the pilot film.

The Curse of Rava aired next. Even though the plot, concerning the desecration of the Kalastanian god Rava, is yet another cliche, this episode uses Spider-Man's powers to the best effect

since the pilot. During the episode's climax, Spider-Man leaps from floor-to-ceiling-to-wall and over furniture avoiding the psychic onslaught of Mandak, an evil Kalastanian priest. The look Spider-Man gives the camera after Mandak is defeated by the idol he sought to protect is priceless and pure comic book Spider-Man.

Night of the Clones takes a far-fetched idea and actually makes moderately effective use of it. Veteran genre actor Lloyd Bochner's portrayal of both the good and evil Dr. Moons is solid, as is the climactic battle between Spider-Man and his own evil twin. On the other hand, the notion of a human clone being created from a blood cell (let alone an evil clone that somehow retains the memories of the host) may have been suspenseful fifteen years ago, but it seems a little trite when current cloning technology is making real headlines. The biggest drawback to this episode however is Morgan Fairchild's portrayal of Lisa Benson; her acting is wooden and unconvincing. Closer observation of this episode also shows that she originally played the role with some kind of false accent, but her lines were re-recorded later minus the accent.

Escort to Danger, the last episode of the first year, ended the season on a low note. Once again an overused plot is resuscitated, and it's a plot that a character like Spider-Man doesn't fit into well. Political intrigue is an acceptable device for a character like James West from *The Wild Wild West*, but for a superhero it falls short. Add to that a flimsy secondary plot concerning a beauty pageant, and a forgettable episode arises. A perfect example of how slipshod **Escort to Danger** is comes from Peter Parker's allergy to tobacco. In a pivotal scene, Spider-Man's location if given away when he hides between sacks of tobacco, and indeed, Peter sneezes in the presence of J. Jonah Jameson's cigar. Unfortunately, this is the only episode where he reacts this way, even though Jameson smokes in many others.

The second season started better. **The Captive Tower** is a tight, action packed episode that pre-dates the plot of the film *Die Hard* by almost ten years. Ellen Bry was added to the cast as Julie Masters, a photographer for a rival newspaper, and a possible romantic interest for Peter Parker. Here, Peter must off her suspicions as he changes to Spider-Man and back again more than once to free the hostages (including himself) trapped by terrorists in a high-tech skyscraper. This episode only aired once on CBS, but it played on the USA Network once over Thanksgiving 1992, albeit edited to add room for more commercials.

A Matter of State was another cliche-ridden, political cover-up episode dealing with double-crossings, mistaken identities and stolen defense plans. It seems that little original thought went into the story, and it turns predictably into a hero-must-save-the-helpless-girl episode; the girl in this case being Julie Masters. It's a routine episode that brings down the high point at which the series started. By this time, CBS was starting to see the light when it came to *The Amazing Spider-Man*. The ratings for the original pilot were very good, but the series itself was struggling. After **A Matter of State**, CBS began airing episodes as specials, usually to fill sudden holes that came up in the schedule. That was pretty much the death knell for the show, which only aired five more times in the next ten months.

The Con Caper aired next. This episode, saddled with a silly title, seems now to be a showcase for actress Chip Fields' (Rita) singing talents more than anything else. The plot, such as it is, deals with a paroled politician who's comeback is a smokescreen for a daring prison break and robbery. Spider-Man is able to foil the plot, but the episode never generates much excitement, and the idea of a free concert set up to quell angry prison inmates is preposterous.

The Kirkwood Haunting is a run-of-the-mill "extortionist fakes haunting" story pulled straight from any episode of *Scooby Doo*, but it's actually fun to watch. It's interesting here to note that a series that postulates that Spider-Man can exist, and that psychic forces (**The Curse of Rava**) are real, also postulates that ghosts are fiction. Spider-Man discovers that the haunting is a fake in a routine fashion, but the scenes of him saving the nosey Julie Masters from wild animals that freely roam the "haunted" estate are enjoyable. The only real problem is that no one at the mansion figures out that

Peter Parker is Spider-Man, even though they continue to pop up alternately throughout the episode.

Photo Finish starts out as an intriguing mystery that quickly unravels and turns absurd. Peter Parker is covering a story about a rare coins collector·when he is struck from behind and the coins are stolen. A photo of the supposed thief turns up on a roll of his film, a photo he could not have taken. The picture implicates the ex-wife of the coin collector, but Peter has serious doubts about her guilt. Up to that point the story holds together. It collapses after Peter goes to jail because he refuses to give up the suspect photo. After he is incarcerated, he periodically escapes from his cell and continues to investigate the robbery as Spider-Man. How did Peter manage to smuggle his costume into the cell with him? How did he manage to leave the prison grounds (as Spider-Man no less) without anyone spotting him? These threadbare plot points make the story lose its mysterious edge and damage the story beyond repair.

Wolfpack is an episode that has its moments, though it suffers from the same affliction as almost every other episode; mediocrity. Some of Peter's college friends accidentally create a chemical that induces a kind of hypnosis. Once exposed to the chemical, a subject will do whatever is commanded, good or evil. A corrupt pharmaceuticals magnate plans to use the chemical for personal gain, but Spider-Man intervenes. The scenes of Spider-Man saving his classmates from a lab fire are exciting, but the rest of the episode loses momentum. At the end, Spider-Man gets the criminal to confess in front of the police by exposing him to the same hypnosis chemicals he had used on Peter's classmates. The police believe what they see without any real evidence, only the word of a man dressed in a red and blue costume. The story strains at the seams when Peter and his friends use real hypnosis to counteract the effects of the drug; they become experts very quickly. College physics must cover a lot more than $E=mc2$.

The final episode of *The Amazing Spider-Man* to air was the two hour movie **The Chinese Web**. It's too bad that this was the final episode, because if this was any indication, the series was in the midst of improving itself. The story was tight and well-paced, with a number of plots coming together at just the right speed. There was some political intrigue, but it was offset by a fair amount of action. Strong performances occur throughout the movie, especially from Nicholas Hammond, who played Peter Parker much more like an adult than in any other episode.

Of course, this is not to say that the film doesn't have its problems. The Spider-Man costume still looks silly, and when Peter and the others arrive in Hong Kong, the film turns into a tourist slide show, padding itself with pretty pictures instead of moving the story along. Still, the story actually works well, especially when it delves into the characters. When Peter leaves an attempt to kidnap Min Lo Chan so that he can change to Spider-Man, Chan's daughter, Emily, berates him and calls him a coward. Peter has developed feelings for Emily, but her scolding hurts him all the more because he can't tell her he's Spider-Man. After she discovers this on her own, she apologizes to him, and promises to keep his secret. Moments like these make **The Chinese Web** a real treat, and a credible ending to a series that struggled throughout its run.

The main problem with *The Amazing Spider-Man* is that is too often relied on lowest common denominators to act as support for flimsy plots. Chances are the producers figured they weren't making much than a "kiddie show" and allowed holes in the plot to remain in place, since kids never notice such things. That's too bad because they could have had a spectacular show on their hands if they had put more effort into it. At least they played it straight, and left out the campiness of the original *Batman* series, or the later *Superman* films. They treated the character of Spider-Man with some respect, even if they never really got him quite right. Rumor

has it that genre film director James Cameron is planning to do a big screen, big-budget version of Spider-Man for a possible 1995 release. Perhaps a major motion picture will be able to do justice to the web-slinger in ways that the series couldn't. But if the film doesn't happen, at least fans of Spider-Man can look back at the series and say that somebody tried.

The Amazing Spider-Man

review by William E. Anchors, Jr.

Production credits:

Executive Producers	Charles Fries
	Daniel R. Goodman
Music and theme (year 1)	Stu Phillips
Music and theme (year 2)	Dana Kaproff
Spider-Man creator	Stan Lee

Regular cast:

Spider-Man/Peter Parker	Nicholas Hammond
J. Jonah Jameson	Robert F. Simon
Captain Barbara	Michael Pataki (season one)
Rita	Chip Fields
Julie Masters	Ellen Bry (season two)

Number of episodes:	1 two hour pilot movie, 11 one hour segments, 1 two hour movie

Premise: The adventures of Spider-Man, the web-swinging teenage superhero with the senses and abilities of a spider.

Editor's comments: Not a bad show, but not a great one either. Unfortunately, CBS never gave the show time to develop, and rarely showed it on a regular basis so it could find a following. The series is seen fairly often now in movie format (see the end of this article). In 1993, for the first time in fifteen years *The Amazing Spider-Man* was shown in its original one hour format by the Sci-Fi Channel. A few episodes have been released in uncut form on prerecorded tape and laser disc.

Spider-Man (airdate: Sept. 14, 1977, two hour pilot movie). Important people are acting strangely all over the city, and are performing crimes under some kind of mental influence. Afterwards, they have no memory of the deeds. Someone later contacts a local tv station and states that unless the city pays a ransom of $50,000,000 he will use his mind control to kill ten important people. Meanwhile, at a lab that Peter Parker works at, a spider is hit with a dose of radiation from an experiment, and it bites the student. The results are amazing: he develops incredible powers and senses similar to a spider. At first he puts his wall-climbing skills to work obtaining great photographs that he can sell to J. Jonah Jameson and the editor's newspaper. But Jameson isn't interested - he only wants pictures of the "spider-man" that winos have been seeing climbing the alley walls - not believing a word of it. So Parker uses this as an inspiration. He makes himself a costume, calls himself Spider-Man, and produces pictures for the newspaper. But Parker's more immediate problem is the madman who, as promised, is killing people all over the city. [This TV movie predated the series by seven months and was titled *Spider-Man*, although the series itself was titled *The Amazing Spider-Man*, and some of the cast were different than the series.] **Cast**: Nicholas Hammond as Peter Parker/Spider-Man, David White [*Bewitched*] as J. Jonah Jameson, Thayer David [*Dark Shadows*] as Edward Byron, Michael Pataki as Capt. Barbera, Robert Hastings as Monahan, Jeff Donnell, Mary Ann Kasica as Aunt May, Lisa Eilbacher as Judy Tyler, Ivor Francis as Prof. Noah Tyler, Hilly Hicks as Robbie Robinson, Barry Cutler as the delivery man, Len Lesser, Jim Storm, Ivan Bonnar, Norman Rice, Harry Cesar, George Cooper, Roy West, James E. Brodhead, Carmelita Pope, Kathryn Reynolds, Robert Snively, Ron Gilbert, Larry Anderson. **Writer**: Alvin Boretz. **Director**: E.W. Swackhamer.

SEASON ONE

The Deadly Dust, parts one and two (airdates: part one, April 5, 1978; part two, April 12, 1978). A woman is about to jump from a skyscraper, but Spider-Man comes to the rescue. Returning to the Daily Bugle, Parker finds an upset editor because the reporter didn't get any photos of Spider-Man saving the jumper. Meanwhile, in Miami a reporter for the *Examiner* is ordered to fly to New York and get the story on Spider-Man - by staying at all times with Peter Parker, the only person to get photos of the superhero! Back in New York at the college Parker attends part time, a Dr. Baylor has brought into the school plutonium oxide over Parker's and everyone else's objections. He rejects their opinion that the material could be stolen and turned into a bomb, or that his security precautions are insufficient. Dr. Baylor ignores all objections and will not listen to reason. Parker's friends talk him into trying to convince Jameson to do an expose, but the editor isn't interested. Instead, he introduces Parker to Gale, the beautiful and wily female reporter from Miami. Unfortunately, this means that Spider-Man will be unable to function at a time he is needed the most, as Peter's college friends have stolen the uranium (which the police believe Spider-Man has taken), and they plan to make a functional atomic bomb to show how dangerous it is to have the material commonly available. **Guest cast**: JoAnna Cameron [*Blade Runner*] as Gale, Robert Alda as White, Randy Powell [*Logan's Run*] as Gregg, Simon Scott as Dr. Baylor, Anne Bloom as Carla, Steven A. Anderson as Ted, Herbert S. Braha as LeBeau, Emil Farkas as Benson, Richard Kyker as Angel, Sid Clute as Di Carlo, Leigh Kavanaugh as Linda, Ron Hajek as the salesman, David Somerville as the singer, Gail Jensen as the singer, Walt Davis as the helicopter repairman, Barbara Sanders as the waitress, Jerry Martin as the doorman. **Writer**: Robert Janes. **Director**: Ron Satlof.

The Curse of Rava (airdate: April 19, 1978). Parker has been assigned to cover an exhibit in town on Rava, an ancient Kalastan god who supposedly places a curse on unbelievers who come in contact with him. Meanwhile, at the Bolt Museum where the artifacts are being shown, a Kalastanian native is complaining that "unbelievers" must not be allowed to gaze at the cursed statue. The curator refuses to stop the showing, so the man begins chanting. Suddenly the statue seems to come to life and cause a sword to narrowly miss the terrified museum operator. Later, Parker arrives to write his story just as a mob of Kalastanian picketers begin attacking the museum. They are run off by the arrival of Spider-Man, but afterwards Jameson shows up, furious that the display he is financing is being wrecked. An associate requests that Jameson send the religious cult statues back to their native land to avoid any further trouble. Jameson refuses moments before the statue of Rava tips over and crushes the man. Jameson is arrested for murder, and may lose his job in four days if he misses a stock board meeting. When Spider-Man/Parker investigates, he finds that the man who threatened the curator has been behind all the events. **Guest cast**: Theodore Bikel as Mandak, Adrienne LaRussa as Trina, Byron

Webster as Rusten, David Ralphe as Dr. Keller. **Writers:** Dick Nelson and Robert Janes. **Director:** Michael Caffey.

Night of the Clones (airdate: April 26, 1978). Jameson is involved with the selection of the prestigous Tovald award, and Parker is sent to attend a press conference of an important scientist who is bitter over never having received the award. The doctor has been doing clone research, the result of which is an evil duplicate of himself who begins killing award judges - without the knowledge of the original Dr. Moon. At the conference, Dr. Moon explains that he has developed a form of rapid cloning that can produce a duplicate of its original within hours. Later, Jameson is furious that Peter didn't get pictures of the elevator crash that killed two judges. The editor orders Parker to cover a costume ball that night that the remaining judges will be attending. Parker can't afford a costume, so he goes as Spider-Man! Unfortunately, the evil clone has had a confrontation with Dr. Moon and knocked him out. Now the duplicate Moon has created a clone of Peter Parker, and that night the cloned Moon and a new Spider-Man put into operation a plan to kill the judges and Peter Parker. **Guest cast:** Morgan Fairchild as Lisa Benson, Lloyd Bochner as Dr. Moon, Rick Traeger as Dr. Reichman, Irene Tedrow as Aunt May. **Writer:** John W. Bloch. **Director:** Ron Satlof.

Escort to Danger (airdate: May 3, 1978). Jameson is upset because Parker spent the evening with a glamorous actress, but didn't get any pictures of her. He is ordered to the airport where foreign President Calderon and his daughter Maria are arriving. Just after Parker reaches this destination, he sees an unknown man being kidnapped. Spider-Man goes to his rescue but the criminals get away. Returning to work, Parker is in trouble again for not getting pictures of the president. But he manages to wrangle the assignment of getting an interview with the president and his daughter, which he does by arranging to be her chaperon in a beauty contest she is appearing at. Meanwhile, he continues to investigate the kidnapping, not yet knowing that Maria is to be the next kidnap victim, perpetrated by a political party from her home country that opposes

her father's rule. **Guest cast:** Alejandro Rey as President Calderon, Barbara Luna as Lisa Alvarez, Madeline Stowe as Maria Calderon, Harold Sakata as Matsu, Michael Marsellos as Sauti, Lachelle Price as Kim Barker, Bob Minor as Curt Klein. **Writer:** Duke Sandefur. **Director:** Dennis Donnelly.

SEASON TWO

The Captive Tower (airdate: Sept. 5, 1978). Parker is assigned to cover a big shindig at a newly-built, ultra-modern building because Jameson is attending. At the high-rise, Parker notices the arrival of Julie Masters, ace reporter for a competing paper who is constantly stealing Peter's scoops. He is interested in her romantically despite Julie putting a kink in his career. They head upstairs to keep track of the boring event, not realizing that the day is going to become exciting very soon: terrorists are at that moment closing down the building and getting ready to hold everyone inside - including Peter "Spider-Man" Parker - as hostage. **Guest cast:** David Sheiner as Forster, Todd Susman as Farnum, Fred Lerner as Duke, Barry Cutler as Barry, Warren Vanders as Hammer, Ed Sancho-Bonet as Ramirez. **Writers:** Gregory S. Dinallo, Bruce Kalish, John Philip Taylor. **Director:** Cliff Bole.

A Matter of State (airdate: Sept. 12, 1978). Arriving at a crowded airport, a government agent carrying a briefcase of top-secret papers is attacked and his documents are stolen. The airport is closed so that no one can leave while the police are looking for the case, and a cover story is released of the airport being placed in quarantine. Reporters Peter and Julie arrive to cover the story, but Peter is suspicious that there may be more going on than the police are admitting to. Meanwhile, the thieves escape with the papers, their only problem being that Julie accidentally photographed one of the three men involved in the robbery. They realize this and follow her. Luckily Peter's spider-senses warn him of danger and he trails Julie too. One of the thieves attacks the female reporter and steals her film. Spider-Man comes to the rescue, but captures the wrong man while the real thief gets away. Peter returns to work only to find that Julie seems to have disappeared. Worse still, one of the three thieves who has the stolen defense plans is also the FBI agent Julie took the photo of, and after finding out that his men took the wrong film from her, he wants Julie out of the way - permanently. **Guest cast:** Nicholas Coster as Andre, John Crawford [*The Powers of Matthew Star*] as Evans, Michael Santiago as Carl, James Victor as Martin. **Writer:** Howard Dimsdale. **Director:** Larry Stewart.

The Con Caper (airdate: Nov. 25, 1978). A paroled politician plans a comeback after being released from prison, even though it is illegal for him to do so. James Colbert claims he still has a desire to serve the people of the state, and Julie Masters gets him to admit that he wants to be involved in prison reform. The ex-politician ends up at the office at J. Jonah Jameson, where he pleads for the editor's support in getting him an official position within the prison system. Not long after leaving Jamison's office, Colbert is informed that a prison riot has occurred and prisoners have been taken. Rita tries to convince Jameson to assist Colbert in getting appointed because he had been helpful to her in the past. The gruff editor finally agrees to do so. Parker falls under the spell of the ex-convict as well, no one realizing that the prison riot is being faked by some of his colleagues in order for him to pull off a scheme - the robbery of $50,000,000 from a high-security vault. **Guest cast:** William Smithers as James Colbert, Ramon Bieri as Cates, Andrew Robinson as McTeague, Fred Downs as Warden Rischer. **Writers:** Gregory S. Dinallo and

Brian McKay. **Director:** Tom Blank.

Kirkwood Haunting (airdate: Dec. 30, 1978). Peter is called in to Jameson's office, where the editor tells him about a friend in the military who was recently accidentally killed. Jameson shows Parker a letter from the dead man's wife, Lisa Kirkwood, who writes to say she is selling her house because her dead husband is haunting it! Jameson thinks that the haunting may be a scheme to bilk the woman out of the fortune she inherited, so he sends Peter to investigate the situation. When Parker arrives at the Kirkwood mansion, he finds a "psychic researcher" at the home, hired by Mrs. Kirkwood - a prime candidate for the person faking the mysterious happenings. **Guest cast:** Marlyn Mason as Lisa Kirkwood, Peter MacLean as Dr. Anthony Polarsky, Paul Carr [*Voyage to the Bottom of the Sea*] as Ganz, Peggy McCay as Dr. Davis, Del Monroe [*Voyage to the Bottom of the Sea*] as the thug. **Writer:** Michael Michaelian. **Director:** Don McDougall.

Photo Finish (airdate: Feb. 7, 1979). J. J. Jameson tells Parker about a story he is working on about rare coins, then sends Peter to one of Jameson's collector friends for information. Weldan Gray explains that he loves old coins, but he must sell his collection because of his ex-wife. While the man is talking to Peter, his spider senses warn him of danger, but he is still knocked out from behind, as is Gray, then $800,000 worth of coins are stolen. After the police arrive, Peter leaves and develops his photos - and finds there is one extra - showing Mrs. Gray with a gun. But Parker becomes convinced of her innocence and will not give the police the photo - a situation that may reveal his secret identity, and lands him in jail. **Guest cast:** Jennifer Bilingsley as Mrs. Gray, Charles Haid [*Hill Street Blues*] as the police lieutenant, Geoffrey Lewis as Weldan Gray, Milt Kogan. **Writer:** Howard Dimsdale. **Director:** Tony Ganz.

Wolfpack (airdate: Feb. 21, 1979). Peter is helping out a student friend on a project he is working on when a soccer ball is accidentally thrown through the college lab window, knocking over vials and starting a fire. Spider-Man arrives at the right moment to save the day, but the project for Sorgason Chemicals to develop a consciousness control drug is badly damaged. When Peter talks to J.J. Jameson later, the editor is suspicious of the project - and the administrator of Sorgason Chemicals, who was once jailed for stealing drug formulas. Back at the lab, Mr. Hansen arrives to tell David that his company is withdrawing all support for the school, as the work being done has not produced anything of commercial value. David pleads with him to examine a new batch of drugs. Hansen stays, but an assistant adds in an incorrect chemical which causes a cloud of smoke - and Hansen is amazed when everyone who hears his voice obeys his every command. The corrupt manufacturer realizes he has the perfect new drug that will make him a fortune - by using it for criminal activity. **Guest cast:** Gavan O'Herlihy as David, Wil Selzer as Art, Allan Arbus as George Hansen. **Writer:** Steve Kandel. **Director:** Joe Manduke.

The Chinese Web (airdate: July 6, 1979, special two hour episode). A man arrives at the guard-surrounded home of a wealthy art collector named Mr. Zeider. He is informed that Min Lo Chan has just left for New York, where new evidence can prove his innocence of charges he is wanted on in China - which will result in Mr. Zeider losing a one billion dollar construction contract. As such, Min Lo Chan must be killed while in the city. Meanwhile, at the office of J.J. Jameson, a friend arrives to talk to him. It is the same Min Lo Chan,

who explains he is looking for three marines who will clear him of the espionage charges that China has against him, as they were witnesses to his refusal to cooperate with the enemy. Jameson agrees to help and sends out reporter Parker to track down the three soldiers. While he and Min go through some records at a government office, Peter's spider-senses detect an assassin coming. He is forced to find a way to change into Spider-Man without his secret identity being revealed, and stop the gun-toting henchman - the first of many sent out to eliminate Min. **Guest cast:** Benson Fong [*Kung Fu*] as Min Lo Chan, Rosalind Chao as Emily Loo T'ao, Hagan Beggs as Evans, Richard Erdman as Zeider, Myron Healey as Lt. Olson, John Milford, Anthony Charnotta as Quinn, George Cheung as Dr. Pai, Tony Clark as Joe, Ted Danson as Major Collins, Michael Mancini as Bertino, Robert Mayo as Lou, Arnold F. Turner as Abbott, Herman Tweeder as the hot dog vendor, Zara Brierley, Peter Wong, Suzanne Vale, Hudson Lueng, Michael Chan, Eric Wile. **Writer:** Lionel E. Siegal. **Director:** Don McDougall.

MOVIES

The following movies have been released for syndication.
Spider-Man (2 hour movie).
The Chinese Web (2 hour movie).
Spider-Man Strikes Back (2 hour movie, released overseas only). Contains **Deadly Dust part one** and **Deadly Dust part two**.
The Dragon's Challenge (2 hour movie, released overseas only). A retitled version of **The Chinese Web**.
Photo Finish/Matter of State (Made up of **Photo Finish** and **A Matter of State**).
The Deadly Dust (Made up of **The Deadly Dust part one** and **The Deadly Dust part two**).
Wolfpack/Kirkwood Haunting (Made up of **Wolfpack** and **Kirkwood Haunting**).
Night of the Clones/Escort to Danger (Made up of **Night of the Clones** and **Escort to Danger**).
Con Caper/Curse of Rava (Made up of **The Con Caper** and **The Curse of Rava**).

The Flash

TV's
The Flash

A Behind-the-Scenes Analysis of the Fastest Man Alive

article by Robert Alan Crick

This writer will never forget the day, some eleven years ago, when a high school pal and comic book fanatic delivered this dire update on *The Flash*: Iris West Allen, beloved wife of police scientist Barry Allen - a.k.a. the Flash, the Scarlet Speedster, the Fastest Man Alive - was dead!

It seemed that several issues back, the evil Professor Zoom, the insidious "Reverse Flash" from the distant future, had vibrated the molecules of his hand at superspeed into Iris' skull and, with a single jab, destroyed the delicate structure of her brain! Barry Allen's sweet, devoted wife - my ideal fantasy mate from the comic book I had once followed with such interest only a few years before - was gone, and I had missed it while my adolescent attention had strayed into the worlds of *Star Trek* and secret agent James Bond.

Surprises like this can happen in the blink of an eye in comic books - especially one like *The Flash*, in which speed is literally "what it's all about". *The Flash* was one of the best in the DC line during the 1970s (a time when DC was rapidly losing favor to Marvel, with its hip, grittier edge). Eventually, it would also become one of the many cancelled network TV series of the year 1990 - and one of its best.

Even so, it had always seemed unlikely that anyone would ever make a movie or television series out of *The Flash* the way they had *Superman*, *Batman*, *Wonder Woman*, and other DC successes. Long-time comic book fans, of course, knew who the Flash was - knew all about his wife Iris, his nephew Wally West (secretly Kid Flash), his friend Jay Garrick (the "Golden Age" Flash from a parallel Earth) and his foes (The Pied Piper, Captain Boomerang, Heat Wave, Captain Cold, The Mirror Master, Professor Zoom, The Trickster, just to name a few). But the average executive or house-wife probably didn't have a clue; somehow the Flash had never become a household name the way DC's *Superman*, *Batman*, and *Wonder Woman* had.

It was doubtful too whether any studio would want to put up the money it would take to make a video version of *The Flash* a reality; the special effects for such a production would surely be murderous. Even as a comic book, the Flash was one of the hardest characters ever to bring to life; just making him run from one end of a room to another in a single panel could be nightmare - all those dozens of little red Flashes drawn in dozens of different running positions in flip-it book style, his jagged lightning bolt and Mercury wing insignias trailing behind like inky yellow ribbons.

Then too, there was the question of whether even clever effects work could make the Scarlet Speedster convincing to the camera trick-savvy audiences of the 1990s. The *Superman* TV series had awed children in the 1950s, but the old actor-lying-on-a-glass-table technique used to make George Reeves fly on TV was considered "old hat" long before the big screen movie with Christopher Reeve was made in 1978.

Yet somebody did make the attempt - and, for a few brief months in 1990, network television was a better place for it. *The Flash* may not have been everything fans of the comic book hoped it might be, to be sure; comic book adaptations almost never satisfy the fans who made the characters famous to begin with. *The Flash* was no artistic failure, however - far from it. Yes, CBS's air time might have been better spent on documentaries, live produc-tions of the great stage plays, educational programming, and news, but for what it was *The Flash* was certainly tremendous fun to watch.

And one really did have to watch the show, too. If all the telephone clicks, rings, and buzzes made playwright Lucille Fletcher's *Sorry, Wrong Number* "pure radio" in the 1940s, the blurs, streaks, and color splashes of *The Flash* made the CBS series "pure television" - a visual feast. Iron the bedsheets or read the newspaper while *The Flash* was on, and one was certain to miss the best visuals the small screen had to offer. Weekly action-adventure TV had never looked so good - or, it must be said, moved quite so fast.

The comic book version of *The Flash* had been the 1940 brainchild of a talented gentleman named Gardner Fox, whose original Flash character had been named not Barry Allen but Jay Garrick. Garrick's super speed came about because - in one of those remarkable super power-endowing lab accidents so fre-quent in comic books - he accidentally inhaled the fumes of a powerful substance called "hard water". Thanks to 1940s science gone awry, the comics' original Flash had arrived.

Fashioning himself a simple, maskless uniform comprised of bright blue trousers and a long-sleeved red shirt with a yellow lightning bolt on its front (sometimes yellow lightning streaks adorned his trouser legs, too), Garrick patterned the rest of his attire after traditional artistic renderings of the Greek speedster Mercury, messenger of the gods - complete with the usual yellow wings affixed to both sides of his rounded WWI doughboy cap (courtesy of comic book "poetic license", it never fell off no matter how fast Garrick ran) and one just above the outer ankles of his Robin Hood-style red boots. Fox's creation was soon one of the most memorable heroes of the 1940s - a period which would eventually come to be known as the "Golden Age" of American comic books.

In his introduction to the book *The Greatest Flash Stories Ever Told*, DC executive Mike Gold credits "the very simplicity" of its basic premise as making the Jay Garrick Flash so popular among 1940s comics fans. "Almost everybody could run, and

The Flash: **John Wesley Shipp as Barry Allen/The Flash and Amanda Pays as Dr. Christina "Tina" McGee.**

anybody could imagine the benefits of being able to run faster," Gold observes. "The ability to run was among the ways boys measured their success in gym class and on baseball sandlots. It was easy to understand the desire of being able to sleep later and still make your classes on time. The Flash showed boys of that pre-war era what might happen if they could only run faster... like he could."

Clearly this "wish fulfillment" factor had a great deal to do with it. What boy or girl (but especially boys, the comics' biggest fans) has not imagined how magnificent it would be to outrun track stars, schoolbuses, locomotives, bullets - or even the snarling neighbor-

hood dog whose house one must silently sneak by on foot for fear of one's life?

Unfortunately for the Flash's most loyal fans, during the 1950s, the popularity of super-hero comics had waned considerably, with only a handful of favorites like Superman, Batman and Wonder Woman surviving at all. The Flash, it seemed, could outrun many things, but not the marketing department. Jay Garrick's exploits, like those of so many great super-heroes, had been crushed by plummeting revenue. Into this arena of floundering sales entered resident DC science fiction enthusiast Julius Schwartz. As editor for some of the key DC titles, the now-legendary Schwartz would play a major role in reviving interest in the few surviving super-heroes and in revamping some who had fallen by the way - including the once mighty speedster The Flash.

It was Schwartz and his co-workers at the "new and improved" DC who took the original great but nearly forgotten Flash concept and helped breathe new life into it. Before long, DC writer Robert Kanigher came up with a whole new identity and origin for The Flash making him more modern and astonishing than even the original from the 1940s. The original Jay Garrick was no more (not dead of course, just in a handy parallel universe the new Scarlet Speedster could pop over to every now and then), and in his place was Kanigher's "Flashier" Flash, a handsome, brilliant - but persistently tardy - young police scientist named Barry Allen.

In Kanigher's original script (for Issue #4 of *Showcase Comics*), the new Flash's origin was as follows: while Barry Allen was working late in his police lab in Central City during a violent thunderstorm, a lightning bolt crashed through the window, striking both Barry and his well-stocked shelves full of hundreds of lab chemicals. Their composition drastically altered by the lightning's powerful energy, the structurally new fluids showered upon Barry's body, drenching him - and transforming his entire atomic structure forever.

It was difficult for even Barry to know precisely which combination of chemicals had soaked his unconscious form (after all, had all the chemicals been transformed by the lightning's electrical heat, or only some?), but the result was soon apparent. Barry found himself with unbelievable super speed, and with virtually complete control over his own atoms. Tardiness need never again be a problem for Barry Allen; he was now every bit as fast as the lightning bolt which had transformed him - perhaps faster.

In fact, if he chose, Barry could vibrate every molecule of his body at such intense speeds that he could actually pass through solid objects - brick walls for instance - or vibrate himself into invisibility if it was necessary to listen in on a villain's plot undetected. If shot at, Barry could vibrate and allow the bullet to pass right through him, or spin like a top to deflect the bullet the way a whirling fan might deflect an object tossed inside. For that matter, he could even catch the bullet before it could strike somebody else, passing his hand on a parallel course with it the way a baseball player might scoop up a baseball moving parallel to the movement of his glove.

Barry's super speed had other advantages as well. Running faster than gravity could pull against him, Barry could race up the side of a building, and blast across the surface of a lake or an ocean. Rushing past a group of criminals with guns, Barry could create a speed vacuum of such incredible suction that he could pull the criminals, arms and legs flailing, right along with him across town and onto the very doorstep of the Central City Police Department. Zipping past a public fountain, Barry could use this speed vacuum the same way to yank along the fountain's contents and then deposit the water on a raging fire to save the day.

And all of this was still just a start! If it all sounds fantastic and like loads of fun, that's because it was; the new "Silver Age" Flash introduced in Showcase #4 was one of the most thrilling comic book heroes of his day.

With Joe Kubert slated as the new comic's original inker, penciller Carmine Infantino was responsible for the Flash's new costume - a magnificent blending of the old with the new altering the future of super-hero costumes forever. The yellow Mercury wings affixed to the boots and temple areas were still there, but this time the boots were yellow and less Robin Hood-ish, and the old doughboy-style hat was replaced by a Batman-like cowl (minus the menacing pointed nosepiece). Except for the tall boots, the whole

outfit had a skintight one-piece look, a bright red long underwear design with the cowl affixed. The Jay Garrick lightning bolt was still there too, but smaller and emblazon atop a white circle, and another jagged lightning design (inspired by the bolt which had given Barry his speed to begin with) encircled Barry's waist like a belt, while another raced around Barry's sleeves just below the elbows.

In his introduction to *The Greatest Flash Stories Ever Told*, Mike Gold describes the unique appeal of the Flash costume, calling it "unlike any ever seen on a super-hero: Capeless, not merely form-fitting but apparently welded to the human body," A costume "at once simple and ultra-modern." As Gold observes, in this sleek red-and-yellow creation, "The Flash stood out in every crowd of heroes."

It was indeed one of the best superhero costumes ever, so perhaps it should be no surprise that it, like Barry, had its share of special tricks. Whenever Barry was out of uniform and trouble broke out, the young scientist would duck quickly out of sight and press a button on his special yellow "costume ring" - an amazing little device Barry had designed himself. In a split second, a spring within the ring would expel a tiny, compressed red-and-yellow package, and in contact with the air it would unfold and expand into Barry's full-size Flash costume. In less time than it takes to read this sentence, Barry would change into his Flash costume, and, now a crimson and gold blur, race off to save the day.

With this formula, *The Flash* soon became a comic book all its own. Barry's girlfriend Iris became his wife; his nephew Wally (in an absolutely mind-boggling repeat of the first "random" lightning-and-chemicals lab accident, which later turned out to be not so random after all) became Kid Flash; Barry discovered he could spin like a top from his own "Earth One" to "Earth Two" to team up with his hero and pal Jay Garrick (a character Barry had originally assumed to be a fictitious comics hero before learning he really did exist on a parallel world); the new Flash joined the Justice League of America right alongside DC greats like Batman, Superman and Wonder Woman; and Central City, soon the home of its own Flash Museum, developed a rogues gallery of costumed villains second only to those created by Bob Kane for Batman's dark and dangerous Gotham City (and, in the newspapers, by Chester Gould for Dick Tracy's big city crime world).

In the early 1980s, of course, Iris was done away with (later, highly complicated science-fiction plotlines somehow managed to revive her), and even Barry himself died bravely in the line of duty outracing the hundreds of times faster than the speed of light beam of anti-matter cannon fired towards Earth. Barry was replaced by former Kid Flash Wally West (who, adopting a larger version of the altered outfit Barry had given him as a young boy, abandoned his later teenager-hip mostly yellow costume for a design once again virtually identical to Barry's). Wally's super-speed abilities were more limited than Barry's - slightly less fantastic and much more physically demanding, though to the delight of long-time fans, even Barry was eventually revived somehow for future storylines (nobody really stays dead in comic books), able once again to dazzle readers with his breathtaking ability to outrun almost anything imaginable.

Fortunately, it was the Barry Allen Flash which first-time TV series creators Danny Bilson and Paul De Meo chose to bring to the small screen for CBS in 1990 (Jay Garrick was always a little too old-fashioned and Wally West too self-centered and cocky to really root hard for). Originally the pair had something far stranger in mind, however. According to Marc Shapiro in "Night of the Scarlet Speedster" - a November 1990 *Starlog* article - in the script they had

prepared (set in the future, its title was **Unlimited Powers**), the offspring of DC heroes The Flash, Green Arrow, Dr. Occult and Legion of Super-Heroes member Blok would team up to do battle with the forces of evil.

The Unlimited Powers script went nowhere, but CBS President of Entertainment Jeff Sagansky thought it was time the network made another stab at a superhero-inspired TV show (it had been

nearly ten tears since their last real hit in this genre, the popular Marvel comics-inspired series *The Incredible Hulk*). It was Sagansky who gave Bilson and De Meo the go-ahead to executive produce a weekly series based on an individual comics character. Fortunately, the team decided that special effects technology had finally caught up with the times, and that the Silver Age version of *The Flash* might make for some exciting - if expensive - small screen visuals.

Stephen Hattman took on the role of supervising producer for the series for episodes two through eleven, while Don Kurt, a producer on episodes one through ten, accepted the supervising producer tasks from episode twelve on. Also credited as producers for the elaborate and costly program were Gail Morgan Hickman, Steven Long Mitchell, and Craig W. Van Sickle, while its co-producers were Michael Lance and (starting with episode eleven) David L. Beanes. Frank Jiminez was assigned the varied duties of associate producer.

Bilson and De Meo personally took charge of the script for the two-hour pilot episode (an important decision, since only they knew how "comic book-ish" they wanted the series to end up), with Ray Quiroz serving as script supervisor through episode seven. Gillian Murphy would take over as script supervisor from then on, while Howard Chaykin and John Francis Moore were assigned the roles of story editors for the full twenty-two episodes of the series.

Perhaps the program's real behind-the-scenes stars, however, were the team members behind the special "look" of the series. Sandi Sissel served as director of photography on the pilot, with Francis Kenny, John C. Newby, and Greg Gardiner accepting the position at various points during the series' run. As production designers, Bilson and De Meo tapped the talents of Dean Edward Mitzner, Richard Fernandez, Peter A. Samish and Francis J. Pezzer. Bill Myer and Rolf Keppler served as make-up supervisors, while the show's costume designers (excluding the special Flash costume, of course) were Bob Miller and Le Dawson.

Aided by conceptual designer Dave Stevens (creator of the comic book feature which inspired Bilson and De Meo's 1990 big-screen film *The Rocketeer*), Robert Short "designed and created" the $300,000 red-and-yellow Flash outfit, which was (thankfully) patterned after the original Carmine Infantino ahead-of-its-time creation for 1956. Fans of the comic book must have been instantly pleased with the resulting outfit. Beyond the slight cowl alteration (in what was, arguably, an ever-so-slightly misguided attempt to make the TV Flash a scowling vigilante of the *Batman* movie variety, a beak-like nosepiece was added), a minor reworking of the original lightning streak chest emblem and the belt and glove markings (they no longer looked like just part of the fabric, and the belt now pointed arrow-like to just below Barry's stomach), and the switch from yellow boots to red (minus the Mercury wings) - the costume looked, from a distance at least, more or less like Carmine Infantino's original comics creation.

On close inspection, of course, the ten-pound costume, with its Spandex and foam rubber (all sprayed with special electrostatic nylon), the suit may have been less impressive. This thick, velvety-looking creation seemed unlikely to fit into even the most ingenious finger ring - or be flexible and thin enough to be worn beneath the hero's costume, the way *Spider-Man*'s Peter Parker often wore his. Still, efforts to emulate *Batman* with the sinister cowl redesign and muscle-enhancing curves notwithstanding, fans who were troubled by the complete overhaul given to the traditional Batman costume in that 1989 movie (the comic's thin tuck-in-your-cape-and-wear-it-under-your-business suit cloth costume became a thick rubber suit of armor so sturdy that star Michael Keaton often seemed stiff as a board even when walking or just moving his head!) were pleasantly surprised. The TV Flash's costume might have to be carried inside an aluminum suitcase, but at least it wouldn't keep series star John Wesley Shipp from doing what the Flash was born to do - run.

Much of the credit for this goes to David Stipes and Robert D. Bailey, the pilot episode's visual effects supervisors who, with special effects co-ordinator Bill Schirmer, helped make The Flash seem to move like lightning. Patrick Clancy and Peter W. Mayer added to the feeling of physical freedom as the visual effects editors, and Philip Barberio served as visual effects co-ordinator. Special video effects came from effects wizards of The Post Group, and certainly the contributions in the pilot of stuntman Dane Farwell and stunt co-ordinator Billy Burton (returning later for episodes two and four, with Fred Lerner taking over for episode three and from episode five on) added much to the belief that Barry had considerably more flexibility in his costume than actor Shipp probably had in real life.

The casting for the pilot was splendid, even if offbeat. Though familiar to some soap opera audiences, actor John Wesley Shipp was a virtual unknown to ninety-nine percent of the viewing audience, but he was handsome, witty, pleasant, and engaging in the role of Barry Allen. Shipp was perhaps more muscular and "beefy" than the comic books' fit but slender hero (he somehow seemed younger, too, and more the "swinging single" type), but he was also too winningly lighthearted and likeable (with great comic instincts) to seem like just another macho monstrosity from Muscle Beach. Watching the series' development, fans noticed that Shipp introduced subtle differences in his "dual role", making the Flash slightly more raspy-voiced, reserved, and businesslike, and Barry more cheerful and talkative. And yet somehow, despite all this, Shipp seldom let anyone forget that it was Barry, an average guy, under the mask - not an easy feat.

In the role of Tina McGee (comics purists must have winced at this one, since Tina is really a romantic interest for the Wally West Flash), talented British actress Amanda Pays was also well-selected. Though some might complain that Pays often seemed to shout much of her dialogue even in low-key moments, her character genuinely seemed like a humane, responsible scientist, as interested in helping Barry stay healthy after his chemical dousing as in researching his bizarre condition. Her accent also lent the series a touch of class not usually associated with "comic book shows".

The one other major character (although several others appeared with rather amazing regularity over the series' twenty-two episodes as Barry's Central City relatives, friends, informants, and co-workers) was Barry's very 1990s lab associate Julio (Alex Desert), the hero's wild-haired but professional pal with more than just an inkling that his friend Barry might be faster than he looks. Very much "into" hip clothing, weird food, "fixing up" Barry with blind dates, and forever talking about his girlfriend Sabrina, the gifted Desert made Julio a good scientist - and a good friend.

The pilot episode Bilson and De Meo scripted (and directed by Michael Okuda) was titled simply **The Flash** and first aired Sept. 20, 1990. The resulting program was, by anyone's standards, certainly one of the most exciting and well-handled science-fiction series pilots ever seen.

Remarkably, the talents of composer Danny Elfman (of the big screen's *Batman* and *Dick Tracy* fame, two movies whose visual styles are often comparably to that of the series) were secured for the project. Elfman, then on the rise after scoring projects for "up and coming" film director Tim Burton (in 1990, Elfman was *the* hot composer), came up with a catchy "speed-and-adventure"-ish title theme which, though seldom heard outside of the show's airings, actually rivalled much of his best big-screen work. Superb incidental music was provided by Shirley Walker, who often matched the mood of Elfman's composition perfectly in many scenes and gave each week's storyline a unique musical

style. Thanks to Walker, each week's show seemed like a little movie all to itself.

While the series utilizes some rather grainy footage when actor Shipp runs on a treadmill before a blue screen (especially during the jogging-when-his-tire-goes-flat bit in the pilot), overall the series' special effects - especially those featuring the Flash as a dizzying red blur just like in the comic book - are truly spectacular, launching the

new show in high style. Just as pleasing, though was the breezy, "hip" sense of humor brought to *The Flash* by Bilson and De Meo, with even the "vigilante justice"-themed pilot is peppered with levity. This was a wise mood, especially for the pilot, since that episode's dark tale of vengeance could easily have become so bleak and oppressive as to antagonize strangers to *The Flash* and alienate long-time fans of the comics (who know full well that the comic book Flash was not born out of desperation or bitterness, and that the comic book Central City, while weird and with quite a crime problem, is generally a nice, friendly place to live).

Still, audiences and critics were quick to complain that the *Flash* pilot suffered somewhat from the decision to turn the comic book into a kind of Tim Burton *Batman* clone: the hero's costume has been changed to make the Flash more like Burton's movie caped crusader; the Flash appears mostly at night just as Batman does in the movie; a wave of fearful speculation hits the city as tales of a "demon... as red as blood - and fast, like a flash" circulate, echoing rumors in the movie's Gotham of a giant bat terrorizing the city; Barry turns vigilante to avenge his brother's murder much as Bruce Wayne dons his cape after the deaths of his parents. There is even a "You made me!" speech from the Flash to Pike near the end, recalling a similar revelation between the Batman and the Joker - and nearly everybody noticed. A few less-than-generous souls even cried "Rip-off!" right away.

But even skeptics had to admit that the concept of the Flash as a blood-red "ghost" appearing from thin air to terrorize criminals by night is a solid, sensible idea. Who among us *wouldn't* be scared by a scarlet figure who seems to materialize and dematerialize at will, leaping in at his prey from out of nowhere like some crimson phantom? Clearly, the comic book really *could* have been done this way, had its creators wished it - and it might have worked just as well.

All such criticisms aside, the opening five minutes of the pilot alone show why the series deserved a longer run than a mere twenty-two episodes. While its beginning is, perhaps, a little too similar to that of Tim Burton's *Batman*, it is also a very exciting one by TV standards, especially with such far better than average music pounding on the soundtrack. For several minutes, one almost forgets one is only watching TV and not a big-budget wide screen movie.

Just as *Batman* begins with a husband, wife and child threatened by criminal elements in a dark, brooding Gotham City, so does *The Flash* open with a "family vs. big city brutality" scenario, this time in Central City. TV's Central City is a dark, Gotham-inspired world both old-fashioned and futuristic environment, illuminated chiefly by streetlamps, looming murals, and neon. The setting is a marked departure from the less stylized (and less unsettling) world of the comic book, in which Central City usually seemed bright, relatively modern, and in many respects even surprisingly tidy (more like Superman's Metropolis or the 1960s TV Gotham than the Gotham of Burton's movie). Granted, one wishes Bilson and De Meo had resisted the urge to emulate Burton's 1989 film so blatantly, but who can deny that the attempt to give the show a unique look is a commendable one? After all, how many shows set even in real cities make even the slightest effort to create a distinct sense of place at all? In TV, it seems, the whole world looks just like Los Angeles.

We soon learn that Central City is a town under siege, terrorized by the vicious Dark Riders biker gang, headed by a deadly former motorcycle cop called Nicholas Pike. Bilson and De Meo's husband, wife and child team scurry for cover as the biker gang approaches (the hat-wearing, impatient father particularly recalls the approach to costuming and characterizations taken in *Batman*, as will the frequent intermingling of classic cars with the newer models), and as they crouch in an apartment building doorway, the bikers bomb their car, then toss another bomb at a pursuing police car.

In a small yet visually effective moment, director Robert Iscove moves from the image of the exploding, fiery police car to the image of lit birthday candles on a "police badge" cake for Jay Allen,

Barry's policeman brother. This "big police fire to little police fire" switch is, of course, a relatively simple transition even for TV, but one has to applaud the show's creative team for such a clever edit. It is the little moments like this one which makes *The Flash* pilot (and the whole TV series) worth watching - those tiny little flourishes of wit, wisdom, big-screen expertise.

Granted, one wishes that Bilson and De Meo had chosen to sidestep the cliched "men on motorcycles = trouble" equation (it is every bit as tiresome as their *Batman* fixation), and many a comics fan must have groaned to find that the best villain the writers could come up with for the Flash's debut was a grungy-looking small-time hood like Pike. Still, even the comic book Flash has been known to foil a simple bank robber or two, and, cliched or not, the biker gang idea does offer a threat which makes use of the show's central motif: speed. Motorcycles are common, yes, but they move fast, and for the Flash to seem a force to be reckoned with, we must see him up against a force that can really move.

One also understands that for "ordinary" little Central City to simultaneously receive a superhero *and* a supervillain in its opening show stretches the credibility factor for even a fantasy show to the limit (the *Batman* TV pilot avoided this problem completely by establishing its hero and the evil Riddler as already familiar faces in Gotham from the start). In addition, Bilson and De Meo hope to avoid repeating the "supervillain of the week" format of the old *Batman* series, most likely viewing it as something of a creative trap, drawing attention away from the hero every week to showcase the latest comic book villain (and whatever ill-chosen "special guest star" is brought in to play him). It is an understandable concern - although, ironically enough, a few more supervillains in the show's first season before tapering off a bit might have helped the ratings considerably.

The pilot includes many other clever touches. Barry's doomed brother Jay is clearly named after Golden Age Flash Jay Garrick (and played by Tim Thomerson, who looks enough like Shipp to make the older brother concept convincing); Tina first meets Barry at "50 Garrick Avenue", another sly homage to the original Flash; Barry gives back Jay's old City Relays medal as a birthday gift just before, as the Flash, Barry takes up running his own "city relays"; the final Flash vs. Pike battle occurs at "Central City Electric", furthering the "fast as lightning" electricity motif; the Flash's lightening bolt-on-a-white-circle chest logo (shrewdly, if not very originally, recalling a similar scene in 1989's *Batman*) appears in the night sky as a power plant electricity burst streaks across the moon; and, in the final scene, Barry's now fatherless nephew Shawn (Justin Burnette) hugs him as the camera pans into the pale blue sky until the Flash logo materializes, surrounded by red, then vanishes as bolts of lightning blast across a black screen from all sides.

Perhaps the most surprisingly "extra" in the pilot show is the depth it gives to its main characters. For example, while much of Julio's quirky personality (his fondness for Sabrina, his love of strange foods, his interest in "fixing up" Barry with new girls, usually disastrously) will emerge with time, he is quickly established here as caring, warm, loyal, offbeat, and funny. True, Iris West (Paula Marshall), so appealing in the comics, comes across as so shallow, spacy, and unreasonable here that even comics fans don't mind not seeing her again, but - for a pilot in which just to see their old friend Barry get zapped, doused with chemicals, discover he can run fast, and don his famous red-and-yellow costume would have made most comic fans dance with glee - an amazing amount of character development comes through too, and naturally the pilot is just that much better for it.

As soon as Barry's father Henry (M. Emmett Walsh), a former cop, makes his birthday party comment about "real cops who work the streets" without even realizing he has made a swipe at his lab scientist son Barry, we realize that the TV Barry Allen is a hero with a great deal of conflict in his private life. When his mother tells him to be careful investigating the site of Pike's latest mayhem, Barry's father jokes, "What's he going to do, stub his toe on a footprint?" We can see that the remark must hurt, and it helps little when, at Jay's grave after Jay has been killed by Pike, Henry shows no faith at all in his surviving son's ability to put Pike behind bars without getting killed too.

Even the press seems to echo Henry's view of Barry's job; "Let's see if we can find a *real* detective," says an impatient reporter at the crime scene. All of this helps tremendously in making us "connect" with Barry as a flesh-and-blood person. *The Flash* pilot doesn't really have to be a story about a man out to avenge the death of his brother and prove his heroism to himself and his dad, but these extra psychological elements add a human quality few who tuned in expecting a mere "comic book show" could have anticipated. Most viewers who had seen the pilot's TV ads demanded only that Barry be able to run fast: they must have been pleasantly surprised that he turned out to be human too.

Star Labs researcher Tina McGee, like Barry, resists the usual "one-dimensional" label given to so many comic book heroines. Though clearly intrigued by Barry's condition, Tina is in no way the stereotypical cold-hearted experimenter that, say, Speilberg movies so often serve up as villains rather than heroes. Indeed, the health-conscious Tina even warns Barry that others will experiment on him if they find out about his super-speed. Recalling that when Star Lab's funding was threatened, her own husband died while foolishly testing a special enzyme on himself after refusing to try it out on other humans as those funding him wished. Tina seems genuinely concerned that Barry's health - and his future - is in

jeopardy from both within and without. "I'm not your husband, Tina," Barry must even reassure her when she becomes overprotective yet another time. "It's not happening again."

Even Pike - admittedly drab biker thug though he is - is at least given a few extra touches of interest. A talented cop gone bad who once penned Central City's *Motorcycle Officer's Handbook*, Pike was tossed off the police force when his partner Jay got wise to Pike's hijacking operations. With a flair for the dramatic which includes updating Genghis Khan's methodology by tying a man to a speeding motorcycle instead of a wild horse, the vengeful Pike - a master of irony, eventually uses the same phony cargo truck trap to destroy Jay that was used on him years ago. An otherwise mundane villain, Pike could easily have turned out much worse without ideas like these (in a later episode, **Fast Forward**, Pike's prestige as a villain will be enhanced considerably).

But probably the most fun of the *Flash* pilot - beyond the skillful acting and often thrilling special effects - comes, as suggested earlier, from the humor of the script. Much of this humor is visual, springing from Barry's adjustment to his new abilities: rushing to keep up with his dog Earl on a romp through the park, Barry overcompensates and slams into a clump of bushes, sending leaves flying; jogging to meet Iris at an art gallery following a flat tire, he can't stop himself until he blasts into the ocean like a torpedo some thirty miles away; policemen buddies pick him up at night and drive him home - joke after he leaves about his funny red boots - then find all the doughnuts left in the back seat are gone, eaten by the ravenous Barry; and, in probably the pilot's single most clever bit, Barry does some super-speed house-cleaning, only to kick up such a whirlwind behind him as he goes that he messes up the whole apartment all over again - and catches his shoes on fire!

But not all of the script's humor is visual. Relying on all kinds of double entendres, clever comebacks and witty asides, Bilson and De Meo have a field day with the dialogue as well. After Barry's lightning accident, for instance, Julio admits, "I though you were done - well done, you know?" Seconds later, when Barry reaches for a coffee mug and knocks it across the room with the impact, Julio says, "I'm switching you to decaf, man," little knowing that too much energy is indeed precisely Barry's problem. Later still, Barry, usually one who never eats food Julio brings to work, finds his need to replace spent energy so great that he now eyes even Earl's dinner. "Now I know I'm in trouble," he frets. "Even the Kibble's starting to look good!"

There are several other amusing lines. Iris, breaking up with Barry, says, "things have just been moving way too fast," to which Barry agrees, "Yeah. No kidding." Sweeping Tina into his arms for a spin around the Star Labs test track several scenes later, he soon apologizes for the prank. "Sorry, I got carried away," he says. "Or you did, I guess." Following a physical encounter with Barry, Iris remarks, "I can't believe it was over so quickly" - though it is swiftly clarified that what she means is a TV boxing match that has ended in just two rounds. And, in a sort of satirical homage to all those squeaky clean "overgrown Boy Scouts" who served as heroes of such tales in the past, Bilson and De Meo even wink at the TV audience near the end of the episode; just before punching out a gang member, the Flash says matter-of-factly, "I realize how an unhappy childhood probably led you to all of this - but that's really no excuse." Not even Adam West's TV Batman could have said it better!

With the pilot offering *The Flash* such a fine start, one might easily expect upcoming episodes to stumble a little - and the series did stumble from time to time, but never really disastrously. About the worst that can be said of the following twenty-one installments of *The Flash* is that, first, they were done so quickly and with such intensity that a few errors popped up from time to time, and second, that the tone of the series was sometimes inconsistent - in other words, that in one show the Flash might be foiling a museum heist, in another show his own clone, and in the next a costumed supervillain like the Trickster or Captain Cold.

Much of this can be explained rather easily. Not surprisingly, considering the number of other behind-the-scenes *Flash* personnel who regularly came and went, in just twenty-two episodes, *The Flash* utilized eleven directors - an average of a new director every two shows. Co-executive producer Danny Bilson himself directed three episodes (among them a Mirror Master and a Trickster installment), as did Gus Trikonis. Bruce Bilson, with five episodes to his credit, directed the most episodes, while Mario Azzopardi helmed four. All the other episodes were directed by individuals who gave *The Flash* only a single try.

As for the show's writing, a total of fifteen different individuals contributed a story idea, a teleplay, or both over the course of the series. Fortunately, however, Gail Morgan Hickman (with six episodes) and the team of Howard Chaykin and John Francis Moore (with nine) were involved very heavily, as were Jim Trombetta and Stephen Hattman (with three shows each) and Jon Vorhaus, David L. Newman and co-executive producers Danny Bilson and Paul De Meo (all of whom worked in some way on two shows apiece). Without a doubt, comic book veterans Chaykin and Moore were the series' chief assets, scripting many of the series very best episodes - including those featuring the Trickster, the Mirror Master, and retired "good guy" crimefighter the Ghost.

Despite all the comings and goings among writers, *The Flash* maintained a degree of consistency in that it usually played more like TV melodrama than like a comic book, utilizing a fairly "serious" cops-and-robbers tone more in keeping with *The Incredible Hulk* than *The New Adventures of Wonder Woman*. Even when a villain from the comic book turned up in Central City, his origin and behavior, however far-fetched, were usually more "earthbound" than fanciful, with his famous comic book costume often dispensed with entirely.

Strangely, many of the episodes involving *Flash* comic book villains (most of these aired in the second half of the series' run) turned out to be among the most entertaining, and one wonders for that very reason if perhaps *The Flash* - delightful "vigilante justice" film noir though it often was - might not have been comic book TV's biggest lost opportunity. Probably more than any other comic in the DC line, *The Flash* offered an outrageous, costumed collection of rogues rivalling those from the old *Batman* TV series: Captain Boomerang, The Pied Piper, The Mirror Master, The Trickster, Heat Wave, Captain Cold, The Top, The Weather Wizard, Professor Zoom, and so on.

And yet, for the most part, the series' creators chose to leave all of this "ready made" material largely untapped. Granted, one would not have wanted to turn *The Flash* into another TV *Batman*, complete with animated "POW!'"s and "BAM!"'s flashing across the screen and lines like "Holy Lightning Bolts!" There is no reason to believe that a campy *Flash* would have worked in the 1990's any better than the semi-serious one CBS delivered. In all likelihood, making *The Flash* a weekly laugh-it-up would have been disastrous.

Still, the original *Flash* comic book is such an out-and-out entertaining one to begin with (amusing *without* coming across as a campy laugh riot) that in retrospect it seems a shame that the only way Bilson and De Meo could think of to make it filmable was to "Tim Burton-ize" it with dim lighting and dark overtones. The film noir look of the series is offbeat and distinctive, and the "Scarlet

Stalker" approach to the Flash himself could be chilling, but still one wonders: would a brighter, less eerie Central City like the one in the comic book *really* have fallen flat? Would it have *really* ruined the show if Central City had seen more Captain Colds and Mirror Masters and fewer Nicholas Pikes? Would the show *really* have fallen apart had that neat red outfit unfolded like a raft from Barry's costume ring? Don't fans of comic books - the one and only sure-fire audience for shows like this - tune in to see just that sort of thing anyway?

Comics are comics, of course, and TV is TV, but few have ever really tried to make a comic book into a TV show without tossing out - or distorting beyond recognition - the very things that made the comic a hit in the first place. The TV Hulk cannot speak because "Hulk smash!" will sound too silly, they reason. Wonder Woman can't fight Nazis in World War II because nobody will watch period pieces. Superman can fight only dim-witted gangsters with guns because supervillains like Lex Luthor and Terra-Man with "super-weapons" will cost more money and time. Somehow TV types always feel compelled to play havoc with the delicate balance of elements that made the original concept work issue after issue to begin with. Perhaps it should be no surprise after all that some CBS executives actually wanted to toss out the famous Flash costume - and have Barry Allen run around in a sweatsuit!

Episode Two of *The Flash*, **Out of Control** was the brainchild of writer Gail Morgan Hickman. Directed by Mario Azzopardi, the episode, like the pilot, begins and ends with lightning blasts and the Flash's chest emblem, but also debuts a weekly opening credits sequence - a terrific piece of dizzying action from the series and rapid-fire graphics beginning, in near *Dick Tracy* movie style, with a sort of vivid "primary colors" comics tone and ending with echoes of *Batman*'s dark power. Elfman's theme offers a perfect accompaniment, blasting away at us almost as fast as the images.

Unfortunately, the episode overall is a disappointing follow-up to the pilot, despite its heavier science-fiction overtones. The tale has Dr. Carl Tanner (Stan Ivar), Tina's old flame, lurking about Central City's slum areas at night injecting street people with an experimental serum. The result each time is a grisly transformation (done with gruesome makeup and inflated balloons beneath latex "skin") right out of *The Howling* and *An American Werewolf in London* - films the episode strongly resembles when a German Shepherd is injected and turns into a nightmarish werewolf sort of creature. The whole affair is a rather repulsive one, unfortunately, and when the Flash quips, "You really gross me out, Tanner", the audience has probably said the same thing about the entire episode forty-five minutes earlier.

Almost as dissatisfying is the fact that, while we do learn why Tanner sees street people's lives as "wasted" and thus useful only as guinea pigs (his real parents were "just like them", the proud scientist confesses shamefully), it never is made quite clear just what his serum is meant to do. In the pilot, Tina says her late husband David's enzyme was to have "stimulated the brain and enhanced the senses", and Tanner suggests that his serum is similar. Even so, while he insists repeatedly that he is nearing a breakthrough, just what that breakthrough is remains hazy even at the episode's end. If he is trying to make human beings stronger, uglier, and more violent, he certainly succeeds; beyond that, it is hard to see any purpose to his experiment - and thus the entire episode - at all (other than giving the special effects department a chance to sicken viewers who tuned in expecting more action-adventure instead of a horror movie).

A few other elements don't quite work, either. Tina and Barry haven't known each other long enough for Tina to accuse Barry of

The Flash: John Wesley Shipp as Barry Allen/The Flash.

being "jealous", for example. So far they are just friends, aren't they? But despite all this, **Out of Control** has its share of fine moments. It is nice to meet Barry's superior, Lt. Warren Garfield (a fairly standard grouch here, but eventually more than that), and some strong continuity with the pilot is present. For example, Barry's brother Jay is mentioned, as is Iris West (who is unlikely to return from her art world life in Paris), and Tina's husband's death from his own research gone awry is important to the plot of the entire episode (Tanner wants to get his hands on the notes). Barry's late arrival at Tanner's lecture is a nice touch too, carrying over the comic book's concept of Barry Allen as a terrific scientist but habitually tardy, especially before his lab accident. ("Sorry," Barry apologizes to Tina. "I got here as fast as I could." Well, not exactly!)

The rapport between Barry and Julio continues to be strong in **Out of Control**, and the Officer Murphy character (Bill Manard), teamed again with the less abrasive Officer Bellows (Vito D'Ambrosio), is a delight, getting off the best line of the episode when the mutated dog runs amuck. "That ain't no mutt!" he cries. "That's Dogzilla!" In addition, Tanner's excited response when he first meets the Flash face to face is perfect for a scientist ("What are your? Some kind of government experiment? Where do you come from?"), and the special effects for the Flash continue to be terrific, with Barry disarming a frightened street person and the officers about to open fire; using a security guard badge to cut an escape hole into a glass vacuum chamber; and catching a hurled bottle of a deadly chemical. Oddly, though, some of the best effects remain some of the show's least expensive ones; when Barry "flashes" into or out of a scene, the hair of anyone present is blown aside with a rush of wind. It's a simple effect (done with a wind machine), but with the added "whoosh" sound effects, it works splendidly on TV.

Probably the single best moment of the episode, though, is one nobody but a comics fan is likely to catch. When police officers call for backup, they direct their listeners to the "corner of Gardner and Fox". Gardner Fox, of course, was the creator of the original Jay Garrick Flash, and thus the spiritual father of everything on screen.

The next episode, **Watching the Detectives**, was much, much better. Written by Howard Chaykin and John Francis Moore and directed by Gus Trikonis, **Watching the Detectives** features a delightful Mike Hammer-ish musical score which provides perfect accompaniment to the antics of its main guest character, no-nonsense lady P.I. Megan Lockhart (Joyce Hyser). Hired by Central City's corrupt D.A. (confidently played by Vincent F. Gustaferro) to uncover the Flash's true identity - he wants a "superhero in his pocket", one might say - Lockhart pops up comically disguised as a klutzy secretary, a cable TV repairman, and even Tina McGee herself. Stubborn, self-centered, and rude - but also quite funny in several key scenes ("Doesn't that weird you out?" she asks Tina when Barry zooms away in the blink of an eye. "Constantly," Tina admits) - Lockhart leaves the audience wanting more by the end of the episode. In fact, actress Hyser is so colorful that she actually "steals" the episode from Amanda Peys, who has only a few brief scenes.

As always, Officers Bellows and Murphy (especially Murphy) make for pleasant comedy relief (Murphy, always the opportunist, is starting a "Where will the Flash show up next?" pool even though he personally has yet to see or believe in the Flash), and the first appearance of streetwise con man Fosnight (the always enjoyable Dick Miller) is a welcome addition. Lt. Garfield makes his second appearance, and skilled but arrogant WCCN reporter Joe Kline (the ever-offbeat Richard Belzer) returns for the first time since the pilot. Guest star Arthur Simonson (Harris Laskaway) makes an effective illegal casino crime boss, and Noble John Spanier (Jordan

Lund), a Bible-spouting arsonist he has hired to torch waterfront property, is a nicely quirky touch.

Continuity, obviously, is again a strong point with **Watching the Detectives**, though it also provides its most noticeable weakness. Barry's relatives, including his late brother Jay, are mentioned constantly in the episode (the greedy Castillo threatens their safety if Barry does not help him gain more control over Simonson), and it is nice to see that Barry's family - unseen so far since the pilot - have not been forgotten. Even so, Barry's fear of exposing them to danger would carry far more emotional weight if the "Mom", "Dad", "Eve" and "Shawn" he refers to were actually visible in something beyond a one-second glimpse of a family photo. Any viewer who hasn't seen the pilot must wonder why he is expected to get "all worked up" with concern for the safety of people he has never met - and, ultimately, he doesn't.

All this aside, **Watching the Detectives** is immensely watchable, and again proves that terrific effects can be achieved even when very little money is spent. When an angry Barry zips into and then out of Castillo's office, the jetlike whooshing sound and the sudden blast of air sending dozens of papers flying off Castillo's desk works just fine even though we don't actually see Barry causing it.

The effects involving speeded up film and similar camera tricks are also well done, however. At one point the Flash blasts onto the scene of a murder attempt, shoving the gun aside just as a woman is about to shoot her husband. It takes less than three seconds, but the energy of the moment is terrific. Two other scenes - Barry "cheating" at Simonson's illegal casino and then, as the Flash, battling the man's hoods inside the casino (he uses a roulette wheel as a shield to deflect bullets, whereas the comic book Flash would deflect them with his own speed) - are more light-hearted, even recalling moments in Disney's 1968 film *Blackbeard's Ghost* (which used ghostly invisibility rather than super-speed to defeat a crooked casino chief's thugs).

The single best moment in **Watching the Detectives**, though, has to be an absolutely dynamite moment when Castillo forces Barry to admit that he is the Flash. In a totally unexpected move, Castillo pulls out a hand grenade, removes the pin, and tosses it across the floor of Barry's apartment. "Four second fuse!" he declares quickly. "Three! Two!" And then, with the tension absolutely explosive, suddenly it is time for a commercial break! There is every reason to believe that this totally unexpected situation makes for the single most exciting cut to a commercial in the entire history of American series television.

And the outcome is almost as good. After the commercial break, the scene is repeated, this time with Castillo's "Three! Two!" countdown slowed mechanically. Barry drops the drinking glass he is holding, grabs the grenade, returns the pin, and - as the glass falls in slow motion - snatches up his glass again just inches from where it was when he let go of it. *This,* in case anyone has any doubt, is precisely why comic book heroes do indeed have a place on TV!

Episode Four, **Honor Among Thieves** is also good. A sort of hybrid between *Raiders of the Lost Ark* and *Mission: Impossible*, the episode (from a story by Howard Chaykin and John Francis Moore but scripted by Milo Bachman, Danny Bilson and Paul De Meo) involves six highly specialized criminals who descend upon Central City just as the local museum is receiving the priceless "death mask of Rasputin". Convinced the plotters are after the mask, a Federal agent and local authorities guard it night and day, then find themselves needed several places at once when, individually, the criminals start a crime wave elsewhere. As it turns out, the chief criminal, Stan Kovacs (the always excellent Ian Buchanan of *Twin Peaks*

fame), is after the mask after all.

The weakest element of **Honor Among Thieves** (capably directed by Aaron Lipstadt) is the Flash's visually exciting but unlikely manner of capturing Kovacs in the museum at the climax. In just a few minutes of screen time, the Flash reveals precision skills at lassoing, discus throwing (with a shield), and archery (the arrows pin Kovacs inside an ancient tapestry). As long as Barry's powers are limited to super-speed, the audience can identify with him in a spirit of wish-fulfillment; we believe that we could do everything he can do if only we could run that fast. When Barry is seen as impossibly good at *everything*, viewer identification weakens a bit - as does the credibility of the overall program.

For the most part, though, **Honor Among Thieves** plays surprisingly well. Barry's sense of humor is welcome in his encounters with the various criminals ("There is a substantial penalty for withdrawal," he tells one, locking the man in the vault he was about to rob), and the dialogue still has at least one good super-speed double entendre (when someone suggests that being cooped up doing research is no more exciting in a lab than it is in a museum, Barry is not so sure. "I do my share of running around," he says).

Some nice character development also appears, seen mostly in Barry's awkwardness around his former mentor, museum curator Ted Preminger (well played by Paul Linke), with whose guidance the lab scientist almost became an archeologist. "Henry Allen wasn't much of a father to me," Barry admits at one point, noting that the more sensitive Preminger understood Barry's intellectual nature in his teen years far better than the boy's street cop father ever could. When Barry gave up museum work at nineteen, the kindly curator felt so abandoned that the two haven't spoken in ten years,

and when it gets patched up at the end, it is a nice moment. (It would be interesting, though, to find out why, if young Barry had little interest in non-intellectual pursuits, he now has the physique of a top bodybuilder. Maybe he pumped iron as a kid to please his dad.)

The episode also has some strong visual effects: The Flash as glimpsed through a speeding auto's side rear view mirror; an exploding billiard parlor from which he just barely escapes; his capture of a thief by constructing a cage made of stacked gold bars. The growing belief around Central City in "The Flash", as the tabloids call him, is well-done too (Officer Bellows still believes in him; Officer Murphy still doesn't), as are the show's gripping opening moments, in which the criminals, concerned only about being "late", create a little nonchalant mayhem on their way into town when detained by police. It is also nice to see Barry's nephew Shawn again at the end of the episode, though it might have helped the "surrogate father" element if his father Henry had appeared. As in **Watching the Detectives** it's hard to appreciate the effect Barry's family has on him if the uninitiated viewer never quite knows who he is talking about.

Writer Jim Trombetta's **Double Vision** (Episode Five, directed by Gus Trikonis) is one of the most flavorful of all *Flash* episodes, with splendid Spanish-style music and opening with a cinema-worthy travelling crane shot moving slowly along the street of a Mexican-American Central City district and eventually delivering the viewer to a close up of a wall graffiti "Help" message meant for the Flash. The travelling shot takes quite a long time to complete, and is such a thing of beauty that a vivid Spanish atmosphere is established long before a word of dialogue is ever uttered.

The "Help" message is a lure for the Flash, whose skull is pierced by a special controlling circuit fired into the back of his neck from a special rifle in a church. One of the community's residents, it seems, is Paloma Aquilar (Karla Montana), living with her aunt and uncle because her undercover agent father is about to testify against drug lord Reuben Calderon (Michael Fernandes). Thanks to Calderon's employee Trachman (Charley Hayward), a mind control genius with circuitry in his head, the girl's whereabouts will soon become known. With the aid of a computerized glove and visor, Trachman uses the Flash as a kind of super-speed puppet to strike fear into the more superstitious of Paloma's protectors in the hope that they will hand her over.

It is all an unbelievably round-about way to force Paloma out into the open, and to prevent her father from testifying, and as a result the storyline of **Double Vision** is more difficult to follow - and swallow - than most. Adding to all the confusion is the sudden presence of *Twin Peaks*-style flashbacks whenever Barry has a blackout or is hypnotized by Tina. The flashbacks (not to mention some oddball "pranks" the Flash has performed during his blackouts, but which we have not seen) do provide some truly effective moments of mystery, but sometimes Barry's mental state makes the already puzzling tale even more perplexing.

Even so, it is gratifying to see that Jay (mentioned fondly here as having taken Barry to fights) has not been forgotten, and there are some witty lines too. "A little early for midnight mass," the Flash informs a church prowler, for example, and later, "No use, Gepetto," he tells Trachman, no longer under his control. "Pinocchio's a real boy now!" The episode also features some great special effects, the best being a terrific slow motion sequence in which a mind-controlled Paloma fires a gun at her father, only to have the Flash catch the bullet in flight inches from Aquilar's chest.

Sins of the Father (episode six, written by Stephen Hattman and directed by Jonathan Sanger), begins, appropriately enough, with a lightning storm, the setting for a chain gang escape by vindictive bank robber Johnny Ray Hix (Paul Koslo). Eventually, Hix (a fairly mundane villain even compared to Pike) is in Central City, his sights set on Barry's ex-cop father Henry (who sent Hix to prison) and on stolen bank money he hid during a chase years earlier.

Sins of the Father has considerable light humor: Barry literally beats the stuffing from a punching bag in the police gym; his nervous super-speed tapping of his spoon on a drinking glass shatters it as Henry embarrasses him with Tina; Tina distracts Henry with golf talk as Barry wrestles with Earl for the Flash glove in the dog's mouth; Henry - ever the physical type - picks *The Babe Ruth Story* when his wife requests a movie instead of sports on TV; and the Flash spins a billiard ball as a threat to a criminal friend of Hix's, drilling it right into the table's surface.

Another plus is one of the show's best homages to superheroes past in the welcome appearance of eightyish actor Robert Shayne (formerly Inspector Henderson on TV's *The Adventures of Superman*), consulted here for the first time as Barry's blind newspaper vendor friend and street informant Reggie. Additionally, the usually grouchy Lt. Garfield shows a sensitive side this time, warmly comforting Henry after Hix murders his retired cop pal Pete Donello (Richard Kuss in a brief but well-handled role), and actress Priscilla Pointer comes through with her usual professionalism as Barry's mom.

But **Sins of the Father** is really about Barry's strained relationship with Henry, who, when reminded that Barry is a cop, feels compelled to add, "in a lab coat". It must be said here that, as scripted by Hattman (and played by the talented M. Emmett Walsh), a little of Barry's dad goes a long way. It probably reflects positively on

both writer and performer that Henry comes across as such an unreasonable, thoughtless sort that it comes as a genuine pleasure when Barry finally tells him off. "Did you ever for one single minute stop and think that I might get a little sick and tired of your endless criticism of me and my work?" he asks. The fact that the viewer can't help thinking, "Give it to him, Barry!" shows what a strong chord is struck artistically here. On the other hand, Henry is often so ornery that it is a tad unconvincing when he decides on a father-and-son talk, telling Barry at last, "As much as I loved Jay, I never loved you any less." We're glad Henry opens up, and we hope he means it, but ultimately the viewer probably builds up more resentment for Henry than he ever does the "bad guy" Hix!

A troubling logic problem creeps into the series with this episode. In the past, when Barry appears as the Flash, we've assumed he has run to his car or bedroom to grab his aluminum briefcase and switched clothes. Here, however, there is a puzzling scene with Barry changing clothes in mid-run. If this were the comic book, we could easily accept this, since - even without a costume ring - his costume there is so thin he could wear it under his street clothes. TV's Flash costume, though - like Michael Keaton's rubber "suit of armor" in *Batman* - looks a little too thick to be worn that way. The "running change" effect is a good one, but again the show often works best if some events occur offscreen.

The Flash's pole-vaulting trick (is there any sport Barry isn't good at?) is also problematic, recalling similar feats of expertise marring **Honor Among Thieves**, and the remote-control machine gun car doesn't seem like Hix's style at all. Also, how is it that, after nineteen years, Henry's pal Pete only now figures out the location of Hix's stolen money? But the weakest element here is the final encounter with Hix, during which Barry pounds away at Hix's face in a wild rage. Does Barry lose control because Hix has attacked his dad seconds before? Is he enraged because of the gunfire launched at his childhood home? Is he beating up Hix to show his dad that he can be a "tough cop" after all? None of this seems particularly likely, ultimately leaving the viewer dissatisfied with the way the whole episode turns out.

Child's Play (episode seven, directed by Danny Bilson) is one of *The Flash*'s most formulaic episodes, even if a memorable one. The moment we meet smart-aleck street kid Terry Cohan and his bratty sister Cory, we know we're in for one of those sappy "he's a good kid deep down, he just needs love" stories television is so fond of. Why is it that TV seems to believe in only two kinds of children - wisecracking irritants who give their parents a rough time, and wisecracking irritants who give cops a rough time?

Child actor Jonathan Brandis (well-received in the Stephen King mini-series *It*) is the main focus of the episode, and he is believable as a kid with a penchant for mischief. Unfortunately, gifted writers Howard Chaykin and John Francis Moore (the story is by Stephen Hattman and Gail Morgan Hickman) give him so many rude and cynical "tough kid" lines that it's hard to care much what happens to him. If an adult character snapped at Barry and the police this much, not to mention picking pockets, snatching a writer's research from his car, and even trying to sell stolen information to a drug lord (!), he'd surely be the episode's villain of the week. Apparently, when a kid does all this, it's just cute.

The episode is not without some solid appeal, however. Concerning a 1960s refugee named Beauregard Lesko (Jimmie F. Skaggs as an amusingly spacey hippie villain) who plans to turn Central City into a city of addicts who'll pay big money for his "Blue Paradise" inhalable spray drug, **Child's Play** uses weird psychodelic camerawork to show the drug's effects. The show also continues the breezy health food vs. junk food and "The Flash exists" vs. "The

The Flash: John Wesley Shipp as Barry Allen/The Flash.

Flash doesn't exist" sparring between officers Bellows and Murphy, and gives the Flash some fun lines. "Never accept rides from strangers," he says in Adam West style after saving Terry from a kidnapper, and he later describes himself as "just a bad flashback" to Lesko.

The direction is also frequently quite good. In one scene, when Barry opens his car trunk to reach for his aluminum suitcase, the screen is blocked by the open trunk for a split second; when he closes it again, he is already dressed as the Flash. In another, the Flash ties up and gags a criminal, and, as the camera pulls slowly back for a long shot, we see that the man has been deposited on the doorstep of the police department! **Child's Play** also offers another clever "in joke"; the sign on a movie theater announces a big superhero movie double bill: *Batman* and *Superman*.

The very best moment of **Child's Play**, though, appears when, as he battles "outlaw chemist" Lesko near the end of the episode, the Scarlet Speedster gets sprayed in the face by a quick dose of Blue Paradise. Soon Barry's image becomes all soft and fuzzy, and as he leans against a wall he falls right through without even damaging the wall. The drug's potency burned off now, Barry observes, "I guess my molecules were vibrating so quickly that I passed right through the wall" - exactly what every *Flash* comics fan hoped had just happened! The Flash purposely performs this feat in nearly every issue of the comic, and to see it on the show makes for a terrific moment. Barry's only comment here is that the experience was "weird", but maybe if the show had lasted longer he could have added the vibrating through walls trick to his repertoire of skills. If the producers feared it would make Barry too invulnerable, they needn't have worried; their writers proved quite well even in the pilot that a good surprise attack is all the leverage a villain really needs.

The Shroud of Death (episode eight, written by Michael Reaves from a story by Howard Chaykin and John Francis Moore) is notable for two reasons: a suspicious Julio almost discovers Barry's secret; and a surprisingly sensitive Lt. Garfield becomes engaged, nearly loses his fiance when she takes a bullet meant for him, and turns vigilante much like Barry (whose "Yes, I do!" answer to Garfield's comment that he doesn't understand how he feels is another reference to the loss of Jay). All ends well, of course. Barry tricks Julio by distracting him with a shout of "Look at that!", a quick appearance as the Flash, and returning to Julio's side again with a casual "I guess he *does* exist"; and Garfield's fiancee Mavis (Lenore Kasdorf, whose character seems good for the gruff old policeman) recovers and marries him.

The main storyline has a judge (whose death, from a neon sign crashing atop his car roof, is particularly well-staged by director Mario Azzopardi, complete with interesting shots from high above the auto), an ex-DA, a secret informant, and Lt. Garfield being stalked by a mysterious "angel of death". As it turns out, the angel is actually a woman named Angel (played with vindictive energy by Lora Zane), whose father was sentenced to death thanks to those she is eliminating.

The Flash gets his usual quota of clever lines in this episode ("Visiting hours are over," he tells Angel as she contaminates Mavis' hospital I.V., then declares, "Three strikes. You're out!" as he avoids three rapid-fire Ninja star assaults from her on the hospital rooftop), as does Barry himself ("Where've you been?" asks Julio. "Oh, out running around," says Barry). The special effects are top-notch as always, with Barry using a hubcap to shield Garfield from Angel's bullets and outrunning the explosion of a device just beneath his feet within the second it explodes. There is at least one slip-up in the script (Garfield "chews out" Barry for

leaving a murder site, but Barry does it again and even phones it in to Julio), and the device of sending one's intended victim a "calling card" (a piece of neo-Fascist necklace symbol) is as old as mysteries themselves. Overall, though, the episode works remarkably well, with the softening of Garfield giving it particular appeal for fans.

Ghost in the Machine (episode nine, written by John Francis Moore and Howard Chaykin) is one of the show's very best episodes yet. The writers and director Bruce Bilson (plus the musical, set design and costuming personnel) give the episode a real comic book/movie serial feel, recapturing the atmosphere of the often-emulated *Batman* movie better than any entry thus far. The second the episode opens in a black-and-white 1955 Central City, with a 1950's TV commercial in a bar interrupted - in true Joker style - by a weird doomsday declaration from a criminal genius called the Ghost, we know **Ghost in the Machine** is going to be something very special.

There is something undeniably *right* about this opening, with the bar thrown into panic as the Ghost (Anthony Starke) declares that at midnight the downtown area will explode. "Nightshade! Where's Nightshade?" someone cries, and in seconds, conjuring up images of the Batman emerging from the Batcave in his Batmobile (Or Zorro on Toronado, The Green Hornet in his Black Beauty, etc.) a dark car emerges from a secret headquarters hidden beneath a cheerful billboard. Soon, the black-cloaked crimefighter Nightshade invades the command center of the video-obsessed villain, and uses a handmade jamming devices to thwart his plans. A fire breaks out, with the Ghost's twentyish lady friend Belle (Sherrie Rose) escaping while the Ghost - believed dead- enters a secret room and activates a freezing chamber set for the year 1999 (when the door seals, the counter trips back to 1990).

When he awakens (still as a young man) in a now full-color 1990, Nightshade has long since retired, Belle is now played by the older Lois Nettleton, the video age foreseen by the Ghost has largely come to pass, and a new superhero - The Flash - guards the city. His cryogenics attempt a success, the Ghost now believes there is nothing he cannot do. With equipment stolen from Star Labs and WCCN, he connects his own body and mind to the city's circuitry, and televises a new blackmail demand for a billion dollars, threatening the city's access to light, water, heat, information and so on.

Naturally, Nightshade (in reality a friend of the unwitting Lt. Garfield, Dr. Desmond Powell, played by Jason Bernard) must spring into action again, but this time the Flash assists. By the end of the episode, both the Ghost and the Flash have learned Nightshade's identity ("A colored guy. Who would've guessed?" asks the Ghost, and comics fans are delighted. There *should* be more black superheroes); Barry, worried about Dr. Powell's safety, learns how Tina must feel when he hurries off into danger; Dr. Powell's retirement suggests that having a normal life while fighting evil may be impossible for Barry also; and the younger and older breeds of hero learn to respect each other's talents and techniques.

Ultimately, this is Dr. Powell's episode, and Jason Bernard is so warm, wise and eloquent that he practically steals the show; one actually wishes Nightshade had his own TV show so the viewer could tune in and watch every week. Also quite good are Starke as the Ghost, whose "ahead of his time" 1950's predictions about the future of video make him an unusually remarkable villain, and Lois Nettleton, whose once-gorgeous Belle arouses considerable sympathy because she has changed so much while her lover has changed so little.

Another plus for the episode is the dialogue, which, as usual, is inventive and fun. "Ah, ah, ah! Don't touch that dial!" says the Flash as the Ghost fiddles with his control panel to continue

tormenting him. When Nightshade offers the Fastest Man Alive a ride to the Ghost's old hide-out, the Flash refuses: "No. Bad for the image."

As illustrated in the joke about image consciousness, the best humor this time around has a decidedly satirical edge. When Murphy, in a cheezy tuxedo, sings *My Way* to Bellows' piano accompaniment on a charity telethon, it is both Las Vegas lounge lizard types and telethons we laugh at, not just Murphy's weak performance. When arrogant reporter Joe Kline tries to "pick up" Tina and gets slapped (minutes later, he will be struck by the Ghost's invading thugs), this is clearly a big of a "slap" at sleazy journalists as well - with charity volunteers even applauding Tina's reaction.

Even television itself - and its viewers - "takes it on the chin" when the 1955 Nightshade tells his arch-enemy, "Too much TV, Ghost. You've got no attention span." The point is further driven home when the Ghost plays a 1990s video game and scores well. "This is how far TV's gotten?" he despairs. "Reduced to a pinball game? I expected more. Much more." Equally good is the moment when a modern youth comments on the Ghost's "bad" score. Once it has been explained that in 1990, "bad" can mean "good", the Ghost understands almost immediately. "Orwellian doublespeak", he realizes. "Like in *1984*." But this is a 1990s youth he is addressing. "Eighty-four?" the young man cries. "I can't remember that far back, man!" Undoubtedly, even in 1955, Nightshade's estimation of the result of too much TV was right on target!

There are some other clever touches: "Thirty-five years from now, who'll remember the Flash?" wonders the almost-forgotten Nightshade, and more attentive fans will note that the Barry Allen/Wally West *Flash* era (begun in 1956) had, by 1990s, lasted almost exactly that long; the 1990s billboard masking Nightshade's secret lair, as if crying out to both Nightshade and the Flash, reads, "Our World in Your Hands. Love it or Lose it"; the Ghost's 1990 broadcast to the city, in a clever homage to TV's *The Outer Limits*,

includes the lines, "Don't bother adjusting your set. I will control the vertical. I will control the horizontal." Even the last few seconds of the show are inventive, with the Ghost, his experiment gone a bit too far, mentally trapped in a staticky world floating past our TV screen after the usual Flash logo.

It is also nice to finally meet Julio's oft-discussed girlfriend Sabrina, and to find that the now-married Garfield, though calling costumed vigilantes "a pain in the keester", is still mellowing. When Barry recalls that the Flash saved Garfield's life twice in the last episode (strong continuity again), Garfield doesn't deny it: "Well, yeah. But the good guys should wear badges. That's the law." Chiefly, only the two attempts to kill the Flash fall flat; the Scarlet Speedster escapes much too easily from the first trap at Star Labs, and the Ghost's "video torture" of the Flash in the climax is handled in such a way that it is very difficult to tell just what is going on.

Sight Unseen (episode ten, written by Jon Vorhaus from a story by Vorhaus and Gail Morgan Hickman) is not a bad show considering it uses the overdone H.G. Wells *Invisible Man* idea. The twist here is that the villain, Brian Gideon (sympathetically played by Christopher Neame), is an oddly honorable foe, a researcher plagued by a brain tumor and rage for Central City, Star Labs, and the government over their support for chemical weapons research. Infuriated because unfeeling Federal Agent Quinn (George Dickerson), responsible for a horrible chemical accident killing thousands and afflicting Gideon, is also behind similar secret research at Star Labs, a well-meaning but unstable Gideon seeks revenge. "We are all responsible," he maintains, and by the episode's end he has killed two men connected with the appropriately named "Project Pandora" and filled Star Labs with the toxin.

George Dickerson's Quinn supplies fine cold-hearted menace, forcing Lt. Garfield out of his role as head decision-maker, handcuffing Barry just for challenging his authority; seeking Gideon's belt like "stealth device" so he can become a "big man in Washington"; and even lethally radiating Star Labs (now in a self-activated "contamination lockdown") even though Tina and chief administrator Ruth Werneke (Deborah May, at first harsh, then growing more human as her fear and illness grow) are still trapped inside. It is the usual government bad guy role, but Dickerson plays it smoothly.

Director Christopher Leitch handles the deaths-by-invisible-killer scenes quite capably, and Lt. Garfield shows again that he can be compassionate around his officers (Barry fears Tina will be dead in just four hours) instead of just yelling at them all the time. In a brief light moment, voice-attuned blind newspaperman Reggie shows that he's not fooled by either invisible men or Barry in disguise, and a still disbelieving Officer Murphy (in a deadly-accurate satire of crass commercialism) reveals to his pal Bellows his plan to cash in on the Flash phenomenon by way of "I Saw The Flash" T-shirts, underwear, and even "Flash Gum"!

Probably the worst moment of the show is the all-too-easy discovery that something in Barry's blood fights the deadly toxin afflicting Tina and Ruth. Almost as troubling, though, is a scene recalling a weak costume-changing moment from **Sins of the Fathers**. The Flash enters a Star Labs truck, then reappears as Barry when Murphy and Bellows arrive. Has Barry retrieved his clothes by exiting through a back door, or was he wearing them underneath his costume?

Beat the Clock (episode eleven, written by Jim Trobetta and directed by Mario Azzoparoli) is probably *The Flash* at its most artistically sophisticated. Little in the show is as distinctive-looking as, say, the black-and-white movie serial homage in **Ghost in the Machine**, but for sheer intrigue and suspense, **Beat the Clock** is well, unbeatable.

As in the movie *High Noon*, clocks are constantly in the background in **Beat the Clock**, and the time they show generally reflects the time it takes to watch the episode. Beginning with a long, slow traveling shot down a prison corridor, the camera stops on a saxophone-playing Wayne Cotrell (sympathetically played by Jay Arlen Jones), set to die in the electric chair that night for murdering his singer wife Linda. The scene shifts quickly to Barry's lab, where Barry watches a WCCN report from Joe Kline, who feels Central City is electrocuting Wayne while far worse criminals walk the streets. The time is 11:00, one hour before midnight.

Julio - a close friend of Wayne's - soon argues with Lt. Garfield over the accuracy of the police investigation, then exits, after which Barry gets a call meant for Julio. The caller, jazz musician Dave Buell (Eugene Lee) has stolen a cassette with proof of Wayne's innocence, but he is killed (a lonely crane shot of the phone booth establishes the risk he is taking) before he can explain. Barry exits, sending desk papers flying. The clock on his desk reads 11:05.

Buell is gone, and the cassette is smashed by a passing truck. Barry calls Julio to meet him at the Take Five jazz club, and as Julio exits it is 11:07. At the club, Julio introduces Barry to Wayne's crooked brother Elliott (a very impressive Thomas Mikal Ford) and his henchman Whisper (an ominous Ken Foree), a one-time singer whose throat has been cut. Several clocks show it is now 11:12. By 11:17, Tina has the tape and is at work deciphering it. The Flash visits Wayne in his cell and gets his story (a slow motion, yellow-tinted flashback is well used here, as is another later). Back at the club, Elliott and Whisper are plotting by 11:22.

At Star Labs, Tina discovers Linda's is the voice on the tape - singing a song not from previously known recordings. It is 11:24. Julio is unknowingly stalked by Whisper at the morgue while reviewing the file on Linda's death, and when we return to the lab, it is 11:27. By 11:32, Tina is trying to get the governor on the phone to stop Wayne's execution, but is stopped by Whisper, who steals the restored recording. By 11:43, a very much alive Linda - stricken with drug-induced amnesia by Elliott - is recording yet another new song in his boarded-up apartment above the jazz club. Attempting to rescue the now-doomed woman, the Flash gets pushed out a window by Whisper, after which Julio and Whisper battle, then the Flash and Whisper again ("I'm gonna teach you about the quick - and the dead," says Whisper). Whisper loses temporarily, and by 11:54, a confused Linda has appeared in the jazz club like a ghost and sings. By 11:55 (five minutes before execution time!) Barry and a desperate Julio are about to rush her to the prison ("Listen, listen! I can make it," Barry starts to tell him, "because I'm...", but Julio won't listen). By 11:58, another battle with Whisper resumes in the club, ending with the Flash smashing the thug into a wall clock, which stops at one-and-a-half minutes before midnight! With just seconds to go, Wayne strapped into the chair, and the switch being pulled, the Flash arrives at the prison, releases Wayne from the straps and electrodes, and rushes him away as the chair sizzles with energy!

Why the Flash doesn't just stop the switch from making its descent instead of wasting those precious milliseconds unhooking straps and fasteners is impossible to explain, of course, and the scheme to keep Linda alive to make new tapes to be sold as old ones has its share of unanswered questions. But the "ticking clock" format is absolutely perfect for *The Flash*, the tension is just spectacular, and the storyline overflows with startling twists and turns. This *Flash* show really seems like a last-minute police investigation, not just science fiction. For continuity's sake, it was also a great idea to bring in Father Michael again (John Toles-Bey, wisely

brought back from **Out of Control** after a ten-episode absence) as Wayne's pre-execution spiritual adviser.

Best of all, the villains are three-dimensional, and the always likeable Julio comes across with more passion, depth, and humanity than we have ever seen before. Julio grew up very middle class, it turns out, but his dad insisted the Mendez family stay in the ghetto, exposing Julio to great pressure to join the street gangs. Wayne, though, helped Julio out. "You had Jay; I had Wayne," Julio tells Barry in one of the series' most bittersweet, reflective moments.

Indeed, in nearly every way, **Beat the Clock** is *The Flash* at the top of its form. Who could have thought that a "comic book show" could offer this much intrigue - or skill?

Guest star Mark Hamill of *Star Wars* fame received some criticism for overacting as an insane multiple personality in **The Trickster** (written by Howard Chaykin and John Francis Moore and directed by Bruce Bilson), but ultimately none of it matters. Hamill's performance is over-the-top, to be sure, but this is also what helps **The Trickster** take *The Flash* to unbelievable heights of ridiculous fun.

Cynics might call the Trickster a mere Joker rip-off from *Batman*, but seeing a supervillain from the *Flash* comic book - even if in altered form - makes thrilling viewing. It is also terrific to see Joyce Hyser again as P.I. Megan Lockhart (to help us recall her **Watching the Detectives** appearance, her theme song is reprised, and the Trickster gets a fine tune all his own - a lilting circus-style tune emphasizing his clownish brand of showmanship). This time Megan calls Barry from 150 miles away in stark terror, and Barry is worn out by the time he arrives as the Flash. He does, of course, show up in time to save Megan from crazed magician James Jesse - who is about to cut her in half with a chain saw in a run-down theatre occupied only by an audience of mannequins! (Megan jokes later to Tina, "Let's just say, if not for Barry, I'd be beside myself.")

The deranged Jesse is captured easily, but, believing the Flash has stolen his latest "one true love" (he has murdered his past twelve), he soon kills two state troopers on his way to prison and heads for Central City. Occupying an empty prop warehouse, Jesse dons a bizarre harlequin outfit (complete with mask and cape), robs a novelty shop (hanging one poor employee), kidnaps Megan, and does his best to destroy the Flash, who eventually defeats him in a showdown at Central City's police costume ball.

Hamill - "letting go" as he never has before - does an astonishing job making Jesse maniacally funny, deadly, and totally unpredictable. One minute he's about to saw Megan in half, the next proclaiming his love for her: he reaches the bizarre conclusion that the Flash has brainwashed Megan to steal her away for no rational reason at all; from scene to scene he's dressed first as a magician, then a harlequin, then an FBI agent; and by the end, he's screaming "I'm the Flash! I'm the Flash!" from the rear of a police car!

Hamill's dialogue is especially quirky. "Move over! I'm driving!" Jesse tells a dead state trooper as he dumps him from the car; rolling an exploding cake towards the Flash at the ball, he shouts, twisting the title of an old song," I knew you were coming, so I baked a cake!"; and, doing his best Bullwinkle and Rocky, he pulls a rabbit from a hat with their famous lines, "Oops! Don't know my own strength!" and "And now here's something we hope you'll really like!"

The references to the old song and Bullwinkle and Rocky are but two of many allusions and in-jokes. The costume ball is held at the Infantino Hotel - named, obviously, after Carmine Infantino, designer of the comic book Flash's costume. Barry is torn between Megalopolitans "intense fleeting passion" and Tina's "complex but true love" - just like Katherine Hepburn in *The Philadelphia Story*,

the film Barry and Tina start to watch when Megan calls. Officer Murphy paraphrases Walter Winchell's classic radio opening when he addresses the press in his Flash costume as a joke. *The Merry-Go-Round Broke Down* - the tune from Warner Brothers' own *Merry Melodies* cartoon shorts plays as Jesse is defeated, and the Flash comments, "That's all, folks." The Flash jokingly refers to the warped Jesse in his magicians' garb as "Mandrake", recalling the amazing comic book magician.

Strangely, Joe Kline is absent, but a new reporter whose name is Arthur Kline (though listed as "Jim Kline" in the credits) briefly appears. Another odd moment occurs when Lt. Garfield says Jesse dumped the bodies of the two state troopers inside the city limits, yet we have seen one dumped on the highway - supposedly on the way *from* Central City (it is their squad car he repaints as his "Trickster-mobile"). Also, Barry is chloroformed before Megan is forced to dress up for Jesse, so what makes him tell Tina later that Jesse now thinks Megan is "his costumed sidekick" Prank? Finally having both Barry and Megan witness the Trickster's Central City middle-of-the-street debut seems a bit too coincidental.

Despite all this, the episode deserves raves for its inventiveness. For instance, commenting on *The Philadelphia Story*, Barry says, "Look, I just hope there's a cartoon with it." In seconds, he gets Megan's call for help and for the rest of the show finds himself *in* one - as Megan observes when she snaps, "Enough! I'm sick of this cartoon crap!" at the end of the show and punches Jesse. Megan's landing in the hands of a lunatic just by trying to repossess Jesse's car is totally unexpected, and the Trickster's exploding statue of a red Mercury is a nice touch also. The show's best running gag, though, is that now Officer Bellows is convinced his partner Murphy - never present when the Flash appears - is himself the Scarlet Speedster; no matter how much Murphy denies it, more evidence just keeps on piling up!

The show's emotional conflicts are also different. As expected,

Barry worries about this week's villain, but mostly because he fears his own outside-of-the-law costumed antics have inspired the Trickster's very existence. "Ever since I became the Flash," he observes, alluding to the **Double Vision, Ghost in the Machine** and **Sight Unseen** episodes, "these eccentric criminals have been coming out of the woodwork - Trachman, The Ghost, Gideon. Now this." If weirdness can breed weirdness, this probably explains a lot about superhero comic books in general. Similarly, Tina is jealous of Megan, as one might predict - but, unexpectedly, largely because now Megan, not Tina alone, knows Barry's secret. (Tina probably should worry more; Barry and Megan do become physical, preceded by a passionate kiss, and Megan's joke, "Wait a minute. It's not over yet, is it?" Such bending of our expectations just adds that much more to making **The Trickster** one of the best *Flash* shows of all.

The old *Dr. Jekyll and Mr. Hyde* tale gets a modern twist in episode thirteen, **Tina, Is That You?** (written by David L. Newman from a story by Newman, Chad Heyes and Carey Heyes). Directed by William A. Fraker, the episode again shows Barry needing Tina's help with a health problem, this time sleep deprivation. Plagued by nightmare about a Tina who alternately declares her love for him and claims to despise him and to want him dead, Barry finds himself trying to achieve relaxation by letting Tina hook their minds together with a Star Labs "biofeedback machine". Thanks to a faulty two dollar part, however, Tina is blasted across the room as it somehow taps into Barry's nightmare.

Tina, Is That You? provides an interesting acting challenge for Amanda Pays, whose normally gentle if overprotective Tina becomes hostile, rude, and dangerous after the accident. Before long, Tina is a miniskirt-wearing, tattooed member of the all-female Black Rose gang who - though she never really harms Barry - must be "reprogrammed" with the same Star Labs mental device to get back to normal.

Unfortunately, none of this "evil Tina" material is particularly well-explained or even very convincing. Tina is certainly unpleasant in her darker persona, but her lines never drip with evil the way we might hope. As a result, she never seems as menacing as the two gang members she joins, thus greatly diminishing the episode's tension - and Barry's need to cure her. In the end, the viewer is left with a show that, for all its potential, never quite works as it should.

Even so, **Tina, Is That You?**, like all twenty-two *Flash* installments, has its moments. Tina can be very funny in her deranged state even if not frightening, especially when she makes life miserable for her nurse and threatens to tell all of Central City the identity of the man in the red suit - and she doesn't mean "Father Christmas", she says. Barry is amusing too, trapped in yet another blind date from Julio and Sabrina (this one is a good one, but Tina purposefully wrecks it, and eventually kidnaps the poor girl), pacing a hole in the hospital waiting room carpet and nervously emptying a vending machine. In addition, the scene in which the Flash - trapped by Tina with Barry's kidnapped date Lisa (Yvette Nipar) - uses a pencil and a metal fan to create a super-speed circular saw is a particularly neat trick, and when the Flash meets Tina, he declares in campy hero style, "Tina, you've been a very bad girl." There are also at least two clever lines about super-speed. "He'll be here in a second - and I mean that!" Tina tells her fellow gang members, and when Lisa tells Barry, "Don't be gone long," he responds, "Oh, I never am." There is also a funny moment during a bank robbery when a little boy is seen wearing an "I Saw the Flash" T-shirt. Apparently Murphy's "get rich quick" idea to cash in on the Flash myth is working after all!

Be My Baby (episode fourteen, written by Jule Selbo and

directed by Bruce Bilson) is a fairly routine segment about a young lady named Stacy (a very appealing Kimberly Neville) whose inane husband, millionaire criminal Philip Moses (Bryan Cranston) has chased her and their baby to Central City. Stacy is, of course, taken in by Barry, who - aided by Tina and his mother Nora (Priscilla Pointer) - finds himself awkwardly caring for the baby and other children throughout the episode. As it turns out, Moses is obsessed with perfection and neatness in every way, and only married Stacy - daughter of an Olympic gold medalist and a Nobel Prize-winning chemist - to father the finest baby possible.

There is a lot of visual humor here, mostly involving babies: Barry uses super-speed to appease a roomful of wailing toddlers, builds a playpen from lab shelves, eats teething biscuits to renew his strength, and - as the Flash - gags tied-up gangsters with diapers. It is also nice to see Barry's mom again, as well as pickpocket/hustler informant Fosnight, and a neatnik villain is a good idea. There are also two lightweight language jokes: having knocked cold one of Moses's men with vegetables in a restaurant alleyway, the Flash explains to the chefs, "Sorry, I guess dinner's on him"; and, encountering the week's villain, he declares, "You've broken your last commandment, Moses!" Beyond all this, **Be My Baby** is a fairly routine, but watchable, show.

Fast Forward, featuring the return of biker cop-gone-bad Nicholas Pike, is much more colorful, even if unpleasant and not particularly logical. Since there is no proof that Pike murdered Jay (his lawyer suggests that perhaps the Flash killed him), he is freed on a technicality, and a fed-up Barry - suspended for punching Pike in public - decides to leave his Flash career and Central City for good. Before he goes, however, Pike threatens to flood Central City with a missile, luring the Flash to the old Devil's Gate Dam from the pilot. Pike fires the missile at the Flash, who tries to outrun it. When detonated, the missile hurls Barry ten years into the future, where his super-speed powers are no more and Pike is the sadistic mayor of a *1984*-style nightmare world.

Written by Gail Morgan Hickman and directed by Gus Trikonis, **Fast Forward** creates a very weird, hostile 2001 with a seventeen-year-old freedom fighter Shawn (Paul Whitthorne); a married Julio and Sabrina; an aging Murphy arrested for selling illegal Flash action figures; a Tina who blames Barry for abandoning his city when it needed him most; and a secret museum honoring the long-missing Flash, whose true identity has been figured out long ago. It also offers strong continuity with the pilot (Jay is talked about a lot, and we see Justin Burnette as Shawn again) and alludes to **Ghost in the Machine** (Barry notes that someone - it was Dr. Powell - once told him the Flash "would be forgotten in a few years"). In fact, the secret museum houses Trachman's mechanized glove from **Double Vision**, the costumes of good guy Nightshade and bad guy Trickster, and much more. It must be noted too that the brief "two Flashes becoming one" scene near the end is one of the series' better effects.

Despite the absolutely breathtaking new look given to Central City by the special effects team (it is a truly startling transformation), something is slight askew about the episode somehow. Indeed, while fans of dark science fiction - and especially time travel stories - will probably like **Fast Forward** a great deal, many others likely won't. The series' trademark light touch is largely missing, for one thing - fine for the 2001 Central City, but somehow even the 1991 segments seem particularly humorless this time around; watching *The Flash* would be no fun at all if it were this oppressive every week. For another, the way The Fastest Man Alive is sent back to 1991 (where WCCN's Joe Kline actually apologizes on camera to the Flash for hinting that the Scarlet Speedster might have

committed murder) makes very little sense. If one explosion sent a super-speeding Flash exactly ten years into the future, why wouldn't a duplicate explosion send him forward another ten instead of backwards?

Equally puzzling is how one city can become so warped without the outside world ever intervening. Why doesn't the government step in? Has the entire U.S. gone downhill along with Central City? There is also a good argument that, while the 2001 Pike is quite formidable, the 1991 Pike - not a particularly exciting villain even in the pilot - just isn't worthy of such a big, sprawling science fiction adventure. A supervillain from the comic book - maybe even Captain Cold, the Mirror Master, or the Trickster - might have meshed better, but when we see a biker hood controlling a missile, however maniacal he might be, somehow it just doesn't work.

Less ambitious but in many ways more satisfying is episode sixteen **Deadly Nightshade** in which a murderous costumed vigilante called the Deadly Nightshade - clearly an admirer of the original, gentler Nightshade, and inspired by his recent re-appearance - starts gunning down criminals left and right. As it turns out, the Deadly Nightshade is the richest man in town, young Curtis Bohanan (Richard Burgi), whose shame for the crimes of his late mobster father is so great he has devoted his fortune to making amends to Central City. The unbalanced Bohanan has gone too far, though, and - knowing the Flash and the original Nightshade will oppose rather than join him - decides he must eliminate both, designing a mechanized exoskeleton suit to help him match the Flash's quick movements when Barry arrives to defeat him.

There is much to enjoy in the episode, especially the return of the marvelous Jason Bernard as Dr. Desmond Powell, as wise, warm and witty as ever. We see Powell's secret "trophy room" again (hidden this time behind a "Crack Kills" billboard), see again that Lt. Garfield is grateful to the Flash for saving his life eight episodes earlier, and we learn that Nightshade "brought down" Fosnight years before. Guest star Denise Crosby (Tasha Yar of *Star Trek: The Next Generation*) scores well too, appearing as Dr. Rebecca Frost, a stressed-out psychiatrist who thinks the city's various costumed vigilantes are unbalanced and dangerous, their behavior usually "triggered by the loss of a parent or sibling" (a sibling, in Barry's case). By the end, Rebecca has softened, making an interesting love interest for Barry, though her suggestions about the Flash's glory-seeking give him reason to seek council from Dr. Powell. "I always finished second," Barry recalls to Tina. "Second to Dad. Second to Jay." Such troubled soul-searching makes for great character development - time after time, script after script, one of *The Flash*'s greatest strengths.

We are disappointed when Garfield learns in a 1955 file that his friend Dr. Powell was the original Nightshade and his identity becomes known to all. The admirable, honorable Dr. Powell deserves the praise of "Fifties Hero Unmasked" headlines, but we had hoped we might see him don the costume again; both the actor and his role are just that good. Even so, Garfield's discovery supplies another strong in-joke for comics fans; the police captain in 1955, it turns out, was a Capt. Julius Schwartz - named after the DC comics editor who, with writer Robert Kanigher, penciller Carmine Infantino, and inker Joe Kubert, helped create the Barry Allen Flash in 1956.

Director Bruce Bilson serves up several really funny moments. Shot by the Deadly Nightshade while saving reporter Joe Kline on live TV, the Flash is asked to comment on being accused of murder. "Get that mike out of my face!" he snaps, echoing the sentiments of many a soul persecuted by the press in times of crisis. When the

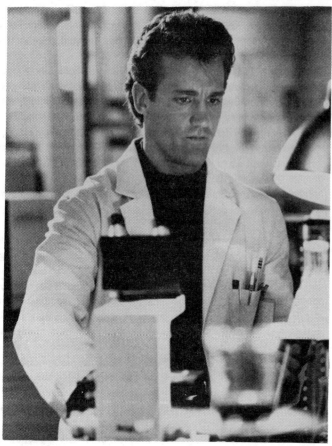

Deadly Nightshade calls WCCN saying he wants to speak to Joe Kline, the snide secretary is a delight; "You and every other lunatic in town," she says, no doubt recalling Son of Sam. "Do you want to leave a number, or the name of the dog who gives you your orders?" Dr. Powell and Barry - whose identity Powell figured out long ago - make a wonderful team, Dr. Powell out-of-breath and exasperated when Barry forgets to slow down for him, and Barry hurting himself being too impulsive. "If you'd wait for me once in a while...!" Dr. Powell complains after Barry is shocked grabbing an electric fence. But writers John Francis Moore and Howard Chaykin's best line goes to Fosnight after the Flash whooshes off again. "He ought to slow down," Fosnight says. "He's gonna give himself a coronary!"

It is terrific to hear the superb musical theme for the Nightshade used again here (Shirley Walker's contribution to *The Flash* is absolutely tremendous), and only one small moment really harms the episode. When Tina admits she can't understand Barry's super-hero situation, she suggests he speak to someone who can - Dr. Powell. Obviously, Barry has told her Powell's identity, and this just doesn't sound like Barry at all. He'd be furious if Powell had been so disloyal!

Episode seventeen, **Captain Cold** (written by Gail Morgan Hickman from a story by Hickman and Paul De Meo) has one of the comic book's best villains. As seen here, Capt. Cold is a overcoat-wearing albino hit man with dark glasses who uses a stolen nuclear powered "portable freezing unit". As played by a polite, soft-spoken, "icey"-voiced Michael Champion (whose performance recalls Liberace, Jack Nicholson, or perhaps Bruce Glover's Mr. Wint character from *Diamonds are Forever*), Captain Cold is an amazingly self-confident criminal who - even after killing his employer for welching on their deal - goes after the Flash just the same. "Once I take a job," he says, "I always finish it - no matter what."

As one might expect, the writers have a grand time toying with

the language for this character. "Cool is my specialty," he says proudly, posing as an air conditioner repairman. Facing the Flash for the first time, he declares, "Even you can't outrun the cold hand of death." Breaking down the door of a tabloid reporter's dwelling, he cries "You ordered some ice?" Seconds later, he gleefully warns "I'll huff and I'll puff and I'll freeze all your stuff!" and then - clearly a Eugene O'Neill fan - "The Iceman cometh!" Other characters like Fosnight, Officer Murphy (who, trying yet another "get rich quick" scheme, is writing a novel about his exploits), and *Inquisitor* reporter Terri Kronenberg get into the act too, tossing out comments about "Frosty the Snowman", "human snowcones", and "the Good Humor man". The Flash gets his share of ice jokes, too. "What's the matter? Didn't you get to play in the snow when you were a kid?" he asks, and then - after freezing Captain Cold solid by reflecting a freezing unit blast back at him from a mirror - he comments, "Those summer colds. They're the worst!"

Humor abounds in this episode. For instance, when Barry (fighting a cold from his first two battles with Captain Cold) sneezes, his jerking motion hurls him backwards in his armchair into a wall, and Murphy's novel about his heroism is hopelessly riddled with nonsense. The allusions to comic books continue as well, with Murphy saying Bellows will have to read the comic book version of Murphy's novel, and Barry calling Terri "Lois Lane" once). As for drama, Tina's desperation to save Barry's life when he has been frozen solid gives Amanda Pays one of her best scenes, and, as presented by the special effects team and director Gilbert Shilton, the special "ice" tricks are virtually flawless.

Not so flawless, though, are two brief moments in the script. When Captain Cold - counting on being present at the last bomb site, where the Flash will be tired and slower - issues three bomb threats to the police, how does he know in what order the Flash will dispose of them? Similarly, why does Barry so eagerly accept a "stabilizer belt" to heat up his body just after Captain Cold has escaped from jail? Does Barry know about the second freezing unit? Still, flawed or not, the episode is great fun, and we hope at the end that we'll see Captain Cold again sometime.

Episode eighteen, the humorously titled **Twin Streaks** (written by Stephen Hattman and directed by James A. Contner) recalls the "weird science" formula of the less than successful **Out of Control**, and unfortunately shares that episode's more erratic storytelling style. More or less a reworking of the equally uneven *Superman IV: the Quest for Peace*, **Twin Streaks** involves two young scientists, Jason Brassell (Lenny von Dohlen) and Ted Whitcomb (Charley Lang), who, after luring the Flash into a trap with a phony bomb threat to injure him, clone a duplicate Barry Allen (well played by Shipp in a dual role) from his blood. Naturally, the naive duplicate (called "Pollux" like the twin in mythology) shares Barry's super-speed abilities but lacks the emotional maturity to use them properly. Just as naturally, both scientists (Brassell is stubborn and harsh, Whitcomb nervous and gentle) must be killed by their impulsive but well-meaning Frankenstein's monster during the episode, since the identity of Pollux's look-alike Barry will be at risk from these two otherwise.

To the credit of actors von Dohlen and Lang, the two scientists, despite their opposing characterizations, both manage to win a small degree of sympathy. The more likeable Whitcomb's death seems truly undeserved, and the formerly aggressive Brassell - eager to market a "race of warriors" like Pollux - falls apart so completely afterwards that when his "just desserts" come they don't seem quite so just after all. Most of the sympathy is reserved for Pollux, however, who seems so childlike and lost that we almost understand his need to eliminate the real Barry and take over his identity.

There is some nice continuity with the pilot here when an earlier clone disintegrates after reaching 347.31 miles per hour on the scientist's treadmill (Barry reaches 347 miles per hour on a treadmill in the pilot). Also appealing once again are Officers Murphy and Bellows (developing a kind of *Odd Couple* routine, Bellows objects to Murphy's unhealthy appetite in much the same way Julio is forever trying to get Barry to try his weird specialty foods). Tina's role as the over-cautious physician has not been forgotten, either; she worries that Barry is overexerting himself and taking too many risks, as if he were invulnerable (he is twenty percent slower in speed tests than three months ago but has a faster heartbeat, and his injuries are not healing as quickly).

The best super-speed moment in the episode is the humorous "windstorm" stirred up by a playful Pollux on a self-propelled park merry-go-round (a hot dog vendor and a picnicking couple are nearly blown away), but the scene is which Pollux catches a bullet in mid-air and hurls it back at the gunbearer at super-speed is a great concept too. As for star Shipp, he gets plenty of laughs with his "wide-eyed child" routine, and is hilarious in the scene in which Pollux appears in the world's gaudiest (and most effeminate-looking) sailor suit freshly swiped from a clothing store window.

Twin Streaks is also plagued by implausibilities, however. When Pollux has his first day out of the lab, who but Barry Allen and Tina happen along to find him there? Also, why the two scientists just happen to base their speed experiments in Central City is never properly explained; it doesn't seem to have anything to do with the Flash, so it might have been wiser to have the pair travel to Central City upon reading about him in the tabloids. And while we're at it, shouldn't a Barry Allen clone whose development has been accelerated in a lab first appear with long hair instead of a neat, short John Wesley Shipp haircut? Somehow it is hard to imagine that Brassell would style Pollux's hair before unveiling him to the sleeping Whitcomb!

Episode nineteen, **Done With Mirrors** (written by Howard Chaykin and John Francis Moore, and directed by Danny Bilson) is the last *Flash* show to introduce a "new" supervillain from the comic book and it is another winner. A complex, tricky tale of double-crossing thieves both out to sell a stolen solar device, **Done With Mirrors** is a tale of illusion from start to finish, with even Barry getting into the act. Clever use is made of the mirror motif throughout - double-crosses, a pair of thieves, a West Coast Star Labs (though in **Alpha** we'll learn of a New York Star Labs as well), two thefts, and so on. The guest cast is also strong, especially Carolyn Seymour as Tina's jet-setting mother, Signy Coleman as Barry's old schoolmate turned thief Stasia, and - of course - *The Partridge Family*'s David Cassidy as pony-tailed, black-garbed criminal Sam Scudder, a.k.a. The Mirror Master.

This Mirror Master flings tiny projection devices as diversions, devices conjuring up over two dozen images during the show, among them a cowboy, a samurai, a priest, a mime, and a cigarette girl. Cassidy is unexpectedly good in his role, even if something of a departure from the Mirror Master of the comic book. At once charming and menacing, witty and wicked, the character is fascinating to watch because the viewer simply does not know what to expect. In one scene, for instance, he first threatens Stasia in the street, then starts kissing her passionately as if nothing has happened!

The comic highlight of **Done With Mirrors** occurs when, as part of a scam to arrest the Mirror Master, Barry must pose as a nonexistent "Professor Zoom", the man who "created" the Flash.

With spiked hair, dark glasses, and a thick Italian accent, actor Shipp is hilarious, especially when Barry's "hammy" side takes over. "You may not know, but I also invented the video camera, the laser disc, the microwave oven, the digital watch," he tells the Mirror Master, his make-believe resentment growing more intense with each item. By the time he is complaining, "Of course others take credit for these...," Barry sounds so outraged by all this imagined thievery that Stasia must punch him in the ribs!

Also funny is Barry's reaction when he finds himself covered with phony snakes thanks to one of the Mirror Master's illusions. Screaming "Snakes!" with such wide-eyed horror that it is hard to believe this is the same self-confident fellow who runs around in a red suit at night, Barry shows a slightly scaredy-cat side we've never witnessed before - and it is great to see. Tina's mother (who left Tina's father to go "find herself" when Tina was only a child) also provides some humor, a classy presence, and a chance for more character development for Tina.

Equally welcome is the fact that even nineteen episodes into the series, the writers (here, Howard Chaykin and John Francis Moore) have not forgotten their source material. When Barry poses as "Professor Zoom" (a made-up mad scientists he has mentioned as a joke to Stasia when asked who "built" the Flash), the name is an obvious homage to the comic book Professor Zoom, the evil Reverse Flash from the future who eventually kills Barry's wife Iris. But there is more. When Barry, Tina and Tina's mother attend an art gallery, the name outside reads "Garrick Gallery" - yet another homage to the comic book's original Golden Age Flash of Earth Two.

Episode twenty, **Goodnight, Central City** (written by Jim Trombetta and directed by Mario Azzopardi) is not classic *Flash*, but it does have its appeal - chiefly *Lost in Space*'s Bill Mumy as Roger Braintree, a "brilliant", bespectacled schoolmate of Barry's. Roger's latest invention - a humming "sleep-inducing machine" - quickly starts his smalltime crook cousin Harry (Matt Landers) into plotting a citywide heist. But Roger, though Harry's partner, refuses to make a bigger machine after discovering that prolonged exposure to its sound waves causes death. Harry is persistent, however, even pulling a gun on his soft-hearted cousin, and in the struggle Roger is abruptly shot and soon dies. Attempting a rescue, Barry - after switching to his street clothes - is struck on the head by Harry and framed for Roger's murder.

Roger is a very sympathetic character with his round glasses, bowtie, and boyish demeanor - gentle, polite, pleasant, yet clearly corruptible where his cousin Harry is concerned. Mumy's performance is so appealing that when Roger dies halfway through the hour, we are genuinely troubled, and for the rest of the show we keep hoping his death, like Harry's in the sleep-inducing test beginning **Goodnight, Central City** is all just an illusion too. Matt Linders is effective too, creating a wildly impulsive Harry who always goes too far in every caper - with "too far" this time meaning murder. Also effective is Victor Rivers as bigtime criminal Stan Morse, who - for all his faults - sees no reason to wipe out a whole city of innocent people.

Goodnight, Central City has a few other strengths. Tina, for instance, takes a more obvious part in the action than usual (we have not seen her leave Star Labs to assist Barry all that often since the pilot, but this time she has to), and Lt. Garfield, still softening, truly seems pleased to free Barry from jail when Harry is captured. There is less memorable action than usual, and once again the Flash changes into Barry's clothes without our knowing where they came from, but the sleep-wave attack on the city using old air raid sirens is a good idea, with the sound effects especially strong. There is also

one visual joke for those who like them: a store being looted is named "Bilson's", after co-executive producer Danny Bilson. Similarly, science fiction fans will note the mention of a "Sturgeon Street" and "Bradbury Arms" and that Terri Kronenberg's last name is awfully close to that of director David Cronenberg.

Unfortunately, the episode also lacks the hoped-for quota of witty moments; it seems double entendres concerning sleep do not come as readily as those about speed, ice, and so on. Of course, Murphy's insomnia makes for a mild grin or two (with Murphy, it's always something), as does Fosnight's appearance as a "nun" as part of a scam. Born loser Harry's belief that he has dynamic big-time crime czar talent earns a faint chuckle too, as do Roger's goofy inventions, and the Flash's remark to Harry as he carries the crook to the police station over one shoulder: "I'm running late, Harry. Why don't you ride with me?" In the end, though, it's all pretty tame stuff for *The Flash* - not bad, just not thrilling.

Alpha (written by Gail Morgan Hickman from a script by Hickman and Denise Skinner) is a fairly predictable "I want to be human" runaway robot story starring Claire Stansfield as Alpha One (Artificial Lifelike Prototype Humanoid Android One). Alpha (pleasantly played by Claire Stansfield), who was conceived as "the ultimate covert assassin", escapes her government creators after her reading how Lincoln freed the slaves inspires her to free herself. Soon afterwards, she becomes Tina's new lab assistant (Tina worked briefly on an artificial limb robotics project three years earlier), and is eager to avoid government reprogramming. Naturally, Barry and Tina do all they can to keep her out of harm's way.

Eventually, after the Flash rescues Alpha from their clutches for the last time, the ruthless Col. Christine Powers (Laura Robinson) activates Alpha's self-destruct command, which will surely kill anyone near Alpha as well as their creation. In just thirty seconds, the Flash carries Alpha ten miles away - too far for the signal to reach the "bomb" in the android's brain. (In a nice visual joke, a traffic sign nearby reads, "Maximum Speed 55".)

Director Bruce Bilson again offers a Lt. Garfield siding with his men against Federal interference, Fosnight scheming to line his pockets at others' expense (this time, though, he has been softened so much that he almost seems part of the team), and references to fantasy and sci-fi (both *The Wizard of Oz* and Isaac Asimov are mentioned). We also revisit the Hotel Infantino for another homage to the comic book.

Much, much better is the final episode, **Trial of the Trickster**, with Mark Hamill every bit as wild, devious and deranged as in episode twelve. Joyce Hyser also returns as P.I. Megan Lockhart, every bit as tough and spunky as we remember her. This time James Jesse escapes with the help of Zoey Clark, a love-hungry fan and Clarx Toys heiress who dresses as Jesse's partner, Prank. Together, they capture the Flash with a chewing gun and epoxy mixture, brainwash him, and turn him into the Trickster's goofy, grinning, gag-a-minute partner in crime. Eventually, they put the whole city on trial on the very site of Jesse's own trial.

As with **The Trickster** the installment is filled with enough zany gags and one-liners for any two regular episodes. During Jesse's escape - courtesy of Prank's laughing gas - a policeman takes a bullet for Jesse's attorney. "Sacrificing yourself for a *lawyer*?" Jesse gasps. "Time to rethink your priorities, Bub!" Later, he sends a dead rat to Megan, and the note reads, "Some Discoloration May Occur After Dying."

Mimicking reporter Joe Kline (in full makeup) on TV, Jesse's commentary is riddled with Kline's pet expressions (calling people "Babe, for instance) and a seemingly endless string of meaningless reporter cliches. Dropping a load of chewing gum on the street to stop the Flash, the Trickster (parodying an old TV commercial) asks, "Who wants gum?", to which Prank eagerly replies, "I do! I do!" He mimicks Fred Rogers too once the Flash is in his clutches. "It's a beautiful day in my neighborhood?" He coos. "Won't you be my neighbor?"

Brainwashed, the Flash can be funny too. "It's not guns that kill people!" drawls the Fastest Man Alive in cowboy style, tossing a bullet at a policeman's feet. "It's these little hard things!" Asked for a match, he checks his costume, and declares, "Left 'em in my other suit." It is fun to watch Barry act so unexpectedly kooky for a change.

But it is Hamill's emotional "hairpin turns", his wacky tightrope dance between murderous and loving, bombastic and nonchalant which gives the show its best moments. "If you touch that mask again, I'll murder you!" Jesse bellows at Prank as she starts to wreck the Flash's image by revealing him. Then, a split second later, Jesse adds, "'Kay?" with such a "cutesey" little voice and grin that only the world's biggest spoilsport could keep from laughing. Likewise, Jesse melodramatically declares to Prank, "You can't begin to understand the depth and genius of my plans!" Then, turning back to the Flash to start brainwashing him, he tosses out the casual line, "Besides - it's guy stuff."

Similarly, when the Flash later suggests, "Hey! I could vibrate my fingers through somebody's brain!" (Aha! So Barry *can* vibrate through objects at will! One has to wonder why on TV he still prefers just to run around things), the Trickster laughs with disgust. "Oh, gross!" he says, but then, without a flicker of hesitation, he adds, "Ah, maybe later." Comics fans, by the way, will recall that the deranged Professor Zoom - the evil yellow-costumed Reverse Flash - actually killed Barry's wife Iris with just the sort of super-speed jab to the brain Barry mentions.

The pleasures of this episode come by the dozens: another mention of the Hotel Infantino; Barry's peculiar glance at a familiar waiter now sporting a Trickster-style haircut who asks him "Would you like another?" (Yes, it *is* the same waiter - played by Brad "Cat" Sevy, then in a ponytail - who asked, "Would you, uh - would you like another one?" in the pilot; we've come full circle!); the return of the music written for the Trickster for his first appearance; Megan's "Good Lord, McGee, is there anything you don't know?" comment (we've asked ourselves that countless times); the Trickster's use of *The Merry-Go-Round Broke Down* as his courtroom theme; the Trickster's various accents, costumes, and toys; Barry's very human misgivings about the Flash being ignored somewhat by the media after just a year while Megan and the Trickster are getting all the attention; Tina and Megan's effective team-up to stop the Trickster and rescue Barry; Tina's moving declaration of devotion to Barry as his partner for as long as he needs her. Even our final view of a strait-jacketed Trickster bouncing around in a padded cell, and spouting his usual "Nobody tricks the Trickster!" threat at us through the glass is a memorable, if unsettling, image.

At the end of the episode, Barry says yet another goodbye to Megan, who is on her way back to San Francisco. Asked to join her, Barry says, "My family is here. My friends are here. I'm just not ready to say goodbye." Neither were fans of the series, and perhaps writers Howard Chaykin and John Francis Moore, seeing "the writing on the wall", wanted to express their own sentiments with this line. Director Danny Bilson seems to express a similar feeling in his closing shot. Order restored once again following the Trickster's vandalism of the city, the camera pulls back on a "Welcome to Central City" sign, revealing a new, narrower sign being hung underneath. This one, using the comic book's famous slanted-letter cover logo, reads "Home of the Flash" (perhaps one day Central City, like its comic book counterpart, will even create its own Flash Museum honoring the Scarlet Speedster). As we ponder the way after a year its masked vigilante has been embraced by much of the city at last, a familiar red blur whooshes past the sign. *The Flash* as an American network TV series may be over, but the Flash's work will keep on going. Lt. Garfield's final line seems to sum it all up: "Hey, Allen! We've got work to do!"

Trial of the Trickster aired in the U.S. on May 18, 1991, just eight months after it began. A short time later, when the 1991-92 fall

TV season was advertised with the usual hoopla, Bilson and De Meo's expensive, difficult-to-produce *The Flash* was nowhere to be found on CBS' proposed line-up. Though the series' twenty-two installments would live on in syndication and home video if there was enough interest in them, for all practical purposes, TV's *The Flash* was gone.

Nobody was really surprised. Time slot changes had done little to boost the show's ratings in any dramatic way (some fans even lost track of the show when it would move to a new spot on the schedule), and while critics pointed out that *The Flash* was improving markedly as the season progressed, but, while their compliments certainly helped, none raved about the series loudly enough to really lure in many new viewers.

With ratings lower than needed for such an expensive program (CBS had put more than $6 million into the two-hour pilot alone, and over a million dollars for each subsequent episode), the network, having admirably stuck it out for a full season, found it very hard to justify renewal. And, since Bilson and De Meo were adamant about the need for a high budget to create the Flash's effects, bringing back the show in a cut-rate version was out of the question. It was a great loss to *Flash* fans, but in the end, even they hated to think of the Fastest Man Alive's dazzlement subdued by network cost-cutting. Besides, there were always reruns - and back issues of the comic book, where the only budget hindering Barry's exploits was the cost of paper and ink.

Looking back over the TV series as a whole, much stands out - the way actor Shipp helps us never forget it is Barry beneath the costume yet often plays the Flash with a subtle difference just the same; the superb effects; the brilliant "new sound every week" musical scores; the complexity of the characterizations; the casual "in-jokes"; the persistent good humor; the magnificent use of neon, darkness, wall murals, and more to give Central City a stylized look. Every network show should be created with such admirable, care and devotion.

But most impressive of all is *The Flash*'s remarkable attention to continuity. Even as late as the last show, Julio still has the same girlfriend, WCCN and its tactless star reporter Joe Kline are still part of the saga, a character first seen nineteen episodes earlier (Megan) is still part of Barry's life, an outdoor restaurant still has the same waiter, and Barry's family is still being talked about with deep affection. While it is true that in some ways *The Flash*'s continuity stumbles a bit on occasion, it must be noted that the personnel behind most network TV programs totally lose track of the saga they are creating. Indeed, the episodes of many shows could be aired in random order without anyone ever once noticing a discrepancy.

In twenty-two episodes, Officers Murphy and Bellows appear in sixteen (seventeen, if the two-hour pilot is divided); Lt. Garfield is present for seventeen; reporter Joe Kline is there for ten; Fosnight is there for six; Barry's dad is around to irritate him twice; his mother is there to comfort him twice; his nephew Shawn appears three times; Sabrina appears four times; Reggie appears twice; Megan Lockhart shows up three times; Father Michael appears twice; the Trickster plagues Central City twice; Pike wrecks havoc twice; and Barry's dog Earl - well, let's just say Earl's around most of the time too. And even when many of these characters aren't seen, especially Barry's family, they're talked about with remarkable frequency. How many other shows persistently pay this much attention to themselves?

The answer, of course, is very few.

There is probably no way a TV version of *The Flash* could ever have satisfied everybody - comics fans, science fiction fans, TV viewers, critics and so on. Television audiences are, after all, an extraordinarily picky lot, and even the slightest departure from a popular comic book formula is bound to raise cries of, "Well, they got *this* right, but why in the world did they have to fiddle around with so-and-so? Why, that was the comic book's very best part!"

But nobody can deny that while *The Flash* lasted it was tremendous fun, capturing better than any other TV show ever made the thrill and sense of adventure we buy comics for in the first place. It was, just as Bilson and De Meo intended, like nothing viewers had ever seen before, except in the multi-colored, multi-paneled artistry of the comics page.

Clearly, if future attempts to bring comic book heroes to the small screen are only half as successful artistically as *The Flash*, then we have a great deal to look forward to. Let's all hope that we will not have too long to wait.

The Rogues Gallery of
The Flash

article by Craig W. Frey, Jr.

The Flash, which aired on CBS during the 1990-91 season, was one of the most innovative shows on television. It reveled in its quirkiness and managed to keep its integrity while being thoroughly tongue-in-cheek. It was brazen entertainment, screaming "Look! I'm a superhero show!" It wasn't as dark as the recent *Batman* films, nor was it as campy as the *Batman* series from the 1960's; it somehow blended both schemes and added a few new twists into the mix. It was pure, unadulterated fun, which in the cold world of network programming is often the kiss of death.

And so it was with *The Flash*. The show lasted only one season, airing 22 episodes, including the two-hour pilot film. But in those 22 episodes some of the most interesting stories were played out and a few nifty super villains came to life. A superhero needs the challenge of top-notch villains, and the Flash certainly had his share. We'll run down (pardon the pun) a few notable bad guys from the series and see how they rate against the Scarlet Speedster and against each other.

Worthy villains are mandatory to any superhero show, but they were even more important to *The Flash* because of the strong performance John Wesley Shipp brought to each episode as Barry Allen/the Flash. Shipp is an extremely gifted actor, and he was capable of bringing subtle facets out of his character. He played both Barry Allen and the Flash not as distinct and separate, but as complimentary identities. The Flash was an extension of Barry Allen, not a flip-side, darker personality. Shipp made the Flash, a character with unbelievable powers, completely believable, and sometimes even vulnerable. Shipp's on-target performance made it all the more critical that the villains his character faced be up to the task of defeating the Flash.

The first villain who should be mentioned is the first one the Flash ever faced, the one who, indirectly, created the Flash; Pike. Although Pike wasn't a super-villain, as he had no super-human powers, his type of dramatic evil still provided a powerful obstacle to the fledgling superhero. Pike was a more dangerous enemy because he had several connections to the hero: 1) He used to be one of the "good guys" (a police officer). 2) He played a part in the hero's creation and resolution to continue being a hero. When Pike, the leader of a band of motorcycle terrorists called the Dark Riders, killed Barry Allen's brother, Jay, he ensured that Barry would use his newfound powers and become the Flash. Barry even told Pike this during their final confrontation. When Pike asked who the Flash was and where he came from, Barry responded "You made me!" In effect, Pike created the instrument of his own downfall and sealed both Barry's fate and his own.

As played by Michael Nader, Pike was a far cry from the typical, nostril-flaring heavy that he could have been. Nader made Pike into an intelligent, calculating schemer. He was a match for the Flash because he had the loyalty of the Dark Riders and because he so easily preyed on the fears of Central City's citizens. Nader played the enigmatic madman to perfection; relishing the role, but not overdoing it. He was bad enough for the viewers to dislike him, but not so flamboyant that his presence diminished the hero, as Jack Nicholson's Joker did in the first *Batman* film.

Pike was a dangerous villain, but his return in the episode **Fast Forward** halfway through the season was both a blessing and a curse. It was good to see the Flash's premiere enemy again, but without the threat of the Dark Riders behind him, some of Pike's nastiness was lost. The idea that in the Flash-less future, Pike became the Mayor of Central City was too far-fetched, but the whole of the story still worked. Michael Nader played Pike competently once again, but while he made a good first villain, he wasn't the most exciting continuing nemesis.

The first real super-villain the Flash faced was Dr. Carl Tanner in the episode **Out of Control** Tanner was continuing the experiments that killed Tina McGee's (Amanda Pays) husband. When he injected himself with a serum designed to accelerate human evolution, he became a beast that the Flash had to stop before his rampage tore the city apart.

As super-villains go, Tanner was pretty lame. The story, a typical "Jekyll and Hyde" yarn, wasn't so hot to begin with; it was slow, hackneyed and predictable. The make-up used to transform actor Stan Ivar from Dr. Tanner to a muscle-bound monster was impressive, but that's about all that was impressive. Ivar brought nothing special to the role, but there didn't seem to be much there to work with. The final confrontation between the Flash and the Tanner-beast was lackluster and carried little emotional weight. *The Flash*'s first on-air super-villain was definitely less than super. As a final note on this villain: Did anyone else notice that Tanner sounds a lot like Banner, and that the Tanner-beast looked a great deal like a certain green-skinned Goliath from another comic company?

The next bad guy of any note was Trachmann from the episode **Double Vision**. Charles Hayward played Trachmann with electronically-hyped enthusiasm. His character's ability to electronically take over another's nervous system played up the dark side of virtual reality, and the story took advantage of the fact that the Flash could be a vulnerable hero. At one point, Trachmann was able to use his powers to force the Flash to help his henchmen kidnap the daughter of a man about to testify in Federal court. This exposed a weakness and reminded the audience that the hero wasn't indestructible; like most of us, the Flash could be corrupted.

Trachmann was definitely a step up from Tanner. He was a super-villain in control of himself, and he enjoyed being evil. He was also in control of his power, knowing how to use it to its fullest effect by taking control of the hero. That is the mark of a great super-villain; the ability to use his enemy's power against him. Trachmann's downfall was his over-reliance on his own technology, but he was a worthy adversary for the Flash because he was the first to exploit the Flash's speed for his own purposes.

There are fans out there who enjoyed the episode **Child's Play**

and they think that Lesko was a great villain. I don't happen to be one of those fans. The episode trivialized recreational drug use and made Lesko more glamorous than dangerous. Drug pushers should never be characterized as corny visionaries; they are insidious killers who don't care at all about the pain and suffering they perpetuate. They don't have dreams about total domination, and they don't live in spacious psychedelic digs with throwback, cultish lackeys. This representation was a major misstep for the series, as a more realistic vision would have given the episode a much needed edginess that was missing and sent a message about drug use more clearly than what was shown.

Lesko, portrayed by Jimmie F. Skaggs, was a megalomaniac with delusions of grandeur; a Woodstock reject too much out of place in the 1990's. When the Flash captured Lesko by playing an electric guitar at super-speed, the episode crossed the line into cheap camp and, thankfully, put the lid on an ill-conceived episode.

Ghost in The Machine gave viewers both another super-villain, the Ghost, and another costumed hero, Nightshade. The Ghost, like Trachmann from **Double Vision** used high technology to aid his evil schemes. Originally a villain from the 1950's, the Ghost predicted the power that television would have over society and set himself into suspended animation until technology caught up with his warped vision. He awakened in the 1990's to find things even more vivid than he had imagined them.

As the Ghost, actor Anthony Starke was like a kid in a candy store; a young genius mad with kinetic energy. Unfortunately, the Ghost didn't quite measure up to the likes of Trachmann. Perhaps today's audiences are desensitized, but the crux of the Ghost's plan, that television really is "the Evil Eye" that it was called so long ago, just doesn't wash today. Trachmann's technology was cutting edge virtual reality; the melding of man and machine. That kind of technology can still unnerve an audience because its so new. Television doesn't scare us anymore, and that fact diminished the Ghost's potential. He was little more than a video hacker, albeit a powerful one. The addition of Jason Bernard as Dr. Desmond Powell/Nightshade, the man who defeated the Ghost in the 1950's, redeemed the episode and gave John Wesley Shipp's Flash a much-needed mentor. The Ghost wasn't the Flash's greatest adversary, but he wasn't the worst either. He ranked about average over all.

Sight Unseen had some great special effects, and it fulfilled the mandatory "hero battles the invisible villain" rule that apparently exists in genre television. Christopher Neame was Gideon, a man who created an invisibility device, and used it to break into S.T.A.R. Labs to destroy some lethal biochemicals. Neame was good in the role, but he was unusually invisible, and its hard to be an on-screen presence when you aren't really on-screen all that often. Still, the idea of an invisible villain taking on the Flash worked well. Gideon didn't need to be fast, and it didn't matter how fast the Flash was. Speed was ineffectual against this enemy and Barry had to find an indirect method to capture him. Gideon was also a more effective villain because he was slightly sympathetic. He was trying to right what he felt was an injustice, but he unwittingly placed Tina McGee in danger, so the Flash had to stop Gideon and save his friend. The star of this episode really was the special effects, however; everything else took a back seat to them, including the stature of the villain.

The next major villain that the Flash faced wasn't superpowered, but she knew the secrets of his super-speed, and that made her doubly dangerous. In **Tina, Is That You?** Tina McGee was zapped by an energy surge from a biofeedback machine and transformed into a ruthless criminal. Amanda Pays took the chance to break out of her limiting role as Tina McGee to the hilt. She played the evil

Tina as vindictive and uncompromising, more than willing to snuff out the Flash, a man she truly cared about.

Since **Sight Unseen** covered the invisible villain requirement, this episode covered the "hero faces off against friend who has become enemy" mandate. It was also based on the gimmick that an all-female band of modern day desperados terrorized the city and after her transformation, Tina took over as their leader. The Flash, who had been tracking the Black Rose gang, had to pull double duty to bring them in and save his friend, who was becoming more evil by the minute. Tina may not have been a super-villain, but she had a hold over the Flash that no other criminal had, and that made her one of his most dangerous enemies.

The evil Tina McGee may have been bad, but no other criminal could ever hope to match the spectacle and anarchy that was the Trickster. He was colorful and crazy; a deadly, mad genius, and the first super-villain to come from the pages of *The Flash* comic book. The Trickster was a cunning psychopath, a madman with a plan to eradicate Central City's Scarlet Speedster.

Mark Hamill took the opportunity to obliterate the lingering stigma of Luke Skywalker by making the Trickster so over-the-top that the rest of the cast had to scramble to reach him. Not surprisingly, John Wesley Shipp kept up with Hamill's bravura performance by making the Flash out to be the Trickster's ultimate straight man. Together they added a tremendous amount of fun to their confrontations. They were silly, but they never crossed the line into kiddie camp, as was done in **Child's Play**. Hamill returned to the role of the Trickster in the final episode of the series, **Trial of the Trickster** making him the only villain to appear twice. His second appearance was hampered somewhat by a convoluted plot that was too big to fit into a one hour episode, but he was just as manic as the first time. Had the series continued, Hamill's Trickster would surely have been inducted into the Recurring Villains Hall of Fame, where the likes of Ceasar Romero's Joker, Julie Newmar's Catwoman, Roger Carmel's Harry Mudd, John Delancie's Q and Micheal Dunn's Miguelito Loveless live on in the hearts of fans.

The next noteworthy villain who faced off against the Flash seemed to be patterned after another well-known DC comics hero. In **Deadly Nightshade**, Curtis Bohannon took on the aspect of the Nightshade, first seen in the episode **Ghost in the Machine**. Bohannon's Deadly Nightshade was far more brutal than the original, however, and his killing spree brought Dr. Desmond Powell out of retirement once more to clear his alter ego's name.

The Deadly Nightshade had more than a passing resemblance to Batman: Curtis Bohannon was a wealthy socialite disturbed by a traumatic childhood event (the discovery that his father was an underworld kingpin), and compelled to become a costumed vigilante to cleanse a guilty conscience. The difference was that the Deadly Nightshade had no problem with killing his underworld targets, something neither Batman nor the original Nightshade resorted to.

The best thing about the episode was Jason Bernard's return as Desmond Powell/Nightshade. Powell made a perfect partner for John Wesley Shipp's Barry Allen, and his wisdom gave real definition to his alter ego. Actor Richard Burgi made Bohannon into Powell's flip-side; a man with the right intentions, but without the morals and ideals needed to keep him from crossing the line from hero to killer. Bohannon's Deadly Nightshade took vigilante justice too far; he wasn't content simply turning criminals into the police, his agenda called for snuffing them out. Furthermore, with his strength augmented by an electronic exo-skeleton, the Deadly Nightshade was able to match the Flash's speed with super-strength. The Deadly Nightshade showed how costumed crime-fighters like the Flash can fall from the tightrope they walk between heroism and criminality, and that made him a worthy adversary.

The Flash's next challenge was the second one pulled from *The Flash* comic book; Captain Cold. Aside from the Trickster and the Deadly Nightshade, the producers of *The Flash* shied away from putting their bad guys in costumes. Perhaps they wanted the Flash to be somewhat of a singularity, since having so many costumed characters might reduce the hero's countenance. Whatever the reason, Captain Cold wore regular clothes, except for his freezing gun. It made sense from a certain point of view: Why would a criminal go through all the trouble of creating an elaborate costume simply to commit crimes? On the other hand, half the fun of watching a show like *The Flash* was seeing the wild outfits the characters would wear.

If it has already been accepted that police scientist Barry Allen was given incredible powers after doused by chemicals charged by a bolt of lightning, and that he dons a costume to protect his identity when he goes around righting wrongs, then why not take things a step further? What has already been accepted is (realistically) pretty far out, so why not give the audience far out villains as well?

At any rate, the producers made up for Captain Cold having no costume by giving the role to Michael Champion, who gave a solid, offbeat performance. He made Captain Cold as frigid on the inside as he made the outside world with his freezing gun. Champion went from quirky to deadly in the space of a heartbeat and he took the story with him when he did it. His performance propelled the episode from start to finish, and, as usual, Shipp kept pace with his co-star, matching Captain Cold's chilliness with the Flash's terse determination to overcome his foe. Fans may have missed Captain Cold's costume, but they got their money's worth with Michael Champion's terrific portrayal.

Every genre television series must have a casting coup, a guest star that no one would expect to see in a role that they'd never be expected to play. *The Flash* had one when David (Keith Partridge) Cassidy was tapped to play the Mirror Master in the episode **Done With Mirrors**. The Mirror Master was the third super-villain lifted from the comic book, and as with Captain Cold, the producers decided to forgo the villain's costume for a long overcoat and nifty special effects.

Surprisingly, Cassidy was up to the role of the Mirror Master. He was actually pretty slimy and seemed to relish being nasty for a change. He may not have played the most dangerous villain the Flash ever faced, but he was certainly the shiftiest. Cassidy slithered through scenes with a smirk, daring Shipp's Flash to guess whether it was really the Mirror Master or just another of his fancy holographic reflections. The episode perfectly mixed danger and fun; it was one wild ride and Cassidy definitely made the role of the Mirror Master his own.

That about covers it when it comes to the worthwhile villains the Flash had to defeat. Of course, there were characters like Pollux from the episode **Twin Streaks**, a clone of the Flash perfectly played by Shipp in a dual role. But Pollux wasn't as much a villain as he was a kind of "lost soul", and the episode filled the "hero battles himself" rule that goes with the other Mandatory Genre Plots listed earlier. The other criminals showcased were either conventional bad guys, or characters so weak that they aren't worth mentioning at all. *The Flash* had a better than average record when it came to super-villains. Even some of the weaker ones, like the Ghost, were at least fun to watch. There is every reason to believe that, if there had been a second season, *The Flash* would have continued to bring great villains to life. Rumors abounded that other villains from the comic like Weather Wizard and even Professor Zoom might have made appearances. Also, the strong performances by Michael Champion, David Cassidy and especially Mark Hamill easily qualified the return of Captain Cold, Mirror Master and the Trickster.

Unfortunately, there was to be no second season. CBS bounced the series from time slot to time slot with very little warning. Viewers had trouble keeping up with *The Flash*, so to speak, and so the ratings faltered. A massive letter campaign from fans was ineffectual and the show fell into single season oblivion. It hasn't vanished completely, though. The pilot film, *The Flash*, is now available on videocassette, and the episodes **The Trickster** and **Trial of the Trickster** have been combined to create the film *The Flash II: Revenge of the Trickster*, also available on videocassette. This way at least fans can reminisce with some of the best action that the series had to offer. It may be a small consolation, but it keeps the show from disappearing completely. *The Flash* may have too quickly run its course on television, but the show is well-remembered and it always came in first place with fans of the hero, and fans of super-villains.

THE FLASH

review by William E. Anchors, Jr.

Production credits:

Executive Producers	Paul De Meo
	Danny Bilson
Developed by	Paul De Meo
	Danny Bilson
Theme Song	Danny Elfman
Music	Shirley Walker

Regular cast:

Barry Allen/The Flash	John Wesley Shipp
Christina "Tina" McGee	Amanda Pays
Julio Mendez	Alex Desert
Henry Allen	M. Emmet Walsh
Nora Allen	Priscilla Pointer
Joe Kline	Richard Belzer
Officer Murphy	Biff Manard
Officer Bellows	Vito D'Ambrosio
Lt. Warren Garfield	Mike Genovese
Fosnight	Dick Miller
Shawn Allen	Justin Burnette

Premise: The adventures of DC Comics super-hero, the Flash, now brought to the screen for the first time in a live action format. Stories revolve around Barry Allen, the fastest man alive, and his efforts to support law and order in Central City.

Editor's comments: Possibly the most brilliantly conceived and executed television show to be put on the air in years. Somewhat reminiscent of the 1989 movie *Batman*, the show, particularly the pilot, is dark and moody, and loaded with atmosphere. Visually the series is portrayed with an unusual time and place perspective, brought about by using cars and trucks from all time periods and from countries around the globe. All of the stories, except for the mediocre "Be My Baby", range from above average to superb. Music composed by Danny Elfman (of *Batman* fame) is breathtaking, as are the top-notch special effects, including the stunningly realistic speed sequences. Direction is also well above average, as are the special villains created for the show (or revised from the comic). *The Flash* has been lucky to include some extraordinarily talented stars, particularly John Wesley Shipp and Amanda Pays (the latter of *Max Headroom* fame). Even guest stars have been above par, especially Mark Hamill's brilliant portrayal of The Trickster in two episodes. About the only flaw is the stories seem to occasionally have been written by committees instead of individual writers. A prime example is "Honor Among Thieves", which is a good episode but it often makes little or no sense, probably the result of no less than *five* separate writers working on the script - something that almost always results in a bad story. Nonetheless, *The Flash* is nothing short of amazing, considering it is being made in a time when we are being assaulted and insulted by junk like *The Munsters Today* or *Dracula: The Series*. Just when you figure TV can't get any worse (and it does) an occasional gem comes along. In this case, the jewel is called *The Flash*.

The Flash (airdate: Sept. 20, 1990, two hour pilot). Barry Allen works for the Central City Police Department in the crime lab, while his brother Jay is the captain of the motorcycle division. Their father, Henry, is a retired street cop who never lets Barry forget that "real" cops work out on the street, not in the lab. At a birthday party for Jay, Barry's beeper goes off calling him back to work. Barry and his partner, Julio, are called in to look over the site of the latest attack by the Dark Riders, a group of motorcycle hoodlums led by ex-motorcycle cop Nicholas Pike, who is now terrorizing Central City because of his being thrown off the force. After making examinations at the crime scene, Barry and Julio return to the crime lab, where, while working late at night, a bolt of lightning goes though the lab window, knocks over a rack of chemicals, then hits Barry. He awakens in a hospital room, having been hit with a strange combination of chemicals and the lightning bolt, but he decides to leave the hospital to help the struggling police department fight Pike and his gang. At the crime lab, Barry's doctor calls and asks Barry to see a specialist at Star Labs to be checked for cell damage. He refuses, at least until he outruns his dog by several hundred miles an hour while giving Earl a walk. Then when he tries to run to catch a bus to see his girlfriend, Iris, he ends up at Crystal Beach, thirty miles away - in a total of ten seconds running time.

Iris shows no interest in Barry's sudden problem, so he agrees to see Dr. Christina McGee, a scientist at Star Labs, a government-funded research facility for top-secret research. Barry is wary of the place after hearing that a scientist had died there under strange circumstances the year before, a scientist who turns out to have been Tina's husband. But he shortly learns to trust Tina as she proceeds to try to understand the chemical change in Barry's body that, after placed on a treadmill, allows him to run 347 miles per hour before the device explodes. After each super-fast movement Barry must consume vast quantities of food to replace burned-up calories. Over a meal, Christina warns Barry that his super speed must remain a secret, as the federal government will turn him into a human guinea pig to experiment on and duplicate. He agrees, but wants Tina to help him be rid of the super-speed ability. At a Star Lab test track, Tina times Barry running at over the speed of sound. He is able to run at this high speed without danger because of a special suit Tina has adapted from an experimental diving outfit. However, Barry collapses after the run, a side affect of his body adapting to his movements at high speed. Meanwhile, Pike makes an additional attack on the Central City Police Department to flaunt that they cannot stop his gang. That night, Pike plans the final attack designed to destroy the police department and kill Jay Allen - the man who had him thrown off the force. [The character of Iris became Barry's wife in the the comic book, and was intended to be a regular in the series but Iris seemed largely superfluous and was dropped after the pilot, giving Barry a much greater freedom in working with other female characters and helping considerably in developing the other personalities in the show.] [This episode was released in Europe and Japan as a theatrical movie and on video tape.] **Guest cast:** Michael Nader as Nicholas Pike, Tim Thomerson as Jay Allen, Lycia Naff as Lyla, Robert Hooks as Chief Arthur Cooper, Paula Marshall as Iris West, Patrie-Allen as Eve Allen [Jay's wife], Wayne Perre as Rick, Eric DaRe as Tyrone, Ricky Dean Logan as Scott, Mariko Tse as Linda Park, Sam Vlahos as Dr. Lawrence, Josh Cruze as Petrolli, David L. Crowley as the S.W.A.T. captain, Virginia Morris as the mother, Richard Hoyt Miller as the young father, Jan Stango as the young mother, Brad "Cat" Sevvy as the waiter. **Writers:** Paul De Meo and Danny Bilson. **Director:** Robert Iscoe.

Out of Control (airdate: Sept. 27, 1990). Street people are dieing horribly, then disappearing, in Central City. Their protector, Father Michael, goes to the police to ask for help, but Capt. Garfield refuses to assign officers to Skid Row, complaining that he lacks the funds to patrol every alley of the city. After giving Barry a hard time for bringing the priest into his office, Garfield tells Barry to stick to his test tubes. Later that night, Barry joins Tina at a scientific speech being given by a genetic researcher and old flame of hers, Carl Tanner. Carl has never stopped loving Tina, even though she married a mutual friend instead. Now with her husband dead, Carl hopes to re-spark some old feelings from Tina, a situation Barry is not overly happy with. Back at the police building, a near-riot occurs when the street people demand protection from the horrible menace that hunting down and killing them in the back alleys of Central City. Barry finally becomes frustrated with Garfield's lack of action, and begins an investigation of his own, where he learns that someone is experimenting on Skid Row bums by injecting them with a mutating drug. The trail of questions leads Barry, unfortunately, back to Carl, who is doing work in gene modifications and is experimenting on the street people since he doesn't consider them to be human beings. As more people die, Barry reveals that he suspects Carl, resulting in Tina accusing Barry of simply being jealous. Meanwhile, Carl himself becomes a monster after taking an injection of the drug he has been using on others, and he takes an additional injection to turn into a super-being to destroy the Flash. **Guest cast:** Stan Ivar as Dr. Carl Tanner, Jeff Perry as Charlie, John Toles-Bey as Father Michael, Robert Benedetti as Dr. Mortimer, Michael Earl Reid as Mickey, Mario Roccuzzo as Sam, Bill Dunham as Jack, Macka Foley as the cop. **Writer:** Gail Morgan Hickman. **Director:** Mario Azzopardi.

Watching the Detectives (Oct. 18, 1990). A large fire has broken out in a warehouse, the latest of many suspicious burnings. The Flash shows up just in time to save two children from the burning building, while nearby in a van is Megen Lockhart, a private detective filming one of the firefighters she suspects to be the Flash. In fact, Megan has been hired to learn the secret identity of the Flash, and his appearance at the fire at the same time as the fireman leaves only one suspect: police officer Barry Allen. Back at her office she meets District Attorney Thomas Castillo, a corrupt politician working for mobster Arthur Simonson, who has just been cleared of charges after the D.A. fails to prove the government's case against him. With dreams of going on to much bigger things, he has hired Megan to find out the Flash's secret identity, so he can blackmail the super-speedster into doing his bidding, and put his mob boss out of business so Castillo can replace him. In the meantime, Barry is trying to find out why the abandoned warehouses are being burned, not yet realizing that the mob is behind the fires in an effort to buy the property at bargain prices and move in a gambling casino and hotels there. He is also unaware that Megan has managed to film him turning into the Flash, which he learns when Castillo arrives at

Barry's home to announce that he knows who Barry is, and the Flash will now help him put Arthur Simonson out of business so he can take his place. With the safety of his friends and relatives at stake, Barry has no choice but to comply. Even worse, while Barry is busy doing Castillo's bidding, the D.A. orders Megan and Tina killed, as he wants the secret of the Flash's identity to himself. **Guest cast:** Joyce Hyser as Megan Lockhart, Vincent F. Gustaferro as Thomas Castillo, Harris Laskawy as Arthur Simonson, Helen Martin as Sadie Grosso, Jordan Lund as Noble John Spanier, Hubert Braddock as the bartender, Pat Cupo as the lounge lizard, Darrell Harris as Gillespie, Manual Perry as Gordo, Brenda Swanson as the slinky dame, Frankie Thorn as Judith, Nicholas Trikonis as Pat. **Writers:** Howard Chaykin and John Francis Moore. **Director:** Gus Trickonis.

Honor Among Thieves (airdate: Oct. 25, 1990). A group of expert thieves and burglars are meeting in Central City, and their arrival has already led to the death of three police officers. Elsewhere, Barry attends a meeting for the officers working at providing security for a special art treasure arriving soon at the Central City Museum. The police are aware that the crooks are in town, but have no idea where they are. Barry knows the museum director, Ted Preminger, who had been Barry's teacher and had hoped the young Barry would follow in his footsteps. Barry turned to the police force instead, resulting in a rift between the two friends that has never healed. Preminger is concerned about keeping his museum alive, and realizes that the visiting mask will bring in desperately-needed income. Before the thieves can try to hit the museum Flash manages to put one of them out of commission, but this makes the group aware of his presence and they plan to kill him. Their first attempt fails just as Preminger's assistant, Celia, meets the gang leader to help him with their plans. Later, Barry identifies one of the gang members and when the Federal officers find out who it is, they decide to pull the exhibit as it is too dangerous to keep it at the museum. But before they can go anywhere Celia reveals the planned move to the gang, causing them to launch their real plan: a city-wide robbery of financial institutions while the police are busy guarding the mask. **Guest cast:** Ian Buchanan as Stan Kovaks, Michael Green as Mitch Lestrange, Clarence Clemons as Darrell Hennings, Elizabeth Gracen as Celia Wayne, Paul Linke as Ted Preminger, Rene Assa as Mark Bernhardt, Jon Menick as Parry Johnson, Ping Wu as Chu Lee, Lydie Denier as Kate Tatting, Sav Farrow as Franco Mortelli, Michael Wyle as Anderson. **Writers:** Milo Bachman, Danny Bilson, Paul De Meo, Howard Chayakin and John Francis Moore. **Director:** Aaron Lipstadt.

Double Vision (airdate: Nov. 1, 1990). At Central City's Day of the Dead Festival, Barry and Tina are celebrating Felix Tomarquin's first year in the U.S. at his restaurant. After eating, Barry is certain someone in trying to contact the Flash, and Barry has received a letter for him to meet a stranger at a local church. Arriving there, he meets a young lady who says she knows nothing about the letter, but when Barry hears someone in the closed church he changes into the Flash and is promptly ambushed. Shot in the neck with a knock-out dart, the Flash collapses as the man who shot him walks up and announces that he is about to take control of the super-hero. The next day Barry awakens in bed, with no idea how he got there, and Tina suddenly arrives and complains that he never showed up at the play they were supposed to see together, and she was unable to find him all night. Before they can figure out why he has a memory black-out, Julio calls Barry and asks that he come down to the small church he was at the previous night. It seems that neighbors, simple peasants

from a foreign country, saw the church's statues walk outside on their own. The description sounds like the Flash may have moved them, but Barry has no memory of it happening. The superstitious neighbors believe it is an evil sign, but the same girl that met Barry the night before thinks their fears are nonsense. Later, after arriving at home, Barry has another blackout, not yet realizing that Trachmann, the man who knocked him out, has given Barry a brain implant that allows him to control the Flash's actions. With the help

152

of the fastest man alive, Trachmann plans to find Sofia Tomarquin, the daughter of a man who is going to be a witness against his mobster boss, and put her on ice so Peter Paul Aguilar cannot testify. **Guest cast:** Charley Hayward as Trachmann, Karla Montana as Paloma, Michael Fernandes as Reuben Calderon, Ricardo Gutierrez as Father Becerra, Zitto Kazann as the Santero, William Marquez as Felix Tomarquin, Richard Yniguez as Peter Paul Aguilar, Elisabeth Chavez as Sofia Tomarquin, Anne Gee Byrd as the official, Clifton Gonzalez Gonzalez as Javier O'Hara. **Writer:** Jim Trombetta. **Director:** Gus Trikonis.

Sins of the Father (airdate: Nov. 8, 1990) Johnny Ray Hix, a felon Barry's father put behind bars years earlier, has managed to escape prison and plans to get the revenge he has vowed to obtain. After Heny Allen has supper with Nora and Barry the phone rings, and on the other end is a threatening Johnny Ray, and who wants Henry to know he has returned to kill him and his former partner, Pete, who was crippled by a bullet from Johnny Ray, who would have killed the cop if it hadn't been for the arrival of Henry. The next day, Henry warns Pete that Johnny Ray is in town, and they prepare for an attack by the killer. Barry and Nora notice Henry's strange behavior, but do not know the reason for it until Johnny Ray blasts the front of the Allen house with machine gun fire. Johnny gets away before Barry can catch him, but he is determined to stop the maniac before his father or Pete are harmed - which he fails to do as Pete is killed then Henry is wounded. Meanwhile, Johnny Ray is looking for the fortune in cash he hid before he was caught, but the hiding place now turns out to be inside a land development project that has greatly changed the appearance of the area, making it very difficult to find the loot. **Guest cast:** Paul Koslo as Johnny Ray Hix, Richard Kuss as Pete Donello, Michael James as Gruber, Ralph Seymour as Danny, Pete Antico as pool player #2, Richard Camphuis as the prison guard, Will Gill, Jr. as the security guard, Chuck Hicks as the senior officer, Fred Lerner as Welles, Cole McKay as pool player #1, Robert Shayne as Reggie, Wes Studi as Roller. **Writer:** Stephen Hattman. **Director:** Jonathan Sanger.

Child's Play (airdate: Nov. 15, 1990). A newspaper writer, Phil Sullivan, has been putting together information about Beauregarde Lesko, a radical and drug pusher from the 1960's that was supposed to have died years earlier. As Sullivan leaves his apartment he drops his bag containing the computer discs with the information on Lesko in the front seat of his convertible, only to have a young street-wise boy on a skateboard steal the bag and get away. Before the reporter can do anything a bomb is set off by one of Lesko's followers, blowing up Sullivan's car with him in it. Later, Barry and Tina, friends of Sullivan and his wife Joan, attend the funeral and vow to find out who killed him. Meanwhile, on the streets of Central City a pusher is lining up the distribution of Blue Paradise, a new drug invented by Lesko, one that is incredibly addictive and destructive. It turns out that his prospective buyers are cops, but when they try to arrest Duvivier they are jumped by thugs. The timely arrival of the Flash wraps things up, and Duvivier soon finds himself behind bars. Later, Barry catches the same kid who stole the bag breaking into his car, and Barry arrests him. Terry Cohen is a thirteen-year-old who ran away from a foster home, and has lived on the streets with his younger sister for nine months. They have survived by petty theft, and now that Terry has been caught he will be sent to juvenile hall. No one knows about his sister, but Barry finds her along with Perry after the boy tries to run away when Barry agreed to take him home so he could avoid juvenile hall. While Barry takes them both home, Lesko is ordering his assistant, Pepper, to get the disc back from

Terry - and kill him to keep the boy from talking. Meanwhile, Lesko plans to release Blue Paradise throughout the city to turn the citizens of Central City into a huge collection of addicts that Duvivier, now out of jail, can sell the drug to. **Guest cast:** Jonathan Brandis as Terry, Perrey Reeves as Pepper, Michael Lamar Richards as Joan Sullivan, Jimmie F. Skaggs as Beauregarde Lesko, Kirk Baltz as Duvivier, Ivonne Coll as Carmen Hijueles, Freddie Dawson as Phillip Sulivan, Remy Ryan as Cory Cohen, Mark Dacascos as Osako, Alec Murdock as the passenger, Awest as the hippy guy, Lance Gilbert as Aliota. **Writers:** Howard Chaykin and John Francis Moore. **Director:** Danny Bilson.

Shroud of Death (airdate: Nov. 29, 1990). As Judge Foster and his wife leave the theater, they find an envelope on the windshield of their car with a medallion inside. Getting in the car, the judge suddenly realizes what it is - just as an explosion occurs and the theater marquis is blown off the building, crushing him and his wife to death in their car. Barry and Julio arrive at the scene and quickly realize that whoever killed the Fosters was an expert at explosives. Lt. Garfield is less than impressed with their detective work, but they get a chance to tease him when they find an engagement ring he dropped that he plans to give to his girlfriend, Mavis, whom he has been dating for three years. That night Garfield pops the question, and she says yes. Unfortunately, Garfield doesn't yet know that he is on the same hit list as the Fosters, from a person with a grudge against several people from her past. Meanwhile, Barry heads to a survivalist shop with a lead on the special explosives used to kill the Fosters. He shows up as the Flash to learn who produced the explosives, but the man refuses to talk even after Barry dismantles every illegal automatic weapon in his shop. Later that night Barry has diner with Tina, who announces she has been offered the job of her dreams in California. Before they can discuss the situation further a disgruntled politician, Frank Dejoy, receives the same part of a medallion as the Fosters. Stopping by Barry's table on the way out he is suddenly hit and killed by two arrows. With Tina now moving away, Garfield on a hit list, and two bizarre deaths to solve, Barry encounters another problem: after changing into the Flash to find the killer, she knocks him out with a ray gun-like device and pulls out a knife to finish him off. **Guest cast:** Lenore Kasdorf as Mavis, Walter Olkeqicz as Calahan, Lora Zane as Angel, Don Hood as Frank Dejoy, Fred Pinkard as Judge Foster, Marguerite Ray as Mrs. Foster, Dani Klein as the reporter, Randall Montgomery as the aide. **Writer:** Michael Reeves. **Director:** Mario Azzopardi.

Ghost in the Machine (airdate: Dec. 13, 1990). In 1955 Central City, a criminal known as the Ghost decides to blow up the city hospital when the mayor refuses to pay a ransom demand. But all is not lost: a mysterious crime fighter known as Nightshade appears from the darkness to oppose him. But the Ghost, an expert who uses video devices for his crimes, is ready for Nightshade, who is ambushed by the Ghost's female partner, Ghostess. At the last second Nightshade pulls out a jamming device, stopping the detonation signal, and as a fire breaks out in the warehouse the Ghost sneaks off into a time chamber, where he will awaken in 1990. Afterwards, no one ever finds the secret room with the capsule, and in 1990 the Ghost returns to haunt Central City. Elsewhere, Barry and Tina go to a tv telethon with Julio and his girlfriend, not knowing that the Ghost, rejoined by his 35-years-older Ghostette is on their way to the very same station. Arriving their, the Ghost takes everyone hostage, and begins a broadcast of his own to threaten the city. The timely arrival of the Flash runs the Ghost's thugs off, but they escape with much equipment while Flash saves several people from harm. Also in the studio is Dr. Desmond Powell, long-retired from his secret identity as the superhero known as the Nightshade, who decides it is time to return to action against his old adversary. Later, just after Ghost announces to the city that he is going to obtain revenge for the city not paying him in 1955, Flash arrives to stop him, but is trapped in a laser web that threatens to burn him to a crisp. The Flash's only hope left is the Nightshade, who arrives to stop the Ghost - but he is gunned down after disarming one of Ghost's men. Now Central City is at the mercy of the sinister Ghost. **Guest cast:** Jason Bernard as Dr. Desmond Powell, Lois Nettleton as Belle Crocker, Anthony Starke as the Ghost, Floyd Raglin as Tex, Sherrie Rose as the young Belle Ian Abercrombie as Skip, Gloria Reuben as Sabrinna. **Writers:** John Francis Moore and Howard Chaykin. **Director:** Bruce Bilson.

Sight Unseen (airdate: Jan. 10, 1991). At Star Labs Barry is upset with Tina because she must break a date to finish up a project that Tina's slave-driver boss, Star Labs chief executive Ruth Werneke, demands that she work all night if necessary to finish. After Barry leaves so Tina can get back to work, an invisible intruder enters Star Lab, kills a guard, and sabotages a top-secret germ warfare experiment so that it will be released into the atmosphere, killing everyone in the Star Labs building, and if the automatically-sealed labs are opened, it will mean instant death for thousands of people in Central City. When the alarms sound at Star Labs, Ruth and Tina try to get out, but don't make it before the building is sealed shut. Minutes later, Barry tries to call Tina to ask her something, and a phone message reveals the lock-down status of the lab. The Flash rushes to the lab, but is unable to enter. He manages to contact Tina through her computer terminal, and Barry learns if he tries to break into the lab it will automatically decontaminate - killing everyone inside. Ruth claims she doesn't know anything about the deadly germ weapon, but she finally admits the truth, and after watching a video tape of the lab they realize an "invisible man" is responsible for the contamination. Tina is furious that Star Labs has anything to do with manufacturing weapons, which also happens to be the motivating factor behind the sabotage by Brian Gideon, an ex-Star Labs employee who is now dieing of a brain tumor because of other weapons work that he was tricked into doing by the people he worked for - and now wants to expose. Meanwhile, an incompetent federal employee named Quinn arrives to say that he can have a neutralizer for the germs delivered to the lab within twenty-four hours - far too late for Tina and Ruth, as the virus in the lab will have killed them long before then. Realizing that there is no hope if matters are left up to Quinn, Barry contacts Tina, who is proceeding to work on an anti-toxin, and Barry plans to go into action as the Flash to find the invisible intruder - but is arrested and handcuffed by Quinn, who has no intention of letting Barry interfere further with his operation. **Guest cast:** Deborah May as Ruth Werneke, George Dickerson as Quinn, Christopher Neame as Brian Gideon, Francois Giroday as Dr. Cartwright, Sarah Daly as Edwards, Robert Shayne as Reggie, James Tartan as Dr. Velinski. **Writer:** John Vorhaus. **Director:** Christopher Leitch.

Beat the Clock (airdate: Jan. 31, 1991). Wayne Cotrell, a jazz musician, is waiting on death row for his execution, which will come in less than an hour. He has been sentenced to death for the murder of his wife, singer Linda Lake, because he was jealous of her having struck it big and was leaving him to move to California where she was to begin producing records for a major record company. Although Wayne admits to having had an argument with Linda and leaving their club with another woman, he denies having

killed her or their breaking up over her career, but the jury still found him guilty in a trial and several appeals. At the nearby Central City police department, Barry's buddy Julio is upset over knowing his friend, Wayne, will soon be killed for a crime he didn't commit. After Julio leaves, a musician named Dave Buell calls the lab and reveals to Barry that he has proof that Linda Lake is alive - but before he can finish the phone call he is killed by Whisper, a thug that has had his vocal cords cut by a gang. Rushing there as the Flash, Barry is too late to save Dave, and all he finds is a mangled cassette tape - the proof Dave spoke of. Barry gets ahold of Julio to meet him at the club Wayne's brother owns, where Linda sang for the first time. At the club, Barry catches Elliott Cotrell lieing when he claims that Dave is in Chicago, so he takes the tape to Tina to have her reconstruct the evidence. Meanwhile, Barry rushes to Wayne's cell to hear his side of the story - but neither they or Julio have yet figured out that Linda is *not* dead, she is alive and sedated in Eliott's apartment, where she is continuing to sing songs that Eliott plans to release later when there is a huge demand for Linda's music, netting Elliott a fantastic profit. Once that is done, he will have Whisper finish her off for real - just like he did the girl whose burned body the police mistook for the very much alive Linda Lake. **Guest cast:** Thomas Mikal Ford as Elliott Cotrell, Ken Foree as Whisper, Angela Bassett as Linda Lake, Jay Arlen Jones as Wayne Cotrell, Eugene Lee as Dave Buell, John Toles-Bey as Father Michael, Joe Bellan as the security guard, Dennis Vero as the morgue attendant. **Writer:** Jim Trombetta. **Director:** Mario Azzopardi.

The Trickster (airdate: Feb. 7, 1991). Barry and Tina are getting ready to watch a movie at Barry's apartment when Barry checks his answering machine and hears an urgent call from Megan Lockhart. It seems that Megan is working in Willowheaven, a resort town one hundred and fifty miles north, where she has been hunting down James Montgomery Jesse, a multiple-personality lunatic criminal, who currently thinks he is a magician and, after Megan calls Barry, Jesse captures her ant ties her down so that he can practice sawing her in half - with a chain saw. Running the longest distance of his career, the Flash arrives at the abandoned theater Jesse is practicing his magic in and saves Megan at the last second. Jesse isn't impressed, and goes after the Flash with the chain saw. The criminal is quickly tied up and picked up by the police, and as he is being dragged away he swears undieing love to Megan, the aggressive girl of his dreams. Megan returns with Flash to Central City where she spends the next few days at his apartment, giving the police time to put James Jesse safely behind bars. But en route to jail Jesse kills his guards and steals their car, then heads for Central City to obtain revenge against the Flash and be reunited with Megan, his one true love. Once in Central City, Jesse's deranged mind looks for a new personality to latch onto, and seeing a prop warehouse that is for sale, he breaks in and becomes inspired to be a super-villan, known as the Trickster. **Guest cast:** Joyce Hyser as Megan Lockhart, Mark Hamill [*Star Wars*] as James Montgomery Jesse/The Trickster, Gloria Reuben as Sabrina, Tim Stack as Jim Kline, William Long, Jr. as Matthews, Christopher Murray as Williams. **Writers:** Howard Chaykin and John Francis Moore. **Director:** Danny Bilson.

Tina - Is That You? (airdate: Feb. 14, 1991). Tina arrives at Barry's apartment at two in the morning, and explains that she cannot hold back the truth anymore: she is in love with him. He is surprised, but admits that he loves her too. Before they can speak further, they look out the window and see an old lady get mugged. Barry goes into action as the Flash and catches up with the thief, who turns out to be Tina! But this is not the Tina he knows, which he realizes as the woman screams how much she hates him, then she pulls a pistol and shoots him - just as he awakens from the same dream he has been having over and over. Going to Tina for help, he doesn't tell her what he has been dreaming about, but explains his problem. She claims that his sped-up metabolism is not producing the Alpha waves needed for a good, sound sleep. She hooks herself and Barry up to a new bio-feedback machine that will take some of her excess Alpha waves and give them to Barry, but the experiment goes haywire when he falls asleep and has the nightmare again, causing the machine to transfer the memories to Tina. She is knocked unconscious and has to be taken to the hospital, and when she wakes up she has completely changed in personality - into the evil Tina Barry has dreamed about. Returning to work, Barry becomes upset because Julio has fixed him up with another blind date, which always turns out to be a disaster. Meanwhile, the Black Rose Gang, a trio of female criminals, is robbing a fur shop, until the Flash catches them and ties them up. Murphy and Bellows arrive to take them in, but are overpowered and the girls are on the lose again, until the Flash makes a second appearance. Unfortunately, they try to run down Barry, and in the ensuing car crash the gang leader is killed, which the other girls blame the Flash for. Back at the hospital, Tina sees slimeball reporter Joe Kline on TV doing a report about the dead Black Rose leader - and is inspired to become their new leader, to not only create a new crime wave in Central City, but to kill the Flash as well. **Guest cast:** Yvette Nipar as Lisa March, John Santucci as Big Ed, Denise Dillard as Shauna Duke, Courtney Gebhart as Janie Jones, William Forward as Dr. Wilhilhite, Ivy Bethune as the old woman, Mary Gillis as Nurse Gladys, Bella Pollini as Harley Lyndon. **Writer:** David L. Newman. **Director:** William A. Fraker.

Be My Baby (airdate: Feb. 21, 1991). On his way home, Barry sees a girl knocked down and her suitcase thrown on the ground. Obviously hungry, Barry tries to help her but she refuses. Moments later, two hoods emerge from a limousine and try to catch Stacy, who gets away because of the timely arrival of the Flash. Barry catches up with Stacy, who still refuses help until Barry mentions that he is a cop. She asks him to take her and her baby - hidden in a backpack - to a street mission. She ends up spending the night at Barry's apartment, and the next day is taken to a street home Nora Allen works at, but the girl is still reluctant to reveal her past. Elsewhere, crime boss Philip Moses is ordering his men to find and capture Stacy's child - his daughter - no matter what it takes, and he could care less what happens to Stacy, the girl he married not for love, but because of her background. [Why this truly horrendous script was ever produced is a mystery, but it is far below the standards of the rest of the series.] **Guest cast:** Bryan Cranston as Philip Moses, Kimberly Neville as Stacy, Robert Z'Dar as Bodey Nuff, David Chemell as Roy, John Hostetter as Mills. **Writer:** Jule Selbo. **Director:** Bruce Bilson.

Fast Forward (airdate: Feb. 27, 1991). After nearly destroying Central City, Nicholas Pike is released from prison because of a technicality that arose after his arrest The public is furious, as is Barry, whose brother Jay was murdered by Pike. Barry grabs Pike on the way out of court and swears that the murderer will pay for his crimes, but he is forced away by Pike's attorney, who threatens to turn Barry in for harrassment. Afterwards, Barry is eating at a cafeteria when Pike sits down beside him and tells Barry what a coward Jay was, and that he plans to get even with Central City and no one can do anything about it. Finally fed up, Barry hits Pike, but this is witnessed by Pike's attorney, and when Barry returns to work

he finds himself in hot water and possibly out of a job. Garfield has to give him a thirty day suspension while the situation is reviewed by Internal Affairs. Meanwhile, Pike is unloading a surprise for the Flash - a heat-seeking missile that will follow him and destroy the super-hero no matter how fast he goes. Back at Star Labs, Barry is fed up with both work and being the Flash, and gets into an argument with Tina. Deciding to leave town for a few days, he turns over Earl to Julio and starts driving out of town. He doesn't get far before he hears that Pike is threatening to blow up the dam above Central City unless the city pays him $1,000,000. Changing into the Flash he races to Devil's Gate Dam, where Pike is waiting for him with the missile. When Pike sees that the missile cannot catch up with the fastest man alive, he detonates the warhead - and the Flash finds himself propelled ten years into the future, the result of his great speed and the force of the explosion. Barry finds that Central City has radically changed - all for the worse. Pike is now mayor and virtual dictator of Central City, now turned into a police state run by Gestapo-like black-clad police. They confront Barry as it is illegal to wear a Flash costume, and he finds that his powers are gone - the Flash is now powerless in a world he cannot comprehend. **Guest cast:** Michael Nader as Nicholas Pike, Robert O'Reilly as Victor Kelso, Gloria Reuben as Sabrina, Beth Windsor as Monica, Hank Stone as cop #1, Paul Whitthorne as Shawn (age 17). **Writer:** Gail Morgan Hickman. **Director:** Gus Trickonis.

Deadly Nightshade (airdate: March 30, 1991). A group of terrorists have taken prisoner the daughter of a wealthy publisher, and will only let her go if the city pays $3,000,000 and releases their comrads in prison. As they are talking to Lt. Garfield, a dark shape appears in the building they are in, pulls out two machine guns, and kills the kidnappers. The murderer is the 1950's Central City costumed hero, the Nightshade. Only it isn't the original Nightshade - Dr. Desmond Powell in disguise - but someone imitating him, except that the new version has taken the law into his own hands and is playing judge, jury, and executioner. At police headquarters, Dr. Rebecca Frost arrives at Garfield's office, where she says her patient, the kidnapped girl, is still in shock and only mentions the Flash, who arrived after the murders and freed the girl. Frost considers anyone who wears a costume to be a nut, and possibly the Flash is the real murderer. No one yet knows that the new Nightshade is at fault, and that night Frost is interviewed by sleezy reporter Joe Kline, during which she states that the Flash is a menace whether he is guilty or not. Barry is furious, and is thinking about giving up his super identity. Tina recommends that Barry talk to Dr. Powell, alias the Nightshade, who happens to be the boss of Dr. Frost, and an acquaintance of Curtis Bohannon, a wealthy man working for the betterment of mankind - and the new Nightshade, an identity he revived to make amends for the criminal doings of his crooked family by killing those who break the law. Barry meets Dr. Powell at Nightshade's secret headquarters, and reveals he is the Flash. Desmond doesn't want to become the Nightshade again, but he finally agrees to work with the Flash to stop the deadly menace when more murders of criminals occur - all done by the new Nightshade. **Guest cast:** Jason Bernard as Desmond Powell, Richard Burgei as Curtis Bohannon, Denise Crosby [*Star Trek: The Next Generation*] as Dr. Rebecca Frost, Will MacMillan as Keefe, Jonathan Fuller as Steve. **Writers:** John Francis Moore and Howard Chaykin. **Director:** Bruce Bilson.

Captain Cold (airdate: April 6, 1991). A new super-criminal is in town, an albino known as Captain Cold, who is knocking off mobsters that oppose the criminal he is working for as a hit man, one

who uses a freeze weapon to kill his victims. Later that night, Barry receives a call from Julio, who asks him to come over to examine the frozen bodies found by the police. Barry is unable to explain their condition, but Garfield reveals that the victims are the cream of criminal leadership in Central City - all ordered killed by Jimmy Swain, a mobster in Central City who wants to take over all the criminal activity. Before Captain Cold leaves town, Swain gives him one more job: that of killing the Flash. Meanwhile, Barry finds himself burdened with a nosy newspaper reporter, Terri Kronenberg, who has been assigned to him. Barry wants nothing to do with the obnoxious woman, but has little choice in the situation since he

does not yet know that she is a fake looking for a story on the Flash to help her land a job. Just after Tina arrives to tell Barry that the killer must be using a nuclear-powered weapon, a call comes in to the police that three bombs have been planted in the city, all of which will go off in five minutes. The Flash finds and defuses them all, but the last one is a trap: Captain Cold is waiting for him and wounds him with the freeze weapon. Before he can finish the Flash off, sirens announce that the police are closing in. Captain Cold leaves, but it is obvious that he will return. With Kronenberg following Barry's every move, stopping Captain Cold won't be easy. **Guest cast:** Michael Champion as Captain Cold, Lisa Darr as Terri

Kronenberg, Jeffrey Combs as Jimmy Swain, Francois Chau as Johnny Choi, Jeffrey Anderson-Gunter as Nicholi Brown, Jerry O'Donnell as Ray McGill, Erni Vales as Luis Vega. **Writer:** Gail Morgan Hickman. **Director:** Gilbert Shilton.

Twin Streaks (airdate: April 13, 1991). At a lab in Central City, secret illegal experiments on genetic research are taking place. Dr. Jason Brassell has managed to produce the world's first clone. But it is more than just a clone, it is a being capable of super-speed. Unfortunately, the clone burns itself out and disintegrates while running at over three hundred miles per hour. Jason's partner, business manager Ted Whitcomb, is aghast that their experiment to produce cheap, advanced workers has resulted in a death, but Ted feels no guilt over the clone's destruction - the clone was only a product, and a defective one at that. Ted knows the answer to the problem of burn-out: he needs a sample of blood from the Flash, whose superior makeup allows him to work at high speed. Meanwhile at Star Labs, Tina is warning Barry that he must literally slow down or he will burn himself out. Barry swears that he can handle the load, but Tina continues to stress that he may die if he doesn't take it easy. Just then, Barry hears a police call about a bomb threat at the railway station - but the call is a fake, as the only thing there is a trap to cut the Flash and obtain a sample of blood, which works as planned. Before the police arrive Jason gets the sample, and later that day a new clone is born - this one an identical copy of Barry Allen/The Flash. Using an advanced growing method, the new Barry, called Pollux after the speedy Roman god, reaches physical maturity in hours, but mentally and emotionally remains a child. Within the next few days Pollux learns to read and absorbs information at super-speed, but remains emotionally immature. Realizing the value of the clone, Jason decides to sell him as a weapon, netting him and Ted millions, although Ted is against the idea. What neither of them realize is that Pollux, who has no sense of right or wrong, is growing beyond their ability to control, and after putting together a blue Flash-like uniform, Pollux escapes. Now there is a mentally-incompetent second Flash loose in Central City, along with a second Barry Allen. **Guest cast:** Charley Lang as Ted Whitcomb, Lenny Von Dohlen as Jason Brassell. **Writer:** Stephen Hattman. **Director:** James A. Contner.

All Done With Mirrors (airdate: April 27, 1991). Stasia Masters, an old friend of Barry's, and her boyfriend, Sam Scudder, break into a California branch of Star Labs to steal a top secret computer chip. After getting the chip Stasia doublecrosses Sam, knocking him out then setting off the intruder alarm on her way out. Back in Central City, Tina is a nervous wreck as she and Barry await for her mother to arrive at the railway station. Just after Jocelyn Weller arrives, so does Stasia, who grabs Barry and gives him a big kiss, much to the embarrassment of Tina and the indignation of her mother. The girl says she is happy to see Barry again after returning to Central City, and that she will see him again, then leaves after stealing his wallet. Barry doesn't notice this until they go to leave, and after the three of them go to Star Labs Jocelyn seems unimpressed with Tina's work, or Central City. Meanwhile, Stasia is in town to sell the chip to a fence, but Sam has phoned ahead and a couple of his men have tracked her down and plan to hold her until he arrives. She manages to make a getaway, and runs right past Barry, Murphy, and Bellows, who are eating but drop everything to give chase to the running armed men. A shootout ensues until the Flash arrives, but Stasia manages a get-away by throwing a coin in the street, whereupon a cowboy with swinging lasso appears. It is only a hologram projected by the coin, one of several stolen from Sam, but it is enough of a distraction for her to leave in a cab. When Barry shows up at the lab, Stasia is there, and she claims she showed up because his wallet "fell" in her purse. She claims she doesn't have anyplace to stay that night, so Barry offers to take her in - a big mistake, as Sam has just arrived in town with a whole bag full of hologram tricks, and he plans to get rid of Stasia and steal another classified laser-site crystal from Tina's Star Lab - and the Flash had better not get in his way. **Guest cast:** David Cassidy as Sam Scudder, Signy Coleman as Stasia Masters, Carolyn Seymour as Jocelyn Weller, Richard Blackwell as the art buyer, William Hayes as Fletcher, Zack Norman as Serge Tallent, Gloria Reuben as Sabrina. **Writers:** Howard Chaykin and John Francis Moore. **Director:** Danny Bilson.

Slumber Party (airdate: May 4, 1990). Small time hood Harry Milkgrim is caught again in a theft by Murphy and Bellows, but while arresting him he suddenly dies. At the morgue, Barry checks the man, and finds a small computer-chip device behind his ear. Barry leaves, not seeing the arrival of Roger Braintree, Harry's cousin and near-genius inventor. It seems that Harry isn't dead at all, but the chip emitted a sound that put him to sleep and simulated death. Now that the device has been proven to work, Harry has plans for building a much larger system, put together by Roger, and used to knock out victims who are being robbed. Roger really doesn't want to go along with it, but he needs research money for his inventions. Meanwhile, Barry is being plagued by bill collectors when a computer swaps his name for another Allen. While they are badgering him on the phone, Garfield and an Internal Affairs representative, Farrow, shows up to tell Barry that Harry has disappeared, and since Barry saw him last the suspicion falls on him. He is told to contact Roger, since he is Harry's only relative, and to inform him of the missing body. Arriving at Roger's lab, Barry finds him very evasive, and after he informs Roger of the missing body he leaves, not noticing Farrow taking photos of him leaving Roger's lab. Later that day, Roger and Harry show up at the Central City Savings and Loan wearing masks and earplugs, and turn on a loudspeaker version of the chip, knocking everyone out. When Barry hears the call come in for the police, he rushes to the bank as the Flash, but he is knocked out as well. Harry starts to kill the Flash, but Roger stops him, and they make an escape. With the device gone the Flash awakens and turns into Barry, not realizing that he is being filmed by bank cameras. Farrow also arrives, finding Barry at the scene of the robbery, and now accuses Barry of being involved in the crime. Barry is told to take a couple of days off so he goes to see Tina, where she has just found out that the sleep device kills if used too long. Barry heads for Roger's lab to straighten things out, but Roger has just made the same discovery, and insists that the jewel heist that he and Harry, along with a couple of thugs, made earlier in the day must be the last. Harry can't take no for an answer, as he plans to plug the device into the city siren system to put all of Central City asleep, not caring that he could kill everyone. He pulls a gun on Roger and during the scuffle Roger is shot and falls to the floor. He is dieing just as Barry shows up, and the speedster is knocked out by Harry's thug pal and the gun that killed Roger is placed in Barry's hand. Now when the police find Barry and the body, Barry will be arrested for murder and robbery, as the thug has placed some of the stolen gems in Barry's apartment for Internal Affairs to find. [This episode was pre-empted in most of the U.S. for a 30 minute news bulletin about President Bush having had chest pains, a situation that could have been summed up in 30 seconds.] **Guest cast:** Bill Mumy [*Lost in Space*] as Roger Braintree, Matt Landers as Harry Milkgrim, Victor Rivers as Stanley Morse, Jeffrey King as Farrow, Pamela Gordon as the morgue attendant, Sven Thorsen [*Captain Power and the*

Soldiers of the Future] [not credited]. **Writer**: Jim Trombetta. **Director**: Mario Azzipardi.

Alpha (airdate: May 11, 1991). In a simulation of an assassination, an android named Alpha has been built and programmed to be an expert exterminator. But she cannot shoot the gun, as her programming has been *too* good. Her ability to make decisions has led her to believe murder is wrong, and has given her an overwhelming desire to live. She knows that the scientists who created her will reprogram her the next day, and since she does not want to become a killer, she escapes the lab. A couple days later, Barry is supposed to go to a club that is raising funds for a charity. Julio, who is running the affair, lines up Tina to go with Barry to the Disco Inferno, but when Barry arrives at Star Labs Tina can't go. While at the lab he meets a new employee, the android Alpha, whom everyone thinks is a bit strange, but no one realizes that she isn't human. Arriving at the Disco Inferno alone, he runs to Alpha, who had ducked into the club to avoid some Federal officers following her. Barry asks her to dance, but she ducks out a door when she sees the officers coming after her. Barry chases her, but they are both stopped by Federal officers working for National Scientific Intelligence Agency, the top-secret agency that created Alpha. While Barry turns into the Flash to disarm the men, Alpha escapes, but only after her arm is hit with a bullet. Arriving at Star Labs with Tina, Barry finds the lab's security system disabled, and Alpha inside, her arm dripping blue fluid where she was shot, exposing her android nature. She explains why she ran away, and that she came to Star Labs because the company had done some of her design work. Alpha wants to learn how to disarm her self destruct mechanism - which the Federal officers can detonate within ten miles. As they talk the Federal officers arrive, along with Col. Powers, the ruthless director of the program that created Alpha. While the officers are at the lab Alpha escapes again, leaving Barry to have to locate her again - and figure out a way to keep her alive and out of the hands of the government. **Guest cast**: Laura Robinson as Col. Kristine Powers, Clair Stansfield as Alpha, Kenneth Tigar as Dr. Rossick, Jason Azikiwe as Costigan, Anthony Powers as Joey C., Sven-Ole Thorsen [*Captain Power and the Soldiers of the Future*] as Omega, Ross Partridge as Wiseguy, Kenneth Tigar as Dr. Jason Rossik, Gloria Reuben as Sabrina. **Writer**: Gail Morgan Hickman. **Director**: Bruce Bilson. Sven Thorsen

Trial of the Trickster (airdate: May 18, 1991). "In your guts you know he's nuts" says t-shirts being sold outside Central City Courthouse now that the day has come for the trial of James Montgomery Jesse, the multiple-personality murderous lunatic now known as the Trickster. The courthouse has become a circus as people pour in to see the trial. Barry waits for Megan to show up, but when she does arrive from San Francisco she is swamped with reporters and Barry can't get a word in. Once the trial starts, Jesse's big-bucks attorney tries to get him under control, but instead he gets out of his handcuffs and attacks Megan Lockhart, who knocks him out in two punches. The trial is postponed until Jesse can get a psychiatric evaluation, but while Jesse is back in his cell he receives a message from "Prank", his imaginary sidekick (whom he had dressed Megan up as during his earlier crime spree). This time there is a new Prank, a pretty, young, and mentally unbalanced girl who manages to break him out of custody in court the next day by using laughing gas. Prank takes Jesse to her toy shop, where she talks him into being the Trickster again and to allow her to be his partner. Now

outfitted with all types of high-tech toys, the Trickster vows revenge on Barry, Megan, the Flash, and Central City. His first move: putting the Flash under his power so he can put the people prosecuting him on trial. [This episode and "The Trickster" have been edited into a two-hour movie and released on video tape in Europe and Japan.] **Guest cast**: Joyce Hyser as Megan Lockhart, Mark Hamill as James Montgomery Jesse/The Trickster, Corinne Bohrer as Zoey/Prank, Marsha Clark as Denise Cowan, Parley Baer as the judge, Gloria Rubin as Sabrina, Brad Sevey as the waiter. **Writers**: Howard Chaykin and John Francis Moore. **Director**: Danny Bilson.

THE FLASH
- The Unfilmed Script
review by William E. Anchors, Jr.

War Wagon (a script by Steven Long Mitchell and Craig W. Van Sickle, dated Aug. 3, 1990). [Note: This early script still contains the character of Iris (Barry's girlfriend in the pilot movie) who never appeared again after the first episode.] It is night in Central City. Outside a government building three figures make their way past complex security systems. The Major watches as Hacker, a wiry black man, gains entrance to the building, enabling him and a menacing looking character, One-Eyed Jack, to follow inside. Nearby in their police car are Murphy and Bellows. The pair are discussing the conviction of master terrorist Hans Schpenk, who killed thirty eight people. Their conversation is interrupted by a call alerting them to a break-in at the Warrick Towers.

As the police close in on the government computer center, One-Eye sets a bomb to go off in thirty seconds. Murphy and Bellows are inside searching for intruders as the Flash hears a police call on the situation and rushes there at top speed. The three intruders are already leaving the building when the two cops encounter the bomb that will go off in only a few seconds. A red blur goes past as the Flash grabs the bomb and throws it out the window only a second before it detonates. The blur rushes out without either officer getting a good look at Central City's superhero.

At Star Labs, Tina is upset with Barry for being so active that night. The stresses on his metabolism have been considerable after appearing a dozen places around the city in one evening. Despite her concern, Barry insists he must use his powers to help others. The next day, Barry is in the government office dusting for prints with the assistance of Julio. While Murphy and Bellows attempt to explain what happened the night before (carefully avoiding mention of the red blur), Julio locates one of the devices used to get past the security systems. A data processor who works at the office, Darlene, enters and is questioned by Barry as to what the thieves might have wanted. Barry is told to mind his own business by Detective Lance Neidmeyer, who insists he can handle the case.

That night Barry is at Tina's apartment where she has cooked up an evil-smelling "re-metabolizer" she wants him to drink. He chugs a mouthful while they watch TV. Disreputable reporter Joe Kline - "Voice of the City" - comes on with a special report. He claims the Flash won't be needed anymore because of the police department's five-million-dollar anti-crime vehicle, the Peace Keeper, which is about to hit the streets. Neidermeyer is interviewed since the vehicle is his pet project. Barry is surprised to also see that

Tina is on the taped interview, where she is attacked by Kline for her stand against using the vehicle. She criticizes Neidermeyer about the secrecy behind the project, wondering what he is trying to hide. He declines to reveal anything.

Barry has to rush back to his apartment to meet Iris, having forgotten a dinner date with her. She is upset over his being terribly late, and believes his forgetfulness to be a result of the accident in his lab (the one that, unknown to her, transformed him into the Flash). She leaves after learning Barry was with Tina. The following day Barry has a meeting with Neidermeyer, and has to make his way through a group of protestors - including Tina. Going inside a warehouse, Barry is among the dignitaries and press as Neidermeyer introduces the Peace Keeper. The armored-car type vehicle demonstrates advanced weaponry and near invulnerability. Just then Tina breaks in and announces that she has learned the vehicle also carries guided missiles. Kline and other reporters demand that Neidermeyer reveal everything. He refuses and leaves as reporters question Tina. In the crowd is the Major, who tells his men that they will continue their operation that night.

Once darkness falls, the Major, One-Eyed Jack and Hacker knock out a security guard and gain entrance to the Peace Keeper. After rendering unconscious two more guards they grab the vehicle as an alarm goes off. The Peace Keeper brushes away arriving police like mosquitos and roars off into the night. Later, Tina is returning home when she is abducted by One-Eyed Jack. Tied and gagged, she is taken to a barn where the three thieves are holed up with their war wagon.

The next morning Barry and Julio are helping investigate the loss of the Peace Keeper. Barry's upset that he's been unable to contact Tina, who at that very moment has managed to get untied and is listening in on a radio transmission between the Major and someone else. It becomes obvious that the vehicle will be used to rescue Hans Schpenk. One-Eyed Jack catches Tina and she is taken to the Major, who insists that she will help in freeing Schpenk.

By that evening Barry has still not made contact with Tina. Searching the city as the Flash, Barry comes across the keys Tina dropped when she was kidnapped. He has no sooner left to continue his search when the Peace Keeper rumbles by with Tina and the three men inside. Pulling up to the Central City Armory, a cannon blast opens the door before a missile is fired inside, leveling the entire building. Elsewhere, Barry returns home where Iris is waiting for him. She says that she is probably going to accept a job in Paris. At that moment Barry sees the Armory on a TV report. Seconds later he arrives at the destroyed structure where Kline is reading a demand supposedly written by Tina. Speaking for the protestors, the letter claims that the police must disarm themselves by the next day or the Central City power station will be destroyed.

In the morning Barry pays a visit to Neidermeyer's boss. Gaining entrance to Chief Cooper's office, Neidermeyer tries to run Barry off, but Allen lets Cooper know that Tina cannot be behind the demand. Although Cooper is far more rational than the raving Neidermeyer, he is unconvinced of Tina's innocence since the letter was in her handwriting. He orders Neidermeyer to destroy at all costs the Peace Maker and Tina McGee. Barry returns to his lab where he finds Iris waiting for him. She has come to tell him goodbye. Unable to reveal his super powers and how they have changed his life, Barry can do nothing to stop her from leaving.

At the barn, One-Eye makes a move on Tina and has to be ordered away by the Major. Elsewhere, Barry pays a visit to Darlene to question her again. Some computer work provides clues that

Schpenk is going to be rescued by the Peace Keeper while being escorted through the area on his way to a Federal prison. The attack on the government building was to learn what route would be used to transport Schpenk. Barry and Julio meet Cooper and try to convince him that the attack on the power station is a ruse to keep the police tied up. Cooper listens to the theory but isn't convinced. Seeing no other alternatives, the Flash goes into action.

At the barn, One-Eye makes a move on Tina and has to be ordered away by the Major. Elsewhere, Barry pays a visit to Darlene to question her again. Some computer work provides clues that Schpenk is going to be rescued by the Peace Keeper while being escorted through the area on his way to a Federal prison. The attack on the government building was to learn what route would be used to transport Schpenk. Barry and Julio meet Cooper and try to convince him that the attack on the power station is a ruse to keep the police tied up. Cooper listens to the theory but isn't convinced. Seeing no other alternatives, the Flash goes into action.

On a dark deserted street, the Peace Maker confronts the group of vehicles transporting Schpenk. Both motorcycles and cars escorting the prison van suddenly blow up from cannon and machine gun fire. The van is stopped and its armored doors blown open. Schpenk is grabbed and placed in the war wagon, which is driven away at high speed when the Flash comes into sight. Barry jumps on top but is thrown off when Hacker hits the brakes. A missile is fired and Barry vanishes in a fireball. All Tina can see is flames everywhere.

Police and reporters close in on the scene after the Major and his group are long gone. All they find is a lone survivor, a guard who tells how the Flash rescued him from certain death. Elsewhere, Barry is bloodied, battered and in great pain as he tries to catch up with the armored vehicle. The combination of using his super speed too long and the injuries from the battle cause him to collapse. He doesn't reawaken until that night, and returns to the lab where Julio gives him a wary look because of his appearance. Ignoring his partner's questions, Barry remembers Tina telling him earlier about different methods of inserting secret messages in documents. Examining her letter, he finds numbers Tina placed in the demand note to the police. Realizing they are a radio frequency, Barry turns on a receiver that picks up a transmission signal from the Peace Keeper. Figuring out that the armored car will meet an airplane landing on a dry lake bed southwest of Central City, Julio alerts Cooper while Barry heads that way as the Flash.

With only minutes before the plane will land, the Flash heads south and soon closes in on the Peace Keeper. Radar on the vehicle picks up Barry and the Major opens fire with the cannon. The Flash keeps dodging until all the ammunition is gone and the computer aboard the vehicle blows a circuit from trying to track Barry's movements. While the Major, Jack and Hacker are panicking, Tina escapes through an escape hatch but is pursued by One-Eye. As he is about to stick Tina with a knife, Barry rescues the female scientist then goes after Major and Hacker. Seeing what is happening below, the pilot radios the Major that he won't land amid the gunfire. The jet starts to fly away as the Major fires a missile at Barry. It begins homing in on him, but the Flash circles around and the missile flies right through the open hatch of the Peace Keeper before exploding.

The next day Barry congratulates Tina for being hired as an adviser to Chief Cooper to replace the demoted Neidermeyer. He wants to celebrate by sharing some champagne with her, but Tina grabs the champagne and hands Central City's superhero some of her chunky re-metabolizer to drink instead. Even a superhero can't win every battle.

Mr. Terrific

review by William E. Anchors, Jr.

Production credits:

Producer	David O'Connell
Music	Gerald Fried

Regular cast:

Mr. Terrific/Stanley Beamish	Stephen Strimpall
Barton J. Reed	John McGivar
Hal Walters	Dick Gautier
Harley Trent	Paul Smith
Number of episodes:	17 one half hour segments

Premise: The United States Bureau of Special Projects invents a Power Pill that can turn a normal person into an all-powerful superman. But for some reason, the pills will only work on the metabolism of auto mechanic Stanley Beamish, who becomes a bumbling superhero working on cases for the government.

Editor's comments: Another *Batman* clone, another flop. *Mr. Terrific* is moderately amusing but has never been syndicated because the hero takes drugs to receive his powers, the studio fearing the possibility of children emulating Stanley Beamish.

Matchless (airdate: Jan. 9, 1967). The director of the Bureau of Secret Projects is in a helicopter following a railroad car transporting a defecting scientist and the top-secret Portable Power Paralyzer, but someone kills the agent following the scientist aboard the speeding train. The director, Barton J. Reed, contacts Stanley Beamish, a mechanic in a gas station, and gives him his Power Pills and next assignment: to catch up with the train and meet the foreign scientist. Once there, he is to pay off the scientist and take the device, but the super-hero is warned that the scientist has been spotted by enemy agents, who will try to assassinate him before he can defect and sell the weapon. **Guest cast:** Luciana Paluzzi as Mala, Harold J. Stone as Shenko, Richard Erdman as Manny, Iggie Wolfington as Petrov. **Writer:** Unknown. **Director:** Jack Arnold.

Mr. Big Curtsies Out (airdate: Jan. 16, 1967). A crime leader known as Mr. Big is actually a woman, but that doesn't help Mr. Terrific, as he left his power pills behind. **Guest cast:** Kathie Browne as Mr. Big. **Writer:** Unknown. **Director:** Jack Arnold.

I Can't Fly (airdate: Jan. 23, 1967). Reed and Walters arrive at the gas station disguised as telephone repairman. They explain to Stanley that the President is in grave danger: the nosewheel on the aircraft he is on is stuck in the closed position, and cannot safely land. Mr. Terrific prepares for action to save the President, but when he tries to take off he falls flat on his face - the pills no longer work. As Reed and Walters check on the pills, Stanley continues to attempt to restore his powers, and ends up in a straightjacket after police see him in a park trying to fly. **Guest cast:** David Opatoshu as the psychiatrist, Ellen Corby as Mrs. Walters, Ned Glass as Dr. Reynolds, Susan Kelly as Betsy, Sheryl Ullman as Linda, Angelique Pettyjohn as Carol. **Writer:** Unknown. **Director:** Jack Arnold.

[Title Unknown] (airdate: Jan. 30, 1967). Hal thinks Stanley may have turned crooked, and his efforts to find out the truth are hampering Stanley's work on a jewel robbery. **Guest cast:** Susan Seaworth as June, Marjorie Easton as the princess, Jay Novello as Count Gregory. **Writer:** Unknown. **Director:** Jack Arnold.

The Formula is Stolen (airdate: Feb. 2, 1967). Enemy agents have stolen the Power Pills, and now they want the only man they work on, Stanley Beamish. They keep an eye on Stanley's gas station after finding out that Mr. Terrific works there as a civilian, and send in a lady spy named Nina to kidnap him. The spies accidentally get Hal instead, but realize their mistake and return for Stanley, whom they kidnap and prepare to force over to their side. **Guest cast:** Joan Huntington as Nina, Lee Bergere as Claude, Richard Dawson as Max. **Writer:** Unknown. **Director:** Jack Arnold.

Stanley the Safecracker (airdate: Feb. 20, 1967). When Stanley discovers he looks just like a certain safecracker, he takes the place of the crook to locate and capture a gang of devious criminals. **Guest cast:** Barbara Stuart as Dolly, Robert Strauss as Carl. **Writer:** Unknown. **Director:** Jack Arnold.

Stanley the Fighter (airdate: Feb. 27, 1967). A crime ring is using a gym as a hideout, so Stanley goes undercover as a boxer to capture the gang. **Guest cast:** Charles Direkop as Tiger, Leo Gordon as Archie. **Writer:** Unknown. **Director:** Jack Arnold.

My Partner, the Jailbreaker (airdate: Mar. 6, 1967). A criminal who was sentenced to jail never revealed where he hid his stolen loot. Wanting to find the money, Stanley goes undercover as a fellow inmate who is placed in the same cell as the thief, and convinces him that he can break the thief out of jail if he will reveal where the loot is hidden. **Guest cast:** Richard X. Slattery as Blackjack, Joyce Van Patton as Margo. **Writer:** Unknown. **Director:** Jack Arnold.

Fly, Ballerina, Fly (airdate: Mar. 13, 1967). When a Soviet ballerina decides to defect, Stanley goes to her assistance. **Guest cast:** Cynthia Lynn as Daschinova, Barrie Chase as Tanya. **Writer:** Unknown. **Director:** Jack Arnold.

Harley and the Killer (airdate: Mar. 20, 1967). Years earlier Harley Trent helped send to prison a knife-throwing circus performer who murdered his wife, and now has escaped from prison and intends to get even with the Bureau of Secret Projects agent. Stanley agrees to stay with Harley and protect him, but the agent may be better off facing the killer! **Guest cast:** Henry Brandon as Herman J. Von Breck, Bonnie Hughes as George. **Writer:** Unknown. **Director:** Jack Arnold.

Stanley and the Mountaineers (airdate: Mar. 27, 1967). When Stanley and Harley get mixed up with hillbillies, Harley finds himself as the groom at a shotgun wedding, while Stanley is spending his time looking for an illegal moonshine still. **Guest cast:** Debbie Watson as Jennie May, Florence Lake as Maw. **Writer:** Unknown. **Director:** Jack Arnold.

Has Mr. Terrific Sold Out? (airdate: April 3, 1967). When a group of dignitaries visit the country, Stanley puts on a demonstration of his powers, but he doesn't realize that one of the group is an

impostor who plans to kidnap him. **Guest cast:** Arnold Moss as Chelsey/Victor, Ned Glass as Dr. Reynolds. **Writer:** Unknown. **Director:** Jack Arnold.

Stanley Goes to the Dentist (airdate: April 10, 1967). Stanley finds himself with a miniature transmitter implanted in his tooth after he visits a spy dentist who is interested in important government secrets. **Guest cast:** John Hoyt as Dr. Travis. **Writer:** Unknown. **Director:** Jack Arnold.

Stanley the Track Star (airdate: April 17, 1967). An important athlete has been kidnapped at a track meet, so Mr. Terrific goes into action to save him - and finds himself sidetracked by a beautiful spy. **Guest cast:** Ziva Rodann as Christina, Christopher Dark as Basil, Don Marshall [*Land of the Giants*]. **Writer:** Unknown. **Director:** Jack Arnold.

The Sultan Has Five Wives (airdate: April 24, 1967). Stanley really goofs on his latest assignment: he is supposed to give fake blueprints to a foreign agent, but he instead gives the spy the real thing. **Guest cast:** John Vivyan as the ambassador, Ulla Stromstedt as Tanya, Michael Pataki as Andre, Cliff Norton as Dr. Schmidt. **Writer:** Unknown. **Director:** Jack Arnold.

Stanley Joins the Circus (airdate: May 1, 1967). Stanley goes undercover again to find a stolen top-secret code book, but ends up fighting performers and a gorilla while trying to find it at a circus. **Guest cast:** Dort Clark as the circus boss, Ted Cassidy [*The Addam's Family*] as Bojo, Susanne Cramer as Teresa. **Writer:**

Unknown. **Director:** Jack Arnold.

[Title Unknown] (airdate: May 8, 1967). Stanley is assigned to be a bodyguard for a visiting sultan, but his super strength gets him into trouble. **Guest cast:** Robert Miller Driscoll as the Sultan, Than Wyenn as Marco. **Writer:** Unknown. **Director:** Jack Arnold.

The Pill Caper (two hour syndicated movie). This movie presently shows up occasionally on television, and is made up of four edited-together episodes: **Matchless, I Can't Fly, The Formula is Stolen,** and **Harley and the Killer.** [See pages 160-161 for synopsis of the individual episodes.] Cast: Stephen Strimpall as Mr. Terrific/Stanley Beamish, Dick Gautier as Hal Walters, John McGivar as Barton J. Reed, Paul Smith as Harley Trent, Luciana Paluzzi as Mala, Harold J. Stone as Shenko, Richard Erdman as Manny, Iggie Wolfington as Petrov, David Opatoshu as the psychiatrist, Ellen Corby as Mrs. Walters, Joan Huntington as Nina, Lee Bergere as Claude, Ned Glass as Dr. Reynolds, Richard Dawson as Max, Henry Brandon as Herman J. Von Breck, Tyler McVey as the general, Robert Cornwaite as the blue boy, Narianne Gordon as Gladys, Jerry Ayers as Marvin, Emily Banks as Carol, Lou Cavaller as the gas station customer, Eileen Wesson as the nurse, John "Red" Fox as the policeman, Russ Grieve as the second policeman, Bill Quinn as the pilot, Will J. White as the co-pilot, Susan Kelly as Betsy, Sheryl Ullman as Linda, Angelique Pettyjohn as Carol, Paul Bryar as Henry, Lori Lehman as the little girl, Hal Smith as the drunk, Dort Clark as Sam, Molly Dodd as the secretary. **Writers:** Budd Grossman, Harvey Ballock, R. S. Allen, David Harmon, Arnold Margolin, Jim Parker. **Director:** Jack Arnold.

Captain Nice

review by William E. Anchors, Jr.

Production credits:

Executive Producer	Buck Henry
Producer	Jay Sandrich
Associate Producer	Al Westen
Creator	Buck Henry
Music	Jerry Fielding
Theme by	Vic Mizzy

Regular cast:

Captain Nice/Carter Nash	William Daniels
Mrs. Nash	Alice Ghostly
Sgt. Candy Kane	Ann Prentice
Mayor Finney	Liam Dunn
Police Chief Segal	William Zuckert
Mr. Nash	Byron Foulger

Number of episodes: 15 one half hour segments

Premise: A chemist working for the police department invents a serum that causes super-powers in anyone who drinks it.

Editor's comments: A cute show by the people who created *Get Smart*. Created to cash in on the *Batman* "craze", the show never caught on with the public and was quickly cancelled.

The Man Who Flies Like a Pigeon (airdate: Jan. 9, 1967). Mild and meek chemist Carter Nash holds a normal job working at the crime lab of the Big Town Police Department. He is experimenting with a special serum that gives the user super powers, but hasn't had time to perfect it, as he spends more time warding off the romantic advances of Sgt. Candy Cane than he does working on the serum. While he and Candy are walking in the park one night they are attacked by a band of muggers, and Carter takes his serum for the first time after Candy is knocked out. In no time at all, the gang is rounded up - the first case solved by Captain Nice. **Guest cast**: Kelton Garwood as Gregory Omnus, Arthur Malet as the crook. **Writer**: Buck Henry. **Director**: Jud Taylor.

How Sheik Can You Get? (airdate: Jan. 16, 1967). A Middle-East sheik named Abdul Beimer is visiting Big Town, and is saved by Captain Nice when an assassin tries to kill him. When the police offer him a bodyguard, he picks Sgt. Candy Cane, she not knowing that the sheik plans to add her to his stable of 108 wives. She turns him down but the sheik won't take no for an answer, and tries to poison Carter when he defends her. When this fails, he sends an assassin after Carter and kidnaps Candy Cane. **Guest cast**: Larry D. Mann as Sheik Abdul Beimer, James Lanphier as Ibid, Fred Villani as Fetta, Jan Arvan as Yebba, Harry Varteresian as Sopar. **Writers**: Peter Myerson and Treva Silverman. **Director**: Gary Nelson.

That Thing (airdate: Jan. 23, 1967). While changing clothes to go after some jewel thieves, Carter accidentally leaves some of his secret formula open. A caterpillar gets into it, turning an ordinary insect into a monster, which the police find out about after a flower shop is eaten. Carter faces down the beast, but is defeated. But he may still be able to win the day - he is going to feed his formula to his pet parakeet and send him against the insect. **Guest cast**: Johnny Haymer as Dr. Von Keppel, Frank Maxwell as Gen. Rock Ravage, Vince Howard as policeman #1, John Neris as the nurseryman, Ted Gehring as thug #2, Jason Wingreen as thugs #1, Kip King as policeman #2. **Writers**: Peggy Elliot and Ed Scharlach. **Director**: Gary Nelson.

That Was the Bridge That Was (airdate: Feb. 6, 1967). Mayor Finney is dedicating a new bridge in Big Town, a structure named after him. When a little old lady hits the bridge with a bottle to christen it, it falls apart and Captain Nice must support the bridge so everyone can get off safely. Carter checks the materials and finds the cement filled with all types of foreign material, including oatmeal. He tells the mayor (his uncle), who contacts the crooked construction company about their shoddy work, but they kidnap him when Mayor Finney refuses to pay for their work. The police cannot find Finney, and it is up to Captain Nice to save the distraught politician. **Guest cast**: Edward Binns as Al Spencer, Phil Roth as Hal Porter, Sabrina Schraf as Miss Schneider, Georgia Schmidt as Harriet Weaver. **Writers**: Al Gordon and Hal Goldman. **Director**: Gary Nelson.

The Man With Three Blue Eyes (airdate: Feb. 20, 1967). When Big Joe Kowalski is about to be released from jail, a crime wave hits Big Town. It seems the thief is the only survivor of a gang that robbed two million dollars from a train. He has never told anyone where he hid the money, so now every crook for miles has arrived in Big Town to grab Big Jo and the loot. The mayor has Carter hire a fake mind reader to find out where the money is hidden, but the thief has a heart attack and dies before he can tell anyone where the currency is hidden. Unfortunately, after the medium is hired, the family of the thief mistake Carter for the Great Medula and kidnap him. **Guest cast**: John Dehner as the Great Medula, Florance Halop as Mrs. Kowalski, Dan Travanti as Lenny, Ross Hagen as Jake, Ernest Sarracino as Joe Kowalski, Barbara London as the check girl. **Writers**: Treva Silverman and Peter Meyerson. **Director**: Charles Rondeau.

Is Big Town Burning? (airdate: Feb. 27, 1967). After leaving a movie with his mother, Carter sees a fire start and, after considerable delay, changes into his costume, saves a damsel in distress, and puts out the fire - but not before seeing the arsonist escaping the basement. The next day Miss Devine, the exotic dancer saved at the fire by Captain Nice, is called into the police department to be interrogated for information as to the identity of the arsonist, who turns out to be the building's landlord, Mr. Lipton. The landlord is rounded up, but Carter finds himself in hot water when Lipton realizes who Carter is and claims that he will reveal his secret identity if Carter testifies against him. **Guest cast:** Victor Tayback as Mr. Lipton, Marilyn Lowell as Miss Devine, Robert Munk as the guard, Hollis Morrison as the prosecuting attorney, Tommy Ferrell as the defense attorney. **Writer:** Buck Henry. **Director:** Gene Reynolds.

Don't Take any Wooden Indians (airdate: Mar. 6, 1967). Anthropologist John Edgars returns from a South American expedition and decides to eliminate the man who was the financier of the trip. When Carter prevents this from happening he gets into deep trouble, as Dr. Edgars has sent a poison-dart armed native to kill him. Meanwhile, the deranged doctor has kidnapped Candy Cane and injected into her a lethal tropical poison. **Guest cast:** Joe Flynn [*McHale's Navy*] as Dr. John Edgars, Joseph Perry as Luna, Ben Wright as Dunbar. **Writers:** Treva Silverman and Peter Meyerson. **Director:** Richard Kinon.

That's What Mothers Are For (airdate: Mar. 13, 1967). Mrs. Nash is furious when budget cuts get most of the police department pink slips, including the now-unemployed Carter Nash. The City Council assumes that Captain Nice will protect Big Town, but Mrs. Nash has other ideas: she will prove the entire police force is needed by pulling off a daring robbery of an expensive diamond. She drinks some of Carter's super juice, but when she tries to take the gem she is captured by criminals who insist that she join their gang. They force her to help them steal the diamond, and after the robbery Nash tries to go into action as Captain Nice to find the culprits only to find his mother has drank all of his formula. **Guest cast:** Felice Orlandi as Lucky, Dennis Cross as Larkin. **Writer:** Martin Ragaway. **Director:** Gary Nelson.

Whatever Lola Wants (airdate: Mar. 20, 1967). Carter is working late at the lab, but the loud music from a nearby bar is distracting him and breaking his test tubes. He goes over to the nightclub to complain, but while there is slipped a Mickey in his fruit drink, causing him to pass out "drunk" in the street. He gets into trouble when a photo appears in the newspaper with him passed out in the gutter, but the next day the same noise is disturbing him, so he goes back again. He finally discovers the real reason for the loud music coming from the bar: it is just across the street from the City Jail, where thugs are using the noise to cover the sounds they are making as they dig a tunnel to free their imprisoned partners. **Guest cast:** Barbara Stuart as Lola, Dick Wilson as the drunk, Ron Foster as Doc Simmons, James Gammon as Milton the Mole, Julie Parrish as the hatcheck girl. **Writer:** Arne Sulton. **Director:** Richard Kinon.

Who's Afraid of Amanda Woolf (airdate: Mar. 27, 1967). Carter has become involved in a case against the syndicate, and is holding a book containing the names of mob members. After police capture the wife of a syndicate leader, they convince her to turn State's evidence. She claims she will testify against her spouse, but Carter doesn't realize that she is really just after the document. After taking Amanda to his home for safekeeping, she turns on the charm to get hold of the book, but he instead studies it to break the code it is written in. Just after deciphering the code, the crime boss breaks into Carter's house, retrieves the book, and announces that he plans to fit the whole family with cement overshoes. **Guest cast:** Madlyn Rhue as Amanda Woolf, John Fiedler as Gunner. **Writers:** Mike Marmer and Stan Burns. **Director:** Hollingsworth Morse.

The Week They Stole Payday (airdate: April 10, 1967). A gang hijacks an armored car, steals the city payroll, then leaves behind a truck containing counterfeit money. Carter later discovers the change, but there is little he can do about it, as he learns that Policewoman Candy Cane and Mrs. Nash, Carter's mother, have been kidnapped by the group of thieves, and they will be killed if Captain Nice shows up to save them. **Guest cast:** Pat Harrington as Arthur, Victor French as Anthony. **Writers:** David Kethum and Bruce Shelly. **Director:** Gary Nelson.

It Tastes OK But Something is Missing (airdate: April 10, 1967). Mrs. Nash races home to tell Carter that she overheard some crooks talking about their plans to rob the post office, but Carter is unable to turn into Captain Nice when he cannot produce any formula for want of a single ingredient. So he experiments with alternate chemicals, which don't produce the desired results - he ends up smelling like hamburger and driving all the neighborhood dogs crazy. **Guest cast:** Simon Oakland [*Kolchak: The Night Stalker*] as Harry Houseman, Dick Curtis as Bostic, Johnny Silver as the small man. **Writers:** Peggy Elliott and Ed Scharlach. **Director:** Gary Nelson.

May I Have the Last Dance (airdate: April 17, 1967). Sgt. Carter accidentally helps four women steal some furs. To clear his name, Candy Cane goes undercover as a dance instructor to try to capture the culprits. Unfortunately, they recognize her, and after Candy phones Carter for help, they are both locked in a room that is having all the air removed so they will suffocate. It looks like the only way for them to survive is for Carter to change into Captain Nice, revealing his secret identity in the process. **Guest cast:** Celeste Yarnall as Rossalind, Marilyn Mason as the receptionist, Burt Mustin as the old man, Deanna Lund [*Land of the Giants*] as Louise, Lindsay Workman as the storeowner. **Writers:** David Ketchum and Bruce Shelly. **Director:** Charles Rondeau.

One Rotten Apple (airdate: April 24, 1967). A nightclub owner, swinger Lloyd Larchmont, believes someone is out to kill him. Going to the police for help, he is assigned Candy Cane to keep an eye on him as she masquerades as a waitress at his club, hoping to find the employee making the threats. But Mrs. Nash's arrival blows her cover and gets them both tied to a time bomb. **Guest cast:** Bob Newhart as Lloyd Larchmont, John Milford as Lionel, Jo Anne Worley as Rusty, Shirley Boone as Ellie, Charles Gordin as the news vender, Margaret Teale as Babsy. **Writers:** Peter Meyerson and Treva Silverman. **Director:** Gary Nelson.

Beware of Hidden Prophets (airdate: May 1, 1967). The return of the Great Medula spells trouble for Carter, who is trying to capture an art thief after the Medula predicts the crook's escape. Carter is fired for allowing him to get away, but later discovers the magician was in on the escape. In Medula's nightclub, Carter finds a tablecloth with the escape plans on it, but the crooks grab it back after stuffing Carter in a washer. **Guest cast:** John Dehner as the Great Medula, Joseph Campanella as Kincade. **Writers:** Peter Meyerson and Treva Silverman. **Director:** Gary Nelson.

My Secret Identity

review by Douglas Snauffer

Production credits:

Executive Producer	Martin J. Keltz
Creators	Brian Levant
	Fred Fox, Jr.
Producer	Paul Saltzman
Theme music & lyrics	Fred Mollin

Regular cast:

Dr. Benjamin Jeffcoate	Derek McGrath
Andrew Clements	Jerry O'Connell
Stephanie Clements	Wanda Cannon
Erin Clements	Marsha Moreau
Mrs. Schellenbach	Elizabeth Leslie
Jeff (year 1)	Robert Haiat
Kirk Stevens (years 2-3)	Christopher Bolton

Premise: *My Secret Identity* is the story of Andrew Clements, a fourteen-year-old boy who finds himself endowed with superhuman abilities after walking into an experiment being conducted by his scientist-neighbor, the kind-hearted Dr. Jeffcoate. Andrew, a comic-book enthusiast, can't decide whether he wants to save the world like the superheroes he reads about, or simply be a normal teenager, so he dabbles in a little bit of both. Needless to say, Dr. Jeffcoate feels responsible for Andrew and tries to instill in the boy the wisdom to go along with his incredible talents.

Writer's comments: There are a few interesting footnotes to this series. It's one of the few superhero shows in which the star doesn't don a costume to fight crime. Being a normal teenager, Andrew wouldn't dare be caught in some hokey outfit. Also, upon receiving his powers, Andrew dubs his alter-ego "Ultraman", but such references are dropped after the first season. It could be the producers received pressure from the creators of the popular Japanese comic book and TV character. In the earliest episodes, Andrew holds an aerosol can in each hand to guide himself in flight. This gimmick was quickly put aside, probably to avoid appearing environmentally inert, since many of the episodes dealt with such issues.

SEASON ONE

My Secret Identity (pilot episode, airdate: Oct. 3, 1988). Andrew Clements is your average fourteen-year-old boy. He lives with his mother Stephanie and eight-year-old sister Erin in the small suburban community of Briarwood. He attends Junior High School and loves contact sports, cars, and of course, girls. The only difference is that Andrew is also an avid comic book collector. When his father died a number of years ago, Andrew filled the void in his life by turning to the superheroes that he so loved reading about. They became his role models. Living next door to the Clements family is the eccentric and secretive Dr. Benjamin Jeffcoate, one of the world's smartest men. He lives alone and spends most of his time in his basement laboratory working on elaborate scientific experiments and curious inventions. Besides an occasional 'hello' or 'good day', the only contact Andrew and the doctor share is the boy mowing Jeffcoate's lawn once a week. One day Andrew enters the lab looking for "Dr. J" and stumbles into the path of a blue photon beam developed to grow bigger and better vegetables. Andrew is momentarily stunned, but shakes it off, and assures the concerned Dr. Jeffcoate that he is fine. The next morning, however, he awakens to find himself floating over his bed. He soon learns he also has superspeed and physical invulnerability - nothing can hurt him, and nobody can move fast enough to catch him. When Andrew tells Dr. Jeffcoate, the doctor is torn between feelings of guilt over the accident and immense curiosity at the scientific implications. But Andrew is simply excited. He dubs himself "Ultraman" and plans on ridding the world of evil, as long as it doesn't conflict with his weekend plans. He and Dr. Jeffcoate begin to develop a friendship and trust. "We're a team" says Andrew. "Like Flash Gordon and Dr. Zarkov, Batman and Robin." But the relationship is put to the test when shortly afterwards, Caroline, the cute girl next door, is kidnapped. Andrew wants to use his superpowers to rescue her, but Dr. Jeffcoate still fears for his safety. **Guest cast:** Alyson Court as Caroline, Kenneth McGregor as Caroline's father, Doug Lennox as the hitman. **Writers:** Brian Levant and Fred Fox, Jr. **Director:** unknown.

A Walk on the Wild Side (airdate: Oct. 10, 1988). Dr. Jeffcoate's lab is broken into and his surface tension abrogator is stolen. The device is an extremely important piece of the doctor's new invention, which can restructure the molecules of anything containing hydrogen and oxygen to produce water. Andrew discovers the culprits behind the theft are the Apache Devils, a local youth gang. Using his superpowers, Andrew saves the life of a gang member and accepts an invitation to join their ranks, in hopes of recovering the abrogator. But when Andrew refuses to commit a serious crime, it leads to a confrontation with Rock, the gang's leader. **Guest cast:** Lee J. Campbell as the policeman, Tracey Davis as the salesgirl, Marco Bianco as the driver, Adam Kositsky as Jimmy, Nicholas Shields as Nick, David Hewlett as Rock. **Writer:** David Cole. **Director:** Bill Corcoran.

Only Trying to Help (airdate: Oct. 17, 1988). Andrew has been keeping a diary of his experiences as Ultraman. Trouble begins when his mother finds it and takes a peek. She starts to worry that the comic book world of superheroes is becoming all too real to her son. So the next day she visits Andrew's teacher, Miss Santini. Stephanie follows her advice and invites the school psychiatrist, Dr. Fox, to dinner, but introduces him as "Mr. Fox". Andrew thinks this is his mom's date and is on his best behavior. The next day, Andrew

Jerry O'Connell as Andrew Clements, Derek McGrath as Dr. Jeffcoate.

spots "Mr. Fox" kissing another woman, but when Andrew tells his mom, she reveals that she invited Dr. Fox to dinner to observe Andrew because of what she read in his diary - which still leaves Andrew the task of explaining the things he wrote. **Guest cast:** Maria Ricossa as Miss Santini, Malcolm Stewart as Dr. Fox.

Writer: Eric Weinthal. **Director:** Al Waxman.

The Track Star (airdate: Oct. 24, 1988). Although Andrew fails to make the Briarwood High School track team, he still volunteers as towel boy. But when the school's star runner begins to intimidate

165

The Track Star: Andrew is impressed with his coach (Clark Johnson).

him, Andrew decides to put his superspeed to use and convinces the coach to give him another tryout. On the track, Andrew easily passes all the other runners and is told to be ready for the next week's meet. Dr. Jeffcoate scolds Andrew for using his powers selfishly, but

Andrew fears if he backs out now he'll lose the attention of adorable classmate Cyndi. The day of the track meet, Andrew faces a dilemma - should he run the race as Ultraman or take his chances as a normal athlete? **Guest cast:** Garth Dyke as David Matthews, Leah

166

Salomma as Cyndi, Clark Johnson as Coach Lloyd, Victor Ertmanis as Frank Matthews. **Writer:** Eric Weinthal. **Director:** Rob Iscove.

Memories (airdate: Oct. 31, 1988). Dr. Jeffcoate is a nervous wreck after an old flame, Susan Anderson, announces she is coming to visit him. It seems a long time ago she left him for another man who Dr. Jeffcoate believes was everything he is incapable of being - handsome, intelligent, smooth, rich, and successful. Stephanie steps in and helps him to purchase some fashionable outfits. Later, she stages a fantasy dinner for the two of them so Dr. Jeffcoate will be ready for the real thing with Susan. The night of the big date, Andrew decides to follow the doctor and his date around and act as a guardian angel for his friend. **Guest cast:** Susan Anton as Susan, Ron Gabriel as the manager. **Writer:** Eric Weinthal. **Director:** Al Waxman.

You've Got a Friend (airdate: Nov. 7, 1988). Andrew is very thrilled when his TV comic book hero, Captain Noble, comes to town on a publicity tour. When Andrew has the opportunity to meet him in person, he's almost speechless. Fred Cooper, the actor behind the Captain Noble mask, is charmed by Andrew and invites him to attend the upcoming rehearsal of his "big stunt". But the experience turns sour when Andrew learns that the stunt is actually being performed by a stuntman. Fred explains to Andrew that he actually did his own stunts forty years ago, but that age has caught up with him. And since audiences expect Captain Noble to stay young forever, a stuntman is now necessary. Andrew finds this impossible to accept, and begins to press Fred into doing his own stunts again. The following day, Andrew, Fred, and Dr. Jeffcoate watch in horror as a young boy accidentally falls from a bridge into the water below. Without hesitation, Fred jumps in after the boy. Is he really up to the rescue, or has Andrew pressured him into a deadly situation? **Guest cast:** Gene Barry as Fred Cooper, Cassal H. Miles as Fred's assistant, Mung-Ling as Melinda, Lisa Yamanaka as Megan. **Writer:** Michael Williams. **Director:** Don McCutcheon.

For Old Time's Sake (airdate: Nov. 14, 1988). When Dr. Jeffcoate reminisces with Ray, his best friend and fellow scientist, Andrew, at first, becomes jealous. But when Ray is kidnapped and a double takes his place, Andrew joins forces with Dr. J to save "their" friend from professional ruin. **Guest cast:** Fred Willard as Ray. **Writer:** Martin Mobley. **Director:** Al Waxman.

The Lost Weekend (airdate: Nov. 21, 1988). Kyle Buchanan, the father of one of Andrew's friends, has to cancel his plans to take the boys on a camping trip. Andrew is able to talk Dr. Jeffcoate into chaperoning the weekend, but the other boys make no bones about their disappointment. Kyle, although forty, is just a big kid who allows the boys to do whatever they want. Dr. Jeffcoate's idea of a weekend in the forest includes orderly nature hikes and bird watching. The kids' spirits pick up when Kyle shows up unexpectedly, and even Andrew's loyalties are tested. But when Kyle nearly drowns and two of the boys eat poison berries, Dr. Jeffcoate comes to the rescue and teaches them all a lesson about acting responsibly. **Guest cast:** Michael Kirby as Kyle, Shaun McCarthy as Jason Buchanan, Trevor Smith as Mark. **Writer:** Eric Weinthal. **Director:** Don Shebib.

Forbidden Ground (airdate: Nov. 28, 1988). Andrew becomes convinced that he's developing superstrength, though Dr. J can find

no evidence to support this. So when Stephanie asks him to look after Erin for an afternoon, Andrew is less than enthusiastic. In fact, he ignores Erin while the two are in the house together as he speculates on whatever superpowers might come next - like telepathy and superhearing. Fed up with her brother, Erin decides to take off with her friend Melissa for a game of hide 'n' seek. She finds the perfect hiding place in a storm drain, but once inside she can't get back out. When Melissa isn't able to find Erin she becomes bored and wanders off. Andrew panics when he discovers that Erin is missing, and he and Dr. Jeffcoate begin searching for her. When they do find Erin, it may be too late. The water level is rising, and to Andrew's dismay he may not have the strength to lift the heavy drain cover to free her. **Guest cast:** Gema Zamprogna as Melissa, Kerry Frost as Mimi, Kelly Frost as Diane. **Writer:** Eric Weinthal. **Director:** Bill Corcoran.

It Only Hurts for a Little While (airdate: Dec. 5, 1988). Andrew tires of watching Peter, the school bully, harass his friends. He challenges Peter to meet him after school to put an end to the bully once and for all. Then our hero heads for the dentist. The dentist discovers an enormous cavity in Andrew's mouth and insists he return the following day to have it filled. Fine, except Andrew realizes he can't have novocaine because the needle won't pierce his invincible skin. Andrew rushes to Dr. J for advice. The doctor instructs him to simply ask the dentist for gas instead of novocaine, and not to worry. But the next day Andrew learns the dentist doesn't use gas, and before he can protest she gives him the injection. The needle goes in! Andrew feels it and is stunned! It seems the X-ray that the dentist took has altered the effects of the gamma rays that originally gave Andrew his superpowers, making him mortal again - perhaps permanently. Which means Andrew must face Peter without the benefits of Ultraman. **Guest cast:** Simon Craig as Peter, Gordon Voolvet as Tim, Megan Smith as Dr. Burns, Richard Hardacre as the teacher. **Writer:** Eric Weinthal. **Director:** Harvey Frost.

Grounded (airdate: Dec. 12, 1988). After Andrew breaks his promise not to fight with his sister, Erin, Stephanie puts her foot down and grounds our hero for two weeks. To make things worse, Andrew has a first date the next night with Jennifer Laughton, whom he considers to be a goddess. Jennifer is so excited about the date that Andrew doesn't have the nerve to break it. Obviously, there's no way he can stay in his bedroom and be out on a date at the same time...or is there? When you're Ultraman, anything is possible, or so Andrew assumes. **Guest cast:** Kathleen Robertson as Jennifer, Hal Johnson as Mr. Johnson, Briar Boake as the vendor, Victoria Evans as the waitress, Doug Kier as the first editor, Janelle Hutchison as the second editor. **Writer:** Eric Weinthal. **Director:** Al Waxman.

The Eyes of the Shadow (airdate: Jan. 23, 1989). With the help of Dr. Jeffcoate's translating device, Andrew asks Mr. Chen, who only understands Chinese, for a date with his lovely daughter, Lea. Andrew is concerned about the Chen family's safety when he and Lea are shadowed by a trio of menacing gang members while going to the local movie theater. After discovering that the thugs have been extorting the Chens for some time, Andrew, as a disguised "Ultraman", teams with Dr. Jeffcoate to get rid of the troublemakers. **Guest cast:** Wendy Chong as Lea Chen, Von Flores as Dan Chen, Herb Lee as Mr. Chen. **Writers:** Fred Fox, Jr. and Elliot Stern.

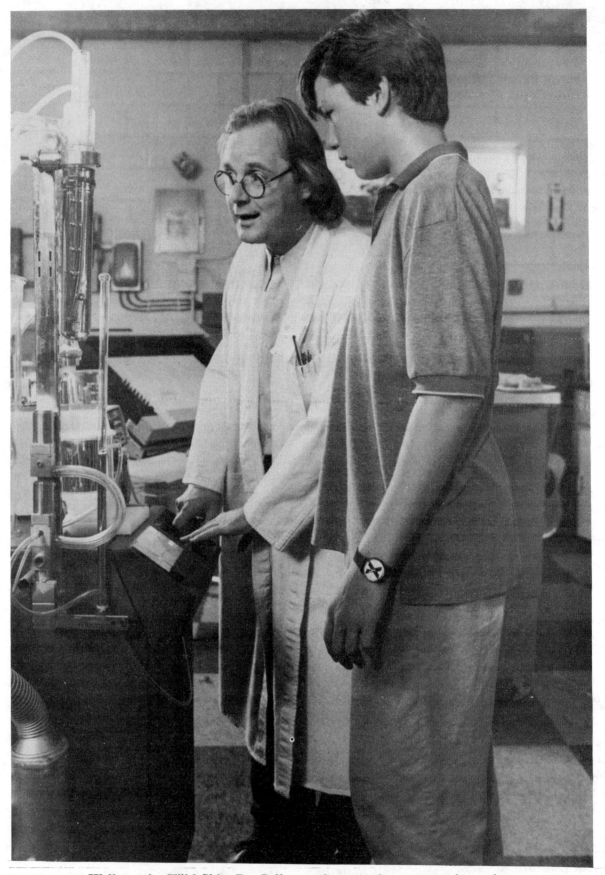

Walk on the Wild Side: Dr. Jeffcoate shows Andrew a new invention.

Director: Alan Simmonds.

Video Connection (airdate: Jan. 30, 1989). Andrew and Dr. J cooperate with the police after Andrew discovers that, as a delivery boy for a local video store, he is dropping off drugs, and not just movies. **Guest cast:** Allison Mang as Cathy, Darrin Baker as Mike, Nicholas Pasco as Nick, Errol Slue as Lt. Fulton. **Writers:** Stephen Witkin and David Cole. **Director:** Jim Kaufman.

Toxic Timebomb (airdate: Feb. 6, 1989). Dr. Jeffcoate thinks his new consulting job at Macro Plex Industries - complete with a healthy paycheck, posh office and pretty assistant - is great, until he discovers the plant is improperly dumping toxic wastes. When he confronts his "stunned" boss, Weston Foyt, Dr. J is told to document any wrongdoings and is given a building passkey so he can gather evidence at night. An apparent setup, Dr. Jeffcoate is arrested when he enters the lab. Harriet, a Macro Plex employee and long-time friend of Dr. Jeffcoate's, approaches Foyt with similar concerns and finds out that she is being framed to take the fall for the company's illegal activities. Fearing that his dumping scheme will now be exposed, Foyt arranges for a bomb to kill Dr. J, Harriet and Andrew. Can "Ultraman" save the day - and three lives? **Guest cast:** Amanda Hancox as Harriet Chase, Dave Nichols as Weston Foyt. **Writer:** Richard Marcus. **Director:** Alan Simmonds.

Two Faces Have I (airdate: Feb. 13, 1989). Tired of his shyness around women, Dr. Jeffcoate invents a device that changes his biochemical makeup. The machine not only builds his courage, but also creates an alter ego, Jeffie, who is both charming and romantic. In no time, Jeffie falls into the unlikely arms of his widowed neighbor, the nasty Mrs. Schellenbach. Andrew, who can't believe what is happening, must convince his good friend Dr. J that he has a split personality before the love-smitten Jeffie springs for a diamond engagement ring. **Guest cast:** none. **Writer:** Elliot Stern. **Director:** Harvey Frost.

One on One (airdate: Feb. 20, 1989). Stephanie has a difficult time finding a celebrity to attend a fundraiser she's organizing for the Special Olympics. When Andrew learns that Dr. Jeffcoate once crossed paths with Rick Downes, a famous basketball player, he hurries to tell his mom that she may have her star. After listening to an irresistible pitch by the scientist and Andrew, Rick agrees to participate in a one-on-one contest at the fundraiser. Andrew, in the meantime, has struck up a friendship with Bobby Spillman, a local amateur hoopster who has given up the game to make a living unloading crates. Can a game of one-on-one between Rick and Bobby encourage Bobby to pursue a professional basketball career? **Guest cast:** Conrad Coates as Bobby Spillman, Phil Jarrett as Rick Downes. **Writer:** Philip Bedard and Larry Lalonde. **Director:** Alan Simmonds.

Stranger in the House (airdate: Feb. 27, 1989). Andrew tries to convince his family that his penpal, John, a man recently released from jail, is trustworthy. But the young superhero changes his mind when John asks Andrew's mother out on a date. Following John to his seedy apartment, Andrew learns that John's obligations to a former cellmate may endanger both his mother and Dr. Jeffcoate's new laser, the perfect counterfeiting tool. **Guest cast:** Alan Jordan as John, Michael Copeman as Crawford. **Writer:** Eric Weinthal. **Director:** Jim Kaufman.

Secret Code (airdate: Mar. 6, 1989). After using his superpowers to save some preschoolers from a runaway truck, Andrew is distressed to learn that the truck driver is taking all the credit for the courageous act. Adding to Andrew's misery, Cassie, a reporter for the school newspaper, tells our superhero that he has been selected as the school's most ordinary student. When Andrew and Cassie are kidnapped by industrial spies who think the teens know the secret of Dr. Jeffcoate's most recent invention, Andrew has the opportu-

nity to show Cassie he is not merely ordinary, but extraordinary. **Guest cast:** Joanne Vannicola as Cassie; Murray Cruchley as Richard, Heidi Von Palleske as Tamara. **Writer:** David Cole. **Director:** Steve Scaini.

Look Before You Leap (airdate: Apr. 24, 1989). After using his superspeed powers without looking to see who might be watching, Andrew receives a stern lecture from Dr. Jeffcoate about carelessness. But the message goes unheeded and is spotted by a shocked Mrs. Schellenbach, his next-door neighbor. Later that day, Andrew once again takes to the sky without hesitation, however, this time it's to save the life of Dr. J. The two panic when they realize Mrs. Schellenbach has taped the rescue with her new home video camera. Can they convince their antagonistic neighbor she is seeing things before she sells the story to the tabloids? **Guest cast:** none. **Writer:** Eliot Stern. **Director:** Don Shebib.

Breaking the Ice (airdate: May 1, 1989). Jeff is busy making arrangements to throw a surprise birthday party for his best friend, Andrew. Unaware of the true nature of his buddy's whispered messages and covert meetings, Andrew begins to feel left out and becomes hostile towards Jeff. Dr. Jeffcoate sees that Jeff is being treated unreasonably and decides to tell Andrew about the upcoming party plans. Anticipating a full house, Andrew is indeed surprised when the lights go on. **Guest cast:** Krista Bridges as Suzannah, Warren Van Evera as Pops. **Writer:** Eric Weinthal. **Director:** Jim Kaufman.

Give the Guy a Chance (airdate: May 8, 1989). Andrew takes it upon himself to coach Doug, an insecure schoolmate, on how to act so that his friend can try out for a role in the community play. Much to everyone's surprise, Doug's reading is very good, and he is cast as the Evil Knight opposite Andrew's part as the Good Knight. Because Doug has as little athletic skill as he has self-confidence, the young man becomes a dangerous, sword-toting leading man. Can Ultraman prevent Doug from literally bringing the house down on opening night? **Guest cast:** Anais Granofsky as Cassie, Eric Richards as Doug. **Writer:** Judith Broadway. **Director:** Jim Kaufman.

When the Sun Goes Down (airdate: May 15, 1989). So that Stephanie and her friend Denise may enjoy an evening together, Andrew and Dr. Jeffcoate agree to babysit Denise's young son, Danny. Stephanie and Denise have fun until two aggressive men approach the women at a local singles bar and begin harassing them. Trying to get out of this tense situation and hoping the men will leave, Stephanie gets up to call home. On the phone, Dr. J senses something is wrong and goes to the rescue, posing as Stephanie's fiance. As things at the bar go from bad to worse, "Ultraman" and Danny swoop down on the scene to lend some extra hands. **Guest cast:** Paula Barrett as Denise, Kyle and Christopher Price-Cox as Danny, Paul Hubbard as Jonathan, Marvin Karon as Paul. **Writer:** Bill Fuller and Jim Pond. **Director:** Don Shebib.

Looking for Trouble (airdate: May 22, 1989). With his mother's birthday only a few days away, Andrew spends his time thinking of ways to earn enough money to celebrate at a chic restaurant. Dr. J agrees to front Andrew the cash and is subsequently invited to join in on the festivities. However, when a sudden surge of robberies takes place in his neighborhood, Andrew's thoughts turn to how

3rd season cast, left to right: Derek McGrath, Jerry O'Connell, Wanda Cannon, Marsha Moreau, and Chris Bolton.

"Ultraman" could be stopping these crimes. Ultraman hits the streets looking for trouble - and gets plenty of it when he forgets his mother's birthday dinner. **Guest cast:** Don Dickinson as Tim. **Writer:** Neil Ross. **Director:** Tim Bond.

The Set Up (airdate: May 29, 1989). Dr. Jeffcoate signs a contract to sell the rights for his new product to Mr. Connally as Andrew consigns two rare comic books with nothing but a handshake from Walter, the local comic book dealer. Concerned that Andrew does not understand how to conduct business, Dr. J has the young man accompany him when he delivers a product prototype - only to discover that he is the one who's been swindled! With some assistance from Walter, who has paid Andrew handsomely for the old comic books, Dr. J and "Ultraman" concoct a scheme to deliver the deceitful Mr. Connally into the hands of the police. **Guest cast:** Harvey Atkins as Walter, Reiner Schwartz as Mr. Connally, Ellen Maguire as Pauline, Bryan Elliot as the punk. **Writer:** Gary Skiles. **Director:** Don McCutcheon.

SEASON TWO

Out of Control (airdate: Oct. 2, 1989). Andrew asks Dr. Jeffcoate to be his partner in a father and son bike race. Thrilled at the prospect, he accepts and becomes determined not to let Andrew down. But during the race, Dr. Jeffcoate's overzealous attitude leads to a dangerous situation and only Andrew and his superpowers can save the day. Later Dr. Jeffcoate apologizes to Andrew for losing the race, but Andrew explains that winning was never as important to him as the two of them being able to spend the time together. **Guest cast:** Michael Kirby as Kyle Buchannan, Jaimz Woolvett as Jason Buchannan, Gillian Steeve as Melissa. **Writer:** Roy Sallows. **Director:** Alan Simmonds.

Not So Fast (airdate: Oct. 9, 1989). Andrew's best friend Kirk Buchanan has just moved back to town with his mother and stepfather. But the happy reunion is cut short when Kirk incurs the wrath of a local bully, Wayne. The two decide to settle their dispute with a chicken race towards the edge of a cliff. Andrew tries to talk Kirk out of the dangerous stunt, but Kirk is determined to show Wayne up. The action comes to a head with both Kirk and Wayne racing their cars toward the steep bluff, and even Andrew may be unable to prevent a disaster. [Note: Kirk's last name changes from Buchanan to Stevens after this one episode.] **Guest cast:** David Stratton as Wayne. **Writer:** Fred Fox, Jr. **Director:** F. Harvey Frost.

Nowhere to Hide (airdate: Oct. 16, 1989). Andrew meets Piper, a mystery girl on the run. He offers her his help, but when he meets the man she's running from he is told that she is actually a dangerous criminal. Protesting her innocence, Piper tells Andrew her side of the story and Andrew must decide whom to believe and whom to help. **Guest cast:** Kathryn Rose as Piper, Maurice Dean Wint as Carl, Richard Chevolleau as Mike. **Writer:** Eric Weinthal. **Director:** Alan Simmonds.

Photon Blues (airdate: Oct. 23, 1989). While Dr. Jeffcoate conducts further research on the photon beam which originally gave Andrew his superpowers, Mrs. Schellenbach introduces Jamie, her nephew who is visiting with a touring rap group. When the group warns Jamie to brighten up the dingy club they are booked into, the young man steals the photon beam. Andrew, Dr. J and Kirk track down the club where the group is to perform and arrive just in time for Andrew to take the beam's impact. As Dr. J retrieves his light, the heavy lighting platform topples. Andrew instinctively reaches out to stop its fall and discovers an amazing new strength. **Guest cast:** Dean McDermott as Jamie, Michie Mee and L.A. Luv as the rap group. **Writer:** Eric Weinthal. **Director:** Otto Hanus.

Heading for Trouble (airdate: Oct. 30, 1989). After helping the school football hero with his stricken Jeep, Andrew finds himself socializing with a new crowd for whom alcohol is an essential ingredient of any good time. Attracted by a cute girl in the group, however, Andrew joins the crowd and soon experiences his first hangover. Later, Andrew admits to his mother that he really doesn't enjoy drinking and promises to stop. When his new girlfriend's life is endangered by the football hero's drunken recklessness, however, only Andrew's superpowers can prevent a tragically sobering lesson. **Guest cast:** Dylan Neal as Sean, Kimberly Mills as Trudy, Elissa Mills as Nicole, Sean Roberge as Josh. **Writer:** A. Stea, P. Lauterman. **Director:** F. Harvey Frost.

Long Shot (airdate: Nov. 6, 1989). Andrew accepts a position on the photography staff of the school paper in order to meet Beth, a cute but very competitive shutterbug whose photos always land on page one. Meanwhile, Dr. Jeffcoate races the clock to finish an article for a prestigious French science journal. Erin's inexplicable knowledge of the subject of his paper causes Dr. J to rethink its publication, while Andrew's natural aptitude for photography results in his overshadowing the girl he would most like to impress. However, when a fire breaks out in school, Andrew's quick action gives Beth a photo opportunity that restores her confidence. **Guest cast:** Krista Bridges as Beth, Joanne Vannicola as Cassie. **Writer:** Bill Murtagh. **Director:** George Bloomfield.

Along for the Ride (airdate: Nov. 13, 1989). Andrew can't decide who he likes better, his pretty schoolmate Leah or her big brother, Jim, a dropout who somehow manages to drive a different exotic car every day. Erin, in the meantime, finds herself charmed by a conniving ten-year-old who is dying to see the inside of Dr. Jeffcoate's lab. Later that day, Erin lifts Andrew's key to the lab, where she and her new friend cause an accident. At the same time, Andrew unwittingly accompanies Jim on a holdup. When Andrew is arrested for the crime, it appears that only his superpowers can keep him from wearing a permanent set of stripes. **Guest cast:** Elliot Smith as Jim, Elissa Mills as Nicole. **Writer:** Elliot Stern. **Director:** Steve Scaini.

Collision Course (airdate: Nov. 20, 1989). Andrew is caught in a dilemma when evidence points to Kirk as the force behind a series of robberies at school and Kirk denies any knowledge of the crimes. At home, Erin, in a bid to score points towards a terrific birthday present, chooses Andrew as the subject of her "The Person I Most Admire" essay. With the help of a new radio transmitter developed by Dr. Jeffcoate, Andrew and Kirk set out to find the true thief. When Kirk confronts the man who set him up to receive stolen property, only Andrew's powers can save his friend. **Guest cast:** Nathaniel Moreau as Cody. **Writer:** Rick Adamson. **Director:** George Bloomfield.

Troubled Waters (airdate: Nov. 27, 1989). Winslow, Dr. Jeffcoate's old seafaring friend and mentor, is back in harbor charming Erin and Andrew with his tall tales of life at sea. But unknown to Winslow his boat was also used to smuggle an ancient and valuable statue into the country. When confronted by the smugglers, Winslow and Erin mange to flick the radio switch to "on"... but only for a moment! The call is finally heard on Jeffcoate's new boat, and with a little help from Andrew's superpowers the two friends now chart a successful search and rescue mission. **Guest cast:** Colin Fox as Winslow, Neil Clifford as Johnny, Dwayne McLean as Frankie. **Writer:** Scott Barrie. **Director:** Steve Scaini.

Don't Look Down (airdate: Dec. 4, 1989). When Dr. Jeffcoate substitutes for Andrew's physics teacher, he runs up against Mitch, a student who never passes up a chance for a laugh by fooling around in class. Meanwhile, Erin shops for a new outfit in a trendy boutique. Later, she decides her outfit is too much for a banquet hall full of real estate agents gathered to honor her mother, and mercifully decides to change. At the same time, Andrew and Dr. J determine that Mitch has the brains but not the stable home life to be a good student. When Dr. J is injured on a class outing, however, Mitch rises to the occasion and comes to his rescue. **Guest cast:** Greg Spottiswood as Mitch, James Mainprize as Mr. Lockett, Gillian Steeve as Melissa. **Writer:** David Cole. **Director:** Otta Hanus.

Caught in the Middle (airdate: Dec. 11, 1989). Enrolled in a police "ride along" program, Andrew and Kirk dream of fantastic adventures until their hopes are dashed by a boring day on the beat with Police Officer Meg. Erin, meanwhile, nervously practices for an upcoming horse show. The boys get their excitement the next day, however, when Officer Meg is taken hostage by, but then later captures, a pair of armed thieves. When Andrew and Kirk ask what kind of recognition she will receive for her bravery, Meg replies that her personal satisfaction at having done a good job is enough. Later that afternoon, Andrew shares this lesson with his sister when Erin does her best but fails to earn first place in the horse competition. **Guest cast:** Julie Khaner as Meg, Chris Benson as the first bandit, Eli Gabay as the second bandit, Steve Baker as Ted. **Writer:** Greg Phillips. **Director:** Stuart Gillard.

Secrets For Sale (airdate: Jan. 22, 1990). Andrew and Erin are apprehensive and Dr. Jeffcoate a bit jealous when Stephanie appears to be romantically interested in her boss, Ted Macklin, a slick talking real estate developer. Their emotions turn to anger and concern once they learn that Macklin is behind a move to bulldoze a local wilderness area which they have been actively trying to save. Things go from bad to worse when Andrew and Dr. Jeffcoate learn that the property has been purchased by Stephco, a division of Macklin's company named after Stephanie, and that she may be involved. **Guest cast:** Barry Flatman as Ted Macklin. **Writer:** Judith Broadway. **Director:** Alan Simmonds.

Running Home (airdate: Jan. 29, 1990). Feeling he is getting too much "grief" from his mom and stepdad, Kirk decides to pack his bags and surprise his natural father, a movie stuntman, by showing up on his doorstep. Andrew, realizing the reunion may not turn out the way Kirk hopes, accompanies his friend on the trip. They find Kirk's dad, Pete, on the set of his latest movie. At first Pete avoids seriously discussing his and Kirk's relationship, but later explains to the boy that he's just not ready to be a full-time parent. The two boys return home, Kirk realizing that running away isn't the answer, and Andrew with a new appreciation for his and Dr. Jeffcoate's relationship. **Guest cast:** Peter MacNeill as Pete. **Writer:** Eric Weinthal. **Director:** Don McCutcheon.

Missing (airdate: Feb. 5, 1990). Dr. Jeffcoate's Jeep is run off the road and the doctor is confronted by mysterious strangers. Later, when Dr. Jeffcoate doesn't return home on time, Andrew and Kirk begin searching for clues to his whereabouts. A blood stained business card, an unmonitored experiment and a cryptic phone call lead them to fear the worst. Eventually, they are able to trace their missing mentor to a secluded mountain hideaway, but before attempting a rescue they must face electric fencing, security guards, and vicious attack dogs. **Guest cast:** unknown. **Writer:** Lou Messina. **Director:** Harvey Frost.

Stolen Melodies (airdate: Feb. 12, 1990). Andrew is able to arrange for a popular band to perform at his school, earning attaboys from his principal and fellow classmates. But later a bootleg tape of the band begins to circulate around the school and suspicion falls upon Kirk. It's only with Dr. Jeffcoate's aid that Kirk is able to prove he could not be responsible for the superior, digitally recorded bootlegs. When the group's manager is identified as the real culprit, he attempts to escape by helicopter, only to be grounded by Andrew. [This episode's B-story, in which Erin relives memories of her deceased father through Clements family home movies, is particularly touching.] **Guest cast:** Tim MacMemamin as Jimmy, Martin Cummins as Grant, Dennis Fitzgerald as Robert Clements. **Writer:** Bill Murtagh. **Director:** Otta Hanus.

Toe To Toe (airdate: Feb. 19, 1990). After hearing how Dr. Jeffcoate used the laws of physics to successfully wrestle in high school, Andrew talks him into participating in a charity wrestling event. Of course, Dr. Jeffcoate is under the impression all he will be doing is ushering people to their seats. After arriving at the benefit, however, "Battling Bennie" Jeffcoate hopes the laws of physics can still triumph over brute force when he accidentally finds himself in the ring with pro wrestler The Yukon Giant (who appears as himself). [Note: **Toe To Toe** is the first collaborative effort of writers Michael O'Connell (father of Jerry O'Connell) and Derek McGrath (Dr. Jeffcoate).] **Guest cast:** The Yukon Giant as himself. **Writers:** Michael O'Connel and Derek McGrath. **Director:** Otta Hanus.

The Reluctant Hero (airdate: Feb. 26, 1990). When Andrew secretly uses his superpowers to rescue a child about to fall off a bridge, his apparent heroism causes Kirk to question his own courage. In an attempt to bolster his friend's sagging confidence, Andrew decides to trust Kirk with the secret of his superpowers. Kirk thinks Andrew's explanation of his heroic deed is the funniest thing he's ever heard, so Andrew promises to demonstrate his powers later that night. When a blast from an x-ray machine temporarily drains Andrew's powers, however, it becomes Kirk's turn to play the hero. **Guest cast:** Sharon Bernbaum as Tracy, Denise Baillargeon as the mother, Craig Sandy as the reporter. **Writer:** Michael Mercer. **Director:** Eric Weinthal.

Split Decision (airdate: Apr. 23, 1990). At his mother's request, Andrew agrees to spend time with James, a troubled young boy from the shelter. After many attempts to win James over, Andrew finally begins to make headway when the two go to a local wrecking yard, a place, where years earlier, Andrew and Kirk became compadres. Unfortunately, the new friendship unravels when Andrew thoughtlessly backs out of his plans with James to go on an eagerly awaited double-date with Kirk and two very attractive girls. Regretting his decision, Andrew rushes off to find James, who no one has seen for quite some time. Andrew's sixth sense and superspeed leads him to the wrecking yard - and to a dangerous situation when he may not be able to rescue James from a perilous perch. **Guest cast:** Marlow Vella as James, Gillian Steeve as Melissa, Charmaine Boyde as Kim, Gemma Barry as Marilyn, Suzanna Shebib as Gloria, Rena Polly as Rachel, Nicole Lyn as Jan. **Writer:** Eric Weinthal. **Director:** Randy Bradshaw.

Misfire (airdate: Apr. 30, 1990). When Andrew tries out one of Dr. Jeffcoate's latest experiments, he has no idea it will make his superpowers go haywire. Unfortunately, he learns of the problem too late and winds up blazing an embarrassing trail down the ski slopes - right in front of the girl he was trying to impress. Meanwhile, back at home, Stephanie has problems of her own when her interview with *Working Mother* magazine does not go exactly as planned. An irritated Dr. J recommends that Andrew stay in his room for the remainder of the trip. But this advice goes unheeded when Andrew sees his pretty ski bunny rushing towards a collision with a snow machine and he decides to take heroic action without knowing if he'll have the use of his superpowers. **Guest cast:** Courtney Taylor as Sarah, Samantha Follows as Jackie, Diane D'Aquila as Diane Mitchell, John Shepherd as George Wilson. **Writer:** Elliot Stern. **Director:** Stuart Gillard.

White Lies (airdate: May 7, 1990). Kirk is upset when rumors about his faltering love life appear in the school paper and assumes Andrew has been leaking the information to the gossip columnist. Meanwhile, Erin mistakes Kirk's friendliness for love and develops a serious crush on him. When Kirk finds a note in his locker asking him to sit down and talk, he thinks it's an attempt by Andrew to patch things up and reacts harshly when he discovers a love-smitten Erin. Coming to the realization that they have all been victimized by the false rumors, Kirk apologizes to Erin, and Andrew tries to put a halt to the gossip. **Guest cast:** Joanne Vannicola as Cassie, Zack Ward as Daniel, Miranda DePencier as Michelle, Michael DeSadeleer as Earl. **Writer:** Eric Weinthal. **Director:** Don Shebib.

Off the Record (airdate: May 14, 1990). Andrew and Kirk become celebrities after landing jobs as teen veejays of a local music video station. The pair work in harmony until they learn that budget cuts will force the station to take one of them off the air and they have one week to prove who's best. Meanwhile, Dr. Jeffcoate is frantic when he discovers he's being audited and his last hope is Stephanie's accountant - who happens to be his archenemy, Mrs. Schellenbach. As Mrs. Schellenbach tries to "wheel and deal" on Dr. J's tax forms, Andrew and Kirk try to outdo one another to impress the station manager. After Andrew secretly uses his superpowers to tape an exclusive interview with an elusive rock star, Kirk decides to stage a flashy and dangerous motorcycle stunt to get attention. But when push comes to shove, the two young men must decide if stardom is worth the price of their friendship. **Guest cast:** Kristina Nicoll as

Jenny Barnes, Richard Sali as Sam Benton, Santino Buda as Billy Ryder, Katie Griffin as Allison. **Writer:** Bill Murtagh. **Director:** Otta Hanus.

Best Friends (airdate: May 21, 1990). After surprising Andrew by purchasing four concert tickets, Kirk further shocks his friend by announcing he has gotten them both jobs at the local burger place to pay for the seats. However, shortly after he begins flipping hamburgers, Kirk turns in his apron and shifts his attention to the pursuit of a pretty customer - sticking Andrew with all the work and also the tickets. Andrew begins wondering what best friends are really for as Kirk continually breaks his plans with him to spend time with Paula. Dr. J gladly takes the extra tickets, but Andrew is slightly taken aback when he finds himself double-dating with his own mother. Striking out with Paula, Kirk seeks out Andrew at the batting cage, only to find him with a pretty new partner. **Guest cast:** Lorne Pardy as Mr. Burger, Andre Roth as Paula, Kim Bourne as Lauren, Ron Payne as Mr. Davis, Diana Rowland as Mrs. Davis. **Writer:** Joe Menosky. **Director:** Rob Malenfant.

More Than Meets the Eye (airdate: May 28, 1990). Dr. Jeffcoate is less then pleased when Andrew invites Kirk to help with a science presentation at the all-girl school where his "straightlaced" niece, Rebecca, attends. Predictably, the boys are more interested in the cute coeds than in the project. Dr. J is shocked when he discovers Kirk, clad only in a towel, in Rebecca's room. Later, Rebecca invites Kirk, Andrew, and one of her schoolmates for a drive in her new car, a careless ride which takes a turn for the worst. Dr. Jeffcoate is not surprised when Kirk claims responsibility for the accident, that is, until Rebecca confesses the truth to her uncle and he must reevaluate his opinion of Kirk. **Guest cast:** Sharry Flett as Patricia, Susannah Hoffmann as Rebecca, Cyndy Preston as Penny, Maryke Hendrikse as Brooke. **Writer:** Rick Adamson. **Director:** F. Harvey Frost.

Seems Like Only Yesterday (airdate: June 4, 1990). A relentless developer decides to tear down the local roller skating rink to make room for condos. With all hope lost of saving the structure, the Clements and their friends can only think back to special moments that occurred at the rink. Andrew remembers his first encounter with Kirk; Stephanie recalls the moment she told her husband she was pregnant with Andrew; Mrs. Schellenbach reminisces about her roller derby days, and Dr. Jeffcoate thinks about his dad's advice to a young, infatuated Benjamin. When the fateful day arrives, it seems nothing, save Andrew's superpowers, can stop the wrecking ball. **Guest cast:** Dennis Fitzgerald as Robert Clements, Les Rubie as Frank, Dan MacDonald as Bill Lanville. **Writer:** Fred Fox, Jr. **Director:** Don Shebib.

SEASON THREE

Ground Control (airdate: Oct. 1, 1990). Stephanie grounds Andrew, which means he's going to miss a big party he was anxious to attend. Later, he rebelliously sneaks out of the house and he and Kirk "borrow" Stephanie's boss' classic red Ferrari, which has been left in Stephanie's care. Out on the road, the boys are feeling pretty hip, until an undercover police officer commandeers the car for use in a highspeed chase and shoot out. **Guest cast:** Cindy Preston as Staci, Robbie Fox as the biker, Gene Mack as the tow truck driver, Jank Azman as the teacher. **Writer:** John May. **Director:** Otta Hanus.

Trading Places (airdate: Oct. 8, 1990). Stephanie is having problems with her self-confidence, so Dr. Jeffcoate agrees to hypnotize her. During the procedure, he instructs her to be more like the person she most admires, in her case, Madonna. Andrew and Kirk happen to walk into the room while Dr. Jeffcoate is placing the hypnotic suggestion and end up with their personalities switched. **Guest cast:** Tamara Gorski as Alison, Edward Heeley as Raoul. **Writer:** Eric Weinthal. **Director:** Don McCutcheon.

Dropout (airdate: Oct. 15, 1990). A school aptitude test threaten to end Andrew and Kirk's friendship. Andrew excels, but Kirk misinterprets his test scores and believes it will serve him just as well to drop out of school. He turns to what he believes to be his only true talent, professional motorcross racing. Andrew agrees to join Kirk's pit crew in order to keep their friendship alive and in hopes of convincing his friend to return to school. **Guest cast:** Dean Hamilton as Bulldog, Sarah Stevens as the arguing girl. **Writer:** Dawn Ritchie. **Director:** Carlo Linconti.

Sour Grapes (airdate: Oct. 22, 1990). Dr. Jeffcoate, Andrew and Kirk are off to the south of France where the doctor is to introduce his new powdered wine at an international festival. It doesn't take long for Andrew and Kirk to hit the beaches and nightclubs, but Dr. Jeffcoate has better luck finding romance. Unfortunately, it turns out his new love may actually be out to kill him. **Guest cast:** Renee Murphy as Michelle, Colombe Demers as Monique, Neil Crone as the desk clerk, Deborah Duchene as Genevieve, Patric Creelman as the first dancer, Jacqueline Graham as the second dancer. **Writer:** Terry Saltsman. **Director:** Harvey Frost.

First Love (airdate: Oct. 29, 1990). Dr. Jeffcoate's new, temporary lab assistant is a pretty college coed, Dusty. Her free-spirited manner captivates Andrew, who soon finds himself head over heels in love with the young woman. For a time, it seems the feeling may be mutual, until Dusty announces suddenly that she has accepted a fellowship at an astronomy outpost in Chile and must leave immediately. Andrew is deeply hurt, but wise advice from Dr. Jeffcoate snaps him out of it and he superspeeds to the airport in hopes of seeing Dusty off. **Guest cast:** Carolyn Dunn as Dusty, George Markos as the bus driver. **Writer:** Paul Ledoux. **Director:** Harvey Frost.

A Novel Idea (airdate: Nov. 5, 1990). [This colorful episode was inspired by the hit feature film *Dick Tracy*.] Andrew must turn out a comic-book style detective story for his Creative Writing Class, which he joined to impress a girl, Jennifer. Once at his word processor, Andrew invents a primary colored world in which hard-bitten cop Nick Nolan (Andrew) is pitted against Underworld kingpin Slimeball Seville (Dr. Jeffcoate), his henchman Knuckles Nichols (Kirk), and the evil Pasta Fazool (Mrs. Schellenbach), who plan to take over the city with organized crime. They kidnap Nick's young friend Freckles (Erin) to lure him into a deadly trap. [Note: Co-star Wanda Cannon, once a performer with Toronto's prestigious Imperial Room Orchestra, has a brief musical number in this episode.] **Guest cast:** Gemma Barry as Jennifer Lindsay, Dwayne McLean as the first henchman, John Stoneham Sr. as the second henchman, Richard Blackburn as the third henchman, Raymund Hunt as the fourth henchman. **Writer:** Aubrey Tadman. **Director:** Stuart Gillard.

David's Dream (airdate: Nov. 12, 1990). Stephanie's volunteer work brings her into contact with David, a ten-year-old boy who is dying from an inoperable brain tumor. Realizing the boy's greatest wish is to fly, she and Dr. Jeffcoate arrange for David to ride in an F-14. In the meantime, David befriends Andrew, who is busy preparing for a windsurfing competition. A conflict arises when David's flight is scheduled on the same day as Andrew's contest, but the young boy chooses to stay grounded and cheer Andrew on. The F-14 flight is rescheduled, but when the day arrives David is too ill to go. Later that night, Andrew takes David in his arms and using his superpowers, they embark on a very special flight. **Guest cast:** Noah Plener as David. **Writer:** Susan Snooks. **Director:** William Fruet.

A Bump in Time (airdate: Nov. 19, 1990). Andrew wants to accept a part-time job at the Briarwood Country Club, but Dr. Jeffcoate would rather he volunteer this time to an environmental tree planting campaign. After they argue, Andrew superspeeds through the park where he runs into a tree and knocks himself out. When he awakens, he finds himself in the middle of a 1960s anti-war demonstration. As police move in, Andrew is saved by Robbie, a young hippie, and the two of them become friends. It seems Robbie's band has been invited to play at Woodstock, but Robbie has backed out. He has learned that Agent Orange is being secretly manufactured by a nearby appliance company, and he plans to break in and expose this fact to the public. The band asks Andrew if he would like to fill in for Robbie at Woodstock, and Andrew accepts. On the way, they hear over the radio that police have cornered Robbie in the plant and sharpshooters are being called in. Andrew rushes to Robbie's side and together they make the public aware of the situation. When the paddy wagon they are being taken away in lurches, Andrew hits his head again, and he awakens to find himself back in the nineties. Andrew apologizes to Dr. Jeffcoate for the argument and later finds out that his adventure in the sixties actually happened. He finds a picture taken of both him and Robbie, only now Andrew has vanished from the photo. Stephanie then points out to Andrew that the person in the picture, Robbie, is actually Robert Clements, his father. **Guest cast:** Nicholas Shields as Robbie, Reg Dreger as the attendant, Larissa Lapchinski as Star, Paul Kaufman as Pick, Christopher Kennedy as Soulman, Dan Buccos as the reporter, Dwyne McLean as the guard. **Writer:** Sanjay Mehta. **Director:** Otta Hanus.

Calendar Boy (airdate: Nov. 26, 1990). Andrew and Kirk sneak into rehearsals for a fashion show, and after one of the male models sprains an ankle, Andrew is chosen to stand in for him. While changing backstage at the show, a photographer sneaks a photo of Andrew in his jockey shorts. Later, when the picture turns up in the high school calendar, Andrew becomes very popular, attracting even the attention of the most popular girl in school. Andrew enjoys being a sex symbol until the next modeling job, where he's treated like a piece of meat. He decides he'd rather be known for who he is rather than what he looks like. **Guest cast:** Cheryl MacInnis as Candace Blushak, Susan Haskell as Lauren Vale, Brendan Statles as the linebacker, Chandra West as the shy girl. **Writer:** Dawn Ritchie. **Director:** Don McCutcheon.

Moving Out (airdate: Dec. 3, 1990). Andrew is having growing pains, and Stephanie has the solution. She's promised a friend to help find someone to house-sit for a few weeks. When Andrew begs for the opportunity, Stephanie agrees, hoping that the experience of living on his own for a while will do him some good. When word spreads that he has his own place, Andrew becomes a big man on campus. But he soon learns a valuable lesson in responsibility when things start getting out of hand. **Guest cast:** Rebecca Wood as Kelly, Karen Hunchak as Katie, Jason Brock as Kyle. **Writer:** John May. **Director:** Otta Hanus.

Teen Hot Line (airdate: Jan. 14, 1991). As a community project, Andrew, Kirk and Dr. Jeffcoate become involved in a telephone distress line for troubled teenagers. Kirk talks to Amanda, a disabled girl who's father is overly possessive because of her condition. Andrew gets a call from a suicidal boy who is being abused by his father. Kirk agrees to meet with Amanda and convinces her to join the hotline as a counselor, which earns her new respect from her dad. But Andrew's advice to the young boy backfires, and the boy decides to commit suicide by jumping from the ledge of a tall building. Now, only Andrew can talk him down. **Guest cast:** Bill Lake as Dr. Hobbs, Noam Zylberman as Julian, Kyra Levy as Amanda. **Writer:** Martin Lager. **Director:** Don McCutcheon.

Trial by Peers (airdate: Jan. 21, 1990). Andrew lands a job as a valet car park at a fancy restaurant. But there's no reason for celebration when he's arrested and accused of copying customer's keys so he can later break into their homes. After being booked, the judge offers Andrew a choice: a normal trial or teen court, a pilot program which allows young people to be judged by their own peers. Andrew chooses the latter. Kirk does surprisingly well as Andrew's lawyer, but the evidence works against him. It seems Andrew's only chance may be to reveal his superpowers to the world, which would explain how he could be in two places almost at once. **Guest cast:** Richard Zeppieri as Tony, Andy LeWarne as Percy, Deb Grover as Judge Daley, David Orth as Norman, Walker Boone as the detective, Samantha McCombs as the "nasty girl". **Writers:** Charles Lazer and Dawn Ritchie. **Director:** Otta Hanus.

A Life in the Day of Dr. J (airdate: Jan. 28, 1991). While the Clements are busy preparing a surprise birthday party for Dr. Jeffcoate, he sits alone in his lab dreading the idea of turning forty. He feels he hasn't accomplished anything with his life. Then the effects of an ongoing experiment hits him and he falls into a dream. In the dream, Mrs. Schellenbach warns him to expect a visit by three others and to heed their warnings. Then Andrew shows up in the guises of a "Fifties Greaser", "Rap Artist", and "Tour Guide". He takes Dr. J into the past, present, and future and teaches him what's really important in life. **Guest cast:** Kyle Labine as Benny, Justine Campbell as Dagmar, Rena Poly as Mrs. Jeffcoate, Joshua Magder as Scooter. **Writer:** Dawn Ritchie. **Director:** Steve DiMarco.

My Other Secret Identity (airdate: Feb. 4, 1991). Andrew is infatuated with a beautiful young actress, Alana Porter. So much so, that he impersonates a woman in order to get a role in Alana's latest movie. Trouble begins when he must deal with the leading man, Tony Fenzi, during a love scene. Later, Andrew invites Alana and her father, Michael, home to meet his mother. Since Stephanie is out of town, Dr. Jeffcoate must bail Andrew out by standing in for her, in drag! Finally, Andrew realizes that the lies have gone too far and that he must reveal his real self to Alana. **Guest cast:** Mia Kirshner as Alana, Alf Humphreys as Trent Garber, Colleen Klein as the first hopeful girl, Norwich Duff as Michael Porter, Dean Richards as Tony. **Writer:** Aubrey Tadman. **Director:** Otta Hanus.

Pirate Radio (airdate: Feb. 11, 1991). Andrew discovers an old radio transmitter in Dr. Jeffcoate's lab. Andrew sets up the old relic in his bedroom, and later he and Kirk put on a mock radio broadcast, unaware they are actually going out over the air. The next day, they learn they have created a "Gonzo Radio" craze and are masters of the airwaves. But a DJ at a local radio station worries he is losing listeners to the two unknown pirates, and reports them to the Federal Broadcast Commission. Soon afterwards, Andrew learns that the water supply to the school has been contaminated, but will the FBC shut him down before he can alert students? **Guest cast:** Murray Cruchley as "Krazy Ken" Kelsey, Peter Millard as Meyers, Rino Romano as Brannen. **Writer:** Wilson Coneybeare. **Director:** Harvey Frost.

From the Trenches (airdate: Feb. 18, 1991). Andrew and Kirk sit down together to write a book entitled *The Ultimate Guide to Dating*. They plan to cover such topics as picking up girls at the mall and double dating. But their research together turns out to be a tribute to Murphy's Law - whatever can go wrong...does! **Guest cast:** Lisa Nichols as Dana, Katie Griffin as Renee, Vince Metcalfe as Doyle. **Writer:** John May. **Director:** Harvey Frost.

The Invisible Dr. J (airdate: Feb. 25, 1991). While assisting in an experiment, Andrew accidentally gives Dr. Jeffcoate an incorrect chemical and the doctor becomes invisible. The two must then work together to get ahold of the chemical cure, which is stored at a high security research laboratory. It soon become a race against time to prevent Dr. J from becoming permanently invisible. **Guest cast:** Steve Mousseau as Burnhamthorpe, Drew Coombes as Slash, James Stewart as Flea. **Writer:** Susan Snooks and Scott Barrie. **Director:** Stefan Scaini.

Three Men and a Skull (airdate: Mar. 4, 1991). While conducting a geological survey for the Monumental Oil Company, Hartley Jeffcoate, Dr. Jeffcoate's younger brother, unearths a fossil skull, which he dubs "Jeffcoate Man." The skull is believed to be the earliest example of homo sapiens ever found in South America. Hartley asks his brother to verify the authenticity of the skull. But someone sneaks into the lab and replaces the real thing with a fake skull, and Dr. Jeffcoate, upon examining it, must declare his own brother a fraud. The man behind the switch is Methey, an executive from Monumental Oil who has promised several private investors their would be no delay in drilling, which would surely be the case if the skull was ruled authentic. When the Jeffcoate and Andrew uncover the truth, Methey decides to eliminate them *and* the skull. **Guest cast:** Geraint Wyn Davies [Airwolf] as Hartley, David Gardner as Griz Hardwold, Alex Carter as Methey, Duncan Ollerenshaw as Brock, Chandra Galasso as the TV reporter. **Writers:** Derek McGrath and Michael O'Connell. **Director:** Otta Hanus.

The Great Indoors (airdate: Mar. 11, 1991). Stephanie breaks the bad news to Andrew and Erin that they can no longer afford to keep the Clements' family cottage. So they head into the mountains accompanied by Dr. Jeffcoate and Kirk to prepare the cottage for prospective buyers. Later, an avalanche traps everyone inside, where they must tough out the isolation and haunting memories until help arrives. **Guest cast:** Billy Van as Rocky Kalish, Joyce Gorden as Irma Kalish. **Writer:** Dawn Ritchie. **Director:** William Fruet.

Dr. J's Brain Machine (airdate: Apr. 22, 1991). Andrew agrees to help test a research project of Dr. Jeffcoate that may some day restore the memories of people who become ill or injured. As a storm rages outside, Dr. Jeffcoate hooks his young friend up to the "Brain Machine", which will manifest memories stored deep inside of Andrew's psyche. Then lightning strikes, and a power surge erases Andrew's memory, including all knowledge of his superpowers! **Guest cast:** None. **Writers:** David Garber and Bruce E. Kalish. **Director:** George Bloomfield.

Slave for A Day (airdate: Apr. 29, 1991). The Briarwood Country Club is holding it's Annual Charity Auction, and Kirk, Andrew, and Dr. Jeffcoate are all up for auction. Andrew is bought by Mr. Blaine for his shy daughter, Linda; Kirk is bought by twins who have vowed to kill him; and Dr. Jeffcoate is bought by Mrs. Schellenbach, who needs a dance partner. Their experiences together make for a sometimes sobering, sometimes comedic, and eventually uplifting day. **Guest cast:** Ron White as David Blaine, Janne Mortil as Linda, Bryan Okes Fuller as Wayne. **Writer:** Glenn Norman. **Director:** George Bloomfield.

Big Business (airdate: May 6, 1991). Andrew gets a job working as a mailboy at the McClafferty advertising firm. One day a client, Quigley, the owner of a running shoe company, asks Andrew for his advice on the product, and Andrew's suggestion gets him promoted to Executive Youth Consultant for the Quigley account. But his reign as a bigwig may be short lived. While giving a presentation to Quigley and account executives, Andrew incorporates his superpowers into the act, which Quigley takes as a sign of cheap theatrics. **Guest cast:** Chris Bondy as Mr. Jamieson, Michele DuQuet as Veronica, J.W. Carroll as Quigley, Gina Clayton as the secretary. **Writer:** John May. **Director:** Ken Girotti.

My Old Flame (airdate: May 13, 1991). Kirk has fallen hard for pretty Christa Stambler. But when he goes to introduce Christa to Andrew, he discovers the two of them were once involved in a relationship. Andrew and Christa begin to reminisce about old times and it soon becomes apparent they still have feelings for one another. Andrew must then decide what means more to him, Kirk's friendship or getting back together with his old flame. **Guest cast:** Andrea Roth as Christa, D. Jon Dawes as Brooke Carlson. **Writer:** Wilson Coneybeare. **Director:** Stefan Scaini.

A Bank, A Hold Up, A Robber and A Hero (airdate: May 20, 1991). The Clements, Dr. Jeffcoate, and Kirk are all eye witnesses to a bank holdup. Later when they're questioned by a police detective no one can remember what happened - until a reward is mentioned. Then each person takes a turn telling his or her version of the story, including how they heroically subdued the robber. The detective isn't sure who to believe. The robber finally comes forward and tells the truth, including how Andrew tripped him up by using his superpowers! **Guest cast:** Ed Sahely as Oberhouse, Tim Lee as the bank manager, Wayne Robson as the gorilla. **Writer:** David Garber and Bruce E. Kalish. **Director:** William Fruet.

The Adventures of Superboy

review edited by William E. Anchors, Jr.

Production credits:

Executive Producer	Ilya Salkind
Character created by	Jerry Siegel
	Joe Schuster
Music	Kevin Kiner

Regular cast:

Clark Kent/Superboy	John Haymes Newton (season 1)
	Gerard Christopher (seasons 2-4)
Lana Lang	Stacy Haiduk
T.J. White	Jim Calvert (season 1)
Lex Luthor	Scott Wells (season 1)
	Sherman Howard (seasons 2-4)
Andy McAllister	Ilan Mitchell-Smith (season 2)
Matt Ritter	Peter Jay Fernandez (seasons 3-4)
C. Dennis Jackson	Robert Levine (seasons 3-4)
Jonathan Kent	Stuart Whitman (seasons 1-2)
Ma Kent	Salome Jens (seasons 1-2)
Dr. Peterson	George Chakiris

Number of episodes: 99 one-half hour segments

Premise: The Man of Steel as a teenager attending Shuster University, where his alter ego Clark Kent has made friends with cub reporter T.J. White and the irresistible Lana Lang, whom he has known since his childhood days in Smallville. During his adventures fighting everything from crime to outer space aliens, he makes one of his greatest enemies, the evil Lex Luthor, who also attends Shuster University.

Editor's comments: OK, it isn't great art. What it is is good entertainment, pure and simple, and is superior to the vast majority of its made-for-syndication competitors. Besides, who could possibly resist Stacy Haiduk?

SEASON ONE

The Jewel of Techacal (airdate: Oct. 3, 1988). Lana Lang's globe-trotting father and his assistant are heading to Shuster University to mount an exhibition of artifacts from their latest archaeological dig. Professor Lang's assistant believes one of the relics is cursed. Their arrival at the local airport seems to support this theory when their landing gear fails to function, and they are nearly killed - except for the fact that Superboy enters the scene in the nick of time and rescues the endangered plane. Reunited with her father after the near catastrophe, Lana Lang tries desperately to smooth out past differences until the curse strikes again, felling Professor Lang with a massive heart attack. It's clear the cursed artifact must be returned to its place of origin or all of Shuster is in danger. Unfortunately, a ruthless upperclassman, Lex Luthor, along with his henchman, Leo, has pilfered the priceless artifact intending to sell it to the highest bidder. **Guest cast:** Peter White as Prof. Thomas Lang, Michael Manno as Leo, Gregg Todd Davis as Haines, Forest Neal as Dean Thompson, Bob Barnes as Dr. Spencer. **Writer:** Fred Frieberger. **Director:** Reza S. Badiyi.

A Kind of Princess (airdate: Oct. 10, 1988). Clark Kent has fallen for Sarah Danner, whose father is a very important man in organized crime. He's come to Shuster University for his daughter's birthday, which doesn't sit well with Casey, the local crime boss. Fearing that Sarah's father is moving in on his territory, Casey orders him killed. All-out war is declared between the two gangsters after Superboy saves Sarah's father. Clark questions his feelings toward Sarah, who accepts her father's work a little too matter-of-factly for Clark's tastes, though it's not long before Sarah herself becomes her father's bargaining chip against Casey. Helpless to do much but wait with his girl's life hanging in the balance, Clark Kent sees what little value Sarah's life has to her father, as he gambles frivolously with Casey. **Guest cast:** Julie McCullough as Sarah Danner, Ed Winter as Matt Danner, Harry Cup as Casey, Antoni Carone as Jake, Steven Anthony as Arnie, Dennis Underwood as the bodyguard, Roger Pratto as Detective Harris, Rebecca Perle as Nancy, Dennis Michael as Henry Oman, Paul J. Darby as the cop. **Writers:** Howard Dimsdale and Michael Morris. **Director:** Reza S. Badiyi.

Back to Oblivion (airdate: Oct. 17, 1988). T. J. White, the son of *Daily Planet* newspaper editor Perry White, is investigating several acts of violence reported at the scrap heap near Shuster University, when he too falls victim to deadly machines constructed by old man Wagner to protect his yard. When Lana Lang hears of the attempt on T.J.'s life, she defends Wagner as a fine, upstanding citizen. She even goes out to his scrap yard to calm the frightened Mr. Wagner. Hounded for years by inconsiderate children and neighbors, the old man's past catches up with him as he begins to relive the Nazi holocaust, surrounding himself with protection. When Lana Lang turns up with some food, the senile old man mistakes her for his murdered daughter Lena. Attempts to reason with him are futile and it takes Superboy to brave the scrap-metal onslaught Mr. Wagner has prepared for the imagined Nazi takeover. **Guest cast:** Abe Vigoda as Mr. Wagner, Dennis Michael as Henry. **Writer:** Fred Frieberger. **Director:** Colin Chilvers.

The Russian Exchange Student (airdate: Oct. 24, 1988). The

Season One: John Haymes Newton as Superboy/Clark Kent, Stacy Haiduk as the beautiful Lana Lang.

college adventures of Superboy continue as Natasha Pokrovsku, a Soviet exchange student, visits the Shuster University campus to work on a joint Soviet/American energy experiment with Professor Abel Gordon. While working in his high-security laboratory, Pro-

fessor Gordon is jolted from his seat by an electrical short in the computer. Knowing that only he, Natasha, and his assistant Jeff Hilford have access to the lab, Prof. Gordon, already leery of the foreign exchange student, suspects Natasha of rigging the explo-

Season One: John Haymes Newton as Superboy/Clark Kent, Stacy Haiduk as Lana Lang, Jim Calvert as T. C. White (son of *The Daily Planet*'s Perry White).

sion. Insulted and hurt, Natasha packs to return to the Soviet Union while Clark, Lana and T.J. try to talk her into staying. Later, another incident occurs that nearly kills Prof. Abel, and Natasha is believed to be the cause. But T.J. and Clark believe she is innocent and become determined to clear her from suspicion **Guest cast:** Ray Walston [*My Favorite Martian*] as Prof. Abel Gordon, Heather Haase as Natasha Pakovsky, Courtney Gaines as Jeff, Tania Harley as Elena, Roger Pretto as Detective Zeke Harris, Chase Randolph as Drake, Ralph Rafferty as the janitor, Rick Defuria as the policeman, Dennis Deveaugh as the thug, Aley Edlin as the second thug.

Writers: Vida Spears and Sava V. Finney. **Director:** Reza S. Badiyi.

Countdown to Nowhere (airdate: Oct. 31, 1988). During a peaceful protest over the development of a dangerous new laser gun for the government, four thieves dressed as Shuster University football players steal the controversial weapon. To protect their getaway, they kidnap the protest's organizer, freshman Lana Lang. Clark and T.J. are at a loss as to where the criminals are headed with Lana and the gun, but the young journalism students decipher a cryptic clue, and they realize that the thieves intend to sabotage the launching of NASA's space shuttle scheduled for that afternoon. Concerned for the safety of his dearest friend and the danger posed to the U.S. space program, Clark Kent has little choice except to venture out into public as the Boy of Steel - Superboy - for the first time ever. **Guest cast:** Doug Barr as Roscoe Williams, Duriell Harris as Theodore, Noah Meeks as Miller, Fred Broderson as the detective, Jay Glick as the security chief, Paul J. Darby as the radio operator. **Writer:** Fred Frieberger. **Director:** Colin Chilvers.

Bringing Down the House (airdate: Nov. 7, 1988). A rash of deadly mishaps plague the boardwalk and baseball amusement park the same week that Shuster University alumnus Judd Faust returns for a rare concert appearance at the college. The introverted rock star sweeps Lana Lang off her feet and appears to make Clark Kent a little bit jealous. While investigating the strange accidents, Clark discovers there is a bizarre link between Faust's return to Shuster and the deadly theme-park threats. Faust's compulsion to collect almost anything is revealed to be a driving force in his personality - and in his profession. When Lana finds out what lengths Faust will go to add to his collection, it may be too late for her to survive her crush on the outlandish celebrity. **Guest cast:** Leif Garrett as Judd Faust, Don Sheldon as Andy, Antonio Fabrizio as Charles, Dennis Michael as Henry, Sabrina Laloyd as Betsy, Ed Montgomery as the umpire. **Writers:** Howard Dimsdale and Michael Morris. **Director:** Colin Chilvers.

The Beast and Beauty (airdate: Nov. 14, 1988). After a jewelry store is held up, the guard swears it was Superboy who melted their vault with his heat vision. Not realizing there is an impostor, the police issue a warrant for Superboy's arrest. Meanwhile, at Shuster University, Clark Kent is interviewing Jennifer Jenkins, a Shuster graduate and contestant in a regional Beauty Pageant. Hugo Stone is the impostor and the would-be suitor of Jennifer Jenkins. Once she jokingly agreed to marry Stone if he "had a million bucks." Armed with high-tech machines and a Superboy costume, he is stealing his million dollar dowry. The girl has no idea that the lunatic Stone will soon be paying a call on her, and Superboy's problems are only beginning as the police arrest him after he saves two officers from a burning car that wrecked in pursuit of the impostor. **Guest cast:** David Marciano as Hugo Stone, Lonnie Shaw as Jennifer Jenkins, Roger Pretto as Detective Zeke Harris, Jeff Moldovan as Rudy, Rick Higley as the cop, Tom Nowicki as the security guard, Dan Barber as the emcee, Tal Millican as the announcer, Cyndi Vicino as the woman. **Writers:** Toby Martin and Bernard M. Khan. **Director:** Jackie Cooper.

The Fixer (airdate: Nov. 21, 1988). Superboy gets involved in a fixed basketball game at Shuster University which is masterminded by Shuster University senior, Lex Luthor. Luthor has bribed the star player to throw the game by threatening to publish some photographs of him smoking grass at a party, which would ruin his pro-basketball career. Clark, Lana and T.J. team up to defeat Lex by convincing Stretch to win the game in spite of the consequences. Stretch eventually comes to the realization that if he does throw the game, he will be in Luthor's hip pocket the rest of his life. He decides to try his best to win, but his every move is foiled by another player who is on the take. **Guest cast:** Michael Landon, Jr. as Stretch, James Hampton as the coach, Curley Neal as the state coach, Michael Manno as Leo, Carl Jay Cofield as Moose, Harry Burney III as the referee, Ron Segall as the umpire. **Writer:** Alden Schwimmer. **Director:** Colin Chilvers.

The Alien Solution (airdate: Nov. 28, 1988). Unknown to Superboy and Lana Lang, they are being monitored by a weird gaseous creature in a spaceship high above the Earth's atmosphere. After inhabiting a lifeless body on board its ship, the alien follows and captures the unsuspecting Lana and subsequently succeeds in luring the Boy of Steel into his clutches. After a pitched battle on the Shuster University campus where Lana is rendered unconscious, it appears that Superboy has indeed defeated the strange alien warrior. But the gaseous being escapes the lifeless warrior form, and enters Lana's comatose figure. Thinking his lifelong friend is on the verge of death, Clark stand vigil over her hospital bed until he is confronted by the alien-possessed Lana. Clark is torn up over Lana being hurt by the alien, until the being regains consciousness and tricks Clark into following the gaseous creature back to its ship as Superboy. Once on board the alien vessel, the creature plans to add Superboy to his collection of lifeless warriors. **Guest cast:** Jeff Moldovan as Alien warrior, Dennis Michael as Henry, Christine Page as Dr. Howard, Ray Muennich as the paramedic, Todd Sealey as the first student, Tom Bahr as the second student. **Writers:** Michael Carlin and Andrew Helfer. **Director:** Colin Chilvers.

Troubled Waters (airdate: Dec. 5, 1988). Clark Kent's father is a prominent and vocal resister to Carl Kenderson, a suspicious land investor, who is mysteriously making bids on their community's modestly valued farmlands. Having obviously chosen an unscrupulous adversary, Jonathan "Pa" Kent soon finds himself in Smallville Community Hospital, the victim of an unexplainable tractor accident. Against Jonathan's wishes, Clark's old girl friend, Ellen Jensen, calls the Kent's son back to Smallville from Shuster University. When Clark arrives, Pa Kent tells Clark of his suspicions that Kenderson plans on buying up the land and mining it. Clark uses his X-ray vision to discover that there is nothing unusual under the soil except an underground river. When Kenderson sets out to torch the Kent farm, disaster is averted by Superboy, who discovers that the underground river is Kenderson's goal - he intends to sell the water cheaply to outsiders. But Kenderson isn't about to quit yet, and part of his plans include the death of Jonathan Kent. **Guest cast:** Julie Donald as Ellen Jensen, Peter Palmer as Cal Kenderson, John Zencda as Jarvis, Daniel Kamin as Borkner, Norman Lund as Bennington, Joe Tomko as Corbin. **Writer:** Dick Robbins. **Director:** Reza S. Badiyi.

Kryptonite Kills (airdate: Jan. 23, 1989). Professor Peterson's colleagues send part of a glowing green meteorite to Shuster University where he displays it in his geology class. Peterson begins to tell what a great source of energy the rock seems to be when Clark suddenly faints before the entire class. In the confusion, Lex Luthor steals the strange, radiating rock from space. With the Kryptonite in his clutches, Luthor sets in motion a plan designed to put the entire city in the palm of his hand. Using the stone's alien energies, Luthor plans to overload the city's power plant, plunging the city into darkness as a cover to rob the town blind. **Guest cast:** Pamela Bach as Veronica Lawlor, Michael Manno as Leo, Cyndi Vance as Anges, Paul Cohn as Oswald, Larry Francer as Felix. **Writers:** Andrew Helfer and Mike Carlin. **Director:** Jackie Cooper.

Revenge of the Alien, parts one and two (airdates: part one, Jan. 30; part two, Feb. 6, 1989). The gaseous alien that opposed Superboy was defeated when the Boy of Steel placed the being in a canister that was then locked in a lab. Unfortunately, a vandal steals the canister from the laboratory and releases the creature, who now wants revenge on Superboy. Disguised as a policeman, the alien

Season One: Lana Lang and Superboy.

tracks Superboy/Clark Kent to Shuster University, where Clark's father, Pa Kent, is visiting his son. Suddenly there is a huge explosion, and everyone, including Clark, is temporarily knocked unconscious. In the confusion, the alien enters the body of Pa Kent. When Pa Kent and Lana Lang leave together, no one suspects that alien has taken over Pa Kent's body and abducted Lana, and is using her as bait to capture Superboy. The alien holds Lana hostage at a building where Kryptonite, the only substance that can kill Superboy, is secretly hidden. The alien knows if he can get Superboy close enough to the Kryptonite, he will weaken the boy of steel and take over his body. Superboy's attempt to rescue Lana may be his last.... **Guest cast:** Glenn Scherer as Johnson, Roger Pretto as Lt. Zeke Harris, Dennis Michael as Henry, Dana Mark as Dean Lockhardt, Alan Jordan as Williams, Mark Macaulay as the crook, Chick Bernhardt as the cop, Jerry Eden as the newscaster. **Writers:** Andrew Helfer and Michael Carlin. **Director:** Peter Kiwitt.

Stand Up and Get Knocked Down (airdate: Feb. 13, 1989). T.J. White and Clark Kent investigate the mysterious death of T.J.'s friend Michael, who had recently performed at a local comedy club. Suspecting that the club is involved in Michael's death, T.J. signs up to perform. That night, he overhears the club owners talking about Michael's murder. They thought Michael was trying to muscle in on their drug running business, so they eliminated him. When the club owners realize T.J. is snooping too much, he decides to get rid of the pesky teenager - permanently. **Guest cast:** Gary Lockwood as Dexter Linton, Hayden Logston as Michael, Cindy Hamsey as Angel, Lester Bibbs as the emcee, Jack Spirtos as the goon, Joe Hess as the goon, Brett Rice as the suit. **Writers:** David Patrick Columbia and Toby Martin. **Director:** David Grossman.

Meat Mr. Mxyzptlk (airdate: Feb. 20, 1989). An evil creature from the fifth dimension named Mr. Mxyzptlk comes to Earth to find the secret of Superboy's powers. Mr. Mxyzptlk turns himself into a Clark Kent clone to win the affections of Lana Lang. When Superboy tries to get Mr. Mxyzptlk away from Lana, Lana believes Superboy is jealous of her newfound relationship with Clark. Meanwhile, Superboy must find another way to get Lana away from the Clark clone before she is whisked away to the fifth dimension by the mysterious Mr. Mxyzptlk. **Guest cast:** Michael J. Pollard as Mr. Mxyzptlk, Russ Wheeler as Prof. Royer, Cindy Vicino as the lady, Steve Dash and Jim Rios as the muggers. **Writer:** Dennis O'Neill. **Director:** Peter Kiwitt.

Birdwoman of the Swamps (airdate: Feb. 27, 1989). A construction project benefitting the poor is halted by mysterious, inexplicable occurrences. The local wildlife is blamed for the acts of vandalism. The spokesperson for the wildlife, an old Indian woman, says the local animals are upset by the construction and they must not be disturbed. The investigative talents of Clark, T.J., and Lana come into play when they try to get to the bottom of the strange attacks on the construction company. The old Indian woman claims the birds themselves are causing the acts of destruction, while Mr. Hogan, the owner of the construction company insists the woman is behind the mishaps. Superboy is called in to upright the huge pieces of fallen construction machinery, only to find himself momentarily succumbing to the Indian woman's ancient magic. Meanwhile, Mr. Hogan, showing his true colors, sends his men out to remove the threat of the Indian woman - permanently. **Guest cast:** Marlene Cameron as the Birdwoman, James MacArthur [*The Swiss Family Robinson*] as Mr. Hogan, Mike Walter as Woody, Ted Science as the accomplice, Jack Swanson as Frank, Kim Crow as Prof. Rogers, Liz Vassey as the student. **Writer:** Bernard M. Khan. **Director:** Reza Badiyi.

Terror From the Blue (airdate: Mar. 6, 1989). Lana Lang shows up at the police station to do an interview for her paper on community relations. Lt. Harris isn't back from lunch, so Lana goes for a walk.

Meanwhile, Harris is outside talking to Detective Jed Slade, a crooked cop who Harris is trying to talk into turning himself in for his criminal activities. Just as Lana walks by, Slade pulls out a gun and tries to kill Harris. Seeing the attempted murder, Lana runs when Slade orders a couple of his cronies to get her. Running from the scene of the crime, Lana hides out in a friend's house far away the location of the incident, but the crooked cop hasn't given up and is still trying to find and silence Lana before she can reveal what she saw. She finally calls Clark for help, but a tapped phone at Clark's house leads Slade and his henchmen to Lana, where they hunt her down. **Guest cast:** Roger Pretto as Lt. Zeke Harris, Cary-Haroyuki Tagawa as Detective Jed Slade, Chase Randolph as Oscar, Michael Stark as Stone, Jim Howard as Gray, David Hauser as Manton, Chick Bernhard as Kinneran, Eddie Edenfield as Baker. **Writer:** George Kirgo. **Director:** David Grossman.

War of the Species (airdate: Mar. 13, 1989). Lana Lang, Clark Kent and T.J. White come face-to-face with a super-powered android at a nearby scientific laboratory. While researching a story for the *Shuster Harold*, Lana and T.J. find the dead body of a scientist in his lab. They also encounter the shocking results of his latest experiment - an eight foot robot who tries to kill them. Superboy crashes through the wall, momentarily obstructing the robot, saving Lana and T.J. But the three discover the robot will multiply into an army of robots programmed to kill all of humanity, unless Superboy can stop it. **Guest cast:** Kevyn Major Howard as Dr. Stuart, John Matuzak as the android. **Writer:** Steven L. Sears. **Director:** Peter Kiwitt.

Little Hercules (airdate: April 10, 1989). While sending a romantic poem to his girlfriend by computer, a thirteen-year-old computer genius accidentally sets off a sequential code which activates secret military weapons. The military can not stop the nuclear chain of events once it has started. The only hope is to call on Superboy, who flies the boy genius to a secret submarine where the missiles are ready to launch. With time running out, the boy decodes the computer while Superboy uses all his super powers to deactivate the nuclear missiles. But unless they can finish in time, it may be the beginning of World War III. **Guest cast:** Leaf Phoenix as Billy Hercules, Allen Hall as Lt. Redman, Mal Jones as the commander, Elizabeth Marion as Amanda, Twig Tolle as Larry, Dean Drapin as Prof. Simon, Robert Hollinger as Heywood, Brian Solako as Lenny, Jason Jacobs as Driggs. **Writer:** Wayne A. Rice. **Director:** David Grossman.

Mutant (airdate: April 17, 1989). While attending a nuclear scientists' convention, Clark sees a prominent physicist being kidnapped by some strange-looking people. He follows them to the top of a skyscraper, where they promptly vanish after walking through a wall into a spaceship. Having been stunned by a ray beam, Superboy cannot stop the ship from leaving, and when Clark and T.J. try to report the mysterious happenings to the police, the officer interviewing them thinks that they are both nuts. Meanwhile, the kidnappers turn out to be dangerous mutants from 24th century Earth. Because the plutonium and other materials they need do not exist in their century, they have returned to the 20th century to force the physicist to help them build a atomic bomb. He refuses, but they insist they have ways to force him into submitting. Back on Earth, Clark, T.J., and Lana try to learn what has really happened to Professor Lipcott, resulting in T.J. being taken prisoner as well. **Guest cast:** Skye Aubrey as Val, Bill Christie as Hol, Edgar Allen Poe IV as Adio, Jack Swanson as Professor Lipcott. **Writer:**

Season Two: Gerard Christopher as Superboy/Clark Kent.

Michael Morris. **Director:** Joe Ravitz.

The Phantom of the Third Division (airdate: April 24, 1989).

Clark Kent and schoolmates Lana and T.J. return to Smallville to visit Ma and Pa Kent. Soon after their arrival, a mysterious phone call leads the Kents to believe Clark was injured in a car accident.

At the hospital, Pa Kent is abducted by the "Phantom", a crazed war veteran who was in the army with Pa Kent. The Phantom blames Pa Kent for his capture during the Korean War and now seeks revenge. Clark must find a way to turn into Superboy and save his father without giving away his dual identity. **Guest cast:** Joe Campanella as the Phantom. **Writer:** Bernard M. Khan. **Director:** David Nutter.

Black Flamingo (airdate: May 1, 1989). A punk-rocker positions his high-powered rifle atop a tall building, waiting for his target to come into view: a senator who is about to be assassinated. Luckily for the politician, Clark Kent is nearby, and he saves the senator and captures the giggling rocker. Superboy notices the boy is wearing a medallion with an emblem from a local club, so he goes undercover in the punk nightclub to discover why the boy was convinced he must murder the senator. At the club Clark comes up against the mysterious Snake-Man, who is using hypnosis to force young punk rockers to perform evil deeds against their will. The Boy of Steel is momentarily mesmerized by the Snake-Man's mind-altering spell but uses his super powers to overcome the brainwashing. Now with the help of Lana and T.J., Superboy tries again to apprehend the evil Snake-Man. **Guest cast:** Fernando Allende as the Snake-Man, Ada Maris as Natasha, Herbert Hoper as Agar, Ron Knight as the senator, Remy Palacion as the punk, Reggie Rierre as the punk, Ron Russell as the bouncer, Scott Gallin as the bouncer. **Writer:** Cary Bates. **Director:** Chuck Martinez.

Hollywood (airdate: May 8, 1989). Superboy arrives to help an eccentric scientist repair his time machine. Superman considers the scientist dubious at best, but his machine is causing power outages everywhere, so he agrees to use his heat vision to repair the device. But when he does so the scientist accidentally hurls them both back in time to 1939 Hollywood. Trapped in the past, Clark saves a beautiful girl from some thugs. It turns out that she is Victoria Letour, a beautiful, famous movie star whom he ends up falling in love with. Meanwhile, he finds the Professor but the odd man reveals that the time machine must be repaired before they can return home - and the necessary parts don't exist in 1939. Superboy enlists Victoria to help him build the world's first electronic calculator, which Superboy hopes he can use to fix the time machine and return the scientist and himself back to the their own time. **Guest cast:** Doug McClure [*The Land That Time Forgot*] as Professor Zugo, Gail O'Grady as Victoria Letour, Fred Buch as Stoddard, Nick Stannard as Willis, Stephen Geng as Gus, Michael Walters as the hood, Jeff Moldovan as the hood, Bill Cordell as the assistant director, Gene Tate as the lawyer, Frank Cipolla as the paper boy, Emmet Fitzsimmons as the truck driver, Arnie Cox as the husband. **Writer:** Fred Frieberger. **Director:** David Nutter.

Succubus (airdate: May 15, 1989). A man asks a beautiful woman author for her autograph, but gets more than he bargained for when Pamela Dare instantly drains his youth and turns him into an old man - a dead one. Later, T.J. White becomes smitten with the sexy romance novelist when she visits Shuster University to promote her new book. She does her best to get in good with T.J., knowing that he is Superboy's friend, but is only using him to find the Boy of Steel - a similar tactic she uses on Clark after meeting him. Unbeknownst to all, the author is a "Succubbi," a centuries old vampire-like creature who drains the youth out of her victims to maintain a youthful existence. Pamela captures Lana and T.J., holding them hostage to lure Superboy to her lair. She plans to drain the life out of Superboy to keep herself youthful forever. **Guest cast:** Sybil Danning [*V, Battle Beyond the Stars*] as Succubus, Rita Rehn as

Professor Myers, T.J. Kelly as the executive, Lee Stevens as Simon. **Writer:** Cary Bates. **Director:** David Nutter.

Luthor Unleashed (airdate: May 22, 1989). Lex Luthor uses a strange electronic device to knock out security equipment and guards to break into an Army base and steal some top secret laser weapon made specifically to kill people. Later, because Lex and his accomplice were wearing ROTC uniforms from Shuster college, T.J. and Clark are called in to find out if students were involved. Although Lex isn't an ROTC student, he immediately comes to mind as the guilty party. Meanwhile, Lex is in a lab working on a chemical weapon when an explosion occurs and he is trapped behind a sea of flames. Superboy saves the life of Lex by blowing out the flames. At first Luthor is appreciative - until he learns that the exploding chemicals being blown around have caused all his hair to fall out. To Luthor's dismay, he'll be bald for the rest of his life. Luthor vows to get even with Superboy for this horrible fate. **Guest cast:** Michael Manno as Leo, Pretto as Harris, Rance Howard as the colonel, Steve Howard as the guard, Larry Francer as Felix, Paul Cohn as Oswald. **Writer:** Stephen Lord. **Director:** David Nutter.

The Invisible People (airdate: June 5, 1989). Superboy becomes involved with a group of homeless people when he comes to their aid after a savage firebombing of their tent city. Chief suspect is a greedy business man, Gerold Manfred, who has agreed to sell adjoining property to a real estate developer for $145 million if he is able to rid the nearby land of the tent city. T.J., Lana and Clark get involved in their plight, attempting to fix up the tent city after the fire bombing. Hired goons, acting as Gerold's "security guards", kidnap Damon, the leader of the homeless workers. In the scuffle, T.J. is knocked unconscious, unceremoniously dumped in a van, and pushed towards a watery ocean grave. Superboy dashes to save him and the kidnappers escape. Superboy teams up with Lana and the destitute families in an inspirational attempt to rescue their missing ally. Lana finds Damon, but is captured herself by Manfred. When Damon rejects Manfred's bribes to move the tent city, both of them face death. **Guest cast:** Sonny Shroyer as Gerold Manfred, Greg Morris [*Mission: Impossible*] as Damon, Cynthia Ann Roses as Alice, Bill Orsini as Gruber, Jack Malone as Baker, Rick Higlet as the cop, Bob Painter as Alex. **Writer:** Mark Evanier. **Director:** Jackie Cooper.

SEASON TWO

Season Two: The second year of Superboy brought a completely changed cast, including the so-so John Haymes Newton being replaced with Gerard Christopher. The character of T.C. was written out, Lana returned, Lex Luthor was played by another actor, and the new character of Andy McAllister, Clark's new roommate, was added (T.C. having left to work for his father). A new opening title sequence appeared at the beginning of this season.

With This Ring I Thee Kill, parts one and two (airdates: part one, Oct. 15; part two, Oct. 22, 1989). Lex Luthor returns, after going through plastic surgery and altering his fingerprints to disguise his identity from Superboy, and he plans to steal a new, top-secret military weapon for use in killing the Boy of Steel. Lex kidnaps Lana Lang and forces her to marry him while using his sinister genius to gain access to the powerful weapons system. Intending to destroy Superboy with the missile launcher, Luthor inadvertently only wounds the super hero, leaving him paralyzed. Disappointed

Season Two: Gerard Christopher as Superboy, with Ilan Mitchell-Smith as Andy McAllister, Stacy Haiduk.

that his weapon hasn't destroyed Superboy, Lex Luthor lures the super hero from his wheelchair by broadcasting a tape of the villain with his captive Lana Lang. After a grueling rehabilitation period, a fully restored Superboy uses his super powers to apprehend Luthor, and the evil genius is sentenced to death - but makes another escape from the hands of justice. **Guest cast:** (part one) Michael Manno as Leo, Douglas Brush as the general, Kevin Corrigan as the security guard, Thom Scoggins as the commander, Linda Perry as the secretary, David Cullinans as the doctor, Jim Greene as the

minister, Janice Shea as the nurse; (part two) Tracy Roberts as Darla, David Cullinane as the doctor, Clarence Thomas as Wally, Richard Lake as the Warden, Jerry Lake as the journalist. **Writer:** Fred Frieberger. **Directors:** David Nutter (part one), David Grossman (part two).

Metallo (airdate: Oct. 29, 1989). Roger Corben, a bungling bank robber, tries to rob an armored car even through he is having extreme chest pains. Superboy arrives and apprehends the bank robber, but the small time crook has a heart attack and is taken to a hospital. After being there awhile he recovers and escapes by murdering his doctor. After he leaves he suffers another attack and his car crashes into a tree and explodes. The police presume he is dead, but journalist Clark Kent is not so sure. Meanwhile, Corben is actually alive, having fallen into the hands of a mentally-unbalanced doctor who turns him into more of a machine than human being, and replaces his failing human heart with a radioactive power source, Kryptonite. The unearthly power source transforms the villain into the powerful cyborg Metallo. **Guest cast:** Michael Callan as Metallo, Paul Brown as Schwartz, Dave Fennel as the mayor, Kurt Smildsen as the doctor. **Writers:** Mike Carlin and Andrew Helfer. **Director:** David Grossman.

Young Dracula (airdate: Nov. 5, 1989). A young man stops a store hold-up single-handedly, but in a strange way. He orders the first thief to knock himself out, which he does. The second one enters the building and shoots the boy twice with no apparent effect, and the boy orders the punk to start beating his head on the floor, and he complies. Later, Clark saves Andy's life by pushing him out of the way of a falling steel girder. It strikes Clark in the head, and although it can't really hurt him, he has to pretend it does. While at the hospital to get checked out, Clark meets the young man from the store, who is actually visiting intern Dr. Byron Shelley by day, and by night is a vampire. Shelley is using his knowledge of modern medicine to find a cure for the dreaded curse, and at the same time, he is being stalked by an older, more powerful vampire, who wishes Shelley to remain among the unliving creatures. **Guest cast:** Kevin Berhardt as Dr. Shelley, Lloyd Bochner as the old vampire, Dennis Neal as the doctor. **Writers:** Llya Salkind and Carey Bates. **Director:** David Nutter.

Nightmare Island (airdate: Nov. 12, 1989). Andy has talked Lana and Clark into going boating with him although they are reluctant to leave when they learn that the "ship" is little more than a dilapidated row boat. Sure enough, it sinks, but the three teenagers are able to make it to shore safely on a small island. Once there, Superboy arrives explaining that he heard their radio signal to the coast guard, but as he tries to fly Lana back to the coast he is knocked out by a strange ray. It turns out that a deranged alien is also stranded on the deserted island, and after knocking out Superboy he kidnaps Lana Lang and attempts to kill Andy McAllister and Clark Kent. The creature robs Superboy's powers with his ray gun, leaving Andy and the now-mortal Superboy to team up to rescue Lana and apprehend the alien. **Guest cast:** Phil Fondacaro as the alien. **Writer:** Mark Jones. **Director:** David Nutter.

Bizzaro...The Thing of Steel, part one (airdate: Nov. 19, 1989). When Professor Peterson gets into a new project it usually spells trouble for Superboy. This time he is trying out a duplicating machine that doesn't work out planned, and he accidentally creates a bizarre duplication of Superboy. The creature, named "Bizzaro," has all the strength of Superboy and warped duplicate memories and emotions. As a result, he gets away and tries to take the place of Clark. Andy sees him and thinks Clark has merely dressed up for a costume party he is supposed to take Lana to. Arriving at the party, Lana is upset over his making her wait so long when he shows no signs of being sorry. She gets mad and slaps him, but he takes the slap as a sign of love. Changing into his Superboy costume, he kidnaps Lana Lang as he too has strong feelings for her. At that moment Superboy arrives to attempt to rescue Lana by exposing the creature to Kryptonite, but while the rock is killing Superboy it has

no effect on Bizzaro, who leaves Superboy dieing near the Kryptonite. **Guest cast:** Barry Meyers as Bizzaro, Valerie Grant as the mom, Billy Flanigan as Todd, Christy Lyle as the girl, Kristian Trueloen as the cop, Andrew Lamoureaux as the kid, Chris Lombardi as the student. **Writer:** Mark Jones. **Director:** Den Bower.

The Battle With Bizzaro, part two (airdate: Nov. 26, 1989). Andy McAlister rescues Superboy from lethal Kryptonite. The Boy of Steel, together with Professor Peterson, figures out that the Kryptonite didn't work on Bizzaro because he is a defective copy, and the Kryptonite needs to be a defective version as well. Meanwhile, Bizzaro tries to explain his love to an unappreciative Lana who only wants to go free, but he insists that they will live together forever. Outside the store they are hiding in, the police arrive to "rescue" Lana, not knowing that Bizzaro is as powerful as his better half. He quickly shows what he is capable of, and a call is put out for Superboy to help. He arrives with the warped style of Kryptonite hoping it will stop Bizzaro, but the attempt fails. Instead, he saves the creature from a natural combustion that results from his duplicate nature. By this time Superboy realizes that Bizarro is not inherently evil, and the strange creature tearfully releases Lana to Superboy once he realizes that she belongs with him. **Guest cast:** Barry Meyers as Bizarro, Tom Norwicki as the police sergeant, Larry Lee as the clown, John McLoughlin as the S.W.A.T. leader. **Writer:** Mark Jones. **Director:** David Nutter.

Mr. and Mrs. Superboy (airdate: Dec. 3, 1989). Mr. Mxyzptlk, the mischievous imp from another dimension, arrives back in town - a sure sign of trouble for Superboy. While Clark, Lana, and Andy are at the pool Mxyzptlk shows up, as does a giant by the name of Vikabok, who is pursuing the impish prankster. They both disappear, and begin causing havoc all over town as the giant pursues Mxyzptlk. Superboy finally catches up with the magical being, who explains that Vikabok is upset with him because of a practical joke: he took everything the giant owned and stranded him on a desert island for 103 years. Superboy agrees to help Mxyzptlk before the whole town is destroyed, but the imp explains their only hope is for Lana and Superboy to pretend to be married, and adopt him so he can be a denizen of their world. According to Mr. Mxyzptlk, Vikabok will quit trying to kill him once he believes Mr. Mxyzptlk has become a citizen of Earth. **Guest cast:** Michael J. Pollard as Mr. Mxyzptlk, Richard Kiel [*Moonraker*] as Vikabok. **Writer:** Denny O'Neil. **Director:** Peter Kiwitt.

Programmed For Death (airdate: Dec. 10, 1989). Andy receives a call from his father, which is bad news as far as he is concerned, as the man is always in trouble, whether it be with the law or the Mob. Arriving at a meeting place Andy agreed to see him at, he finds a van containing not his father, but a high-tech robot with Jack McAlister's voice, who knocks Andy unconscious. The next day Jack shows up at Shuster University and meets Clark and Lana, whom he tells about his prison record and criminal activities, during which time Andy was sent to live with an uncle. Jack claims he is looking for Andy, who hasn't been seen since the day before, and he wants to contact Superboy to report a murder in order to save himself from being killed. Later, Superboy finds out about the "killer", which is actually an evil mechanical robot - called a "Dreadbot" - which has a sinister, human-like brain. The evil machine reflects the dark side of the mind of Jack McAlister, and intends to kill Superboy. After it absorbs all the electrical power in the city, the Dreadbot aims a lethal charge at Superboy as Andy and Jack look on helplessly. **Guest cast** George Mahari as Jack McAlister, Bryce Ward as the detective, Eric Whitmore as the cop, Ottaviano as the security guard. **Writer:** Cary Bates. **Director:** David Nutter.

Superboy's Deadly Touch (airdate: Dec. 17, 1989). Superboy stops to help a pair of nuns whose bus broke down on the way to a benefit. Superboy gets behind the bus to push it, not realizing that one of the nuns is Lex Luthor, who sprays a gas out of the bus and knocks out the Boy of Steel. When he awakens, Superboy is unaware that he has been infused with a deadly and uncontrollable power source. He finally realizes that something is wrong when he tries to stop some bank robbers and nearly kills them in the process. The destructive energy makes his super powers run amuck and now everything he touches seems to fizzle and burn. Dr. Peterson unsuccessfully tries to cure Superboy, whose last hope seems to be Lex Luthor, who offers to reverse the effects if the governor gives him a full pardon. **Guest cast** Tracy Roberts as Darla, Ken Grant as the cop, John Robert Thompson as the governor, Barry Cutler as the government official, Janis Benson as the nun, Gay Fry as the nun, Denise Norgaras as the technician. **Writers:** Mark Jones and Cary Bates. **Director:** Den Bowser.

The Power of Evil (airdate: Dec. 24, 1989). An evil, shapeless monster escapes from its containment in a far away country, bent on destroying Superboy. Sensei, an inhabitant of the mystical land, travels to America to warn the super hero of the impending danger. Meanwhile, Andy and Lana practice karate after a pair of punks nearly beat Andy to a pulp. The instructor keeps asking Andy how to reach Superboy, as Andy, always a braggart, claims he can contact the future Superman at any time. Actually the instructor, Seth, is the beast in disguise, and he insists Andy take him to Superboy. Lana notices how strange Seth has been acting, as she has been dating him. Meanwhile, Sensei arrives to talk to Superboy, and explains that the creature will find him soon, and it must be stopped before it kills again. **Guest cast:** Keye Luke as Sensei, Michael Champlin as Seth, Bret Cipes as the old man, Jim Becke as the cop, Michael Marzello as the voice of the creature. **Writers:** Michael Prescott. **Director:** Danny Irom.

Superboy... Rest in Peace (airdate: Jan. 7, 1990). In the distant future a scientist learns that a deadly android has escaped and traveled back in time, where it is due to arrive at 20th century Shuster University. It seems that in the future it is known that Clark Kent was Superboy, although the android that intends to kill Superboy is not aware of the super hero's secret identity. In the future, Serene, a girl chosen to go back and destroy the android before it can change history, is aware of who Clark is and looks forward to meeting her idol. The beautiful scientist arrives to find Clark Kent and warn him without divulging the future. However, Lana Lang and Andy McAlister are confused by the sudden appearance of Serene, who they think has romantic eyes for Clark. **Guest cast** Betsy Russell as Serene, Andreas Wisniewski as the android, John Swidels as Professor Henderson, Lamont Lofton as the scientist, Judy Clayton as the lab assistant, Gayle Nadler as Gloria, Alison Dietz as Debbie, Harry L. Burney III as the campus guard. **Writer:** Michael Maurer. **Director:** Danny Irom.

Super Menace! (airdate: Jan. 14, 1990). While Professor Peterson is out of the country, the Army experiments with deactivating a sample of deadly green Kryptonite, doing away with the rays that hurt Superboy, but retaining the energy it produces. Instead, they inadvertently convert it into mysterious red Kryptonite. Superboy is invited to look over the new form of Kryptonite, since the rock - now

turned red - should be harmless. Instead, the new Kryptonite proves to be equally deadly to Superboy by making the Boy of Steel purely evil. Metallo is enlisted to combat the super-hero - now a super menace - but instead he tries to team up with Superboy and take over the world. **Guest cast:** Michael Callan as Metallo, Jim McDonald as General Swan, Richard Vaigts as Warden Ordway, Barry W. Mizerski as the first scientist, Henry J. as the second scientist. **Writer:** Michael Maurr. **Director:** Richard J. Lewis.

Yellow Peri's Spell of Doom (airdate: Jan. 21, 1990). Clark, Andy, and Lana meet Loretta at a local club where she works. The rather plain-jane girl whom no one takes seriously has a yen for Superboy, so Clark delivers an autographed photo of the Boy of Steel to her. That night, Loretta practices some Black Magic and raises an evil spirit named Gazook. The demon realizes that Loretta wants the love of Superboy, so he turns her into "Yellow Peri", a beautiful woman that no one recognizes as the homely classmate of Clark's. With the help of Gazook, Yellow Peri puts a spell on Superboy, forcing him to fall in love with her. But she realizes that Lana Lang's true love for Superboy can break her spell, so she sets out to kill Lana. **Guest cast:** Elizabeth Keipher as Loretta/Yellow Peri, Georgia Sattele as the student, John Glenn Harding as the bartender, Steve Latshaw as the newscaster, Steve Hansen as Gazook, James Detmar as the voice of Gazook. **Writers:** Mark Jones and Cary Bates. **Director:** Peter Kiwitt.

Microboy (airdate: Jan. 28, 1990). Superboy confronts "Microboy", a would-be super hero, who has romantic eyes for Lana Lang. The new super hero is secretly a student inventor who has created a machine which infuses his body with remarkable powers from microwave radiation. His energy goes haywire causing a life-threatening situation that only Superboy, with the help of Professor Peterson, can safely resolve. **Guest cast:** Frank Military as Microboy, Tony Faozzi as the derelict, Larry Francer as Felix, Tim Powell as Orville Wright, Steve Kelly as Wilbur Wright, George Colangelo as the drama teacher, Stacy Haiduk as Julie Ann. **Writer:** Cary Bates. **Director:** Richard Lewis.

Run Dracula, Run (airdate: Feb. 4, 1990). Dr. Byron Shelley, who was helped by Superboy to develop a drug that would keep his alter-ego of a vampire under control, is jumped by two thugs and his anti-vampire serum is stolen, forcing him to revert back to the evil dark ways of his ancestors. Lana receives a call from Byron where he pleads for help, and asks her to send Superboy before he changes into a vampire and kills again. Not knowing where Superboy is, Lana leaves to help him on her own, but the vampire attacks her, turning Lana into a vampire. She uses her new evil powers to turn Superboy into a vampire as well, and they both team up with Shelley, who plans to sneak out of the country with his newly converted vampires. Unless Superboy can use all of his super powers to resist the dark powers, he and Lana will be doomed forever. **Guest cast:** Kevin Bernhardt as Dr. Byron Shelley/Young Dracula, Louis Seeger Crune as the sheriff, Ivan Green as the old man, Leslee Lacey as Lorranie, Ed Amatrudo as Moe. **Writers:** Llya Salkind and Cary Bates. **Director:** Richard Lewis.

Brimstone (airdate: Feb. 11, 1990). Andy asks Lana to help him with a project, but she doesn't know that what he has in mind is selling fake Kryptonite rocks at a game. As the fans are leaving the game a wild man begins running amuck, a hideous-looking person with rotten, decaying flesh hanging from his face. He strikes and scratches several people before being shot by the police, but even this doesn't stop him, as he only gets up and runs off. A bleeding Andy gets ready to go to the hospital when a strange man claiming to be a doctor approaches Andy and Lana. He finally reveals that the berserk man is possessed by a powerful, mad magician, and that every person scratched will become a horrible-looking creature under the magician's power. Andy is given a foul-tasting liquid to "cure" him, but Superboy is not so lucky: he corners and tries to stop the wild man, but, incredibly, the possessed individual overpowers the Boy of Steel and scratches his face - which almost immediately places him under the control of the evil sorcerer Prodo. **Guest cast:** Philip Michael Thomas as Brimstone, Carlos Gestero as Prodo, Marc Macaulay as the maniac, Antoni Carone as the commanding cop, Michael Leopard as the security cop. **Writers:** Mike Carlin and Andrew Helfer. **Director:** Andre Guttreund.

Abandon Earth (airdate: Feb. 18, 1990). Two police officers see some unusual lights, then two strangely-dressed people appear. They are none other than Jor-el and Lara, the biological parents of Kal-el, now known as Superboy/Clark Kent, ever since they sent their son to Earth and the Kents found and adopted the boy. They state that they have arrived for their son, a message that is soon on the radio and tv, and Clark learns when he hears the newscast. Changing into Superboy, he leaves the Kent to meet them, while Ma and Pa Kent agonize over the possibility that their adopted son may be gone forever. Arriving where his real parents are waiting, Superboy refuses at first to believe that they could be his mother and father, but finally accepts it as true. As he spends more time with Jor-el and Lara, they convince him to return to Krypton, much to the heartache of the Kents. Meanwhile, Jor-el and Lara a pair of frauds, who are only masquerading as Superboy's parents, kidnap Andy and Lana to take them along on the return flight. **Guest cast:** Britt Ekland [*The Man With the Golden Gun*] as Lara, George Lazenby [*On Her Majesty's Secret Service*] as Jor-el, Ken Grant as Officer Campbell, Emily Lester as Officer Woods, Eric Whitmore as the police officer, Michael Preston as the second police officer, D.J. Kaussar as the FBI agent, Michael Mass as the terrorist, Steve Latshaw as the newsman, Bob Wells as the newscaster. **Writers:** Cary Bates and Mark Jones. **Director:** Richard Lewis.

Escape to Earth (airdate: Feb. 25, 1990). Arriving on an alien planet, Superboy is immediately imprisoned along with Lana and Andy, and learns that "Lara" and "Jor-el", are not his true parents from Krypton, but deadly chameleon-like aliens able to change their appearance at will. After luring the super-hero away from Earth, the aliens reveal their plan to imprison Superboy and the kidnapped Lana Lang and Andy McAlister in a bizarre space-zoo. **Guest cast:** Britt Ekland [*The Man With the Golden Gun*] as Lara, George Lazenby [*On Her Majesty's Secret Service*] as Jor-el, Frank Tranchina as Studd. **Writers:** Cary Bates and Mark Jones. **Director:** Andre R. Guttsreund.

Superstar (airdate: March 11, 1990). Andy arrives with his girlfriend, Clark, and Lana, at a Jessica James concert with some back stage passes. Unfortunately, he actually bought them and the guard won't let them go in as their passes are expired. Only Clark gets past the guard by using his press pass. Once near the stage, Clark sees a driverless, automated car heading towards superstar Jessica, and after changing into Superboy he saves her. Jessica takes Superboy home with her, but he refuses to spend the night. The next day someone contacts Clark to see if he wants an exclusive interview with Jessica, and he leaves right away. Once he gets to the studio, he finds a 70's rock star named Venus, who was supposed to have died in an aircraft crash. Actually she survived but was horribly mutilated, so she got the beautiful Jessica to pretend to sing new songs that Venus actually recorded. Venus explains that she is telling Clark this to let the public know the truth, but actually she plans to kill Jessica, as she was already behind the car incident. **Guest cast:** Ami Dolenz as Jessica James, Kimberely Bronson as Venus, Kevin Quigley as Tucker, Deborah DeFrancisco as Tiffany, Joe Candelora as the maitre D', Bradford Dunaway as the security guard, Steve Latshaw as the engineer. **Writer:** Toby Martin. **Director:** Ken Bower.

Nick Knack (airdate: April 9, 1990). A remote-controlled toy truck enters the room of Nick Knack, a demented electronic genius who Superboy put behind bars in a mental asylum. The truck contains a device he uses to cut the bars on his cell and escape to the waiting arms of Lily, the assistant that helped him escape. Nick Knack has promised to marry the plump Lily (which he has no intention of doing), but he has a heist to pull off first, one that will require the talents of Superboy. The criminal takes his revenge against the super hero with an ingenious device that will absorb all of Superboy's powers and transfers it to a mechanical suit. After rendering Superboy powerless, Nick-Knack will use the suit to become the richest man in the world - if everything goes according to plan. **Guest cast:** Gilbert Gottfried as Nick Knack, Donna Lee Betz as Daisy, David Hauser as the soldier, Andrew Clark as the security guard. **Writer:** Mark Jones. **Director:** David Nutter.

The Haunting of Andy McAlister (airdate: April 16, 1990). Andy, Lana, and Clark drive to Andy's great uncle's mansion, where he has asked them to spend the weekend. Because Andy can't read maps, they end up lost and only accidentally find the huge home. Once inside, everyone is impressed with the old mansion, and Andy tells them how his ancestors built the house when they were wealthy from selling rifles. The last fifty years his distant relative, a sheriff out of the old west, spent his entire fortune building more and more rooms onto the house, and for some reason was terrified that the outlaws he killed would return to haunt him. The decrepit home is full of secret passageways and trap doors, one of which Clark falls through. Meanwhile, Andy playfully shoots an antique rifle creating a mysterious rift into another dimensional plane allowing evil spirits from the past to escape, including Billy the Kid, who plans to kill Andy as revenge for his imprisonment in another dimension. **Guest cast:** Thomas Shuster as Billy the Kid, Fred Ornstein as Uncle Nate, Dan Kamin as the bullethole outlaw, Sandy Huelsman as the woman outlaw, C. Rand MacPherson as the hangman outlaw, Ricardo (Papy) Rogers as the toothless outlaw. **Writers:** Andrew Helfer and Michael Carlin. **Director:** David Nutter.

Revenge From the Deep (airdate: April 23, 1990). In the 1960's a strange man is at a party, and is approached by a woman who tells him that he cannot remain with "their kind". They go outside to the ocean shore, where he - actually a creature hiding in human form - uses a strange power to turn her into a piece of coral before throwing her in the ocean. Many years later, Andy is using a metal detector at the beach to find buried treasure. A skeptical Lana goes walking in the surf, where she sees the coral that was once a woman, and takes it home with her. Unbeknownst to her, it contains the spirit of Ariana, a magical creature from the sea. The creature proceeds to take over Lana's body to seek revenge against the fellow being from Atlantis that now lives on land in human form under the name of Charlie. She is forced to use fantastic powers to track him down, but once she finds Charlie Superboy has to try to intercede as the two use

their incredible powers to do battle. **Guest cast:** Donatella as Ariana, Michael Shaner as Charlie, Steve Latshaw as the announcer, Judy Johns as Heather, D. Christain Goushaw as the bartender, Connie Adams as Susie, Steve Zurk as the beach patrol officer.

Writer: Toby Martin. **Director:** Andre R. Guttfreund.

The Secrets of Superboy (airdate: April 30, 1990). After being put back in prison by Superboy, the evil toy genius Nick Knack escapes from jail to take revenge against the boy from Krypton. Once out of confinement, he builds a mind probe device that he first tries out on Daisy, his assistant. He drains Daisy's brain until she dies, all of which happens in less than a minute, giving him the idea of trying it out on Superboy. First he uses an electronic device to lure Lana and Andy to his lair, then once there, he uses his deadly brain scan which is designed to uncover Superboy's weaknesses which are hidden in the recesses of their brains, and kill Lana and Andy at the same time. **Guest cast:** Gilbert Gottfried as Nick Knack, Donna Lee Betz as Daisy, Roxie Stice as the girlfriend. **Writers:** T. Gilmour and Mark Jones. **Director:** Joe Ravetz.

Johnny Cassanova and the Case of the Secret Serum (airdate: May 7, 1990). Clark, Lana, and Andy are practicing their tennis when another player asks Lana for a date. She turns him down, as there is something she doesn't like about Johnny. When the young man arrives home, he finds his criminal brother dying from a gunshot wound, and before Stanley dies he gives Johnny a special liquid chemical he stole. The secret serum is designed to have the power to make someone irresistible, and after he takes the serum, Johnny is instantly transformed into the irresistible Johnny Cassanova. Meanwhile, the gangster who really owns the serum, Mr. Gore, is searching for the liquid and will do anything to get it back. He learns that it has fallen into the hands of Johnny and his new girlfriend, Lana, and it will take Superboy and his super powers to save them from Mr. Gore, who will stop at nothing to obtain the serum. **Guest cast:** Mark Holton as Johnny Cassanova, Glenn Maska as Johnny Avonasac, Robert Reynolds as Stanley, Michael Marzella as Mr. Gore, Dan Hanemann as the Cabbie, Steve Dash as suited man #1, Nich Stannard as suited man #2, Gregory Ashburn as the manager, Conrad Goode as the bouncer. **Writers:** Liya Salkind and Mark Jones. **Director:** David Nutter.

A Woman Called Tiger Eye (airdate: May 14, 1990). An old hag of a woman kills a man after he declares that she has double-crossed him. Returning home, she takes off a disguise that reveals her to be a middle-aged woman, a female named Tiger Eye who has just completed a set of crystals of great magical powers. Now all she needs is Superboy's heat vision to fuse the crystals together. Knowing Lana's special relationship with Superboy, Tiger Eye kidnaps her to use her as bait, so that she can lure Superboy to her lair and force him to fuse the crystals together. Once this is done, they will imbue the sexy villain with incredible magical powers which allow her to control Superboy to perform her bidding. **Guest cast:** Skye Aubrey as Tiger Eye, Erik Freeman as Peter, Erik Lindshield as Denny, Tony Dimartino as Phillip, Danny Wynans as Bobby, Peter S. Paik as the Asian man, Ilse Earl as the teacher. **Writer:** Michael Maurer. **Director:** Andre Guttfreund.

SEASON THREE

Season Three: Year three started off with another new opening sequence, and another cast change: Lana and Clark have gone to work for the Bureau For Extra-Normal Matters, and on their new job they work with an agent, Mack (Peter Jay Hernandez), and for their boss, C. Dennis Jackson (Robert Levine). Thankfully, the abrasive character of Andy was dropped, and Stacy Haiduk returned to continue playing the beautiful Lana Lang.

The Bride of Bizzaro, parts one and two (airdates: part one, Oct. 7, 1990, part two, Oct. 14, 1990). The sinister Lex Luthor returns to seek revenge against Superboy with the help of the Kryptonite-powered duplicating machine responsible for creating Bizzaro, the imperfect double of the Boy of Steel. The creature, yearning for a mate, is coaxed into helping Luthor destroy Superboy with green Kryptonite, in exchange for a female Bizzaro. After Lex Luthor creates a Bizzaro duplicate of Lana Lang, Bizzaro agrees to kill Superboy. But the scheme backfires as the newly-created Bizzaro Lana convinces Bizzaro not to kill Superboy and instead annihilate the sinister genius, Luthor. Not one to be caught unprepared, Luthor unleashes a whole army of Bizzaro duplicates of himself to destroy both Superboy and Bizzaro. **Guest cast:** Barry Meyers as Bizzaro, Tracy Roberts as Darla, Wendy Leigh as Jody James Donatello, James Zelley as Mike, Leith Audrey as Bizzaro Darla, D. Christian Gottshall as Artie, Bruce Hamilton as the reporter, Shanna Teare as Bizarro Lana, Eric Whitmore as the bartender, Bill Orsini. **Writers:** Michael Carlin, Andrew Helfer. **Director:** David Grossman.

The Lair (airdate: Oct. 21, 1990). Matt Ritter is kidnapped while investigating rumors of a monster in a dense forest near the Lakeside Nuclear Power Facility which is operated by Patrick Kenderson. Lana Lang and Clark Kent search the forest and discover the tragic origins of the creature. With all his super powers, Superboy is not able to save the creature from the guns of local hunters. **Guest cast:** Jordan Williams as Patrick Kenderson, Michael Pniewski, Antoni Carone, Tom Nowicki as Bob, Dennis Neal as Ed, Robert Small as Ron, Paul Vroom as Hal, Buddy Staccardo as Jerry, Kathy Nell as Mrs. Carter, Joe E. Ring as the bartender, D. Christian Gottshall as Arnie. **Writer:** Stan Berkowitz. **Director:** David Grossman.

Neila (airdate: Oct. 28, 1990). A female extraterrestrial, Neila, arrives on earth in search of a perfect mate. Of royal descent on her own planet, Neila seeks a man who is equal to her strength and powers, and finds him in Superboy. She realizes, however, the Superboy is devoted only to Lana Lang, and tries to disguise herself as a human in order to attract him. When her attempt fails, Neila threatens to destroy Earth in her rage, and Lana may be asked to sacrifice herself to save the world. **Guest cast:** Christine Moore as Neila, James Van Harper as Lee, Arnie Cox as the proprietor, Mike Goughn as the officer, Barry Mizerski as the clothing store owner. **Writers:** Gary Rosen and Stan Berkowitz. **Director:** Mark Vargo.

Roads Not Taken, parts one and two (airdates: part one, Nov. 4; part two, Nov. 11, 1991). A scientist has created a dimension travel machine which allows entry into alternate worlds. By watching the device, people in our world can see how their lives would have changed if they had taken alternate paths. Lex Luthor is accidentally sent into another dimension through this machine and finds himself in a world where the alternate Superboy is a criminal and has murdered the alternate Lex Luthor. Meanwhile, in the present dimension, Lex's girlfriend, Darla, kidnaps Lana to force Superboy to bring Luthor back. Lex schemes to resurrect himself and become the new messiah to the people of the alternate world. In his attempt to take Luthor back with him, Superboy is hurtled into yet a third world, in which his third alternate has become a sovereign. Trapped in this third dimension, Superboy learns that in this world he is a dictator who rules with an iron fist. The counterparts of Lex Luthor and Lana are freedom fighters who are part of an underground movement to overthrow the Sovereign and achieve democracy. Superboy faces off with the Sovereign Superboy in an attempt to stop him from destroying the freedom fighters. **Guest cast:** Kenneth Robert Shippy as Dr. Winger, Tracy Roberts as Darla, Robert Reynolds as the farmer, Robert Floyd as the messenger, Jason Paddell as the kid, Brian Grant as the fan, Edgar Allen Poe III as the

Michael Callan as Mr. Corben/Metallo.

derelict, Maureen Collins as the mom, Paul Matthew as the Superboy double, Jacob Witkin as Advisor #1, Jack Swanson as Adviser #2, Steve DeMouchel as the driver, Jason Padgell as the kid, Tim Powell as the man. **Writers:** John Francis Moore and Stan Berkowitz. **Director:** Richard J. Lewis.

The Son of Icarus (airdate: Nov. 18, 1990). Clark and Lana are amazed to see a man flying high in the sky. Changing into Superboy, Clark catches up to the man, just before he is killed by flying into a high-voltage wire. As he dies, he mumbles some clues to the Boy of Steel, leading him to Matt Ritter, a man who is being drawn into a cult made up of American descendents of a lost African tribe, who practice a ritual that gives them the power to fly. Each time they practice the ritual, an imbalance in nature occurs and a fire creature is created as a result. The creature sets off fires in its path, causing havoc and destruction - and even Superboy is unable to stop it. Clark and Lana learn of the cult's secret and try to warn Matt before it's too late. **Guest cast:** Brent Jenning as Teo, Lou Walker as Joseph, Alice McGill as Marinda, D. Christian Gottshall as Artie, Robb Morris as Malcolm, Annelle Johnson as Jasmine, Wayne Brady as John. **Writer:** Paul Stuberrauch. **Director:** Richard Lewis.

Carnival (airdate: Nov. 25, 1990). When people start to mysteriously vanish, Lana's investigations lead to a small time traveling carnival, run by a satanic stranger, Deville. She discovers that Deville and the carnival date back 108 years and there is a history of people reported missing whenever the carnival shows up. Lana is captured by the sinister Deville who transforms himself into the likeness of Samuels, a scoundrel who has once before caused Superboy to lose his temper - all part of Deville's plot to taunt Superboy into giving up his soul. **Guest cast:** Gregg Allman as Samuels, Christopher Neame as Deville, Claudia Miller as Beth, George Colangelo as David, Shavonne Rhodes as the bearded lady, John Edward Allen as the dwarf, Janice Shea as the fortune teller, Billy Gillespie as the cop, Elizabeth Fendrick as the woman hostess, Leslie Lacy. **Writer:** Toby Martin. **Director:** David Grossman.

The Test of Time (airdate: Dec. 2, 1990). Lana and Clark are out tramping through the woods while working on a story. Suddenly Clark sees something strange with his super-vision: what looks like a miniature tornado quickly approaches them, and picks up, spins, and throws Clark to the ground. When he stands up, Clark sees Lana frozen in position, and he goes for help - only to find the rest of Smallville frozen in place. After some investigation he learns that the town isn't frozen in place, but is just moving extremely slowly, but then decides that the world has remained the same, he is just moving fast. Eventually he discovers the truth: two aliens come to Earth in search of a new planet to invade, and are subjecting Clark to a series of tests, using their power to control time, in order to learn the weaknesses of humans. Keeping his true identity a secret, Clark uncovers their schemes and misleads them into thinking all humans have supernatural strength. **Guest cast:** Eric Conger as Alien #1, Bryce Word as Alien #2, Rex Benson, Danny Haneman as the driver. **Writer:** David Gerrold. **Director:** David Hartwell.

Mindscape (airdate: Dec. 9, 1990). At the end of a typical workday at the Bureau for Extra-Normal Matters, a construction worker brings in a strange stone which he claims is making noises. As the stone begins to glow and crack, Clark rushes to change into Superboy who then fuses the rock back together, but to no avail. The rock explodes and a transparent oozing creature launches itself onto Superboy and wraps itself around his neck. The Bureau must watch

helplessly as even lasers are not able to cut the creature away. Superboy floats in and out of bizarre dreams, while the alien feeds on the adrenaline these dreams cause, growing larger and larger. Finally, it appears that Superboy is truly dying, and in his dreams he travels outside of himself and through a tunnel of light. At the end of the tunnel, he meets his real parents, who are dead, and they tell him it is not his time. Feeling more confident, Superboy goes back into himself, now renewed with the strength to battle the alien. **Guest cast:** Lex Luger as Superboy Mark II, Judy Clayton as Stern, Sonya Mattox as staffer #1, Chris Calvert as staffer #2, Rod Ball as the worker, Jacob Wilkin as the man, Kathy Polling as the woman, Cliff O'Neal as the Superboy double. **Writers:** Michael Carlin and Andrew Helfer. **Director:** David Nutter.

Superboy...Lost (airdate: Dec. 16, 1990). While trying to deflect the comet which is hurtling toward Earth, Superboy is knocked to the ground in the Florida Everglades, stricken with amnesia. He is found by Marissa and her son Jeremy, who have long been living in the swamp and do not recognize him. The three of them are constantly surprised by his powers which he soon must call on to save Jeremy from his father, Damon, the leader of the Satanic cult to which Marissa once belonged. Superboy foils the cult's first attempt to kidnap the boy, but their second attempt is successful. While with the cult, Jeremy sees a newspaper with Superboy's picture and a headline about the comet. When Superboy rescues him, Jeremy shows him the clipping which begins to trigger his memory. Superboy rushes after the comet and recalls, just in time, what went wrong before. He tries a different strategy and hopes that he can deflect the comet before it crashes into Earth. **Guest cast:** Sara Essex as Marissa, Kevin Quigley as Damon, Juan Cejas as Jon, Kevin Corrigan as the ranger, Paul Sutera as Jeremy, Shaun Padgett. **Writer:** David Gerrold. **Director:** David Hartwell.

Special Effects (airdate: Jan. 6, 1991). Jackson overhears Lana and Clark complaining that they are never given any real work to do so he decides to do them a favor. He sends them to interview a 10 year old child - the only witness to the murder of a film director. Their investigation brings them to the late director's movie set where they encounter Max Von Norman, the special effects man who created the monster, Caliban, which the child claims was the murderer. On the set, Clark and Lana also encounter their old friend, Andy McAlister, who is an intern on the film. The trio is on the set when the film's leading man is killed and the monster responsible, Ajax, is seen fleeing the crime. Superboy's attempt to catch the creature is foiled by Max, who destroys Ajax with a futuristic flame thrower. Suspicious of Max's motives for killing Ajax, Lana accepts an invitation to a party at Max's house and discovers a door to another dimension from which Max has been obtaining the monsters and using them both as models for his work and as killers - sending them after all the film people that once scorned him. **Guest cast:** Richard Marcus as Max Von Norman, Barry Meyers as Caliban, Ilan Mitchell-Smith as Andy McAllister, Bill Cardell as the writer, Denise Locca as Risa, Jim Cardes as Lou Lloyd, Rob Burman as Ajax, Caria Kneeland as the ingenue, Bodie Piecas as Robin Melville, Andrea Lively as Mrs. Watson, Danny Gura as Teddy, Candice Miller as the script girl. **Writer:** Elliot Anderson. **Director:** David Grossman.

Neila and The Beast (airdate: Jan. 13, 1991). Neila, the alien princess who once had designs on Superboy, has come back to Earth for his help: the "commoners" of her planet have killed all the other aristocrats and are intent on her death as well. As she asks Superboy

to help her, a beast appears which they kill, and its body is taken to the Bureau for study. Neila then goes to Lana who agrees to help her and tries to give her some advice - Neila must learn that all people are much the same, no matter what their background. Lana takes Neila to a bar and encourages her to return the friendliness of Mitch, who is actually one of the commoners sent to kill Neila. Mitch invites Neila, along with Lana and a date, to his house for dinner. When Lana's date, Clark, is delayed because the beast's carcass which he is examining comes back to life, she leaves so that Neila can be alone with Mitch, but once Lana is gone he and his cohort attack Neila with a ray machine. Meanwhile, Superboy follows the beast who explains that he loves Neila, and she is in grave danger. **Guest cast:** Christine Moore as Neila, Terence Jenkins as Mitch, Chris McCarty as Peter, Judy Clayton as Stern, Danny Dyer as Hank, Christopher Oyen as the first scientist, Tom Akas as the beast. **Writer:** Lawrence Klavan. **Director:** Jefferson Kibbee.

Golem (airdate: Jan. 20, 1991). An old Jewish man, Levi Hirsch, distressed at the amount of bigotry in the world, creates a golem - a creature formed from clay which is brought to a human-like life through prayers from a mystical book of ancient Judaism, the Kaballah. But Levi is unable to control the creature when he sends it after some neo-Nazis which live in his neighborhood. In the Golem's haste to do Levi's bidding and attack the neo-Nazis, he accidentally kills Levi. Distraught, the Golem has only the original purpose Levi gave him for guidance - he must kill all bigots, which, in his illogical mind, includes anyone in a uniform. **Guest cast:** Paul Coufos as Daniel, Brian Thompson as the Golem, Victor Helou as Levi, Darren Dollar as Mike, Larry Bucklan as Jonah, Matt Battaglia as Darryll, Chris Vance as the first kid, Kris Kazmarek as the second kid. **Writer:** Paul Stubenrauch. **Director:** Robert Wiemer.

A Day in the Double Life (airdate: Jan. 27, 1991). Jackson can't understand why Clark is always running off on "little emergencies", so he has him keep a diary for a day. Since he spends the day changing from Clark to Superboy and back, he's forced to make innocuous entries to conceal his identity. And when agents Harris and Keller spend the day fighting with each other, Superboy discovers that their real problem is that they care for each other and neither wants to be the first to admit it. At the opportune time, Superboy does "a small favor for some friends...", using his super breath to blow Harris into Keller's arms. At the end of the day, Jackson declares, after looking at Clark's diary, that he knows the truth about him - he has no life. **Guest cast:** Allyce Beasly as Agent Stephanie Harris, Tom Kouchalakos as Agent Frank Keller, Jeff Maldovan as the leader, Billy Gillespie as cop #1, Bill Painter as the traffic cop, Jesse Stone as Eddie, Carl Campeon as man #2, Jack Carrol as the hunter, Barry Cutler as Doug, Dan Fitzgerald as the sheriff, Allison McKay as the farm woman. **Writers:** Stan Berkowitz and Paul Stubenrauch. **Director:** David Nutter.

Body Swap (airdate: Feb. 3, 1991). Knowing Superboy's desire to discover where he came from, Lex Luthor uses Dr. Oliver Deland to trick Superboy into an experiment which is supposed to help him find his past. In reality, Superboy is hooked up to a machine which allows Luthor to switch bodies with him. Superboy, in Luthor's body, tries to make Lana believe that it's really him. She doesn't trust him at first, but after a visit from Luthor (in Superboy's body) during which he suggested they make their relationship more intimate, Lana begins to realize that neither Luthor nor Superboy have been behaving in character. After Luthor captures the real Superboy, and has him put in jail as Luthor, Lana gets him out and together they set out to trap the real Luthor. **Guest cast:** Nathan Adler as Dr. Oliver Deland, D. Christian Gottshall as Artie, Ken Grant as Dad, Valerie Grant as Mom, Carrie Ann Reiter as the girl, Ryan Porter as the bob, Randy Heim as the burly man, Bob Barnes as the warden, Joe Candeiara as the governor, Lamont Lofton as the cop, Ann Morsello as the newswoman, Kurt Smildsin as the guard, Shawn McAllister as the jailer. **Writer:** Paul Schiffer. **Director:** David Grossman.

Rebirth, part one and two (airdates: part one, Feb. 10; part two, Feb. 17, 1991). When Superboy stops a gang newly arrived from the Caribbean from raiding a military truck full of weapons, it seems that he accidentally causes the death of Winston, the gang's leader. An eye-witness, Mayall, swears that Winston was in an abandoned car when Superboy crashed an out-of-control truck into it, although Superboy had first x-rayed the car to make sure there was no one in it. Superboy is suddenly in doubt of himself, a doubt which in-

creases when the gang's new leader, Llewellyn, later uses a female hostage to get away from Superboy, whose hesitation puts the woman at risk. Needing time to think, Superboy goes home to Ma and Pa Kent, convinced that he should give up using his powers. But, when Clark has to use his powers to save his father, he realizes that he cannot turn his back on the gifts with which he was born. He must return to Capital City and use his powers for justice. Back in the city, as Llewellyn plans to raid a military depository of its latest weapons and is setting up a buyer for the goods, Mayall's greed is too much for him and he again approaches Llewellyn for more money. This time, when Mayall leaves, Llewellyn orders Desmond to kill him. But Lana has been checking up on Mayall and, finding he has spent an exorbitant amount of money since the "accident", is suspicious. Clark arrives at the Bureau to find Lana has gone to question Mayall. Lana arrives at Mayall's apartment just as Desmond is tying him up, about to leave him with a bomb. She hides in a closet while Desmond questions Mayall, who explains that Llewellyn knocked Winston unconscious and threw him in the car when it was already in flames. Desmond hears Lana and ties her up as well, leaving both her and Mayall to be blown to bits. **Guest cast:** Gregory Millar as Llewellyn, Michael Owens as Mayall, Kevin Benton as Desmond, Kevin Benion as Desmond, Joseph Pickney as Winston, Bob Sakaler as the reporter, Robert M. Rodriguez as Hector, W. Paul Bodie as Lemont, Paul Darby as Capt. Quentin, Steve Roulerson as the sergeant, Rita Rehn and woman, Michael Balin as Lt. Fulton, Roger Pretta. **Writer:** Paul Diamond. **Director:** Richard J. Lewis.

Werewolf (airdate: Feb. 24, 1991). A distraught woman, Christina Riley, brings a videotape to the bureau which she claims shows a werewolf, which she has been tracking for months, attacking her. Although it is blurred, Clark, using his super-vision, claims he can see something so Jackson gives him the case. Together, Clark and Christina try to track down Canaris, the man whom Christina believes is the werewolf. Christina, armed with a silver dagger, and Clark trace Canaris to his office on the night of a full moon. Starting to make the change, Canaris locks himself in his office, while Clark turns to find Christina has mysteriously vanished, leaving the silver dagger behind on an ashtray. Canaris, as the werewolf, bursts out of his office. Clark turns into Superboy and the two begin to fight until the werewolf falls onto the dagger and dies, turning back into his human form. When Clark sees Christina the following day, she is relieved that it is over and the two go to the University City Studio Tour. After they leave, the Bureau gets the report that here was another werewolf attack the night before and they reason that Canaris must have scratched Christina the night she made the videotape, passing the curse along to her. **Guest cast:** Paula Marshall as Christina Riley, Robert Winston as Canaris, Jay Glick as the jeweler, Barry Cutler as Doug, Kelfus Matthews as the security guard, Ray Russell as the office guard. **Writer:** Toby Martin. **Director:** Bryan Spicer.

People vs. Metallo (airdate: April 8, 1991). While Mr. Corben is on trial for Metallo's numerous crimes, he has a chunk of Kryptonite smuggled into the courtroom - just as Superboy is taking the stand. Placing the Kryptonite in his chest, Mr. Corben transforms himself into Metallo, takes over the room, and decides to use the jury to prove that Superboy is the guilty one for leading him into the life of crime. Metallo tells the jury about Superboy talking Metallo into helping him raid a military base. When Metallo asks Superboy if the events are true, he must answer "yes" and the jury is shocked. Lana insists Superboy have the right of defense and Metallo agrees - appointing Lana as Superboy's defense counselor, whereupon she

Stacy Haiduk as Lana Lang, Sherman Howard as Lex Luthor.

shows that Superboy was under the effects of red Kryptonite. When Metallo claims that he was not in his right mind either, Lana shows an important difference - even under the influence of red Kryptonite, Superboy wouldn't kill. Reminding the jury of all that Superboy has done for them, and invoking the principles he fights for and which the court represents, Lana so persuades the jury and the rest of the people in the courtroom that they all turn against Metallo and charge at him. **Guest cast:** Michael Callan as Mr. Corben/Metallo, Janis Nenson as the judge, Tim Powell as Nichols, Paul Brown as Prof. Schwartz, Kurt Smildain as the doctor, Jim McDonals as Gen. Swain, Barry Mizerski as scientist #1, Henry J. as scientist #2, Doreen Chalmers as the older woman, Joann Hawkins as Greta, Ric Reitz as the Sloane defense attorney, Greg Paul Meyers as Gunther. **Writers:** Andrew Helfer and Michael Carlin. **Director:** Richard J. Lewis.

Jackson and Hyde (airdate: April 21, 1991). Gail Peyton brings a bottle of her grandfather's "Health and Strength" elixir in to the Bureau. Although Dennis Jackson is convinced it's just snake oil, he agrees to send it to the lab, but forgets to drop it off. When he later gets in an accident and is trapped in his car, he drinks the elixir. Amazingly, it gives him the strength to break out of the car, but it also makes him wild and mean. The next morning, his personality is still strange - he is pleasant and jovial - and decides to go out in the field with Matt. As they leave we learn that a man was beaten to death very near where Jackson had his accident. While Matt and Dennie are on a call, they meet Elissa, and later that nhat night, Dennis goes to the club Elissa sings at to meet her, first going to Gail for more elixir. Suspicious, Gail follows him and watches as he drinks the elixir for courage, then bursts into Elissa's dressing room and chases her into the parking lot. Elissa hides in a car and, though Jackson seemingly passes her by, something crashes in and kills her. **Guest cast:** Heather Ehlers as Gail Peyton, Juice Newton, Barry Culler as Hank, Kelly Muilis as Brenda. **Writer:** Toby Martin. **Director:** John Huneck.

Mine Games (airdate: April 28, 1991). As Superboy follows Lex Luthor, who is dragging the kidnapped Lana Lang into a mine, he finds himself in a trap. Luthor has lured Superboy into the abandoned mine where he plans to kill him with Kryptonite. But just as his evil plan is unveiled, the roof of the mine begins to collapse. Lex and Superboy are trapped together in a chamber of the mine while Lana is trapped on the other side, near the mine entrance, by a fallen rock. As the two men begin to run out of oxygen, Superboy convinces Luthor that the only way he'll get out alive is to take the Kryptonite as far away as possible. The far end of the chamber is still not far enough, but Superboy remembers seeing a battery, now covered by fallen rock and dirt. Together, Superboy and Luthor dig for the battery, hoping the lead in it will be enough to shield Superboy from the deadly rays of the Kryptonite - otherwise, they are both sure to perish. **Guest cast:** None. **Writer:** Sherman Howard. **Director:** Hugh Martin.

Wish For Armageddon (airdate: May 5, 1991). Clark is having a problem with dreams. He keeps dreaming that terrible things are happening to the Soviets - things for which they are blaming the U.S. But when Clark wakes up, he finds out that these things are real. What he doesn't realize, is he's the one who's doing them. Garrett Waters seems like an upstanding citizen, well known for his activity in charitable causes. He has even gotten Superboy to help him out by collecting donations and signing a Declaration of Principles advocating rights for the homeless. Trouble is, it's also a contract with the devil. For Garrett Waters was once a Medieval monk, cursed to live until the end of the world. Throughout nine centuries, he has used this Satanic contract to try to cause Armageddon and it seems this time he may be successful. **Guest cast:** Robert Miano as Garrett Waters, Marc Macaulay as Lee Woods, Peter Palmer as the President, Gailna Loginova as the Russian officer, Rebecca Staples as the tortured woman, Walter Hook as Anatoil, Lewis Crume as the judge, Frank Hilgenberg as Dave, Angy Harper as the waitress, Peggy O'Neal as the wife, Craig Thomas as the construction worker. **Writer:** Gerard Christopher. **Director:** Bob Wiemer.

Standoff (airdate: May 12, 1991). The Bureau is having a get-together for an employee leaving to return to college, when a stranger in the club begins asking questions about Clark and the others. Suddenly, he pulls a gun on the bartender to rob him, and when Clark starts to change into Superboy he is met by the hood's accomplice. Unable to transform into his super alter ego, Clark becomes one of two dozen prisoners in the restaurant, being held by two convicts who escaped from a courtroom that morning. Police are searching door-to-door for the pair, and it's only a matter of time before they arrive. Unfortunately, when they do show up, Mack is forced to run them off. Now, with Clark unable to change into his secret identity, they are at the whims of the two convicts. **Guest cast:** Tom Schuster as escaped convict #1, Philip J. Celia as escaped convict #2, Frances Peach as Fran, Barry Culler as Doug, Alan Landers as the cop, Sharie Doolittle as the screaming woman, Jim Greene as the bartender, Ralph Wilcox as Sergeant Barker, Lou Bedlord. **Writer:** Joseph Gunn. **Director:** John Huneck.

The Road to Hell, part one and two (airdates: part one, May 19; part two, May 26, 1991). A large, menacing snake approaches a young child in a thick forest, but the child - obviously gifted with super powers - picks up the snake and throws it hundreds of feet. Watching the child through a dimensional portal, two strangers say that the child must not grow up on his own in the wilds, but it may be to late to help him. They then begin watching Superboy save a helpless car accident victim, and as she starts to kiss the Boy of Steel as a reward, he disappears and finds himself transported to the building he works at - except no one knows him now. What's more, much has changed in this new world, such as the lady he saved was killed, Lana has now been working in the field for two years, and no one has ever heard of Superboy! Realizing that he is another dimension, Clark goes to see Dr. Winger, who, in Superboy's world, had created an inter-dimensional travel device. But the Winger in the dimension didn't have Superboy's help and couldn't complete it. Later, meeting a changed Lana who cares about nothing except a big story, she admits she doesn't know Clark, but has heard of a young boy who lives in the wilds with super powers. Meanwhile, while Superboy tries to figure out a way home, a radically different Lex Luthor has tracked down the young Superboy in Africa, where he plans to use the child to achieve his own selfish goals. **Guest cast:** Kenneth Robert Shippy as Dr. Winger, Tracy Roberts as Darla, Joel Carlson as the alternate Superboy, Carla Capps as Serena, Justina Vail as Dr. Winger's assistant, James Zelly as the man, Arron Schnell as the three-year-old Superboy, Jesse Stone as the newspaper vendor, Ron Ely [*Tarzan*] as Superman, Manuel Depina as the second doctor, Doug Dobbs as the short cop, Kent Lindsey as the reporter. **Writer:** Stan Berowitz. **Director:** David Nutter.

SEASON FOUR

A Change of Heart, part one (airdate: Oct. 6, 1991). Lana has been

waiting for Superboy for a long time and now, tired of loving a superhero, begins to date Adam Verrel, one of Capitol City's richest bachelors. But he's also the most evil. While Adam is busy dating Lana, he is also planting suggestions of malcontent in people's minds. Throughout the city, there are huge television monitors which Adam has set up at his own expense, to broadcast messages encouraging people to care for their city. Unfortunately, although what is heard are such motivating sayings as "A clean city is happy

196

city," the subliminal message plays quite a different tune. People begin to act more and more strangely, while becoming more violent as well. Superboy is warned of Verrel's intent by Tommy Puck, once an evil criminal who had developed the technology Verrel is using, but had a change of heart since contracting a fatal disease after volunteering for a medical experiment in jail. When he learns of Verrel's duplicity, Superboy rushes to protect Lana, only to have Adam frame the boy of steel for Lana's death. But can she really be dead? **Guest cast:** Michael DesBarres as Adam Verrel, Bill Mumy [*Lost in Space*] as Tommy Puck, Carla Copps as Deana, Frank Eugene Matthews, Jr. as Ernie, Bill Cordell as Dr. Connelly, Jim McDonald as Lt. Walker, Don Fitzgerald as the mayor, Jay Glick as the priest, Kathy Poling as the smiling woman, Robert Reynolds as the security guard, Danny Haneman as the prison guard, Bob Norris as the man, Dennis Neal as the first reporter, Tricia Jean Matthews as the second reporter, Chris Calvert as the gang leader, Bob Sokoler as newscaster. **Writer:** Paul Stubenrauch. **Director:** David Nutter.

A Change of Heart, part two (airdate: Oct. 13, 1991). Adam Verrel, a prestigious citizen who just happens to be manipulating the minds of everyone in Capitol City, has framed Superboy with the murder of Lana Lang. Superboy agrees to go to jail and await trial while Adam uses Lana, whose death he simulated, to lure Tommy Puck into helping him destroy the people of Capitol City. Tommy, afraid for Lana, agrees while the city gets crazier and crazier. Finally, Superboy decides he must break out of jail to save his city and, as he does so, learns there is a cure for Tommy's disease. Superboy realizes the monitors are to blame for the growing insanity, and begins to smash them. Using the monitors, Verrel shows Superboy that Lana is alive in his power and Superboy must try to save her. With the help of Tommy Puck, who kills Verrel, Lana is freed. But when Puck hears there is a cure for his disease, he appears to have another change of heart and runs off - perchance to experiment again? **Guest cast:** Michael DesBarre as Adam Verrel, Bill Mumy [*Lost in Space*] as Tommy Puck, Carla Copps as Deana, Frank Eugene Matthews, Jr. as Ernie, Bill Cordell as Dr. Connelly, Jim McDonald as Lt. Walker, Don Fitzgerald as the mayor, Jay Glick as the priest, Kathy Poling as the smiling woman, Robert Reynolds as the security guard, Danny Haneman as the prison guard, Bob Norris as the man, Dennis Neal as the first reporter, Tricia Jean Matthews as the second reporter, Chris Calvert as the gang leader, Bob Sokoler as the newscaster. **Writer:** Paul Stubenrauch. **Director:** David Nutter.

The Kryptonite Kid (airdate: Oct. 20, 1991). While trying to find a cure for Superboy's weakness to Kryptonite, a young genius, Mike Walker, gets blasted with the green stuff, which begins to take over his body. Mike, scared, dying and angry, breaks out of the military institute where he so recently worked and begins a rampage across the city as the "Kryptonite Kid", a green man who can blast energy from his fingertips. Superboy, unable to approach the Kryptonite Kid, enlists some help from a look-alike, Vic Ferraro, who had been jailed for impersonating Superboy. Vic approaches the Kryptonite Kid, trying to convince him to return to the lab where a cure for his condition has been found. When the kid realizes Vic is an impostor, the real Superboy has to step in, despite his weakness to Kryptonite. While all the military stand and watch, only Vic, who has just lately learned about heroism, steps back in to help save the day. **Guest cast:** Jay Underwood as Mike Walker and the Kryptonite Kid, Leo V. Finnie, III, Sharon Camille as the babe, David Carr and Dawn McClendon as the reporters. **Writers:** Michael Carlin and Andrew Helfer. **Director:** Thierry Notz.

The Basement (airdate: Oct. 27, 1991). When Lana takes a field call to investigate a basement for ghosts, she finds none - only an alien that takes over the identities of others. The alien takes on Lana's form and is about to take her entire identity when it is interrupted. Lana uses the distraction to damage the identity stealing device. The creature, however, is able to get enough of Lana's memories and behavior before the device breaks to pass for her at the Bureau. The alien realizes that she needs Lana in order to lure Superboy to her. But she makes the mistake of telling Clark she'll be back. When she does not return on time, Clark, concerned because Lana is always punctual, goes to the basement as Superboy. There, he is confronted with two identical Lanas. He chooses the wrong one until the alien, not knowing that Lana lied to her, tells Superboy to kill the real Lana - just as he always kills his enemy. Now knowing which is the alien - Lana knows he always tries *not* to kill - a struggle ensues. The creature attaches her shape-changing device to Superboy but he is able to dislodge it, and the alien is transformed to the substance her device is now attached to - thin air! **Guest cast:** Cassandra Leigh Abel as the girl. **Writer:** Toby Martin. **Director:** Hugh Martin.

Darla Goes Ballistic (airdate: Nov. 3, 1991). While Lex Luthor is feverishly working on a potion to make himself an even greater genius, Darla is getting more and more annoyed. Lex barely spends time with her as it is, and now it's her birthday! He won't pay attention and, finally, she destroys his experiment to get him to react. He does - and tells her to go ahead and kill herself it that's what she wants. Instead, she unknowingly drinks his experiment and becomes a human supercomputer, with psychokinetic powers as well. Darla sets her sights on Superboy, and kidnaps Clark and Lana to lure the boy of steel. Clark convinces Lex to let him go - that he can get to Superboy, who will help Lex create an antidote. Armed with the antidote and a bottle of champagne, Lex tries to get the cure into Darla. She guesses his intent, and is willing, but can't let down the force shield she has subconsciously built around herself. But there is an even simpler antidote - all Lex has to do is give her what she wanted in the first place - a little love and understanding. **Guest cast:** Tracy Roberts as Darla, Ronald Knight as the bank CEO. **Writer:** Sherman Howard. **Director:** John Huneck.

Paranoia (airdate: Nov. 10, 1991). Just as reports of a U.F.O. come in, Jackson's superiors show up at the office, claiming that one of the field operatives knows something of interest to national security. They begin gruelling interviews with all the staff, making them all paranoid. Though the little group is normally quite loyal to each other, they now begin to look at one another with suspicion. Particularly vocal are Lou and Alexis. That night, when one of the superiors, Flynn, is seen by Lou and Clark, dead and bleeding, yet minutes later Lana sees him alive, the group gets to thinking. They realize that the two superiors, and the two policemen who came to investigate the murder are aliens, trying to cover up evidence at the bureau. Clark is able to slip out as the aliens decide to leave and captures them all in the elevator. More aliens show up and explain that the captured four are convicts and that their race generates emotions, in this case paranoia, the way humans generate heat. **Guest cast:** Jack Larson as Lou Lamont, Noel Neill as Alexis Andrews, Jordan Williams as Flynn, Kevin Corrigan as Mel Stuart, Elizabeth Fendrick as Margaret, Max Brown as the leader, Jeff Breslauer as the cop, Tony Shepperd as Charlie. **Writer:** Paul Stubenrauch. **Director:** David Nutter.

Know Thine Enemy (airdate: Nov. 17, 1991). Lana wakes to the voice of Lex Luthor on her radio, telling all of Capitol City that they

197

Seasons 3-4 cast, shown clockwise: Stacy Haiduk as Lana Lang, Gerard Christopher as Superboy, Robert Levine as C. Dennis Jackson, Peter J. Fernandez as Matt Ritter (head of the Bureau For Extranormal Matters).

only have six hours to live. To Darla's chagrin, however, this is not yet another ploy for ransom money. Lex is determined to blow the two of them up with the rest of the world. Luthor lures Superboy to his old lab, where he and Lana find a contraption which, when he puts on the attached headset, plunges Superboy into Lex's memories as Lex himself, There, he learns that Lex was the victim of a physically and mentally abusive father and that the only light in his life was his younger sister, Lena. Lana, seeing Superboy suffering, tries to discover how to break the trance and, finding none, enters Luthor's memories herself. As Darla pleads with Lex, we discover

that Lena has recently died and that Lex has created Lex and Lena androids that will live together forever, as he once had promised her - alone in the world. **Guest cast:** Jennifer Hawkins as Lena at twelve, Denise Gossett as Lena at twenty-three, Kathy Gustafson-Hilton as Lex's mother, Edgar Allen Poe IV as Lex's father, Ryan Porter as the bully, Bob Sokoler as the newscaster. **Writer:** J.M. DeMatteis. **Director:** Bryan Spicer.

Know Thine Enemy, part two (airdate: Nov. 24, 1991). Lana is able to break Superboy out of Luthor's memory loop before he becomes embedded in it forever. They look for information on Lena, only to find the article on her death. After further investigation, however, it seems that she may have faked it. Lana continues her search as Superboy follows a signal he believes is coming from Lex. Instead, he finds Darla, who has shot Lex in the arm and is seeking Superboy's help. She leads Superboy to Lex's new lab where Lex insists there's no way to stop the bomb. When Lana shows up with Lena - who explains to Lex how much she's hated him - he is determined to go ahead with the destruction. But the Lex android, whom Luthor programmed so well with his love for Lena, stops the countdown as Lex, forever hurting, insists he never loved his sister. **Guest cast:** Jennifer Hawkins as Lena at twelve, Denise Gossett as Lena at twenty-three, Kathy Gustafson-Hilton as Lex's mother, Edgar Allen Poe IV as Lex's father, Ryan Porter as the bully, Bob Sokoler as the newscaster. **Writer:** J.M. DeMatteis. **Director:** Bryan Spicer.

Hell Breaks Loose (airdate: Dec. 1, 1991). As construction is being done at the Bureau, workers begin to notice strange things. Tools are found twisted and mangled, they hear unexplained noises and voices, and see phantom lights. Clark and Lana, working late one night, hear something strange as well. Investigating, a strange wind from *inside* the room nearly blows Lana out the window. The next day, the workers find a second wall behind the one they were breaking down and, between the two, a clarinet. (In the Thirties, the building housed a grand ballroom called the Trocadel.) Lana decides to call in paranormal specialists, and that night they discover a gun where the clarinet had been. Later, it shoots itself into the wall which Superboy then crashes down, revealing a human skeleton. It is the remains of a clarinet player, Johnny Carino, who once worked with the mob that owned the Trocadel. In love with Lisa, Johnny decided to go straight. His boss doesn't see eye to eye, and had Johnny shot and stuffed in the wall. But Johnny's spirit can't rest easy as he had promised Lisa that that very night they would go away together - she was to meet him back at the Trocadel. He had told her that he would wait for her - forever if he had to. Lana finds Lisa who, though elderly, is still alive and brings her to the Bureau where the spirit of Johnny has created a wind tunnel and is jeopardizing the lives of everyone there, even Superboy. The disturbance subsides when Lisa approaches and Johnny's voice tells her that he waited, and he will still be waiting when she's ready. His mission over, the Bureau rests at peace once more. **Guest cast:** Gerard Christopher as Johnny Carino, Phyllis Alexion as Lisa, Bever-leigh Banfield, James Delmar as Ben, Fred Ottoviano as Jeno, Michael Edwards as the officer, Paul Vroom as the henchman, Frank Eugene Matthews, Jr. as Eddie, Chris Labban as the young Eddie, Jim Candelora as the band leader. **Writer:** James Ponti. **Director:** Bo Wiemer.

Into the Mystery (airdate: Dec. 8, 1991). Superboy is haunted. Haunted by the vision of Azrael, a mysterious woman who seems to bring disaster wherever she appears, yet he is the only one who sees her. And he is haunted by the memory of his Aunt Cassandra, a favorite relative whom the rest of his family never understood. As Clark tries to track his Aunt Cassandra, he becomes convinced that there is some relation between his aunt and Azrael. He finds Cassandra in a small town, stricken with cancer, and wishing that death would take her soon. Yet she prayed to see her nephew, Clark, once more. Death, in the form of Azrael, heeded her prayer, and led Clark to his aunt. While once we were able to see only the destruction death could bring, we now see the solace it is capable of as Azrael welcomes Cassandra into her open arms and she is engulfed in light. **Guest cast:** Peggy O'Neal as Azrael, Frances Peach as Aunt Cassandra, Edan Gross as the young Clark, Tina Dean Taylor as Cody, Andy Isaacs as Andy, Jack Carroll as the hardware store owner, Gayila Cole as the elderly beautician, Debra Anne Gay as Miss Cooper, Kurt Smildsin as the driver, Bob Sokoler as the anchor. **Writer:** J.M. DeMatteis. **Director:** John Huneck.

To Be Human (airdate: Jan. 19, 1992). While listening to a newscaster describing the panic and confusion created by a super-terrorist called Chaos, we open on a touching scene, in a quaint but misshapen cottage, where Bizarro Lana is lovingly serving an equally bizarre breakfast to Bizarro. The mood is not to last, however, as Bizarro Lana's body begins to smoke, and she bursts into flames. As Bizarro later grieves beside her grave, Superboy comes to comfort him, and decides to take him to a research doctor to see what can be done to make Bizarro more human. The doctor concludes that the only hope is to transfer Superboy's brain-waves to Bizarro. She knows that Bizarro will gain intelligence, but lose his powers, rendering him almost human. The effect it will have on Superboy, however, is unknown. They go ahead with the procedure, and Bizarro does indeed gain intelligence. The doctor begins the process of teaching him as Superboy leaves, feeling only slightly dizzy. Bizarro makes great progress and, once his skin has been altered to look human, visits Clark who christens him Bill. But Clark/Superboy is not so fortunate and his dizziness and weakness gets worse. When Superboy attempts to stop Chaos' latest terrorism, he is struck down, and Chaos throws Superboy's limp body into his car and speeds away. **Guest cast:** Barry Meyers as Bizarro, Paul McCrane as Chaos, Patricia Helwick as Dr. Lynn, Leith Audrey as Bizarro Lana, Russ Blackwell as the first policeman, Michael Monroe as the second policeman. **Writer:** J.M. DeMatteis. **Director:** John Huneck.

To Be Human, part two (airdate: Jan. 26, 1992). Superboy awakens to find himself still in a weakened state and trapped in Chaos' hideout, an old abandoned hotel. Chaos, seeing Superboy conscious, begins to kick and beat him in front of cameras set to televise the event to the world, as Chaos preaches the futility of hope. Bill/Bizarro sees what is happening to Superboy and becomes confused. Bill knows the only thing that can save Superboy is for him to reverse the process and become a freak again. Though at first he refuses to do this, he realizes Superboy would never allow him to suffer, and Bill asks the doctor to change him back to Bizarro. While Bill is transforming back into Bizarro, Lana finds Superboy's trail and goes to the hotel alone. She struggles with Chaos for his gun and is thrown off the roof of the building. But before she can be hurt, Bizarro catches Lana and carries her to the roof where he confronts Chaos, who tries to convince Bizarro that the two of them are brother-freaks. Bizarro sees the truth in this, but is still attached to his brother Superboy, and therefore must fight Chaos. Afterwards, although Bizarro cannot be changed back into Bill, the research doctor begins the slow but rewarding process of teaching Bizarro as he is. **Guest cast:** Barry Meyers as Bizarro, Paul McCrane as Chaos, Patricia Helwick as Dr. Lynn, Leith Audrey as Bizarro Lana, Russ Blackwell as the first policeman, Michael Monroe as the second policeman. **Writer:** J.M. DeMatteis. **Director:** John Huneck.

West of Alpha Centauri (airdate: Feb. 2, 1992). A small titanium colored cube, which a young boy saw drop out of the sky, is brought to the Bureau for Extranormal Matters. When it begins ticking, and the police bomb squad can't penetrate the cube's surface, Superboy is called in. As Superboy breaks the cube's surface and disarms the bomb, an alarm goes off inside and a man appears in a bolt of

Gerard Christopher as Superboy/Clark Kent, as of season 3 an intern for the Bureau For Extranormal Matters.

lightning. He grabs Superboy and, much to the boy of steel's surprise, the other man is stronger. When Lana interferes, she is transported along with the other two into a space ship. She and

Superboy are then put into the ship's prison where they find many others whose grandparents were put there for mutiny. The present captain brought Superboy there because one of the prison factions believes a savior will come symbolized by what looks much like Superboy's S-shield. The captain hoped that once they saw that Superboy couldn't get out of the prison, they'd stop plotting. Superboy tries to convince the prisoners to band together - there are several factions fighting amongst themselves - but they seem unable to do so. Finally, Superboy challenges the captain's right hand man - the same one who caught him before - and, as they fight, manages to convince him that the captain is lost. When it's obvious that Superboy's opponent believes him, the guard won't let him out either. Finally all the prisoners band together, free themselves, and leave the captain alone in the prison, still shouting out orders. **Guest cast:** Gregory E. Boyd as Ta-El, Andrew Clark as Capt. Vladic, Kevin Quigley as Sage, Darren Dollar as the first mate, Angie Harper as Zoren, Patrick Cherry as Orek, Michael Monroe as the bomb squad man. **Writers:** Mark Jones, Paul Stubenrauch and Stan Berkowitz. **Director:** Jeff Kibbee.

Threesome, part one (airdate: Feb. 9, 1992). Dr. Odessa Vexman, a psychiatrist, harbors deep resentment against Superboy. She once helped him, with the hope of capturing his attention, but when he was oblivious to her, she felt rejected. Now, a prison psychiatrist where both Metallo and Lex Luthor are kept, she manages to set them both free, hoping to convince them to work together to destroy Superboy. Meanwhile, while Lana feels homesick and goes home to Smallville, Clark stays in Capitol City to keep tabs on the now at large Metallo and Luthor. When Superboy sees that Odessa worked at the prison and is now missing, he suspects her, but it isn't until Clark is looking at her files at the Bureau and Matt tips him off about Odessa's feelings for Superboy - something he was previously unaware of - that he's really suspicious. When Superboy follows the path of destruction which Odessa has left to lead him on, he is met by Metallo and Luthor who has rigged a device to affect Superboy's hearing and, therefore, sense of balance. As Superboy stumbles, overcome by Luthor's creation, the three villains (including Odessa) move slowly toward him. **Guest cast:** Justina Vail as Dr. Odessa Vexman, David Hess as Donnie, Bob Barnes as the warden, Ed Amatruda as Trenton, James Zelley as Ray. **Writer:** Stan Berkowitz. **Director:** David Nutter.

Threesome, part two (airdate: Feb. 16, 1992). Superboy just manages to escape the three villains as they approach him for the final kill but, unable to counteract the effects of the sound machine Luthor has built, he goes to Smallville to find a away around it. When he arrives, he finds Lana upset with the way Smallville, hit by the worsening economy, is being turned into a pit of gambling, with X-rated theaters on the way. When Superboy steps into the picture, the owner of the casino calls on Luthor, Metallo and Odessa for help. The three arrive as Superboy discovers that he can counteract one sound machine with another and they'll cancel each other out. Armed with his machine, and a lead sheet to take care of Metallo's kryptonite, Superboy heads for a showdown. He takes care of Metallo first, then uses his sound machine against Luthor's, which he then destroys. But as the villains scatter, he forgets about his own which Odessa later retrieves. Lana has a few plans of her own though, and ducks into a thrift shop where she manages to get an outfit just like Odessa's. When Metallo sees her with Superboy, he thinks the doctor is double-crossing him, and Metallo tries to strangle Odessa. Luthor stops him by removing the kryptonite from Metallo's chest and approaches Superboy, who is already fading fast from the sound. Ignoring Odessa's warnings to be careful, Luthor is gloating at the kill when Superboy uses his heat vision to make a sign drop onto Lex and knock him out. As Odessa tries to

grab the dropped kryptonite, Lana goes for her and, just as Superboy crushes the sound generator, Lana uses the kryptonite to knock Odessa out and she and Superboy walk away together leaving the threesome together, unconscious, in their wake. **Guest cast:** Justina Vail as Dr. Odessa Vexman, David Hess as Donnie, Bob Barnes as the warden, Ed Amatruda as Trenton, James Zelley as Ray. **Writer:** Stan Berkowitz. **Director:** David Nutter.

Out of Luck (airdate: Feb. 23, 1992). A two-bit thief, Charlie Carmichael, pulls a job on an old coin shop and makes off with a cursed coin that gives him good luck while giving bad luck to all who come near him. As Clark and Lana see Charlie driving recklessly, Clark becomes Superboy and tries to stop him but before he can get to Charlie, a telephone pole is struck by lightning and begins to fall towards Lana. In the interference, Charlie gets away while, after catching the pole, Superboy himself is struck by lightning. The proximity to Charlie and his coin starts a string of bad luck for Lana and Superboy, who can't seem to get his rescue missions right. Superboy himself comes to believe in the curse and, when he arrives in the nick of time to save Lana who's been kidnapped by Carmichael, is unable to act. Lana tells him she's learned the incantation to counteract the curse and Superboy, using it, gets his confidence back and is able to defeat Charlie. When Lana later tells him the incantation was just some Latin she remembered from high school, it seems the curse isn't real until we see that Charlie was no longer in possession of the coin when Superboy overcame him. Charlie dropped the coin at the last job he did, and it has now been picked up by someone else - to start the chain again? **Guest cast:** Pat Cupo as Charlie Carmichael, Jack Swanson as Corrigan, Larry Bucklan as Bob, Sam Ayres as Andrew, Steve Oumothel as Phillip, Donald Fergusson as Bennett, Kathy Neff as Mrs. Berger, Kathy Bronston as the woman, Trisha Colligan as the first nun, Kim Gabriel as the second nun, Mindy Bronston as the woman, Craig Thomas as the director. **Writer:** Sandy Fries. **Director:** Bob Wiemer.

Who is Superboy? (airdate: Mar. 1, 1992). A new computer is brought to the Bureau that is capable of recreating incidents when given pictures of the location and the participants, and an eyewitness account. The salesman leaves it there until the next day so they can try it out, giving Lana and idea - she'll come back that night and try to find out who Superboy is. Very apprehensively, Clark goes with her and as Lana goes through the Superboy incidents she remembers, we see a montage of clips from past episodes. In the final analysis, it seems Clark is the only one who is always there at an incident, but never there once Superboy shows up. Clark tries to point out all the things that could be wrong with the analysis - all the incidents were recreated from Lana's memory, Superboy could have more than one alter identity, etc. - when she decides to combine all the events and let the computer decide who Superboy is. The machine goes into action, and we see another montage of clips, when Lana suddenly deletes the program. If Superboy doesn't want anyone to know who he is, she decides to respect his wishes. As the two start off to get a pizza, they hear the squeal of brakes and a loud crash. Clark, of course, has to beg off on their meal and Lana, obviously still suspicious, kisses him and lets him go. **Guest cast:** Brett Rice as Whitehead, Joe Candelora as the governor, Bob Barnes as the warden, Barry Meyers as Bizarro, Shanna Teare as Bizarro Lana, Gregory Miller as Llewelyn, Christine Moore as Nella, Bill Painter as the police officer, Kellus Mathews as the security guard, Kelly Erin Welton as the werewolf, Rod Doll as the worker. **Writer:** Stan Berkowitz. **Director:** Bob Weimer.

Cat and Mouse (airdate: Apr. 19, 1992). Clark is greeted at the office with some good news and some bad news. The bad news is, because of government cutbacks, his job has been eliminated. The good news is he's being promoted so he can keep working at the Bureau. But the bad news is he's got to have a psychiatric evaluation first. Clark is understandably concerned - will he be able to go through the evaluation without giving away his identity or refusing to answer any questions? He decides to go ahead and is examined by Dr. Samantha Meyers who finds him a bit frustrating, although interesting. With every question she asks, a montage of clips from past shows is triggered and he must answer with a qualification. Dr. Meyers begins to believe he must be hiding something, but has faith that the lie detector test will unearth it. Even on the lie detector test, although Clark gets some difficult questions, he again is able to qualify them. For instance when asked if he's ever willingly destroyed public or private property, he answers "Only in emergencies." The machine stays steady throughout all the questions except the last - "Have you ever used an alias?" The needle of the lie detector goes wild as Clark tries to figure out how to answer this without lying or giving himself away, until it finally smokes and catches fire. He has only one more test to go - she tells him her recommendation will be against his promotion. Determined, Clark tells her that he'll appeal her decision - he's an asset to the Bureau - when she smiles. That was the answer she was waiting for - proof that he is not too meek for the job. **Guest cast:** Erin Gray [*Buck Rogers*] as Dr. Samantha Meyers, Michael Owens as Mayall, Paul Daray as Capt. Quintin, Michael Balin as Lt. Folton, Kevin Benton as Desmond, Christine Moore as Neila, Robert Miano as Garrett Woods, Michael Des Barres as Adam Verrell. **Writer:** Gerard Christopher. **Director:** Peter Kiwitt.

Obituary for a Super-Hero (airdate: Apr. 26, 1992). As we watch a montage of clips from past episodes of Superboy, we hear the voice of a news anchor talking about the boy of steel - in the past tense. As the reporter continues his story, he explains what little is known at this point. The Coast Guard had received a distress call from a yacht near Capitol City. Just as they neared the yacht, they saw Superboy landing on the deck only to disappear seconds later during an enormous explosion. As the reporter continues his coverage of the event, including man on the street interviews, and a direct link with the Coast Guard who are searching for Superboy's body, Lex Luthor calls in. When the Coast Guard captain says his sonar's found something shaped like a human body, but that the sonar bounces off it like it was made of steel, it seems the guessing is over and Superboy is really dead. Luthor pops the cork off his champagne a little early, however. He has now taken over one of the TV monitors, and begins to gloat to Lana, who is in the studio, about how he planted the kryptonite bomb aboard the yacht. But as he is gloating, the captain shows the news anchor what the sonar really found - an old brass figurehead. Superboy had seen the bomb in time and gone underwater, moving the figurehead under the yacht to fake his own death so that the murderer would step forward. As Luthor sputters over the raising of the figurehead, Superboy steps up behind him, surprising Luthor and the rest of the country except for one little boy who just knew Superboy couldn't be dead. **Guest cast:** Bill Mumy [*Lost in Space*] as Tommy Puck, Barry Meyers as Bizzaro, Michael Callan as Metallo, George Sarris as Mandel, Elizebeth Rothan as the female reporter, Lesa Thurman as the bureau worker, Jesse Leipter as the boy, Joanna Garcia as the girl, Kristin Trueison. **Writer:** Stan Berkowitz. **Director:** John Huneck.

Metamorphosis (airdate: May 3, 1992). The bureau has a new mystery on their hands. It seems that old people are dying with the IDs of young people in their wallets - young people that are missing. As Clark and Matt investigate one of the latest deaths, an old woman seems to be constantly on their trail, a trail which finally leads to a health club owned and run by Adrian Temple, a man who is much older than he looks. As Matt talks to Temple, Clark sees the old woman outside and rushes out to catch her. He is forced to turn into Superboy to stop her from being run down by a truck and when he does he finds the woman is none other than Lana. She explains that the transformation began not long after she was at Temple's health

club and fell asleep during a rub down. Lana went to a doctor who, after finding traces of gold in Lana's blood, began to look into the history of alchemy. The doctor shows up at Temple's office just as Lana and Superboy go back to find it in a shambles, and they take the vial of gold liquid which they find in Temple's refrigerator to analyze it. The results lead the doctor to believe that Temple uses the blood of young people, along with the gold liquid, to keep himself young. When he gives them his own blood in return the age passes on to his victims. Temple follows their trail to the doctor's office and bursts in on them, in search of his elixir. He's willing to strike a deal - he'll give them the antidote to save Lana for some of Superboy's blood. They agree but, instead of Superboy's blood, they transfuse Temple with the blood of an old man and when he returns to his proper age, Lana is given back her own. **Guest cast:** Rowdy Roddy Piper as Adrian Temple, Robin O'Neil as Sasha, Judy Clayton as Dr. Stern, Bret Cipes as Nathan Steeps, Stacy Black as the receptionist, Valerie Bastilone as the woman body builder, Roger Floyd as the first kid, Joe Bradley as old Jeff Olson, Billy Gillespie as the pathologist. **Writer:** Paul Robert Coyle. **Director:** Bob Wiemer.

Rites of Passage, part one (airdate: May 10, 1992). As Clark celebrates his birthday, a series of events occur: the ship in which he arrived on Earth begins to hum and glow, the purple crystal which was taken from the spot where his ship landed begins to hum and glow, and Clark begins to lose control of his powers. Ma and Pa Kent call him when the ship begins its manifestations and Clark rushes home. At the same time, Jackson, who investigated Superboy's landing site twenty years earlier is called into go back to Smallville. Afraid to go back in the field alone after all this time behind a desk, Jackson takes Matt along with him and Lana, knowing something strange is going on with Clark, insists on going as well. When Clark gets back to Smallville and enters the ship, he is greeted by a holographic image of a Krypton elder who instructs him to place the purple crystal in the receptacle or emergency measures will be taken. Of course, Clark does not have the purple crystal and he soon finds out just what those emergency measures are - his powers are taken away. **Guest cast:** Unknown. **Writers:** Mike Carlin and Andy Helfer. **Director:** David Grossman.

Rites of Passage, part two (airdate: May 17, 1992). The holographic image of the Krypton elder explains to Clark that his powers were taken away because he can not control them until he gets the purple crystal and completes the rites of passage. If this is not done within eight hours, his powers will be gone forever. Meanwhile, Jackson, Matt and Lana arrive in Smallville and visit the scene of Jackson's investigation twenty-odd years earlier. He remembers passing a pickup truck, and they decide to question area residents, starting with the Kents who own the closest property. Ma and Pa Kent are not very helpful, but Jackson sees their old truck which they admit is twenty-five years old, while the Kents learn that Jackson is waiting for the purple crystal to be delivered to his hotel at any moment. Matt takes the car and heads off to the hotel to get the package, while Lana and Jackson walk off to continue their questioning. Clark takes the truck to try and head Matt off but, though he is successful, an old bully from his Smallville days works at the hotel and will not relinquish the package to anyone but Jackson. Clark goes home and, as Matt arrives to get the same song and dance from the hotel clerk, Clark returns in the Superboy suit and succeeds in scaring the bully off. He convinces Matt to let him have the package and returns to the ship just in time to place the crystal in the proper receptacle and undergo the rites of passage. His powers are returned and Clark is ready to return with the others the next day - until the next time of the passage. **Guest cast:** Unknown. **Writers:** Mike Carlin and Andy Helfer. **Director:** David Grossman.

Super Force

review by Tony Bell and William E. Anchors, Jr.

Production credits:

Executive Producer	James J. McNamara (year 1)
	Roderick Taylor (year 2)
Producer	Michael Attanasio
Developed by	Larry Brody
	Janis Hendler
Created by	James J. McNamara
Producer	Michael Attanasio
Music	Kevin Kiner
	Joel Goldsmith

Regular cast:

Zachary Stone/Super Force	Ken Olandt
F.X. Spinner	Larry B. Scott
E. B. Hungerford	Patrick McNee
Buddy	Marc Macaulay (year 1)
Carla Frost	Lisa Niemi (year 1)
Zander Tyler	Musetta Vander (year 2)
Merkle	Antoni Corone (year 2)

Number of episodes:	48 one-half hour segments

Premise: It is the year 2020, and the world has changed. Astronaut Zach Stone has returned from a two-year mission to Mars. Armed with a prototype space suit adapted to the streets, Stone is given the power to fight crime and establish order. In 2020 times are tough, but this man is tougher.

Editor's comments: *Super Force* seems to be sort of an updated version of *Streethawk*, with Ken Olandt portraying a futuristic cop who has the double identity of Super Force. As the disguised hero, Super Force uses a super cycle, futuristic weapons, and a force-field equipped protective suit. The first season seemed reasonably entertaining considering the budget of the series. However, the second season brought many changes under the helm of a new executive producer, Roderick Taylor (creator of the infamous *Otherworld*), including cast changes and Zach obtaining several powers, one of which is psychic abilities. As could be predicted, the series took a nose dive in quality and believability in the second season thanks to the uninspiring writing and production skills of Taylor.

SEASON ONE

Super Force (airdate: Sept. 22, 1990, two hour pilot). Police officer Frank Stone chases two crooks into the Satori Enterprises building, but becomes trapped and is killed by a gas vented into the room. Meanwhile, returning from two years in deep space is the capsule *Columbus*, a space vehicle containing Commander Zachary Stone and four fellow astronauts who are trying to make it home after a meteor storm disables the vehicle's engines. Miraculously the capsule makes it to Earth, where the international crew are welcomed home as heros. Once the parades are over, Zach finds things less pleasant. It seems that his father has died while he was gone, and his brother Frank is dead as well, after which Frank is accused of being a crooked cop. To clear the family name, Zach quits NASA and joins the police academy. Meanwhile, Hungerford, an old acquaintance of the Stone family, is killed as he leaves his apartment by an assailant he recognizes moments before he dies. Later that night, after Hungerford doesn't show up at his police graduation, Zach takes a cab to the Hungerford Industries building, which has been broken into. He finds what he believes is an intruder, but it turns out to be F.X. Spinner, one of the engineers who works there. Looking around, F.X. and Zach find Hungerford's body, and Zach becomes fed up with what he perceives to be a crime-ridden world. He starts to go after the killer, but F.X. explains that he wouldn't stand a chance, at least he wouldn't without the "suit". The suit turns out to be a prototype space-suit, with a powerful external skeleton, state-of-the-art electronics, body armor, and other advanced features. Using it, he tracks down the killer and is shocked to find that the assassin is his "dead" brother Frank, who is now out to kill Zach.

Zach manages survive the encounter, and F.X. nurses him back to health at the Hungerford Infirmary. F.X. is sceptical that is was Frank who killed Hungerford, despite Zach's testimony. Frank was the one who helped F.X. out of a life of crime and into Hungerford Industries, to use his genius for science. Both men, however, are sceptical of the future of Hungerford Industries without E.B., especially with such men as Teo Satori (whom Zach's father had once put behind bars) waiting to take over. As F.X. ponders the situation, Zach heads to his first day on his beat in the Crime Zone - the toughest precinct in the city, and the same beat Frank walked. Doing some investigating into the unusually rampant vandalism going on, Zach discovers that all the buildings are owned by the same realtor. He is interrupted in his investigation by a message from Hungerford to come to the lab. When he arrives, Zach finds out that F.X. has solved the problem of Hungerford Industries - he has programmed everything about Hungerford, including voice and memory, into a computer which will be capable of handling the business. The problem solved, Zach turns back to his concern for Frank, and asks F.X. to modify the suit for street use. Some time later, F.X. and Zach go to visit the realtor who has been experiencing all the bad luck. Leaving a bug in the realtor's office, Zach learns the next target for vandalism and he and F.X show up as some punks are torching the place. Zach puts on the new suit which F.X. has just completed and Super Force makes his first appearance, forcing the vandals into early retirement.

Zach confronts the realtor who owns all the buildings that have recently been vandalized, and learns that he's just a front for Satori. Meanwhile, the Hungerford Computer has tapped onto the F.B.I.'s computers and learns that a group of businessmen with Satori at the head is planning this violence to undermine the nation's confidence in the government so it can be overthrown. When Frank Stone, Jr. disappeared, he was unofficially investigating Satori, and Hungerford believes that Satori is behind his disappearance. As Satori

Ken Olandt as Zachary Stone/Super Force (top), Larry B. Scott as F.X. Spinner.

moves his wave of violence to the suburbs, F.X tells Zach he's made the Super Force suit more accessible - he gives Zach a police badge and tells him to press the red star in the middle and the suit will come to him. When Satori's punks take a suburban woman hostage in her own home, Zach presses the star and, dressed in the suit and on the Super Force motorcycle, heads for the scene of the crime. Super Force arrives just in time as one of the punks is threatening to hurt the held woman and, although he scatters the punks and saves the woman, the gang gets away.

While Zach and his captain, Carla Frost, are talking, they are interrupted by a call - there is a riot in the Crime Zone. While they are taking care of that, Satori is holding a conference, announcing that the city needs a leader capable of taking care of the spreading violence, and that he would be the ideal choice. While the conference is taking place, Satori has his gang burst in and take everyone in the room hostage. Meanwhile, after Carla, Zach and the rest of the police finish quelling the riot, they are called in to help at Satori Enterprises. The police chase off the gang which escapes in a helicopter that Zach later traces to a company owned by Satori. He goes to the company, takes care of the gang, then confronts Satori who has Zach's brother Frank fight him. Super Force is hesitant to hurt Frank, but is forced to fight for his life. A vicious struggle ensues in Satori's factory and, at the end, when Frank is decapitated by some of the machinery, it turns out to have been a robot all along. Super Force continues after Satori and, seeing him taking off in a helicopter, shoots him down. **Guest cast:** Marshall Teague as Frank Stone, Jr., G. Gordon Liddy as Satori, Cec Verell as Patty Pretty, Sandra Perry as Miranda, Max Brown as Sgt. Anderson, Bill Orsini as Ed Maxwell, Jordan Williams as Gilardi, Michelle Fleisher as Susie Maxwell, Robert Small as Elton Charles, Leroy Mitchell, Jr. as Kareem Feldman, Judy Clayton as police chief #19, Sen. Edward J. Gurney as police chief #2, Ronald Knight as police chief #3, Nichele Adams as the police aide, George F. Colangelo as St. Germain, Lamont Lofton as the anchorman, Carmen J. Alexander as the business man, Carol Hilliburton as the business woman, Grant Ford as Gen. Frederickson, Sandy Fox as the pretty girl, Shanna Teare as the teenage girl. **Writers:** Larry Brody and Janis Hendler. **Director:** Richard Compton.

Battle Cry (airdate: Oct. 7, 1990). A war veteran from the Secret War in Germany, Sam Sargasso returns home to find his beloved wife has been murdered. Sargasso turns into a maniacal killer, determined to get revenge on all of the witnesses to his wife's murder. From the clues surrounding the slayings of two of the witnesses, Detective Zachary Stone uncovers Sargasso's trail and, as Super Force, arrives just in time to save the next victim. **Guest cast:** Richard Hatch [*Battlestar Galactica*] as Sam Sargasso, Rebecca Renfroe as Louise Dvorak, Barry Cutler as Henry Valenz, Gordon J. Noice as Kelso, Maureen Collins as Julie Sargasso. **Writers:** Larry Brody and Janis Hendler. **Director:** Chip Chalmers.

As God is My Witness (airdate: Oct. 14, 1990). Jesse Caldwell, a psychotic evangelist who is out to "save" the world, escapes from the state mental hospital. When his doctor, Dr. Christa Traynor, reports a threatening phone call she received from Caldwell, Carla takes the threat more seriously than Zach and orders him to investigate. Zach finds that Caldwell has been preaching in an abandoned church, converting punks into "squeaky clean" members of a new religion. When it becomes apparent that this new religion is responsible for the string of crimes committed by "clean cut" youths, Super Force blasts into the old church and puts an end to Caldwell's sermons. **Guest cast:** Michael Des Barres as Jesse Caldwell, Heidi Payne as Dr. Christa Traynor, Carla Capps as Alberta, Antonio Fabrizo as Gemullich, Nina Lebidensky as the Russian woman, Paul Allen Skye as Carson. **Writers:** Larry Brody and Janis Hendler. **Director:** David Nutter.

U-Gene, part one (airdate: Oct. 21, 1990). U-Gene is a genetic experiment who has escaped from a laboratory in Germany. Gunther, posing as a German Inspector, convinces the police chiefs that

U-Gene is a dangerous killing machine that must be stopped. When Zach Stone is told to investigate the case with Gunther, he investigates the "inspector" as well. Suspicious, Super Force traces Gunther and finds him in a confrontation with U-Gene, about to be shot. Before he can stop his programmed response, U-Gene shoots Super Force with such a high-tech gun that he is left bleeding on the ground. **Guest cast:** Lou Ferrigno [*The Incredible Hulk*] as U-Gene, Tom Nowicki as Gunther, Nancy Duerr as Ambassador Chalmers, Tom Kouchalakos as Craig, Tim McCormack as the security guard. **Writers:** Larry Brody and Janis Hendler. **Director:** Chip Chalmers.

U-Gene, part two (airdate: Oct. 28, 1990). After Super Force is seriously wounded by U-Gene, the genetically engineered giant takes him to his hideout and repairs both Zach and his suit. There Zach learns that U-Gene is indeed an experiment gone awry; he cannot be the perfect killer machine his creators desired because he has a conscience. Gunther, the true killing machine, tracks U-Gene to the hideout, upon which Super Force convinces the police to let U-Gene give himself up for diplomatic immunity. When he discovers that Gunther has tricked him, and means to kill U-Gene, Super Force helps the giant escape from Gunther, allowing him to choose his own life. **Guest cast:** Lou Ferrigno [*The Incredible Hulk*] as U-Gene, Tom Nowicki as Gunther, Nancy Duerr as Ambassador Chalmers, Tom Kouchalakos as Craig, Tim McCormack as the security guard. **Writers:** Larry Brody and Janis Hendler. **Director:** Chip Chalmers.

Prisoners of Love (airdate: Nov. 4, 1990). A cruel businessman, Huff, plans to use penetic experiments to create a perfect female...but needs models. When beautiful young women begin to disappear from nightclubs, Zachary Stone and Carla Frost go undercover, only to have Carla chosen as Huff's perfect candidate. F.X. is kidnapped along with Carla and as a result, Super Force is able to track them by the homing device in F.X.'s watch. He arrives at the newly abandoned hideout just as F.X. is about to be shot, then catches up to the fleeing criminals and rescues their cargo of kidnapped women. **Guest cast:** Mike Preston as Huff, JoAnn Hawkins as Amanda Hayes, Katie Finneran as Allison. **Writers:** Larry Brody and Janis Hendler. **Director:** John Nicolella.

The Crime Doctor (airdate: Nov. 11, 1990). While F.X. is with a date at an outdoor cafe, a man disguised as a cop arrives and opens up with automatic weapons fire, killing F.X.'s date. Seconds later Super Force arrives, and disarms the cop-turned-killer. Later, F.X. and Zach investigate the situation and discover that this is the second police officer to go berserk and attack the public. Other people given positions of public trust have also gone berserk and attacked people as well, but before F.X. and Zach can determine the source of the problem, Zach is kidnapped after he tries to help a hit-and-run victim. The ambulance operators take the knocked-out Zach to the evil Dr. Verona, where he undergoes a mind-altering operation that compels him to pursue and kill his alter-ego: Super Force! It seems the sinister doctor has been performing surgical experiments on innocent people, turning them into vicious killers. Now Zach has become her latest test... **Guest cast:** Sara Douglas [*Superman - The Movie*] as Dr. Verona, Juan Cejas as Mikhail. **Writer:** Roy Thomas. **Director:** David Nutter.

The Gauntlet (airdate: Nov. 18, 1990). Mel, while attempting to put an end to her brother's thievery, witnesses his diamond heist, as well as his subsequent demise at the hands of a mysterious man in a trenchcoat. She and Zach Stone soon discover that the killer is really

a much honored detective and friend of Zach who has turned to a life of crime. Mel, determined to avenge her brother's death, stalks the renegade detective to his lair, only to be caught and disarmed by the villain and his thugs. As they are about to open fire at Mel, Super Force bursts in takes them by storm. **Guest cast:** Sydney Penny as Mel, Tom Schuster as Ferrett, Curt Smildsen as Sgt. Foyt. **Writers:** Warren Murphy. **Director:** David Nutter.

Come Home To Die (airdate: Nov. 25, 1990). A gang robs an armored vehicle of a Photocomet Launcher, a weapon so advanced it is even capable of breaching the defenses of the Super Force suit. When F.X. sees the symbol left behind at the scene of a bank robbery committed using the Launcher, he realizes that Brick Boss, the leader of the gang to which F.X. used to belong, is behind the crime. Feeling to blame because he could have once testified against Brick Boss and didn't, F.X. tries to dissuade him from continuing his actions. Brick Boss, however, is uninterested in changing his ways, and gives F.X. an ultimatum - join me or die. But F.X. fails a test of loyalty and Brick Boss is about to shoot him with the Photocomet Launcher when Super Force arrives. With the help of F.X., Super Force defeats Brick Boss who is ultimately vaporized. **Guest cast:** Denis Forest [War of the Worlds] as Brick Boss/Neal, Kareen Germain as Niko, Carl Compean as the gang member, Robert Reynolds as guard 32, Sonya Mattox as Miss PVC, Bob Sokoler as the reporter, Jesse Stone as the old man. **Writers:** Larry Brody and Janis Hendler. **Director:** Les Landau.

Gravity's Rainbow, part one (airdate: Dec. 2, 1990). A string of unusual robberies leads F.X. and the Hungerford Computer to conclude that someone is planning to build a Gravitational Fusion Device, or Gravity Bomb, capable of destroying the world. Knowing this, Super Force is able to stop the criminals as they try to steal the final component needed for the bomb. While terminating the robbery, Super Force finds his missing brother, Frank Stone, Jr., who was part of the criminal team. Frank's mind has been controlled by the evil Satori, but he assures Zach that a shot from his stun gun destroyed the link. But the link between Satori and Frank is still effective and, while Zach is out on police business, Frank knocks F.X. out and puts on the Super Force suit. **Guest cast:** G. Gordon Liddy as Satori, Marshall Teague as Frank Stone, Jr., Anthony Corone, Peter Palmer as Taggert, Paul Vroom as guard #1, Roger Floyd as the prisoner, Wendy Chioji as the TV newscaster, Greg Anderson as the S.P.L.A.T. member. **Writers:** R.L. Taylor, Bruce A. Taylor, Jeff Mandel. **Director:** Les Landau.

Gravity's Rainbow, part two (airdate: Dec. 9, 1990). Frank Stone, Jr., wearing the Super Force suit, retrieves the final component Satori needs to build a gravity bomb. Satori, through Frank, issues an ultimatum to the world which now thinks Super Force is evil. Satori's next assignment for Frank is to kill his brother, Zach. Zach, determined to save his brother, as well as the world, puts on his old suit and faces Frank with a Hemispheric Synchronizer designed to sever Satori's mind-hold. Once Frank's mind is restored, he and Zach, in the two Super Force suits with force shields activated, surround the bomb, forcing it to self-destruct. Frank then leaves Zach to plan revenge on Satori, and the Governing Council formally thanks Super Force for saving the world. **Guest cast:** G. Gordon Liddy as Satori, Marshall Teague as Frank Stone, Jr., Anthony Corone, Peter Palmer as Taggert, Paul Vroom as guard #1, Roger Floyd as the prisoner, Wendy Chioji as the TV newscaster, Greg Anderson as the S.P.L.A.T. member. **Writers:** R.L. Taylor, Bruce A. Taylor, Jeff Mandel. **Director:** Les Landau.

Water Mania (airdate: Dec. 16, 1990). There's an extortion racket on "The Strip" and protection money is being demanded from all the businesses, including Bobby Monroe, Zack's friend who owns a dance club. Zach traces the extortion ring to Mink Navarro, a mob leader. When Bobby can't meet Mink's monetary demands, Mink's goons attack the club. Super Force drops into the party, foiling their attempt to destroy the club. **Guest cast:** Jackie Gayle as Bobby Monroe. **Writers:** R.L. Taylor, Bruce A. Taylor, Jeff Mandel. **Director:** Jerry Lewis.

Sins of the Father, part one (airdate: Jan. 6, 1991). A prison gang escapes, killing two armed guards, and taking an unwilling convict, Chris King, with them. For the killing of the guards, each of the escapees has a $100,000 price on his head and is declared D6-14 - wanted dead or alive. Chris' father, Bud King, enlists Zach's help to save his son from Dr. Lotar Presley, an ex-secret agent turned bounty hunter, who is hunting the escapees with armor and weapons even Super Force has never seen. Zach is unable to reason with Presley or to have Chris removed from the D6-14 list, and when Bud explains that it is his fault that Chris turned to crime, Super Force takes over. As the black knight steps between Presley and the last of the other escapees, the bounty hunter throws a small weapon which temporarily allows him to penetrate Super Force's force shield. Super Force is thrown into the wall by Presley's blow and lays motionless. **Guest cast:** Richard Lynch [*The Phoenix*] as Dr. Lotar Presley, Cecil Stone as the captain, Jeff Philips as Chris, Gary Elliot as Bud, Sharon Camille as Brook, Rob Bollinger as Billy, Mark Salem as Freon, Fred Ottaviano as Wink, Michael Kelly as Mr. Clifford, Steve Zurk as the guard, Ralph Wilcox as prisoner #1, Judy Clayton as Justice Vytek. **Writers:** Larry Brody and Janis Hendler. **Director:** Tom Desimone.

Sins of the Father, part two (airdate: Jan. 13, 1991). Super Force is only momentarily stunned by Presley's blast, and regains consciousness in time to save the escapee from certain death. Then, Zach pays a visit to Presley's lab, where he slips a homing device into his bag. Following the device, Zach is able to arrive on the scene to keep Presley from killing Chris. Although Chris gets away from Presley and Zach, he calls his father from the penthouse where he and his girlfriend are hiding out. Tracing the call through the tap that Zach put on Bud King's phone, Super Force reaches the penthouse just in time. There is a showdown with Presley, and Super Force must destroy him to save Chris. **Guest cast:** Richard Lynch [*The Phoenix*] as Dr. Lotar Presley, Cecil Stone as the captain, Jeff Philips as Chris, Gary Elliot as Bud, Sharon Camille as Brook, Rob Bollinger as Billy, Mark Salem as Freon, Fred Ottaviano as Wink, Michael Kelly as Mr. Clifford, Steve Zurk as the guard, Ralph Wilcox as prisoner #1, Judy Clayton as Justice Vytek. **Writers:** Larry Brody and Janis Hendler. **Director:** Tom Desimone.

Of Human Bondage (airdate: Jan. 20, 1991). Super Force, while out apprehending diamond thieves, happens upon three strange circular impressions in the ground giving off a type of radiation unknown on Earth. The Hungerford Computer immediately guesses it is extraterrestrial. When several local high school students disappear, Zach's police investigation leads him back to the area. Witnesses to two of the disappearances describe two unusually strong females spraying something on their friends, drawing a green glowing door in the air, and dragging their friends through it. Meanwhile, Hungerford, excited over the prospect of getting evidence of extraterrestrials, sends F.X. out to get dirt samples of the area where Super Force spotted the circular impressions. Hungerford is right, these impressions are made by an invisible space ship carrying two aliens who are collecting human specimens for an interplanetary zoo and F.X. becomes their final addition. Just as the ship is about to take off, Super Force finds it, blows a hole in the side, and rescues the students and his friend. **Guest cast:** Traci Lords as the first alien, Grace Phillips as the second alien. **Writers:** R.L. Taylor, Bruce A. Taylor and Jeff Mandel. **Director:** Sidney Mayers.

A Hundred Share (airdate: Jan. 27, 1991). A manipulative TV news reporter, Randi Rae Face, can't resist the offer of Bennett Herd to help her get one hundred percent of the viewing public watching her show. Herd plans to achieve this by using subliminal messages telling people to tell all their friends to watch Randi. Once Herd gets everyone watching her show, he plans to insert a subliminal message instructing the special guard for the Ambassador of the United Nations to assassinate the Ambassador. All would be lost except that Zach and F.X happen to watch the news with the Hungerford Computer. Since the computer is not affected, but Zach and F.X. obviously are, they determine that there are subliminal messages in the newscast which only affect humans. Hungerford figures out a way to monitor the messages so that he can find out what they're being told to do. On the night of the planned assassination, Hungerford discovers the message for the guard just in time for Super Force to save the Ambassador - and humiliate Zach's constant nemesis, Captain Merkel. **Guest cast:** Barbara Treutelaar as Randi Rae Face, Tristan Rogers as Bennett Herd. **Writers:** William Micklberry, R.L. Taylor, Bruce A. Taylor and Jeff Mandel. **Director:** Tom DeSimone.

Come Under the Way, part one (airdate: Feb. 3, 1991). Super Force saves a family that is attacked by a group of men in a van. When Zach's investigation leads him to the address the van is registered to (a bikini club called "The Plush Pony"), he encounters his old girlfriend, Crystal. Crystal disappeared while Zach was on his mission to Mars and, feeling scared and alone in Zach's absence, she joined a cult led by a Dr. Landru. Little information is available on the doctor, except that he writes fantasy books revolving around an island, and that he runs a string of places that attract those who are lonely and need help, preferably with money. Hungerford also comes up with the address of one of Landru's ex-wives. She invites Zach to a meeting for those interested in learning Landru's way but, feeling suspicious, she covertly takes his picture. Landru and his followers identify Zach as a cop and, when Zach is on his way out

of the meeting with Crystal, a car is waiting for him. The car plummets straight towards Zach and Crystal from four flights up, crashing and blowing up in a great ball of flame. **Guest cast:** Zander Berkeley as Dr. Landru, Ginger Lynn Allen as Crystal, Tim Powell, Catherine Hader as Cadet Kline, Peggy O'Neal as Mrs. Landru #4, Rita Rehn as Mrs. Landru #5, Justina Vail as the hostess, Tom Kouchalakos as Francis Merkel, Ed Amatrudo as Butch. **Writers:** Rod Taylor, Bruce Taylor, Jeff Mandell. **Director:** Russ Mayberry.

Come Under the Way, part two (airdate: Feb. 10, 1991). Zach gets himself and Crystal out of the way just as a car is about to crash into them. An autopsy of the driver shows some strange brain alterations, but the body is too badly destroyed to get any workable data. Zach continues to try to get Crystal to give him a chance to prove the truth to her, but she is unwilling to listen. Meanwhile, Dr. Landru decides to step up his plans and use his brain altering machine on more of his followers, rather that wait for them to "achieve enlightenment", rendering them completely helpless to his will. When three of Landru's followers are sent on a robbery, one is killed, and the autopsy shows a strange brain pattern, similar to that of the man who tried to kill Zach. He realizes that Landru is behind this, and that he must get Crystal away from him at all costs. Zach rushes to the club where she works, only to find that she is due to "come under the way" that night. F.X., who has been reading one of Landru's books, figures out where his hideout must be, and Super Force crashes through the shield around Landru's island just as he is modifying Crystal's brain. It looks as if Super Force is too late to save her, but using his force shield he is able to bring Crystal back from the hell to which Landru had sentenced her. **Guest cast:** Zander Berkeley as Dr. Landru, Ginger Lynn Allen as Crystal, Tim Powell, Catherine Hader as Cadet Kline, Peggy O'Neal as Mrs. Landru #4, Rita Rehn as Mrs. Landru #5, Justina Vail as the hostess, Tom Kouchalakos as Francis Merkel, Ed Amatrudo as Butch. **Writers:** Rod Taylor, Bruce Taylor, Jeff Mandell. **Director:** Russ Mayberry.

Tales of Future Past (airdate: Feb. 17, 1991). A black political leader is assassinated by three members of the People's Liberation Army, a group whose purpose is the destruction of democracy and the implementation of a fascist police state. Just after Super Force kills the three responsible for the murder and leaves the scene, Hallor S1 appears in the prop warehouse where Super Force caught two of the assassins. Hallor, a genetically engineered warrior from the future, was created by the People's Liberation Army and sent back to the past for the sole purpose of killing Super Force who is otherwise destined to kill the leader of the PLA, rendering them powerless in the future. Having missed Super Force at the warehouse and, knowing his dual identity, Hallor goes to the police station to leave a message for Zach. Hallor kills all the police officers in the station, then leaves a cryptic message which F.X. and Zach figure out is telling Super Force to meet Hallor at the prop house. Super Force goes to the warehouse but Hallor stays out of sight and follows him back to the Hungerford lab. Hallor breaks into the lab seconds after Zach has left and, thinking F.X. is Super Force, kills him instead. Zach, hearing the shots, runs back, finds F.X. dead and, seeing Hallor about to return to the future, shoots at him. When his bullets don't stop Hallor, Zach dives for him and they are both transported to the same site, 150 years in the future. Hungerford, still present in his computer form is able to electrocute Hallor but knows he must be killed in the past as well, to undo his slaughter of the police officers and F.X. Realizing that Hallor must have arrived at the prop house just after Super Force killed the PLA assassins (because of the message he left for Zach), Hungerford sends Super

Force back to that time. Super Force finds Hallor and they have a tremendous struggle ending with Super Force shooting Hallor through the eye, causing him to internally explode. **Guest cast:** Sting [pro wrestler] as Hallor, Tom Kouchalakos as Francis Merkel, Billie Gillespie as Taggert, Bryce Ward as Eckhart, Micha Espinosa as Rhea Nine, Angie Harper as the reporter. **Writers:** R.L. Taylor, Bruce A. Taylor and Jeff Mandel. **Director:** Rod Taylor.

Yo! Superforce (airdate: Feb. 24, 1991). A young girl disappears at a carnival, Candyland, while F.X. is there with his three cousins, L.X., G.X. and Otis X. When Zach investigates the disappearance, he learns that L.X. and G.X. disappeared (momentarily) at the same time as the girl and becomes suspicious. The Hungerford Computer can find no criminal record of F.X's cousins, but does find that this was not the first disappearance from Candyland. When Zach goes undercover at the boardwalk with Cadet Kline, she too disappears, taken as the first girl was, by Prof. Usher, the boardwalk's "Guess Your Weight/Age" man, to be frozen in time in his Hall of Beauty. While searching for Kline, Zach runs into the X's only to find that they are undercover police. Working together back at the lab, everyone realizes that Professor Usher must be behind the disappearances, and that one of them must go to Candyland in drag. They decide that F.X. is the only possible choice and he goes along with the scheme, very reluctantly. It turns out, however, that F.X is the image of Christine, the love of Professor Usher's life, who died 25 years ago. Of course, the Professor must add him to the collection. F.X.'s cousins and Zach follow the tracking device planted on F.X. while Hungerford tells them to wait, but the cousins won't stop. Hungerford manages to convince Zach that if he doesn't come back to the lab, he will not be able to save F.X. As the cousins are getting frozen by the Professor, Zach gets his Super Force gear and, returning in the suit, is able to withstand the immobilizer. As Super Force frees the women and the X's, he and the Professor fight it out, trading energy between the Professor's molecular immobilizer and Super Force's Gravitronic Shield. In the blast of green light, the battle ends as the Professor turns grey and lifeless, then disintegrates into dust. **Guest cast:** Dr. Dre, T-Money and Brian Perry as F.X's cousins, Rex Benson as Professor Usher, Catherine Hader as Cadet Kline, Jennifer Hawkins as Jennifer. **Writers:** R.L. Taylor, Bruce A. Taylor and Jeff Mandel. **Director:** Russ Mayberry.

Breakfast of Champions (airdate: March 10, 1991). When Zach stops a group of thugs from raiding a store, he realizes that one of them, Darrow, is different. Because Darrow seems to truly want to make something of himself, Zach takes him under his wing and brings him to an ex-fighter who will train Darrow to realize his dream - becoming a gladiator. But Darrow can't wait, and after a few months of practice, he joins a television gladiator show run by Kareem Feldman, in which the accent is on beating and maiming in the name of high ratings. When Darrow ends up losing a match, becoming paralyzed in the process, Zach investigates. The Hungerford Computer discovers a depressant drug, Toramine, in Darrow's system, leading Zach to believe that the fights are fixed by drugging whichever gladiator Feldman determines should be the loser. Zach goes undercover as a reporter for a video magazine about fighters and gets behind the scenes before a big match in which Hollander, the champion, will go against a female gladiator, Alexander, whom Zach has befriended. On the sidelines during the match, Zach sees Alexander slipping, and realizes that she must have been drugged just before the fight. He is able to get out the door to retrieve his suit and cycle in time to save Alexander, but first he must contend with the other gladiators. During Super Force's final fight, his opponent, the champion Hollander, falls onto an electrical grid and is killed. Super Force then collars Feldman, as we see the ratings soaring ever higher. **Guest cast:** Aaron Vaughn as Darrow, LeRoy Mitchell as Feldman, Dennis Alexio as Hollander, Corey Iverson as Alexander, Julia Michaels, Dennis Alexio as Hollander, LeRoy Mitchell, Jr. as Kareem Feldman, Joe Hess as Cominskey, R. Emmett Fitzsimmons as Casey, Aaron Vaughn as Darrow, Frank DeVito III as Bradley. **Writers:** Larry Brody, Robert L. Henry, Janis Hendler. **Director:** Jefferson Kibbee.

The Carcinoma Angels (airdate: March 17, 1991). A letter to Zach's brother, Frank Jr., addressed to the precinct is forwarded to Zach. The letter is from Mary McAdams, a woman whom, although Zach has never met her, was involved with Frank. Zach and F.X. set out to find Mary, but discover that they are not the only ones searching for her. Before Frank turned her away from a life of crime, Mary rode with an outlaw biker, Ginnis, who has just gotten out of prison after a five year sentence, and now wants to find his wife. Although Ginnis finds Mary first, Zach is right behind him and he and F.X. help break up the reunion which Mary definitely did not want. While the three of them have dinner at Mary's house, and she tells them about her relationship with Frank, Ginnis and his two cronies attack the house, kidnapping Mary. Mary tries to reason with Ginnis, to no avail. However, by interfacing with the central police computer, Hungerford is able to predict where Ginnis took Mary and Super Force is able to find them. He stuns Ginnis's two companions, but finds Ginnis more difficult to deal with. After a chase, and a showdown in a junkyard, Ginnis is pinned under his motorcycle which explodes into flames, taking him with it. **Guest cast:** Don Stroud as Ginnis, Carla Ferrigno as Mary, Marshall Teague as Frank Stone, Jr., Michael Walters as Torrey, Darlene Deacon as Elvin. **Writer:** E.B. Swirkal. **Director:** Robert Short.

There's a Light (airdate: March 24, 1991). Super Force is badly hurt and F.X. takes him home to the Hungerford Lab, the only possible place where he can be saved, but F.X. and Hungerford are in a quandary. Zach cannot be kept inside the suit, yet the suit is the only thing keeping him alive. F.X. and Hungerford work up a system through which they will disconnect Zach from the support system of the suit, one tier at a time. Meanwhile, although he is unconscious, Zach is dreaming, and Super Force has become a separate entity and the two of them are debating over which one of them is a monster. Super Force contends that Zach puts everyone around him in jeopardy, forcing Zach to think about the past as we see a montage of clips from the past episodes. Although Zach protests that he's helped a lot of people, Super Force corrects him - he's the one who's doing the helping - and we see another montage of clips to prove his point. The two of them continue to argue, while F.X. and Hungerford fear they are losing Zach. Indeed, although Super Force and Zach come to an understanding that together they've done the right thing all along, Super Force tells Zach their time is over, and Zach's vital signs go flatline. **Guest cast:** None. **Writers:** R.L. Taylor, Bruce A. Taylor and Jeff Nandel. **Director:** Michael Attanasio.

A Hero's Welcome, parts one and two (airdates: part one, April 21; part two, April 28, 1991). This is a two part edited version of the first half of the Super Force two hour pilot.

Too Late the Hero, parts one and two (airdates: May 5; part two, May 12, 1991). This is a two part edited version of the second half of the Super Force two hour pilot.

SEASON TWO

At the End of the Tunnel, part one (airdate: Oct. 6, 1991). As F.X. grieves over Zach's death, Hungerford tells him there's still hope. Zach is technically dead but Hungerford has connected himself to what he speculates is Zach's soul. Hungerford hooks F.X. up to Zach, to have his mind bring Zach back. F.X., however, only succeeds in having a lucid dream; he never enters Zach's mind. Hungerford then sends F.X. to get Zander Tyler, who has worked with Hungerford before. She is a pretty, intelligent police captain in the Esper Division, a low profile, psychic department. She uses her powers to project her mind into Zach's, a life threatening process, and something most psychics can't do. She enters his mind and convinces him that he wants to remain among the living - he has work to do. Alive once more, Zach wants to know how it all happened. F.X. blames himself for the helmet failure that caused the accident, but Zach absolves him, mysteriously saying he knows the helmet had been sabotaged, though he's not sure how he knows. Zach seems to have changed from the experience. He feels different, more aware - he's actually somewhat psychic. F.X. discovers that the helmet was indeed sabotaged, and believes that means someone else must know Zach is Super Force. **Guest cast:** Kevin Quigley as Crase. **Writers:** R.L. Taylor, Bruce A. Taylor and Jeff Mandel. **Director:** Tom DeSimone.

At the End of the Tunnel, part two (airdate: Oct. 13, 1991). F.X. discovers that Super Force's helmet was indeed sabotaged. F.X. and Hungerford tell Zach about the neurolink between him and Hungerford, though the origin and extent of his increased powers are still partially a mystery. F.X. and Zach go to Aerodyne Tech to investigate the helmet malfunction, where the sabotaged component was manufactured. They meet Beagle Crase, who says that the component had been made a long time ago and no one would remember much about the part - it's a unique piece and very few people would be capable of understanding it. Back at the lab, Zach displays amazing mathematical skills and an ability to see the entire electro-

magnetic spectrum. He also has the strength of 4.2 average men. Zach gets fed up with the tests and storms out to a bar, where Zander meets him. Zach reveals that he sees he has a mission now. His "death" and resurrection had a meaning. He is back to battle evil on a much grander scale than before. Meanwhile, Crase tells F.X. he knows who sabotaged the helmet. F.X. goes to Aerodyne where Crase reveals himself to be the saboteur. At the bar, Zander "picks up" that F.X. is in trouble. Crase, who once was to Hungerford what F.X. is now, sabotaged the helmet to get revenge on F.X. and is now going to kill him out of jealousy. He puts F.X. into a exquisitely painful torture machine. But Zach, as Super Force, is able to save him in time. Back at the lab, Zach explains to F.X., Hungerford, and Zander that he has foreseen many battles ahead and he needs his friends by his side. They are with him. **Guest cast** Kevin Quigley as Crase. **Writers:** R.L. Taylor, Bruce A. Taylor and Jeff Mandel. **Director:** Tom DeSimone.

Love Slaves of Outer Space (airdate: Oct. 20, 1991). In an episode from last season, two aliens in the shape of beautiful women were hired to go to Earth and capture humans for a menagerie. Super Force, of course, stopped them, damaging their ship in the process. As this episode opens, the two aliens are being sued by their former employer for breach of contract. They offer to go to Earth to retrieve Super Force but, if unsuccessful, they must become their former employer's love slaves for life. Upon arriving at Earth, the women begin their investigation to find Super Force. When they learn that he comes when there's trouble, naturally, they cause some. But what they get is Police Captain Merkel and his Splat team. They knock the team unconscious and take Merkel thinking, because of his uniform, that he is Super Force's child (his "shell" isn't hard yet). Super Force broadcasts a "1000 number" for the aliens to call and Merkel arranges the meeting, warning him (in police code) of danger. The aliens, however, are unsuccessful in capturing Super Force and end up at his mercy. They do not want to return to their planet to become love slaves, but Merkel wants to arrest them if they stay. Super Force talks Merkel into granting them field probation (he threatens to walk away and let him deal with the aliens alone otherwise) and the aliens are ready to begin their new life on Earth, with Zach Stone assigned as their probation officer. **Guest cast:** Grace Phillips as the first alien, Micha Espinosa as the second alien, Larry Bucklan as the manager, Philip Garcia as the first guy, Carl Erie Jahnsen as the prisoner. **Writers:** R.L. Taylor, Bruce A. Taylor and Jeff Mandel. **Director:** Sidney Hayers.

Light Around the Body (airdate: Oct. 27, 1991). Zander Tyler is haunted by visions of a woman being buried alive by a faceless man. Her superior, a psychiatrist named Sincara, appears concerned. Members of Esper are not supposed to have uncontrollable visions. Knowing this, Zander seeks help from Zach Stone. Zach and F.X., with the help of the Hungerford computer, search all reports of disappearances hoping to find a clue. The reports seem endless when Zander gets a vision of a street sign: Orange Drive. Zach has her go back to her office while he and F.X. cross reference "Orange" with the reports of missing people. They come up with no answers. Zach, still worried, finds that Zander never returned to her office. He begins to get visions of her, that she's in danger and he sees the street sign "Orange Drive", while Hungerford points out that Sincara means roughly in Spanish "without a face." Indeed, it was Sincara all along who was putting visions into Zander's mind to lure her to a place on Orange Drive, there to punish her for spurning his advances by burying her alive. He has set the building, including the coffin he puts Zander into, with booby traps. It is also he that lures

Zach to her thinking she is in love with him. And Zach, afraid that arriving as Super Force might precipitate disaster, goes without the suit. He finds that his new powers allow him to see Zander beneath the ground. He sets off a trip wire but is able to duck in time as Sincara comes out from hiding. They exchange shots. Zach then senses a mine just as he's about to step on it. He triggers it with a brick and, when Sincara pops up to see if Zach is dead, kills him. As Zach approaches the spot where Zander is buried, she sends him images of explosions - she too is booby trapped. Carefully, Zach brushes the dust from atop the coffin and sees the explosive attached to the lid. It will detonate just :04 after he touches it. Zach gathers his powers and tosses the lid aside, jumping in to shield Zander. The bomb goes off harmlessly as Zach repays Zander for saving his life. **Guest cast:** Ed Amatrudo as Dr. Sincara. **Writers:** R.L. Taylor, Bruce A. Taylor and Jeff Mandel. **Director:** Sidney Hayers.

Instant Karma (airdate: Nov. 3, 1991). Zach investigates a cult leader who's been having rich people sign their wills over to him. It seems routine; the leader Max Offal gathers people and has a woman "channel" an ancient spirit who talks through her to the audience. It does not seem like an unusual case until Zach sees that the channeller is Crystal Chandler, his old girlfriend whom he'd previously saved from a cult [in an episode last season]. Zach convinces Crystal to come to Hungerford Labs. There she channels the spirit Bobakava who is able to beat Hungerford at chess. F.X. and Hungerford wonder how the trick is being played, while Zach insists he feels a presence inside Crystal. Zach goes to investigate Max's headquarters where he finds the hypnotizing machine that Max has been using to control Crystal. Zach returns to the lab, thinking he was wrong about the presence, where F.X. and Hungerford tell him there really was a spirit inside Crystal. The chess moves she made correspond exactly to the logic used by a first century poet and mathematician Bobakava. It seems that Max unknowingly has been having Crystal channel a real spirit, convincing rich people to turn over their wills to Max, then using his hypno machine to make them commit suicide. But when Max sees Crystal converse with Bobakava, he thinks she's crazy and decides it will be safest to eliminate her and plans for her to commit suicide on stage at a cult meeting. Just as Crystal grabs a bodyguard's gun and is about to shoot herself, Zach arrives and appeals to Bobakava to come and save Crystal. Bobakava, realizing that Max has used him to cheat people of their money and their lives, decides to kill him. Bobakava is about to use Crystal to shoot Max, when Zach reminds him that if he does, she'll have to stand trial. Bobakava then enters Max and makes him shoot himself saying with Max's last dying breath that people aren't ready for his wisdom yet. **Guest cast:** Ginger Lynn Allen as Crystal Chandler, Jordon Williams as Max Offal, Ron Russell as the bodyguard. **Writers:** R.L. Taylor, Bruce A. Taylor and Jeff Mandel. **Director:** Tom DeSimone.

Hank's Back, part one (airdate: Nov. 10, 1991). A country singer, Hank, was cryogenically frozen in the 70s, he claims so that he could be thawed when country music became popular again. In reality, Hank was frozen by his manager, Col. Partridge, to get Hank away from the Mob from whom the colonel had borrowed a large sum of money. But the Mob's collection agency still has records of the debt, and sends two henchmen, Gunnar and Ratso, to thaw Hank out and get the money. Hank gets away from the two Mob men, goes to a bar and meets Zach and F.X. They take Hank back to the lab, and Zach leaves Hank in F.X.'s care while he investigates the singer's story. While Zach is out, Hank insists on leaving, so F.X. goes along to watch him, making sure he has the Emergency Telemetry Cartridge

with which he can call Super Force. As Zach returns to the lab and Hungerford explains what he's found out about Hank's financial difficulties, Hank and F.X. are enjoying themselves at another bar - until Gunnar and Ratso show up. F.X. sends off a signal to Super Force as he and Hank fight with the two "collectors". When Super Force shows up, Hank gets away from Gunnar and Ratso but they take F.X. hostage, dropping a plasma grenade, capable of killing everyone in the bar. **Guest cast:** Keith Joe Dick as Hank, Kelley Mullis as Gina, Jill Schumacher as the young girl, James Zelley as the security guard, Marc Macauley as Ratso, Ralph Wilcox as Gunnar, Mal Jones as Col. Partridge. **Writers:** R.L. Taylor, Bruce A. Taylor and Jeff Mandel. **Director:** Roderick L. Taylor.

Hank's Back, part two (airdate: Nov. 17, 1991). Super Force covers the grenade with his body, allowing it to detonate harmlessly. Hank reveals that he has the Telemetry Cartridge, so there is no way to track F.X. Hank returns to Zach and Hungerford, where they get a call from Ratso and Gunnar giving Hank twenty-four hours to find the money. In his anger at getting F.X. in trouble, Hank smashes his guitar (which had been frozen with him) and finds a map which his manager, the colonel, placed there. Zach and Hank follow them and find a suitcase, empty but for a note from the colonel saying that since Hank had the talent, he needed the money. Hank is not ready to give up so quickly, however, and is determined to see if the colonel might still be alive. He recalls that the colonel always swore by a quart of "Slow as Black Strap" molasses a day, and believes he knows where the colonel might be. First, however, he must meet with Ratso and Gunnar, and explain that he needs more time to get the money. While Zach goes to the Precinct, Hank takes it upon himself to meet the two mobsters, and they give him another twenty-four hours. As Hank goes to find the colonel, Zach returns to the lab, where Hungerford has traced the location to which a case of the colonel's favorite molasses has been delivered each month. Indeed, at 110 years old, the colonel is alive - sort of. All that's left is his head, which is hooked up to a device that keeps him alive - and he's still eating his molasses. Hank confronts him and he explains that he would have left Hank everything, but there's no cash. Just then, Ratso and Gunnar arrive, having followed Hank to the colonel. Luckily, Super Force is not far behind and, although the colonel is temporarily disconnected from part of his life support, he lives through the event. Hank knocks Ratso unconscious while Super Force shoots Gunnar. And, after it all, the colonel is still eating his molasses and Hank is back on stage - now he has a fifty year old tax debt to pay off. **Guest cast:** Keith Joe Dick as Hank, Kelley Mullis as Gina, Jill Schumacher as the young girl, James Zelley as the security guard, Marc Macauley as Ratso, Ralph Wilcox as Gunnar, Mal Jones as Col. Partridge. **Writers:** R.L. Taylor, Bruce A. Taylor and Jeff Mandel. **Director:** Roderick L. Taylor.

Ghost in the Machine (airdate: Nov. 24, 1991). Dr. Richard Olcott, the obnoxious psychic host of a radio call-in show, is attacked by a mysterious green energy over the phone and then kills himself. Zach Stone and Zander Tyler investigate. Olcott is a true psychic who had applied for Esper Division at the same time as Zander but decided to do the radio show instead. Zander takes over the show (since she's a psychic) hoping to find a clue. F.X. studies the tapes of the show after which Olcott committed suicide. He hears a weird noise much like a fax machine come over the air right before Olcott killed himself. He has Hungerford analyze it. Meanwhile, Zander is attacked by the same green energy via the same phone noise and her personality begins to change. As Zach and F.X. wonder what's going on, Hungerford determines that the noise on the tape con-

Bruno, Jim Greene as Nathan Phillips, Roger Floyd as Biff, Jim Cordes as Winston. **Writers:** R.L. Taylor, Bruce A. Taylor and Jeff Mandel. **Director:** Richard Compton.

Made for Each Other, part two (airdate: Dec. 8, 1991). Zach detects the bomb in time to alert the office and no one is hurt by the explosion. Zach has Winston pretend to be dead so whoever tried to kill him (it was his wife) won't do it again. Then Zach and F.X. go undercover at the college posing as rich students who want to take Caesar's course. He wants to date one of the women to find out how they are being controlled and made to marry and kill wealthy men. He meets one of the coeds and follows her to Caesar's lab. There he overhears Caesar say she knows Winston's still alive and must be killed. Zach investigates the lab and sees that the computers are controlling the girls. He returns to Hungerford lab where they decide the best way to save Winston, since they don't know where he is, is to go back to Caesar's lab and destroy her computer. Zach, as Super Force, returns to the lab and, after struggle with the controlled girls, Caesar, and her two male henchmen, destroy the computer. The girls are freed but Dr. Caesar meets her untimely end, killed by one of her men's stray bullets. **Guest cast:** Candace Critchfield as Dr. Calphurnia Caesar, Maria Canals as Lori Wechsler, Tamara Glynn as Nikki Philips, Von Von Lindenberg as Bruno, Jim Greene as Nathan Phillips, Roger Floyd as Biff, Jim Cordes as Winston. **Writers:** R.L. Taylor, Bruce A. Taylor and Jeff Mandel. **Director:** Richard Compton.

Illegal Aliens (airdate: Feb. 2, 1992). Two aliens were allowed to remain on Earth rather than return to their own planet and become love slaves for life. Zach was assigned as their probation officer and he's finding that they have a great deal of trouble assimilating into Earth's culture. But the trouble gets worse when an alien law enforcer, Nomad, comes to take the aliens back to their planet to serve their sentence. Zach manages to put him off the track long enough for Hungerford and F.X. to come up with a weapon to defeat Nomad - his true form is pure energy and any conventional weapon will only make him stronger. Super Force and Nomad meet in the field near the other aliens' ship and begin battling while F.X. tries to analyze Nomad's energy spectrum so that Super Force can use a negative energy gun on him. Just as F.X. gets the proper reading, Nomad knocks the weapon out of Super Force's hand and it is up to F.X. to fire off the fatal blow. When all is over, the two aliens arrive and insist on leaving earth. They reason that more enforcers will show up, and they must hide in another dimension until they can decide what to do. **Guest cast:** Grace Phillips as the second alien, Micha Espinosa as the first alien, Jeff Moldovan as Nomad, Peter Paul de Leo as the biker, Larry Bucklan as the manager, Buddy Reynolds as Jack. **Writers:** R.L. Taylor, Bruce A. Taylor and Jeff Mandel. **Director:** Sidney Hayers.

The Viral Staircase, part one (airdate: Feb. 9, 1992). Brigette, a woman who went through astronaut training with Zach, is part of an eco-terrorist group which infiltrates Hungerford Industries. Super Force stops them before they can do damage, but one of the group is missing. Later at the precinct, Brigette tells Zach that she quit the astronaut program to help save the Earth from biological weapons, which she insists are being produced at the Hungerford compound. Zach and F.X. check out her story and find suspicious supplies being ordered by a new researcher, Dr. Biggs, who, along with his assistant Megan, is supposedly looking for a cure for cancer. After Zach and F.X. leave their lab, we find out what happened to the fifth member of Brigette's group - the two researchers have given him a

tained a computer virus so sophisticated it could attack a human with psychic powers. Zach, realizing that the virus must have caused Zander's personality change, goes to the station and finds Zander about to shoot herself. Zach subdues her and takes her back to the lab where F.X. hooks her up to Hungerford who will try to draw the virus from her and destroy it. If he fails, he'll die and Zach, who is connected to him via a neurolink, will die as well. Zander, empowered by the virus, unhooks herself and attacks. Zach pleads with the virus that's taken over her personality to infect him instead. Zander kisses Zach, transferring the virus to him. F.X. quickly hooks Zach to Hungerford and, after a violent electronic struggle, the virus is destroyed. **Guest cast** Jacob Witkin as Dr. Richard Olcott, Raynor Adams as Bowie, Jack Swanson as Dr. Morris, Stan Lee Rice as One-eyed Jackson. **Writers:** R.L. Taylor, Bruce A. Taylor and Jeff Mandel. **Director:** Chip Chalmers.

Made for Each Other, part one (airdate: Dec. 1, 1991). A female college professor, Dr. Calphurnia Caesar, is implanting electronic devices into the brains of pretty young coeds, allowing her to control them. Zach, unaware of this, is assigned to find one of these women, Nikki Philips, who has disappeared (because Caesar needed to readjust her implant). Just after Zach finds Mrs. Philips on campus, she returns to her husband, only to kill him. Zach discovers that a great many older, wealthy men have been taking one of Dr. Caesar's classes "Wealth Without Guilt" and have been marrying women from Caesar's "Thinking about Thinking" class, whom she has used for her brain devices. Then he learns that Philips' widow has left all her inherited money to the Caesar Research Institute, run by none other than Calphurnia. Zach phones Philips' best friend and lawyer, Clark Winston, and asks him to come to the precinct. Winston has also married one of Caesar's students via the wealth class. As Zach talks to him, he sense heat from Winston's briefcase and rips it open to find a time bomb that's ready to explode. **Guest cast:** Candace Critchfield as Dr. Calphurnia Caesar, Maria Canals as Lori Wechsler, Tamara Glynn as Nikki Philips, Von Von Lindenberg as deadly virus. When the body is found, the autopsy clues Zach and F.X. in on what the doctor is up to as he prepares his next victim - Brigette! **Guest cast:** Tristan Rogers as Dr. Biggs, Janet Gunn as Bridget Cross, Carrell Myers as Dr. Megan Gardner, Thomas McNamara as the apprentice Coroner Biddle, Jack Swanson as Dr. Morris, Eddie Earl Hatch as Ray. **Writers:** R.L. Taylor, Bruce A. Taylor and Jeff Mandel. **Director:** Michael Attanasio.

The Viral Staircase, part two (airdate: Feb. 16, 1992). After doing some research into Biggs' past, Hungerford finds out that he is one of the world's most-wanted criminals. Hungerford is discovered trying to break into Biggs' computer, who then manage to trace Hungerford's tap back to his secret lab, just as Hungerford fries the scientist's computer. While Biggs and Megan try to find the exact location of Hungerford's lab, F.X. and Zach pay a visit to Biggs' lab. They find nothing but a dying Brigette and hurry back to Hungerford whom Biggs was unable to locate. Biggs is able, however, to penetrate the Hungerford computer and he explains to Zach and F.X. that the virus is his plan to destroy the weaker humans which technology has allowed to survive. When Biggs releases the virus into the air system, Hungerford seals off their area, and Zach puts on the Super Force suit, which will protect him against the virus. At the same time, Ray and the remainder of Brigette's group are preparing to blast their way into the facility. While Hungerford and F.X. search for their own antidote, Super Force goes in pursuit of Biggs and his formula. He downs Megan, but Biggs gets past him and heads out. Biggs is not so lucky with Ray, however, who manages to shoot the scientist even though the virus began taking control of his body as soon as he entered the building. In all the destruction, though, there is a breath of fresh air - F.X. and Hungerford discover that sunlight kills the virus, which is now dying even as it breaks forth into the outside air. **Guest cast:** Tristan Rogers as Dr. Biggs, Janet Gunn as Bridget Cross, Carrell Myers as Dr. Megan Gardner, Thomas McNamara as the apprentice Coroner Biddle, Jack Swanson as Dr. Morris, Eddie Earl Hatch as Ray. **Writers:** R.L. Taylor, Bruce A. Taylor and Jeff Mandel. **Director:** Michael Attanasio.

The Big Spin (airdate: Feb. 23, 1992). Zach is sitting at a bar with his old girlfriend, Crystal Chandler, as she fills him in on her latest kick - astrology. She insists that she's going to win the lottery which is up to a billion dollars because her horoscope predicts she's going to have a great "financial opportunity." She and Zach buy a ticket and he returns to the Hungerford lab with it in his wallet for safekeeping. When he gets there, F.X. is on a ladder working on the Super Force suit and drops a wrench on Zach's head. Zach is knocked unconscious and begins to dream, turning the Super Force set into a sitcom, complete with audience. In the dream, Zach finds he has the winning lottery number only to discover he's lost the ticket. Zach, F.X., and Crystal go on to search all over for the ticket in what amounts to a typical slapstick comedy. At the end, Zach learns there is a 101% tax on the winnings, and he actually owes the government ten million dollars. When he finally wakes, and F.X. tells him what happened, he realizes it was all a dream - then the ticket falls out of his wallet! **Guest cast:** Ginger Lynn Allen as Crystal Chandler, Phil Card as Wink, Kristian Truelson as the tax man, Siobhan McNamara as the little girl. **Writers:** R.L. Taylor, Bruce A. Taylor and Jeff Mandel. **Director:** Tom DeSimone.

The Luddite Crusade (airdate: Mar. 1, 1992). Patricia Luddite, of the District Attorney's office, has decided to make her career move and she's basing it on putting away Super Force as a criminal. To help her convince Police Commissioner Pfister of Super Force's guilt, she uses computer generated imagery, taken from the memories, brain scans, and statements of witnesses. Also present at the demonstration is Merkel, who has always had it in for Super Force, and Zach, who was invited along with any other officers who cared to attend, though the invitation was purposely sent out after midnight. Throughout the demonstration, Luddite has clipped out parts of the reenactments, so that the footage clearly condemns Super Force as behaving illegally. The information is so stacked against Super Force that Pfister is ready to sign a warrant for his arrest allowing officers to shoot to kill if necessary. Zach runs out to get F.X. who shows up just as Pfister has received the necessary forms to sign. He agrees to wait until he sees F.X.'s demonstration during which Spinner takes Luddite's computer disc and retrieves the information which she purposely blanked out, now showing the whole story. Super Force is seen to be the hero he is, and Luddite herself is targeted for the next investigation. **Guest cast:** Timothy Leary as Police Commissioner Pfister, Julie Austin as Patricia Luddite, Jackie Gale as Bobby Monroe, Richard Lynch as Lothar Presley, Rob Bollinger as Billy, Ed Amatrudo as Butch, Tim Powell as the father, Steve DuMouchel as the first cop, Robb Morris as the second cop. **Writers:** R.L. Taylor, Bruce A. Taylor and Jeff Mandel. **Director:** Robert Short.

King of the Trees (airdate: March 23, 1992). A scientist, Dr. DeNunzio, and his assistant Katy are examining some samples from a dig when they discover a humanoid creature. Although they believe it is some kind of a preserved missing link, it comes to life and breaks out of the lab. The police are alerted and Merkel is ready to take it in dead or alive - preferably dead. Zach and F.X. try to find the creature first, and pay a visit to Dr. DeNunzio where F.X. steals one of the blood samples that DeNunzio had taken before the creature got away. As they analyze the blood and decide that the creature cannot be from Earth, Zach gets reports of strange breaking and enterings during which the creature has stolen old rocks and twigs. Zach arrives at the scene where Merkel has the creature cornered and tries to reason with it, but it misunderstands and Merkel captures it before it can seriously hurt Zach. Once the creature is behind bars, though, Zach is able to communicate with it and learns its name is Iau. Iau is from another dimension and, because of rivalries between priests in his world, their sacred flame was transported to Zach's dimension, Iau, as the most powerful priest, transported himself to retrieve the flame which had broken into the pieces of rock and wood that he had been retrieving. As the court rules to allow Dr. DeNunzio to have the creature for research, Zach and F.X. pretend that F.X. is the doctor's assistant, and Iau is released into his custody. They immediately free Iau, allowing him to collect his sacred flame and go back to his own dimension. **Guest cast:** Tom Nowicki as Dr. DeNunzio, Angie Harper as Katy, Kevin Nash as Iau. **Writers:** R.L. Taylor, Bruce A. Taylor and Jeff Mandel. **Director:** William Mickleberry.

A Rainbow at Midnight (airdate: Apr. 26, 1992). As three punks trash an old bum's shack and start going for Bartok, the bum, F.X. and Zach happen by and break things up. While Zach is arresting them, they hear a volley of gunshots and one of the punks goes down. And although the kid is clearly dead, he wasn't hit by a bullet. Later, back in the lab, Zach sees a cop who is bleeding from a horrible stomach wound. He believes the apparition is real until it vanishes into thin air. Confused, Zach goes to his psychic friend, Zander, for help. Piecing together clues from the apparition, they discover the cop died twenty years earlier in an incident dubbed the

Tower Massacre. His name was Rathman and he, along with his partner Bartok and a rookie cop, was attacked in the same alley where Zach found the bum, Bartok and the punks. While Zach and Zander make this discovery, one of the punks is talking to Merkel, seeking immunity in exchange for fingering Zach as the one who killed his friend. As Merkel fills Zach in on the situation, the kid begins to clutch his chest and falls to the floor, dead. Only Zach sees the image of Rathman leaving the office. When the third punk, Rammer, comes into the precinct to seek asylum, Merkel hands him over to Zach, who has an idea. He takes Rammer and Zander to the alley where Rathman reappears and together they convince him to forgive himself and his

Taylor, Jon Ezrine, and Jeff Mandel. **Director:** Chip Chalmers.

The Monkey's Breath (airdate: May 3, 1992). A mysterious woman, Mariah Black, steps into a bar and hypnotizes a young girl with psychic powers, convincing the girl to leave with her. Black

murderers. As Bartok, lucid for a moment, forgives his partner, Rathman feels the weight and guilt of the last twenty years fall off and, bathed in a rainbow of light, he passes on to a better place. **Guest cast:** Tom Schuster as Rathman, Michael George Owens as Bartok, Javi Mulero as Rammer. **Writers:** R.L. Taylor, Bruce A.

brings the girl before a shrine in her apartment featuring a monkey's head and paws. Chaining the girl to a pole, she begins a ritual which ends with her biting the girl's neck and draining her life force. Investigating the bar, Zach feels great evil and enlists Zander's psychic help. While at Zander's office, Zach meets her new commanding officer, none other than Mariah Black, yet he does not feel the same evil. But Mariah feels his power, and decides that with the life force of Zander and Zach, she will remain strong for a long time. She is able to overcome Zander, whom she brings back to her altar and chains to the pole. Then, Black goes after Zach, who does not resist. When he sees Zander, though, he recovers. The two join minds and, between them both, are able to overcome Black and destroy her. **Guest cast:** Peggy O'Neal as Mariah Black, Donna Rosae as Patrice, Jack Swanson as Dr. Morris, Carla Maria Kneeland as Anna. **Writers:** R.L. Taylor, Bruce A. Taylor and Jeff Mandel. **Director:** Sidney Hayers.

The End of Everything, part one (airdate: May 10, 1992). A break-in at Epsilon Corporation puts Zach on the case and he is given a list of the stolen items by Eve, the assistant to the president. When F.X. goes over the list with the Hungerford Computer, it seems to point to nanotechnology - machines the size of atoms that take molecules apart and put them back together any way they're programmed to. Nanotechnology is illegal, however, because if there's a programming error, they might not put the atoms back together at all. And if they went haywire, they could turn the whole world into grey goo. When Zach goes to talk to the president of the company, Slate, he meets up with Eve again. Later, over drinks, she admits to him the real story. The people who stole the equipment, Joe, Carl and Mary, are plasmoids, synthetically created humans with real thoughts and emotions. They were created at Epsilon Corporation so that they would die after a short lifespan and customers would have to buy the latest model. The plasmoids hope that they can use nano machines to undo the death program within them. Zach agrees that the plasmoids deserve a chance at a longer life, but if the nano machines get out of hand, he fears they could destroy the world. When the plasmoids reenter Epsilon in search of the nano machines, Slate's trap which Eve warned them about is waiting. Just as they get past a team of guards, Super Force shows up. He stuns Carl, and is trying to talk Mary and Joe into giving him the stolen canister of nanomachines when more guards show up shooting. **Guest cast:** Bryce Ward as Slate, Tamara Tibbs as Eve, Rob Richards as Joe, James Short as Carl, Robin O'Dell as Mary. **Writers:** R.L. Taylor, Bruce A. Taylor and Jeff Mandel. **Director:** Tom DeSimone.

The End of Everything, part two (airdate: May 17, 1992). Super Force protects Joe, Carl and Mary from Slate's guards, then takes the canister of nano-machines from the plasmoids. Then, distraught that he is resigning the three to die, Zach tries to figure out a way to save them that won't compromise world safety. Finally, he decides that the programming of the nano-machines should be done by F.X. and Hungerford, so that it can be achieved in a controlled environment. Though Eve has told him that the pituitary gland is the key to the death program, they are concerned that, like all living things, it might be interlinked with other biological systems. They need the specifications of the plasmoid anatomy, which can only come from Slate. When Zach goes to Slate to try to threaten him with his knowledge of the illegal nanotechnology, Slate informs him that not only is he authorized to work with those materials but that Eve,

whom Zach is falling in love with, is a plasmoid as well. For the time being, they must be content to buy time with the programming that F.X. can do on his own. Carl's not willing to wait however and, after attacking Slate, they both wind up dead. When Zach meets Eve at the plasmoids hideout, he is forced to tell her what she really is. They find that both Mary and Joe are dead as well and, though Eve injects herself with the nanomachines, there is no telling if they'll actually work. **Guest cast:** Bryce Ward as Slate, Tamara Tibbs as Eve, Rob Richards as Joe, James Short as Carl, Robin O'Dell as Mary. **Writers:** R.L. Taylor, Bruce A. Taylor and Jeff Mandel. **Director:** Tom DeSimone.

Long Journey Home (airdate: May 24, 1992). Zach and F.X. saved Iau, a creature from another dimension. Iau was trying to find the pieces of a religious icon, so that he could return to his home, but he must wait for a specific alignment of the planets. In the meantime, he goes to the lab where he was found and steals some plutonium, upon which he feeds. While waiting in the woods for midnight to arrive on the day he can return, he meets a young boy, Jamie. Jamie has a crystal which his mother found in the woods which Iau needs to reach his dimension. As they talk, Merkel, who is bent on finding and killing Iau, use the plutonium to trace him and his team closes in. Iau is forced to grab Jamie and run, as the cops begin to open fire, endangering the boy. Both Jamie and Iau have been shot but, after eating the rest of the plutonium, Iau is able to heal himself and Jamie. When Zach checks out the woods later, he finds all of Iau's religious artifacts and gathers them so no one will steal them, knowing Iau can trace them to the lab. He shows up there with Jamie and F.X. learns that Iau also cured the boy of his formerly incurable cancer. Jamie surrenders the crystal to Iau and together they all go back to the woods at midnight so Iau can return home. As Iau is transporting, Merkel shows up but it is too late. The giant healer has passed through to his own dimension, leaving the crystal for the boy. **Guest cast:** Kevin Nash as Iau, Tino Dean Taylor as Jamie. **Writers:** R.L. Taylor, Bruce A. Taylor and Jeff Mandel. **Director:** Sidney Hayers.

A Hundred Years A Second (airdate: May 31, 1992). F.X. has a new toy - a device which allows a person to relive memories with complete realism. When Zach interrupts him during a two-hour session of memories about women, F.X. insists that Zach try it out. He reluctantly agrees, but the affect is disastrous. Zach goes into a seizure and passes out. When F.X. is finally able to revive him, he has amnesia, and tries to choke F.X. Finally, Spinner gets Zach strapped down, and Hungerford reconfigures the machine to reconstruct Zach's identity. Again, the affects are unexpected. Zach is unable to separate his identity from that of others in his memory. They continue their efforts, hoping he will get himself straight, but after numerous flashbacks from past episodes, he is left catatonic. There is biological brain activity, but no functional activity. The last thing they can try is to use the link Hungerford has with Zach and re-input all his neural information, a process which may completely alter Zach's personality. The procedure drains all the power from the lab and fearing for the worst, they revive Zach only to find that he has no knowledge of what happened and thinks he's only been using the machine for five minutes. **Guest cast:** Musetta Vander as Zander Tyler, Sting as Halar, Kevin Quigley as Beagle Cross, Grace Phillips as alien #1, Micha Espinosa as alien #2, Peggy O'Neil as Marian Black, Ginger Lynn Alan as Crystal Chandler. **Writers:** R.L. Taylor, Bruce A. Taylor and Jeff Mandel. **Director:** John H. Radulovic.

Lois and Clark
The New Adventures of Superman

season one review by Jim Faerber

Production credits:

Executive Producer	Deborah Joy LeVine
Music	Jay Gruska
Superman created by	Jerry Seigel and Joe Shuster

Regular cast:

Superman/Clark Kent	Dean Cain
Lois Lane	Teri Hatcher
Jimmy Olsen	Michael Landes
Perry White	Lane Smith
Catherine "Cat" Grant	Tracy Scoggins
Jonathan Kent	Eddie Jones
Martha Kent	K Callan
Lex Luthor	John Shea

Number of episodes:	1 two-hour pilot,
	20 one-hour segments

Premise: The adventures of Lois Lane, ace reporter for the Daily Planet, and Clark Kent, recent transplant from Kansas, who harbors that familiar super-secret. Unlike any other comic book series to make it to television, this series favors an emphasis on whimsical romance and snappy banter rather than science fiction and action-adventure. The rest of the cast includes Perry White, the Planet's Editor-in-Chief; Jimmy Olsen, a cub reporter; Cat Grant, the society columnist; Johnathan and Martha, Clark's adoptive parents; and Lex Luthor, the richest man in Metropolis, and secretly a criminal mastermind.

Writer's comments: This series has caused more of a stir in the comics community than the casting of Michael Keaton as Batman. While comics fans want a virtual recreation of their favorite comic on the small screen, series like that have almost always failed. While I thoroughly enjoyed the syndicated *Superboy*, I'm still amazed that it lasted for four seasons, considering it was probably the truest interpretation of a comic book to ever grace the small screen, including *The Flash*, which I believe had too much emphasis on the Flash's life as a cop. At any rate, executive producer Deborah Joy LeVine decided to make her focus the relationship between Lois, Clark and Superman, even going so far as to promote the show as "The First Love Triangle Between Two People." With this slant, Superman is reduced to basically cameo appearances in some episodes. Still, comics fans are evenly split: they either love or hate the show; there seems to be no middle ground. I, for one, enjoy the show, mainly because of it's many brilliant touches. For instance, in one episode, Clark plays baseball-against himself. In another, he talks to his parents on the phone while standing on the ceiling. When he's bored, he paces back and forth, up and down the wall. When he

sees Lois all dressed up for the first time, he unconsciously floats a few feet off the ground. He calls his mom for advice on how to get a stain out of his uniform. But people who were initially turned off by the show should take another look next season. Deborah Joy LeVine has been replaced as executive producer with James Crocker, formerly Deep Space Nine's Supervising Producer [LeVine will be kept around as Executive Consultant, however]. Crocker's main goal will be to bring in the action adventure aspects that were sorely lacking in season one.

SEASON ONE

Lois and Clark (airdate: Sep. 12, 1993 two hour pilot movie). Clark Kent arrives in Metropolis and lands a job with the Daily Planet, a large newspaper. When the space transport, Messenger, explodes, Clark is teamed with ace reporter Lois Lane to interview Dr. Samuel Platt, a scientist who worked on Messenger and predicted disaster. But Platt has since been fired and now lives in poverty on the waterfront. He tells the reporters that he knew Messenger was unsafe and stated so in his report. He soon found, however, that his reports had been altered. Later, the reporters talk to Dr. Toni Baines, head of the Eprad space program, who dismisses everything Platt said.

That night Clark escorts Lois to reclusive billionaire Lex Luthor's extravagant party, where Luthor unveils plans to fund a privately owned space station, Station Luthor. The following day, Clark saves a city worker who was caught in an under ground explosion, and while doing so, ruins his business suit. This prompts him to wonder if there isn't a better way to perform his good deeds. Upon returning to Platt's for another interview, Lois and Clark find he has committed suicide. Meanwhile, the United Nations has turned down Luthor's bid to fund Station Luthor in favor of trying to salvage their own Prometheus Program. After Perry White refused to publish Lois and Clarks's story about the unproven sabotage of Messenger and murder of Platt, Lois and photographer, Jimmy Olsen, go to Eprad in hopes of finding evidence of Platt's theory.

Unfortunately, Dr. Baines (secretly in league with Luthor) manages to capture them. When Clark arrives and finds them in danger, he allows himself to be captured with them so he won't reveal his powers. When Bains starts a chemical leak which will explode, Clark frees himself and rescues Jimmy and Lois. As Baines makes her escape aboard a helicopter, Luthor triggers a bomb, which kills her. The following day, a new transport is set to launch and Lois sneaks aboard to get the scoop. Meanwhile, in Smallville, Clark and his mom go through a variety of different costumes before hitting upon the right look.

While on board, Lois notices a bomb and tampers with some equipment to alert the space personnel. This delay is shown on TV, and, knowing that this is the last chance for the space program, Clark flies to the launchpad in his new costume. He finds Lois, and, with

(top) **Lane Smith as Perry White, Michael Landes as Jimmy Olsen,** (bottom) **Teri Hatcher as Lois Lane, Dean Cain as Clark Kent, Tracy Scoggins as Catherine "Cat" Grant, John Shea as Lex Luthor.**

seconds to spare, swallows the bomb. He then lifts the entire transport into space, where they link up with Prometheus. Later, Clark flies Lois back to the Daily Planet, where the entire newsroom is awestruck. When he leaves, Lois dubs him Superman, based on his "S" insignia. **Guest cast:** Elizabeth Barondes as Lucy Lane, Kenneth Tigar as Dr. Platt, Kim Johnston Ulrich as Dr. Baines, Mel Winkler as Inspector Henderson, Maggie Bly as Mrs. Platt, Lindsay Berkowitz as Amy Platt, Gloria LeRoy as Beartrice, Shaun Toub as Asabi, Jean Montanti as Newspaper Worker, Persis Khambatta as Chairperoson, Clyde Kusatsu [*Bring 'Em Back Alive*] as Launch Commander, Gerry Black as Head Colonist, Gregory Miller as Homeless Man, Kamala Dawson as Carmen Alvarado, Jim Wise as Man #1, Sean Moran as Man #3, Greg Collins as Man #2, Robert Rothewell as Security Guard, Lee Weaver as Supervisor, David Fury as Cop, Anne Wyndham as Reporter #2, Yolnda Gaskins as TV Announcer, Christopher Darga as Man with Binoculars, Timi Prulhiere as Soap Opera Actress, Scott McCray as Soap Opera Actor, Marco Hernandez as Worker, Jerry Hauck as Reporter #1, Gregory Paull as Elderly Woman, Adrian Ricard as Older Woman, Mark Frazer **Writer:** Deborah Joy LeVine. **Director:** Bob Butler.

Strange Visitor From Another Planet (airdate: Sept. 26, 1993). The Daily Planet is invaded by a group of FBI agents led by Jason Trask, who demand access to all information regarding Superman, as well as interrogation sessions with Lois and Clark. During Clark's debriefing, he is strapped to a polygraph, but is able to sweat it out by giving very vague answers, as well as using his powers. After the agents are called away, Perry realizes that their credentials are totally false, and no one in the government has ever heard of

Trask. Lois and Clark then visit with George Thompson, who has come to Metropolis to get to the bottom of Trask's mission. While Lois talks, Clark uses his X-Ray vision to peek inside Thompson's briefcase. What he sees is a file marked Smallville, 1966, the year Clark was found by the Kents.

Later, Lois follows Thompson to an abandoned warehouse. Once inside, Thompson orders Trask to surrender all authority of Bureau 39 [which investigates alien threats], but Trask has gone rogue, and kills Thompson. Meanwhile, Clark has returned to Smallville, where he questions his parents regarding his arrival. Johathan and Martha then take him to where they buried the rocket, but it's gone. The following day, Lois and Clark learn of Thompson's death. They then visit General Newcomb, who worked with Trask on the old project: Bluebook and Bureau 39. He disliked Trask, and gives the reporters a passkey to the warehouse. Once inside, Clark is shocked to find his rocketship among the many UFO's. When he picks up a strange orb, it somehow tells him he's from Krypton.

But before he can learn more, Trask and his men arrive and abduct the reporters. They are taken aboard a fighter jet, and Trask intends on dropping Lois, hoping Superman will come to her rescue. When Lois and Clark fight back, they both fall out of the jet, and as they fall, Clark swithces to Superman and saves Lois. Trask and his men, however, get away. After Trask has escaped, Lois and Clark take Perry to the Bureau 39 warehouse, but find it deserted, leaving Clark no ties to Krypton. **Guest cast:** Terrence Knox [*Tour of Duty*] as Jason Trask, Elizabeth Barondes as Lucy Lane, Joseph Campanella as George Thompson, George Murdock as Gen. Burton Newcomb, Tom Dugan as Soldier #1, Jeff Austin as Soldier #2, David St. James as Polygraph Technician, Randall Boffman as Government Agent, Alex Wexo as SWAT Leader, Steven E. Einsphar as Young Johnathan. **Writer:** Bryce Zabel. **Director:** Randall Zisk.

Neverending Battle (airdate: Oct. 3, 1993). Perry calls a special staff meeting, where he announces that the search for Superman will take precedence over all other stories. This outrages Lois, who considers Superman "hers." Meanwhile, Luthor holds a meeting with three other scientists, and they decide to put Superman through a series of tests designed to measure his powers. He has one scientist pose as a desperate man threatening to jump off a building. When Superman arrives to help the man, a second scientist jumps off a building clear across town. Superman sees this and catches her. Luthor had surveillance equipment set up and was able to time Superman's flight.

Later, Superman arrives at a bank to investigate a bomb threat. As soon as he goes inside, the bank explodes, having been detonated by Luthor. Lois and Clark then talk to a policeman, who says that there were surveillance cameras set up inside that didn't belong there, and that the bomb was detonated by remote control. Lois then realizes that someone purposely tried to kill Superman. Clark looks over the psychoanalytic profiles on the two jumpers and discovers that both of them worked for Luthor. Changing into Superman, he flies to Luthor's penthouse and confronts him. He goes on to demonstrate, in a rather threatening manner, some of his powers. While Luthor doesn't admit to anything, he says that, should Superman stay in Metropolis, people will be hurt. Superman then goes to his parents and tells them of his dilemma. Ultimately, he decides to quit being Superman for awhile.

Later, Lois and Clark talk about Superman and she convinces him that Superman will be missed and is needed. This inspires Clark and he goes back into action. Meanwhile, Luthor has found Superman's weakness: he has morals. **Guest cast:** Elizabeth Barondes as Lucy Lane, Larry Linville, Roy Brocksmith, Miguel A. Nunez, Jr., Tony Jay as Nigel, Brent Jennings, Mary Crosby as

Monique, Lou Cutell as Maurice, Ritch Brinkley as Stan, Shaun Toub as Asabi, Will Albert as Businessman, Yolanda Gaskins as Lnda Montaoya, Rosa Li as Japanese Woman #1, Saimi Nakamura as Japanese Woman #2, Louise Pellegrino Rapport as Grandmother. **Writer:** Dan LeVine. **Director:** Gene Reynolds.

I'm Looking Through You (airdate: Oct. 10, 1993). When Superman is awarded the key to Metropolis, he is overwhelmed by all the attention, and Lois is overwhelmed by the fact that Superman seemingly ignores her. Meanwhile, the city is being plagued by the Robin Hood-like crimes of a seemingly invisible man. Lois and Clark visit with Helene Morris, who claims to be the invisible man's wife. She shows them his lab and explains how his suit makes him invisible. Unfortunately, a nosey neighbor sells Helene's story to the tabloids, and Barnes, an escaped gold thief, steals the invisible fabric from the Morris' lab.

STAR labs, meanwhile, has figured out how Alan Morris becomes invisible: his suit reflects light to appear ultraviolet, the invisible part of the spectrum. But Barnes has since initiated his own crime spree, and his is geared toward violence and greed. In an attempt to clear his name, an invisible Alan Morris visits Lois late at night. Clark has since returned to Smallville and tells his parents that he's afraid he's losing himself to Superman. They encourage him to remember that there's a "man" in Superman. Barnes has recently sprung his old gang from jail, and they plan on robbing the Metropolis Gold Repository. After some detective work, Lois and Clark are able to determine that Barnes is the thief, and where he will strike next. Lois and Alan wait at Clark's apartment and Superman arrives.

While Alan sleeps, Superman assures Lois that she'll always stand out in a crowd for him. Suddenly, Superman realizes how to make Barnes visible, and flies off. But Lois and Alan want in on the action, and so they don invisible suits and head to the Gold Repository. Unfortunately, they're caught and thrown in the vault. While the invisible gang has a shoot out with the cops, Superman arrives and dumps phosphorus on the gang, making them visible again. He then plows through the vault and rescues Lois and Alan. In the end, Alan retires from the Robin Hood gang and gets a job-at Luthor Technologies. **Guest cast:** Leslie Jordan as Alan Morris, Jack Carter as Murray Brown, Patrika Darbo as Helen Morrris, Jim Beaver as Barnes, Thomas Ryan, Miguel Sandoval as Eduardo Friez, Shaun Toub as Asabi, Yolanda Gaskins as Linda Montoya, Francine York as Mistress of Ceremonies, Lelie Rivers as Deputy Mayor, Cliff Mendaugh as Old Man, Nancy Locke as 1st Woman, Teresa Jones as Debutante, Bob McCracken as Invisible Man, Estelle LeVine as Matronly Woman. **Writer:** Deborah LeVine. **Director:** Mark Sobel.

Requim For a Super Hero (airdate: Oct. 17, 1993). While covering an upcoming boxing match, Clark is shocked to learn that Lois is the daughter of reputed reconstructive surgeon Sam Lane. That night, Lois receives a call from Allie Dinello, the gym manager. However, when Lois arrives, she sees Allie get run down by a speeding truck. Lois goes to her father for information on why Allie was killed, but he's no help. That night, Lois and Clark break into Dr. Lane's office, and find a secret lab, which contains state-of-the-art cybernetic devices. This makes them realize that he's cybernetically enhanced four of Metropolis' favorite fighters. Realizing that by printing the story they'd be endangering Dr. Lane's life, Lois and Clark conceal the truth from Perry. Meanwhile, Dr. Lane feels guilty and gets evidence on tape from Max Menkin, the promoter who had Allie killed. With Dr. Lane's permission, Lois and Clark then run their story. Luthor, who has secretly been bankrolling the operation, is outraged. He decides to kidnap Lois as a way of getting to Dr. Lane.

John Shea as Lex Luthor, Teri Hatcher as Lois Lane, Dean Cain as Superman.

The night of the fight, Menkin kidnaps Lois at gunpoint. Superman arrives to rescue her but is distracted by three of the bionic boxers. While he subdues them, Luthor shoots Menkin, thereby "saving" Lois and tying up his loose ends. Meanwhile, in the arena, the fight has been cancelled, but Garrison, a loud-mouthed cyborg, refuses to leave until he's had his shot at Superman. Superman then arrives and beats Garrison-by poking him with his index finger. **Guest cast:** Denis Ardnt as Dr. Sam Lane, Matt Roe, Joe Sabatino, John La Motta as Allie Dinello, Dave Sebastian Williams as Ringmaster, Jean Speegle Howard as Elderly Woman. **Writer:** Robert Killebrew. **Director:** Randall Zisk.

I've Got a Crush on You (airdate: Oct. 24, 1993). As a rash of fires burn the West River District, Lois goes undercover as a singer in the Metro Club, which is run by the Metro Gang, who control everything in West River. Lois thinks they're behind the fires as well. Little does she know that Luthor's involved as well, with plans to build Lex Harbor over the ruined buildings. Clark gets worried about Lois and goes to the Metro Club with hopes of getting a job as well. It's fortunate he's there, because the club is attacked by the Toasters, a group of punks using hi-tech flame throwers to cause the fires. Clark saves the life of Toni Taylor, the sister of Johnny Taylor, leader of the Metros. When Toni orchestrates a coup and forces

Johnny into retirement she finds Clark a job as a bartender. That night, while Lois is on stage singing, Luthor arrives to talk with Toni. Both Lois and Clark see Luthor, but he only see Lois. This forces Clark to blow Lois' cover, since Luthor would have anyway. This way, he scores more points with Toni for his loyalty.

That night Lois follows Toni to an alley near West River, where she meets with the Toasters, whom she hired to create a situation allowing her to assume control of the Metros. But the Toasters have grown too powerful to control, and they plan on burning West River to the ground. They then tie up Toni before carrying out their plan. Lois rushes to Clark's to call the police, but it's too late; West River is already in flames. When Lois leaves, Clark switches to Superman, and drops in on the Toasters. He uses his supercold breathe to freeze them, then manipulates a thunderstorm to help put out the fires. Lois then tips off the police to Toni's whereabouts. **Guest cast:** Jessica Tuck as Toni Taylor, Michael Milhoan as Johnny Taylor, Johnny Williams as Lou, Audrey Landers as Toots, Alexander Enberg as Toaster #1, David DeLuise as Toaster #2, Shashawnee Hall as Bartender, Gregg Daniel as Newscaster, Tom Simmons as Reporter #1, Piper Perry as Girl #1. **Writer:** Thania St. John. **Director:** Gene Reynolds.

Smart Kids (airdate: Oct. 31, 1993). Four orphans escaped from the Bechworth State School after stealing some vial of Metamide 5, an experimental intelligence-boosting drug which had been tested on them by its inventor, Dr. Carlton. Later, the people of Metropolis are held at bay by the Smart Kids, who demand that all authorities stop looking for them. At the Bechworth School, Lois befriends Inez, whose older sister Amy is one of the Smart Kids. When Amy is caught trying to free Inez from the school, Lois is able to get custody of her. After another visit to the school, Clark is able to snag a sample of Metamide 5, and has it analyzed at STAR labs.

That night, Superman is seen changing into Clark by one of the Smart Kids' surveillance cameras. Lois and Clark then learn that Dr. Carlton has vanished without a trace, but he's actually at Luthor's, who paid him to invent Metamide 5. He even went as far as inventing Metamide 6, which increases intelligence even further, eventually leading to mental overload. Luthor tested this on Carlton, who became a vegetable. Meanwhile, Clark has received a note from the Smart Kids, who want to talk to him via a two-way camera set up in Clark's apartment. When they talk, Clark is able to use some super-speed trickery to convince them that he isn't Superman. Lois, on the other hand, has a tough time when she finds Amy in hysterics when she realizes the drug has worn off. The following day, STAR labs has discovered that prolonged exposure to Metamide 5 results in slower mental activity, and Lois and Clark convince Amy to take them to the Smart Kids' hideout.

Meanwhile, the Smart Kids have kidnapped Luthor, along with a huge supply of Metamide 5 and 6, in order to blackmail the city into leaving them alone. Clark switches to Superman and confronts the Smart Kids' leader. He is able to convince him that being normal isn't all that bad. **Guest cast:** Courtney Peldon as Amy Valdez, Michael Cavanaugh [*Starman*] as Dr. Carlton, Scott McAfee as Phillip Manning, Jonathan Hernandez as Dudley Nichols, Emily Ann Lloyd as Inez Valdez, Sheila Rosenthal as Karen, Margot Rose as Mrs. Powell, Ralph B. Martin as Cabbie, Bergen Williams as Helga. **Writer:** Dan LeVine. **Director:** Robert Singer.

The Green, Green Glow of Home (airdate: Nov. 14, 1993). Jonathan and Martha are visited by their neighbor, Wayne Irig, who has found a strange green rock in the wake of a violent storm. He shipped a piece off to be analyzed and now some government operatives are on their way to question him. He gives Jonathan the remainder of the rock to hold. Clark tells Perry the injustice being

dealt to Wayne, and Perry sends the reporters to Smallville to investigate. When they get to the Irig farm, they find a horde of government people, who claim to be testing for insecticides, but no sign of Irig. Little do they know that Irig is being questioned by Jason Trask [from **Strange Visitor From Another Planet**], who believes that the rock is connected to Superman.

Later that night, Lois and Clark stay with the Kents, and, after Lois has gone to bed, Jonathan shows Clark the rock, with disastrous results. Clark immediately becomes weak and passes out. When he awakens, he slowly regains his strength, but not his powers. The following day, Lois and Clark are again denied access to the Irig farm, but Trask forces Irig to phone Clark and tell him nothing's wrong. Back in Metropolis, Perry sends Jimmy down to Smallville to check on Lois and Clark. On their third visit to the Irig farm, Lois and Clark are captured and separated. Lois is simply held captive, but Clark is interrogated by Trask. When he fails to budge, Trask goes to the Kent farm and abducts Jonathan and Martha and retrieves the rock. He then threatens to kill the Kents if Clark won't reveal his connection to Superman. Clark tells the truth, but Trask won't believe him since he has no powers.

Meanwhile, Jimmy and the Sheriff have found Lois and they all head to the Kent farm. Jimmy tries contacting Superman with a special ultrasonic watch from STAR labs. Suddenly Clark's powers kick back in, with the shrieking of the watch, and he escapes to confront Trask. Clark attacks Trask, But Trask has the rock, which again weakens Clark, thus evening the odds. When Trask pulls a gun, the Sheriff shoots and kills him. In the end, Lois and Clark dub the rock kryptonite. **Guest cast:** Terrence Knox [*Tour of Duty*] as Jason Trask, Joleen Lutz as Rachel Harris, Jerry Hardin [*The X-Files*] as Wayne Irig, Lt. Scott Caldwell as Carol Sherman, Sharon Thomas [Dean Cain's Mother] as Maisie, Patrick Thomas O'Brien as Barker. **Writer:** Bryce Zabel. **Director:** Les Landau.

The Man of Steel Bars (airdate: Nov. 21, 1993). It's over ninety degrees in mid-November in Metropolis, and Lois and Clark attend the Mayor's press conference addressing the heat wave. During the conference, Dr. Saxon steps forward with his opinion of what's causing the heat: Superman. He believes that every time Superman uses his powers, it draws energy from the sun, making it hotter. Back at the Planet, the reporters look over a chart of all Superman's super-efforts, and, on those same dates, the temperature rose. When Superman saves some worker and the temperature rises again, the DA asks Superman to appear at a special hearing. Superman agrees not to use his powers until the problem is solved. However, he isn't even out of the courthouse when he stops a felon form escaping, and Judge Diggs now has no choice but to arrest him. Superman is then placed in Perry white's custody.

Meanwhile, Saxon meets with Luthor, who is secretly manipulating a controlled leak at his proposed nuclear plant, thereby causing the heat. Once he gets rid of Superman, he'll stop the temperature increases and the city will approve his facility. Clark is forced to break the law by stopping a runaway train from colliding with the station. The following day, Superman announces that he'll leave Metropolis. Clark then has to tell Lois that he got a job offer back in Smallville, and will be leaving also. Once he leaves, Lois meets with Dr. Goodman, who doesn't agree with Dr. Saxon's opinion of the heat wave. She and Lois look into Metropolis' underground system of waterways, and find them boiling. They, then, investigate a new chart of Superman's activities and the temperature boosts are the same, the hottest spots in the city have no relation to Superman. In fact, the hottest spot is Luthor's Nuclear Plant. Lois, then, makes a televised plea to Superman to meet her at Luthor's Plant. Just as Luthor is preparing to activate the plant, Superman arrives and shuts it down. He then announces to the city

that he is back. **Guest cast:** Sonny Bono as Mayor Berkowitz, Richard Fancy as Dr. Edward Saxon, Rosalind Cash as Judge Angela Diggs, Haunani Minn as the DA, Elaine Kagan as Dr. Katherine Goodman, Tony Jay as Nigel, Tom LaGrua as Murray Mindlen, Miguel Sandoval as Eduardo Friez, Scott Burkholder as Prisoner, David J. Partington as Sgt. Stahl, Hartley Silvera as Cabbie. **Writer:** Paris Qualles. **Director:** Robert Butler.

Pheremone, My Lovely (airdate: Nov. 28, 1993). As a way of proving to Luthor that her special perfume is a success, Miranda sprays the newsroom of the Daily Planet with her concoction, causing them to fall hopelessly in love with anyone to whom they are even remotely attracted. Everyone is affected but Clark, and he is stunned when Lois begins coming onto him with all the subtlety of a locomotive. Clark later comes across a photo of Miranda in a magazine, and recognizes her as the woman from the Planet who is probably the cause of all the confusion. But Lois comes by and literally throws herself at Clark. The next morning, however, she is returned to normal. Lois and Clark then head over to Miranda's shop, where she denies any involvement. But Clark is able to swipe a sample of her potion.

Later, Miranda visits Luthor, and sprays him with the potion. Oddly, he is unaffected. Meanwhile, Lois and Clark deduce that, for the potion to work, there must be some physical attraction. That night, Luthor dines with Lois, and the potion kicks in, making him hopelessly in love with her. The next day, Miranda is furious over being shunned by Luthor and increases the potency of her potion, making its effects deadly and permanent. She then sends a note requesting a meeting with Lois. When Lois goes to meet Miranda at the airport, she is captured and put in danger. Miranda intends on spraying all of Metropolis with her potion. Meanwhile, Luthor arrives at the Planet, requesting that they contact Superman because he fears that Miranda will do something rash. Superman figures out Miranda's plan and speeds to the airport, where he rescues Lois and grounds Miranda's plane. Later Luthor has a startling revelation: he is hopelessly and eternally in love with Lois, and not because of the potion. **Guest cast:** Morgan Fairchild as Miranda, Tony Jay as

Nigel, Sophia Santi as Rehalia, Courtney Taylor as April, Jeff Austin as Phil, Conrad Goode as Hans. **Writer:** Deborah Joy LeVine. **Director:** Bill D'Elia.

Honeymoon in Metropolis (airdate: Dec. 12, 1993). When Lois sees Congressman Ian Harrington involved in shady dealings with a mystery man, Perry sends Lois and Clark into the Honeymoon suite of the Metropolis Inn to spy on them, as their meeting place is across the street. A taped conversation reveals the mystery man threatening Harrington that his vote had better go the right way. The following day, the reporters have learned that the mystery man is Thaddeus Roarke, an international arms dealer and weapons specialist. It also turns out that Harrington is involved with the House Defense Committee. That night, Lois and Clark watch as Roarke shows Harrington what will happen when their plan comes together. While Lois and Clark can't see what happens, it's obvious that it's horrible. After Harrington and Roarke leave, Lois sneaks into their office and starts snapping pictures of their files. She doesn't realize that they're on their way back, and Clark has to create a diversion to save her.

The following day, while reviewing Lois' pictures, the reporters come across something called Tsunami, but Lois wasn't able to get the rest of the report. Perry takes the reporters to meet his government contact, Sore Throat. Sore Throat tells them of the Navy's own Star Wars Program called Project: Shockwave. It sets up a sound barrier and adjusts itself to the scope of the attacker attempting to breach the sound net. Later, Lois goes poking around a warehouse on the waterfront owned by Roarke, but she gets captured and tied up with Harrington. Meanwhile, Luthor arrives at the Daily Planet. He designed Shockwave, and reveals that Roarke designed a different system, but the Navy opted Shockwave. They then theorize that Roarke intends on sabotaging Shockwave by tricking the system into thinking it's being attacked by something huge so it overreacts. Clark races to the waterfront and frees Lois and Harrington. Suddenly, an immense tidal wave moves towards the shore, and Clark switches to Superman in time to dig an underwater trench, letting the water rush back out to sea. **Guest cast:** Charles R. Frank as Congressman Ian Harrington, Charles Cyphers as Thaddeus Roarke, Richard Libertini as Sore Throat, Fred Stoller as Phil, Andrea Stein as Ingeborg. **Writer:** Dan LeVine. **Director:** James A. Contner.

All Shook Up (airdate: Jan. 2, 1994). Superman meets with Professor Daitch, who tells him about an asteroid called Nightfall; it's seventeen miles wide, and heading straight for Earth. He figures that if Superman plows into the asteroid at full speed, he'll fragment it. Superman agrees and flies into space. However, when he hits the asteroid, it fragments, but he is sent hurtling back to Earth where he lands in the Suicide Slum section of Metropolis. In the reentry, Superman's costume was vaporized and impact caused him to loose his memory. Lois finds Clark at the police station, and he has no clue who he is. She takes him back to the Planet, and, following the doctor's advice, gets him back in the swing of things. First, they attend a press conference in which officials report that, while Superman was partially successful, there is still a three mile wide chunk of Nightfall heading for Earth. They plan on using a nuclear warhead, since Superman has vanished.

Meanwhile, after some homeless people reported seeing a falling star, Jimmy and Perry head over to the Suicide Slum where they find a piece of Superman's suit. Lois then gets an offer from Luthor to live in his underground bunker which will survive the impending doom. She is tempted, but refuses. Meanwhile, Jonathan and Martha have arrived in Metropolis and are shocked when they realize that Clark doesn't know he's Superman. After convincing

224

him otherwise, he still can't remember how to fly or use his other powers. The government launches its Asgard missile at the asteroid, but it misses. After a failed attempt at flying, Clark runs into Lois who tells him how she feels about Superman. This jogs him memory, and, with minutes to spare, Superman flies into space again, this time pushing the asteroid out of harms way, instead of hitting it. **Guest cast**: J.A. Preston as Gen. Robert Zykling, Richard Belzer as Inspector Henderson, Richard Roat, David Sage, Matt Clark, Jenifer Lewis, Suanne Spoke as Dr. Jerri McCorkle, Rick Fitts as Frank Madison, Shaun Toub as Asabi, Lee Magnuson as Ground Controller, Eric Laneuville as Vendor. **Writer**: Bryce Zabel. **Director**: Felix Enriquez Alcala.

Witness (airdate: Jan. 9, 1994). While conducting an exclusive interview with Dr. Vincent Winninger, Lois witnesses the doctor's death at the hands of an assassin. Luckily, the assassin doesn't know Lois is there, and she escapes with one of Winninger's notebooks. Later, at the crime scene, Lois identifies Dr. Hubert as the killer, but Hubert was Winninger's friend and has a solid alibi. By this time, Clark has deemed himself Lois' protector, and he is able to foil an attempt on her life. Unfortunately, Lois didn't see the gunman and isn't convinced she's in any danger. The following day, Jimmy has deciphered Winninger's notebook, and it contains a formula for increased male potency as well as a map of Brazil. Meanwhile, Lois recalls Winninger mentioning an old acquaintance, Sebastian Finn, who was a master of disguise. The reporters then realize that he's the killer. The following day, Lois and Clark attend a press conference held by Dr. Barbara Trevino, who is soon to be appointed to the Rain Forest Consortium.

After the conference, Lois is lured up to the roof where Finn again tries to kill her. This time Superman shows up and captures Finn, who won't reveal who hired him. Later, Lois learns that Winninger and Trevino used to be a couple, and, when he dumped her, she began dating Finn. Dr. Trevino then calls Lois and threatens her, prompting Lois to spend the night at Clark's. The following day, Lois and Clark meet with Dr. Hubert, who reveals that Winninger spent considerable time in Brazil where he discovered a plant that increases male potency as well as rich mineral deposit. Trevino tried to convince him to exploit the land for commercial value, but Winninger refused. With him dead, there would be no one to stop Trevino from exploiting the land, especially once she became head of the Rain Forest Cosortium. That night, Trevino infiltrates the Planet, and attacks Lois, but she is foiled by Lois and Jimmy. Superman, meanwhile, flies to Brazil and puts a stop to the mining. **Guest cast**: Elliot Gould as Dr. Vincent Winninger, Phil Michelson as Himself, Charlie Dell, Richard Belzer as Inspector Henderson, Claudette Nivens as Barbara Trevino, Brian George, William Mesnik as Sebastian Finn, Julie Araskog as Reporter, Hal Sparks as Skateboarder, Roz Witt as Teacher, Bradley Pierce as Kid #1, Ahmad Stoner as Kid#2, Megan Parlen as Girl #1. **Writer**: Bradely Moore. **Director**: Mel Damski.

Illusions of Grandeur (airdate: Jan. 23, 1994). Children of wealthy or famous Metropolitans are being kidnapped and are only returned after a huge ransom is paid. Even then, they remember nothing. Lois and Clark interview Chris Moskal, the most recent intended victim, who saw his friend Nicky get abducted instead. Nicky got into a magician's trunk, closed the lid, and vanished. Later, Lois and Clark attend a posh party at The Magic Club and notice that famed magician Darren Romick's magic boxes have a similar design to the one Chris mentioned. When Lois tries to question Romick, he vanishes in a puff of smoke. That night, Lois and Jimmy follow Mr. Moskal as he goes to deliver the ransom to Nicky's kidnapper. However, when Superman arrives to help, he is hypnotized into

recapturing Nicky. The kidnapper also plants a post-hypnotic suggestion that will cause Superman to commit crimes whenever he hears the trigger words.

The following day, Clark has no memory of being hypnotized, and only learns of this through Lois. He then flies to Smallville to consult his parents, who remind him that if he concentrates, he can overcome anything. Later, Clark meets up with Lois at The Magic Club, and she has learned that Romick has experienced a recent windfall. When Lois is forced into volunteering for one of Romick's tricks, she is sent into the basement where she comes across Nicky, who is being held spellbound by a mesmerizing television broadcast. Lois, too, falls under its spell. When Superman comes crashing in to save the day, he confronts Romick, who pleads innocent. It is then that Romick's assistant Constance, reveals that she is the mastermind behind the kidnapping schemes. She then hypnotizes Lois, Nicky and Romick to position themselves into various threatening places. Superman is directed to fly into space to hook up a satellite through which Constance can broadcast her messages. But, once in the clean night air, Superman recalls his parents' words of wisdom and snaps back into his own frame of mind. He then streaks back and rescues Lois, Romick and Nicky and captures Constance. **Guest cast**: Ben Vereen as Dr. Andre Novak, Penn Jillette as Darren Romick, Marietta Deprima as Constance, Eve Plumb as Rose Collins, Jarrett Lennon as Nicky Collins, Stephen Burleigh as Mr. Moskal, Adrienne Hampton as Mrs. Moskal, Christopher Miranda as Chris Moskal, Whitney Young as Little Girl, Vince Brocato as Florist. **Writer**: Thania St. John. **Director**: Michael Watkins.

Ides of Metropolis (airdate: Feb. 6, 1994). After covering the murder trial of Eugene Laderman, Lois is shocked when the pronounced-guilty Eugene escapes and winds up at her apartment. Lois is convinced of Eugene's innocence, so she allows him to stay. Detective Betty Reed, on the other hand, has been assigned to track him down, and question Lois, who denies having any contact with Eugene. Eugene was convicted of the murder of his boss, computer mogul, Henry Harrison, because he was having an affair with Harrison's wife, Lena. However, after Lena admits to Lois that

Eugene killed her husband, Eugene is forced to reveal that he only took the blame to protect Lena, the true murderer. Jimmy then follows Lena and sees her go into a hotel and into the arms of a man whose face is hidden by shadows.

Meanwhile, Eugene tells how Henry got irate when Eugene stumbled across his new computer program, called the Ides of Metropolis. Reed again questions Lois, who informs Reed of her theory that Lena is the murderer. But Lena has a solid alibi. While Lois and Clark are out investigating, Eugene notices a slight defect in Lois' personal computer, and, after hacking into more sophisticated systems, finds a similar problem. He then realizes that the Ides of Metropolis isn't a computer program, rather, it's a computer virus. With the virus expanding nationwide, Reed tells Lois and Clark that she dug up Harrison's body, but found only that of a homeless man. Clark then takes Eugene to the University, where he can work on a cure for the virus, and Lois and Reed head to Harrison's office where they find Henry alive and well with Lena. It seems he designed this virus to cripple the nation and force them into using his products, and he faked his own death to eliminate himself from suspicion. He and Lena disarm Reed and Lois and lock them in a room.

Meanwhile, Eugene has formulated an antidote, but it has to be manually distributed at three key points nationwide. So, Clark switches to Superman and flies the computer disks to their locations. Once he vanquishes the virus, all power in Harrison's office goes out, allowing Reed and Lois to free themselves and arrest Harrison and Lena, thus clearing Eugene's name. **Guest cast:** Todd Susman as Eugene Laderman, Melanie Mayron as Det. Betty Reed, Paul Gleason as Henry Harrison, Jennifer Savidge as Lena Harrison, Tony Jay as Nigel, Richard Gant as Judge Cobb, Myrna Niles as Miss Bird, Yolanda Gaskins as Newscaster, Ben Bolock as Ben the Bailiff, Debbie Korkunis as Aerobics Trainer, Richard E. Whiten as Bodybuilder, Lee Mathis as Technician. **Writer:** Deborah Joy LeVine. **Director:** Phillip J. Sgriccia.

The Foundling (airdate: Feb. 2, 1994). The Kryptonian globe Clark pocketed [in **Strange Visitor From Another Planet**] begins to glow and an image of Clark's Kryptonian parents, Jor-El and Lara, appears before him, initiating a series of messages that will soon appear. However, soon after this first message, Clark's apartment is robbed and the globe is among the items stolen. The thief, a young street punk named Jack, is mystified when the globe glows and a message appears. He snaps pictures of it and eventually arranges to sell it. Unbeknownst to Jack, the buyer is Luthor. Meanwhile, Lois has contacted Louie, a local hood who has a soft spot for her, and he has fingered Jack as the thief. So, Lois and Clark interrogate Jack.

Once alone, Jack tells Clark about the globe and how he sold it. He promises to notify Clark if he has any more contact with this mysterious buyer. That night, Luthor manages to activate the globe, triggering another message. But this time, Clark is able to see the hologram as well. Luthor activates the globe a number of times over the next few days, and, since the messages are also visible to Clark, he is able to learn about Krypton and the circumstances which brought him to Earth. Lois knows Clark is hiding something about the theft in his apartment, and eventually he is forced to tell her about the globe. She is outraged that he deliberately kept it from her when he stole it from Bureau 39, but he is too busy to deal with that at the moment, because Jack's younger brother, Denny, has called, and Jack's been abducted. At Luthor's bunker, Luthor and Nigel try to get Jack to reveal from whom he stole the globe, theorizing that its owner must be Superman. But Jack won't budge. Clark has since taken to the air, and as he zeroes in on Jack's location, he sets off alarms in Luthor's bunker. Luthor and Nigel prepare to escape, but the globe senses Superman near, and levitates out of reach. Super-

man finally arrives, but Luthor and Nigel have escaped. After seeing that Jack and Denny get put into nice foster homes, Clark returns to Smallville, where he puts the globe to rest in his treehouse, which is labeled the Fortress of Solitude. **Guest cast:** Chris Demetral as Jack, Richard Belzer as Inspector Henderson, Robert Costanzo as Louie, Tony Jay as Nigel, David Warner as Jor-El, Brandon Bluhm as Denny, Eliza Roberts as Lara. **Writer:** Dan LeVine. **Director:** Bill D'Elia.

The Rival (airdate: Feb. 27, 1994). Lois is green with jealousy when her old college rival Linda King arrives in town and goes to work for the Metropolis Star, the Daily Planet's fiercest rival. To make matters worse, Linda scoops Lois out of a story when Superman rescues a woman from a burning building. With the Metropolis Star continually scooping the Planet, Perry is forced to announce budget cuts and even lay-offs if the reporters don't get cracking. Lois is furious when she realizes Linda has set her sights on Clark, and Clark won't take Lois' advice about Linda's shady side. In fact, Clark has lunch with Linda and they just happen to be in the right place at the right time to witness an elevator accident, which is averted by Superman. Clark later notices that the elevator cables had been cut. Meanwhile, Preston Carpenter, the wealthy publisher of the Star, reveals his plans for power to Linda. As he slowly edges out the Planet, he will soon control most of what the American public reads, thereby controlling what they think. Clark begins to get suspicious of Carpenter when he realizes that he called Linda seconds before the elevator accident just to see where she was. With this in mind, he quits the Planet and gets a job as Linda's partner at the Star, much to Lois' chargin.

While covering a press conference, Clark's suspicions are confirmed when Carpenter calls Linda seconds before armed thieves attempt to steal some jewels on display at the conference. That night, Lois arrives at Clark's apartment and finds Perry and Clark, who reveal to her that Clark never actually quit the Planet, but is working undercover. The three of them then decide to team up with Linda in order to prove that Carpenter is creating the news, instead of just reporting it. Linda uses Carpenter's attraction to her to lure him out of his office long enough for Lois and Clark to snoop through his computer. What they find is an already-written editorial about the assassination of Secretary Wallace, which hasn't happened-yet. Clark, Lois and Linda go to the hotel where Wallace is staying to try and warn him, but it's too late. Lois and Linda are captured by Carpenter's men, forcing Superman to rescue them and stop the assassins. In the end, Carpenter is exposed, and the Planet is back on top again. **Guest cast:** Dean Stockwell as Preston Carpenter, Nancy Everhard as Linda King, Bo Jackson as Himself, Kevin Cooney as Secretary Wallace, Mike Savatino as J. Harvey Stark, Dana Chelette as Fire Chief. **Writers:** Tony Blake and Paul Jackson. **Director:** Michael Watkins.

Vatman (airdate: Mar. 13, 1994). Clark is shocked when Superman begins making miraculous rescues in Europe, when Clark hasn't left Metropolis the entire time. Eventually, Superman meets the imposter: a perfect double of himself, who acts like a large child. The imposter tells Superman that his time is up, and he is being replaced as Superman. After a dizzying chase through the Metropolis subway system, the imposter returns home to Luthor's penthouse. It seems that Luthor and Dr. Fabian Leek "created" this new Superman through genetic engineering, and he considers Luthor his "father," since he has the mind of a child. When Lois sees the new Superman in action, he is immediately smitten with her, and accepts a dinner invitation. When the new Superman arrives at Lois' apartment, he tries to make out with her in the manner of any thirteen year old. Luckily Clark shows up, and the two face off, with

Superman leaving and promising to see Clark again.

The following day, Lois and Clark visit Dr. Leek, who wrote a famous article on cloning. But, in person, he downplays his own prowess and claims that cloning is still in the developmental stages. Convinced that Leek is lying, Lois and Clark suddenly recall Superman donating a lock of hair to a charity auction and how the lock was stolen soon after. This would provide enough material to make a clone. That night, Leek tells Luthor [and, unbeknownst to them, the clone] that the clone is imperfect, and that he is dying. So, Luthor directs the clone to kidnap Lois and use her as bait to kill Superman. The clone does this and takes Lois to a studio lot, where they await the real Superman. When he arrives, they duke it out, until Superman convinces his double that they shouldn't be enemies. The clone then flies to Luthor's lab and destroys it, along with the lock of hair. He then tells Superman that he's dying, and he wishes to be thrown into the sun, thereby preventing Luthor from using him to create another clone. Regretfully, Superman complies and gives his brother a Viking funeral. **Guest cast:** Michael McKean as Dr. Fabian Leek, Sam Rubin as Newscaster, Ira Heiden as messenger, Wil Albert as Delacroix, John McMahon as Cop, Cynthia Ettinger as Tour Guide. **Writers:** H. B. Cobb and Deborah Joy LeVine. **Director:** Randall Zisk.

Fly Hard (airdate: Mar. 20, 1994). With Clark, Jack [introduced in **Foundling**], Jimmy, Perry, Lois and Luthor all at a the Daily Planet for one reason or another on a quiet Saturday night, a gang of armed terrorists enters the newsroom and seizes the building. Only Jimmy, who was not in the newsroom at the time, isn't captured. Instead, he escapes through the air ducts in hopes of finding help. Fuentes, the group's leader, totes a nuclear device, which he claims he will activate if anyone misbehaves. With the Planeteers safely locked in the conference room, Fuentes orders his group to begin their operation. Clark uses his X-Ray vision to determine that Fuentes is reading the blueprints to the Planet. When Clark is able to use his heat vision to activate the sprinkler system, Willy, the bumbling security guard [who doesn't know anything is wrong], tells the fire department that it's a false alarm. While Clark tries to determine just what Fuentes is up to, Luthor tries to slip out the door, but is shot. To prevent further escape attempts, Fuentes handcuffs Luthor to Lois and Clark to Jack, further hampering any chance Clark has of acting. Clark is able to use his vision to see them digging on the floor below. When he overhears the name "Dragonetti," Perry recalls the Daily Planet building's history. It was once a nightclub during Prohibition, and Dragonetti was the notorious gangster who ran the speakeasy.

Rumor has it that his vast fortunes are buried somewhere in the building. Finally, Jack has had enough, and he and Clark slip out to find Willy and have him notify the police. He agrees to do so. Later, Jimmy exits the air duct system only to be held at gunpoint by Willy. He escorts Jimmy back to the newsroom, where he is revealed to be the mastermind behind the entire operation. Willy tells the Planeteers that he was Dragonetti's partner and is entitled to the fortune. But Fuentes doublecrosses Willy and locks him up with everyone else. Taking Lois as his insurance, Fuentes and his group prepare to leave with their fortune after executing their witnesses. After shorting out all the lights, Clark breaks his handcuffs and systematically takes out all the crooks, with Fuentes escaping with Lois, to the roof. When they both fall off, Superman catches Lois, then Fuentes and the nuclear detonator. Fuentes and his group are then taken into custody. **Guest cast:** Chris Demetral as Jack, Macon McCalman as Willy, Robert Beltran as Fuentes, Alexandra Hedison as Remy, Cole Stevens as Schumak, Anthony Leonardi as Blackman, Don Fehmel as George. **Writer:** Thania St. John. **Director:** Phillip J. Sgriccia.

Barbarians at the Planet (airdate: May 1, 1994). At the headquarters of the now-defunct Bureau 39, a gang of thieves break in and steal a sample of kryptonite. Meanwhile, after a romantic evening in Paris, Luthor proposes to Lois, who gives him a firm "maybe." Meanwhile, the Daily Planet is having a financial crisis, and, after numerous budget cuts, Luthor buys the ailing paper. While everyone else sees this as a godsend, Clark fears the worst is yet to come. The changes occur quick, with Perry forced to retire and Jimmy and Jack [last seen in **Fly Hard**] demoted to working in the printery. When a bomb hidden in a replica of Jack's lunch box explodes, Superman flies in to action, but even he isn't able to save the Planet, and Luthor announces that they won't rebuild. Luthor cites Jack as the saboteur and has him arrested.

Meanwhile, he gets Lois a job at Luthor News Network. Although she tries to get Clark to accept an invitation to be her partner, he refuses. Instead, he admits his true romantic feelings for her, but she does not reciprocate. That night, in a secluded spot, Luthor begins to purchase the kryptonite from a crook named Devane, but instead, kills Devane and keeps his money and the kryptonite. Meanwhile, Superman visits Lois, who wants to know if there's any hope for them romantically, because if there is, she'll turn Luthor down. Reluctantly, Superman admits that it wouldn't work. In light of this, Lois tells Luthor she'll be his wife. **Guest cast:** Chris Demetral as Jack, Patrick Kilpatrick as Devane, Castulo Guerra as Steve, Beverly Johnson as Mrs. Cox, Alex Nevil as Chip, Darby Hinton as Firechief, Barbara Beck as Sandra Ellis. **Writer:** Dan LeVine. **Director:** James R. Bagdonas.

The House of Luthor (airdate: May 8, 1994). Having overheard another young felon brag about how he set Jack up, Jack escapes from Juvenile Hall and meets up with Clark, Perry and Jimmy. Together, they decide to find out, once and for all, just what happened to the Daily Planet. Meanwhile, Luthor and his assistant, Mrs. Cox, set off a bank burglar alarm as a way of getting near Superman. Once he arrives, they test out their kryptonite, which proves to be the genuine article. Finally, after some intensive detective work, the gang gather enough evidence to conclude that Luthor had numerous insurance policies on the Planet, leaving him with more that enough money to rebuild. Instead, he walked away with 75 million dollar profit. Clark goes to Lois with this information, but she refuses to believe it, and won't break off her wedding to Luthor. Luthor requests Superman's presence and then traps him in his basement using a kryptonite-laced metal cage. Later, Lois questions Luthor about Clark's insinuations, but he lies his way out of it.

Meanwhile, Perry goes to see wealthy media mogul, Franklin Stern, and asks him to buy the Planet. Alas, Stern turns him down,. The day of Luthor and Lois' wedding has finally arrived, and the gang from the Planet boycotts the ceremony. During the wedding, Lois has second thoughts and refuses to marry Luthor. Suddenly, Perry, Jimmy and Jack burst in with Inspector Henderson. They have given him their evidence, and he wants to arrest Luthor on countless charges. Luthor snaps and flees to his basement to kill Superman before he is jailed. But, to his horror, Superman has escaped, using his super-breath to draw the key close enough to the cell to grab. Luthor then leaps off the penthouse balcony to his death. However, his corpse is subsequently stolen from the morgue. The Planeteers are overjoyed when Franklin Stern announces that he has, indeed bought, the Daily Planet and will rebuild. **Guest cast:** Chris Demetral as Jack, Beverly Johnson as Mrs. Cox, Richard Belzer as Inspector Henderson, James Earl Jones as Franklin Stern, Phyllis Coates [*The Adventures of Superman*] as Ellen Lane, Richard Stahl as Archbishop, J. Madison Johnston as Guard. **Writers:** Dan LeVine and Deborah Joy LeVine. **Director:** Alan J. Levi.

Rex Smith as Jesse Mach.

Streethawk

review by William E. Anchors Jr.

Production credits:

Created by	Bruce Lansbury Paul M. Belous Robert Wolterstorff
Produced by	Burton Armus Karen Harris Stephen Cragg
Music	Tangerine Dream

Regular cast:

Jesse Mach	Rex Smith
Norman Tuttle	Joe Regalbuto
Commander Leo Altobelli	Richard Venture
Rachel Ward	Jeannine Wilson

Number of episodes:	1 ninety minute pilot movie, 12 one hour segments

Premise: A crippled motorcycle cop is given another chance to hit the streets when he is chosen to ride Streethawk, a highly-advanced motorcycle, used unofficially by the Federal Government to fight crime.

Editor's comments: It isn't as bad as it sounds, and probably would have lasted longer if ABC hadn't insisted on airing it on Friday night, the same evening that led to the cancelation of *Star Trek, Dark Shadows, The Phoenix, Starman* and so on. Although Friday has traditionally killed all fantasy/sci-fi series, the networks still insist on putting them on on Fridays, and it finished off *Streethawk* in only thirteen episodes. *Streethawk* is a moderately entertaining program in the same vein as *Knight Rider* and *Blue Thunder*.

Streethawk (airdate: Jan. 4, 1985, 90 minute pilot). A police van hauling fifty pounds of cocaine is robbed by two thieves on motorcycles who appeared out of nowhere, and disappear despite being chased by a number of police cars. Nearby, a motorcycle cop named Jesse Mach is jumping a line of police cars in "The First Annual Harbor Jump," an unofficial contest sponsored by a group of cops. The contest comes to a halt when Commander Leo Altobelli flies overhead in a police helicopter, and he puts Mach and a friend on suspension for two weeks.

Putting their unplanned free time to good use, Mach and Marty go dirt bike racing. When Mach's bike won't start, he is left behind by Marty, who rides out into the desert and accidentally stumbles onto a drug transfer by the same men who had stolen the cocaine a few days earlier. Finally getting his bike started, Mach goes out looking for Marty, only to find him dead. Suddenly hearing someone behind him, Jesse turns to see a black 4-wheel drive truck heading towards him just before he is run down.

Weeks later, a crippled Mach returns to work only to find that the death of his fellow police officer and friend is not being investigated, and that he has been transferred from the motorcycle department to Public Affairs. Returning home that night, he is met by Norman Tuttle, who had tried earlier to get Jesse interested in the

Streethawk project. Norman claims that he can have Jesse's bad knee fixed. Tuttle takes him to the Streethawk Command Center, and convinces Mach to join the program. In the next few weeks Jesse begins a comprehensive fitness course and training on Streethawk.

In the meantime, Jesse continues to ask questions about the death of his friend, and the owner of the black truck that ran him down sends one of his men out to try to kill Mach. Failing to shoot Mach while the cop is walking in his parking garage, Mach and fellow officer Sandy McCoy continue to ask questions until McCoy is kidnapped by Police Commissioner Miller when she discovers that he is the killer's partner.

As a trial run for Streethawk, Norman sends out Jesse to watch over another police drug shipment that they believe will be hit. When the police van is attacked, Mach spots the black 4-wheel drive belonging to Corrido, but loses it when he chases the attacking motorcycles, which he discovers are using drain tunnels for their getaway. After catching the motorcycle riders, Mach returns to Command Center where he ends up stealing Streethawk after getting into an argument with Norman over using the super bike for personal reasons. Riding to Corrido's estate, Mach is nearly killed when he is separated from the bike, but he manages to free Sandy and pursues an escaping Corrido who is being chased by the police. After the police are run off the road, Mach continues to follow the truck alone in a now-malfunctioning Streethawk. When a machine gun opens up on him, Mach maneuvers around the truck, which begins chasing him. Knowing that a cliff is ahead, Mach heads for it, and at the last second uses his jet thrusters to do a 360 degree loop, landing behind the truck, which goes over the cliff and is destroyed with Corrido still in it. **Guest cast:** Jayne Modean as Sandy McCoy, Lawrence Pressman as Thomas Miller, Robert Beltran as Marty Walsh, Christopher Lloyd [*Star Trek III: The Search For Spock*] as Anthony Corrido, Raymond Singer as Bernie Golbert, John Carter as Elliott Kirby, Doug Cox as Eddie Williams. **Writers:** Robert Wolterstorff, Paul M. Belous. **Director:** Virgil W. Vogel.

A Second Self (airdate: Jan. 11, 1985). On patrol late at night, Streethawk responds to a stolen car report and becomes engaged in a wild chase with the stolen vehicle and a "block" car following it, which ends up crashing and killing the driver. The owner of the car theft ring, the older brother of the man who was killed, vows to get revenge on Streethawk by obtaining a hit man. Meanwhile, Jesse receives a visit from an old friend who is in town for the first time in eight years. What Jesse does not realize is that his friend is the pro hired to kill his secret identity - Streethawk. **Guest Cast:** George Clooney as Kevin Stark, Robert Lipton as Burton Levine, Marco Rodriguez as Pauley, James Welch as Mouse, Sal Landi as Nicky Levine, John Wesley as Keith, Jim McKrell as the TV commentator, Larry Mango as the officer, Jason Corbett as Officer Dell. **Writers:** Nicholas Corea, Bruce Cervi. **Director:** Virgil W. Vogel.

The Adjuster (airdate: Jan. 18, 1985). Jesse trails Mitch Elkins, a jewel fence, to an abandoned warehouse where two thieves try to sell some stolen gems, but they are delayed by Mach on Streethawk

until the police show up. Arriving from New York to extradite Elkins, Vincent Cannon, a ruthless NYC cop, loses the fence after threatening to kill him at the L. A. airport if the thief didn't come up with the money that he stole. After losing the man in the airport, Cannon returns to police headquarters, where Altobetti assigns Mach to be his partner to assist him in finding Elkins. During the next two days the New York cop manages to alienate Mach and his fellow police officers during the search for the escaped suspect. Later that night, without Mach's knowledge, Cannon meets and beats information out of one of Jesse's regular informants, information that leads him to Elkins - whom he would almost kills before Streethawk intervenes.

The next morning, Cannon is told by Altobelli that Elkins has been spotted at a local amusement park. Getting to the park before Mach, he kills the fence. At the same time, Norman finds out through a computer search that the man working with Mach is not Cannon (the real detective turned up dead in New York) but a hit man hired by a big-time underworld figure. Believing that Streethawk was responsible for inadvertently delivering Elkins to the killer, Jesse is determined to bring the sadistic murderer to justice. **Guest cast:** Marjoe Gortner as Vincent Cannon, Milt Oberman as Mitch Elkins, Bernie White as Bobby, Michael Horsley, David Wells, Robert Dryer. **Writer:** Nicholas Corea. **Director:** Virgil W. Vogel.

Vegas Run (airdate: Jan. 25, 1985). A Las Vegas showgirl, Linda Martin, is being forced to testify against her former Mob boyfriend. Now Martin is on the run after some of her boyfriend's men try to abduct her in Vegas. After escaping to Los Angeles, Martin encounters the thugs again when she tries to visit her sister. Running into the street seeking help, she is nearly run down by Jesse and Norman who happened to be driving by. Giving her a ride, they become involved in trying to get her to Chicago alive to testify against the Mob leader, as well as working to free her sister, who is being held prisoner by the thugs. **Guest cast:** Sybil Danning [V] as Linda Martin, Christie Houser as Donna Martin, Christopher Thomas as Jimmy Pinard, Stephen Liska as Mike, Robert Miranda as Harry, Edward Bell as Raymond Elliot, Leslie Bevis as Annie, Gregory Itzin as Harvey, Jay Fenichel as Bobby, Barry Berman as Stick, Hal Havins as Biff, Rebecca Perle as the car hop, Teri Hayden as the old lady, Clay Williams as the mugger, Bill Capizzi as the cabbie. **Writer:** Deborah Davis. **Director:** Virgil W. Vogel.

Dog Eat Dog (airdate: Feb. 1, 1986). Jesse is given the job of attempting to persuade rock star Deborah Shain to appear in a public-service ad for the police department, but she refuses the offer. After talking with Jesse, she leaves with her boyfriend. He is killed by two thugs hired by her manager because of the boyfriend's outrageous blackmail demands - $5,000,000 to destroy a tape showing Jacobs killing a former partner. After narrowly escaping

the scene of the murder, Jacobs hires a professional assassin to kill the singer. Despite her objections, both Jesse and Norman get involved with trying to find the assassin, and to prevent Deborah's death. **Guest cast:** Daphne Ashbrook as Deborah Shain, Lee Ving as Virgil Powell, Charles Lampkin as Artie Shank, James Whitmore, Jr. [*Black Sheep Squadron*] as Neil Jacobs, Kai Wulff as Bingham, Michael MacRae as Hooper, Theoplas Forsett as Anthony. **Writers:** Nicholas Corea, Bruce Cervi. **Director:** Daniel Haller.

Fire on the Wing (airdate: Feb. 8, 1985). An arson scam operating in three different cities has both the police and Streethawk baffled. Altobelli calls into his office Will Gassner, an important local businessman whose warehouse was torched, but the man refuses to co-operate with the police department. Later, while re-examining the film of the burning warehouse taken by Streethawk during a stakeout, Norman spots an ultralight aircraft landing in the dark. He decides that the arsonist must be silently using one of the aircraft (by turning off its engine and gliding to a landing) to reach his targets. Mach begins checking out local ultralight aircraft dealers for someone who might fly them at night, and is nearly killed while test-flying a sabotaged aircraft.

Investigating the case further, Mach finds that Gassner and other businessmen are being extorted by a professional arsonist, but discovers that Gassner refuses to co-operate because of his wife being killed in an earlier business fire set in retaliation for his helping the police. Shortly after learning this, Mach is called by Norman when he detects a low flying aircraft on a radar system he has set up. Using hyperthrust, Mach catches up with the ultralight aircraft seconds after it firebombs Gassner's home - with a visiting Rachel Ward inside. Streethawk manages to free Rachel and Gassner after they are trapped inside the burning home.

Because he still refuses to buckle under to the demands of the arsonists, Gassner's daughter Diana is kidnapped by them to force him into paying. The criminals do not know that the man is almost bankrupt and cannot possibly pay their extortion demands. Finding out about Diana's kidnapping, Mach picks up Streethawk and leaves for her most probable place of imprisonment - the ultralight airport where Jesse was nearly killed earlier, and whose owner has been connected to the burnings by Norman's computer. Arriving at the airport, Mach learns that Diana has escaped and is being chased by a missile-armed ultralight that is about to destroy the car she is in. **Guest cast:** Clu Gulager as Will Gassner, Kristen Meadows as Diana Gassner, Jere Burns as Eddie Watson, Tige Andrews as Morgan Harkness, Raymond Singer, Hank Brandt as Nick, Earl Boen as Peter Reiger. **Writers:** L. Ford Neale, John Huff. **Director:** Virgil W. Vogel.

Chinatown Memories (airdate: Feb. 15, 1986). Returning home from a jog on the beach, Jesse finds his former fiancee (Lili) waiting for him. She requests his help for a friend in trouble with several

Chinese gangs because he stole an ivory statue from their safekeeping - a statue they consider so vital to their interests that they will do anything to have it returned. Investigating the case puts Jesse and Streethawk in the middle of a gang war, and reveals a disturbing fact - Lili's "friend" is actually her new fiance. **Guest cast:** Shelagh McLeod as Lili, James Saito as Joe Ching, Beulah Quo as Auntie Pearl, Keye Luke [*Kung Fu*] as Mr. Ming, Sab Shimono, Nelson Machita as Chang, Rob Kim, Aki Aleong. **Writers:** Deborah Davis, Hannah Shearer. **Director:** Paul Stanley.

The Unsinkable 453 (airdate: Feb. 22, 1985). After being sentenced to twenty years in prison for a bank robbery in Chile, Eric Gault is transported aboard a prison bus to a Federal penitentiary. While on route the bus is attacked in an attempt to free Gault, who, during the confusion, is switched with a double to cover his escape. In the area on a test ride, Streethawk responds to the police call and upon arriving Jesse sees what the guards have missed: Gault escaping in a nearby van. **Guest cast:** Bianca Jagger as Simone Prevera, Mayf Nutter as Eric Gault, Greta Blackburn as Francine, Conrad Bachmann as Warden, Morgan Lofting as Judge Hanover, Raymond Singer. **Writers:** Paul M. Belous, Robert Wolterstorff. **Director:** Paul Belous.

Hot Target (airdate: March 1, 1985). While on the lookout in the desert for an illegal arms sale, Streethawk witnesses the murder of the would-be buyer of a high-tech laser weapon. Using hyperthrust, Jesse catches up to the killer's helicopter and identifies the craft as one belonging to Marpell Industries, a research facility specializing in medical lasers, and where a former flame of Norman's is head of medical research. **Guest cast:** Joanna Kerns as Mona Williams, Charles Napier [*Outlaws*] as John Slade, Sam Ingraffia as Alfred Molina, Sandy Lipton, George McDaniel. **Writers:** Sheldon Willens, Deborah Davis. **Director:** Harvey Laidman.

Murder is a Novel Idea (airdate: March 8, 1985). Stefanie Craig - a former police officer and good friend of Jesse - quits the police force to become a best-selling author. Her latest book (an expose of a famous twenty-year-old unsolved murder case) is nearing completion and will reveal the name of the killer, whom she believes to be long since dead. After a local TV broadcast discussing the upcoming book, Craig finds out that the killers are not dead after all when they try to murder her to keep their identities secret. **Guest cast:** Belinda Montgomery [*The Man From Atlantis*] as Stefanie Craig, Don Hood as Howe, John Di Santi, Robert Carnegie. **Writer:** Karen Harris. **Director:** Harvey Laidman.

The Arabian (airdate: March 15, 1985). When Rebel's Choice, an

$8,000,000 thoroughbred, is found to be suffering from a fatal illness, he is put to sleep by the attending vet. Shortly thereafter, the owner's boyfriend and the horse's trainer kill the doctor to hide any news of the death of the valuable animal, and the next day they fake a kidnapping of the horse to cash in on the insurance policy. Streethawk is drawn into the case when Jesse encounters the escaping van while on a test ride. **Guest cast:** Barbara Stock as Elizabeth Morgan, Bibi Besch [*Star Trek II: The Wrath of Khan*] as Mrs. Collins, Jeff Pomerantz as Harry Stone, Tom Simcox, M. C. Gainey, Walker Edmiston, Jourdan Fremin. **Writer:** Joseph Gunn. **Director:** Richard Compton.

The Assassin (airdate: March 22, 1985). A senator's son - who has received numerous death threats from terrorists - is escorted by the police and Federal officers from his plane through Los Angeles International Airport, where a man dressed as a nurse opens fire on him, but misses the target. On the scene to provide additional security, Streethawk pursues the escaping assassin until called off by Norman, who wants the job handled by Airport Security.

After the man escapes, Jesse is assigned by Altobelli to assist the Federal officer covering the case in providing security for the terrorists target. After several botched assassination attempts, both Jesse and Norman suspect that the son isn't the target at all. **Guest cast:** Dennis Franz [*Hill Street Blues*] as Frank Menlo, Ann Turkel as Melanie, Marc Alaimo as Truman, Paul Rossilli as Steven Cavanaugh, David Oliver, Naomi Serotoff, Raymond Singer. **Writer:** Karen Harris. **Director:** Harvey Laidman.

Follow the Yellow Brick Road (airdate: March 29, 1985). Phil Simpkins, a Vietnam vet, is fed up with local street violence and crime and decides to do something about it: He forms the 12th Street Protection Association, a group of vigilantes. After one of the member's children is attacked by a local gang member, the Association goes after the gang at their headquarters. On his way back to Streethawk's base, Jesse encounters the fight and stops it just as the gang is about to open fire with their guns on Association members. Meanwhile, as police arrive on the scene of the brawl, a heist team hits a local gold storage facility and robs it of twenty bars of gold. With the police tied up with the 12th Street fight, the thieves escape capture. Realizing that the street battle saved them from being caught, they plan another gold theft from the Federal Gold Depository, and use two of their men to start a running battle with Simpkins to delay the pursuit of the police - and Streethawk. **Guest cast:** Robert Costanzo as Simpkins, Catherine Parks, Phil Rubenstein as Abe, John Aprea as Dumos, Bert Rosario as Joey, Don Swayze as Pug, Gamy L. Taylor as Mrs. Scroope, James Emery as Albert. **Writer:** Burton Armus. **Director:** Daniel Haller.

Swamp Thing

review by William E. Anchors, Jr.

Production credits:

Executive Producers	Benjamin Melniker
	Michaele Uslan
	Andy Heward
	Tom Greene
Producer	Boris Malden
Created by	Len Wein
	Berni Wrightson
Developed for TV by	Joseph Stefano
Music	Christopher L. Stone

Regular cast:

Dr. Anton Arcane	Mark Lindsay Chapman
Jim Kipp	Jesse Zeigler
Tressa Kipp	Carrell Myers
Oboe	Anthony Galde
Swamp Thing	Dick Durdock
Sheriff Andrews	Marc Macaulay
Will Kipp	Scott Garrison
Abigail	Kari Wuhrer
Dr. Hollister	William Whitehead
Graham	Kevin Quigley

Premise: "The swamp is my world. It is who I am. It is what I am. I was once a man. I know the evil men do. Do not bring your evil here, I warn you. Do not incur the wrath of Swamp Thing." So says the man-turned-beast, a creature who is a victim of an experiment sabotaged by the evil and cruel Dr. Anton Arcane, who now desires to destroy the creature that opposes his power-mad schemes.

Editor's comments: A show with much promise, but hit-and-miss on delivery. Swampy is such a lovable, friendly creature that you want to enjoy the series, but it takes awhile to really appreciate the show. If you only watched the first few episodes you might want to catch it again, as the series was given an overhaul in **The Shipment**. I wouldn't say the newer episodes are any better, but they are different.

The Emerald Heart (airdate: July 27, 1990). Jim Kipp is rowing his boat through the swamp when he sees a small man hanging upside down on a pole. He releases the man, who claims that the "monster" who put him there will soon be after him. Jim tells his mother, Tressa Kip, about the dwarf later, but she doesn't believe him. Minutes later, the sinister Dr. Arcane arrives. While he and Tressa talk, Jim returns to the swamp to take some food to the man he saved, but he encounters a real-life monster. Luckily, the warm-hearted Swamp Thing arrives to scare off the creature created by Arcane, but as Swamp Thing tries to show Jim the way home they encounter the dwarf, Humphrey, who has been killed. Swampy restores the dwarf to life, then catches up with the would-be-killer, and for committing violence in his swamp he is turned into jungle vegetation. Meanwhile, Arcane finds Humphrey in town, and kidnaps him to use the man for some horrific genetic experiments. Back at the swamp, Jim's divorced mother decides it wasn't such a good idea to move back to her old home near the swamp, but Swampy secretly presents her with a gift that may just change her mind. **Guest cast:** Patricia Helwick as Savanna Langford, John Edward Allen as Humphrey, Glenn Wilder as Hurd Fitch, Beth Johnson as Heather Jo, Bobbie Porter as the toad boy. **Writer:** Joseph Stefano. **Director:** Fritz Kiersch.

The Living Image (airdate: Sept. 7, 1990). Dr. Arcane performs plastic surgery on a girl to make her look like the wife of Alec Holland, a man considered to be dead, but in reality he is now known as the creature called Swamp Thing. It has been ten years since the accident that "killed" Alec, and his "wife" holds a memorial service for him, which Swamp Thing watches from the woods. Seeing her reminds Alec of his last days as a human being, when Dr. Arcane demanded that the scientist develop his virus restorative work for him, which Alec refused. Arcane needed the formula to restore the life of his dead wife, whom he has kept frozen in cryonic acid until he can find a way to cure her. But Alec knows that Arcane will use the formula for evil purposes as well, and he has no intention of finishing the work for fear that Arcane will obtain it. Not long after the meeting, Alec and Linda are caught in an explosion thanks to Arcane, resulting in the death of Linda and Alec's change into Swamp Thing. Not knowing that Arcane is trying to make him believe Linda is still alive, Swamp Thing follows the fake Linda into town, and corners her to find out who she really is - not yet realizing that she is in on another of Arcane's schemes to obtain Alec's formula. **Guest cast:** Marsha Smith as Linda Holland, Lonnie Smith as Alec Holland, Rex Benson as the minister, Robert Small as the real estate salesman, Billy Gillespie as the home buyer, Doc Duhame as intruder #1, John Hoye as intruder #2. **Writers:** David Braff, Judith Berg, Sandra Berg, Joseph Stefano. **Director:** John McPherson.

The Death of Dr. Arcane (airdate: Sept. 14, 1990). Arcane's thugs follow and kidnap Jim. Later, Arcane enters the swamp and releases a creature that he claims "will devour anything in its way", an act witnessed by Swampy, who is told that if he interferes with Arcane's new project, Jim will be killed. The evil scientist claims that five more creatures will be released into the swamp, resulting in the death of every living creature - including Swampy. Meanwhile, Jim is in an air-tight container and he will die in a matter of hours from a lack of oxygen. **Guest cast:** Pat Cherry as the coroner, George Colangelo as the assistant, Darren Dollar as the deputy, Kevin Quigley as thug #1, Andrew Clark as thug #2. **Writers:** Joseph Stefano, Judith Berg, Sandra Berg. **Director:** John McPherson.

The Swamp Maiden (airdate: Sept. 21, 1990). Late at night, Jim takes his sleeping bag and sneaks out of the house. He heads into the swamp to look for the legendary "Swamp Maiden", and meets Swampy, who only wants Jim to go home as it will not be safe in the forest that night. Jim goes on and meets Oboe, who is sure the Maiden, a vivacious, naked female creature whose mere kiss can turn you into a monster, will appear that night. While in the swamp, Oboe and Jim run into a journalist, who claims he is not in the woods to find the Swamp Maiden, but another legendary swamp creature all together - and he'll do anything to capture the half-man/half-beast he has heard about. **Guest cast:** Tom Nowicki as Greg, Heide Paine as the Swamp Maiden. **Writer:** Lorenzo Domenico. **Director:** Yuri Sivo.

Spirit of the Swamp (airdate: Sept. 28, 1990). Several of Arcane's creatures are chasing another of his monsters, until Swamp Thing intervenes. Arcane is furious that all his work is "down the drain" now that the beast has gotten away into the vast swamplands. Elsewhere, an old man enters the swamp looking for "something of the creature", then he magically appears in Arcane's lab. It seems that Arcane has summoned the powerful master of the mystic arts to destroy Swamp Thing, since all of his efforts have failed. In return for delivering Swampy by using his voodoo magic, Arcane will pay Duchamp with a magical black rose that he owns. Entering the swamp, Duchamp prepares his voodoo for a final show-down with Swamp Thing - but the voodoo master doesn't appreciate the magic of the swamp. **Guest cast:** Roscoe Lee Brown as Duchamp, Sandy Beach as mutant #1, Tony Marini as mutant #2. **Writers:** Judith Berg, Sandra Berg, Michael Reeves. **Director:** Yuri Sivo.

Blood Wind (airdate: Oct. 5, 1990). One of Arcane's assistants invents a new formula that fails to work, but Arcane believes he can get the mind-altering drug to function by adding some cells from a living donor. Elsewhere, Tressa is upset that Jim seems to have disappeared, and as she walks into the woods looking for him she is unaware that the assistant is getting ready to dump the deadly toxin - which he claims is a cure for hatred - into the swamp. Swamp Thing runs off the assistant, but accidentally drops the top of the formula's container and the fumes blow out towards Tressa, just a short time before she finds her son. Before long, the chemical that Arcane swore didn't work begins to have profound effects on Tressa, and after she goes into town everyone - including Arcane - who comes in contact with her immediately hates her. **Guest cast:** Michael Champlin as Crown Prince, Laurie Logan as Mrs. Spitzler, Jay Glick as the pastor, Bill Orsini as the gardener. **Writer:** Marc Scott Zicree. **Director:** Walter Von Huene.

Grotesquery (airdate: Oct. 12, 1990). Someone is dumping rusted barrels of toxic chemicals into the swamp, killing off nearly everything that it comes in contact with - including Swampy. The dumping was Arcane's doing, and after neighbors begin complaining, he agrees to send some workers to clean up the mess. Incapacitated by the fumes of the substances, Swamp Thing is found by the workers, and they sell him to a "grotesquery", a freak show of sorts in a travelling circus. Jim sees some signs advertising the traveling freak show, and the rancid owner offers him a job feeding his "animals". Jim accepts mostly out of curiosity, but his feelings turn to ones of horror when he learns that his best friend, Swampy, is in one of the cages, and is slowly dieing. Swamp Thing begs to be released and returned to the swamp, or he will die. Jim promises to get the creature home, but the circus owner has no intention of letting that happen. **Guest cast:** Patricia Helwick as Savanna Langford, Jacob Witkin as Simon, Joshua Susman as Amos, Kathy

Mark Lindsay Chapman as the evil scientist Dr. Anton Arcane.

Gustafson-Hilton as Clair, Christopher Alan as the kid brother, Brad Abrel as worker #1, Dennis Neal as worker #2, Judy Clayton as Gardenia. **Writer:** Michele Barinholtz. **Director:** David Jackson.

Natural Enemy (airdate: Oct. 19, 1990). Swampy is escorting Jim through the swamp, explaining how people are destroying the wilderness. They come across a very dangerous place, which Swamp Thing tells Jim to stay away from, but he won't say why. Jim later returns to the area on his own, and is bitten by a mutated insect, resulting in his becoming extremely ill after returning home. Tressa has him rushed to the hospital, and the doctor there tells her that Jim's condition in serious, having been injected with a deadly venom that has never been encountered before. Dr. Arcane arrives later, acting as if he knows nothing about the situation, but the insect was actually created by him. Later, Swampy arrives at the hospital to help after learning of Jim's condition. But he isn't alone: the insect has arrived at the hospital and is trying to make Tressa its next victim. **Guest cast:** Chase Randolph as Dr. Cass Muir, Bill Cordell as Dr. Bloom, Carolyn Jett as the nurse. **Writer:** Robert Goethals. **Director:** Tony Dow.

Treasure (airdate: Oct. 26, 1990). Swampy is looking for something hidden among a pile of garbage someone has disposed of, and manages to find it: a briefcase full of currency. Meanwhile, a man passing by says he was born in Jim's house. The man suddenly doubles over in pain and asks to use Jim's bathroom. While this is going on, a woman is asking where the Langford house is. Bucky, who claims to be Tressa's brother, explains that he is dieing, and, knowing this, he stole a large sum of money to give to his girlfriend, but decided not to let her have it. He slumps to the floor, so Jim runs to get Swamp Thing for help, hoping he can revive his uncle so Tressa can see him before he is arrested for the robbery - or is killed by his girlfriend, who is on her way to the Langford house and will do anything to obtain the money. **Guest cast:** Cynthia Garris as Eleanor, Kevin Corrigan as Buckholt. **Writer:** Jon Ezrine. **Director:** Tony Dow.

Dick Durock, who starred as the Swamp Thing in the theatrical movies, reprised his role in the new USA series.

New Acquaintance (airdate: Nov. 2, 1990). Jim is feeling lonesome so he goes to see Oboe, but the teenager is getting ready to leave on a date with a girl he recently met. Jim leaves and continues to walk along the lake shore, where he meets a girl his own age, named Lilly. They decide to go to Jim's house, and along the way, three boys say to themselves that Jim will soon learn Lilly's secret. Arriving at his house, they don't notice Swamp Thing watching them, nor does Jim realize that the girl is stealing Tressa's belongings while Lilly is in the house. After Tressa arrives home, she asks Lilly to stay for supper. She does, then goes home, only to return in the middle of the night, so Tressa allows her to sleep in the guest room. However, the following morning Tressa finds a bloodied, dead rabbit in Lilly's bag, and she realizes that something is very wrong with the girl, so she calls the sheriff when she learns that Jim and Lily are alone in the swamp. **Guest cast:** River Phoenix as Lilly, Chris Lobban as boy #1, Danny Gura as boy #2, Jordan Kessler as boy #3. **Writers:** Lawrence G. Ditillo, Wade Johnson, Daniel Kennedy. **Director:** David Jackson.

Falco (airdate: Nov. 9, 1990). While Arcane is at the funeral of Tressa's mother, a man sneaks up, pulls a gun, and shoots at him. He misses, and runs off when two police officers give chase. He manages to allude them, but all of this has not escaped the observation of Swamp Thing, who hides the man's rifle after he leaves it behind. At Tressa and Jim's house the mourners have returned after the shooting, and Arcane shows up to ask Jim if he saw the man, and what the would-be assassin looked like. Jim can only tell him that he had a broken arm, but apparently that is enough for Arcane to deduce who the man was. In town, Falco sees Arcane arrive in front of a building, and he follows. Falco, standing in front of a pet store, releases a pigeon on display, and the bird flies around until it has found Arcane so as to show his hiding place to Falco, who now has Arcane cornered - but leaves the scientist behind to return to the swamp. Arriving there, he meets Swampy, and explains who he is:

another of Arcane's mutants. Pulling his arm from the sling it turns out not to be broken, but feathered - it seems that Falco was once a Falcon, But Arcane has turned him almost entirely into a man. Even though he now possesses human form, Falco retains a Falcon's thirst for killing - and for revenge against Arcane. **Guest cast:** Peter Mark Richman as Falco, Jay Glick as the minister, Doc Duhame as the mutant. **Writer:** Joseph Stefano. **Director:** Fritz Kiersch.

From Beyond the Grave (airdate: Nov. 16, 1990). Jim and Tressa visit the grave of Savanna Langford, Tressa's recently-deceased mother, and remark about how much they miss her - not realizing that her death is about to have another profound effect on them both. Later that day, an attorney named Everett Baxtor arrives to say that Savannah willed everything, including the home and property that Tressa and Jim live in, to the county, not Tressa. Tressa cannot believe her mother would do this, particularly because she had hated the way the area had gone downhill since Arcane and his monstrosities moved in. Tressa knows that the will is a fake and has an idea where the real one is, so Arcane, who is behind the scheme to get ahold of the Langford property, tells his flunky Everett to kill Tressa before she can find the real will. **Guest cast:** Patricia Helwick as Savanna Langford, Brett Rice as Everett Baxtor, Jamie Cuffe as the young Tressa, Lisa Miller as the young Savanna. **Writers:** Wadre Johnson, Daniel Kennedy. **Director:** Tony Dow.

The Shipment (airdate: Nov. 23, 1990). Sheriff Andrews picks up a hitchhiker, puts hand cuffs on the teenager, throws him in the back of his squad car, and claims that the boy is "about to take his last ride". During all of this, Swampy stands by helplessly watching, but he correctly figures that Arcane is behind the kidnapping. Later that day, young Jim comes to the same conclusion when he sneaks into Arcane's lab and sees the hitchhiker locked in a cage along with other prisoners, while elsewhere are standing the mutated products he manufactures by crossing humans and animals in his evil experiments, which he now sells to special customers. Jim is seen so he runs outside screaming for Swamp Thing, while Swampy is at that moment freeing a truck load of the imprisoned mutants. Sheriff Andrews nearly catches Jim as the boy returns home, so he runs again, as his mother is not home to help. Jim gets to a phone and calls his brother Will for help, but just then the sheriff catches him and returns him to Arcane, who plans to ship him to South America for safe keeping so that he can blackmail Swamp Thing into discontinuing his interference in Arcane's schemes. [Note: Scott Garrison makes his first appearance as Will Kipp, Jim's step-brother, in this episode. Unfortunately, the character of Jim was written out, after Arcane fakes his death and transports him to South America.] **Guest cast:** Janis Nenson as Mrs. Blake, Roger Floyd as the hitchhiker. **Writers:** Judith Berg, Sandra Berg, Joseph Stefano. **Director:** Walter Von Huene.

Birth Marks (airdate: Feb. 1, 1991). Tressa's step-son Will has a strange dream about a boat exploding, and a teenage girl swimming away from it, while a new-born child floats away in a box. Waking up, he looks out his apartment window and sees a girl who looks just like the one in his dream running down the street. He runs outside and invites her in, even though it is in the middle of the night. The girl is very strange, mentioning that she can read thoughts, and was blown off of a boat that very same night. Will starts to call the sheriff, but she stops him and assures Will that she is OK. He notices that Abigail has a bar code on her leg as if she were a product, not a person, but she insists that it is just a tattoo. Meanwhile, in the swamp, the unearthly alter-ego of Alec Holland finds a floating cradle with a baby. At the same time, Dr. Arcane is contacted by General Sunderland, whom Arcane informs that he has destroyed the experiment - including a child and a cloned teenage girl - of a competing scientist, and now plans to go to work for Henderson, working on a project he hopes will return life to his cryonically-frozen, deceased wife. [Note: Kari Wuhrer debuts as the clone-girl Abigail in this episode.] **Guest cast**: Doc Duhame as Keefer. **Writer**: Tom Greene. **Director**: Walter Von Huene.

Dark Side of the Mirror (airdate: Feb. 8, 1991). District attorney Matthews states on tv that he plans to put Arcane out of business for good, but the evil doctor has plans of his own: to create a duplicate of Swamp Thing that will do his bidding, including murdering the district attorney. Meanwhile, Tressa has started a boat rental and swamp tour company, and one of the customers has eyes for the divorcee. At the same time, romance is blossoming between Will and Abigail. That evening, while Matthews is dining with Tressa and a friend, Arcane arrives and gives him a bottle of wine and says he will comply with the D.A.'s investigation. But as they leave the restaurant a hideous creature - the copy of Swamp Thing - attacks and kills Matthews. With dozens of witnesses around, the crowd decides to arm themselves and head for the swamp - to kill Swamp Thing. **Guest cast**: Jordan Williams as Eric Matthews, Danny Hanemann as Hammett. **Writer**: W.M. Whitehead. **Director**: Bruce Seth Green.

Silent Screams (airdate: Feb. 15, 1991). Tressa and a couple of friends she went to college with are having a reunion by camping out in the swamp. While busy in conversation Tressa doesn't see a snake nearing her until it bites her. Ilene and Melissa panic and go running off into the swamp, but don't go far before they disappear. When the wounded Tressa tries to find them she runs into an invisible energy barrier, and can get no closer. On the other side of the barrier Ilene and Melissa can see Tressa, but she cannot hear them screaming. The "invisibility cloak" is one of Arcane's inventions that he is working on for General Sunderland - and he could care less what happens to Tressa or her friend as he uses them for his experiments. **Guest cast**: Catherine Hader as Melissa, Elizabeth Fendrick as Ilene, Roger Pretto as Commander Hammer, Michael Champlin as Alexander. **Writers**: Judith Berg, Sandra Berg. **Director**: Walter Von Huene.

Walk a Mile In My Shoots (airdate: Feb. 22, 1991). Swamp Thing comes across Will, who is tied to a tree and hooked up to an explosive charge that is ready to go off. He saves the boy, but then is trapped himself by Arcane, who uses a transformation process to place his mind in Swamp Thing's body, and Swampy's in his, so that he can perform research on Swamp Thing's body unhindered. Arcane returns to a remote lab, but finds that he cannot get into his computer system because of his altered voice. He does, however, manage to answer a communication from Gen. Sunderland, whom he tells that he has perfected the process of placing the General's mind into a body Sunderland has chosen. Elsewhere in the swamp, Will finds Swampy in Arcane's body and it takes a lot to convince the young man of the truth. Returning to Tressa's home, Will gives him first aid, and he spends the time experiencing again what it is to be a man. Before long, though, he realizes that he now has the perfect opportunity to destroy Arcane's operations. **Guest cast**: Robert Reynolds as Gurley, Doc Duhame as Wilkes. **Writer**: Jonathan Torp. **Director**: Bruce Seth Green.

The Watchers (airdate: March 1, 1991). Tressa takes a pair of

Cast replacements: Scott Garrison as Will Kipp and Kari Wuhrer as Abigail.

fishers out into the swamp, but while one of the men is cutting some bait he accidentally cuts off the end of his finger - and doesn't bleed. They are actually cyborgs built by Arcane, but now that Tressa knows their secret they decide to kill her. Luckily Swampy happens to be nearby, and he saves her. The cyborgs return to Arcane's lab, where Arcane and Graham are trying to get out of trouble with Gen. Sunderland. The General wants Arcane to find him a body, and since the scientist's last scheme was foiled by Swampy, now they are looking for the survivor of the boat explosion caused to destroy a competing scientist's work [see **Dark Side of the Mirror**]. Arcane is not yet aware of Abigail's existence - she having survived the boat explosion - but he does know that an adult survived the explosion, and can be identified by a bar code on the leg - which Abigail has. With the clones out searching the area, it is only a matter of time before they find Abigail. **Guest cast**: Scott Higgs as Lamar, Peter Palmer as Orvis, Steve DuMouchel as Officer Donnelly. **Writers**: Tom Greene, W.M. Whitehead. **Director**: Lyndon Chubbuck.

The Hunt (airdate: March 8, 1991). Will is walking home when he realizes that he is being followed, and suddenly he is grabbed by a total stranger. But once he gets loose the stranger turns out to be his father, who claims he was only joking. Will, who hasn't seen his father in five years, isn't amused and figures that his old man is only after something, which is normal for him. It turns out that he has been hired to photograph a swamp flower that only blooms at night for one week a year. Swamp Thing is well aware of the plant, as is Arcane, who, the next day, is telling his assistant, Graham, that a new flower he has developed can produce enough defoliant to wipe out an entire forest. He, of course, has an antidote that he will sell for the right price. As a test, Arcane takes one of the plants to a nursery, where it will release its poison that night. Unfortunately, the girl taking care of the flower at the nursery plans to return that night to feed it plant nutrients, and she will be in deadly danger if the plant releases its gas while she is there. Meanwhile, Tressa is as unhappy as anyone about her ex-husband's return - and she doesn't yet know that he is working for Arcane. **Guest cast:** Paul Coufos as Brydon Kipp. **Writers:** Wade Johnson, Daniel Kennedy. **Director:** Bruce Seth Green.

Touch of Death (airdate: March 15, 1991). Graham and Arcane kill a hunter at night, then use a new drug the scientist has created to bring him back to life - except that it doesn't work. They bury him in the woods and return to the lab, but unknown to them the drug has had a delayed reaction and the man suddenly bursts out of the ground very much alive. Meanwhile, Doc Hollister and Will are working on a new boat, and Will is unhappy that Doc wants to finish up the next day. Seconds later the "dead" hunter bursts through the door and falls on Will, then runs away. Later, Will begins to feel ill, and everything he comes in contact with dies, starting with all the fish in Tressa's aquarium. Arcane and Graham have also found out that the hunter is alive, after discovering the grave is empty. Still in the swamp, they see Will running and yelling for help from Swampy, but he is jumped by one of Arcane's men, then is saved by Swamp Thing. Then another of Arcane's men is killed when he is touched by the hunter. Swampy realizes what has happened, as Arcane has stolen and altered a drug - an extremely dangerous one with deadly side effects - from Alec Holland. While Swampy tries to find a cure for Will, the hunter shows up at the Kipp house the next day and Abigail hires him for some odd jobs, not realizing the danger she and Tressa are in. **Guest cast:** Mark McCracken as Abraham MacCyrus, Ralph Wilcox as the sentry hunter. **Writers:** Torn Greene, W.M. Whitehead. **Director:** Walter Von Huene.

Tremors of the Heart (airdate: March 22, 1991). Arcane has invented a new weapon for Gen. Sunderland: a device that can artificially produce earthquakes. But as they test the device, it continues operating longer than it should, sending shockwaves through the swamp, one of which opens a fissure and drops Swampy into a deep cave. Among Arcane's staff is the newly-hired Sienna, a tough female that takes no lip from the scientist. As she helps Arcane control the earthquake device, Swamp Thing is still stuck in the cave, which, while exploring, he finds opens up into an underground lab containing the earthquake machine. He tries to destroy it, but the lack of sunlight has weakened him - and it will kill him if he is underground much longer. Above ground, Tressa isn't in much better condition, as a tremor has knocked lose some heavy beams from her dock that have fallen on her. Now she is trapped in the water, far from anyone who can help - and the water is rising fast since the nearby dam is releasing water because of the quakes. **Guest cast:** Sandahl Bergman as Sienna, Steve DuMuouchel as the guard. **Writers:** Wade Johnson, Daniel Kennedy. **Director:** Mitchell Bock.

The Prometheus Parabola (airdate: April 5, 1991). Someone has unleashed the Prometheus Parabola, a force devoted to the destruction of Arcane, but possibly may obliterate the forest and Swampy with it. At the Kipp home, Doc Hollister has lined up Tressa for another blind date, and when the date arrives on horseback, Malcolm Neddington turns out to be a hulking brute of a man. While Malcolm is in the kitchen, Doc arrives to say that Tressa's date will not be coming, having been in an accident. Suddenly, the fake Malcolm shoots Doc in the chest, handcuffs Abigail to the unconscious Doc, then reveals that he is actually J.J. Dax, the brother of the man who created the Prometheus Parabola before he was killed by Arcane. Dax takes Tressa into town and on the way explains that he is starting a war against Arcane and he doesn't care who gets in the way of his destruction of the scientist. While in town, Graham sees Dax and Tressa together, and he reports to Arcane, who plans to make an all-out assault against the Kipp home, where Dax is now staying with Tressa, Abigail, and the dieing Doc Hollister. **Guest cast:** Terry Funk as J.J. Dax. **Writers:** Tom Greene, W.M. Whitehead. **Director:** Walter Von Huene.

SEASONS TWO-THREE

Synopsis and credits for seasons two and three are not currently available. However, this is a checklist of episode titles for all three seasons:

The Emerald Heart	The Living Image
The Death of Dr. Arcane	The Swamp Maiden
Spirit of the Swamp	Blood Wind
Grotesquery	Natural Enemy
Treasure	New Acquanintance
Falco	From Beyond the Grave
The Shipment	Birthmarks
Dark Side of the Mirror	Silent Screams
Walk a Mile In My Shoots	The Watchers
The Hunt	Touch of Death
Tremors of the Heart	The Prometheus Parabola
Night of the Dying	Lost Love
Mist Demeanor	A Nightmare on Jackson St.
Better Angels	Children of the Fool
A Jury of His Fears	Poisonous
Smoke and Mirrors	This Old House of Mayan
What Goes Around Comes Around	
Tatania	Swamp of Dreams
An Eye For an Eye	Heart of the Mantis
Sonata	Special Request
Dead and Married	Powers of Darkness
Pirador's Brain	The Chains of Forever
Changes	Destiny
Patient Zero	Fear Itself
Future Tense	Vendetta
The Handyman	The Hurting
Easy Prey	Rites of Passage
A Most Bitter Pill	The Burning Times
The Curse	In the Beginning
Cross-Fired	Brotherly Love
Eye of the Storm	The Lesser of Two Evils
Revelations	Never Alone
The Return of LaRoche	Yo Ho Ho
Hide in the Night	Judgement Day
The Spectre of Death	Payday
Romancing Arcane	That's a Wrap

236

If you have enjoyed this book and want to read about other classic television series, you may wish to look over our listings for *Epi-log*, *Epi-log Journal* and *Epi-log Special* magazines (see pages 238-241). *THE SUPERHERO ILLUS-TRATED GUIDEBOOK* is a compilation of articles, episode guides and photos that have appeared in back issues of all three magazines.

Epi-log magazine is available at better book stores, comic book shops, mail order retailers, or directly from the publisher at P.O. Box 1332, Dunlap, TN 37327 USA.

Thank you for your purchase of this Alpha Control Press publication!

- William E. Anchors, Jr.;

Editor and Publisher

Epi-log Magazine

Each issue of our magazine features up to 100 pages packed full of photos (some in full color) and episode guide reviews of sci-fi, fantasy, horror, suspense, and other TV series! Issues #18-42 have glossy paper and are perfect bound with a cardstock cover. Backissues are $5.95 each, or four for $20 plus postage. See page 242 for ordering instructions.

Issue #1: Out of print since June 1990, we have located a few copies of the rare first issue. It covers: Next Generation seasons 1-3, Star Trek, Star Trek Animated, The Phoenix, Fantastic Journey, Logan's Run, Streethawk, The Invaders, The Starlost, Automan, Buck Rogers, Otherworld, Planet of the Apes, Voyagers, Knight Rider. **Available only at a collector's price of $10 each.**

Epi-log #2: Covers Beauty and the Beast, Lost in Space, Land of the Giants, Voyage to the Bottom of the Sea, The Time Tunnel, Swiss Family Robinson, The Return of Captain Nemo, Battlestar Galactica, Galactica: 1980

Epi-log #3: Covers The Night Stalker, Thriller, The Outer Limits, Night Gallery/Sixth Sense, The Twilight Zone, New Twilight Zone, One Step Beyond/Next Step Beyond

Epi-log #7: Limited copies left! Covers: Alien Nation, Gemini Man, Hard Time on Planet Earth, Science Fiction Theater, Men Into Space, Next Step Beyond, The Invisible Man, Powers of Matthew Star, The Highwayman, Time Express, Max Headroom, My Favorite Martian, Quark

Epi-log #8: Covers The Munsters, The Addams Family, Beyond Westworld, Q.E.D., Red Dwarf, Manimal, Something is Out There, Freddies Nightmares, Tales From the Crypt, Project UFO, Journey to the Unknown, The Hitchhiker, Werewolf

Epi-log #9: Covers Friday the 13th: The Series, The Darkroom, Tales From the Darkside, Ghost Story/Circle of Fear, Hammer House of Horror, Hammer House of Mystery and Suspense, Dark Shadows (1966), Dark

Shadows (1991)

Epi-log #12: Covers Dr. Who years 15-26, Supercar, Terrahawks, Thunderbirds, Quatermass, H.G. Well's Invisible Man, Captain Scarlet, The Secret Service, Hitchhiker's Guide to the Galaxy, Blakes Seven, Doomwatch, Chocky

Epi-log #13: Covers Black Sheep Squadron, Combat, 12 O'Clock High, The Rat Patrol, Dirty Dozen - The Series, McHales Navy

Epi-log #14: Covers China Beach, Tour of Duty, MASH, Aftermash, Call to Glory, Supercarrier

Epi-log #15: Covers MacGyver (years 1-6), I Spy, T. J. Hooker, Barbary Coast, The Six Million Dollar Man, The Bionic Woman, **Untold Tales**: The Barbary Coast

Epi-log #16: Covers Adam Adamant, Out of the Unknown, Star Maidens, The Storyteller, Into the Labyrinth, A For Andromeda, Andromeda Breakthrough, Supercar, Terrahawks, Thunderbirds, UFO, Quatermass, The Saint (part 1), Return of the Saint

Epi-log #17: Covers Mission Impossible (1960s and 1990s), Alfred Hitchcock (NBC/USA), Tales of the Unexpected, Tucker's Witch, Misfits of Science, The Saint (part 2), **Untold Tales**: Mission Impossible

Epi-log #18: Covers Magnum P.I. (years 1-2), Spenser For Hire, The Fugitive (year 1), The A-Team (year 1), SurfSide 6, Bourbon Street, Coronet Blue, Michael Shayne, P.I., 77 Sunset Strip, Hawaiian Eye, **Untold Tales**: The A-Team, Magnum P.I.

Epi-log #19: Covers Tarzan, New Tarzan, Sheena, Ramar, Jungle Jim, White Hunter, Maya, Cowboy in Africa, Daktari, MacGyver (season 7), The A-Team (years 2-5), Fugitive (year 3), Magnum, P.I. (years 3-4)

Epi-log #20: Includes Cover Up, Twin Peaks, Magnum, P.I. 5-8, The Fugitive 3-4, The Young Riders, Man and the Challenge, Dow Hour of Great Mysteries, Inner Sanctum, Captain Midnight, Mystery Show

Epi-log #21: Extensive coverage of Hill Street Blues and Hawaii 5-0

Epi-log #22: Covers Red Dwarf seasons 1-5, Superboy years 1-4, Super Force years 1-2, Lightning Force

Epi-log #23: Covers I Dream of Jeannie (part 1), The When Things Were Rotten, The Ghost and Mrs. Muir, My Secret Identity

Epi-log #24: Covers I Dream of Jeannie, (part 2), Bewitched, (part 2), It's About Time, Alf

Epi-log #25: Covers The Jetsons, Journey to the Center of the Earth, Danger Mouse, Land of the Lost (new and old), Jonny Quest, Pink Panther, Ark II, Adventures of Flash Gordon, New Adventures of Zorro, Ant and the Aardvark, Misterjaw, The Inspector, The Texas Toads

Epi-log #26: Covers Vegas, Land of the Lost, (part 2), Jonny Quest, (part 2); Riptide

Epi-log #27: Covers Land of the Lost, (part 3); Hawkins, The Rookies, Shaft, Ripcord, Then Came Bronson, Jericho, Chips

Epi-log #28: Covers The Unexpected, Hunter, ABC Mystery Movie, Return to the Planet of the Apes, Nightmare Cafe, She Wolf of London, Love and Curses

Epi-log #29: Covers Aliens in the Family, My Partner the Ghost, The Protectors, Man in a Suitcase, The Persuaders, Star Cops, Mystery and Imagination, Blakes 7, Stingray, Robin of Sherwood

Epi-log #30: Covers Stingray (U.S. series), Matt Houston, Sledge Hammer

Epi-log #31: Covers Tombstone Territory, Bat Masterson, MacKenzie's Raiders, How the West Was Won, Cheyenne, Wanted Dead or Alive

Epi-log #32: Covers: The Golden Years, Sable, The New Adventures of Beans Baxter, Mann and Machine, Kung Fu, Wiseguy (part 1)

Epi-log #33: Covers The Fall Guy, Ultraman, Wiseguy (part 2) Battlestar Galactica, Galactica: 1980, Buck Rogers

Epi-log #34: Covers Route 66, Werewolf, 21 Jump Street (part 1), Booker, Mork and Mindy

Epi-log #35: Covers Harry-O, O'Hara, U.S. Treasury, 21 Jump Street (part 2), Kraft Suspense Theater, Kraft Mystery Theater, Highlander

Epi-log #36: Covers Forever Knight part 1); Kolchak: The Night Stalker, The Twilight Zone, The New Twilight Zone, Target the Corruptors, Cain's Hundred

Epi-log #37: Covers Renegade, Forever Knight (part 2) The Munsters, The Addams Family, New Breed, Young Indiana Jones (part 1), Something is Out There, Hard Time on Planet Earth

Epi-log #38: Covers The Detectives, Banacek, Shadow Chasers, Cool Million, Madigan, Darkroom, Misfits of Science, Faraday and Co., Snoop Sisters, Remington Steele (part 1), P.S. I Luv U, Tenafly, Young Indiana Jones (part 2)

Epi-log #39: Covers Crossroads, Ghost Story, Circle of Fear, Remington Steele (part 2), Sword of Justice, Freddy's Nightmares, The Aquanauts, Malibu Run, Young Indiana Jones (part 3), Beverly Hills Buntz, Matt Helm, Untold Tales: Remington Steele

Epi-log #40: Covers Supercar, Terrahawks, New Tomorrow People, The Tomorrow People, The Secret Service, Kinvig, Ace of Wands, Hammer House of Horror, Hammer House of Mystery

Epi-log #41: Covers Quatermass, Journey to the Unknown, Chocky, UFO, Pathfinders, Target Luna, Red Dwarf 6, Thunderbirds, Space: 1999

Epi-log #42: Covers Hardcastle and McCormick, Street Justice, Columbo, McCloud, McMillan and Wife, Lanigan's Rabbi, Amy Prentiss, Hec Ramsey, Baywatch (part 1), The F.B.I. (part 1)

Epi-log #43/Journal #16: Covers Star Trek: The Next Generation (year 7, part two); The Flash; Kolchak: The Night Stalker (part 2) Lucan; Hat Squad; Baywatch (part 2); Charlie's Angels; Gavilan; Thriller; The F.B.I. (part 2); Untold Tales: The Flash, The Night Stalker

Epi-log #44/Journal #17: Covers the X-Files (year one); Lois and Clark; Deep Space Nine (year 2, part 2); The F.B.I. (part 3); Medical Center; Dr. Kildare; Young Dr. Kildare; Baywatch (part 3); Buck Rogers (part 1); Untold Tales: Buck Rogers

Epi-log Journal

Each issue features up to 100 pages packed full of new, never-before-published photos (some in full color), episode guides (greatly expanded over normal *Epi-log* issues), articles, reviews, interviews, and in-depth information on sci-fi, fantasy, horror, suspense, and adventure series! Backissues are $5.95 each, or four for $20. See page 242 for ordering instructions

EPI-LOG Journal #1: An Irwin Allen special, covers Lost in Space, Land of the Giants, Voyage to the Bottom of the Sea, The Time Tunnel, Swiss Family Robinson, The Return of Captain Nemo, **Untold Tales**: Lost in Space

EPI-LOG Journal #2: Irwin Allen special part 2, Lost in Space, Land of the Giants, Voyage to the Bottom of the Sea, The Time Tunnel, Man From the 25th Century, City Beneath the Sea, Time Travelers: **Untold Tales**: The Time Tunnel

EPI-LOG Journal #3: Covers Voyage to the Bottom of the Sea, The Invaders, Otherworld, **Untold Tales**: Voyage to the Bottom of the Sea

EPI-LOG Journal #4: Covers Beauty and the Beast, The Greatest American Hero, **Untold Tales**: Beauty and the Beast, Greatest American Hero

EPI-LOG Journal #5: A Gene Roddenberry Special, covers Star Trek: The Next Generation 1-2, Star Trek Classic, Genesis II, Planet Earth, Strange New World, **Untold Tales**: Star Trek II (unmade series)

EPI-LOG Journal #6: Roddenberry Special (part 2), covers Star Trek: Next Generation year 3, Questor Tapes, Battleground Earth, Spectre, Tarzan, Magna 1, Genesis II, other Roddenberry shows; plus coverage of Voyagers, **Untold Tales**: Voyagers

EPI-LOG Journal #7: Covers Star Trek, Star Trek Next Generation years 4-5, Star Trek Animated, plus extensive features on The Outer Limits, **Untold Tales**: Outer Limits

EPI-LOG Journal #8: Covers The Outer Limits, War of the Worlds, Fantastic Journey, **Untold Tales**: Fantastic Journey

Epi-log Journal #9: Covers Quantum Leap (years 1-2), Planet of the Apes, Return to the Planet of the Apes, **Untold Tales**: Planet of the Apes

EPI-LOG Journal #10: Covers The Wild Wild West, (part 1); Quantum Leap (years 3-5)

EPI-LOG Journal #11: Covers Next Generation, year 6; The Wild Wild West, (part 2); **Untold Tales**: Wild Wild West, Star Trek (classic series)

EPI-LOG Journal #12 Covers The Wild Wild West (part 3), The Man From Uncle (part 1), Star Trek: The Next Generation, year 6, Deep Space 9, **Untold Tales**: Man From Uncle

EPI-LOG Journal #13: Covers The Man From Uncle (part 2), The Girl From Uncle, Deep Space 9 (part 2); Werewolf, **Untold Tales**: Man From Uncle

EPI-LOG Journal #14: Covers Star Trek: The Next Generation (year 7, part 1), Spider-Man, Werewolf (part 2); Battlestar Galactica, Galactica: 1980, **Untold Tales**: Battlestar Galactica, Galactica 1980

EPI-LOG Journal #15: Covers Deep Space Nine (year 2, part 1), Kolchak: The Night Stalker, (part 1); Robin Hood (reviews of all movies and TV shows with episode guide), Battlestar Galactica; Galactica: 1980 (part 2); **Untold Tales**: Galactica 1980

Golden Years * Wiseguy * Sable * Mann and Machine
Kung Fu * The New Adventures of Beans Baxter

Tarzan (1991) * Tarzan (1966) * Ramar * Jungle Jim
White Hunter * Maya * Sheena * Cowboy in Africa * Daktari
* Magnum, P.I. * The Fugitive * The A-Team * MacGyver

The Avengers * The New Avengers * The Champions * Danger Man
Secret Agent * Get Smart * The Prisoner * The Professionals * Honey West
The Man From U.N.C.L.E.   * The Girl From U.N.C.L.E

Land of the Giants * City Beneath the Sea * Man From the 25th Century
Lost in Space * The Time Tunnel * Voyage to the Bottom of the Sea

Epi-log Special

Each issue features up to 100 pages containing out-of-print *Epi-log* issues with additional and/or revised information and new photos. Each backissue is $5.95, or 4 for $20.00 plus postage. See page 242 for ordering instructions.

Epi-log Special #1: (Summer Special) (revised issue #10): Covers: Star Trek Next Generation season 4, Alfred Hitchcock Presents, Alfred Hitchcock Hour, Quantum Leap 1-3, Superboy, Super Force, Swamp Thing, Dracula, The Flash

Epi-log Special #2: (Winter Special) (revised issue #1): Covers Star Trek: The Next Generation seasons 1-3, Star Trek, Star Trek Animated, The Phoenix, Fantastic Journey, Logan's Run, Streethawk, The Invaders, The Starlost, Automan, Buck Rogers, Otherworld, Planet of the Apes, Voyagers, Knight Rider

Epi-log Special #3: (revised issue #5) Covers The Man From Uncle, The Girl From Uncle, The Prisoner, Secret Agent, Danger Man, The Champions, The Avengers, The New Avengers, The Professionals, Honey West, Get Smart

Epi-log Special #4: (revised issue #6) Covers

Batman, The Green Hornet, Superman, Incredible Hulk, Captain Nice, Mr. Terrific, Captain Power, Wizards and Warriors, Spider-Man, Wonder Woman

Epi-log Special #5: (revised issue #7) Covers Gemini Man, Science Fiction Theater, Men Into Space, One Step Beyond, Next Step Beyond, The Invisible Man, Powers of Matthew Star, The Highwayman, Time Express, Max Headroom, Planet of the Apes, Alien Nation, Project UFO

Epi-log Special #6: (revised #11) Covers Dr. Who years 1-13, Sapphire and Steel, The Tripods, Fireball XL5, Joe 90

Epi-log Special #7: (revised issue #12) Covers Dr. Who seasons 14-26, Captain Scarlet, H.G. Well's Invisible Man, Hitchhiker's Guide to the Galaxy, Doomwatch

Epi-log Special #8: (revised issue #4) Covers Salvage One, A Man Called Sloane, Starman, The Flash, The Man From Atlantis, The Immortal, Blue Thunder, V, Bring 'Em Back Alive, Outlaws, Dracula: The Series

Instructions to order issues of *Epi-log*.

Please note new shipping rates (effective 1/1/95):

POSTAGE: Our shipping rates (including handling) are:
From $5.95 to $11.90: $4.00 $11.91 to $29.99: $6.00
From $30.00 to $39.99: $7.00 $40.00 to $49.95: $8.00
From $50.00 to $74.99: $9.00 $75.00 on up: $10.00
Canada/Mexico add $1.00 to the above rates.

UPS shipping: Available to 48 U.S. states only, add 50% to the above rates. **Issue prices:** All issues of our magazine are $5.95 each or 4 for $20 + postage. Postage rates (U.S. only) are listed above. Overseas postage: **Overseas:** double for surface mail, triple for air mail. All overseas orders must be in U.S. funds on international money orders - no checks. Make checks or money orders payable to **Star Tech.** Subscriptions are no longer available (#44 is the last available issue). Please do not send cash.

For best service please use this order blank or a photocopy. Minimum refund is $5.01 - credit slips only issued for $5 or less. Allow 4-6 weeks for delivery. Enclose a self-addressed stamped envelope (overseas send two international reply coupons) for replies to all letters - no exceptions.

EPI-LOG MAGAZINE
ORDER FORM

PO Box 456, Dunlap, TN 37327

NAME (please print clearly)

ADDRESS

CITY   STATE, ZIP

Use your ❑ VISA   ❑ MasterCard

| Mastercard Interbank # | | Expiration date required |

Signature_____

$20 minimum on charge orders (excluding tax/postage).

All charge orders MUST be signed for by the card holder and sent only to the card holder's address. The service charge to return orders for a signature is $5.00.

Please indicate issues desired (one only per line):

	Qty. EACH	PRICE TOTAL	Date sent:	Other info:

FAX Order Line:
615-949-4443

For orders only please - no letters (see above)

Abreviations: OOS Temporarily Out of Stock, NA = Not Available, NYR = Not Yet Released	Qty.	PRICE TOTAL	Date sent:	Other info:

7 3/4% TN. sales tax - applies only to persons living in Tennessee.

Shipping:

Order filled by:

Order checked by:

ORDER TOTAL:

Date we received your order: